OF ASH AND BLOOD

THE ASCENSION RISING SERIES
BOOK 3

K. R. RAINBOLT

Of Ash and Blood

Book 3 of THE ASCENSION RISING SERIES

Set in the NATURAL UNIVERSE

Copyright © 2025 K. R. Rainbolt

Cover design by *Artscandare Book Cover Design*

Editing by *Your Best Book Editor*

Proofing by *Book Witch Author Services*

ISBN (paperback): 979-8-9863026-5-2

ISBN (ebook): 979-8-9863026-4-5

To my momma. Thank you for always having my back and believing in me when I didn't believe in myself. I love you.

To all the readers out there who just need a second away from the real world, I hope you can find that here.

Authors Note

Hey, all you tortured souls. I'm happy to have you here, and I have a few things to note before you dive in. This is a slow-burn, dark-themed, paranormal, 'why choose' novel. This book and the others in this series contain content that may be triggering to some people. If you think you may need a bit more information on the cautions/triggers of this book, please check my website or Linktree.

Said website: https://krrainbolt.com

Or my Linktree: https://linktr.ee/k.r.rainboltauthor

If you're ever confused about something or just want to know what something means, I've included all translations and general information at the end of the novel. I've also added a list of important characters that were mentioned in books one and two, so if you're looking for a reminder on who's who, give that a read.

No AI was used in the making of this book. Please note that you can pry my em dashes from my cold dead hands.

That's all from me! Kick back, relax, and enjoy the read.

Chapter 1

Aaliyah

*D*eath always *wins*.

Those were the cursed words that brought me back to consciousness.

They were subtle, like a breath, almost nothing more than wind against busted shutters that could be played off as a voice. But they didn't *feel* like sound; they didn't ring in my eardrums or make me turn to search for them. They echoed, as if they'd been played directly into my head, and when I opened my eyes, *nothing* greeted me.

Not the frigid dark or the harshness of overhead lights that used to glare down at me from the ceiling at Ascension Rising. Nothing but an endless floor of rolling silver that stretched around me as I stood on what should have been shaky legs. *Nothing* but an obsidian sky littered with millions of pin-prick stars, and when I opened my mouth to scream ...

Nothing greeted me then either.

It only took a second for me to realize where I was, the Void greeting me with all the softness of an old friend, picking at my soul as if reaching a hand out to shake. That was where my recognition ended, my memory a haze as I took a stumbling step forward. There were hints of what brought me here, hints of people that became blurred in my mind's eye, before the subtle plucks of the Void stole them from me.

My name was Aaliyah, and someone had taken me from ... from who again?

I wasn't breathing, but that didn't stop my chest from heaving like I was. The names and the faces of men I knew were important but couldn't quite grasp slipped by. There one second, gone the next, the memories so distant I could no longer reach them.

An overwhelming feeling of dread surged into my chest, grabbing my heart and squeezing it. Though, it didn't beat. Another pluck, another memory gone. I needed to leave, needed to get home.

But what was home?

The endlessness of the silver room was a daunting feature, and unsure what to do, I walked, one step after the other, faster and *faster*, until I was running.

I had to get out. That was the only thing I knew. Those faceless men, they *needed* me. I was ...

What was my name again?

"You seem to be in quite the bind," a voice echoed, sounding off like a cannon and bringing my hopeless run to a stop. A chill filled the air, the bitter cold the first thing that had felt real since I'd opened my eyes. "I wasn't expecting to find anyone else, well, *here*. It's not what you would call an ideal vacation spot. Considering you're dead and all."

I turned, looking back at where I'd just been running from, and found a man, much closer than he should have been. He had his arms crossed tightly over his chest, standing only a couple of inches taller than me. There was a familiarity in the cock of his hips and the way his head tilted. He had striking white hair that was broken only by a small patch of black in his bangs that laid over his forehead in a soft wave; the end twining toward one of his slightly pointed ears.

Then there was the lavender of his eyes, swirling with patches of gold that clashed with the vibrancy of rich violet, and when he smiled, it was another's face I saw. I wasn't sure how I knew, but that face was ingrained in me, one I shared.

My mother. He looked just like my mother.

I opened my mouth to speak on instinct, but nothing came out like it should.

"This is supposed to be my getaway spot, you know, and I'm not much a fan of sharing. Do me a favor and pass on, would you?" the man pressed with a callous wave of his hand and a souring to his thin lips.

The silver under my feet shook, vertigo sending me into a tailspin of dazed confusion, much like the taste of iron that suddenly flooded my mouth. The Void flexed, as if the ground just below it had fissured, and for a moment, surprise replaced the mirth in the unknown man's eyes.

"Well, this *is* interesting. Seems the Void has picked a favorite Reaper," he mused, setting his chin in an open palm. The Void pulsed at his words, as if gleeful to hear them. Was that what I was? A *Reaper*? "Guess it's your lucky day. Do try not to get killed out there again. Would be a shame if we couldn't talk next time."

I got no more, just his smile and the brush of his final parting words, before the ground fell out from under me, and I plummeted.

"And remember, baby Imperial. Death *always* wins."

I held on to those words for as long as I could. They were a serenade, a subtle nothing that pulled me away from what I could hear, smell, and taste. They were the peace of quiet.

But I'd never *liked* the quiet.

Never make noise.

The breath that seized my still lungs was brutal, and I choked on the metallic liquid that was forced down my throat, thick like a viscous syrup, clogging my airway as my body tried to register life again. It was rotten and ancient, smelling sharply like bottled fury, a potent mix of magic and decay.

My sight came next, then the ache, and the *pressure*.

I jolted, another mouthful landing in my stomach like a rancid weight. Useless thoughts rattled my brain as my memories filtered back painfully slow. I tried to focus on what I remembered last, on the hazy thoughts of a dusty piano, and a man's gentle voice ... until eventually, *brutally*, a face came into view.

They get more violent when you make noise.

It was the sharpness of his features, the deep red of his eyes, and the chaotic frizz of his ink-black hair that finally chipped through the haze.

It was the face of a man that had gotten me through more experiments than I could count. My heart jolted as I reached for him, desperate for the comfort of his embrace and the steady beat of his heart under my ear. I waited, eyes clouding with tears, for him to call me his *ab* like he had when I was a child, to remind me I was always safe when he was nearby.

Only the hair on my arms stood, my heartbeat quickening, as if my body knew instinctively that whoever I was seeing wasn't what he seemed. He was feral, his lips and chin covered in his own blood, from where he'd ripped out a chunk of the arm he'd held to my mouth. There was an eerie silence to him that matched his lack of breath and the haunting whites of his wide eyes.

Sebek, my mind finally supplied, and my hand dropped. My uncle by blood, the man who'd turned the Vivas Crypt into the Vampires they were now. The man who'd been my ruin.

This *wasn't* my father, even if he shared his face.

This was a monster.

The lingering traces of his blood were like sour soot on my tongue as I stared up at the gray sky. I couldn't avoid the memories forever, even as I tried to fight them. It was too much, too painful to come to terms with.

Who he was, *really* was.

The leader of Ascension Rising.

The doctors and scientists that had torn into me and destroyed any semblance of peace I'd had in my life had done so at *his* whim. He was behind my endless torment and years of pain. That realization, that this man who'd populated my father's stories with such grace and heroics was nothing more than the demon that haunted my nightmares ... broke something in me.

The frost-bitten rocks dug into my back, and Sebek hovered over me, a freshly bloodied hand cupping my cheek. For a second, I could have sworn he looked worried, beyond the crazed fire in his eyes and the blood that still ran down his neck and arm. I should have been panicking, thrashing, and trying to run, but my mind was still catching up, and I didn't want to leave the fog that cradled me, didn't want to see what was beyond it.

He was my uncle, and he'd done this. *Stole* me, tortured me … and snapped Osiris's neck.

Oh God, *Osiris.*

"No—" I started, the word drowned out as my eyes rolled back, and the pressure behind them stole my voice, never leaving me a moment of peace, even now. My body bowed, darts of fire racing from my head to my fingertips. The *Rends* that had fallen into little more than forgotten history came rushing back to me. The pull, the Void, the *memory.* The brutality of the last one had ripped me clean from my body, torn me into the Void.

The last one should have killed me.

Being away from the Vivas Crypt before had already brought them back once … and it'd taken everything my guys had to bring me back. The taste of Osiris's blood still lingered if I thought hard enough.

I could only wonder, in horrified silence, how Sebek's blood did the same this time.

The need to run, to do *anything* to get away, was so strong I nearly pushed my way up, regardless of the weight that still held me down. Osiris was hurt, and we'd just left him there. On the floor, alone. "Osiris—"

"You're fine. *You're fine,*" Sebek whispered, carefully brushing the hair away from my face, across the chilled blood that stained my cheek. His expression contorted when I didn't give some affirmation back. "I won't let you die again, Glass."

His nickname made me flinch. I didn't have any words for him, nothing that could escape the crushing pressure in my skull and the taste of blood in my mouth. There was only the *Rend.*

My last sight, before it pulled me unwillingly into it, was his red eyes. So familiar, yet so lost to me. So filled with a rage that should have been foreign to them. But this monster wasn't my father, even if they shared a face, and with each savage breath, that only became clearer.

Before the memory took over.

Red eyes.

That was what I was supposed to see when I looked at the man in front of me, whose powerful arms were crossed defiantly over his chest, as if he were unmovable. Red eyes that crinkled at the corners when he smiled, shining with the barest hint of mischief and love.

In the world of ghosts, color wasn't something we had. This place, between the living world and the Void, was a blank slate. Just like my father's eyes and my mother's usually flushed cheeks.

Why'd they show up now, when I couldn't tell them how much I'd missed them? Why now, after Donavan and Nilus had already finished burying me, before my body was even cold?

My mother's soft smile stretched her slightly pursed lips, and for a moment, nothing else mattered. She didn't attempt to say anything, likely because she already knew nothing would happen if she tried. Her appearance was exactly as I last remembered it. From her soft flowery dress to her cooking apron, which was still stained with whatever she'd been making that night. I imagined her hair vividly, long white and down to her lower back, the silky strands wrapped around my fingers as she hugged me tightly.

I'd thought about her hugs a lot, the warmth of her arms and the strength they used to give me. I wanted to be hugged again, to hear my mother's soft voice as she sang her foreign melodies to me. To listen to one of my father's epic tales, of knights and princes, of war and love.

I took a tentative step toward them, as though I still needed to walk. It brought me some comfort, made me feel alive, even though I knew I no longer was. I was afraid to blink. If I did, they might disappear, and this fever dream would fade.

A new brush of emotion filled the air, this time the distinct warmth of love. My mother and father stood like sentinels, waiting for me to process.

Another step.

I was eager for the touch I knew I wouldn't feel. I wanted it, if only to imagine them close to me again.

My mother's trembling hand slipped into my father's own just as I reached them, an arm's length away. A pulse echoed as their hands touched, skimming over my skin. It was strange when the pull wasn't originating from me, almost like I was an onlooker in a game I'd made. Their emotions flickered, fear and uncertainty slipping through the cracks, burning me down to my core. I dropped my arms and took a hesitant step back.

Would they disappear? A tremor forced its way through my frozen limbs as I stared at them, their sunken expressions that suddenly mirrored mine, but that didn't stop them from following my retreating step.

I lifted my hand, trying to ward them off. I didn't want them to leave me. Not yet. I needed more time. I could survive if I got one more second; I was sure of it.

Just a second longer.

My words were empty on the wind, never breaching my lips, no matter how loudly I screamed them.

They reached me before I could back up again, their arms circling me in a tight hug, their hands still firmly clasped together. If I could breathe, the pressure would have pulled the air from my lungs. Inaudible sobs filtered through me, and my body trembled. It was too late. I could feel the pull more clearly now, the familiar tug at my soul breaking down every barrier I had. I clung to them as tightly as I could, surprised my limbs didn't fade right through them.

"No." The word was sharp in the air, my lips forming it as it resounded through the forest like a demand spoken by the trees themselves. It took me a moment to register that I heard it.

"Please." Another whisper. My parents relaxed against me, as though they were hoping for the sound. Then, far too soon, they faded from my view, their souls finding their way past me. To the place they belonged.

The Void didn't take prisoners; it didn't discriminate. It took, and it took, and it took.

Because death *always* wins.

It felt final, the Void uncaring as it claimed them. I fell to my knees, unable to stop the soundless scream.

Only it wasn't soundless.

The violent, hoarse noise echoed through the trees, ripping its way through me. I couldn't stop the shudder that racked my limbs as my eyes landed on the mound of dirt that held my body. I reached out hesitantly to the pile, my right hand grazing over the top. My mouth dropped open, but I was afraid to try to speak.

"Please." *I mouthed the word, and the body beneath the disturbed soil responded with the sound. A crisp chill gripped every exposed nerve I had, and all at once, it hit me again. I could feel the earth on my skin. The sting of my lacerations as the dirt dug into them. Even the rich scent of the forest washed over me, settling on my tongue.*

When the pain overwhelmed the awe, I closed my eyes, falling forward into the earth where my body resided. I could no more stop the scream than I could stop myself from pulling in a first, rasping breath. Unconsciousness licked at my mind, though I tried desperately to stop it. I wanted to hold on to this feeling because agony aside ...

I was alive.

CHAPTER 2

PRINCE

It took two days to get a flight to the States, to the home that my brothers and I had built so many decades ago. A home that was little more than déjà vu in the scattered mess that was my fucking head. Mags had found the address in a book that looked *almost* more ancient than they were, and complained the entire time about my incessant nagging, warning about the "consequences of meddling too soon". Of course, each word went in one ear and directly out the other. This wasn't something I was willing to wait for—fate be fucking *damned*—I needed to get home before *he* could.

I couldn't stand the thought of being too late. I spent the last several decades being too *fucking* late. The memories I'd recalled so far were little better than acid on open wounds that wouldn't stop festering. Every knife those depraved doctors had put to her skin, *my Aaliyah's skin,* every broken bone, and every scream ...

I could save her this time. I *would* save her. After years of being absolutely fucking useless, I could finally be her *Prince.* I could earn that name *and* keep my brothers from falling to the hands of a madman at the same time.

There wasn't any other outcome I'd accept.

I half stumbled onto our property through a ward that felt like home. Osiris's magic, something I only vaguely remembered, welcomed me as if it were him lending me a guiding hand. That gave me hope enough to hurry my steps. The thick foliage was grayed from the winter weather, the chill in the air a refreshing change in pace that felt entirely foreign, even as my feet guided me forward with ingrained certainty. It was strange being back in the flesh. The memories I had of this place were minimal, but they were there. A constant whisper in the back of my mind, telling me that *this* was home.

Home was a moss yard and delicately trimmed bushes, with a forest that scented like mountain air hinted with the freshness of the close sea. *Home* was lavender eyes that made my heart thunder in my chest like it had never stopped, and that was enough to ease every hardship the last couple of weeks had thrown at me.

"Et in domum suam in solem." The words slipped quietly past my lips as I walked up the familiar black steps to the front door.

Before I ran *directly* into it.

I grunted as my nose hit first, a pained ache to add to the humiliation. I hadn't even reached for the handle, like I was just expecting to walk right through. *Bastard.* I brushed it off as Mags chortled behind me.

"Haha, very funny," I said, rubbing the abused bridge, one that felt crooked *before* I'd taken the unexpected hit. "Let's just pretend you didn't see anything."

There was a silence that was borderline deafening, only broken by the sounds of creaking floorboards as Mags came to my side. "Didn't see it, just *listened*. Maybe you should do it again. Mags *swears* they won't miss it this time."

My mouth dropped open, shocked at the mirth that still lingered in their weathered eyes. They crinkled at the corners, crow's feet almost making them seem *slightly* younger than dirt.

"Oh, they have jokes! Remind me why you decided to come again? Weren't you busy, I don't know, cursing some poor farm boy, or pretending to turn passersby into sheep?" I asked, crossing my arms, watching as Mags rolled their eyes.

They were dressed in drab robes, gray abominations that stretched over the porch, trailing behind us on the stairs. Their hair, still scraggly white, peeked out from under their hood as they pushed it back. Dust plumed around them as they shook their head. Or rather, *sand*.

"Mags is exactly where Mags *needs* to be," they said, staring at the door with a vacant, bored look. "Or did you forget your promise already?"

Consequences.

Mags hadn't helped willingly, not really, though I doubted anything they did was by their own will. I needed them to get me to the States. They needed me to stay in Rome. I wouldn't budge, so I did the only thing I could. I made a deal, a *promise*. One I was conveniently trying to forget.

Mags was owed *one* favor at a time *they* felt was right to ask, and I'd be their dog to do whatever it was they wanted.

Bound in blood, literally tied to my shambles of a soul. *Dammit.*

"No, got it locked away, right here. Ready for a rainy day," I grumbled, tapping my head before brushing them off, turning my attention to the door again.

Something nagged at the back of my mind, a warrior's intuition that told me something was wrong. Osiris should have known I was here long before his wards let me in, but on the off chance he was out, Eirik would have been able to scent me the moment I'd hit the steps. He would have greeted me at the door and pulled me into one of his godforsaken bear hugs I knew damned well I missed.

Someone should have realized I was here by now. At the very least, they should have heard me crash quite literally into our home.

But they weren't here, and as I sucked in a hard breath, searching for a scent that my mind would recognize, I realized they hadn't been for a while. Through the quiet, I could hear a heartbeat. *One.* Dread quickly replaced my hope. *Fuck this.*

"Knock, knock, assholes. Daddy's home." I walked in, turning the fucking handle this time and burying my fear as I swung the door open.

Whatever follow-up retort I'd planned died the moment I saw the chaos of the living room. It was in shambles, a struggle clear from the damage: from a ridiculously obnoxious red couch that had been ripped up and knocked on its side to the muddied prints on the floor that burrowed deep, like needles in my eyes.

"The Butcher beat us here," Mags mumbled, skimming their hand along the dried tracks.

I didn't give them my attention as I moved to the staircase, hand trailing a splash of intricate stonework among the gray, *begging* that they'd leave things be and not try to sacrifice a goat or anything while I wasn't there to watch them.

I took the stairs two at a time, hyperfocused on the heartbeat that led me to an open mosaic door that had a full-body shiver racking through me. Just past it was something I couldn't quite place but knew was important. I *flitted* in, the state of the room barely registering as I saw the first hint of a slick tailcoat on a still body. Somewhere in my head, the thick gold embroidery around the edges rang like a bell. It was devious and almost ridiculously gaudy.

Osiris.

I was by his side in a breath, my hand going immediately to his twisted neck. My blood went cold, and all I could do was stare as my lungs constricted in my chest, my vision growing narrow as I ran shaking hands through my hair. Everything in me had warned me this might happen, even Mags's incoherent rambling.

Not all paths lead to redemption.

I refused to believe it, even as all signs pointed toward one thing: Sebek had been here. I could smell him in the air, ancient, sour, and fucking disgusting, something I hadn't been looking for before.

Even the faintest traces of lavender were hours old, *too* old.

Where in the hell was Aaliyah?

I shook Osiris's still body, desperation clinging to me as I fought off the will to scream.

"Wake the fuck up, Osiris." I rotated his head, setting his neck so it could heal. I might have been a touch too rough, wincing as I heard his spine shuffle and pop. But luckily, after an eternity, his eyes opened. "You managed to choose the worst possible time to nap."

There was confusion in his mismatched blues, a twinge of wonder hiding there. The guilt came after, and his head fell back against the floor with a thud as he closed his eyes again. He seemed to have aged from how I remembered him. His skin was dulled, his eyes lacking the fire I recalled so vividly from the night I'd been turned.

His hands went to his face before dragging through his disheveled black hair, disrupting the perfect waves. "I don't have time for night-mares of you today, *frater*."

I could feel his pain, and for a second, I lost the vindictive force that had slowly overcome me. This was my brother, the man I seemed to know better than myself, even with the few memories I had of him. The man who'd left me to *die*, and who I could tell with barely a look, was still haunted by that. I remembered the fight, and the screamed words that led in to the last day I'd seen him before the pyre took me. He'd used my own failings against me that day, so I'd do his bidding, played me like he'd done to kings and peasants. It soured the warmth I held for him.

I wanted the good memories, the ones I felt in my chest that brought prideful joy I knew were buried there, but right now, all I felt was that betrayal. It would be something to fix after we figured out whatever this mess was.

A sickening feeling told me I already knew what was coming.

"Not a nightmare this time, brother," I said. Osiris flinched, his head tilting to look at me again and eyes shooting back open as his jaw dropped. I didn't give him the chance to speak. "While I realize it's been a while since you've had the pleasure of seeing my beauty in the flesh, you need to get yourself together."

Still, Osiris sat silent and stared at me with a slack-jawed expression that showed no sign of moving. It would have been hilarious under any other circumstance.

"Admire. Later." I snapped my fingers over his face before tapping his chin. That seemed to get him, his mouth cracking shut.

He finally focused, narrowing his eyes and scowling at me. When he reached up, brushing a shaking, ungloved hand across my cheek—something that threw me off in a way I couldn't place—that scrutiny exploded into surprise. The hesitancy to his touch faded away, his free hand coming up to match its twin on the other side of my face. "Nero?"

"No, I'm his evil twin, Herbert." I scoffed, sitting back on my heels and crossing my arms over my chest. "Who the fuck else would I be, Osiris?"

I gestured to my body, waving my hands in a circular motion.
"But—"

"But you're *dead*!" I gasped, putting on a show like I was *very* surprised by that fact, even clutching my cheeks at the shock before I rolled my eyes. "Been there, heard that. We have something far more important to deal with than my resurrection."

Osiris's eyes landed on my lips, taking in the smirk I couldn't seem to get rid of, even now. Years of trust, life, and bonds passed between us, and even with the warring anger in my head, I calmed.

At least, until pressure built in my skull. It started low and heavy, as though someone had placed a weight on my neck at the start of my spine. Like a fire had been lit under my ass, I jumped to my feet. "Oh, now is *not* the fucking time."

Osiris was quick to follow me, stabilizing me as nausea took over my thoughts. My teeth gritted, blood sliding down my nose, into my mouth as I coughed.

"What's wrong?" Osiris asked, grunting as he moved to take more of my weight. His arms shook, and I knew it wasn't from the strain.

"Fucking *Rends*." I bit hard, grinding my teeth as I gripped Osiris's shoulder. "Listen. I'm about to drop like a sack of extremely pissed off potatoes. Treat me just like you would have treated Aaliyah. I'm *not* actually dead, all right?"

My words were clipped, boiling down to a groan as tension grabbed at my soul. They never got any easier, even after Mags gave me their *vile* miracle cure that had dragged the *Rends* to a drizzle. It had slowed them, the endless memories that made up my life, but nothing would stop them.

Not until I remembered.

I shuddered as the pressure hit again, more insistent this time. The weight was gone, replaced by a red-hot iron that jabbed into my temple, and I stumbled as vertigo slammed into me.

"How do you know about Aaliyah?" His question echoed in my mind, bouncing off the walls of my skull.

Aaliyah.

Like always, it was thoughts of her that got me through the worst of it, the pain fading as I chuckled, shaking my head at the twist of fate that had led us here. *My* Aaliyah, the one I'd follow into the depths of hell, was the same one that had mended the bonds of the family I'd left behind. Somehow, she'd found her way to us all.

Ours, then, but I'd be damned if she wasn't mine first.

"Because, brother." I held on to the last strings of my consciousness as I flashed him a smile, dragging my tongue across my bloodied lips, my fangs extended and on display. "You weren't the first Vivas to meet her."

My eyes rolled back, and I was stuck in my personal definition of hell: watching my body fall, as I could do nothing to stop it.

Chapter 3

Osiris

I didn't dare to breathe as the figure in front of me grew clammy, and sun-kissed olive skin paled. Mischievous silver eyes that no longer felt familiar dulled, and *Nero's* body swayed, before falling limp. I barely caught him before he could hit the ground.

I blinked, expecting the apparition to disappear like he always did when he came to me in my memories, but he didn't fade, didn't slip away. I *had* to be dreaming, or maybe I'd died myself. How else was this possible?

I homed in on the steely Roman fire that clung to his scent and highlighted the amber in his brown hair. The same fire that had stuck to his words like a brand, a distinction that none could have faked.

The popping crack of shifting bones filled my ears as my spine worked to fix itself. The shards moved, splitting skin and muscle, and the pain that came with it was the only thing leaving me grasping onto the hope that this was more than a fever dream.

That *Nero* was here.

Alive.

Exactly as he'd been before he'd died. Down to the characteristic arc that framed the curve of his lips as he scowled.

His words trickled into my mind until one stuck. A *Rend*.

He had no heartbeat, just like Aaliyah had explained before. The lifelessness of it made me sick to my stomach, and all I could think of was him stuck to a pyre in the middle of a frigid Russian winter.

Charred. Dead.

I swallowed that pain, keeping Nero standing as I waited for it to end. Several minutes passed, long enough that I had to question if he'd died *again,* before he sucked in a gasping breath.

"God, that's so much worse than she'd made it sound." He groaned, spitting a mouthful of blood onto the ground, and dragging himself away from me as he stood on shaky legs. "I will say, of all the things to remember, why did it have to be *streaking*?"

"How—" I started, my mind racing through my own memories to try to catch up.

Nero waved me off with a bat of his hand, his eyes searching the room once again.

"Where is she?" he asked, his tone as unyielding as the steel he used to wield. His face hardened, and his years as a gladiator shone in his eyes as he rocked his head from side to side, popping his neck with a grunt.

I didn't recognize his question until he was snapping his fingers in my face.

"We don't have time for this, Osiris," he pushed. I could only shake my head, another pinch at the back of my neck as more shards of bone shifted into place. My hands went numb, my chest constricting like a noose had just been placed around my neck when he snarled, "Where. Is. *Aaliyah?*"

Muddled memories kept the answer from me. I took in the room's chaos, the strewn hints of volatile magic and the scent of ancient decay. The pool table was in pieces, and chunks of the wall were strewn across the floor. The reason why came with sudden clarity.

Sebek had arrived unannounced. He'd been in a *rage,* one like I hadn't seen in centuries, mumbling something about the crypt in Rome.

"She was here. I was with her by the piano when I felt the wards force open and let him in. Sebek snapped my neck before I could react." Fear laced my throat, strangling me as Nero's face crumpled, eyes wide with terror.

I sucked in a hard breath, not realizing I hadn't been breathing, but now I had a reason. I searched the room for traces of her blood, any hints that he'd done what rattled my nightmares, but there was only stale air and the lingering scent of her fear ... had he *taken* her? If he'd seen her as a weakness, he would have killed her, so what made him do this? Some understanding that she was of his blood?

"No." Panic welled in Nero's voice, choking his words and cracking his façade open. "No, no, *no*."

His eyes searched frantically around the room again. As though disbelieving.

"Tell me you're lying, Osiris. Tell me Sebek didn't see her." He took a step forward, erasing the space that had been between us, his eyes alight with fear and ire. The hairs on the back of my neck stood. "Please, Osiris, he didn't see her, right? He didn't take her?"

I couldn't answer. She wasn't here, and the only option that made sense was that. My silence was enough, like the deafening call of failure. I couldn't defend my weakness, my inability to combat our Maker.

Sebek had Aaliyah, my light.

Tears bubbled to the surface of Nero's eyes, the desolation in them matching my own. He ripped his hands through his hair, and when he opened his mouth, I nearly dropped to my knees.

Nero's scream made my insides seize, as fight or flight suddenly stole my limbs. Magic churned deep in my stomach, mixing with the acid that swirled there. It was the same sound he'd made as he was burned alive, and we were left unable to do anything as the sun consumed the ground and our brother. That same desperation, the same *fear*.

He flipped the couch, the one he'd picked all those years ago, and I watched it crash into the wall, shattering, adding to the destruction of the room.

"Nero—" I was cut off by a hand around my neck. Nero, with a strength that outmatched my own in a way that shouldn't have been possible, lifted me off my feet and slammed me against the nearest wall.

The snapping of my ribs ripped a grunt from my lips. My body reacted on instinct, a *Charm* wrapping around my vocal cords. The need to throw him off me was only outweighed by the understanding that I deserved every bit of his anger.

I let my arms drop to my sides, nails digging into exposed palms. I hoped he could see my worry and my shame ... my *joy* at the fact that he was here.

That I'd take anything he deemed fit to give.

"No. You don't get to speak." His lips were pulled taut against bloodied teeth, his snarl absolute. The *Flame* burst along my skin, reacting to his touch, sparking along his exposed arms. He didn't even flinch. "I can forgive what happened to me." I didn't fight his hand as it squeezed, cutting off the air I didn't need, leaving bruises. "But you did *not* let Sebek take her."

"I didn't let him." The words came out past a choked breath. "I *never* would have let him. I'm sorry, *frater*."

Rage morphed in his eyes, breaking down, until all that was left was simmering regret. The tears that had been there fell, and his hand tightened one last time before he dropped me.

The ground felt colder now, the silence in the air weighing down on me.

"How are you—" I paused, a sudden burn aching in my chest. The words were hollow, broken. "How are you alive?"

Nero kept his eyes on the ground, like he might fall into it himself.

"She brought me back." There was a laugh on Nero's lips, the sound hoarse. His hands ran across his face, fingers leaving red trails. "She gave me a gift I could never even dream of paying back ... just for me to fucking *fail* her again."

One by one, his words gave clarity.

His eyes held a love that I'd never seen there before. Nero had known many things when he was alive: rage, pride, *lust*. But this was something else entirely, something that had swallowed him so completely that he'd found a way past death.

You weren't the first Vivas to meet her. That was what he'd said ... before he'd *Rended*.

He would do anything for Aaliyah, and the reason he would had unjust jealousy burning in my veins. She was ours, *mine*.

Because she couldn't have him.

"You're Prince," I said, keeping my tone even, hiding the distraught feelings behind a wall of numb. How had we not seen it? Her steadfast protector. The man who'd gotten her through Ascension Rising.

"The one and only," he said, chuckling dryly. The way Aaliyah had described him, from the charm of his smirk to his sheer devotion to her, made sense now. All of her descriptions of him rang true. It had *always* been him. "Back in the flesh ... mostly."

"Your memories?" I asked, a part of me breaking when he looked away.

"Nonexistent. I know pretty much fuck all about everything except for *her*. The only reason I'm here now is because I happened to get lucky with my last one ... and remembered you."

It was as if someone had ripped my heart directly out of my chest, the understanding that he was *here* ... but not at the same time. It felt like a cruel joke. I swiped at the blood that had slid from my ear, a remnant of the trauma Sebek had inflicted.

"Look, none of that matters right now. We need to get Aaliyah from Sebek before—" Nero seemed to rethink his words, shuttering as though *haunted* by them. "Osiris, there's something you need to know."

He looked sick, like the mere thought of our maker made him ill. A sentiment I shared. "Sebek is Amoun."

The way he said it confused me, the rattling rage in his voice misplaced. Of course, he was Amoun. It was his given name, one that Nero knew, though there was a chance he didn't remember that.

"Yes, he always has been." I held my pain closer when he sneered, forcing my shoulders back.

"No. Osiris. Sebek is *Amoun*," Nero said with a shake of his head. His pause made my heart jump in my chest, the declaration pained. "And Amoun is the leader of Ascension Rising."

My blood turned to ice in my veins, freezing me solid as I choked on my breath. The surety in his eyes told me he wasn't lying. The fear for Aaliyah, the instant rage at knowing Sebek had seen her, been *here*.

He hadn't just taken her away. He was her uncle, and the master of her worst nightmares. I tried to think the same, to put myself in her shoes, but the idea of ending up back in Darius's hands was too much. Too cruel. It wasn't something I'd wish on even the worst of my enemies, to be forced back into the hands of the people that broke them.

I'd let it happen to her, let him take her. I failed again.

Again and again and *again*.

"No." I shook my head, unable to believe it, even when seeing the truth in Nero's eyes. Sebek couldn't be the leader of Ascension. He'd held Arvand with a sickeningly high regard. Pity overtook Nero's expression when I spoke again. "No. This can't be. He wouldn't have done this. Arvand wouldn't have let him."

"Osiris, he killed Iris and Arvand." Nero completed my thought, even when I tried to reject it. "He *did*, and now he has Aaliyah all over again."

He'd been with her for years ... seen *everything*. "I couldn't stop him before. You didn't see it. You barely had to hear about it. But I'm not dead anymore, and I plan to make Sebek *intimately* aware of that fact."

Nero's hand ran across his face, and once again, the look of a warrior took over. His eyes, filled with a rage that was seemingly unending, met mine.

It was still lost to me, that I was looking at the man that I'd begged the gods to give back to us. He was Nero, to the bone, yet there was something else in his eyes now, a wariness that had never taken root before. A fear that had never held a place amongst the silver.

"Now, we need a plan. Any bright ideas?" he asked, crossing his arms over his chest. "This is probably going to get ugly fast."

Not Osiris, but brother. It was more than I deserved, and it was wrong of me to bask in the forgiveness I didn't earn.

"I would do anything for her," I answered without hesitation.

Anything meant *anything*. I'd been nothing but a burden to her, to this family for the last hundred years, but this was my last straw. I would save Aaliyah.

Or I would die trying.

Chapter 4

Eirik

Blood filled my mouth, my own and that of the guard that bounced off the marble floor, thrown away as the light faded from his eyes. The taste of honey tinted ash lingered, reminding me too much of the Mer that I'd eaten at Valen's. Saliva followed the sickness in my stomach, my eyes blurring as my body tried and failed to absorb the foreign blood.

It didn't matter, not now. The pain was irrelevant, the splintering of my skin nothing more than a push forward. My wrist pulsed, driving my urgency and erasing any rational thought, leaving me with just one goal. *Get* to Aaliyah.

Archon's home became a war zone, my senses honing as the skin of my face pulled taut. My wolf watched on with gleeful ferocity, his hackles raised as I bared my teeth at those left, the soon-to-be-dead men that still circled me with their weapons raised.

As if they thought to threaten *me* with them.

I was moving before any of them could rise to strike me down, my teeth in another throat, a growl buried by the gurgle of blood under my fangs. My wolf howled, screaming our victory with my own as I released the body and charged at the next.

Each one gave way to another, an endless stream that Archon had no issues with sacrificing to me, as he hid behind them. Whatever magic he'd spelled his home with kept my wolf locked away, and I felt that fact with every inch I conceded to his mob of toy soldiers.

The room seemed to close in, the aged marble of the floor warping as my vision went fully red and my shoulders cracked in preparation for a shift that would never come. I was cornered, my lips pulled back, exposing teeth, gaze snapping to the door when Archon clicked his tongue.

"Leaving so soon? Without your brothers?" Malice distorted his words. The smug resonance behind them was infuriating ... and distracting enough for a guard to sneak past my defenses. His blade struck my side, digging through muscle and hitting my ribs.

I barely noticed, too horrified by the sight of watching my *brothers* fall, overwhelmed by the guards that descended on them.

Pain coiled behind their eyes, rolling them back as they clutched desperately at the lavender marks on their wrists. My own seared a hole straight into the core of my beast, the monster going feral beneath my skin.

A tortured groan spilled out of Fallon, matching the writhing cry from Adrian. My beast's attention split between them.

Pack.

Another man came running in loud metal armor that clattered and creaked as he drew a sword high. There was a fear in him that he couldn't hide, the scent like a drug.

He died at my feet.

The burn, the *ache*. My wrist felt like someone had taken a hot iron to it, and that pain sank into my nerves. I couldn't take it any longer. My wolf tipped his head back, his howl deafening my ears as my soul revolted inside my body.

Mate.

"***Move***," I snarled.

The part of my mind that knew to step back had faded away, trapped behind the push of a wolf looking to hunt, behind the drums of war that pounded in my ears like Archon's stuttering heartbeat.

My rational side would have urged me to consider my options carefully, would have lit the *Flame* and roasted the remaining guards alive, but this wasn't me, not anymore. Right now, only the beast remained.

Only the beast mattered.

I rushed Archon, not even getting close before I was snagged to a stop. I fought every second that led to my knee on the ground, collapsing under the weight of gold as Archon's magic tipped the balance in the air. The rush of Archon's men surrounding me fell into the background as my wolf's cries grew so loud they were all I could hear. A shock hit my side like a cattle prod, sending me the rest of the way down.

Then the tap of heeled boots across an aging floor, slow and meticulous.

The mark on my wrist shuddered, ripped away as I let out a scream before it slowly faded back in.

Archon hummed, crouching down. I knew the eyes of a coward, the eyes of a man that held nothing but slime beneath his skin, and Archon wore them both well.

"Such a proud *Úlfhéðinn*, with the strength of a monster and the loyalty of a *dog*," he said as my drive for blood spiraled.

I wasn't able to form words, to rip him apart with my hands or with the thoughts that tore through my mind, only a snarl finding a voice. My skin stretched painfully. Adrian's cry echoed, followed by the wet squelch of a blade slicing through skin.

"Take them below." Archon stood, looking at Adrian and Fallon, and I watched in horror as their slumped bodies were dragged away. Blood trailed under Adrian, his eyes closed. Fallon still fought; his cries were the last I heard before they faded entirely. My wolf's rage turned to a sharp whine, the agony in my *smár Valkyrja*'s bond akin to a severing of my heart from my chest. I had no fight to push against it when Archon brushed me off with a flick of his hand, that gold in his eyes seeming to glow. "Take *him* to the waiting suite. I have someone who wants to say hello."

Then he was walking away, his steps as hollow as the beat of his heart. The guards dragged me to my feet, and I was powerless to fight against it. What little strength I had ended with a few more dying, my claws ripping them to shreds, just to be replaced by more.

The halls passed by, seemingly fucking endless, and by the time I was forced into a room, lit by candle fire and smelling like smoke and burned cedar, I was barely conscious.

Another cry echoed from my chest, and I wasn't even sure if it was the wolf or me that let it go. What an unholy fuck-up ... tonight put every single mistake I'd ever made to shame.

It was my job to protect them. Adrian, Fallon, and *Aaliyah*. It was built into my genetic code somewhere, right alongside the bonds that flared in my chest and the one that sat aching on my arm. They were my pack, my family, and I'd failed at the one thing I'd always sworn to do.

I couldn't protect them like this.

Dust sat on every surface, the reds and flashing golds sticking out as I was chained and collared, metal shackles at my wrist strung to the ceiling as I thrashed.

The magic of Archon's home was stronger than I'd ever given him credit for, built into the chains, and short of chewing off my own arm, I wouldn't be getting out of them. Even if I was at full strength, I doubted my ability. My wolf slammed against my mind, rattling my teeth, a partial shift making me scream as we fought the spell.

My senses sharpened, my vision homing in on the flicker of the flames burning from the table.

The first crack of the whip was barely a thought, the slash of it as muted as the sound of a door opening before clicking closed. It tore through my shirt, dragging me back to the last time I'd been strung up, the vicious memories I'd shoved down now rearing forward. The next strike made me snarl, arching as I looked over my shoulder at the boy doling out the blows. He was young, a Lycan like me, with a collar around his neck that made my wolf pace. His face was shining with sweat, his sunken pale-blue eyes wide as he swallowed.

The deliberate use of a Lycan tipped me off to who Archon sent my way. The scents in the room filled with iron, then to honey as the cedar turned to oak. Familiar and fucking *revolting*. I looked forward again.

The last time I'd smelled it was the day I'd died, a rusted saw accompanying the distinct scent as I'd slumped to the ground like garbage to be thrown out. Which was why I wasn't surprised when Brazen walked in front of me, stopping with his hands behind his back as the slash of the whip echoed in the air again. His face and body were lithe, a telltale sign of a man who'd never seen a hard day's work. And he hadn't, not once in his long life had he had anything that wasn't given to him on a silver platter, me included. His Tiger rolled behind his eyes, the feline grace was wasted on a snake, the raging of a beast feigning power ... even now shying away as my wolf bared his teeth.

I watched as his fury rose when I didn't cower, and just like every time, Brazen's jaw clenched when our beasts went head-to-head.

Mine had always won, and I'd been on the wrong side of his whip more times than I could count because of it. It was worth every beating to see the fire toil in his eyes, the rage he couldn't help but flash with a crack of his palm.

"Mutt," the voice of my old master called, that condescending power to it enough to make me see red. Even through the magic, my fangs fell. "After Sebek took you, I figured that'd be it. I'd lost my favorite mule."

My eyes flashed, my skin straining in an instant. For a second, not even the magic held as I jerked forward. The ceiling cracked, and my voice barely came out past the growl as it shook the floor, and when it did, it wasn't mine. "**We are *not* yours.**"

My wolf's hatred for him was nearly as strong as mine, his fury settling in my stomach as he paced behind my eyes. The intense, predatory hunger that overwhelmed me promised carnage.

"I'm not crazy enough to think I could own a Turned of the *coveted* Sebek Ra," Brazen said, chuckling.

My wrist burned, my chest aching as the bonds in it quivered. I strained against the chains binding me again, snarling when they didn't give. He wasn't worth the response, so I kept my head down, rolling my neck as the wounds on my back closed. I felt them stitch shut, grunting when a dull ache was left behind.

"But this I do enjoy," he said, not hesitating to lean in close, growing some spine, and I had to fight my instinct to flinch. His hand came to my neck, hovering over the scar that stretched across it. I ripped my head back when he touched the gnarled skin, snarling low. I should have known better than to take my eyes off him as his hand wrapped around my wolf emblem necklace.

The one Nero had given me, which I'd held on to like a lifeline, a final reminder of my brother. The metal bent under the force of his hand. I struggled, furious under the weight of my weakness.

My growl stuttered as he ripped it off my neck.

"I hope you don't mind. I want a souvenir to remember this

moment," he said, tucking it into his coat pocket as I thrashed against the chains again. The door opened, and another scent filled the air. Something freshly cooked and spice heavy, obnoxiously intricate. "Seems my dinner is here."

I couldn't form words as my wolf howled and screamed. Brazen sat as a dish was served in front of him, the clattering of silverware following the sound of him humming contently.

Torture was useless, especially now that I had a couple of centuries to live through, and Brazen knew that. The one thing he'd never broken was my pride, even at my lowest. This was his way to combat that.

It made me feel like a beast to be poked and prodded while he watched. He liked to see me beaten, liked the humiliation he knew it brought.

I steeled my mind, closing my thoughts and letting myself drift into my own head. I'd dealt with pain, with torture. It was only a matter of time before I got out, then I would destroy this place for thinking it could hold a Vivas.

Then I'd save Adrian and Fallon, like I was meant to. This was nothing new. Nothing I couldn't handle. I closed my mind to the world and focused on the only thing I could.

Aaliyah, my Valkyrie. I held onto her; the lingering remains of lavender that now sat muddled by the scent of blood. I let the fires of her mark burn me to ashes and I embraced that pain, refusing to give up even that. It was *mine.*

My fear for her blended with the keening cry of my wolf, a fear I had to beat down with vicious intent. Whatever was wrong, Osiris would handle it, and it was on me to get us through this. Protect my brothers and get *out.* So we could get back to her.

"Gadlen, if you would?" Brazen asked, his mouth full as he took a sip of what smelled like red wine.

I shivered, closing my eyes, blocking it all out. Locked away where it couldn't be a problem ... before the whipping began again.

Chapter 5

Aaliyah

The last time I woke, consciousness came slowly, dragging like a weight through tar. It had been muddled and broken, the only bit that I could truly cling to being that moment in the Void, and the strange man that haunted it. Part of me wondered if everything else hadn't all been some sick dream.

This time, my eyes shot open, my mouth again on Sebek's wrist as he snarled from where he had me pinned to the ground. All I could smell, all I could *taste* was iron and soot, the ash from his blood growing even as he pulled back, and I choked the rest down.

On instinct, I jerked away, my head bouncing against the frosted, snow-laden earth. I bared my teeth, still tasting metal as I lashed out like a frightened animal and tried to come to *any* thoughts rationally.

But Sebek didn't flinch, his eyes hollow voids as he dragged me up to my feet.

I forced myself to watch him, always keeping the threat in sight even as my brain tried to get me to look away. He held me steady, his hand on the collar of my shirt, close enough to touch my skin. Still, I watched him, one breath, another, as if time had dragged to a trickle ... before stopping entirely.

His face blurred, and the sight of what was behind him was enough to force me to pause. I couldn't speak as he turned, pulling me with him. I covered my mouth, choking on a scream as my mantra fought to keep me silent.

Never make noise.

He began speaking, the words nothing more than gibberish, a mess that my brain had no chance of following as my vision tunneled, and I found myself gasping for breath.

My eyes traced the desolate parking lot, and the dirtied white exterior of a building that looked long since abandoned. I'd only seen the outside a handful of times, my memories fueling every bit of the desperation that sank into my chest, weighing heavily on my heart.

I stopped breathing entirely as my adrenaline spiked, sending me into a tailspin, and just like before, a cold arm stopped me from running, forcing me to face my demons even as they taunted and *screamed*. Any hope I'd had that somewhere deep inside of Sebek was the man my father used to talk so highly about vanished ...

They get more violent when I make noise.

Sebek hadn't just taken me from the Vivas's house. He'd brought me back to *Ascension Rising*.

"No," I whispered, but Sebek was so lost in his own world he didn't hear me. He mumbled something again as he tugged me forward.

My scream caught in my throat, and I found myself staring at the ground so I wouldn't have to see it.

I couldn't ... I *couldn't*—

"Not here," I gasped, and Sebek's attention snapped to me. I knew I should say something, should *do* something. I reached for that well of darkness in me, searched for the Void, but the sheer sight of Ascension had stolen even that. Tears burst into my view, and I choked on a sob. "Please, not here. *Not here!*"

I didn't allow myself to take another step as I fought against his hold. When I wouldn't move, he pulled me across the road, leaving me to stumble over my feet or fall, and something told me either way he wouldn't stop.

Why here? Did he ... did he plan to continue the experiments?

I nearly blacked out, my eyes rolling back, suddenly seeing white as the fight fled with the rest of my sanity. When he tugged again, everything fell out from under me, my legs caving. This *wasn't* happening.

I'd escaped once and had to die to do it.

I'd die *again* before I let him cut me open. Before I heard the perverse sound of Castillion's laugh, or the click of Nox's pen. Before I had to stare into the nothingness of the overhead lights, and question if this life was even worth it.

I would die before I had to face this alone, without even Prince by my side.

He snarled, bending to pick me up, and I *lost* it. The scream started low in my chest before echoing like a banshee around us. I screamed like he was dragging me to the doors of hell themselves, pulling and yanking with no real plan ... beyond staying the fuck away. I ripped so hard against his grip I felt my wrist pop, then my elbow, pain lacing up my entire arm. It was trivial, an ache that hid behind the rush of adrenaline through my veins. I tried to guess what he'd do, prepare for a strike as he turned entirely toward me.

I braced on instinct, flinching so hard it rattled my teeth, but he didn't swing at me with his free hand, something I knew would at the very least knock me unconscious. Instead, his eyes went wide as he let go of my wrist. His hands, cold and still covered in blood, cupped my cheeks harshly. There was a frantic gleam in his eyes I couldn't place that paired with the manic way he inspected me and the mumbled words I couldn't make out.

But that look on his face didn't leave my mind, the *worried* one he made while rubbing my throbbing wrist.

He used to hate it when I screamed.

He held some affection for me, some kind of instinct to not hurt me, at least not himself. That had to count for something.

"Please, let me go," I asked, voice hoarse as I tried to keep the shake from it. "You don't want to do this."

There was a long pause as he flipped my hand over, pressing his thumb into my palm.

"I'm not done with you yet, Glass. You're *mine*," he whispered, the contrast giving me whiplash as his grip hardened before he dropped me entirely. The shift on his face destroyed me, that deranged calculation in his eyes as he brushed his hand through his hair, spreading blood along his pale forehead. "I allowed that troublesome Turned of mine to live."

It was the first time he'd said something that hadn't been *completely* unhinged, and I lifted my aching hand to my chest as he tilted his head to the side. Goosebumps rose on my arms, and I struggled to breathe. I looked behind him at the door that sat at the top of the concrete steps.

"If you continue to defy me, know that I can go back on that."

A warning, one that was left to ring in my ears as he went deathly silent. He'd let Osiris live ... but going back *wasn't* something he'd be willing to do, not right now.

I'd thrown a wrench into his plans. His words from before suddenly rang, the last moment before he'd dragged me out of my home.

You aren't supposed to be here.

The subtle weight of the charm around my neck soothed me, and I reached up, grabbing the small lavender gem that hung there. It was a promise, a piece of protection from Osiris that I held close to me, always.

A piece of his power.

While Osiris couldn't fight Sebek, he would obliterate *anyone* Sebek sent to him. Osiris was strong, and I was facing the one of the only men alive that could fight him, I was sure of it.

I gritted my teeth, baring them at Sebek as if I were nothing but a feral animal. I channeled Eirik, a growl in my chest. "I'm not scared of you."

It was silent for several long seconds, and I was left taut on the ground, waiting for his words. It was strange to see the way his face softened like the man I *knew* he wasn't ... but I saw in him, anyway. I saw my father's tilted grin, and my blood ran cold as he kneeled in front of me.

My dear ab. My dad's words, the ones my mind swore to me I was about to hear.

"So, I won't go back for *Usire*, clever." Was what reached me instead as he leaned closer, the smell of him acidic. There were traces of blood still lingering in the air between us. "You care for him."

I didn't answer, because it wasn't a question.

"And you care for the others," he whispered, another statement.

The marks on my wrist, the ones that tied me to the Vivas Crypt, itched as his attention landed on them. Dark ink against alabaster skin that stung as his eyes lingered. I wanted to hide them, shield them from his sick appraisal.

The others hadn't been there when he'd shown up, but they had to be home by now. He'd missed them, and they weren't people he could threaten either.

"Do you know where they are?" he asked with a sardonic sneer. "You *assume* home, picking up my insolent Turned. Mourning the loss of you, if he even realizes who took you. Plotting a plan to get you back?"

They *had* to be home.

That shallow look of rage in his eyes deepened before vanishing completely. The cold sank in, and I shivered both from that look and the chill that suddenly wrecked me.

"What are you getting at?" I snapped, overwhelmed by his barrage.

The woods had grown quiet, deathly so. The dark of the early night bled into the forest, hitting the ground and building in front of me in a mirage of inky shadows, but the cold wasn't from that, the brushing press of it more intentional. Like a comforting hand. The telltale hint of a spirit calmed me, and when the familiarity of that touch came, I relaxed even further into it.

Red.

I sagged with relief, taking in the comfort of his presence greedily. He didn't have a physical form; he never had. He was like little more than dust in the wind, a feeling you couldn't shake but knew was there all the same. The ghost that had clung to the armory, that had been my saving grace after losing Prince. He must have followed when Sebek had taken me. I stopped the urge to reach for the cloth that was still tucked away in my pocket, the little red strip he was attached to. He'd come for me and knowing that I wasn't alone helped me sit a little higher.

"Do you think they enjoyed their stroll to Archon's?" Sebek asked, standing again.

My hope crumbled one unsteady breath at a time. Red flashed, the hint of a soft emotion in the air that was meant to help me but only had me sinking back more. Sebek knew. He *knew* where they'd been going.

"I told him to summon them. *All* of them. Usire was supposed to be there as well. So, he might rid me of them before the Eternium—"

"They wouldn't lose to someone like him!" I broke in, unable to even consider another option.

How had this all gone *so* wrong?

"Are you willing to risk it? I could tell him that this sunrise is their last." He crossed his arms over his chest, a glimmer of triumph in the way he stood. Like he'd already won. "Or you can follow me willingly. And I'll allow my meddling Turned to survive the day."

Because he *had* already won.

I'd die again before I walked into that building. Or I *would* have. Six months ago, before I'd met *them*, that had been true. If this would save them, then I would face it.

A thousand times, I would walk through the doors of this wretched building again.

For them.

"You'll tell him to let them go?" I asked, a barter I had no leverage to make. There was another reassuring brush from Red, leaving me shaking. Anxiety filled the air, tasting curdled on my tongue. I looked past Sebek, to the building of my nightmares, and tried to find some comfort in it. Tried to focus on Adrian's laugh or Eirik's soothing purr. Fallon's gentled eyes and Osiris's captivating voice as he read to me.

Prince's all-consuming smile.

"No," Sebek said, surprisingly level. I half expected him to laugh at me, to prod and jab in any way he could. Instead, he just stood there, silently watching me on the ground as my palms pressed onto the frozen earth. "But I will not kill them."

He didn't reach down to pick me up, simply waited for me to stand. To walk myself back into my living hell like he knew I would.

Because I couldn't let the others die for this. Wouldn't even risk it. Not when I could still see Osiris's crumpled form on the ground back at the house, his neck twisted so unnaturally.

So, I stood, my legs shaking as that blissful numbness that had kept the experiments from destroying me clouded my mind. I let my hands fall to my sides, categorizing the steady ache in my wrist, filing it away for when I had the energy to deal with it. Blood dripped down over my lip, egged on by the subtle push of pressure as my nose flooded.

Sebek looked pleased enough, turning and walking up the steps. He didn't even hold my wrist to stop me from running.

For them.

I had to force the first step, nearly crumpling again. My breathing became shallow as I passed through the doors. I waited for them to cave in, for the sounds of vicious laughter to follow my slow steps, but it was silent. There were no grand screams or mocking laughter, just the sound of my footsteps on the tiled floor. Part of me wondered how I was moving at all. But I didn't stop as I followed behind Sebek.

The walls were familiar, from the cracking paint to the smell of bleach, but it was the blood that I noticed first. It was old, decaying, and staining the harsh white a sickly brown. We passed the experiment room, the sight of it alone making me sick, vertigo causing me to stumble. I kept it together even as I saw the bodies strewn about the room. There were no ghosts, a fact I took some comfort in as I began to sweat.

It was like it wasn't really happening, each step a hollow torment. I spent the walk staring at the back of Sebek's black suit, pretending he wasn't this monster, until we came upon a door. The glass that met me was the same I'd stared out of for years. Behind it—the threadbare mattress and the stale scent of uncirculated air.

My cell.

Never make noise.

"Please," I started, shutting down my mantra even as it sat like acid on my tongue. The plea was cowardly, but I couldn't go any farther. My knees locked, my throat swelling until I could barely breathe. "Not here."

He raised an eyebrow as he opened the door. It creaked on rusted hinges, sliding into the room as he carefully lifted his hand, brushing back my matted hair. "I don't have the time to track you down should you run."

He toyed with a strand before tipping my head toward him.

None of my father showed in his eyes, even though I kept begging to see him there. The harshness to his scowl said enough, and I hesitated again.

"Do I have to remind you why you're listening?"

I shook my head, taking the first stumbling step through the open door. I couldn't watch, nearly puking as tears came to my eyes.

So, I closed them.

I saw Osiris, his hands against the old ivories of his piano. I saw Adrian in his kitchen, wearing one of his many frilly aprons, cooking something I'd never forget. Fallon painting with that soft smile he tried to hide. Eirik, lying under the stars, using our joined hands to show me the memories of his past.

I saw Prince standing under that ray of sunshine in Eliza's shop. His tilted smile and grounding presence like a balm.

For a second, there was a brush of cold, one I knew to be Red. He helped me take that step, then another.

Until the door closed behind me.

I sank to the ground, my legs no longer strong enough to hold me. I didn't turn around, instead curling up as I tried to convince myself this was all a nightmare. If I dreamed hard enough, maybe I would wake up between the men that I was growing to love. They would hold me close and tell me everything would be okay.

Never make noise.

I curled tighter as the temperature dipped again, and the faintest brush of a hand showed in the air, making a symbol I didn't recognize. The sobs came quickly but quietly.

Even as I tried to let them out, no sound ever came.

They get more violent when they hear noise.

Chapter 6

Adrian

"Christ, does Archon not feed you here?" I wheezed as I spoke, each word making me want to curl up and die as I pulled the damp, soiled air into my lungs.

The guard doling out my current beating seemed to take offense at my joke. He was short and on the heavier side, wearing a gaudy piece of shining steel armor like he'd walked directly out of the twelfth century. That bulk was more than just for show, though. His next hit slammed into my cheekbone, my head snapping to the side as I tried and failed to avoid the blow. It hadn't worked once since I'd been strung up by my wrists, and the guards started treating me like their own personal pinata. They hadn't even had the *decency* to give me a cell with a view.

Instead, I was forced to focus on the decrepit walls that seemed to literally fall apart around us as the bricks crumbled under years of watered down days. Even the smell was distracting, like unkempt paintings and sour mold, or the rust that ate at the chains that held me. They creaked and groaned as I swayed.

It was disgusting, even by dungeons standards. Osiris would be having a fit.

I spit, grimacing as blood and the broken remains of one of my teeth clattered to the ground. I felt around with my tongue, mourning the loss of one of my molars. The bit of joy I had left stemmed from the smile I had to force, staring through one good eye as the guard snarled behind his mask, the one that made it impossible to hit him with a *Charm*. I shouldn't have goaded him, shouldn't have given him the time of day or the ammunition to try to split my skull again.

But I was nothing if not a people person.

"You hit like a bitch." Each word was a farce, one I poured my heart and soul into as the next blow struck my ribs. The snap of one of them was audible, almost as loud as the cry I hid with a deranged laugh, one meant to veil a truth I didn't want them to see.

I *hurt*.

Every part of me, every bone and muscle. Every tendon that flexed under my skin as I tried to brace for the next blow, coming from a hand laden in silver that found a convenient home in my kidney.

Every breath as blood dribbled down the side of my face, slipping past torn lips and sticking to my battered neck.

The guards didn't have any reaction beyond that first slip of a snarl. No words to distract me or secrets to horde for later. I tried to remind myself that this was temporary. I may not be Fallon, but I could handle a little *light* torture. Right?

After all, everyone in this building would be dead soon. Either I'd make it out, or Osiris would come for me, come for *us,* wherever the others were. We had to have been gone long enough for worry to start in him. Start in *Aaliyah*.

Ah, my little love. The light at the end of the tunnel that kept me going as the next hit cracked something along my sternum. Her lavender eyes, the soft way she smiled. I could almost feel her touch, mending the parts that had broken, her kiss a balm that would wipe away the hurt.

The next blow caught my eye, my distraction not giving me time to evade as his hit landed true. Red covered my vision, blood exploding around me.

Asshole.

I flexed my hands, fingers numb and wrists torn open where the metal sank in. Breathing became a struggle, and it took far too long to remember that I didn't really need to. I held my breath, head tipping back as I tried to keep the smile on.

This wasn't my game; it never had been, but I *had* to play it. For my own sanity, if nothing else.

Keep the façade, hide the weakness.

Fallon would have been laughing by now. Would have scared the guards so shitless they wouldn't have dared to even get close enough for him to *spit on them*. I could feel him even now, in my chest, along the bonds that I reached for every few minutes to make sure he and Eirik were still kicking.

Because I couldn't stand to think about how badly it hurt.

"No response? And to think, we could have had such riveting conversation," I babbled, half choking on my blood as I coughed. "As it is, this is kind of a snooze fest, don't you think? If you're going to resort to torture, the least you can do is make it less boring."

The guard in front of me tensed again as I grimaced and had to be dragged back as the scent of rotting flesh spread from him, just enough to catch. A hint of what he was, something to grab onto.

I let out a breath, tipping my head back up to look at him.

They hadn't spoken, *not one of them*, since they'd walked in those hours ago. Barely made any sound at *all*. This was a tell, if nothing else. A weakness, a *secret*, I could use.

I may not be able to go blow for blow, but I knew how to trade in secrets. I grabbed onto the scent, locking it away.

"Ah, an Undead." The way he froze kept me guessing, pushing on as the others seemed to shuffle nervously. Knowing what someone was could be deadly in the wrong hands. Naturals weren't rare per se, but with his scent and knowing what he was? I could do some real damage with that, and he knew it. "Like that of an old crypt. Not quite the sweetness of trona that a Mummy might have ... a Ghoul, maybe?"

I knew I was right when he flinched, stepping away from me. My own moniker came in handy, the fear of what the *Collector* might do enough to get them to back off as I chuckled. If I got out, I could find him. He knew that. Thank *God* he knew that. "What, cat got your tongue?"

He snarled again, the sound drowned out by the clicking of the cell door behind me just as he rushed forward, only to be held back by his fellow guards again ... before they *all* went silent.

The fear in his stance was a living thing, the way he trembled as he looked over my shoulder enough to make the hair on the back of my neck stand. Any trace of his attention on me faded, every ounce of it following the sound of boots on a sodden ground that slowly grew louder behind me.

I'd never really thought of sound as ominous before, not in a visceral way, anyway. Fear was nothing new. It followed the worry of things that lurked alone in the dark, the fear of death and of loss. I recalled the moment I was turned, and the creeping anxiety that came with being hunted.

Or the panic that came when Ali's mark had started to burn upstairs, before I'd been dragged down here, and every thought I'd had on her since. Hoping, *begging*, that she was okay. That the sinking feeling in my stomach wasn't real.

The sound of the steps was different, almost like I was a fly caught in a spider's web, and while the magic that tied into the binds at my wrist locked the *Flame* in my chest, it didn't stop me from scenting the change in the air.

Fool's gold: bitter and fake. Like a thousand lies and the products of a snake oil salesman.

"They can't respond to you, *Collector*. I made sure of that." The words were followed by the sharp press of fingers into my back, toying with battered ribs. I jolted away from the touch that sought to sink the pain deeper as he searched for the spot that made me squirm the most.

I wasn't Fallon. I *wasn't* a fighter; I never had been. I could barely deal with a burned finger because I tried to eat a cookie that was a little too fresh out of the oven. I couldn't handle pain like he could.

And that showed when I screamed.

It was the first one I'd really let out, the first one that felt real. It slipped past, and no amount of me trying to hold it in would have stopped it as Archon kept digging. When he pulled away, I sagged forward, held only by the chains.

"Well, if it isn't tall, dark, and scraggly. Can it wait for a bit? Can't you see I'm busy?" I bit out, out of breath, sweat sliding down over my face, landing in the fresh lacerations as he walked the rest of the way, until he was in front of me. He didn't have the same fear the guards did, his face a mask of smug authority that I'd grown used to seeing in men like him. He was dressed for a party, all dolled up in a fancy new suit that looked like it damned well might have been sown onto him—a golden-rimmed white atrocity with a fluffed cravat peeking out around his collar. "You look nice, *very* cleaned-up. I'll warn you now, though, Sebek is more preferential to bows. Might consider getting one in red to put on the back of your head so he has something to look at while you kiss his—"

A blow came out of nowhere, cracking into my ear hard enough to make my head spin, blood splattering over the front of that *pretty* white. I wasn't fast enough to mask the pain.

"I was going to say boots," I wheezed, my head ringing.

Archon didn't react how I was expecting, no indignation or petty pride. His eyes didn't light up with that same fearful hint I'd seen when we'd first gotten to Fellow Manor. Gone was the man who seemed to almost hunch over himself, replaced with someone who knew they'd played a rigged game.

One they'd already won.

My instincts were rarely wrong about people, and with just that one look, I *knew* I'd missed something. My mind raced back to the letter he'd sent, to the way he'd invited us into his home, seemingly with no real resistance. The timing was suspicious, so close to the Eternium ... and now paired with the *burning* in my wrist, the ache of fresh marks that still stung.

My little love's marks. The thought of something wrong with her was enough to send fresh adrenaline straight into my veins.

Archon would bend over backward to lick his own ass if it would make Sebek happy, and Sebek, if nothing else, was meticulous and obnoxiously prideful. He'd kill us himself before he let someone else do it and risk being seen as weak.

So, *why* were we still here? We'd been set up, but we'd known that coming in. I hadn't expected more than a little show, maybe a slap on the wrist, and a direct transition to Kri'Valta's Gala. Had we been too cocky to realize the ramifications of this visit because we'd always assumed we were invincible? Either behind Sebek or behind Osiris.

Which meant Sebek had given Archon the go-ahead to do with us as he pleased ...

Or Archon hadn't told him we were here.

"What? *Cat got your tongue?*" Archon goaded, returning my own words back to me, as if watching my thoughts unfold in front of him.

I wasn't a fighter.

"I can see that mind of yours turning, searching for an answer that isn't there, *begging* to be wrong about why you're still here." Archon's words broke in.

"You're really good at dancing around a point," I said, voice now hoarse and cracked. "Why don't you cut to the chase so I can get back to entertaining these lovely gents, hmm? What do you want?"

The silence was almost as harrowing as an answer as Archon watched on. Seconds went by, time passing so slowly I half wondered if I'd ended up in hell. The anticipation of another blow fucked with my head.

It never came.

"Of all the things to ask. I was expecting you to worry for your kin. I never saw you as the selfish type." I flinched when he leaned in. "You Vivas have always been obnoxiously close-knit."

My heart stalled, my breath stolen from me again as dread sank down into my stomach. Acid built up, and I nearly puked as I searched for the bonds that held me to Eirik and Fallon.

There, tense, but there. Alive at least, for now. So why did he look so smug? *What was I missing?*

"Where are my brothers?" I asked, horror siphoning my hope as Archon crossed his hands behind his back.

"All in good time," Archon said, watching me with apt interest. "I believe you asked something else first. Didn't you?"

I wheezed, looking to the ground, unable to keep my head up. His answer didn't come in the form of words, as a hand sank into my hair, forcing my head up as I yelped. The strands snapped, some pulled directly from the root as I was forced to keep my eyes on the Djinn.

"What do I want?" Archon asked, keeping his eyes, that brandished gold, on me. The way he watched, the way he smiled, like he was waiting for me to fill it in myself. "What about I tell you over a game?"

The sinister curl to his words was accented by the power that suddenly lingered in the air. The walls crackled, my chains cinching tight. I didn't have any thoughts beyond how badly it hurt to move. The piercing pain of broken bones and split skin.

"All you have to do is answer a question for me, one simple question," Archon said, raising a finger, wagging it in my face.

A game? The cruel tell in his words told me it wasn't one I'd win. Not as I was now. Not even with a *clear* mind. You didn't take bets or make deals with Djinn, because it was never something you'd come out on top of.

The next hit from the guard behind me struck somewhere in my spine, my legs going numb before a vicious fire shot down them. I choked, a beg caught behind my teeth. A plea for this to end.

I wasn't the fighter.

"But I don't think you deserve to hear it yet. After all, what fun is it if you don't have to work for your information? It wouldn't be fair to just give it to you," he mused, walking back behind me, the click of his boots against the ground no longer audible, as the guard unloaded another fierce hit. "Or you can hope and plead for Osiris to free you. But he won't come, not soon enough."

My bones shifted under my skin, healing just enough for an ache to settle in them before they broke again.

I couldn't do this.

I couldn't do this.

Osiris had to come, or Fallon and Eirik. I wasn't abandoned here. They would find me. There was no way they wouldn't.

I wasn't the fighter.

"Enjoy your time at Fellow Manor, *Collector*. Oh, the fun we'll have in the meantime."

My screams followed him out the door.

Chapter 7

Fallon

There was a fragile peace that came with the sound of crashing waves against endless beaches, one that I'd been missing since I'd turned. It made it easy to fall asleep while being just loud enough to keep me alert in the long nights, something I'd struggled with since I was a boy. It was like an itch that I hadn't realized wasn't being scratched, until I heard the push and pull of the tides again, the heat-filled breeze bringing me groggily awake.

I shook my head, dislodging whatever dream had been lurking before I opened my eyes, blinking several times as narrow rays of light shone through a straw-laden ceiling ... some touching the bare skin of my chest.

I sat up, quicker than I should have, brushing at the spot that should have been scorched, nearly hitting the wall that I was only inches from, in a daze that blurred my vision and made my head *throb*. The hut, small and ... familiar, smelled a mix of earthy wood and soft mint. There was barely anything in it, just a few small trinkets and a pile of paper bark covered with fur that I lay on. My hand shot to my wrist, the corroding ache that had been there dropping off like I'd been doused in icy water, my breathing harsh as I searched the room for Archon and his pathetic guards.

But he wasn't here.

I blinked again, trying to find hints of Fellow Manor in the small space before rubbing my eyes as my hands shook. The illusion stayed firmly in place no matter how much I scrubbed.

What the *fuck* was happening?

"Good morning, Taz," a vibrant voice called as a shadow cast over the room. The nickname hit me in the chest, shredding me open at the singsong tone that danced with a melodic accent I hadn't heard in *centuries*. I arched forward, staring at the entrance to the hut as the small hide covering over it swayed open. "You're missing the festivities. Avata had her baby last night, and everyone's been in high spirits all morning."

Endless black eyes matched the cadence of her voice, a curious spark that brought her rushing back to me almost as smoothly as the nickname she'd given me after I'd tried to shoo away a wandering Tasmanian devil that had gotten too close to our home one night, only to be bitten by it.

Aislinn was dressed in simple leather bands that covered her chest and waist—the ones she used to wear in the hot summers—with small ornate beads braided into her frizzy, full hair. I recalled her making them with my mother just after her fifteenth birthday, and I couldn't remember a time she'd been without them since. She was sweating, sepia skin flushed as she grinned down at me.

I was too lost for words to do anything but stare as Aislinn let the covering over the entrance fall closed.

"Good morning," I whispered, staring dumbly at her as she chuckled and came to my side.

Her hands were warm when she pulled me to my feet, brushing me off as bits of paper bark stuck to me. I was wearing much the same as she was, my chest bare, my waist covered in an animal hide skirt. It was shoddy, something I'd made myself with my first kill, with uneven stitching that rubbed against the side of my leg. She mumbled something under her breath as she pulled away, practically floating through the room, fiddling with one of the few things on the floor.

"Aislinn? Where ... where are we?" I asked, my head a disjointed mess.

The dread in my stomach exploded, nausea making my mouth

water as I flexed my hands, a distinct impression that I was ... *lost*, making them shake.

Aislinn, my old home.

This was a dream. That was the only explanation that made any fucking sense. But I hadn't dreamed of Aislinn in decades. At least not kind ones like this, where she was alive.

It was jarring, realizing that I'd forgotten her face and the range of expressions she made. I soaked them in as she walked in front of me, a carefree sway to her hips, before she tossed a cap on my head that spread out from all directions. It was one she'd made me wear every day after the first time I'd been sunburned when I was just a kid. It had taken me out for days, and Aislinn had sat dutifully by my side, making sure I stayed cool and hydrated.

She'd made the hat in between taking care of me and her other duties, intricately weaving together some dried grasses with a craftsmanship that still stunned me, so I'd have a little more protection outside.

I ran a hand over it, testing the give of the straw, the grit of it under my fingers telling me it was real.

"Home. Where else?" she asked, tsking with a click of her tongue as she straightened the hat, giving the brim a tweak. She scowled at me, planting her hands on her hips with a raised brow. "I *told* you to go easy last night with father. You know how your memory gets when you drink too much. You're still going to help with the first hunt, yes?"

The first hunt, to help a new family after the birth of a child. Aislinn's words before filtered back slowly. Avata, she'd said. The name came up blank, no matter how hard I thought on it. Aislinn looked at me expectantly, so I nodded. "Of course."

The creeping feeling in my chest that made me sick turned into tension as I reached up to rub my sternum. The headache only got worse, the pain almost *real*.

This is a dream.

"Are you all right? You seem stuck in your thoughts today," Aislinn said, going still as she studied me with pursed lips.

Looking at her, I saw every bit the beautiful woman she'd been the day I married her ... but something was missing. A rawness that sank in bone deep, making my skin crawl when she got too close. I didn't *want* her close, something I only realized when she reached for me again and I pulled away.

The *only* person I wanted to touch me was Ali.

Every second I was awake seemed to numb my memories, wrapping them in a haze I couldn't get away from. This was a *dream* ...

Right?

"Just a nightmare," I muttered, turning away from her when she frowned and raised an eyebrow like she didn't quite believe me.

I didn't blame her, but I also didn't give anything else.

"All right ... don't push yourself," she said, her expression further souring when I didn't let her take my hand. She shifted, instead motioning me to follow her outside.

I flinched as the sun touched my bare skin again, the heat scorching. I couldn't remember the last time I'd seen it. Even in a dream, I expected it to burn. Summers had always been borderline unbearable, but today seemed more so.

Aislinn guided me forward to the little patch we'd set aside to have our meals on, the path we'd walked weathered and worn, closer to the water than most of the others in our tribe preferred. There were already a few bowls and a small white canvas set up on it.

I was drawn to it immediately.

It wasn't any bigger than a picture frame, held onto a wooden base with a few straps of leather. I picked it up, running my thumb over the still-drying paint of a small *unfinished* portrait ...

It was the same one I had in my room, hung up next to a beautiful Van Gogh, its brush strokes immortalized in a simple frame. Though, the one I touched now was much less complete.

"You like?" Aislinn asked as she walked up behind me. One of her arms wrapped around my waist as she reached out to touch the painting with her free hand. Her fingers danced carefully over the surface as I unwound myself from her again, but she didn't seem to mind this time, moving closer to her masterpiece. "Been working all morning on it. You're so calm when you sleep. Though ... I do think I prefer you awake. You have the most expressive eyes out of anyone I've ever met, Fallon."

She hummed a familiar tune just as a sharp pain surged behind my eyes, Aislinn's voice warped, the undertones shifting from the rich, accented candor to a softer cadence. The wind shifted, the quiet sea turning to lavender in an instant.

Aaliyah's face came to mind just as Aislinn's hand skimmed over a swipe of drying green paint—my portrait's eyes. My wrist ached, forcing me to look down at the *bare* skin.

I nearly puked.

Aaliyah's mark was gone. I couldn't feel it or the warmth of her I'd grown so used to having, and I'd never felt more alone than in that moment.

Just a dream.

Something in my gut told me there was more to it than that. This was suspicious, directly after we'd gone to Archon's and *lost* to him.

What was his goal with this?

Aislinn pulled away, walking in front of me. She picked up one of the plates she'd laid out and I was too busy holding my wrist to register she was back until she was sitting gracefully next to me again, snorting a laugh as she tapped me on the nose. "Don't look at me like that. I've always had a soft spot for your eyes. Next time, we should paint together. You know, you don't have to be good at something to have fun with it."

Her motto rang in the air as she tore the bread in half and handed me a piece. She took a bite as she spoke. "Ah. Here, from mama. She's busy helping Avata with the baby, so you probably won't see her today. But she sends her love, as always."

Sighing, she leaned back, closing her eyes to bask in the sun.

I rubbed my temples again, idly listening to Aislinn talk about her plans for the day as others started to come out of their own huts. Chatter filled the air, a notable joy clinging to everyone at the announcement of the new baby. They nodded, smiling as though they knew me, whispering greetings that I ignored.

Whatever this was, I just needed to get through it. Maybe I'd wake up in Archon's dungeon, and I'd have to figure out a way to get us out from there. The mark was gone because this was a dream. The bonds were gone because this was a *dream.*

That was all.

I took a bite of the bread, the dense thing drying my mouth out, sending a wave of nostalgia through me. I ate every last bit.

Breakfast went fast after that, the other men and I heading out shortly after to hunt. It was successful, and the day was washed away by the excitement of a fresh kill. It was almost enough to clear the haze of the morning, and when I came home, Aislinn was waiting for me.

I hugged her willingly, just long enough to remember she was here, to memorize her face again. My first love, the wife I'd *killed*. She was a part of me I didn't want to forget. One I'd leave behind in a *heartbeat* for Ali.

And Ali was waiting for me.

"Good night, husband," Aislinn whispered, and I lay in bed next to her, keeping my distance, waiting for her to drift off to sleep.

I was quick and eager to follow, my hand on my wrist the entire time.

But when I opened my eyes, *nothing* had changed. I was still in the hut, still wearing the hides I'd made myself.

My wrist was *still* empty.

The air, the room, the nauseating headache that spawned behind my eyes. Aislinn walked in, just as she had the day before, with the same flushed skin and unapologetic smile.

"Good morning, Taz," she called in a vibrant voice, as her shadow cast over me. Unlike the day before, I didn't lean in to see her face, the shadow more like a cage as her arms came up, binding me in. "You're missing the festivities. Avata had her baby last night, and everyone's been in high spirits all morning."

She said it exactly as she had yesterday, the same cadence, the same sway to her hips as she dragged me outside. The same painting that *haunted* me with imperfect strokes and drying ink. My mother's bread.

Oh, *fuck* me.

The day passed in a sickening blur. The same hunt. The same kill. The *same* celebration that ended with me in bed next to a woman that I knew wasn't real, even as I touched her cheek and felt the heat behind it.

This had to be a fucking dream.

"Good morning, Taz," Aislinn called, my head still on the bed as I stared up at the ceiling. Whatever game this was, Archon had planned it well. *This* was his prison, his hell. I'd expected dungeons and torture, whips and blood. That I could have handled. Pain wasn't something I was afraid of, but this? This was something I damned well couldn't fight my way out of. "You're missing the festivities. Avata had her baby last night, and everyone's been in high spirits all morning."

"She had him yesterday," I said, watching as she snorted and shook her head.

"I mean, *technically*. She had him late last night. I'm surprised the cheering didn't wake you," she said, crossing her arms over her chest as she toyed with one of her braids, the bead on it rattling against another. "Are you all right? I told you to go easy last night with father. You know how your memory gets when you drink too much. You're still going to help with the first hunt, yes?"

I swallowed hard, shaking as I rubbed my temples, the ache in my head furious. "Where am I?"

She bit her bottom lip, her shoulders drooping. My chest constricted at the sight. The need to fix whatever this was warred with the need to try to comfort her.

"Home? Did you—" she started, the same scowl she'd had the last two days.

"I didn't drink last night. Where am I, Aislinn?" I knew she didn't understand what I asked when she grimaced, her head tilting as if to say *sure you didn't*.

This wasn't fucking real, and yet it hurt every single time I saw her face. Every easygoing expression and smile I damned well already stole away.

"Are you still tired? You're acting strange, even for a late night," Aislinn said, for the first time not dragging me outside as she tried to direct me to the bed. "Do you need to lay down?"

Her gentle hands moved me to sit, and I pulled away from her again, moving to the opening that led outside. She was close on my heels the entire way.

"I need to get out of here," I said, yanking back the shade, stunned by the brightness of the sun again. I grunted at it, gritting my teeth as I stormed out into the crowd of people that had beat us out this time. Urgency rushed me, my head swarming with a hint of pain. "I need to find the others. I need—"

"Others? Do you mean Avata? I told you already, she has a new baby, born just last night—" Aislinn said, still trailing close, managing to grab my hand, stopping me from going any farther.

"My *brothers*," I cut in, the holes in my chest where their bonds were supposed to be crippling. Eirik and Adrian had fallen, too. Were they stuck like this?

Or worse?

"You have no brothers," she said, laughing awkwardly, narrowing her eyes as I ripped my hand out of hers. "What's going on, Fallon?"

The crowd filled out around us, the people faceless and *nameless* looking on with distorted expressions that bordered on hateful.

Until only one showed. It was barely enough time for me to catch the paleness of ivory skin and the mark of a scar on the tip of an upturned nose.

"Aaliyah," I whispered, her head tipping to the side, her mouth opening. She smiled at me, her hands joined together as she anxiously looked around the bush clearing. Her mouth opened, as if to speak, though I couldn't hear any of the words.

We were in danger. *She* was in danger, and I couldn't fucking do this right now. Wherever she was, Aaliyah needed me, and I was here instead. The image of her in the crowd grew more frantic the longer I looked, her lips moving desperately as her arms raised above her head, and I was too fucking stupid to understand what she was trying to say.

I reached for my wrist, the one that felt empty without that thin lavender ring.

"Aaliyah? Who's that, Fallon?" Aislinn asked, looking into the crowd as Aaliyah disappeared. Aislinn took her spot, standing in front of me, grabbing both cheeks, forcing me to look at her. "You scare me."

The way she said it brought me back to her for long enough to really look at her. She was Aislinn; she had the features, the strong face and tenacious curve to her lips when she was agitated. She was every-thing she'd always been ...

"I don't know what's happening, Aislinn," I said, shaking my head again. "But I know I can't stay here."

Aislinn's eyes went so wide the whites glowed, her lips pulling back into a bitter sneer. As if the mirage had broken, the other villagers stopped, their heads snapping to look at me before they went eerily still as all their conversations went silent.

"I don't understand," she whispered, the crack in her voice nearly breaking me.

But I'd lost the right to comfort her, to look her in those eyes that I'd loved before my turn. My human life had been good, one full of joy and happiness. That was gone now, and nothing, not even this dream, would change it. I'd accepted that.

"You're not real, Aislinn," I said, brushing the hair away from her face.

"Not real?" she whispered, letting go of my cheeks.

Her laugh filled the clearing, as the villagers began to drop, one by one. They didn't make any sounds as they did, just crumpled like dolls that had lost their strings. The sun blotted from the sky, and the huts around us burst into flames as day turned to night. Engulfing the tribe with screams and fire.

The image was a visceral memory. A night I remembered *too* well ... a dream turned into a nightmare. I shivered, my throat seizing on me as a bite of pain sank into my bottom lip. I raised my hand to brush it away, blood covering my fingers when I pulled them back.

Aislinn was next. Red streaked down her face, out of her mouth and eyes, her head tilting to show a throat ripped out. My mouth watered against my will, my vision shifting to crimson as my stomach wound tight.

Feed, a voice whispered—Sebek's, dark and perverse, my eyes going red.

Blood coated the barren sand beneath Aislinn as she reached her hand out to me, smiling as wide as her mouth would let her. The waves crashed behind me, splashing against a ground that was painted red, brushing my feet as I took a step back.

"Say it," she whispered, smearing the blood over her face, the whites of her eyes glowing. "Why am I not real, Taz?"

Her hand came to my chest, leaving a bloody print there. Even then her touch was soft, gentle, like the way she used to look at me while I held her ... before she'd bled out in my arms, staring at me like I hadn't ripped out her throat, holding me close like she wasn't dying.

"Because I killed you," I whispered, choking on my tears as Aislinn's eyes cleared, kindness there for just a second, before they rolled back in her head.

Her heart stopped, the beat stuttering out, mine following as I forced myself to watch her body slump before she was ripped away from me. The fire dulled, and there was only the rhythmic splash of the waves on bloodied, sandy beaches.

Darkness swallowed my vision, consuming me. The scent of blood was replaced with mint and woody bark. I sat up, clutching my throat, gasping for air.

Light streamed into the small hut, a cold sweat coating my body as I heaved heavy breaths. A hum filled the room as a shadow cast over the door. Just like before, Aislinn walked in, smiling vibrantly as she saw me ...

"Good morning, *Taz.*"

CHAPTER 8

AALIYAH

Arid summer heat beat down on me. Fallon's eyes were wide, horror lining his face as I tried to scream at him to wake up. No matter what I did, he couldn't hear me.

I opened my eyes as the last hints of Fallon faded, a cold sweat sticking to my skin and making me sick to my stomach. I came to a sitting position on the ragged mattress, hugging my knees to my chest, holding onto him, even if it was just for a moment longer. I reached for my wrist like a lifeline, my connection to them weak but there, and that had to be enough for now.

They had to be okay.

I squinted, rubbing my eyes at the headache that came on, looking through the glass walls that haunted me even now, glaringly clear as I searched the hallway for guards that no longer patrolled it.

I was alone, and the silence was almost worse.

My only saving grace was the soft chill that fluttered around the cell, a presence I knew to be Red. He'd stayed, and that was more than I could have asked for. For a second, I could have sworn I saw the impression of him in the glass, like a phantom. My mind filled in the blanks it couldn't see, imagining him like I once had with Prince. Something told me he'd have black hair, or maybe that was just wishful thinking. Maybe he'd smile like Prince, always finding humor in the world around him. He'd laugh well, too. *Deeply.*

I'd used Red as a crutch ever since Prince died, leaned on him even more than the others. It wasn't fair to him; it wasn't fair to Prince's memory either. Yet he was still here, offering what support he could, even if it was just the brush of a comforting hand and the warmth of hope.

"It's going to be okay, right, Red?" I asked as I reached up to scratch the marks on my wrist, one intricate black band for each of the men I held so close to me. They burned slightly, only calming when I touched them. The silence sank down a little deeper, drowning me in poison until I could barely breathe.

"Thank you for staying with me," I whispered as his figure morphed, and I squinted. His form grew more solid, cleaner. For a second, I thought I could see his *eyes.* His emotions lost their sporadic edge, the harsh twists that came with a soul so close to the Void dulling. One peeked through, settling on me, making my heart ache and fill at the same time.

Affection. The caring kind, the loving touch of a warm summer's day. It was soft, pulling the weight from my shoulders as I leaned into the wall. Hope grew, even in this cell. Something that even Sebek couldn't take away from me. "We'll get out of this, one way or another. My guys, they're strong."

My vision clouded as pressure built behind my eyes and nose, blood slipping over my lips. A *Rend* always waiting. I'd forgotten how brutal they were, how unrelenting. I'd been spoiled by my time at the Vivas's home.

"Strength is only measurable by what you're willing to sacrifice," a voice whispered, a chaotic quiet to it that had me tensing. "That is something my troublesome Turned will never understand."

Red disappeared at the callous words, and in his place stood Sebek.

He was still covered in dried blood, a streak against his cheek as he tilted his head curiously. That crazed look that never left his eyes was something I never knew I could fear, but there was nothing behind them beyond that mania. There was no softness or warmth that I sought, like with my father.

There was *nothing,* and he knew nothing. Sacrifice wasn't new to my men, and it wasn't something they took lightly. Sacrifice wasn't their means to power, but they were powerful all the same. Their bond, their *loyalty*. They didn't have to win with fear, not anymore, and that was something Sebek knew little about. He didn't have anyone that would stand by his side if they thought for even a second he would lose.

"Aren't you afraid?" I asked suddenly, almost curious. He was terrifying in all the ways a man with power could be. But did he really think he could fight us all? Not even just me and the men I called mine. The others that grew tired of his games, his tricks and his *killings*. "That you're wrong about them?"

Or did he just not fear death?

"No. Even if they all come, it won't matter," he said after a moment, another spark of clarity showing what I imagine he was like before he went mad. "They've already lost."

He stood on the other side of the glass door that led to my cell, looking down at me. When he reached for the handle, then clicked the lock, I shot up. It was no use, of course, as the door creaked open. He didn't rush me, instead just stepped into the room as I inched away, until my back hit a wall.

A buzz filled the air, the dust between us picking up as Red took a stance in front of me, nervous energy replacing the warmth as Sebek continued his slow march forward. He filled the space, a presence that couldn't be ignored. Fear wasn't a new emotion for me, but the one I felt with him this close was more potent than I'd felt in a long time.

"You underestimate them," I whispered, flexing my hands.

There was a brush of something, a gift that I still didn't know how to control. A power that was as dangerous as my blood.

You underestimate me.

There was no more mocking, just that stony gaze. He took another step forward, and I had nowhere else to go. He reached me in a few long strides, lifting his hand to cup my cheek.

Nausea flooded me just as my mantra did, and I bit back my startled gasp as I tried to turn away from him. "You can't fight me, Glass. It's best you stop trying."

I sucked in a forced breath, swallowing hard, claustrophobic in my skin. My power burned again, just below it. Singing to me, pushing and surging.

But never coming forward.

I gritted my teeth, looking him in the eyes as I called it again. It stayed dormant, even as I fought tears and reached for it with a begging hand, willing it forward with the knowledge of what it was and what it'd taken from me.

Sebek let go of my cheek, pausing to run a finger along the bottom of my jaw, eventually tapping at the skin behind my ear. It was raw, and I jerked as a sharp burst of pain shot through my head.

"You can stop trying to call on your gifts. They're suppressed. Did you think I'd let a Reaper wander around unsupervised?" The chastising words fell just like his hand as he straightened his suit. "Come."

I didn't have much choice, as he grabbed my wrist and tugged me along. My entire body protested, the joints along my arm screaming at the sudden movement. I couldn't stop the flinch that nearly froze me solid. His words were little more than a buzz in the numbness that had become my brain. The realization that he had well and truly trapped me here was a fight I didn't have the energy to take. He'd brought me back to Ascension, and he'd threatened my men. He'd taken the gifts I still struggled to see as mine, but they *were* mine.

Each piece he grabbed stole a little more of my fight, and each calculated move brought another level to the game he was building.

The one I was losing.

"Why here?" I asked, having to close my eyes as he pulled me into the experiment room.

The white backsplash was covered in dried blood, the bodies that were strewn about unrecognizable. The smell still lingered, and I had to fight the urge to puke. I skimmed over the bones, over the broken equipment, and the drip of what I hoped was water somewhere far away. I almost missed it, the mass on the ground that twitched and groaned as it tried to get free from its bindings.

Tied up, gagged, and bleeding was a *man*. He thrashed against his chains, screaming behind the wrap on his face, his eyes going wide as he realized he was no longer alone. Somewhere in the numb, I recognized him.

He was the Gargoyle, the one I'd seen with Fallon and Adrian before we'd gotten to the arcade. It had only been a moment, but I remembered his smile, the way he'd looked at the woman he was with. That thought of them had me jerking against Sebek's hold, pulling enough to back away and stand in front of him and put myself between them.

Whatever Sebek had planned, it couldn't be good.

"What are you doing?" I asked, and Sebek tilted his head.

"What I paid those incompetent doctors to do."

My breath caught, and I struggled to keep my eyes on him as he turned to the table on his left. By a set of familiar tools, familiar *night-mares*. I shook, suddenly finding it hard to breathe.

"Get on the table, Glass," he said, simply turning away from me like he wasn't asking more than I could ever give.

I'd come back into this building; I'd stayed in my old cell. But I couldn't do this. I *couldn't*.

The man behind me made another sound, a tortured one that had me swallowing and balling my fists. Sebek didn't even turn around.

"No," I whispered, shaking my head. "Not this."

He stopped what he was doing, finally looking at me over his shoulder. Whatever warmth was there when he saw me died the moment he looked at the man on the floor. It was like he was looking down at an ant, at nothing more than a bug to be squashed.

"Does his life mean more to you than theirs?" he asked, and I nearly screamed. He knew the answer. "Get on the table, *now*."

Frozen, I struggled with what to do.

Sebek turned back, fiddling with whatever he had in his bag of horrors. I took that second to look back at the man. The one who begged with his eyes for me to let him go, and I wanted to. It hurt deep in my chest, like I was being torn apart when I couldn't. And it hurt even worse when I turned away and took a step toward the table.

"You're a monster." Each syllable slipping past my lips was a condemnation. Of him, and of this place. Of everything he'd ever done to me and to the men I sought to protect.

It was cold, the metal a shining reminder of where I was.

For them.

"You expect me to be weak?" His words collapsed into detachment, the even tone unsettling as the final one ground into a snarl. "I'm not *him*, Glass. You'd do well to remember that."

I crawled onto the table, lying down like I had a million times before. The lights above, flickering, burned my eyes. When Sebek shifted, sending something to the ground, I flinched so hard the table creaked.

Memories flooded my brain, even as I fought to keep them at bay. Reminders of knives biting into skin, of hammers striking vulnerable flesh. I broke out into a cold sweat, my vision blurring as my breath came out in shallow pants. Everything faded away except for the blaring lights above me.

Noise at my side, and I jerked away when Sebek came into view again. His face was so reminiscent of Castillion's it made my mouth flood with saliva, my throat closing instinctively.

Never make noise.

I didn't search for the bag of tricks he had with him, tools and toys he was planning on ripping me apart with.

"Hold still," he said, grabbing my arm. His cold skin was a shock, a pull that dragged me out of my disorientation with vicious efficiency. I waited for the inevitable blow, for him to rip open my veins. Maybe I would get lucky, and he would die from the very blood he was so intent on getting.

He pulled out a needle, one that looked surprisingly sterile. He examined it, swabbing my arm with a napkin that made the skin tingle. It slid into my vein with a quick pinch, and he only pulled enough to fill a vial. When he pulled the needle out, he covered the wound.

Quick. Efficient. *Painless.*

I was shaking, trying to will the panic away that still told me he planned to do worse. I waited ... Waited for the pain he'd watched his doctors inflict on me for years.

He walked around me, not even glancing back, that same vial in his hands. I sat up as he crouched in front of the man. I didn't have enough time to say anything as he mixed my blood with another liquid, until the concoction became a viscous black that clung to the vial's walls. He filled another syringe and injected it into the man's arm.

The gagged man's eyes rolled back, black lines stretching across his skin where his veins were. He choked on his blood before he stopped moving.

The next thing I knew, I was staring at his corpse.

Sebek didn't stop, pulling out another vial. The liquid inside was almost clear before he shook it, glimmering flecks of silver fading in and out inside of it. He did the same again, filling a syringe and injecting the man.

I waited in horror as Sebek stood. I couldn't tell if this was what he wanted, if this man's death was worth it. But eventually Sebek turned around, pulling me down from the table.

"We must go." There was no hesitation in his tone as he pulled a familiar silver sphere out of his pocket. It looked like the one Eliza had used to teleport me out of the Vivas house, and that was only confirmed as the smell of burning metal followed.

I was caught, and I knew wherever we were going was going to be even worse than this. I didn't have a choice as he hauled me toward him, the teleportation spell dragging us away. And we were gone.

Leaving Ascension Rising, and my chance at escape, behind with a final thought on my mind.

The man, the Gargoyle who'd died.

His ghost never left his body.

CHAPTER 9

OSIRIS

It had been centuries since the mere sight of a building bred contempt inside of me. In the life before my turn, that contempt came in the form of picturesque royal architecture that hid monsters behind gold and valor. It had been beautiful, like a nightshade that bore thorns and wore the petals of a rose to fool curious passersby.

If I ever were to set foot in Darius's estate again, I'd rip it apart. Tear it down, brick by brick, even if it might lead to my death to do so. I'd have sworn I'd never hate a place more than those wretched halls, but nothing could have prepared me for the rage that flooded me when Nero and I finally came to a stop in front of a desolate building deep in the depths of the woods, after hours of endless *flitting*. The seemingly harmless building was shaded by the surrounding trees, the dusty white paint dirtied from months of neglect. I knew what hatred was, but this was something that flew beyond my thoughts of the word.

Darius had destroyed me in ways I'd thought nothing else would, but seeing this place now, the one I knew had held Aaliyah and left those shadows in her eyes. That carnage ran to the deepest parts of my soul, found the bits that weren't already broken and shattered them.

My muscles screamed, every inch of me pushed too far as we raced to get here. We'd left as soon as we were able, and we'd barely made it before the sunrise. We had maybe a half hour, at most, and I hadn't even thought of how we might get back yet.

I didn't have the spare mindset to focus on such trivial things. Our escape route could be decided later. The need to get here before Sebek could move on was paramount. Doing anything else, and we risked losing them. Losing *her*.

The only thing that kept me standing was the fact that Nero was by my side. He didn't look on with the same wretched confusion.

"Is this truly Ascension Rising?" I asked, needing to hear the words out loud.

I trained my ears on the building and heard nothing inside.

"It was," Nero said, hard lines tracing his once carefree face.

The man that I'd grown to know as Nero didn't show in this stranger's eyes. There was darkness there now, a dread that stalked the silver depths. Nero had never been one to back down from a fight, not in the centuries that I'd known him.

And he *never* lost.

It was viscerally wrong when he dipped his head, looking beaten as he took a defeated step forward. He'd been the glue that'd held us together, the one who could always pull us back when things spiraled.

Had the Nero I'd known better than myself been lost on that pyre in Russia?

"The beast again lies barren," Magelav mumbled, somehow not out of breath after having followed us.

I hadn't seen the Chronomancer since the early sixteenth century, during one of our feuds in China. At that time, their disguise had been a beautiful woman parading the streets, working for a pleasure house. The time before that they'd been a striking pirate, a man feared as much as respected. This was the first time I'd ever seen them like this, looking so aged and worn, with heavily wrinkled skin and eyes that spoke to their age.

"You're wrong," Nero grunted, flipping his head to glare at Magelav, the heated rage only growing as he turned back to the building. He looked on as if the pitiful structure held every sin he'd ever committed, and even if it were to be burned to the ground, he wouldn't be free of it. "No, you're wrong. She has to be here."

Magelav didn't react to the frothing beast that Nero morphed into, their eyes holding a steady disinterest that felt all too familiar. The sight of them made me sick, as it had every time before. Their relation to Kali was enough to fuel my hatred for them, but I ignored it, for now. As long as they offered help in finding Aaliyah, I would tolerate their presence, and their cryptic words so far had been at least productive, leading us here. Even as they grumbled their insistence that we needed to leave for Kri'Valta's Gala.

It was only hours away now, our one chance to defeat the Horror of the Depths before the Eternium. Before all our work was lost.

"The magic is fresh, *too* fresh. Tastes wrong. *Gone.* As Mags said it would be." Magelav narrowed their eyes as they stepped forward and continued to mumble incoherently. We were given no more explanation as they hobbled toward the white building, leaving Nero and I behind.

Rising failure crippled me, and a blistering rage threatened to consume me.

Sebek had taken Aaliyah, my light—*lux mea*—right out from under me, and now he was well and truly gone.

We followed slowly after Magelav, eyeing the fresh tracks on the ground. The door opened to the smell of antiseptic and rotting flesh, so pungent it curdled in my nose and made me gag.

I followed Nero anyway as he stalked in front of me, trailing after Magelav through a dimly lit hallway that was splattered with dried blood. Followed him as we approached a room that held the brunt of it, and horror greeted us both.

A shiver of disgust coiled in my stomach, demanding I release it. The room was clinical and open, with drab white paint peeling where blood had splattered. Various pieces of equipment were strewn about, most destroyed beyond recognition, like the bodies that littered the ground. The state they were in proved Sebek had been the one to kill them. He liked his tricks, his torture.

Enjoyed making them rip themselves apart, before going in for the kill.

Only one body differed, one that was crumpled to the ground with no outward signs of damage. There was a heavy scent of old stone that gave him away. Gargoyle, bound at the hands. He told me exactly what I hadn't wanted to be true.

Aaliyah had been here.

His body held traces of her blood, the crisp lavender likely what had ended his life. Why? I never knew, not with Sebek. It could have been an experiment, a test, or even just something he did for the fun of it, to draw our attention away while he did other horrid things.

But what stood out wasn't the bodies or the lingering hint of magic in the air. It wasn't the realization Magelav was right, that Sebek and Aaliyah were long gone, a spell the only indication they'd been here.

It was the table that lay in the middle like a sick altar, the metallic sheen stained a rusty brown that still held onto a scent I'd never forget. *Lavender*. Most of it was stagnant, having sunk into the steel through years of use. It had shackles for the wrists and ankles, and another strap to hold someone's head down. So they couldn't fight.

So Aaliyah couldn't fight.

She'd told us of her horrors, of the doctors and of the experiments that had defined her early life, but seeing it? Suddenly, everything burned, from my blood to the mark on my wrist. The singular lavender band was a beacon.

"This was where they did the experiments," I said, under my breath, committing the table to memory, needing it to hurt so I'd never forget it.

Nero didn't hesitate, his eyes closing as he reached up and ran a hand through his hair as he spoke, "Yeah, most of them. The more intensive ones, anyway. There's another room down the hall where they liked to do smaller scale tests."

He reached out, touching the table before his hand tensed, and he dug gouges into the metal. A spark lit in the air seconds later, tasting like fire, before it turned molten under his hand.

"What did they do?" I asked.

I hadn't wanted to ask Aaliyah, didn't want her to have to relive it. At first, I didn't think Nero would tell me—he'd always been the protective sort—but he leveled me with a fury-filled gaze, one that sizzled like the steel that had dripped onto the floor.

"What didn't they do? Electrocution. Fracture resistance. Regeneration. Amputation. And that's just what I've remembered since I woke up." He grunted, pulling away, flexing his hand where the metal stuck and burned him. "Everything. They did *everything* while I stood by and *watched*."

Magelav mumbled something across the room, suddenly throwing a chair and crawling onto the ground with the muck. Nero rolled his eyes at them, brushing his hand on his shirt. That look as he grimaced. I recognized it.

Had this been what the others had seen? When I'd worried over Nero's death and questioned what I could have done differently.

Nero walked in front of me, cutting off our eye contact as he stalked farther in. He didn't look surprised by the sight as he homed in on one of the many bodies. The corpse he selected was in pieces, the skull mostly picked clean, lying on the ground, missing its bottom jaw.

"Well, you've seen better days," he said, eyeing it like he wished the man was still alive, if only to kill him again. One swift kick later, and he was watching with glee as it shattered against the far wall. "Sebek's handiwork really is something, isn't it? Fucker didn't even give me the satisfaction of getting to kill Castillion myself."

The empty room held no hint of relief, and the silence only grew louder as Nero's breath became audible. Both hands came to his hair, and he pulled viciously at the strands.

"You couldn't have done anything, Nero. You cannot blame yourself for this," I whispered, trying and failing to bury my own guilt.

"Couldn't I? I could've gotten here faster, remembered the bastard that did this and found you *before* it happened." He gritted his teeth. "I shouldn't have been dead. Then maybe I could have saved her, instead of being just another fuck-up in her life."

"We never would have found her, had you not been by her side. She wouldn't be Aaliyah if not for you. Stop thinking of the past. It only burns you," I said evenly. "I've spent the last hundred years toiling over your death, and you know what I've learned?"

Nero's eyes cleared enough for me to catch that Roman fire, and even then, I fought to find him there, his past, his life. I fought to find the brother who'd traveled with me through lifetimes, but this was a different man. The same in many ways but changed in many as well. He was Nero, my brother.

And he was Aaliyah's Prince.

"The past doesn't control us. *We* do. Anything less is an insult to the lives we were given. Aaliyah taught me that." And so much more.

She'd snuck into the cracks that Nero's death had caused, like liquid gold, mending the pieces of me until I was almost whole again. She'd filled me with something other than loathing and rage, and now I had Nero back. The man I'd seen do the impossible more times than I could ever count. She may not be here, but we *would* find her. Sebek wouldn't risk harming her, not if he had plans for her blood, and he'd been distraught, thrown off by her appearance, no doubt. Perhaps even more likely to misstep due to her connection to Arvand. We had the upper hand. Now we just needed to get her and the others.

Get through this damned Eternium and go home. So we could *live*. Something I hadn't wanted for decades. I wanted to see her flourish with us, see her smile, and teach her everything she wanted to know. Give her every book she wanted to read, spend every hour I could with her, curled up in the library, enjoy the feel of her in my arms.

To feel her *touch*, the one she gave me freely, the one I'd treasure.

"She's changed you, Osiris," Nero whispered suddenly. His eyebrows drew close before he rubbed away the growing tension. "Everything I've seen of you, every piece of information I've gotten back, has shown you as cold. Cruel, even. That's not you anymore. Is it?"

I only nodded as Magelav crawled their way off the ground.

"She has," I agreed and turned just in time to watch Magelav lick the *wall*. They glowered at it, running aged fingers along the peeled paint, before they turned to face me. "I take it you know what they used to leave here? How can we follow?"

Magelav scoffed, brushing me off to study the wall again. "Oh, now you want to work with Mags, you silly, *silly* boy? Where are your manners?"

Nero set a hand on my shoulder, as if sensing my wrath and seeking to quell it. A move that most people wouldn't have dreamed of doing, he did without hesitation. His touch didn't burn. It hadn't for centuries, but that didn't stop me from jolting at it. It was only a moment before that touch settled me, and he snickered. "Trust me, they don't get any easier to deal with."

Magelav chuckled then, when suddenly their magic was in the air, tastable. It was like freshly washed silk, and the brush of a breeze from a time long passed. It threatened to drown me with the endless flow of time. "Oh, calm yourselves. Magelav is here to help. Here to *teach*."

It was that word that made the power drop, landing on my shoulders. I expected the weight to fall to my wrist, but instead the ache was soul deep in a way that my *blood* knew. It was a pain that shredded my insides and threatened to come out in vile waves.

It was the pain of *loss*.

"But Mags is not your only teacher. Are they?" Magelav asked as I stumbled away, slamming into a wall as I covered my mouth. Nero was much the same, curled up against the closest counter, holding his chest like his heart might try to leave it.

As soon as it started, it snapped to a stop, and that at least helped to calm me.

That was a pain I'd felt only once before. When *Nero* had died. It had lasted for days then. Whatever happened wasn't one of our brothers dying yet, but they were close to it, hovering over death's door, knocking at the gates. My mouth flooded with salt, like I'd tried to drink a vat of sea water.

Eirik.

"What the fuck was that? It felt like ... dying," Nero groaned because he didn't know. He hadn't been the one to feel it.

"One of the others ... Eirik," I started. "But Archon wouldn't *kill* them. He couldn't."

Not without specific orders to. Sebek wouldn't make that call, not after he'd left me alive. He wouldn't kill them without reason, if only because he didn't see the point of spending energy on something so trivial.

"Sebek has that man so far smashed under his thumb he's practically Djinn flavored jam, Osiris. He'd piss on the Hallowed of Death if Sebek asked him to," Nero said with a scoff, his eyes squinting after he spoke, like he was trying to figure out how he knew that.

It wasn't something that I could rule out, but that left us at a crossroads, one that suddenly felt far too heavy. "What do we do?"

"Do, do, *do.* Like you have a choice. The fates play their strings, and all you can do is *choose*," Magelav chimed in, and when I looked at them again, I noted the blood on their hands, now splayed across the wall in a sick pattern. The spell reverberated, pulsing like a heartbeat as the red molded to the darkness that this room still held.

"Lose the brothers?" they said before slashing another bloody mark across the wall. When they lifted their head, it was like looking into a void. Their next words weren't their own. "Or lose your lover?"

"We aren't losing anybody, Mags!" Chaos broke out, Nero seething as he stepped forward, only stopping when Magelav hissed as he touched the blood on the floor.

"Then what are you to do? The Butcher has gone to find friends in a dead man's graveyard, where horror waits for you. You must kill him before the Eternium, or you lose *everything*." The cryptic words sank as deep as a knife. Magelav lifted their hand, showing two bloodied fingers. Then let one fall. "One cannot kill the depths; one cannot free the brothers. All or nothing, nothing or *all*. Fickle be the fates, no?"

Nero looked on in shock, and I focused on the cold that built in my chest. The situation was laid out, a decision that should never have to be made.

"Kri'Valta. Sebek took Aaliyah to Kri'Valta's Gala," I said on a breath.

They were allies, and Sebek was likely going to make sure Kri'Valta made it to the Eternium. With him alive, our plan would crumble. We couldn't pass an Exilium vote with both on the playing field, which meant I'd be forced to Challenge. Sebek had the upper hand there, and our chances of success would go down exponentially. I held my chest, where the ache had vanished, but looked at the mark on my wrist, the one that Aaliyah's soul had burned into my skin. Over the one Darius had forced me to wear.

It was a choice I never would have considered making. Save her, the woman who'd stolen my soul for herself. Or save my brothers, whom I'd promised to give my life for should it ever come to it.

Every failure was again placed at my feet, every choice that led here, to this horrid moment.

"How long do we have?" Nero asked.

"The Gala is today," I responded, brushing my hair away from my eyes before I pulled on the cuff of my shirt, covering the marks on my wrist. "We were to leave once the others returned from Archon's."

It was quickly growing too late for us to go. The Gala was likely already underway, and the sun was set to rise soon. Soon enough that I questioned if we'd even make it there as it was. Silence again, broken only by the sound of sloshing as Magelav continued to refine their bloodied spell.

"We can't just rule them out. They're *our* brothers." Nero's optimism was addictive, and that fire in his eyes something I'd forgotten had burned so brightly. "They're strong bastards. They can make it until we can get to them."

"The fates are uncertain. But the sun ... the sun always rises," Magelav said.

Their eyes dulled with a melancholy I almost missed, that graying white clouded with emotion. They shook their head, refusing to look up from the ground as if avoiding my gaze. My stomach sank.

Nero groaned, rubbing his hands against his face. "Can you please just speak clearly for once, Mags?"

"He plans to let them burn," I supplied, voice steady.

Because Sebek knew that I would only have *two* choices. He did this deliberately, to split my attention and hope that I wouldn't chase him. Part of me paused, in awe of his ability to always keep the upper hand ... and under normal circumstances, he would have been exactly right.

But Nero coming back from the dead was anything but normal. I would no longer allow those I loved to suffer and die. I would not make the same mistake twice, given the opportunity to fix it. "You will go for the others, Nero. I will handle Kri'Valta."

Nero's hands were suddenly at my shoulders again, and I was met with his wide silver eyes.

"When one fights, *we fight with them!*" The mantra on his lips was a prayer, a promise. "I have your back, brother. *Always.* I can take out Archon and get the others. Are you sure you can handle Kri?"

I wasn't sure if *we* could do it. It had been a risk with all of us. By myself, it was likely suicide, but I would not leave another brother to die, and I would not leave Aaliyah in the hands of that devil.

"If Kri'Valta lives through the night, everything is lost. Sebek stays Eternal, and whatever he has planned for Aaliyah goes forward. Our only chance at bringing this down on his head is this Gala. I *will* kill the Horror of the Depths."

The clap of hands broke the tense air that had built. Magelav clicked their tongue. "Fickle *be*. So, you have chosen death? One or the other. Brothers *or* lover. This is a choice dipped in fool's gold. One that has consequences far beyond a simple promise."

Nero let me go, the gladiator I knew suddenly shining as he turned to glare at the Chronomancer that looked on like we were nothing more than passing time in the grand scheme of whatever it was they saw. The fight would always be there, and I had to pull back not to fall to it. Not to falter.

"No. We save them all." Nero breathed. "I won't settle for anything less."

"We head for home. I need to get our preparations," I said as I turned, leaving him and a mumbling Magelav behind me, who whispered something about not going far.

Their magic had grown, the wall becoming a large spell that now sank into my bones. Teleportation. They'd repurposed the magic that Sebek had left from his. It lingered in the air, the faintest traces. It wasn't enough to follow, but it would be enough to get us home and let me grab the items we'd prepared. Hopefully, Magelav would have the strength to get me to the Gala as well.

"Wait for us," I said, sinking my nails into my palm. Nero came to my side, resolute and unspeaking. "*Fratres.*"

We both turned just as Magelav walked out, and we were quick to follow. The spell still sang on their skin, and when they reached their hand out, a small blue circle grew around our feet. I lifted my hand, snapping, the brush of the *Flame* lighting up my soul as it hit the building, but it wasn't enough. Nero joined in, reducing the place that had sought to destroy Aaliyah to dust.

We left it like that. My thoughts split between saving Aaliyah, the woman who'd resurrected my soul, and the brothers I'd promised to always save. I hadn't known Nero was going to die. I hadn't expected it. With the others, I couldn't say the same. I was given a chance to save them, and I wouldn't fail, not again. Sebek underestimated what I was willing to lose for my family, for my light.

What would I do to save them all? A silly question.

What *wouldn't* I do?

The answer to that left me far more hollow.

Magelav's spell dropped us into the living room of our home.

The house was empty, bland without the bustle of our brothers and Aaliyah to give it life. There were marks of struggle that I hadn't seen before, signs of a fight that I'd ignored in our rush to go after her, like the demolished furniture and white hairs that were strewn across a black floor.

It was too much to look at.

"What did you need to get?" Nero asked, his eyes downcast.

It was so strange seeing him again. I'd memorized his picture and swore the nuances of his voice into the deepest parts of my mind, but there were subtleties about him that I hadn't realized had been lost to time.

The quirk of his eyebrow, and the shadow of freckles that spread over his high cheekbones. The flaring grit in his voice that was buried under a haughty tone. So many things I swore I'd never forget, yet I had.

There was a glow on the moss yard, a hint of a rising morning sun. A reminder of what could be lost if we failed. The knock of Adrian's hand against the cabinets as he cooked, the crinkle of chocolate candies in Fallon's pockets, the steady rasp to Eirik's voice when his beast came out. Would I lose those small things, those moments that made them *them?* I tried not to think of it.

"A potion of High Fae Mana, in case we're not back before the Eternium. I wanted to get it in advance," I said, and Nero nodded.

Kri'Valta's Gala was tonight, which meant we had barely a week before the official start of the Eternium. The bringing of the New Year, two hundred and fifty years since the last gathering.

Coming back home should have been feasible, but I wasn't going to take any chances.

His gaze traveled around the room, taking in the space the same as I was. The trace of another intruder that lay sizzling in the air. There had been a press against our wards, someone coming to see us. The lingering smell of gold gave Archon away.

"Seems like someone was here," Nero mused, voicing my silent thoughts as he ran his hand across our kitchen table, his fingers stalling on the claw mark Kali had left there.

"Archon sent men to collect me. I sensed the push against the ward on the way to Ascension." The words came easily but felt like poison. I didn't even recognize myself in them, so shallow and numb.

They hadn't gotten through, not until I let them. I'd felt the moment they'd touched the barrier, so why had Sebek been able to slide past?

The numbness was the only thing holding me together. It was the only thing that kept me focusing on what mattered, on getting as many of us to safety as possible.

When the air lit and dark magic swelled, even Magelav paused next to us, their head tilting to the side as the scent of sulfur hit. I almost ignored it, convinced it was a play on my tired mind as I struggled to keep my magic in check.

It didn't fade, and rage bubbled up.

Not now. *Why* now? I was on a thread, barely keeping everything contained, and yet she was *here*.

Kali.

"Well—" was all she got out, materializing in front of me, before I had her pinned to the wall. My magic, the one I'd forced down into the bowels of my soul, built, starting in my stomach, growing like a fire that had just been fed dry tinder until it raged hot under my skin. It pushed against Kali's, breaking hers down until I couldn't feel it anymore. Only then could I breathe. "What a welcome."

I snarled, my hand tightening. I knew I should step back; we didn't need another Eternal down our throats, and Darius would not take kindly to my harming of Kali. I'd endured her constant presence for that one simple fact. Even after all she'd done, after I'd watched Adrian and Fallon crumble under her corrupt magic ... and faced the onslaught of her cruel words.

I'd done everything to make sure I didn't ruin this Eternium for us before it even began. So, why? "*What* are you doing here?"

That got her attention, and even with my hand at her throat, cutting off her airway, she didn't look scared. She tipped her head, blond hair spilling around us as the ivory bone that had been keeping it up fell loose and clattered to the ground.

"You were supposed to be at the Eternium by now, my reckless little pet. Kneeling at Darius's feet and begging for forgiveness." That furious tint to her words didn't hide the crack in her voice nearly as effectively as she was hoping. Her eyes dilated, her throat constricting under the press of my palm. "Do you have any idea what he's going to do to us now?"

Us? *Us?*

"He'll do *nothing* to me!" I screamed it in her face, and she went red.

Her magic shattered again, snapping against my skin as she brought her hand up to my wrist. Her claws bit in, but the pain was nothing compared to the sickness I felt at the touch of more of her skin.

"Nothing? He's angry, Osiris! More so than I've seen in centuries." Panic. I wasn't used to seeing it on her face, but she was damned near manic with it. Her nose bled, and she thrashed in my grip. "He's waited long enough for you to come back to us. You've had your fun. I've gotten rid of your distraction, and now there's nothing else holding you here. *Come home.* Please."

Her words were met with silence, the begged nature paired so sweetly with the hint of violence. They were so pointed and driven, I almost missed it.

My ward had been breached again, allowing Sebek to pass through. It had been done effortlessly, cleanly, after I'd spent *hours* fortifying their defenses. Only one Sorceri would have been able to slip past them that quietly ... because she'd taught me all I knew.

Because she'd done it before.

Clarity came swiftly. Kali hadn't left my wards in tatters this time, because she hadn't broken them, just invited herself in. The hole, the pinprick opening, that was just enough to allow someone inside before it sealed shut. My eyes bled red. "What did you do?"

The words were quiet, a breath, like a soft question in a dark room. I dropped her, like fiery coals, trying to process and keep my rage in check.

"I   " She stumbled, and my human gifts, the press of Echomancy, destroyed the peace around us. It was a violent wave, every bit of magic that I knew swarming inside of me. The heating of my blood as it flexed, as if waiting to join a fight. The walls creaking as the atoms inside of them struggled to reach me. The crackle in the air as the oxygen burst into micro flames.

"What did you *do?*" I pressed, and she stood.

It hit every inch of the house, keeping her pinned against the wall and snuffing out her power. I was stronger than her, much stronger, more than ever with the blood of the *Butcher* in my veins.

"I got Sebek inside, of course," she said, waving her hand like she hadn't just dropped the ax aimed at her own neck. My fingers dug into my palms. "Got him to the door through your ward, just long enough so you wouldn't have time to deal with it. Though I will say I was impressed. Had I been anyone else, I wouldn't have managed it."

The chime of the clock above the table was all I could focus on. Someone called my name, a hand on my shoulder that left me recoiling.

"Why?" I asked. "Why would you do this?"

"Because that little thing you had stowed away was a distraction, Osiris. One that's ruining you, all of you. I was taking care of it," she hissed. "You have more pressing matters than a *mortal* to deal with. She was going to get you killed."

Any semblance of control I had devolved into nothing more than ash. Careful years of reining in the thunderous instincts that came with being what I was. A moral code that I'd lived by so I would never become like the monster that turned me. A monster that had slipped past my defenses and stolen the one thing that had stood between me and a rope after I'd resigned myself to death.

Kali *let* Sebek in.

"You'll be punished for these bruises. You know Darius doesn't like them on me," Kali mumbled, rubbing her neck.

I took a step forward, brushing off the hand that had found my shoulder until I was a breath away from her.

She threatened Aaliyah before, when she'd first come to our home. I, foolishly, thought I'd sent her away. My misguided attempts to form a better version of myself. One that pulled away from the monster I'd been before.

A fool's path. She'd meant for Sebek to kill Aaliyah.

Kali let Sebek in.

"Osiris?" Kali asked, and I caught the first real hint of fear in her eyes. Too little, too late.

She didn't get another word out as I lifted my hand, just inches from her face, stepping back from her in the same instant.

She'd meant to kill my light, and I'd almost let her.

I snapped my fingers.

Blood exploded around her, so hot it charred the wood at her back. It spilled from her nose, ears, and eyes, as surprise was swallowed by an agonized scream. I did what she had done before to my brothers, to *me*, and boiled it inside of her. I didn't let go as she had, didn't feel any compulsion to show her any mercy she didn't deserve, adding to the waves that battered her. The *Flame* blended with my human magic, morphing until the fire lit blue. Her scream was swallowed only by the next snap.

And another.

"Stop!" a voice yelled, but I was too far gone. The heat of my power torched my clothes, dragging deep fissures into the ground around me as the fire arced into the wooden floor.

Another snap, another burst of blood as she slumped to the ground, her veins growing against her skin before breaking open. My own blood fought in my veins to do the same, a trail sliding down over my top lip.

"Osiris—"

Another. *Another.* Until she'd long stopped screaming.

"Fuck, Osiris!" someone screamed, and I suddenly realized where I was again, with a bloody mess of a body at my feet. The flames died instantly, and shame flooded me at the sight of our house, of the damage I'd caused. "She's dead, Osiris. You can stop now."

Kali ... was a mess of smoldering bones and blood, gone so quickly it was almost like she hadn't been here to begin with. I waited for her to get up, to punish me again.

Such a bad pet.

She didn't stir, and what I'd done truly crashed around me. I'd killed Kali, an Eternal, a close ally to Darius the Great. We were already going to be facing backlash for Kri'Valta; this would *damn* us.

What had I done?

"Hey, whatever you're thinking, stop. She had that shit coming," Nero said, somehow getting in front of me, pushing me away from the carnage I'd created. I tried to center myself, to breathe as I realized my heart thundered like hellfire in my chest. "But that look? Brother, you need to focus."

"What look?" I muttered, and Nero shook his head.

He clapped both hands on my shoulders. A show of support as much as it was an anchoring force.

"Like you don't care, like life doesn't mean anything. I may not remember much, but I remember that look," he said, the words striking like a blow I couldn't get away from as he grimaced. "You look like Sebek, brother."

I froze, suddenly stumbling away from him, but I couldn't deny his words as I stared at the body on the ground, which was still smoking. I wasn't sad about it, not her life. If anything, I wanted to bring her back just to do it again.

That wasn't what we stood for, not now. Vivas, our namesake, meant *to live*. I might have just killed us.

"This was not in the cards," Magelav mumbled, looking at the body like they might try to dissect it. The second Rourovic didn't seem fazed, more interested in the patterns the blood made than whose it was. Still, they were a threat, a wild card, and more likely an enemy than an ally.

"Do you intend to avenge your sister?" I asked.

Magelav shook their head, brushing their hands on their clothes.

"Mags lost their sister long ago. Before you were a thought. Before the fates called on me. But blood knows blood," Magelav hummed, as though speaking of the weather. "Kali was of no importance, little more than sand. Your other sins weigh much heavier. You will pay for them before the end."

Their eyes, frosted like a winter storm, caught mine. It was like watching the clouds clear, the haze falling away for the first time since I'd seen them, showing the beast beneath the banter. They searched for something they wouldn't find, remorse for a death I was no sorrier about than Kali's.

This fight had been centuries in the making, a feud that had been bubbling beneath the surface since I'd learned of their name.

"Our quarrels are long buried, Magelav. I've tolerated much, and I'm willing to put them aside for this," I said, stilted words freezing the rest of the room as magic flooded it. I was on edge. My instincts and emotions ran raw. Vengeful pride threatened to rip the words out of my throat, the *Flame* clinging to them much like the *Charm* I held back. "Do not mistake my hospitality."

Magelav's lips pulled back in a snarl. "Oh, scared I am of the *Kingslayer*. A boy made rotten. Again and again, you *take*. I will follow, because it is demanded. Because I am owed. I will watch you fight and fall to the depths, like the boy you are, because Bronimir didn't deserve to die for his tie to me. Your debt is alive until the day you stop breathing."

Magelav's words were full of the pain I'd felt when I'd lost Nero, their eyes shadowed with the grief of loss. My eyes blew red, and my lips pulled back to expose fangs. Magelav's old lover had been a thorn in my side for centuries before his death. Haughty and full of an ego that he did not have the power to back.

"I didn't kill Bronimir because of who you were, Magelav. Not *once* have I ever held your relation to that *monster* against you. Bronimir tried for my life and almost killed Eirik. I did what I must to protect my brother."

"Pitiful excuses. Not even an apology," Magelav hissed. "Own your wicked thoughts, or drown in them—"

My hands flexed, the air turning to cinders as a burst of lightning shot across it. "An apology? *Never*. Bronimir died because he was a fool, and I'd do it again in a heartbeat."

Sickening calmness, like the gentle breeze before a devastating storm as the magic that lingered on my tongue turned molten.

"Such hatred in your eyes. That folly is what will fail us, *monster*. That emotion, that panicking, writhing thing, will be the end of us. Kali—" Magelav pushed and pushed and *pushed*.

I'd seen the edge of my breaking point before. I'd had many over the years since my release from that hell, but that name ... even on someone else's lips? Her corpse was smoldering at my feet, and still she haunted me.

Every touch, every breath. The barbarous tilt to her lips and the savage cruelty that still clung to my life now. I struggled to breathe, the room collapsing around me until I was locked away in my own mind. In another room, another hell.

Another bed. Bound and bloodied, touched by hands that I couldn't get rid of even now.

"Kali raped me!" I screamed it, a broken cord, a shot to my heart that would linger there as my voice cracked and the dam burst. "I was stuck in the hell that was Darius's harem for years. Kali used me like a doll and broke me until I was nothing but a shell. There are bits of myself I'm still finding centuries after the last time she took what she had no right to. *Hate?*"

I could barely breathe.

"*Yes*, I hate her more than anything in this world save for Darius himself and the monsters that harmed my light. Had I killed Bronimir because of your relation to Kali, I wouldn't have been so kind as to give him a quick death."

I tried to conceal the frantic weight of my breaths as sweat pooled on my brow. My lips trembled, hands flexing, as my eyes grew unfocused.

"His death is still on your hands. You hold your resentment close; it will be your downfall—"

"*Enough!*" Nero butted in, his face a mask of simmering rage as he bared his teeth. Fangs had fallen, his eyes shimmering silver before they flushed red. "Mags, you say one more fucking word, and I'll gut you and leave your body next to Kali's. *Consequences* be damned."

Magelav took a deep breath, another flush of magic brushing against us, against their will. For the first time, it wasn't craze I saw in their eyes. Pain, loss, and a knowing that their fate was as locked as the rest of ours.

"If you despise me so much, then *leave*, Magelav. We will fight this without you," I said, staring down at the withered person that deflated in front of us.

"Mags is not here for you, *Osiris* Vivas. I am here because it is written for me to be," Magelav grumbled, shaking their head viciously. "I am here, because I am owed. My help is not free, and it is not optional."

"Then what's your price?" I mocked as Magelav sneered.

"It is not for *you* to know." They made a pointed look at Nero, and he narrowed his eyes, like it wasn't the first he'd heard of it as well.

The three of us stood in silence, understanding that one way or another, this was the only way forward. There was no other reason they'd suffer my company, and I was feeling the same.

"Consequences are many, and threats are petty and small. No longer are our plans unfrayed. Though ... benefits may also come. I will take Kali's place." Magelav shook their head, bony fingers caked in blood as they ran them across their aged face. "And I will speak no more of Bronimir."

It was an olive branch, the only one we'd have. For Aaliyah, I accepted it, even as more fire caught in the back of my throat.

Without even a further glance, Magelav turned away. "We can dally here no longer. I prepare the spells, you *prepare.*"

I struggled to come to terms with that statement, but I also knew I didn't have a choice. Something nagged at the back of my brain, further damning me.

Nero took up a spot at my side, an unwavering sentinel. He didn't speak, but he rarely had to. He searched my eyes, taking the brunt of my own sins long enough for me to breathe.

"Come on, Osiris. Sun's rising," Nero said as he grimaced, looking at the door. "Are you sure this is going to work?"

I reached for my wrist, an action that had become second nature over the years, but it wasn't Darius's mark that I ached to cover. It was Aaliyah's. I ran my fingers over the *Hallen Bond*, admiring the lavender that stood starkly against the black ink of my brand. It hummed under the attention, as if it were her own hand I touched.

"Have faith, Nero. We are Vivas," I managed.

Come hell or high water, we'd make it through this alive.

CHAPTER 10

ADRIAN

Insanity came from silence; I was sure of it. Ever since Archon had come that first day, the guards had been using it more and more. These few moments alone were somehow worse than anything else they'd thrown at me.

It had been a prominent torture method in the weeks since I'd been here, and it had been *weeks*. No matter what way I sliced it, the days kept coming.

And I was still hanging here.

They'd been gone for hours now, my stomach aching with a hunger that had started several days ago and hadn't let up since. They hadn't fed me, not that I expected them to. It wasn't like it would kill me.

Just another ache, another reminder that I was alone here. That Archon was right ... no one had come.

It was just me and the silence.

This was all part of Archon's plan, no doubt, to make me go crazy in my wait for him to come back. To get me desperate so I might make a deal with him, for whatever it was that he craved so deeply. If he came back at all. It was likely that the Eternium had already come and passed, so now he had to be just biding his time.

Or he died. That would be nice.

There hadn't been a change in the bonds, Osiris's still beating strong in my chest, a constant presence that helped to soothe the aches. Maybe we'd won. Maybe Sebek was already dead and gone, too. Maybe Osiris was working on a plan to get us out as I hung here, wallowing.

I held on to that hope, desperately clinging to it like Fallon with his goddamned chocolates.

"Nine hundred ninety-nine ... One thousand," I sang softly to a tune my mother used to hum, breaking the silence the best I could with busted vocal cords.

When the cell door creaked open, I hated myself for being relieved.

"Ah, back for more already? You spoil me, Eugene," I said in a singsong tone, calling out the Ghoul that had been in charge of my beatings by a name that just seemed to fit him too well. He hadn't told me his real one. None of them had said *anything,* but it seemed to fit.

And it pissed him off, so that helped.

I blissfully ignored the cracking of my words as anxiety came rushing back in. I waited for the fingers at my back, for salt in open wounds. For the strike of a fist against my blatantly exposed skin. Familiarity was the last thing I expected, the brush of lavender sweetness and the warm worried hands that cradled my face something Archon's prison could have never produced.

It was a vision; it had to be because there was no way I was looking the love of my life in her gentle, worried eyes.

"Aaliyah."

The tilt to her stubborn nose, the way her hair fell over her shoulders, braided across the left side of her head in that Viking pattern she loved so much. I barely believed she was real as she glanced frantically around the cell, but the heat of her hands didn't lie, her scent identical to the one I cradled in the depths of my mind. I'd hoarded it, a reminder of her that had gotten me through some of the worst beatings. The euphoria from seeing her shattered at the realization that she was *here.*

In this hell with me.

"Oh, my God, love. What are you doing? You need to—" I coughed on the words, sagging forward. I strained to look over my shoulder, homing in on the sounds that leaked in from the hallway, begging that the guards would stay away a while longer.

"We're here to get you out, Adrian. Just hang on. Osiris is going to break the chains." I didn't quite understand how, but Osiris was nothing if not a man of many skills. It was a tense few moments as we waited, before the chains that held me crumbled to dust. I fell to the ground with all the subtlety of a rock. Aaliyah was quick to move, pulling one of my arms over her shoulder as I sank farther into the muck.

"Come on, there isn't much time. Osiris is getting Fallon and Eirik. We have to move before Archon realizes I'm here."

I couldn't hold back the cry when she tried to hoist me up, the humerus in my left arm still mending from Eugene's last round with the bat.

"I'm too heavy," I grunted, trying to force myself to hold some of the weight and failing rather miserably. Quite pathetic, if I did say so. I'd be taking Fallon up on his request for a sparring partner once we were out, after all. "I can wait here, *go.*"

I hunched on the floor, rubbing my wrists as the blood flow came rushing back to them. Pins and needles turned into knives as I hissed out a cursed breath.

But Aaliyah didn't leave, her warm touch once again finding my face. She tilted me so I could look at her. So I was able to see every inch I've been dreaming of. So ... resilient. The way she put my arm over her shoulder again. Even the way she tensed, like she was unmovable, when she went to lift.

"No. I'm never leaving you again," she whispered, determination set in the line of her jaw as she moved to stand me once more. I couldn't very well say no to being rescued like some damsel in distress. "Come on, one. Two."

I braced for the pain, gritting my teeth as my eyes flashed red just briefly enough to give her some strength.

"*Three,*" she grunted, shaking under my weight as I tried my best to force myself to my feet for her.

The efforts bore fruit as we stumbled up, eventually finding support against one of the brick walls. I leaned into it, trembling legs barely doing anything to keep me standing. Aaliyah was my saving grace, my single point of focus in the room as my body tried to sort through all the wounds that had been inflicted on it. The ones that were still healing, courtesy of my lack of blood. My vision wavered, my breaths sharp gasps that I struggled to keep steady.

I wasn't a fighter, but I'd rather die than be any more of a burden to her.

I had so many questions, so many things on my mind, all of them pushed back as I focused on moving.

The first steps we took were slow, and I listened as closely as I was able to the hall outside the cell. Anxiety rolled in my stomach until nausea took over, but no one came. She opened the door, looking left, then right, before gently leading me outside.

The hallway didn't hold the same spell as the room, and a rush of power flooded back into me as soon as I was past the threshold of the door. It was like the hood that had been covering a fire had been pulled off, and the flood of oxygen ripped through the ashes, growing until they were out of control.

Getting it back gave me enough strength to take my weight off her, still keeping my arm wrapped tightly around her warm shoulders so I could protect her if someone did come. I wasn't powerless now, less likely to be a hindrance, and that let me breathe a little easier. My senses sharpened, and even the *Flame* spiraled down my veins. I breathed it in. Losing it had felt like losing a limb. Seemed all that practice I'd been doing on Fallon's paintings had its merits.

Hope flared as we set a steady pace down the hall, toward what I assumed was Osiris and an endless stream of chaos. Hopefully my other brothers, as well.

Fallon was going to be so proud when we rescued him. I wasn't going to let him live it down.

Aaliyah stopped us at an intersection, looking around before closing her eyes. I watched her carefully, worry building when her face scrunched in pain. Her lavender scent washed over me, tinted with something I couldn't quite place. It was almost acidic, and I brushed it off as a marker of these disgusting conditions.

"This way," she said, suddenly opening her eyes and pulling us off to the right.

My ears trained on the whimpers of those around me. The dank, soiled air that bled into my nose. Everything hurt, *everything*.

Aaliyah gentled her grip around my waist, releasing some of the pressure there, allowing me to breathe easier. She watched me closely, gauging every reaction and adjusting accordingly.

God, I loved her.

Every turn led to more cells, every inch as unfamiliar and untrace-able as the last, but there were no guards, no hints that they'd ever been there. Not even footprints on the muddied floor, none beyond the ones we'd left behind us.

The sheer emptiness of it unnerved me, my senses telling me to pause when my heart just kept pushing me to go.

Where was everyone? This place was a maze, but I'd still expected to see *someone*. If not the guards, then the ones making those noises. The screams and the wails. Prisoners like *me*.

I tightened my arm around Aaliyah's shoulders as she took another turn. The hall we'd been in came to a rigid halt, with nothing at the end but another blank space.

Fuck me.

The euphoria began to wear off, the unease around everything growing as Aaliyah led us farther down the hall. Her steps were unsure now, her head jerking to look fearfully around the narrow space.

"Love, what happened at the Eternium?" I asked softly, tilting my head at her.

The way she looked at me, with those wide eyes, broke my heart. Her arms shook, sweat sliding over her face. With all the time she'd spent at Ascension, I knew she didn't have the muscle mass to carry me. Yet she tried anyway.

"We don't have time for this right now," she whispered, curling close to me as someone screamed behind us, back from the direction we'd just come. "We need to get out of here."

From the empty cells at our backs. The ones I'd let my gaze linger on. I'd searched every inch, not even finding bones. I listened again, hunting for a heartbeat to go with the scream, but there was none.

There was only the quiet. The *dreadful* quiet.

"Please, Ali," I begged, hoping I was wrong, that the little inconsis-tencies I was starting to notice about her weren't real. The scars on her face seemed more vibrant, the braid to her hair intricate and styled in a way I'd *only* ever seen Eirik do for her. I pulled away from her, standing on my own, even as my legs protested and shook. "What happened?"

But she didn't answer. The Aaliyah I knew dropped off this person's face. Her expression soured, her eyes going blank as the color deviated.

That vivid lavender was suddenly lighter, the nuances of them lost in my mind's eye. The hint that had snaked into her scent hammered at my thoughts, hidden inside of it, souring the memory of her.

Fool's gold.

"You're not her, are you?" My vocal cords protested, tears caught in the back of my throat, Archon's latest game seeming to be a breaking point.

The walls wobbled around us, Aaliyah flinching as she jerked away, as if she'd been ripped from my arms. The force was enough to drag me to my knees, my eyes blotting as I tried to force myself back up. One was still sealed shut, the other struggling to focus as I registered the loss of her touch.

"Now, why the long face?" Archon's voice echoed, and I looked over my shoulder, finding an empty hall behind me.

I flexed my hands, focusing on where I'd been, keeping my words close to my chest. Aaliyah was a dirty trick, but I should have seen something like it coming. He'd used my own hope against me, and I'd already given him enough by showing how off center it'd made me. The last thing I needed was to say something that could be used. Archon was a Djinn, and this proved if nothing else, he was crafty enough to force a deal out of anything I might say. The reminder of his last talk, of his game, sealed my lips shut.

"It was quite fun, watching you bounce about, thinking you can get out of my game just because you got out of your cell." Archon's mocking words grated on my eardrums.

"I don't care about your fucking game!" I growled it, sucking in a breath, my eyes going red, fangs dropping as a shiver went through me. It was as vicious as the *Call,* my emotions reigning over my actions like they'd been whispered by Sebek himself. The anger ignited inside of me.

There was no calm to be had, no amount of breathing was going to bring back my mask. Archon had already stripped it away and found exactly what I'd wanted to hide.

Weakness. Fear.

How badly it hurt.

"That's not how this works, Collector. And you're not asking the right questions," Archon taunted, and I gritted my teeth. "My game. One question. One answer. And you can get out of here."

I felt decidedly like a trapped animal as I struggled to get myself standing. I covered my ears so I couldn't hear anything else he said.

"Where are you, Collector?" The words were whispered directly into my head.

I moved again, keeping to the wall at my left, turning as it did, tracking my steps and falling further and further into madness as the cells grew more warped. No exit in sight. The screams grew louder, more empty cells greeting me.

No relief to be found in a place like this, as if it were crafted to be my worst nightmare.

Where was I?

Such a simple question, or it should have been. I was in the basement of Fellow Manor, the dungeon that I'd heard his guards whisper about on occasion when I visited before, searching for information. The weeks of torture built, each moment clearing as the air went silent again.

I stopped moving, hands dropping to my sides. The screams had stopped at the drop of a pin on the soiled floor.

I'd been here for *weeks*.

He wasn't asking for any other reason than to remind me of what he'd said before. His game was as much a tactic as it was another trick. Archon was a Djinn, a proud one, an *old* one. The logical side of my brain that had been flipped off as I'd spiraled into fight-or-flight came back just enough for me to look around again. Really look.

The walls, made of that crumbling stone, the drip of water. Aaliyah's scent, lavender now rotten. It clung to the air, settling in with the muck and soiled cells.

Archon had never assumed he'd lose, had never even shown worry. That was a tell in itself. And he'd been so sure Osiris wouldn't come.

No.

That he wouldn't come soon enough.

"Ah, there it is," the voice echoed, and when I turned around again, the hall that I'd just come from had narrowed. No more twists and turns, only one path, and one room at the end. I could see it from here, the slight glow and sour scent of bleach, daunting in the way it seeped into the hall.

I wasn't in Fellow Manor anymore. Not really.

"So, Adrian. Where are you?" Archon asked, his voice disembodied, that smug tone following me as I moved with slow steps toward the door.

"I'm in your *lamp*," I whispered, dread all consuming.

It was a process to get people inside of a Djinn's lamp, one that took up far more power than it was worth. If Archon did this, he did it with reason and strict intent. This was never just a trap to get us here. This was decades' worth of planning ... something that had to have stemmed from more than just a little grudge. "This can't be happening."

The snap of the *Flame* disappeared from my blood once again, and the safety it brought bled out. The same invisible chains that had tied me down in the cell hit me in the chest, binding me with sickening efficiency as I gasped for breath.

"Congratulations, Adrian. You won the game." Archon clapped, the sound echoing in the air. The hallway warped, the room around me fading away into nothingness tinted with gold.

The first thing I registered was how cold I was, the rigid bite of steel under my exposed back as I opened my eyes. The lights above me beamed down, the intensity enough to stun me.

Archon came into view, looking down over me with a tilted head. "See. You're out of the lamp, just as promised."

He turned the light away, exposing more of the room. It was medical, with machines flashing against the wall, a sterile white seeming to cover every surface.

"Now, what do I want, Collector?" I was trapped like a pig destined for slaughter, and my thoughts raced with the implications. Archon was never supposed to go this far. Nothing I'd ever found suggested he would, that he'd have the spine to. "Nothing less than the fall of Osiris Vivas. I can't kill him. He's too powerful for that, even with Sebek's approval to remove him ... but *you*?"

He ran a hand down my cheek, gently, almost kindly.

"The brothers he values so highly. I saw what the death of that bastard Nero did to him. Tell me, what will another death do?"

We weren't supposed to die here.

Aaliyah's smiling face crossed my mind, the feel of her hand in mine as we danced, the tender brush of lips I would have kissed a thousand more times had I thought it'd be the last.

"Do you know how he got the name *Rex Inferectom?*" Archon whispered, rageful as he clenched the table by my head, his power crackling against it. The gold in his eyes darkened, shimmering dust slipping off his skin. "He was the first deal I ever lost—the *only* deal I've lost—and it damned me and my closest kin. I spent six hundred years in my lamp because of his actions, because of his name."

He stepped back, and another man took his place. One whose face was covered in a surgical mask, a dark pair of shades over his eyes as he grinned down at me wide enough to see even through the cloth. There was a clock on his shirt, one facing me, displaying a timer marked at zero with chilling intent.

"When we get out of here—" I started, flinching away as Archon's hands cupped my cheeks in the most reminiscent way. Like Aaliyah had.

Or like I'd imagined she had.

"You'll what? Barely an hour has passed since you walked through my door, and you've already experienced being trapped for *weeks*. One snap of my fingers, and you're back in my lamp. You're mine, as long as I see fit," Archon said, and snapped his fingers just as he'd said. I flinched so hard the table rocked. "Be glad I want you to truly experience what comes next."

The timer started, and the man above me produced a knife. The gleaming blade glowed under the horrendous lights, and Archon walked away. "You know, there are worse fates. Like being the brother he *does* save."

Hope turned to despair in my stomach.

The sound of a door opening and clicking closed forever tied itself to the first slice of the knife, and the haunting laugh that followed Archon's final words. "A brother that's going to be nothing more than a shell of himself when I'm through with him."

Chapter 11

Fallon

"Taz, please," Aislinn begged through choked tears at the entrance to our hut. Like always, it made my chest cinch up, the crack in her voice making it hard to breathe. It hurt *so fucking much.* I didn't know how to handle it, how to get her to stop or understand. "Mama is worried. *I'm* worried."

I was sitting on the bed I'd woken up in for the past two years. To the same morning greeting and ruthless summer heat. To the waves I'd loved so much in my youth, that were now the siren call of hell. It had been *two years* of the same conversations and repetitive attempts at getting out of whatever the fuck this was.

No matter what I did, either the day went as planned and ended in a dread-filled sleep that no amount of begging would fix ... or everyone died, crumpling into smoldering embers like the remains of their homes.

Aislinn was always last, most of the time dying in my arms with ragged gasps, clutching the wrecked skin of her neck. Other times, she'd stand, mocking, telling me exactly what I already knew ... that this was my fault.

She was right. She *always* was.

A small fire built in my palm, Aislinn's cries growing frantic, picking up in pitch. I held my free hand up to keep her from getting too close. I didn't want to risk her getting burned. The sparks traced my skin, and I shivered, flexing scarred knuckles as the embers hit the dirt floor. The *Flame* danced in my blood, singing a forgotten tune as it crackled.

My head pounded as I rocked it from side to side, popping my neck. I wasn't proud, as my mind cracked under the weight of unease and tension. I'd done everything else I could to try to break this cycle. To leave this day behind.

I couldn't talk my way out of it. I'd tried that until I was blue in the face. I couldn't *fight* my way out, either. I would never do that to Aislinn ... so this had been my most recent attempt, my new morning every day for the last *three weeks*.

Killing myself, because at least it was better than watching Aislinn bleed.

I snapped my fingers, and the fire slipped to the paper bark that made up the walls and bedding, igniting it in a burst of violent flames. Their heat stole the oxygen from the air, scorching to the point that I nearly rushed out of them. This place may be hell, but it was consistent, and it was *painful,* and if there was anything I could handle, it was the pain.

It was easy, letting it swallow me whole. It was physical, not like the bits inside of me that broke every day I woke up here. And it was *real,* something I could grab onto when things were a little too seamless, a reminder that this was a dream.

That I had to get out, while I could still separate right from wrong, and real from fake.

"Fallon?" my mother started, her voice filling the void from outside the hut. It was scattered, broken bits of what it should have been, like my mind wasn't able to fill in the missing pieces. I could barely hear her over the fire. "Fallon, don't do this!"

I closed my eyes as the flames swallowed me, and I sank into them, letting them rip me away from my mother's voice. Darkness grabbed me, like hands pulling me down, filling my lungs.

Her screams mixed with Aislinn's, growing faint until they faded away entirely. The pain lingered, bad enough that if I had any control, I probably would have puked or passed out.

I waited for the familiar pull of the next day, dreading waking on that same bed, watching as Aislinn walked in with a smile that still haunted me. But for the first time, the dark didn't let me go.

"It's not working," a voice whispered, a break to the monotony, so out of place whoever said it might as well have *screamed* it. Enough to shoot adrenaline directly into my veins as I stopped breathing, like that might help me hear more. "If we push too hard, he'll break."

Whoever it was, her voice was quiet and gentle. I tried to flip around and find her, as if she might be in this pit, but I couldn't move. Trapped like an animal in a cage with a blanket thrown over the top.

"Good. I want him broken," another said, twisted and vicious, familiar in a way I couldn't place.

"I can't *hold* broken," she bit back, a gurgle in her voice before a crash filled the air, a wounded yelp following the sound of flesh cracking against flesh.

"You'll find a way. I don't have to remind you what happens if you fail, *Hadlie*."

I strained to hear more as a buzz filled the air, but nothing else came. Seconds passed before I opened my eyes again, blinking a few times to adjust to the low light of the moon through a glass window. My lips were numb, like my body was still trying to figure out how to feel.

The haze followed me like a plague, even here, and I almost forgot to breathe when I realized where I was.

In bed. *My* bed. The sheets were a soft silken comfort I'd spent days picking out. The pictures that surrounded me were lit by the glow of a full moon, familiar ones—Picasso, Michelangelo ... *Aislinn's*. The same one she'd painted for me every day, though now finished. The colors were faded with age and smeared where our fingers had traced.

The grim black room slipped away with the voices that had been in it, my eyes adjusting instantly, the headache that had destroyed me for the past two years fading into a dull ache like the pulse of my fangs in my mouth. I let out a breath, falling back on the sheets as I rubbed my face. I felt like me for the first time since this shit show started.

Home. I was *home*.

"Fal?" a voice whispered, and I flinched, looking for Aislinn on instinct as the body next to me shuffled.

Groggy *violet* eyes peeked up from under the blanket, and Ali rubbed them as she crawled over to me. I didn't move as she laid her head on my bare chest. She was so warm, letting out a breath as she snuggled in close, tucked perfectly into my side, exactly where she should have been.

I'd struggled through the memories with Aislinn, but at least with her there'd been a detachment, an understanding that what I was seeing was wrong. Her voice was something I'd forgotten, the quirks to her personality something I could play off as just another trick in the dream.

Aaliyah was a fresh presence, a breath of lavender-filled air that made my chest hurt at the thought of her being here.

She wasn't. I *knew* she wasn't. But two years of hell had been enough to break me, and even if this wasn't my Ali ... I couldn't help but take comfort in her. I reached for my wrist, grazing the mark that showed there again, the purple band pulsing when I touched it.

"Aaliyah," I said, desperately trying to keep myself sane. Even then, I couldn't stop from leaning in, kissing the top of her head when she inched her way up.

She laughed, looking up at me with gentle eyes, crow's feet at the corners, before she leaned in fully. It caught me by surprise, as she kissed me, running her hand up my chest as my own found her bare hip. There was a tremble in my hands I couldn't stop.

Fuck, I'd missed her so much.

I grunted as she moved, straddling my bare waist as I arched into her touch. My eyes shot wide as she rolled her hips, and the sensual motion dragged me out of my thoughts as she grinned mischievously down at me. Her soft, breathy moan was practically a drug.

I was ashamed of how hard I got, guilty at knowing this wasn't really her.

"I'm not going to be able to walk tomorrow at this rate," she said jokingly, leaning down to bite my ear. I damned near came in my nonexistent fucking shorts and had to physically lift her to give myself some room to think.

The shift from the last day to now was whiplash. Ali giggled, and the sound went straight through me.

"We haven't had sex yet," I said through a groan as I tipped my head back, trying to dislodge the trick, no matter how good it felt. Reality crossed with this nightmare.

I would have remembered our first time. There was no fucking way I'd forget it.

Aaliyah laughed again, and the spark of heat that came with her touch turned molten when she trailed a leisurely line across my abdomen, sticking to the divots on my hips while she hummed. "What would you call last night, then?"

I shivered, halting her moves with my hands, grunting as I stopped myself from arching up to meet her again. Control was something I savored, and I held it with every ounce of strength I had as I took steady breaths.

This wasn't Ali.

Not *my* Ali.

"Osiris, Eirik, Adrian. Where are they?" I asked, taking a deep breath when she stopped moving. She crossed her arms over her chest, blushing brightly as she looked away from me.

"In their rooms, I'd assume," she mumbled, rubbing the back of her neck. "Why?"

"Not here?" I grunted, taken aback by that. There was no way Adrian wouldn't have taken the chance to be here for this, and Eirik was practically her lap dog. "Adrian wouldn't miss the chance to steal the spotlight."

"Fallon."

A voice whispered as Aaliyah curled onto my chest, hiding her face from me. But at least she'd stopped gyrating. The softness of her lavender scent hit me like a wave.

"Why would they be here? I'm *yours,* Fallon. After the Eternium, you made me choose ... I chose you," she said, her voice firm.

Mine? Aaliyah was mine?

Adrian's face flashed through my mind, echoing the hints of a heated conversation that suddenly didn't seem real anymore. The fight in the training room lost its bitter edge.

No, that couldn't be right.

"You have to wake up."

It was almost like Aaliyah had said it, her mouth moving just slightly enough to see the words form. I jolted out of her arms, putting distance between us as the voice ripped me away. A cold sweat started on my forehead, my breathing spiraling as Aaliyah covered her chest with the blanket.

"The Eternium," I said, gasping for breath. "What happened at the Eternium?"

Aaliyah tilted her head to the side.

"You don't remember?" she asked, drawing toward me. The blanket fell, exposing every inch of her smooth skin as she reached for me again. I couldn't even see Aaliyah in the way she moved now, like the softness had been a mask. "What happened at the Eternium, Fallon?"

The voice wasn't hers, instead warped and broken, shifted. There was a sharpness to the words that I couldn't ignore.

"Fallon, wake up!" the Ali in front of me screamed, cracking her soft expression for just a second before she was back to touching my chest. Her hands grabbed my necklace, the one I hadn't realized I was wearing.

The one Osiris had made for us after our wards had been cracked open. The one I'd *forgotten* about, ignored. *That* was it.

That was my way out, and somehow, this Aaliyah warned me about it. I reached up, grabbing the necklace, as she was torn away from me. The room melted, cracks appearing in the floor and walls, like the illusion had been shattered.

"I lost him," a voice whispered, straining through the sound of metal and glass crashing to the ground.

"Then get him back, Hadlie!" another snarled.

I strained against whatever bindings held me down, and for a second they quivered. My finger twitched, and I sucked in a gasping breath I could *taste.* Then the cold touch of what felt like metal, under me and wrapped around my wrists. It was the first real impact I'd seen on this dream world, the shock waves like a ripple that broke open the dark.

An instant of bright lights blinded me, and the feeling of sweat-slicked steel under my back made me grunt.

The woman gasped, choking on a pained cry as my arm shot up, the thick chain at my wrist snapping at the connection joint, clattering as more voices filled the air. The light wobbled, knocked away as blurred faces surrounded me, and hands fought to hold me down.

I lashed out, catching one of the many bodies, sending them to the floor. I was close, *so* close. My other arm tingled, feeling slamming back into it as I clenched my hand into a tight fist.

Freedom was a breath away. One fight, one struggle. I had to get out. I wouldn't have another chance. I snarled, screaming until I went hoarse, using brute force against the magic that held me down. I opened my eyes long enough to see two faces. The girl, an Unseelie Fae from the ashen gray of her skin and the scattering of stars across her face, stretched her hands out in front of her, fingers splayed wide as she set them on my chest. The other belonged to *him*. Archon. The one we'd come to find. The coward who'd hid behind his own guards and used them like cannon fodder.

The one we'd *lost* to.

"I'm trying. He's—" Hadlie grunted, eyes closed in concentration, whatever spell she had me under flexing as I fought. The necklace Osiris had given me strained, heating against my chest until it burned, helping to force the magic open. She gasped as I ripped my arm away from the guards keeping me steady, sweat sliding down her face as she paled. "Something else got in, broke him out."

Archon's hand came to my wrist, forcing me back down to the table as the sickening sweetness of gold filled the air. I snarled, unable to get any words out, my body still only partially mine. I gritted my teeth until I felt one snap. The mark on my wrist glowed, Aaliyah's lavender giving me enough energy to move.

I had to get to her.

Hadlie made a distressed sound, and I felt another crack in whatever held me. A scream ripped through the halls, flexing like the bonds in my chest as I arched off the steel again. At first, I thought it was *mine*.

But it was softer, higher pitched, and doused in a voice I knew well. The rippling bond in my chest strained like cooking wire strung too tightly. It shocked me to my core, enough to let Hadlie's magic sink in and freeze me. My arms fell to the table, the guards no longer having to struggle to keep me down.

Adrian, that was *Adrian's* scream.

I ripped my head to the side, just barely catching a glimpse of him. He was a mess of blood, his skin flayed open, the man above him toying with his organs. His voice went hoarse as his scream ripped at the walls.

"Let him go," I croaked, grunting as I strained against my chains.

I'd never in my entire life felt weaker than when Archon's magic cradled the room. It hit my skin like a blow, and I was too drained to fight it. For one brutal second, I feared him.

"*Now*, Hadlie," Archon snarled, all ice in his voice as his eyes hit mine.

I gritted my teeth, blood filling my mouth as my fangs fell.

"Let him go!" I managed, as another blade sank into him.

He choked, gurgling as blood pooled in his mouth. Vacant eyes stared back at me, going blank as the bond in my chest tightened. It was like an electric shock hit every nerve, and I jolted off the table, screaming with him.

Archon's hand found my necklace, the one that still sat against my chest. I smelled burning flesh as he grabbed it, his hiss pure joy to my ears. Osiris's magic fought him, and there was a war in his eyes that bordered between pain and fear.

Until he ripped the charm away.

The loss of it ravaged me, tore me apart from the inside out, and for a second, I swore I could taste torched lavender. Blood flooded my nose, and the unspeakable sounds of Adrian being ripped to shreds were all I could hear as I seized, and my brain turned to mush in my skull. Delicate hands touched the sides of my face.

Any fight I had died, any will in my muscles fading away as my eyes slid closed. One second dragged into two, and Adrian's screams followed me back to the fucking dream, haunting me. My skin trembled, viciously cold ... before the dark swallowed me, and I was sitting up with a grunt.

The haze followed, the brightly lit room fading back until there were only silken sheets and lavender. I sucked in a hard breath as I brushed my hair back. I reached for my chest, for my wrist, and felt nothing.

Aaliyah stirred next to me, looking at me with groggy eyes as I panicked, flipping the sheets off me.

"Fal?" she asked, touching my chest softly, her brows cinching together as she laid her head over my heart. "What's wrong?"

Everything, *everything* was wrong. Tears came to my eyes, the sound of Adrian's scream destroying me.

"Nothing," I whispered, looking at the wall, trying to sort through what to do. Osiris's magic wasn't here to help me anymore, and I was on my own. Adrian was being ripped apart, and I was here ... next to Ali.

I looked back at her, taking comfort in her eyes, even if it wasn't real. Even if this was my *hell*.

"Just a nightmare."

Chapter 12

Aaliyah

I wasn't sure what I'd been expecting after the teleportation spell left me wobbling on my feet, my head suddenly throbbing, but this little apartment, with a quaint rustic kitchen and freshly cleaned furniture, wasn't it.

Ascension had been akin to a war zone, between the bodies that had been ripped apart and strewn about it, to the hauntingly familiar rooms now painted with aged blood and gore.

Where we'd landed was clean, almost *too* clean, the entire place smelling slightly like bleach in a way that made my stomach turn. When I swayed again, Sebek grabbed my shoulders, keeping me upright even as I jolted away from him.

His hands were icy, a brush of warped power still stinging where he touched as he directed me to the island in the middle of the kitchen. I kept waiting for the bite of pain, for his fingers to sink too deep and leave welting bruises where he held me, but every move was done with methodical intent.

There were four tall chairs in front of the island, and he lifted me onto one before I could protest.

I hated being dragged around, feeling like a puppet that he could toy with. It put me on edge, and I struggled to stay in the seat, even when he shot me a frigid glare as I shuffled. He was gone in a flash, leaving an audible pop in the air. He appeared again just a breath later, this time in front of me, with a first aid kit.

It was unopened, and he cracked it as he pulled at the lid. Those crazed mumbles began again as he reached out and tilted my head left and right, up and down, while I stiffly tried to stop the mantra as it burned in my skull.

Never make noise.

I didn't want to give him any reason to go feral again, to take back his word of letting the others live. The contrast between the two parts of him I'd seen had been blindingly confusing. Hot and cold, concerned and filled with brittle fury. So, I stayed silent as he moved down, lifting my arms so he could check the range of motion, pressing on the joints that had strained when I'd tried to get away, and placing bandages where my palms were scraped.

"There. All better," he said, finally pulling away, giving me room to breathe as I shrank away from him.

He didn't notice, or didn't care, heading toward the kitchen just to fumble with the fridge and the ingredients inside it. He kept his back to me, and I looked around the room, taking the temporary reprieve from his gaze to get an idea of my surroundings. With more time to look, I realized how *little* the room actually had in it. It was missing things I'd grown used to, decorations, and signs of life. Everything felt startlingly bare. There were two main doors, one leading to what looked like an enclosed balcony. The other, I assumed, was the door outside. There was also a long hallway that disappeared into darkness.

I itched to move, glancing quickly at Sebek before turning back toward the balcony.

"You won't make it." Sebek suddenly cut into my musing, the sound of chopping filling the room along with the steady scents of fresh garlic and onion. "Get it out of your head, Glass. You're *mine.* I won't let you escape me again."

The calculated frost had returned to his voice. No hint of the worry that had been there just seconds ago. Again, he turned, the crazed look in his eyes sharpening into dagger-like points that meant to cut.

Eirik had called me that once: *his.* It had meant everything to me then. It made my stomach flutter and my knees weak, made me feel safe in a world where safety had always felt like nothing more than a lie.

Hearing Sebek say it damn near had me gagging.

Was Eirik okay? Were he and the others safe, had they made it back from Archon's, or were they truly trapped there? Had they found Osiris?

I reached for the itching marks on my wrist that ached like the pressure behind my eyes.

"What are you going to do with me?" I asked.

It was a question I hadn't had much time to ponder with everything that had happened. It had been chaos after Sebek had taken me, but now, in this *quaint* room, with a man that radiated feral, dangerous power, I needed to know.

He'd been the leader of the same group that had torn me apart time after time. What would I endure to make sure my men stayed safe until the Eternium?

"What should have been done to start with," he said simply, turning away with the same grace he'd faced me with as he tossed his mixture of cut vegetables into a sizzling pan. "Bring back order to the Eternals."

One moment, he was a mumbling mess, screaming into the void like it might respond. The next, he looked like he could pick me apart, like this was all a puzzle he'd already solved, mixing the pieces together to throw me off.

"How?" I pressed, and just as quickly, he threw his head back and *laughed*.

Laughed belly deep as his fangs dropped, and he *flitted* to me, his food abandoned on the stovetop, still sizzling until the scent of burning oil filled the air. I nearly fell off the chair as his hand shot out to keep me stable. His grip was tight but not painful. "The only way I can. The only way that will last."

The still-lingering smell of iron that had absorbed into his skin had my stomach turning. My mantra rang furiously in my ears, but I returned his look with a glare anyway.

"You have the same look in your eyes, the same fire. *Usire* will be proud." That name burned me, and he let me go to brush a hand over my cheekbone. It was said in a moment of clarity, one that lit his eyes as he spoke so softly.

Then his hand dropped, and that feral expression took over again like he realized what he'd said.

"What?" I whispered.

At first, I didn't understand, the name leaving just a touch of pressure building in my skull. But when he ripped his hand through his hair, that confused, angry panic again rearing its head as he spoke, I understood. "You are so like *him*."

Pain laced the words, giving them a softness he didn't have the right to use. So like the man who'd raised me, died for me, at *his* hands. Without a shadow of a doubt, I knew he was talking about my father.

He had the audacity to say he'd be proud? He should be proud *now*. He should have been proud of me my entire life, from the moment I took my first breath to my first heartbreak, to every *first* he didn't get to see. My father lost so many things when he'd died, so many wonders that I would never have him to guide me through.

I lost him because of the same man that currently stood rigidly in front of me, his rambling trying to convince either me or himself that his brother wouldn't hate him for what he was doing to his child.

"My father is dead," I snarled, suddenly losing my sense.

I should have stayed quiet, kept it in so I didn't risk the others, but I couldn't stand the look on Sebek's face. The way he smiled so calmly, as if remembering a kind moment between him and the man he'd killed.

"He's *not* dead," Sebek said, that look back in his eyes, calculating, *crazy*, as if he believed it. I shot to my feet, and he stepped back gracefully, his head tilting to the side.

The flash of the memory that had come to me in the forest felt raw now, the sight of my mother and father fading from view. Their souls passed on, *gone*. I remembered the steady thump of their emotions, the way it'd felt like a heartbeat, and the fluttering silence that had followed.

My magic tried to flare, burning hot in my stomach like molten lava, trapped under the surface of my skin, and suddenly I tasted blood as I bared my teeth. The spot behind my ear that was still tender throbbed, and I knew whatever he'd put there to suppress my powers was fighting me. Pushing and shoving, the magic that was bound tried to come to my aid but withered under the magic that held it captive. This time it didn't lie low and refuse my call. This time, my power stretched inside me, and there was a whisper of a dark voice. The one that had been *mine* at the hot springs came forward again, this time indignant in my head.

Make him regret caging us, it whispered.

"My father is dead because *you* killed him," I snapped, my vision shifting between clear and clouded black.

A sharp look of surprise, and then he took another step back, but there was no fear in the way he moved. That darkness in me didn't like that; it wanted to see him cower, and I forced another step toward him. "Then you stole me from him, you experimented on me, *tortured* me!"

His eyes, already a familiar red, flushed with the color, swallowing it from iris to sclera. He bared his teeth, fangs catching his lip. Blood slipped over them, dripping down his chin, hitting the floor as he bent. He snarled, like a wild animal. "I did nothing of the sort!"

"You didn't stop them!" I cut in before he could continue. The power in me raged, flowed, and that molten lava in my stomach spread everywhere else. The blood in my mouth turned to ash, as my vision dimmed to a dark gray, and stayed that way this time as the burning behind my ear grew into an inferno. "Do you think he'd be proud of *you*? That he wouldn't be disgusted with what his own brother did to his family?"

One more push, *one more*, and I'd have control. But what would I do with it?

Kill. A whisper. A *promise* that caught in my throat and dug like the daggers in Sebek's eyes that reminded me so much of my father.

"Silence, do not speak of—"

I cut him off, screaming. "You will not stop my voice! Never again!"

The dam shattered, and the gates to my gifts that had been forced shut exploded open. Blood was at my nose, pressure hitting me so harshly that my eyes rolled back. Before I could hit the ground, the distinctive flavor of rotten blood was on my lips, the taste now uncomfortably familiar.

The power that had come to my call had fallen just as quickly to the pressure, the walls that held it building back up, brick by brick. Until I was bound again.

Sebek held me like he was a comfort. He brushed the hair from out of my face, carefully. I could only offer a glare. "I hate you."

His final words were as much of a conundrum as they were agonizing, compounding on the pressure that crested in my skull. "I didn't mean to kill him. Not him, *never* him. *He wasn't supposed to die.*"

The *Rend* swallowed me whole.

Chapter 13

Prince

E*t in domum suam in solem* had been built on our dreams. That much I remembered.

There were hints of me in every piece that I looked at, from the gold speckled décor to the dents and blemishes in delicately carved woodwork. Hints of a life that I couldn't remember, hints of those I knew somewhere deep in my chest, those I *loved*. The rooms felt colder now than what my mind told me they were like before. Aaliyah wasn't dancing down the stairs, light on her feet with a book in one hand and a chocolate in the other. There were tells of my brothers, too. Faded glimmers of Adrian creating chaos in the kitchen, the aroma of something delectable that I could no longer name. The creak of the floor as Eirik stalked the halls, his brutish frame making it impossible for him to sneak. The scent of a freshly tailored suit or two.

My memories were just as broken, just as lost, but it was those that had kept me functional after my rise from the crypt that I had been so desperate to see when I got here. It was supposed to be a reunion, all tears and snot and a doggy pile of a hug that I'd have even dragged Osiris into.

Now, it was empty, *dull*, and painfully blatant in its meaning. If we failed, then either we risked losing Aaliyah. Her smile, her joy, the way she hummed under her breath as she walked. The woman I loved more than all others, who, if she were standing here, would wonder why we weren't *already* at Archon's.

Or we risked losing our brothers. The family that had taken root in my soul, their bonds strong enough that I could still feel them in my chest. Something even death couldn't fully break. The men who'd no doubt lay down their lives to make sure we got Aaliyah home safe.

That made the answer to what we had to do simple. There was no way in hell, come Hades or high water, I was going to let *either* happen.

"I'm going to clean up," Osiris said, brushing a streak of drying blood off his face, stalking away without another word.

"You play with thin strings, ones far more fragile than you can see," Mags mumbled, pulling me from my thoughts as they kneeled next to Kali's still smoldering body.

They seemed bitter, their face screwed into a pout. Their age showed in the wrinkles in their skin and the lost look in their eyes. I'd expected to see something warm, considering their kinship to the pile of coals, but all Mags did was dip their hand in the blood, bringing it to their lips before licking it off. It smelled like an ancient forest, muddled with the thick scent of rotten wood and mulch. Hidden by the greenery and washed away by the subtle scent of rain. *Deceptive.* Mags did it again, this time dipping both hands in, smearing it around.

"Mags, now isn't the time for your riddles," I said, shaking my head as I turned away. I wasn't in any kind of mental state to deal with them right now, especially not after what they'd said to Osiris.

But Mags had never been one to shy away from uncomfortable physical contact, as they grabbed my face with one of their putrid hands, flipping me until I was forced to look them in the eye. I grunted, already biting out a scathing retort, when they spoke. "They won't stop. Never stop. *Never stop.* Death still clings to you, *Prince.*"

Mags didn't say anything else as they let me go, dropping back to the floor with a splash as they continued to play in the blood, fingers moving in a pattern I wasn't sure meant anything, like it was some kind of morbid mud puddle.

They'd spun enough words to make me sick, and fear wasn't an emotion I liked all that well. Especially when I knew they were right. I could feel it, the stutter of my own heart, the way my blood didn't seem to know how to flow correctly. Everything about me felt *off.*

"Thanks for the support, Mags. I do love our chats," I grumbled, flipping away, wiping what blood I could from my face.

Worry of my own death could wait. The sun was rising, maybe ten minutes from cresting at most, taunting me as the shutters closed over the large floor-to-ceiling windows in the kitchen. I'd make it to Archon's faster with a spell, so as much as I ached to get this show on the road, I had some time to kill. I washed my face—*twice*—before I made my way up the stairs. I kept my hand on the cool gray walls, stumbling over the stone accents that lined it, only stopping when my hand hit a divot.

An unfamiliar door in a familiar spot. I ran my fingertips along the wood, searching for a crack that was no longer there, hand falling to the doorknob to my room. *Aaliyah's* room. I'd seen it in more than a few memories, and the smell of it, like rich lavender and the deep breath of mountain air ... It overwhelmed me.

I'd caught bits of her scent around, bits of Aaliyah that I hadn't been privy to, this person who had stolen my heart directly from my chest. It was like proof she was real, that I wasn't crazy.

I stumbled forward, landing on the bed, crawling into the sheets that were drowned in that scent. I could see her now, buried in them, her unruly white hair tangled as she woke, groggily smiling at me.

Good morning, Prince.

"I will save you, Aaliyah," I whispered, digging deeper into the sheets. I felt the burn at the back of my throat before I could get another word out, suddenly choking. Tears branded at my eyes, and I curled into a ball, wishing she were here. Wishing that everything hadn't gone to shit. "I wasn't able to before, and I will *always* regret that. So, please, stay safe for me until I can find you."

I stayed there, wound in those blankets, buried so deep I would have sworn I could hear her heartbeat and subtle breaths. When I pulled back, it was just me in an empty room I'd dreamed of what seemed like a million times. I stood, fixing the blankets so they'd be ready for when we got home.

I'd give her the life she deserved. We *all* would.

I walked out, but rather than turning down the stairs, I moved the other way. To the large mosaic door I'd crashed through when I'd first gotten here. The game room barely stopped me as I moved to my little masterpiece, the sound of swirling whisky pushing me to open the door that had Thoth so beautifully carved into it. My hands lingered on the unfinished woodwork, on the delicate details that I wouldn't have bet were mine if my mind didn't search them out. The room it opened to was cozy, warmly heated from the fresh fire, comforting organic wooden colors and textures accenting the packed space. I singled in on the man who stood in it.

Osiris was gaunt, somehow looking *worse* than he had covered in blood, his eyes far away as he put down his glass, then poured another from the decanter above the fireplace.

His suit was torn, his fresh tie abandoned on the floor. The skin of his wrist was exposed, healing from what looked like his fingernails clawing at it and streaking black lines that seemed to etch into his veins.

I came to his side, using the time to stare into the fire with him. I grabbed the decanter and took a swig, smirking when he glowered at me. It was a reaction, though, one I hadn't realized I'd been looking for. "You look like shit."

He huffed, shaking his head as he downed his next glass. It wouldn't do much. Alcohol didn't affect us the same, I recalled, but he took comfort in it, regardless. He looked me up and down, narrowing his eyes on what was likely the remains of the bloodied handprint on my face.

"And you sound like Adrian," he whispered.

Now *that* made me laugh, my head tipping back. Adrian, he'd still been so new when I'd died, and I could practically feel him on my heels as we ran down the halls, away from Fallon after a prank gone wrong. What we'd done, I couldn't say, but he'd been a partner in crime, a younger brother who reminded me of my human years. "No, Adrian sounds like me, you *ass*."

He'd taken to me like bees on honey, though the memories around him were the fuzziest. God, the things we used to do to poor, *poor* Fally. I'd have to sit down with him and have him recount some once I got him out.

Osiris didn't reply for a moment. His eyes were on the fire, the dead numbness in them only growing as he poured another glass and took another drink. "What was it like, being dead?"

Part of me itched to dig in to that look and ask why the veins in his hand had turned an ashen black. It seemed like something I would have done before.

But I wasn't that same Nero. I *wasn't* Nero, not anymore. I was Prince, and that meant something. I wanted to be the brother he lost, but balancing that with the man I was now seemed so daunting.

"I don't remember much. To be honest, most of my memories are of Aaliyah." There had been moments with them, ones that had shadowed their faces and left me scrambling to learn them all over again. They were the ones that had hit the hardest after I'd finally realized who Osiris was. With Aaliyah, though, I'd remembered a lot, from torture sessions to game nights. To soft singing and endless conversations. The way we'd dance around her cell until the early morning hours, and I'd spend all my time thinking of ways I might get her out. She'd talk about what she wanted, a life outside those glass walls, and I'd dream I could follow her, live that life *with* her. The imprint she had on me was infinite. "It was ... haunting, and the most powerless I've ever felt, having to watch her go through that and not being able to help."

I tapered off, looking away as Osiris's hands flexed, the veins drawing my attention again, sharp like a blade to the ribs. He brought his glass up to his lips, taking a small sip of his drink.

"I couldn't imagine." He didn't turn away, nodding his head for me to continue.

I didn't think I was the "talking it out" sort. Never would have guessed that I'd be the one to spill my guts. But keeping it all inside seemed to just make it hurt worse, and this man who felt so much like a stranger seemed like the only one who would understand.

"Knowing that the same man that had Turned me was the one pulling the strings ... nothing has ever hurt worse, and I *died*." I choked that part out.

I'd died, faced the sun with a shit-eating grin and knew how *badly* it hurt. Had thought nothing would ever compare. Then I saw her, heard the *first* of her bones break.

Then another. *Followed by her screams.* The same ones she'd held in for my sake, behind gritted teeth that were stained with her blood because she didn't want me to worry.

"We'll get her back, Nero," Osiris cut in, a stable voice to the chaos as my mind wandered, and those screams gained volume. "Her and the others."

His hand flexed around his glass. The fire glowed, showing the faint lines of determination on his face and the numb in his eyes. Kali's blood may have been gone, and he may have changed suits, but he looked just as feral now as he had when he'd destroyed her.

"Damn right we will," I grunted, shaking my head. I turned, setting my hand on the back of an obnoxiously red couch, one that I lingered on. There was something familiar about it that had me smiling.

It was like a small reminder that this was my home. My *life*. Now I just had to get everyone back *and* maybe remember what made me Vivas.

"Oh, I haven't forgiven you for killing me yet, you know. Pretty sure you owe me a stiff drink and several uninterrupted piano hours," I joked before swiping his half-full glass away from him. He raised a brow but didn't reach to take it back as I downed the rest. "That's the interest. Be ready to pay up in full when we're back home."

His lips tilted up, his eyes clearing for a moment before he smiled, huffing what could be considered a laugh.

"I wouldn't dream of denying you that, Nero." It was small, but that hint of Osiris still lingering behind those eyes was enough to keep me moving. "Together, then?"

I grinned before I reached out, something my soul told me I'd done a million times, and Osiris did the same, grabbing my forearm as I pulled him into a hug. He shuddered against me for a moment before accepting the contact. "Always, brother."

A throat cleared. I looked over, finding Mags covered head to toe in blood, grinning like a feral beast. Ah, please just let that be Kali's.

"We are ready. The *depths* await amidst your palace of fool's gold. Best not keep fate waiting."

***

Magic had an innate warmth to it, a comforting hold that dragged lazily over the skin, like the touch of a gentle lover. There was a kindness to be found in something so vast and powerful.

When it wasn't pointed toward *you*, that was.

Mags's teleportation spell *spit* me out, like some phlegm that had been caught in their throat, and I dropped directly to the ground. I grunted, slamming into stone and sliding down my fair share of cobblestone steps, swearing up and down as I searched for the asshat of a Chronomancer so I could give them a piece of my mind.

Only to realize *they* weren't fucking here. Which meant, to my great amusement, they'd gone with Osiris. God, I was sad I was going to miss that party.

I stood up, cracking my back with a groan, shaking off the dirt and grime that had stuck to me from the steps, scrunching my nose at the scent of rotten plant life barely veiled by the crispness of winter. If there was anything I missed about being dead, it had to be the fact that I didn't hurt. Now, my muscles screamed, my head close after, like something had knocked loose when I'd landed. I reached up and swiped away a stray dash of blood that slid out of my nose.

A tingling sensation shot down my spine as I looked at the dreary streets behind me. The streetlights were still on, almost mocking me, and the first hints of the orange glow of the sun started in the sky.

Plenty of time to cause a little mayhem.

"Don't worry, guys, Nero's here to save the day. Back from the dead, *completely* healthy!" I said, out loud when it really should have stayed inside, hopping up the steps two at a time. I clapped my palm against my ear as the pressure moved there, chasing its own tail in the midst of my skull. What a *mood* kill. I'd been so ready for this fight, so geared up to break in and save the day.

Just for Mags to go spoil it all and remind me I was dying.

"Damn it. Why did you have to go and ruin my vibe, huh?" I said out loud again. Words just seemed to slip out now that I had a body to voice them.

I took the last step, hands in my jean pockets, nearly crashing into the door before I clicked my tongue. I set my palm down on it, pressing into the metal, weighing my odds as I considered knocking. "Not this time, you bastard."

It felt like standard iron, heavy and resilient. I cracked a smile, pulling my hand back before I slammed it forward, knocking the heavy thing clean off its hinges, and sent it flying into Archon's home.

The tumble was followed by the shattering of glass, a slew of cries coming from the now mangled hall, one man seemingly crushed beneath the weight in a way that made me cringe as I peeked inside, stepping through with a shiver as the house seemed to recognize that I'd already been here. "That looks like it's going to leave a mark."

He was bent at an odd angle, his arm underneath him, contorted in a way that could, under no circumstances, be labeled as correct. His face was a bloody red, head tipped back as he screamed.

The other guards, seeming to snap out of their haze, rushed at me with the coordination of a drugged-up lion, panic stealing their steps. The first, a man with a hearty, earthen scent and muscles that looked like he could take gold in the Olympic hammer throw, swung high with a spear, and my body *moved.*

I grabbed his arm, wrenching his wrist as he tried to bring it down on my head. The weak point caved, and his hand opened, the spear hitting the ground. All within the space of a second.

I threw him to the side, grinning as he crashed into what looked like a *very* fancy sculpture of a man overlooking the hall. It seemed to be the only thing in the drab, dusty place that hadn't been hit by the door.

Oops.

Adrenaline *lived* in my veins, the thrill of a fight a drug I never could have replicated.

Another trickle of blood slid down from my nose, my vision blotting as I cracked my neck again. My hands went numb, my tongue, too, as I fought back the approaching *Rend.* I'd never managed to before, but maybe Mags's sock potion would keep it at bay long enough to get through this.

Or I'd give these boys a lovely show before I died.

The others were more wary than the first that had come running, less rushed as I brushed my hair back, the ominous threat of a wayward memory hot on my heels, pushing me forward.

The guards created a wall between me and the open hall, spears pointed my way. If I wasn't on such a time crunch, I might have taken the time to play a bit.

"Gentlemen, gentlemen. Please, there's enough of me to go around," I said, as I reached down and picked up the spear the other man had dropped, twirling it a few times to test the balance. On instinct, I lowered my grip closer to the wooden end, to accommodate its off-weighted center of gravity from a slightly too heavy head.

My nose flared as I took in the scent of battle. "Oh, I *missed* this."

I hadn't even known I did, but now that I was here, face to face with a slew of enemies ... I knew there was only one place I'd rather be. In Aaliyah's arms, whispering her name, breathing in all that lavender sweetness.

And to get there?

I needed to get through *them*.

They dashed, all at once, looking to take me by surprise, and it was almost comically easy to dispatch them. One by one, bodies fell around me. A spear to the eye, a broken arm leading to a cracked neck.

The *Rend* came hard and fast, slamming into the back of my skull as I grunted, eyes rolling back. I barely managed to jam the spearhead into the wall, ducking below it as another guard swung at me. I collapsed to my knees as wood splintered around me from where his weapon struck mine, and a memory tore through my brain.

The crack of bone and the scream Aaliyah hid behind her lips as she looked me in the eye. I'd taken to hovering over her, blocking out Castillion's face as he leaned over, leering. He was lucky I wasn't alive.

The guard jolted forward, planning to strike again. I was dazed, barely able to keep myself from separating completely. I felt the tug at my soul, like hands reaching inside my chest to pull me out.

So, I made a perfectly logical call and punched him *directly* in the dick.

He flew back several feet, his eyes rolling, and even I cringed as he reached to cover the family jewels before he crashed to the ground. A moaning mess that quickly descended into tears.

Another pulse of pressure, another memory sneaking up on me. My hands shook, my skin going clammy as my body revolted against itself. The shard of a memory that crept past was more familiar, more open as Osiris's face switched with the next guard that ran at me, snarling.

Towering marble pillars filled an expansive ballroom. A black piano that called to me along the far wall, and my brother at my side as we played a song that my fingers twitched along to. The room went silent, masked faces watching on in awe and contempt. Their jealousy was as alive as the beat of my heart.

Blood flew, some of it mine as his sword sliced through the flesh of my arm, most of it his as his body dropped in between memories I couldn't stop, *Rends* I held back with the grit of my teeth. Until I was left panting in a sea of fallen men.

Osiris offered me a hand, gloved in black, his eyes cold as he looked at the bodies in the streets around us. The ones who'd thought it'd be a good idea to fight. I'd been more than happy to entertain them while he meandered.

I turned, just as three more crept into the hall. They stopped short, paling, faces a mask of horror as I picked up a sword that had clattered to the ground. It was weighted nicely, the blade a little dull, but even with that I knew *this* was my true calling. The spears had done their job, but a sword?

It felt right in a way nothing else I'd held had.

A daunting smile on a dark, faceless man, the hints of a fight I couldn't remember. The laugh of a best friend, of a brother in all but blood. We sparred on the sandy beach of his home, his sword shattering on mine.

The blade sang as I sliced it through the air and stalked forward, tripping over my feet. One stepped up, bigger than the rest, his body seeming to be made of stone and scales, fire slipping past his nose as he narrowed eyes with red-slitted pupils.

"What? Scared?" I said, raising the blade in what I imagined made me look like a bit of a psychopath. "Come on, I won't bite that hard. Do it, make my fucking day."

I flashed fangs, my vision dusting red as the veins along my face popped. Another rush of hot fire down my nose. I wouldn't be able to hold on much longer.

Watching him lose all the blood in his face was comical as his sword crashed to the ground.

"Vampire."

Like the monster that haunted his childhood dreams. He waited all of a few seconds before he ran back down the hall. Leaving a trail of dust and piss in his wake.

I hummed, slashing the sword again, planting it tip first into the ground as I leaned over it to look at the remaining two. My useless fucking legs were little better than overcooked noodles, as wetness clouded my ears. No doubt more blood there now, too. I'd need another shower. Hopefully, this next time I could enjoy one without bodily injury.

I snorted at the thought of Mags taking on these beasts with their lovely frying pan.

"His loss," I said, shrugging my shoulder, pointing between the two of them before landing on the one on the left. "You."

I was on him in the next second, hand around the collar of his horrendous armor. I lifted him from the ground, grunting when he tried to land a hit ... then laughing when he did, a dull ache in my cheek, ending in the blood I spit up. That got his attention. "Where are my brothers?"

His eyes flared, lips curling back to show little baby fangs. His ears shifted, stretching long as gills sprouted on the side of his neck. "I'm not telling you shit—"

I snapped his neck and let him drop with the rest.

The last man standing wasn't what I would have even called a man. A boy in soldier's clothing, more like. He'd dropped, as well, staring at me from where he sat like I was the devil himself. To him, I might as well have been.

A Vampire. A monster that stalked the night, even to other monsters. I reached down, hauling him up the same way I had his buddy.

"Let's try this again," I said, cracking my neck from side to side. The pressure pulsed, and I grunted as I stumbled, tasting a hint of salt at the memory of a ship on an open ocean. "I don't think your friend heard me, and I'm kind of on a time crunch here. So, *where* are my brothers?"

A simple question, a simple answer. That was all I needed. I really wasn't *that* unreasonable.

"Wh-who?" he asked through trembling lips and tear-soaked cheeks.

A child, nothing more than a whelp. Seeing him made me almost irrationally angry. This was a boy, and Archon seemed more than happy to throw him to the wolves. He shouldn't be fighting like this yet. Learning to fight, sure.

Who didn't want to earn their first battle scar?

But this wasn't a game. He could die here. If I were anyone else, he likely would have.

"Can't miss them. Tall, dark, wicked with fangs? One may be a little more wolfy than fangs? Seriously, *can't* miss him," I said, chuckling at the thought of Eirik.

The boy narrowed his eyes as he opened and closed his mouth several times, before eventually saying, "The Vivas brothers? But you're not Osiris."

"Wow, very astute of you. You're right, I'm *not* Osiris. He does wish he was me, though. Who wouldn't want this face?" I flashed a grin, shaking my head. Pain shot through my ear, and I grunted as I slapped my spare hand against it to stop the ringing. "You got me off topic. Where are they?"

The boy shook his head, tilting to the side, but he didn't have the same quarrel as the one before him.

"Eirik is with Brazen. He's the only one we were told to watch. The others Archon dealt with personally." He pointed down the hallway, one that likely held several more guards from the sound of it. The name he said made the ringing worse, a deep-seated rage I couldn't quite comprehend ripping down my spine like the snarl that built in my chest. The boy paled. "D-Down there, to the right, then past an ornate door."

"Appreciate it," I said with a grunt, letting the boy slip to the ground as I hauled the sword up again. I could get Eirik, then he could use his bond to lead me to the others. "Do yourself a favor and play dead, then get the fuck out of here, yeah? It's no fun fighting a kid."

I stalked off down the hallway, my body a mix of priming for another fight and wanting to find a nice hole to die in. I licked my bloodied lips, grimacing at the bitter tang, pushing back the pressure as I slammed my palm against my ear one more *fucking* time. It gave me enough focus to walk, which was all I needed.

Onc more step, one more second. I had people to save, people I couldn't afford to let down. No *Rend* was going to stop me, not here.

"I love you, Prince," Aaliyah whispered, her hand in the air like she might reach out to touch me. "Forever."

I *flitted* down the hall.

The next stint of guards was barely child's play, and I sliced through them one after another. Yet no matter how many I killed, there always seemed to be another to take their place.

"Better hurry, Prince. You've got damsels to save." I grunted, the blood flying off the sword and hitting the ground with a splash as I swung it hard.

Precious seconds passed as more funneled in, the guards stockier, a hardier breed than those that came before them. They lined up, spears pointed in my direction, shields held up in a way that made my brain itch.

Pressure. It expanded behind my eyes, blurring my vision as I swayed on my feet. The walls tried to collapse in, a cold sweat starting as I steadied myself against one. The *Rend* was no longer in the mood to let me control it.

I cracked my neck again, tossing the sword in the air, catching it with the tip of the blade facing them, before I *threw* it. The steel edge bit into a guard, his body falling to the floor. I wasn't sure how much time had passed since I'd shown up, but I could only guess true sunrise was right around the corner. Which meant this had to go quick.

"All right then," I whispered, the veins on my face swelling as my eyes went red again, my vision swallowed by it as I raised my hands in a fighting pose. These guards weren't planning on making my life easy.

Too bad for them, I didn't know how to lose.

I smiled like a madman, a feral dog about to feast. "Let's *play*."

CHAPTER 14

OSIRIS

Extravagance was the weakness of Demons. They liked to flash their power and wealth, as though it were a measure of who they really were, to hide their horns and pretend to be something beyond devils. Kri'Valta was no stranger to it.

I stood in the front hall of his home, the building perched precariously on a cliff side that overlooked the Atlantic Ocean, made of stunning marble that had likely taken decades to carve. It was littered with gaudy décor and seemingly endless, priceless pieces of work. Paintings, scriptures, statues ...

Fallon would be so disappointed to know he missed it.

Their age showed in the faded paint that was expertly maintained in gold-framed glass displays. Guards were stationed between the priceless pieces of art, standing like sentinels as I walked through, eyeing each one.

Van Gogh, Monet, Vidal, Rodin ... The list grew.

What wasn't covered in art was bathed in gold, from elegantly hand-carved pillars that stretched to the ceilings, to the guards themselves. They were dressed in flashy armor that screamed of wealth, to an extent that would have been excessive for a *Greed* Demon. It was even more concerning knowing that Kri'Valta was a Lust.

He had decades to amass this fortune, this life, this *power*. Still, seeing it was an entirely different experience. I let my hand fall open at my side and kept walking.

"Welcome, Vivas Crypt," the usher at the door to the end of the long hall said when I approached, his voice a steady monotone. He was unassuming, dressed in a white suit, his dipped head covered in a shawl hiding his face from me. "The master has been expecting you."

The sound of waves crashing against the rocks down below echoed, barely hiding the questionable music that could be heard coming from past him.

I nodded as the man stepped to the side to allow me through, when someone clicked their tongue behind me. I tensed, jaw popping as I fought the need to snap at them for the disrespect.

It only took me one breath to realize it was Magelav. Their swampy stench had grown muted but was still there. I sighed, looking over my shoulder at them to find someone completely different from the witch they'd taken the shape of.

They were lithe, standing a couple of inches shorter than me, with short, unruly black hair and almost sunken gray eyes that felt out of place on their pale face. The high rise to their cheekbones gave them an almost feminine flare that was alluring in the same way poisoned apples were. They'd taken many shapes over the years and seeing another now barely fazed me.

I'd assumed, apparently naively, they'd gone with Nero and left me to my own mission. After their spell had dropped me here, I hadn't even thought to see if they'd followed. What a nuisance to find they had. Part of me wanted to turn away and pretend I hadn't seen them, maybe hope that the usher would stop them at the door.

But if I was invited, so was the Bog Sorceri.

"You dally and dawdle, almost like a child," they said, like they didn't notice me staring.

"Magelav. I see you've dressed for the occasion," I responded dryly.

There was a grunt and an angry stomping of feet. Almost in a flash, their face morphed, flashing to the familiar withered one they'd been using, wrinkled and dull.

"Would you prefer Mags's old form? In such an establishment, no less," they chided, brushing their hair away from their forehead as their façade fell back into place, keeping that vicious scowl.

It was short, the curled black strands waving around their head, their eyes suddenly mirroring Kali's ashen gray. I tensed, and a brush of power slid out from under my skin at the sight. It made me itch, the feeling grating on every nerve.

Mags chuffed, rolling their eyes, and looking at the door I'd been primed to walk through. A line had formed behind us, everyone watching but refusing to get any closer. I turned fully toward the sound of slowly growing sin, ignoring them instead to prepare for whatever I'd find on the other side. I reached for my cuffs, tugging them down to cover as much skin as possible, before stepping through the threshold.

The entire room was a work of art, bodies on display, much like the paintings and sculptures in the hall. Some were strung from the rafters, intricate shibari tracing exposed forms in golden-lined ropes. The vibrant reds of their blindfolds were the only splotches of color. All of them were gagged, those closer to the ground being poked and prodded by the guests. The sound of sex was suddenly the *only* thing I could hear, blending with the music as it became a lust-filled symphony.

I avoided the people in the room as we walked, and they reacted in kind, flinching away when we got too close. Most parted, giving us a clear path through the debauchery. It should have been an easy task, finding the host. Kri'Valta was flashy, if nothing else, and he'd always liked being the center of attention.

But my gaze caught someone else instead, a man who stood out from the others in the room. He was attractive, extremely so, a telltale sign that he, like many of the guests, was a Demon of Lust. He smiled sweetly at a couple that had drawn his way, expertly playing them with every manipulative move he made, but it wasn't that which caught me. There were plenty of attractive Naturals, plenty of other sights to stick to, a Demon to hunt.

This man had hair like snow, a kind that wasn't necessarily rare, especially when marred by a black stripe that twirled over a pointed ear ... but I'd only ever seen it paired with *lavender* eyes once, and that had me taking a step forward.

"Play not, with matters of the grave," Magelav said, their voice a cracked whisper that had me whipping my head to face them. They were normal, or as normal as the Bog Sorceri could be, for all of a second, before their eyes rolled back to show the whites. Pulses of

Chronomancy so strong those around us paused lashed out, freezing in the air as though suspended in time. As soon as it had happened, it stopped, and they were shaking their head, dusting fresh sand off their suit. "The fates have changed, such a fickle, *fickle—*"

"Well, isn't this a surprise? If it isn't *the* Osiris Vivas."

Magelav sucked in a hard breath next to me, mumbling the rest of their thought, as a towering man stepped forward through the crowd. He held an air of potent ancient magic, one that made me sick. His long black hair was styled delicately around his head, with interweaving charms and gems scattered throughout, matching the gold of his eyes. Beyond that, he wore little, only gold chains wrapped over black cloth that covered the most intimate of places. As flashy as he was dangerous.

Kri'Valta had found us, it seemed.

"You know, when I heard that you'd be coming to my little art show, I didn't believe it. That you'd grace me with your presence, and pull yourself out of that hole you'd locked your Crypt in ... I'm *honored.*" His teeth were a row of dangerous fangs, mocking when he smiled. "Well, do tell. How are you liking the party?"

Silly pleasantries were drowned out by the noise around us. I longed to get away from it, to get on with the fight that might well determine how the Eternium would play.

"I'm not here for the party, Kri'Valta," I said, shaking out my hands. The room had lost its color, and I wasn't sure if it was a magic of his or a dimming of my own perspective. My wrist throbbed, as if reminding me why I was here. "Don't pretend otherwise. It's insulting."

Kri'Valta was quick to move, like a viper in shallow water, as he raised an eyebrow, his face scrunching up before he rolled his eyes. "Always spoiling my fun. Come, then."

Every event that had led to this moment flashed in front of me as I stared at the Demon Eternal's back. My body prepared for a fight, a flash of fire lingering on the tips of my fingers, the roof of my mouth burning as fangs threatened to fall.

My mind was the last to catch up, the crippling numbness less like a shield and more like a shadow tonight. The days I'd spent with Aaliyah had cracked it, warping the feeling until it was nothing at all. I'd felt alive, human, and now she was gone.

And I was left with the numb once again.

Magelav and I were led through the crowd, the sensual music reverberating through the floor. Everything was too confined, too *loud*, and I snapped out at those that drew close. The only reprieve came from the fact that no one touched me. Even with the sheer amount of distraction, those on the floor parted as Kri'Valta moved, allowing us through. They watched in awe and in fear.

Kri'Valta was a startling presence, and though I'd been in it before, it was different now. More pronounced, the nuanced brushes of his magic were like markers for what I needed to prepare for, but knowing what was coming didn't stifle the adrenaline as it flooded. It clashed with the hollow part of my soul.

We entered a private room on the far side of the dance floor. Two guards flanked, standing at the door's sides just as it clicked closed behind us.

Tonight, either I fulfilled my end of Drakon's bargain, or I died here.

Aaliyah was gone because of me, in the hands of a monster. My strangled thoughts went to Eirik, Fallon, and Adrian, and the fate I could only pray they'd escape.

The weight of my failures lingered on my shoulders, like the pull of the sun. I searched in my chest for my brothers. Their bonds had wavered, strung tight, but at least they were still there, for now.

I scanned the room. After the ordeal at *The Altar*, I'd expected to walk into much the same decor, but Kri'Valta's space held none of the stoic accent Alderi'Vidius had curated. The room was mostly comfort; the floor was made of soft padding, couches lining the walls, and lush gold silk covering everything else. It was messy, with articles of clothing, jewelry, and other bobbles littering the few tables and the floor. Even the air was a distraction, filled with sex and a hint of Fae drugs strong enough to make me dizzy even as I forced myself to stay alert.

Kri'Valta hummed a tune under his breath, picking up a random bottle as he passed through the room, the amber liquid inside sloshing as he popped the lid. He glanced at us over his shoulder with a mocking smile.

"Magelav? Is that you?" he asked, appraising the surly Chronomancer with an indulgent smirk. He took a swig from the bottle. "You look delectable. Maybe I can convince you to grace my sheets again after this is done with. I'd love to—"

Magelav snorted before gagging, face paling as they covered their mouth. "Speak not to me, Horror. I have no kind words for swine shit."

Kri'Valta raised an eyebrow, swirling his bottle with a dramatic flair, before he rolled his eyes.

"Well, aren't you just charming, as always," he said, taking another sip. Magelav fell into the back of the room, out of Kri'Valta's sight. He turned to me again, shaking his head. "Might I offer you a drink? Before you try to kill me, that is."

Word of my arrival was expected; even so, having the man you were planning to kill say it out loud never got smoother. It would have made things easier if he hadn't seen this coming, but it would have been cowardly.

Had this happened a year ago, I would have told him of it myself. Given him the fight he deserved, and I knew somewhere inside of him he craved. There was honor in a fair fight.

But I couldn't lose, not now. I couldn't let my brothers die in vain. I couldn't abandon Aaliyah to whatever fate Sebek had in store for her. I'd told her once, when we'd first met, that I liked to think we were more than just Vampires.

More than savage beasts with no moral code, like so many others that shared the name.

I'd strip that all away tonight, throw my pride to the ground and lie and cheat if it meant killing this man would save her. Even if it didn't, I was still going to try. Because I could only be more now if she was by my side. Nothing else mattered. I was her monster, her devil, *hers. Lux mea.*

My light.

"I take it *he* told you I was coming?" I asked, and Kri'Valta nodded.

I took a step toward him, veering slightly toward the gold-tinted walls. I waited until his head tipped and he took another drink before I moved. I was careful as I let my hand drift until my palm was against the gold paint.

"Yes, but I would've figured it out the moment you stepped through my door. Why else would I be allowed the pleasure of a visit from the infamous Osiris Vivas? It's insulting, if I'm honest. I'm far too old to fall for assassination attempts, much like you, I'd imagine," he said, watching me with veiled interest, still sipping his drink.

There was a terrifying grace to him, one that reminded me of the sea he was named after. Horror of the Depths. He was every bit the powerful man legends told him to be, a fact that only grew more prominent as he swirled his drink. Gold dust shimmered on his skin, behind his eyes, a physical manifestation of lust.

"Yet you invited me in anyway. Even knowing what I'd come for," I stated, and Kri'Valta's lips curled, exposing two rows of jagged teeth.

Long before he'd become an Eternal, he'd spent his days ruling the ocean, his own Atlantis building until he grew bored with it and sank it down in those same depths. Danger radiated off him, every flourishing wave as likely to be a strike as it was a caress.

"Of course, Sebek and I have been allies for longer than the Eternals have been in control. He told me I could expect a wayward child tonight, and that he'd appreciate it if I removed them for him," he said with a wave of his hand before setting down his glass. The swirling gold in his eyes deepened, his long black hair lifted slightly, as though affected by a soft breeze, and his head tipped to the side. "But I'm curious. Why don't you humor me before you die? What made him snap? He's been *crazed* for centuries, but something happened recently that has sent him over the edge. Having another kill his prized spawn just proves that. Doesn't it, *Usire*?"

Hints of veiled malice shone in his eyes, a curiosity that was bred through lifetimes. Sebek was a brutal enigma that everyone wanted to watch fall apart, even if it meant watching the world break with him.

It was the hubris of immortals. They grew complacent, disregarding any life that wasn't their own.

"He would have found a way to get rid of us regardless," I answered, keeping Kri'Valta in my sights as he clicked his tongue and rolled his eyes.

"That we can agree on, but leaving it to someone else? *The* Sebek Ra admitting the weakness of his own Turned? Not likely. Come now, don't be so *boring*. Give me something believable," Kri'Valta said dully.

My focus was still on him, on the beat of the heart in his chest that was little more than a prop. "Because he found something to obsess over. Something so out of his grasp he couldn't help the spiral," I added.

Kri'Valta's grin grew sinister, and his head tipped back in a laugh. "Now that is a theory I enjoy. Thank you. It will be fun to ponder later."

"Enough of this. You know why I'm here, Kri'Valta?" I asked, avoiding his answer and the rage it sparked as I shrugged off my suit coat.

Magelav stayed back, watching from afar like some twisted emissary of fate. I knew without asking they wouldn't dabble, wouldn't intervene, however this went.

"Didn't care enough to learn. All you petty ants want the same. Power, revenge," Kri'Valta mused, humoring me for a moment. I heard the click of a lock, the door behind us sealing us in. "It matters not which it is."

I'd been watching him since the moment he appeared at the party, the way he moved, looking for hints of guilt that weren't found there. That I hadn't expected to find, but I searched for anyway, because somewhere in the nagging parts of my mind, I wondered if what we'd learned was true.

It didn't matter in the end what his answer was. Either way, he would die here tonight.

"So, you don't recall helping Teviticus murder his son's Pearl?" I asked, and for a flash, surprise took over Kri'Valta's face. It was just as quickly masked with a devious smile.

"Now, *that*, I didn't do," he started. "I haven't had dealings with Teviticus in millennia. Quite the accusation."

Drakon hadn't seemed to think that, yet the rage in Kri'Valta's response was enough to convince me otherwise. If he was wrong, it was still a sour wound to poke, based on the fire in Kri'Valta's eyes.

"Such lies—" I added, noting the flash of red on his face, the indignation.

"I do *not* lie, Vivas," he growled, brushing the hair out of his face. "As fun as this has been, I have a party to get back to, and you've overstayed your welcome."

The change in the air started slowly, the dust that had been brought up sinking to the ground as Kri'Valta's eyes grew wide and flushed with a deepened gold. My hackles raised at the sight.

I took a deep breath.

"You don't consider me a threat, Kri'Valta?" I asked.

This was a dance I had perfected centuries ago, a sway that had been lost to the sands of time when I'd thrown out our violent ways. Kri'-Valta saw himself as invincible, untouchable.

A king. A *god*.

"I'd have to go with no, Vivas, you're not," Kri'Valta said, shaking his head. "Does that change your path tonight?"

Thoughts of Aaliyah flitted through my mind, her soft eyes and the touch I longed for. The same breath brought images of my brothers, the ones I'd abandoned for this goal, to save her. The numb was my only company.

A million times I'd do it again.

I let my hand rest easily by my side. "No, it does not."

"Figured. Don't suppose I can convince you to die quietly? I don't want to interrupt my guests," he said, a flash of fire arcing toward me. Little more than a parlor trick that stopped as soon as it started, swallowed by my *Flame*. Kri'Valta grinned. "You won't win, you know. Even if you kill me, and that spry upstart Alderi takes over. You don't have all the pieces to this puzzle, Osiris, and even the *Kingslayer* can't stop what he can't see."

Kri'Valta moved then, every ounce of his power, every year that had led to that strength behind him as he charged forward.

Every battle he'd seen and conquered.

Every war he'd waged on the winning side.

Every *victory* that led to his inevitable defeat.

A year ago, this fight would have been his. Tonight, it would be mine. *Lie. Cheat. Steal. Whatever it takes.*

This was no longer his game, and I saw the moment Kri'Valta realized that, too.

My fingers twitched, the magic I'd placed throughout the room exploding inside of me. Kri'Valta's eyes went wide with a horror that was befitting his name.

I never used my magic; I abhorred it. I'd always preferred my fights head on, and that was the exact reason Kri'Valta lost before I'd even entered the building. Because he didn't think he had to prepare for this.

He didn't know how much I'd sacrifice to make sure tonight went in my favor. How much I'd *already* sacrificed.

My lungs burned, and I clung to the bonds in my chest as I lifted my hand. Even with so little in the room, my human magic spread. It had started as nothing but sprouts, Hemomancy digging into the wood, my blood sliding along the floor as it traveled its way into the roots of his home, planting a trap in the fiber of the walls. I pulled on Forgemancy next, searching for weak points in the building, for hollowed-out holes that might be hiding something of use. It plucked through the brick, the paint, and the mortar, deconstructing it and breaking it down until it was just parts to be used. I pushed it to go further, allowing it to pick apart the room until the walls quaked, and threatened to fall.

Every bit that I forced out of me added more tension to my spine, the sour taste in my mouth growing as it searched his palace, looking for what I knew to be hidden.

Kri'Valta's pretense of civility fell, horns sprouting from his head, wicked things that stretched around, twisting into spirals. His eyes bled solid gold, and his teeth sharpened into dangerous points. Lust slammed into me; the full brunt of his powers no longer hidden away. He struck out like a wild animal caught in a trap. It sliced through the air, striking me in the side, across my arm. It tore into flesh and ripped all the way to bone.

I was a force of my own. I lifted my hand, snarling as his magic fought against mine, forcing my ring and pinky finger down. I was rot, and my mouth flooded with blood, my eyes bleeding red. My skin split as I kept the pressure on.

I'd fought kings. I'd fought *gods*.

None of them had threatened Aaliyah. None of them had to worry about my full wrath, didn't have to face me while I was so desperate to win.

Kri'Valta had *already* lost. Because if I was trapped under the weight of my own detestable human magic, then I'd be sure he was the first to drown in it.

I caught Kri'Valta's surprised gasp just as my magic spiked, the wretched pull of Hemomancy blended with the Forgemancy I'd bled into the walls. My entire body was drained in an instant, a cold sweat pooling down my spine as the magic I'd kept locked away came barreling out of me. Kri'Valta didn't move, couldn't, as blood rose from the ground, winding around him like an enchanted rope. My veins pulsed, my nose bleeding as I swiped it away.

Kri'Valta struggled against his chains, and I tightened them, imagining them cinching against his skin until his breaths came out in tortured gasps.

"How—" he started, choking on the words as his blood slowed to a crawl in his veins. His eyes rolled back. "You don't use Sorceri magic. You've *never* used your magic."

I'd never needed to. I'd made sure that my infamy was far greater than the supposed weakness of not using my gifts. I was feared ... but it was well known my distaste for my blood. Had it been any other fight, any other time, he would have been right. I would have died before I used it. A part of me died now, knowing that I had.

I leaned into Kri'Valta. His face paled, the bonds tightening on him. The false humanity had flooded away, and I tipped my head, unbreathing as his heart rate picked up.

The quick intake of breath, the dilation of his eyes as fear truly came to him ... It was all more addictive than any drug.

"You've grown cocky, Kri'Valta. Soft," I said, barely more than a murmur. I saw what I'd seen every time another had crossed my path. A man, nothing more. Trapped by his own petty desires, his own faulty reasoning and inescapable fate. "I've learned something over the last few months, that *decades* of life spent in a past that tortured me couldn't."

Aaliyah's soft expression kept me going, even as the magic in me grew to violent heights. The potent rush of it, like hands dancing along my skin, was enough to make me gag. Still, I held the reins, unwilling to let go of our key to victory now.

For my light, the one that had brought me back from the edge of damnation. Who I fought for now.

"I would do anything to keep the one I love safe, and if that means using the magic that eats me alive? Then so be it. There is nothing I would not do for her. Nothing too vicious, too far, or too cruel. *Nothing* that will ever stand between me and her safety again."

I was Osiris Vivas, fourth Turned of Sebek Ra. *Rex interfectorem.* I was a monster, but above *all* else.

I was *hers.*

"Not even myself," I said with a finality that freed as much as it damned.

Kri'Valta balked at me, chuckling with a sour pinch of dread wrinkling the skin between his eyes.

"One problem with that. You can't kill me, Osiris. So, what, you keep me chained up until your magic runs dry? Quite the feat. Do you plan to bore me with your tales then? What about more monologue?" His dry words ended in a huff as I let my hand flash in the air, my hard work showing in my palm. His eyes grew wide as he paled, seeing what I held.

A small gold marble, the weight of it enough to make my arm shake. It was what I'd been searching for, what I'd pushed my magic so hard to find. Kri'Valta had been a pain to subdue, but this was my ace.

A Demon's Core was their life force, what kept them tied to the mortal realm. It had to be kept close, not necessarily on their person, but *close*. I'd been searching for the signature of his magic since the moment I walked into his home.

He jolted against the chains, cursing in an ancient language even I didn't know. The thing binding him to this plane pulsed in my hand.

I squeezed it between my thumb and pointer finger.

"Wait, *wait*!" Kri'Valta cried, jolting, his blood hitting the ground like liquid gold as my bindings tore into his skin. "We can talk about this. Don't do anything rash, Osiris!"

He wasn't mocking anymore, his joyful attitude torn away, exposing the man for what he was. Being faced with his own death had stripped him down to base instincts, to fear and panic, to *bargaining*. I hadn't planned on listening.

"Your death is all the help I need from you," I said, putting more pressure on the ball.

It resisted the fracture, sending a wave of pain up my arm, sharp enough to make my fangs drop.

Kri'Valta screamed as if I'd removed a limb.

"Information then!" he cried, his face blotchy as tears streamed down it. The essence finally cracked, and he shrieked. The gold in the air pulsed, some of it dropping to the floor. "Please, don't break it!"

I clicked my tongue. "Information is a grain of sand on a windy beach, Horror. You're going to have to be more specific—"

"Darius. *Darius*! You want him to fall at this Eternium." A bait, one that I'd expected him to go for, but there was nothing about Darius that

I didn't already know. His fall was something I'd thought about many times in my life. Something I'd dreamed of, and one more Eternal that supported Sebek out of the way would only benefit us. Kri'Valta took a shuddering breath, his eyes closing. I pressed the Core again, and he jolted with a gurgled cry. "I know his weakness!"

I froze, eyes tracking Kri'Valta's panicked gaze as he watched helplessly from the floor. He rocked back and forth, letting out weak gasps as he did.

Darius had many things, but a weakness had never been one. I'd searched *endlessly*. He was untouchable.

It was why he was still alive.

"What weakness?" I asked.

"Promise you'll let me go," he whispered, and I shook my head.

I let the Core roll to a stop on my palm, running my pointer finger over it. It pulsed with life, the inside flowing as it moved. A little pressure, and Kri'Valta was screaming again.

This time, his eyes rolled back, and it took a few moments for him to regain his breath.

"It's not that easy, Kri'Valta. You dying tonight is the only way we can get the support needed for the Eternium, but I can make this painless," I hummed. A small crack echoed in the room, Kri'Valta's broken moan following it. "Or I can make you suffer. Either way, you don't get to live."

I wasn't expecting him to sob, for his head to drop in such poetic defeat. The broken part of my soul reveled in it, and for just a moment, I let that sink in. I swallowed the fear he bled, my fangs aching in my mouth. Instincts I'd thrown away came rushing back.

All for Aaliyah, I tried to tell myself.

"I'll leave, stay in the hell's and let my title as Eternal go without fight or fuss. Everyone will assume I'm dead. At least for the next couple centuries, and I'll tell you everything I know about Darius. *Please,*" he cried, the noise growing louder the longer I stayed silent. I knew what desperation looked like, and Kri'Valta's eyes flashed like a beast with nowhere else to run. "*A binding vow!*"

His words sucked the air from the room. Even my powers dulled as the shock of them hit me. A binding vow, a *true* devil's deal.

"You must be truly desperate," I said, allowing the reins enough room for Kri'Valta to sag forward.

The room shuddered under the weight of our combined power until even the human mask that Kri'Valta held started to flicker. His human form, so beautiful and extravagant, faded away. The Demon that kneeled at my feet was little more than a grotesque beast that heaved heavy breaths. His thick coiled horns tucked close to his bald head, wide golden eyes frantically searching the room for an out he would not find, his sickly yellow skin lit with veins and demonic glyphs that pulsed with his heartbeat. The same one that moved the Core in my hand.

I considered it. "You will tell me how to fell Darius. You will never take the spot of Eternal again. You will *never* bring harm to those of the Vivas Crypt, or those allied with them. You will disappear."

I took a step toward him, ignoring the part of me that purred at his flinch. I reached down, tipping his head up so I could stare into his eyes. Disgust followed the touch that I endured as I started the vow. "Swear it and speak your terms."

The move was instant as Kri'Valta's eyes went fully gold again. When he started to speak, that same gold flowed over his skin, igniting the glyphs that burned into him, one at a time, like dry tinder. The scent of torched flesh soured the air. "I, Valta, Horror of the Depths, Lust of the Kri Horde, swear by my word I will follow the rules outlined by this vow."

He shuddered once, the ancient ruins glowing before setting in that gold. They stretched over his right eye, from his hairline down to his jaw, unfading. "Bound by Infernal Conviction and the fires that made us. *Meus sermo obligat.*"

He sagged, still held up by my magic.

I mulled over his words, tilting my head before I nodded. His posture relaxed, his eyes dulling as pain set in. "Well, speak."

"I'm not that daft, Osiris. I've sworn my part. Now you have to uphold your half," he mumbled, the chains tightening around him, but he didn't relent. "You will not kill me. That is my term."

I hummed low under my breath, letting go of his chin and dipping until I was eye to eye, tilting my head when he shrank away. "I, Osiris

Vivas, *Kingslayer* and eldest of the Vivas Crypt, swear by my word that you, Kri'Valta, shall not die by my hand."

The sealing of the binding vow lit the air like the *Flame,* sparking along our skin as his golden magic wound between us. It crawled up my veins as I finalized the pact. *"Meus sermo obligat."*

My word is binding.

His magic faded away, sealing my vow in the fabric of it. To go against it was a death sentence, and now Kri'Valta held the cards. He took several hollow breaths before his words came crashing down around us. "Darius's luck is tied to an angelic artifact, bound by a pact older than the Eternal's. The only records of it were destroyed some years after he took over, but I've seen *proof.* If you fight him now, you will lose. Just like everyone that has fought him since."

"If Darius held a bond like that, I'd have felt it," I drawled.

"I *don't* lie!" Kri'Valta screamed, his voice shaking the room as he shook his head. The ruins covering his body glowed when he spoke, showing that, at the very least, he believed what he said. "No. It's not magic. It's older than that, forged by the first Angels. The method lost to time, a ritual that's nothing more than dust now. Darius *cannot* die with the idol still intact, and luck will always be on his side as long as it's unbroken. How do you think he took the spot from the original Eternal Atlas to begin with? Darius was a lesser Mythic, *leagues* less powerful. He shouldn't have won. Without the binding, he wouldn't have."

Hints of doubt sprouted.

Darius had taken over as Eternal just decades after they'd first been introduced. He'd been young and had stolen it from a Mythic ages ahead of him in power. I hadn't known of Atlas, but his feats lived on even today, to the point of almost legacy status among the Griffon Mythics. But even then ...

"Where is it?" I pressed.

The room was silent besides the wheezing and the still-sizzling of Kri'Valta's skin.

"The one place no one would look," he said finally. "Trapped under the Eternium, bound in chains where none come back from, it's in the *Pits.* The Eternium holding ground. But if you get it out, and destroy it? Darius wouldn't be able to handle a Challenge. *Or* Retaliation. Even one he places."

A shiver shot down my spine, one full of promise.

The idea of revenge had always been on my mind. After Kali, watching her finally die by my hand ... I craved the same with Darius. To see him brought so low before his heart stopped. With Kali dead, he would seek Retaliation, and I would be the first he'd blame.

A win for him either way.

If this idol truly existed, it was the key to the fall of my old master. In a way that could not be turned against us at the Eternium.

"You did well, thank you," I said, lifting the Core so I could gaze in it once again.

The bindings on Kri'Valta tightened as I stepped forward.

"What are you doing? We had a deal!" Kri'Valta hissed, straining against the magic ropes, helpless as they bit into his skin. His blood hit the ground in a golden, sizzling splash. "You'll die, too, you lunatic!"

Something dark inside of me relished it, the power, the fear that the *Horror* of the Depths felt.

"A deal *is* a deal," I said, standing straight. I'd always been a fan of games, especially ones like this. Ones where the victory tasted so much sweeter. "My magic, however, was bled into this room long before I agreed to it, a failsafe to make sure you didn't walk out of here. A failsafe that I no longer control."

Hemomancy coursed through the room, and his arm jerked crudely, like an unwilling puppet. I set the small pearl in his hand, placing his fate in his own action. Kri'Valta's eyes shot wide, the stark mix of betrayal in them making me feel things I shouldn't.

"I swore not to kill you with my own hands." I put them behind my back, and he struggled against the magic that had already beaten him, choking on a cry as he squeezed until the pearl shattered. "But that's not to say you can't die by *yours*."

I like to think we're more.

It was like watching a switch flip behind Kri'Valta's eyes, his ruins glowing hot gold before he smiled and stopped struggling. One by one, they faded from his skin, as though they were being erased. The cruel expression only distorted further as his head tipped back, and a broken laugh came cracking from his chest.

"You're just like him, *Rex interfectorem*," he choked out as his body turned to dust, disintegrating into nothing more than gold that fluttered in the stagnant air of the room. His last words were nothing more than a haunted whisper. "Sebek would be proud."

They lingered, ringing in my ears, dragging me along as I looked to where he'd been. The rush I'd felt at his death didn't fade, nor the remnants of power that still held on to me like a drug. I'd never been one to fight so dirty, to go for the throat while parading a conversation.

It was cowardly. It was *slimy*.

My stomach cramped, the rush of adrenaline fading with each breath. The power turned to lead, my head spinning as I tried to convince myself that he was wrong ... but Kri'Valta hadn't lied, not throughout our conversation and not now.

It was *exactly* what Sebek would have done.

CHAPTER 15

ADRIAN

Osiris hadn't come.

No matter how much I begged and pleaded, no matter how much time passed or how strong I tried to stay as hit after hit came, bones cracking like what was left of my will to fight.

Osiris *hadn't* come. *No one had come.*

Then again, when I looked at the clock that shone on my torturer's chest ... I wasn't sure why I'd even expected someone to. Three hours and thirty-six minutes. That was all the time it took for me to reach my limit. The invincibility surrounding me had faded. The Vampire stripped away to nothing more than a scared boy lost in the streets of London all over again.

That was how long I'd been ripped apart, how long I'd had only the company of my screams. I missed the silence; I missed the quiet guards and the *weeks* that had passed in Archon's lamp.

The sharp bite of a serrated knife dug into the flesh of my arm, reaching bone with a pinpoint accuracy. My throat had gone raw, my lungs seizing as the air was ripped out of them yet again.

The man above me hummed, his face obscured behind a bloody doctor's mask, slicing through me as if I were nothing but butter.

"Fuck!" I managed, bowing on the table, the restraints unyielding. "No one's ever accused you of having a light touch. Have they?"

The mock humor was the only fight I could manage.

I'd stopped pretending to be unfazed as the methods grew increasingly sadistic. I stopped holding back screams and pleas when he'd stopped using his hands and started bringing in tools, devolving into a begging mess the first time he'd torn me open.

Hysteria the next.

How long had Ascension had Aaliyah for, again? How long had they kept her strapped to the table, knives digging in? If we made it out of this, they were dead. Every single fucking one of them. Just like the man who hovered over me, a halo of light around his head like he wasn't holding a bloodied knife in his hands.

"So soft," he whispered, dragging a gloved hand over my arm, digging his finger into the hole he'd just made there before it had the chance to heal.

"You can't just say it like that, you fucking psycho!" I shrieked, panting when he finally pulled his hand back.

No response, just more fiddling as he set the knife down.

It clattered against the table, and already the wound was closing. More fresh skin for him to fillet like I was a fucking fish. I didn't watch to see what else he might pull up, didn't want to have the anticipation. I closed my eyes and thought of better things.

Of my kitchen, the soft scent of fresh food. Aaliyah, as she danced around me. Burned risotto that tasted better than any meal I'd ever had.

The soft flow of her white hair, and the little hums she made when she sat at the table, her nose in a book. She did it often, a cup of tea by her side sweetened with copious amounts of sugar as she glanced at us over the cream-colored pages. She wanted to be near us while still being lost in her own little joys. I treasured every moment of it, sneaking kisses when I could, savoring every adoring look she'd send my way.

"Easy, we're just having fun," the doctor's voice broke in, cracking my little distraction, ripping me back into the real world as something touched my neck.

I'd never before questioned what it was like to stick my finger in an outlet, but I imagined it'd be just like this. I contorted in the bindings that held me down, writhing so hard I felt a pop in my leg as the bone broke and electricity torched my nerves. I couldn't even scream, my mouth foaming as my eyes rolled back far enough that I worried I might tear something in them.

When it finally pulled away, I gasped.

The reprieve was short-lived, as the device trailed a path down my exposed chest, and I jerked away from it, waiting for the shock to begin again. I wanted to be brave, to throw another joke or spit in his face.

It came to a jerking stop between my third and fourth rib before it started up again. I choked on my own spit, twitching and squirming in the worst kind of agony.

I wasn't the fucking fighter.

I was going to die here ... or worse, I *wasn't*, and this would only continue.

"I can't! I *can't*—"

"You know ... I can take it all away, if you ask," a sinful voice whispered through the wretched agony.

Shaggy brown hair dusted over gleeful eyes, and the scent of sour gold replaced the stench of blood and fear. Archon's hands came to my shoulders, rubbing the muscles there that still quaked from the aftershocks.

The tempting press of a deal was almost too much. I sucked in a breath, biting back the need to beg that had stolen my voice. It was everything my pain-riddled body wanted, and it was everything I couldn't accept. A deal with a Djinn, with the Djinn *Eternal*?

It was stupid. The *stupidest* thing I could do.

My mind was a haze, too disjointed to come up with a plan that could use it to my advantage. The risk outweighed the reward ... I *knew* that.

Sweat came to my skin, my fangs permanently down as they sliced into my lips when I tried to thrash against my bindings again.

"Did your information not warn you about this, Collector? Did your power as a Vampire cloud your mind so much you thought you were the top of the food chain?" he asked, goading me as he squeezed until I yelped.

I wasn't made for torture.

"Ask, and it can stop." A promise that tempted me, that destroyed the walls I'd built around myself.

Another shock, this one lingering until I smelled the burning of flesh in the air. The limit that I'd ridden so closely to now seemed like it was a breath away.

Three hours.

The plea burned in my throat.

Thirty-six minutes.

I wanted to be strong like Fallon. I wanted to growl and snarl at him like Eirik. I wanted to stand unmoving, even in the face of the sun, like Nero. I wanted to kill them *all* until even Osiris was silent in shock. I wanted to spit in their face, and laugh, to be the man who would do anything to stay strong.

I wanted to smile, to hold on to myself and not fall apart at the very seams as the next shock went straight through me. I wanted to live, to not lose a part of me I'd never get back in the face of something worse than death.

I wanted to be a survivor, like Aaliyah.

But I wasn't that man, wasn't a fighter, and coming to terms with that was almost as terrible as the pain. This was all I could take, all the torture my body could endure. It weighed down on me almost as much as the whisper of a begging, *cowardly* word.

One I held back until steps echoed in the air, the sound of a body moving away from the table while another hand reached for me, a knife once again held in deft fingers. It went for my face—the blade gleaming in my eye like he planned to cut it out.

"Please." It was drowned out by the bubble of blood in my mouth as I coughed. My left lung had been punctured some time ago, and the bone sat wedged inside of it, unable to rectify itself and heal.

My voice was a sham of what it had been, the sound so muddled by the tears in my vocal cords that I wondered if they'd even heal right again.

"Please what?" Archon asked, back in a blink, leaning over me. The voice was a curse and a blessing, a cease to the onslaught, a moment to breathe as I tried to see through red-rimmed eyes and a bloody haze that had covered my face. "What, no more snide remarks?"

No deal was worth it. Even in death, it could ruin us.

Tears wet my eyes. I *couldn't* handle more.

I was past the time for pleasantries. Even the need to jolt back with a quip of my own tempered down beneath the pain. Archon had stripped that away until I was exactly what he wanted.

Broken.

"What do you want?" I asked, sagging into the table.

Silence, his favorite means of control. That silence was a tactic all on its own, the anticipation of pain mind numbing as I sucked in sharp breaths that seemed useless as my vision blotted.

"Ah, but I told you what I wanted. Didn't I?" Archon asked, tapping the table by my ear.

Nothing less than the downfall of Osiris Vivas.

"Please." I hated that I begged, but I couldn't find it in me to keep it back anymore.

I needed the pain to stop.

"My, how the great Vivas Crypt has fallen." The clank of steps around the table would haunt me for the rest of my life, the shuddering feeling of a hand on my ruined shoulder nearly making me puke. His squeeze was a warning, like the heat of his breath on my cheek. "But I'm nothing if not a merciful man. All you have to do is ask. I don't need all of you broken. I can free you, Adrian."

Archon's grin was gold foil on nuclear waste, but the man that had been carving me up for hours pulled away, and in that moment, I knew I'd do anything to get him to stay that way.

Pathetic.

"A deal. I want to make a *deal*," I whispered, sealing my own fate with words I hoped would be enough. "Stop the torture."

"And what's in it for me? I can't very well make a deal with nothing in return." Archon's words were honeyed, jabbing at me with a fake concern that made me want to gag. "Tell me, what do you have planned for the Eternium? This is my price."

Our plan, the one that depended on Exilium. The one that already teetered on the edge of success. The fact that it was still a secret was a trump card, one I couldn't give. "Not that."

"Are you in a position to bargain, *Collector*?" Archon clicked his tongue, grabbing my hair and forcing me to look him in the eyes. When he glanced up, I shivered, already knowing what he was signaling for. "Maybe you need a few more hours to think it through."

I was silent for a moment, staring into the lights that blinded me, before I caught on the clock that still counted down on my torturer's chest. Three hours and thirty-six minutes. It was likely approaching sunrise.

I couldn't last through the day, and there was no way Osiris would be here any sooner than just after dusk. I wouldn't last that long.

I wasn't a fighter.

"No," I whispered, closing my eyes as my head sank into the steel. "Fine, you'll get a word. One."

The ramifications were heavy, the pain in my throat sour.

Archon pulled away, and I was left strapped to that table, questioning my own worth as he waited. Everything else that I could have done, everything else that could have been said, flashing over my mind now that the chance was over.

"Fine, one word. What are your plans for the Eternium?" he asked.

And I gave him exactly what he wanted.

"Exilium."

It gave him everything. It was enough to satiate him, hopefully, without completely ruining our plans. A final brush of gold sank down from the air, dusting over the exposed skin on my chest as the pact sealed. I felt the deal like it was a physical thing, a branding on my skin, in the space over my heart. It seared, no doubt leaving a golden mark in its place.

It traveled down my veins, lighting a fuse on the bonds in my chest, down to my wrist where Aaliyah's mark kept me functioning. It was like it ate them, swallowing the ties to my family whole, destroying the last of what made me *Vivas.*

The first one to snap felt almost worse than the blade I'd fought so hard to get away from. My breath was stolen on the next, and the *next.* Until only Aaliyah remained, and I was left staring in horror at those obnoxious lights as I felt it fizzle away. Ash filled my mouth, my body going lax against the table as all my strength left with that mark.

I was split off from the others, completely isolated in my own head, forced into silence ... stuck with only my own broken thoughts. I'd made a deal with Archon, with a *Djinn.* I'd known it wouldn't be that simple.

And I'd fallen headfirst into his trap, anyway.

Archon's laugh was a mockery as the man that had torn into me for almost *four hours* leaned back in. My heart caught, my mind racing as the knife touched my skin. There was a brief moment of disbelief, the fear unlike anything else. I'd told him what he'd wanted, sold out our plans.

"No, we made a deal!" I hissed, jerking away as the blade sank bone deep.

There was a spray of blood, the deafening slice of flesh, but there was no pain.

My vision blackened, and I nearly laughed at my own stupidity. Archon was a Djinn that preyed on weakness, that wanted to break Osiris. He'd told me how he planned to do it. The knife sliced again, easier now that I wasn't struggling.

And he was going to use us exactly like he'd said.

"Oh, but we did, Collector. A deal is *a deal.* No more torture. That *is* what you asked for. I took away your pain," Archon said, nonchalant. I choked on my breath as he walked away, still laughing. "It's *mine* now."

I'd made a deal with a Djinn, breaking one of my many rules in doing so. The knife slid deep again, the color of the room fading as the clock I was forced to watch continued to track each second I was trapped here.

I'd made a deal with Archon.

And it was a deal I'd *lost.*

Chapter 16

Fallon

"I still think we should go with blue. It's calming. Might help you sleep," Aaliyah said, her chin perched on her open palm. She was lying on her stomach, watching me with innocent curiosity, the upper half of her body covered only with a red sheet, her legs kicking idly through the air.

I sat against the headboard, staring ahead, pretending I couldn't see her. Pretending I couldn't still hear Adrian's screams while I lay next to a fake of the woman we both loved, stuck like a fucking rat in a cage.

I'd tried to get out countless times since I first saw that bleach drenched room, *tried* to gather some inner strength to break through whatever magic was holding me in, or find a crack in whatever hell this was. But observing had always been Adrian's shtick, and I was more inclined to start my questions with a closed fist. If I were in any other situation, that was exactly what I would have done.

I looked at Aaliyah's serene face, the delicate arches that defined her high cheekbones and pointed nose. She smiled softly at me, like I was everything she'd ever need, a trust in her eyes that made me look away.

I wouldn't take a chance to try to get myself out of this with force. It wasn't worth the risk if somehow Archon had wrapped her up in this. Even if it wasn't, there was no way I could stomach hurting her. The thought alone made me physically ill.

Archon had done a fucking fantastic job at putting me in a situation that I had no chance of getting out of.

"Fallon doesn't need sleep. He needs answers," Aislinn whispered from beside Ali, leaning over her, grinning broadly until I closed my eyes.

She'd been like a ghost, here to haunt me, and I couldn't tell if she was another part of this cozy cell, or if she was something all of my own making.

Ali waved her hand in front of my face until I opened my eyes again, her nose tilting up in what I'd normally call an adorable glare. Her cheeks were flushed slightly, like they were every morning, dusted with freckles so soft I could barely see them.

"Fallon?" she pressed, touching my hand with a soft fingertip. I took a selfish second to sink into the feeling of her, the spark that jolted across my skin, needing it to ground me even if it was fake. "Hey, what's going on with you today?"

She pulled my face to look at her, the same way she had every morning for the past two years. The same worried expression, and the same hints of lavender in the air that had me pulling in greedy breaths. Until it burned, and until the lavender was washed away just enough to get a hit of something else. Bitter and old, like oil that had been sitting too long in the sun.

Like gold turned to sulfur.

I pulled away gently, shaking my head. "You aren't real."

I'd said it so many times it was practically habit, and Aaliyah laughed as she fell against the bed, a rare deviation from the standard façade of this place. I might get something out of her. A different response, a different reaction. I wasn't so naïve as to believe it had really changed anything.

Tomorrow would be the same.

"Why not?" she asked, stretching out with an indulgent groan, toying with the white strands of her hair. She lifted herself, crawling close, until she was lying over my lap. "Seems pretty real to me."

She traced the skin on my abdomen until the muscle quivered, and I grunted. I let her linger, didn't push her off or make to move like I damned well knew I should have.

Another selfish fucking moment.

I craved that warmth, the touch of her skin on mine more than anything else. I wanted it to be Aaliyah, wanted to know she was safe and protected. It destroyed me every time she touched me, just as much as it gave me the will to keep going.

Day after day after *day*.

"It's not that bad, is it?" Aislinn asked, suddenly at my other side, sepia skin exposed as she leaned back. She wasn't wearing anything, exposed from the waist up as she brushed her hair out of her face, the beads that laced it clinking gently together.

Aaliyah looked at her for a second, as if she saw her, before looking back at me.

"What *is* real, anyway? You could be happy here, with me," Aaliyah whispered, trailing a hand down my bare chest.

She scraped gently with her nails, kissing the lines she left with tender lips. It was torture.

"And me," Aislinn followed, skimming my jaw with her lips, her breath warm on my cheek.

I shook my head, pulling out from between them as my mind warred with my body again.

Aaliyah made a worried noise behind me when I stood up, wrapping her arms around my waist to stop me from moving. I stole another comfort in that touch, another hint of warmth that was enough to get me to close my eyes. It was the only thing that kept me going, that kept me searching for a plan.

For a way out.

"I can help with that."

Hands already raised, I took a stance to fight at the unfamiliar voice. It was the easiest thing I'd done since I was trapped here, the motion as familiar as breathing. My wrist burned, pulsing to the beat of my heart as a woman stepped away from the wall, seeming to almost peel out of the shadow there, her face shrouded by them.

She was tall and lithe, with crystal white hair that cascaded over her shoulders and the shoddy amalgamation of twelfth century armor she wore, a mash of silver and gold.

Stars dusted her face, some glowing more vibrantly than others in a pattern I couldn't place, broken by two silver slashes that stretched from her forehead over her cheeks and down the hollow of her neck. They were a direct contrast with the slate gray of her skin and the black of her eyes that were lit by a single white ring where her pupil should have been. I didn't know as much about other Naturals as Adrian, but I knew an Unseelie Fae when I saw one.

But that was *all* I knew.

The Fae were secretive even among Naturals, and viciously protective of their people and ways. Which made it even more shocking to find her *here*.

How had Archon managed to get an Unseelie in his grasp?

"Who are you?" I asked, stretching my arm out to try and hide Aaliyah, who huddled at my back.

The woman didn't rush forward or prepare for a fight I was itching to dive into, just watched with a defeated expression. She was gaunt, her cheeks sunken as she wiped her hands over her face. There was a splash of yellow I hadn't seen before under her eye and across one of her sharp cheeks.

"Hadlie," she said, tired even in her words. "Nice to meet you in person, Fallon."

Her voice was familiar, the tone of it hitting me in the chest, taking me back to the moment I'd woken up in once before. The one that had washed away as the days passed, one by one. My mind associated her with the scent of bleach and the chill of cold steel.

With her hands over me, grazing my temples, locking me in my own fucking head.

She was the one who'd put me under. The one keeping me here, with whatever magic Fae could do. This was *her* spell.

"You can't hurt me here. It's really not worth the energy to try—"

I pinned her to the wall in an instant, hoisting her up so her feet didn't touch the ground. She didn't struggle, barely moved as she rolled her eyes at me. "Okay."

I tightened my grip against the protest of Ali and Aislinn behind me. Hadlie's skin burned like dry ice, my hand going numb against her neck as my palm blistered. I gritted my teeth. "Get me out of here."

It was like watching her patience drain away as she looked at the ceiling. One second, she was pinned, the next she was gone, and I was hitting the wall where she'd been with a grunt.

"The longer you take to calm down, the less time I'll have to explain," she said, unbothered from behind me. I looked over my shoulder at her, jaw clenched as she picked up an apple from the end table by the bed. She tossed it into the air a few times before taking a bite and speaking through it. "I'm here to help."

She extended the apple like it was a peace offering, wiping her mouth with the back of her other hand. I sneered, keeping my distance, and not even considering looking at the food she offered. I wasn't Adrian, didn't know the intricacies of Fae life and culture, but I damned well fucking knew you didn't take food from them.

"Talk," I gritted out, eye twitching when she smirked. The apple disappeared from her hand a moment later, and the white splashes of stars against her cheeks glowed as it did, flickering.

"You're in Archon's lamp. He put you and ... Adrian?" she said, like she was searching for his name before she shook her head and looked me in the eyes again. "In here, after you tried that grand revolt in the main hall. I'll be honest, I was expecting more from the fabled Vivas Crypt."

That made two of us.

I reached for my wrist, the soothing mark almost mocking. What a fucking mess we'd found ourselves in. I'd expected something radical, something crazy, but in his *lamp*?

Fuck, Osiris was going to *kill* us if Archon didn't first.

"Eirik?" I asked, and for once her pause didn't seem to be solely to irritate me. She looked to the side, biting her lip and swallowing hard. The bonds in my chest were strong, but I didn't trust that, not here. "Where the fuck is Eirik?"

My voice rose, cracking as Aaliyah gasped from the bed. The cold chill of the floor under my feet grew worse, my lips going numb as I waited. Hadlie seemed to mull over her thoughts, her long ears twitching.

"*Alive,*" was her simple answer, as she toyed with a stray ring on her hand.

I let out a breath, my lungs burning. At least alive was something.

I could work with alive.

"Well? Get me *out*," I said, rage growing to fury when she shook her head.

Even more so when I realized there was nothing I could do beyond *talk.*

"Not yet," she said, scratching her neck as she looked over her shoulder at the far wall. Her eyes flicked to the open window, the light breeze fluttering her hair. Her next words were a whisper. "I need your help."

The fear, the panic. The fact that she was here and still looking over her shoulder like Archon might jump out and bite her.

"You're a Fae, a strong one at that. Just kill him and be done with it," I said, watching as closely as I could. The fact that she had me and Adrian under her spell said enough about how much power she had. It showed when she breathed; the air distorting in front of her as she looked at me again.

I *wasn't* Adrian, but I saw the way she froze, holding her breath like it might make her smaller. "Unless you can't. Why?"

"Because I'm *his*," she whispered, biting the words out, her lip curling in a snarl as she grimaced. A shiver rocked her, like even saying that much hurt. Her eyes dulled, agony splitting across them as blood pooled in the corners, only to be wiped away as her hands slid over her face.

Her shoulders bunched, like she was steeling herself, strengthening her stance as she watched me with jaded eyes. I'd fought many like her before ... and I knew that look. I'd never known a more dangerous opponent than one that didn't have anything to lose.

She needed an out, and that was *me.*

The stars on her face twinkled, glittering like little diamonds when she bared her teeth, and showed me the exposed collum of her throat.

A tattoo stretched up her neck, like the limbs of a tree cut off just below her jaw. They moved, as though flowing in the wind, magic ingrained in the wayward branches. Some kind of spell, or ...

"A Fae Bargain?" I asked, sighing when she nodded, her head jerking like even that was going against it.

Wonderful. Caught between a Djinn and a Fae.

I looked over my shoulder at Ali, who was watching us with cold, beady eyes. So different from how she was just seconds ago, like whatever action she'd been told to make had been cut off. Hadlie's doing, without a doubt.

Two years I'd spent by Ali's side, trying to force my way out of this. Four years total, I'd *failed.* I wasn't getting out of here without help.

This wasn't my game, and it was abundantly clear that Archon had built it that way. We were easier to control if we were out of our element. So, he trapped me here, in my own head.

Strapped Adrian to a table and cut him open.

Did God knows what to Eirik.

"And you can get me out of here?" I asked, carefully.

She nodded her head, wobbling slightly, using the wall as a brace as she let out a long breath. "Get you out of the *lamp*, yes. The rest is on you."

Which meant whatever was waiting on the outside was going to be a fight. I cracked my neck from side to side, keeping my face carefully blank.

"Well, what do you need me to do?" I asked.

She shook her head before her entire body twitched. She slammed against the end table, her head snapping back as she let out a gurgled cry. The few things on it clattered to the ground, a lamp and an open book that had no words on the pages. "No, just *agree*."

The room wobbled, and a pain shot down my throat as my fangs fell. I grunted at the weight of it, rubbing my arms as a heat built there. "I'm not agreeing to shit without knowing what you want."

The wall behind Hadlie cracked, her lips opening on a cry as the world around us seemed to crumble. The room I was so attuned with melted, the wallpaper dripping onto the floor, leaving stark white walls behind. Aaliyah clattered off the bed, like a doll that had been dropped, and I jolted to help her just as Hadlie spoke again. "Then you die here. If nothing else, I can promise you that. I'm your only way out, Fallon, and we're out of time."

The room seemed to agree, bits of it flaking away, like the ache that started in every bit of my body. I fell to Aaliyah's side, knees hitting hardwood, just for her to turn to dust when I touched her.

One way or another, I was fucked. At least this way, I knew the terms. I weighed my options, weighed every second I spent in this fucking room. I couldn't get out by myself.

Was it worth it? Unlikely.

My stomach rolled, something like acid burning at the back of my throat.

Worth it or not, I didn't have a choice.

"Fuck," I mumbled, as a fissure opened under me, and nothing but that blank void stared back. "Fine. I agree to help you."

The deal sealed in seconds, a flush of power shooting over my skin, burning down across my chest and side. I grunted, watching as the mark etched into the skin. A *tree*. It grew along me, branches thick with thorns and the pink hint of flower blossoms. Just like the one that stretched under Hadlie's jaw. It crawled up my hip to my side, ending just under my floating rib.

It wasn't the only thing it did; as my chest clenched, my entire body seizing as I arched forward into a fetal position. The air dusted with bits of atomized floor that I kicked up, and in an instant, the bonds in my chest closed off. "What the *fuck*?"

The flickering mark on my wrist was next, mocking me as it stuttered, the color dimming to gray, before it faded entirely.

"You already ate my food, in my realm," she said, producing a piece of bread in her hand, the one my mother used to make. There was a detachment to her words that betrayed the kindness she'd seemed to have before, replaced with a furious expectation. "Agreeing sealed the deal. You're mine until your part is done. Sorry, but I needed to make sure you would do what I asked."

I snarled up at her, fighting through the pain as my head spun.

"You never even told me what I have to do!"

She had the gall to look guilty as she rubbed her eyes again, blood pooling there. This time, she coughed, covering her mouth as more slipped from the corners down her chin. "You have until the end of the Eternium. If you can't succeed by then, the thorns on that branch will pierce your heart."

I pulled in a hard breath, curling into the floor. My veins pulsed, the blood in them dragging to a stop as the temperature dropped again. "You—"

She paused for a minute, as if struggling to find her words, before answering. "You can trust the Fae Eternal."

There was a softness to her tone that oozed warmth. She rubbed her neck again, and I knew that was all I'd get.

Her next breath let out a fog that surrounded the room, dissolving the comfort until we were left in darkness. Her hands brushed over my face, her fingers closing my eyes before her palms were dancing over my temples. I wasn't even sure I heard her right when her whisper echoed in my head. "Tell him my name and he'll know what to do."

When I opened them again, I was blinking at a partially shadowed Century Side of Oakridge. Disorientation was nothing new, and I was quick to take in my surroundings, from the crisp winter air to the bite of shackles at my wrists. My hands were bound above my head, my chest bare as I sucked in steady breaths.

Another dream?

"What—" I said, gritting my teeth, when another rustled beside me.

I flipped my head, finding Adrian looking at me with a bloodied, crooked grin. He was ripped apart, his skin so shredded it was *still* mending at a snail's pace. He barely looked like my brother at all.

"I was wondering when you were going to wake up. Thought I'd die alone out here." He chuckled, his voice cracked and hoarse, looking toward the horizon with a fear I felt in my bones. The reddish hue slammed into me, the weight of where we were as heavy as the emptiness in my chest and the blank space on my wrist. I was out of the lamp, just like Hadlie had promised. So was Adrian, no matter what shape he was in.

But this wasn't free. This was an entirely different kind of hell, one that came with a ticking time bomb that sizzled like my skin.

The sun was rising, and we were on the fucking *roof*.

I pulled against the restraints, fire-like pain starting at my wrists where the bones broke and ending in my strained shoulders until I felt the muscle give way. Until I was panting, shaking like a fucking leaf.

"Yeah, no use on that. Archon had some *serious* magic put into his restraints. Pretty sure he meant to hold Osi with them," Adrian said, his head tipping as he spit out a mouthful of blood. "We don't stand a rat's chance in hell."

Fear was a powerful thing. It bound you up and locked away your sense of self. It folded you into a person who lived for self-preservation and would do *anything* to avoid it.

My crutch had always been control, the need to have everything in place so nothing could surprise me. Fear had swallowed me after I'd lost Aislinn, then again when Aaliyah had stormed into my life, and *again* when I'd almost lost her, too.

Now, the fear was tangible, alive in a way I never expected on the day I'd die. I didn't fear for myself. I never had. I wasn't worried about what death would bring, or if there'd be anything after it.

I was scared for Ali. The idea of her finding us like we had Nero was revolting, like a final "fuck you" from the gods as punishment for being Vivas.

"You know, of all the ways I expected to go out, this was probably at the bottom of the list," Adrian whispered, shaking his head and pulling at the restraints that held his wrists to the wooden cross. My instincts screamed, telling me I should be running. "I would have hoped for something flashier, like in that fight with Kri'Valta, or a magical exploding cake."

His normally cheery character was drowning in a terror he couldn't hide. His eyes were blown wide, his breaths coming out in shallow pants that ended in a crackling in his chest.

"This wasn't supposed to happen, Fallon." Adrian's words ended with a choked laugh, like now that they were spilling out, he didn't have any chance of stopping them. He pulled on his bindings again, the same feeble attempt I'd made, the sour scent of fear-laced blood filling the air. "God, I just want to put up that Christmas tree with Ali. Like we promised we would."

The image gagged me, the thought of missing it enough to make me wrench my hands again, until blood cascaded across the roof. One of my thumbs popped out of its socket, and I yanked down, trying to rip my hand free, just for the shackle to cinch tighter. "It's not over yet. We can get out; we just have to ... We *need*—"

We needed a miracle.

Gritting my teeth, I bit my tongue, screaming through a snarl as the rays began to light up the houses on the horizon of Oakridge, inching up over the brick. I flinched, my flesh sizzling.

Not like fucking this.

"You don't have to lie," Adrian whispered, almost serene, as he tipped his head back. "I just ... Do you think she's okay, Fal?"

I couldn't even tell. The binding of my soul to that Fae Bargain stealing the last touches I'd have with Ali. I swallowed that pain, too. Hopefully, it was one sided, and she'd just been cut off.

I'd hate myself if she felt me die.

"She will be." I *hoped*. I kicked myself at the short phrase, too locked up to give him anything else.

Something deep in my gut told me something was wrong. Osiris would have come for us otherwise. Or he went after Kri'Valta without us. Either way, it was to save her. That much I knew, and I couldn't ever fault him for that. I would have done the same.

Hope was a dying thing, something that slipped away, bit by bit, as the vicious light began to touch us.

"Fuck," Adrian hissed, turning away from it.

His skin started to smoke, and the unmistakable dark lines painting his skin told me what I didn't want to believe. It affected him quicker than me by just a bit, his age making him burn faster.

He'd be the first to go, and I'd have to watch him die before succumbing myself. I flexed my hands, fighting the chains, the magic.

None of it gave, not even enough to hope.

"Adrian," I whispered, trying to get his attention.

This time he sobbed, his eyes still held shut. The burn started on my face, then down my exposed chest, my skin peeling as the blood in my veins fought to get out.

I nearly vomited.

"Was this how Nero felt? Strung up? God, I can't even imagine being alone. He had to have been so scared." Adrian's words were nothing more than a mumbled mess, tears now matching his veins, ashen black as they boiled off.

His skin pulled taut as those thin black lines grew deeper, pulsing to the beat of his heart. They stuck to his features, clinging to high cheek-bones which twisted with a grimace instead of his usual haughty smirk.

"*Adrian*," I tried again.

"I mean, he was strong—*the strongest*—and he still died." Adrian either didn't hear me or was too gone to listen, and when he opened his eyes, the resignation was what got me. Blood pooled in the corners, sliding down his cheeks as he blinked, the familiar brown-lit hazel slowly shifting to black, matching the marks that now consumed his face. "I don't want to die, Fallon, not like this. *Not yet*."

His eyes closed again, and the sun peeked over the lip of the roof. It was like lava, burning and seizing. I held on to a scream, just barely.

"Look at me, brother," I hissed, and he did, even as his skin bubbled.

At least Ali was safe. She had to be safe. Osiris made it to Kri'Valta's. Exilium was going to work, and they'd be free. Maybe Eirik would get out, maybe it would just be *us*.

Another pair of Sebek's Turned lost to time.

Adrian kept his head high, shaking like he had that first night after we'd found him on the streets of London, marveling at the sun he'd wanted so badly to see again, even as it ate him. He was a man who'd gotten on my nerves every second for the past hundred years. He'd stolen my paintings, goaded me into fights like it was second nature to piss me off and pranked me every way he could, most of the time with Nero there to egg him on. My brother, in the truest sense, and if we were going to die like this, then I wouldn't let him die thinking he was anything *but* my brother.

I couldn't let him die afraid. I *wouldn't* let him die alone.

"We are Vivas. When one fights, we fight with them," I whispered, body seizing. Agony. Like Kali had lit a match and boiled my blood in my veins all over again. "I love you, brother. I'll see you on the other side."

Adrian froze as I choked on the words, tilting his head to look at me one last time. He smiled through the pain, the one I'd seen a million times, that I used to roll my eyes at. His grin tipped the corner of his lip, splashed with black and red. "Figures you wait until the end to be sappy."

His eyes rolled back, his breath coming out in a quiet huff, before no more followed. I could still recall how it felt to lose Nero, the pain so visceral it had torn every ounce of breath from my lungs. That same pain ripped through me now, nerves dying so fast it stopped for just a second.

"I love you, Fal."

Then Adrian was gone.

And I knew I'd be quick to follow.

Chapter 17

Eirik

It had been a cold several hours between seemingly endless whippings and having to listen to the *obnoxious* sound of Brazen chewing with his mouth wide fucking open. Most of it had flashed by in a haze alongside the lingering scent of a steak cooked well done, and the shrill cries of a wolf caged. *Mine.* It was because of that haze that I hadn't realized Archon had shown up until the door was already closing, and Brazen was standing from his seat.

They left in a rush and a flurry of words, faster than I was able to follow, tripping over themselves like the devil himself was on their heels. In a rare show of fear, Brazen didn't even bother to finish his drink: a half glass of warm bourbon that made my nose twist. It was almost comical, enough to dull the edge of panic and pain, bringing me back enough to *feel* as I popped my jaw. If I was more coherent, I might have laughed.

Took Osiris long enough to come pay Archon a visit.

I was bloodied, beaten down by the burning on my wrist and the thrumming in my chest, like an unending pulse that roared almost as loud as my other half. He howled again, the sorrowful sound making my head hurt, the echo of it loud in the room as the keening cry slid past cracked lips. I'd expected to hear voices, the begging pleas of a dead man as Archon brought Osiris to us and put an end to whatever this fucking game was.

Instead, a chill filled me, sweat clinging to my skin, the salt from it stinging in the open wounds on my back. The first hints of something wrong started with silence. My wolf went deadly still, only the crack of the fire sounding as I held my breath. My ears strained, listening for the threat my body seemed convinced was just behind me ... when I felt the first fissure open in my chest.

Losing a brother was much the same as losing a limb.

When Nero died, he tore out a part of my heart and took it with him, and I still felt that pain along the jagged remains of his bond. I never could have guessed that what would bring that horrible grief rushing back ... was the feeling of it hitting all over again.

My teeth clashed, and the feral red of my eyes bled into nothing but rage. I didn't have the lucidity to scream, foaming at the mouth as a growl bubbled from my chest.

That part of me that made me *Úlfhéðinn* thundered against my skull, teeth grazing my consciousness, claws digging at my sanity, vicious and cruel with every attempt to crack through Archon's nullification spell. He pushed until my wrists broke in preparation for the shift that wouldn't fucking come, the old metal shackles barely creaking.

Brazen had already tried, already forced more than I had to give. It was his favorite game, and if even he couldn't bring it forward through this hell ...

I fell into a frenzy, my wolf and my mind melding together as we crashed against the chains again. Until more bones broke, until my beast was panting, and any hint of hesitancy bled away, staining the floor like the blood that rained from my wrists. The magic that seeped into the aged iron was potent, lying over my skin like sludge.

But no matter what I did, it didn't break.

Thirty seconds passed. Dread pooled inside of me, eating me alive as the drag of sleep came with the rising of the sun, more telling than it had ever been as I shivered.

Shifts were never comfortable, but I'd grown over the years to look forward to the pain. To the rearranging of bones and descent into a more animalistic nature. My chest expanded, filling with air that was let out in another vicious growl that broke down into a scream.

There was no joy to be found now, as I heard the start of it, the rise of the sun, and the panicked cries. I was *sure* it was them. A fear of my own death had stopped me when it happened to Nero; the thought of the sun on my skin freezing me even as he'd screamed. I'd had a brother die once. I'd never recovered then, and this would *damn* me. How would I look my *Elskan* in the eyes and tell her I'd lost them?

How would I look at myself?

The sound of crashing and cursing filled the space, replacing the screams I hadn't realized had started. Voices cried before being cut off with an abruptness that paired with the slicing of steel through flesh, before the scent of fresh blood filled the air. The clattering of the door flying open at my back was followed by silence.

My heart damned near fucking stopped, and I sagged, pulling in a breath, filling my lungs with what I expected to be coffee-lined mint. My wolf cried again, low in my chest.

I was met with a face I was sure was here to haunt me, covered in red and brimming with feral emotion. His scent hit me as his hands burned against the chains, the spell fighting to keep him off. Sandalwood, the heady scent of Rome and molten steel. Strength, grit. *Gladiator.*

His chest heaved, his face pale and covered in a layer of sweat that made fissures in the red, *silver* eyes honed through years of vicious fights and brutal victories. Osiris wasn't here.

Nero was.

What a shitty time to hallucinate.

"Holy fuck, what did they do to you, Eirik?" he asked, his voice cracking as he hissed, shaking his smoldering hands.

"Nero?" I asked, almost too hopeful. Something in my brain must have shorted, the torture getting to me.

No matter how many times I blinked, he stayed there. Strong shoulders, the same crooked nose and hardy eyebrows. Standing, *breathing*, like he'd never died.

My heart jolted, my beast howling with a renewed energy. Nero flashed a smile, the familiar crooked grin the final smoking gun. "That's me, or so I'm told. Help me out here."

The shackles had burned rings into my wrists, searing the skin. Nero struggled with them, the room draining his strength. I wasn't sure how he was here, or if he really even was, but it was enough to get me moving again.

"Where—" I started, the word bitten off as another ripple of a shift tore through me. I arched in the chains, grunting as my chest contracted, a few ribs snapping. "Fallon and Adrian. We need to find them."

He cursed, raising a bloodied blade—a *sword*—with an ornate golden handle wrapped in delicate red thread. In one fell swing, it sliced through the chain attached to the shackle on my first wrist. Sparks flew at the meeting of steel and iron.

"On the roof, I'd guess. We have to go *now.*" Nero grunted, as shrapnel flew around us, his pain echoing mine, ripping through the last chain holding me captive as the *Flame* coiled in me.

Everything ached as I crashed into the ground, agony welling in my fucking bones. It was inconsequential, a nuisance. I steeled myself, wasting no time before flying through the halls of Fellow Manor. My beast raged in the back of my head, but didn't push to take control, lending me strength to race faster. Only one goal in mind.

We had to get to the roof.

I heard Nero behind me, and together, we caught the remaining guards by surprise, ripping out throats as we climbed. There was no plan, no discussion, but that didn't stop us from falling into a formation as old as the bond between us. The tie in my chest told me where to go, and Nero made sure no one followed us. With each kill, each move that played out like the most well-rehearsed choreography, I let myself believe.

Nero wasn't just here. He fought with me as if he'd never died.

Another bond in my chest exploded, dropping me to my knees with a scream. It ruptured, fizzling into dust so abruptly it had me puking onto the ground. My entire body revolted, a hand on my back the only thing keeping me moving. I struggled to my feet.

Fallon.

Grief had never been something that I'd handled well. I didn't fall into numbness like Osiris or seek a pound of flesh like Fallon. I didn't hide my sorrows behind smiles and affection like Adrian. I shut it down, locked it away where it couldn't be a threat. I didn't have time for something so trivial as grief when my brothers needed someone to lean on. I locked it up, chained and beaten, buried so deep that I might force myself to forget about it.

Until moments like this. Moments when death became too real. My thoughts went to Nero, to the moment we'd pulled him off the pyre in Russia. I could remember that day so clearly, the smoke in the air, and the hint of singed flesh. It was here again now, and it brought every sick memory back to me.

The box I'd kept that trauma in came roaring forward, snapping open, unraveling everything I'd kept in it: my life before my turn. Nero's death.

Brazen's heavy fucking whip.

I reached for the necklace that sat around my neck, the steel that used to burn into my skin like a monument to my brother ... *missing*. The scar there caught under my fingers instead, pushing me just as hard, and I didn't stop to think as I reached the top of a long set of spiral stairs. Fallon's bond pulled tight, my throat closing as it shriveled. The fear of the sun, of death. It was there, biting into me, threatening me with immobilization.

I wouldn't lose another brother.

I was already barreling outside when Nero's scream of protest reached me. The sun hit without remorse. My skin immediately revolted, peeling back, my blood turning to ash in my veins.

I kept moving, kept fighting.

Because it was what *Nero* would have done, what I wanted to do the day he'd died. I couldn't save him, was too scared and too fucking cowardly. So be it his ghost that came to me, or something else entirely ...

I wouldn't fail another one of my brothers again.

CHAPTER 18

AALIYAH

Each memory I had stemmed from an instance of déjà vu. A scent that brushed against the air, hinting at a perfume I knew I'd smelled before. A facial expression that twisted just a bit too much like my father's lips when he used to catch me sneaking cookies at night.

The way I moved or the way my body ached when I did, scars constantly reminding me there was more horror to relive.

Memories were consistent that way, and I'd grown rather good at noticing when I was in one. Which was why I was so confused when I opened my eyes.

I wasn't at Ascension, strapped to a cool steel table with Castillion leering down at me, or in my childhood home, with checkered walls and white tiles that would always be red in my mind.

No, I was in a room of rolling silver, and an endless obsidian sky ... The Void. It was breathlessly silent as a scene that didn't quite register as real played out in front of me.

My mother lay over a body that was unmoving, my father's pale skin seeming ashen in the dull, colorless light.

She pressed her ear to his chest, sobbing when it didn't rise.

"I remember this day," a voice called, echoing as if it had come from everywhere. My mother didn't hear it, still pressed over my father as I jolted, rushing to cover my ears, jerking my head away from the scene.

The air behind me wobbled, as though it was nothing more than water, the sky above seeming to melt as it dripped to the floor in inky black splashes. The Void recoiled, enough to make me turn fully, stepping away as the hair on the back of my neck rose. Slowly, as if parting, those mounds of black took shape, one my brain didn't fully register as a person as the need to run made my legs tense.

Some people had an air about them, one that warned you to keep your distance. Whoever this man was, from the way he towered over me yet kept his posture relaxed to the soft glow that hugged his snow-white skin, had that uncanny air. He radiated light in a place where darkness lingered, watching me curiously, with two of his four arms crossed behind his back, the lower two pressed palm side down against each other over his abdomen. His head, mostly human shaped, ended in familiarity there. A halo of light extended above it, made from the two horns that poked from his skull, connecting again at the tips. He had no defining features beyond that. The eyes I was expecting to see were instead strewn about the large white wings that stretched almost ominously from his back.

My soul wavered in my chest, and the Void seemed to actively avoid him. The shadows slipped away, the ground of silver solidifying beneath his feet, while it remained fluid under mine.

There was something about him, a nagging feeling in my head telling me I'd seen him before.

"Call me Davi," he whispered, his voice echoing again, this time with a hint of mirth.

Maybe that was why I didn't panic when he continued to stare, his head tipping to the side as he studied me, his wings fluttering as the eyes on it blinked lazily. I didn't feel dug into, like he was on the other side of the glass at Ascension, but rather, like he was curious.

Genuinely curious.

"She first came here after Arvand was struck down by Escandric. She tried to save him, give him a part of her soul so he may continue to live," he said, abruptly, turning his head toward my mother. "Come, watch with me."

A strained few seconds passed, filled only with the sound of her sobs, something that had been blotted out before. I hesitated, feeling like it was a mistake to give this man my back, something he seemed to notice as he walked forward, not pausing when I tensed, moving so my only option was to follow him, until my parents came into view again.

My mother's head still laid against my father's unmoving chest. She clutched his shirt, which turned to ash in her hands, the burn marks on his body suddenly glaringly visible. Her eyes shadowed over, the ones underneath her seeming to take notice as they stretched a little further across the floor.

Then she spoke, the words muddled and lost to translation, almost like Eliza's when she used her Siren's Call to coerce people into doing her bidding. Except, I knew them, somehow. Understood their meaning in the depths of my soul, even if it sounded barely more than gibberish. A shudder went down my spine at the thought of them from my own lips, and suddenly it was as if I were in the forest again.

The warmth of a hot spring at my back, Prince's eyes going dull for the last time before he faded away under my touch. The voice that had become a nightmare to me, one that still whispered in my ear, like the devil on my shoulder.

My mother spoke the same words I had to Prince, that wicked voice hers now, too. She whispered them until she went hoarse, and tears filled her eyes, the shadows in them dropping away as blood took their place. Her skin split, breaking open as she sucked in gasping breaths. She covered the open wounds with her hands until they healed, just to watch them split again.

I was too afraid to move, to breathe and risk breaking her concentration, even in this dream. Another gut-wrenching scream slipped out of her before my father's eyes shot open.

I released a breath, realizing the numbness in my hands was from how tightly I'd clenched them.

"One could not be without the other. She tied herself to him, bound their lives. She was the first to mend souls, the first to bring someone back that had fallen to death's call," Davi said, as his wings spread out wide, the rustling drawing my attention.

The scene of my mother faded, leaving us alone in the Void. I could feel the ache where my nails had dug into my palms, and my senses were sharp enough to catch the hint of iron in the air. Whatever this was, a dream or an illusion ... I saw it because Davi wanted me to. I clutched my *chest, letting out a shaky breath when he continued to watch me, waiting for a response I didn't think I had it in me to give.*

"This isn't one of my memories," I said, struggling to find my voice in a place where it normally didn't exist, surprised when his head tipped back and a laugh filled the Void. "I don't know why you'd show me this."

The sound echoed again, and he sank to the floor gracelessly, crossing his legs as he planted his chin in his palm. His wings went almost lax behind him, before tucking close to his back, only the eyes at the bend at the top, staying open.

"Than said you were direct," he hummed, as if bonding us over an inside joke, and I racked my brain, searching for the name I was sure I hadn't heard before. "This is your memory, though. Isn't it?"

I looked around again, chewing on my lip until I tasted blood. I could feel the Void, just like every other time, but there wasn't a feeling of urgency to leave or the gentle pluck against my soul to check if I was dead. I wasn't watching like a guest in my own thoughts. I tried to recall the scene again, my mother over my father ...

My memory. One I was too small to remember.

"Are you saying she's pregnant with me? But that doesn't make sense."

Only silence, before a buzz started in the air. Davi lifted his hand, and even from sitting on the ground, it reached several inches above my head. Sharp talons lined the end of his fingers. The sky slowly crawled down until it was sliding through them, liquid onyx. "Doesn't it?"

The testing pressure of the Void was closer now because of it, and I shivered as it poked at me. The familiar touch made my stomach twist.

"Unless this was a long time ago," I whispered.

All of his eyes were on me as the halo above his head glowed, pulsing to the beat of his wings as they lifted him to his feet again. I struggled to find ones to look at as his head tilted to the side. "The Void should have killed you, especially with only part of a soul. It almost did. Keep watching."

Just as before, a scene faded into view, my mother appearing with a bundle in her arms. One that wiggled and cried. She looked haggard, panting, with white hair stuck to clammy skin.

"That's me?" I said it more than asked, hesitatingly taking a step forward.

My mother held the bundle close, cradling the tiny infant in her arms. For a second, I could feel her warmth, get a hint of that lavender scent that had defined her and that she'd passed down to me.

"The night your mother revived your father, it claimed a piece of you she didn't realize in return. You were the soul that brought him back, a link to them, and a link to here."

She sank to the ground, holding me to her chest as Davi spoke.

"The Void claimed *you*, raised *you*, until you were strong enough to survive without it. Placed a part of itself in the little slot your missing soul left."

The silver floor morphed, and the bits of the Void that had been prodding me did so again. This time excitedly, this time lingering, *like it was waiting for me to acknowledge it.*

I was going to be sick.

"Are you telling me I've been alive since the Natural War?" I asked. "That I lived in the Void?"

"You should have died that night, but you didn't. Not until the Void called you home." Davi nodded, his wings tucking close as he watched me carefully. That same excitement lived in him, a subtle softness sinking into his hum. "Over three thousand years now. You are *the* favorite, without a doubt."

The weight of the words didn't sink in, not really. I remembered my home, being barely tall enough to reach the counters or the light switches on the checkered walls. I remembered my mother cooking on a stove and the smell of gas in the air every time she lit the pilot. Recalled walking the streets of a city with my father's cold hand in mine.

But that was it. I remembered being a child and remembered Sebek taking me. There wasn't a before that, at least not yet. And the idea of it, that my mother had brought my father back ...

Could I ... have done the same?

I reached for my chest, suddenly hopeful in a way I hadn't been in weeks. Prince had been sent on after I'd touched him, or ... at least that was what I'd thought.

What if I hadn't killed him?

Even the thought brought warring emotions surging forward, ones I knew I couldn't afford to think about right now. I shoved it down, locked it away with the fear, to deal with later.

"But I don't remember that?" I said, uncertainty cracking the edges of my words.

"You spent most of it in the Void. Unaging, but a babe. Your mother stayed with you as much as she could, most times at the cost of her own soul," Davi said, pointing to my mother.

She twitched now, still holding the little bundle—me—close, still breathing that song that used to lull me to sleep, that whispered like a long-forgotten memory that teased the back of my mind. Tears gathered in her eyes before she set me down. She did so with trembling arms and an expression that didn't betray the agony she felt.

The dark shadows under her body stretched wide, pulling her into the floor as she sucked in a surprised breath. One moment here, the next, nothing but Void. Nothing but me.

The Void moved around my tiny body after, when I started to cry, touching my fingers as I reached up to grab it as Davi had. It played, strips of obsidian black crawling along my skin, keeping the tiny me occupied until my eyes slid closed, and I yawned.

"Don't fight the Void, Aaliyah. You risk more than your soul by doing so." Davi's words felt like a warning I couldn't afford to ignore. His posture softened again, and he reached a hand out, not quite touching as he fussed. I couldn't have missed the hint of pity there, a look that twisted his featureless face. I didn't have time to ask as he slashed his hand down, and pain shot through me like a wave. The kind I'd felt when I'd first woken in my grave.

This time, it didn't end with the sound of a voice or the scent of dirt and rain.

This time it ended on my wrist.

"Now. It's time to wake up."

I sucked in a hard breath that shattered the haze just long enough for the pain to fully register.

"What—" I started, the word ending on a coughing fit that seemed to seek out the empty spaces in my lungs, filling them with the same blood that splattered white sheets and slid over my lip to the beat of my heart. My vision went next, blurring as my breath frosted in front of me, shiver bumps lining my arms. Red's emotions were a lull, sneaking up from thin air. It was almost like he was stretching after a long nap before he recognized my panicked state. Panic that quickly swallowed rational thought. "It hurts—"

I choked as a fear so nerve-racking that it took my breath away tore through me, fighting my own emotions as I realized that it wasn't *mine*. There was barely a second between that all-consuming fear ... and the fracture of the bonds on my wrist, the abrupt torment leaving me clutching at my chest, gasping as sweat stuck to my skin.

The black ink that had kept me going the past few days was nothing more than a memory on the canvas of my arm. Bits and pieces of the once flowing designs scattered like stained glass across an ivory floor. Incomplete, and *broken*. It seared where they'd been, leaving nothing behind but *scarred* skin.

Coiled artistry with a gentle flow like the waves of the ocean, once rich black ink now a muddied gray. Spilled coffee grounds graced with little tea leaves that seemed to move when I covered them.

Fallon and Adrian ... I couldn't *feel* them anymore.

Every inch of me itched, and I pushed away from the sheets, struggling to get away from them as the temperature continued to drop. They wrapped tighter, tangling in my legs, nearly dragging me to the floor as I finally freed myself.

Anxiety filled the air, then unease as Red danced over my shoulders. My feet hit cold hardwood first, the abrupt chill on the bare soles enough of a shock to clear some of the nerves that had me shutting down as I stumbled.

Breathing became painful, my eyes growing hazy until all the color in the room had faded to a sharp gray. The dim walls were bathed in dark patches of shadows, the bed tucked neatly in the corner I'd just staggered away from. The silence that followed was deafening. That silence was my answer, the one I couldn't even stand to voice.

Adrian was gone. Fallon was *gone.*

But that couldn't be right ... there was no way I'd lost them. Not after everything I'd done to get here. I walked into Ascension; I curled up in my old cell and begged for the day I'd see them again.

I'd lain on the table of my *nightmares*, a needle in my skin, staring into the overhead lights that haunted memories I couldn't even *begin* to call real and what had it gotten me? I touched the blank spaces on my wrists, the ones that seemed to wobble, the black fraying at the edges.

Only two remained now, Eirik's, which strained just as tightly, shuttering like it might well be the next to go ...

And Osiris's, the only point that I had left to grasp onto as I crumbled.

Life wouldn't be so cruel as to take them away, too.

They *couldn't* be gone.

I reached for my chest, shivering, and gasping for a breath I had no chance of steadying. Red grew more sporadic, more intense as I stumbled forward, hitting a cold wall. My legs continued to shake, and I forced my weight into my palms to try to stay standing.

Gone. *Gone.*

In an instant, the chill disappeared along with the remains of fractured emotions that had clung to the air, as though lifted away. I managed a breath, my vision clearing for a moment. A hint of warmth wrapped around me next, like a cocoon, as I sagged. The gentle sparks that flashed across my skin reminded me of the Void: pressing, *prodding* ... almost playful, and starkly familiar.

"*Red*," I whispered, unsure how he was managing it and too tired to question it. He was touching me, in a way, though not fully. There was no whisper of death's uncanny call, but he was close enough that it helped me breathe.

"Grief is beneath you, child of Ra," a voice echoed behind me.

Red tensed, a ripple moving through him as I caged a cry behind closed teeth. Sebek's voice, a steady monotony, was somehow more intimidating than any threats that had ever been screamed at me at Ascension.

I covered the remains of the marks, pretending I couldn't feel them digging into the skin, pulsing as an ache continued all the way up my arm, ending in my shoulder.

"What did you do?" I whispered, steeling my nerves as I looked at him, flinching when I saw how close he was, barely a step away.

He was dressed in the same simple black suit he had been before, the white cuffs still stained a deep brownish red. The black of his hair was greasy, almost appearing wet as he held his hand out, a draping fabric slipping over his fingers. It flowed easily, with little frills along the sleeves and the long bottom of what I recognized as a dress. The sheer white of it seemed out of place, a mockery as I searched for splashes of red I was sure I'd find where he touched it.

"We're late," he said, lips twisting in a disparaging sneer.

It fluttered in his steady hand, as though affected by a soft breeze. Red lingered by it, the barest hint of a hand on the white silk, before a bitter anger filled the room. A spark flashed in the air, the only physical reaction I'd ever seen from him, enough to leave a small singe mark on the otherwise perfect fabric. He danced around me, pushing me to reach out and take it from the monster's hands, though there was no mistaking his intent.

Destroy it.

"*What* did you do?" I pressed again, refusing to take Sebek's offering, shrinking back when his stare turned savage, his fingers clenching until they paled.

One moment I'd have sworn I could see compassion in his gaze, the next he wouldn't even look me in the eye, as if I were so far below him it would be a chore for him to drop his chin. He didn't answer, as he looked over my shoulder.

I'd been too caught up with the burn that still sizzled at my wrist to notice the soft glow that scattered across the floor, lighting up the previously colorless tile. It stretched across the tops of my feet, ending at the black leather of Sebek's shoes. I squinted as it crept up my legs, growing brighter and more vibrant ... until I looked behind me.

The light was coming from what I assumed was a window, boarded up so it couldn't get through, but there *were* cracks, places where it could slip by through the pale brown boards. The burning on my wrist grew into a frenzy. My body ached, the pressure that I'd hoped I'd finally escaped once again building behind my eyes.

Sebek was quiet as the understanding of his silence hit me.

He wouldn't do this. They couldn't *be gone.*

I'd only seen the sun rise a handful of times. It was something I'd avoided if I could, like it was bad luck to look at after so many years without it. Dread rose like bile, and I covered my mouth as my stomach sank.

I stumbled away from the window, right into a set of chilled arms, flinching as Sebek's fingers tightened on my shoulders. His eyes narrowed on the marks on my wrist, some whole and some fractured, a look of disgust crossing his face. There was nothing in his familiar red eyes, no remorse, no worry, *nothing.*

I jerked away, another jolt at my wrist sending a wave of pain down my spine.

"I did what you asked. I didn't run. You promised they'd be safe ..." I whispered through gritted teeth, fighting the tears as the words caught in my throat, silenced by a mantra he'd started.

Never make noise.

I'd walked into Ascension Rising, laid back on the table that was as much a part of me as my scars. He promised he wouldn't hurt them, and I trusted him.

"I did nothing but allow them to fumble. Their mistakes led to their capture. Their weakness is what led to their deaths," he said, cutting through me.

I'd trusted a monster that wore my father's face and destroyed my life one horrid action at a time. I'd held on to some hope that he'd been lying, that when he told me he'd let them live, he'd meant it.

They couldn't be gone.

It was a foolish mistake, one that would cost me ... *everything.* Sebek was a man of cold calculation, of feral power and a lack of morals that stemmed back to the first death of my father. He couldn't be reasoned with because he didn't feel empathy for the ones he harmed.

There was only him, his goals, and the obstacles between them. Me. My men. Everyone that had died and would die because he viewed them as expendable.

"Do you see now, Glass? You're *mine.* Exilium will not save you. Usire will do nothing but die at the Horror's Gala."

I froze, holding my breath as I looked up. Sebek's face was angled toward his watch, like he hadn't just spilled our plan onto the ground like dirt. The bleakness of what awaited us at the Eternium sank down fully, weighing on my shoulders.

"Now dress. We're late."

He was always a step ahead, rigging the board while we stumbled, laughing at every move we made.

And still Osiris fought anyway.

He could have gone for the others and made sure they made it out of Archon's. They could have regrouped, found me at the Eternium where no doubt Sebek planned to take me. Even knowing what he was up against, he came.

I didn't like to think of the world as evil, even with the things I'd been through. It made it hard to want to live when you didn't have something to believe in, even if that was just a smile from a passing stranger.

Or a piece of chocolate from a stoic Vampire who couldn't stand to hear you cry.

Sebek had been there at every turn. Tearing down my hope and my life. There wasn't any doubt in my mind anymore. I *hated* him. For what he'd done to me, for the scars that he'd seen carved into my skin and for the blood that stained his hands.

Fallon. Adrian. Eirik.

I ignored the ache in my chest when I saw his face, the hope I held that there might still be reason to be found in him.

He was going to try to kill Osiris, too.

"I won't let you," I hissed, a familiar black sheen coating my eyes. It was brief, barely a flash, but Sebek saw it.

His eyes widened a fraction before going fully red.

The power drained just as fast, like dumping a glass of water into a bottomless well. Sebek took a step forward, boxing me against the window. I heard a sizzle of flesh as the light hit his hand, but it didn't stop him, and I had nowhere to go.

"You will listen," he said, his body seeming to grow, his presence filling the room like a plague.

I struggled to keep my head up, fighting the instinct to look down when he glared at me. I dug my nails into my palm to center myself, pushing until the skin broke.

Never make noise.

"I said *no*." I lifted my hand, showing my abused palm. Sebek snarled at the sight, that flash of mania driving him again as he jolted forward. "Beat me, drag me, kill me. I don't care. I won't do another thing you ask."

I wouldn't be able to stop him, but I could slow him down. Maybe give Osiris enough time to get in and out before we got there. He had to be there already, the sun at my back telling me as much.

I reached up with my other hand, grabbing the charm that sat around my neck. It was warm to the touch, the little lavender gem glowing as Sebek's eyes flashed to it.

"You will, Glass. We are *late*," he snarled.

Years I spent in Ascension, hours strapped to the same table he'd forced me back on. But I had power here, however little it might be. Sebek valued structure, that much was obvious, and I was happy to throw a wrench in that.

"I'm not afraid of what you can do. I've been through worse, but you know that already, don't you?" I asked, and it was like a switch flipped.

I tried to stumble back, hitting the boards as he shot forward. I wasn't expecting the way he grabbed me, one hand in my hair as he jerked my head to the side.

The gem around my neck sizzled, the power of it nearly choking me as I heard his fangs fall. The charm that Osiris had made for me kept him away for all of a moment.

Before Sebek sank his fangs into my neck.

A gurgling cry was my only sound as he pulled a mouthful of my blood out. It sent an immediate chill through every limb, my veins turning to ice so quickly my teeth chattered. There was no gentleness in the merciless clench of his jaw, no end in sight to the pain that blinded me.

A sluggish brush of fear lingered in the air as Red made himself known. His panic blended with mine, his hysteria falling on my chest as I struggled in Sebek's arms.

Osiris's magic came forward, trying to defend me. The gem at my neck vibrated, like it was desperately trying to keep him out. With each hit of power it threw at him, Sebek bit down harder, sank deeper, looking to hurt. A show of dominance that proved his point with every mouthful he stole.

I sobbed, my hands falling limply to my sides before the gem shattered, its pieces falling to the ground like little shards of glass. I was too stunned to speak as he pulled back, face covered in my blood.

He should have died. I waited for it, even as my heart thundered, and he continued to stare. He brushed his hand over his mouth, licking his lips as his eyes went back to normal. Five seconds passed, then ten. Still, he didn't fall. He leaned in with sickening intent, his jaded expression holding nothing but rage. His eyes flared wide, and he reached up, tearing at his wrist.

I was forced to take his blood, a final insult that made me sick, as I was too weak to even turn my head. Red pushed comfort, grounding me as I coughed and sputtered. He was the only thing keeping me lucid as I felt the flicker of the *Hallen Bond* again.

"Understand, Glass. You're a means to an end. A means to a life, and I will not be denied my peace," he snarled before he dropped me, watching me slide down the wall with a sneer. He tossed the dress at my feet, red splotches covering the white, one distinctly in the shape of his hand. Then he turned away, leaving me broken on the floor, clutching my savaged neck. "This is your last warning. Dress, while I still have the patience to let you."

CHAPTER 19

AALIYAH

I'd seen dead bodies before. Some haunted my memories, consisting of the others that had been at Ascension, living in moments that left me shattered as I woke screaming. I'd seen more in the last few weeks than I dared to count. The dead *weren't* new to me, but this one, the one sprawled on the ground, his throat ripped into ribbons, with Sebek hovering over him like a feral beast?

He was new. Blood pooled beneath his body, staining the golden floors and his once-white clothes.

Sebek had dragged me here, damned near kicking and screaming, through another teleportation spell. The room was covered in gold and red, bleeding a luxury I'd never seen before. Lavish velvet bindings traced bodies that hung from the ceiling, weathered but obviously cared for paintings that made my heart ache at the thought of Fallon decorating the walls.

My neck still throbbed, my head spinning from blood loss. The wound had healed, but the impression of his fangs was a constant reminder of his cruel words and dead eyes, a pain that lingered like a burden I couldn't get rid of. One that paled in comparison to the bonds that fractured on my wrist.

The man couldn't have been much older than early twenties, his blue eyes now open in permanent shock, adorned with flashy green make-up that accentuated the color, with wispy blond hair that had been styled meticulously. His features were soft and inviting, like he was the kind of person you could talk to for hours, with a smile that would light up rooms.

Sebek had killed him in an instant because he got too close, because he'd brushed against my arm as I was dragged through the throng of people.

The room had gone sickeningly quiet in the moments since it happened. Even the music stopped as the others around us turned to look on in horror. Sebek paid them no mind, not even bothering to glance at the body he'd left on the ground as he wiped the blood off his own face.

I couldn't look at him either, bile in my throat as I choked down the tears that burned behind my eyes. I held it all in, jolting closer to Sebek to keep from getting too close to the others in the room, frantic gaze sweeping over them. The rush of gold and red, screams and cries.

A flash of mismatched blue eyes that I knew like the back of my hand. My heart skipped, my mind denying it even as Osiris came into focus. The need to see him again, whole, was overwhelming.

I took a half step forward, if only to see him a little clearer. He was clutching his chest, his face slick with sweat as he seemed to stare vacantly into the crowd, the same desperation in his eyes I felt as I reached for my wrist.

A hand on my arm pulled me violently back into the present. I jolted away at the slosh of blood under my foot. This wasn't a dream, which meant Sebek hadn't taken me to the Eternium.

He'd brought me to Kri'Valta's Gala ... to make sure Osiris didn't walk out of it.

"It seems Osiris has won his fight," Sebek mused, his fingers biting into flesh hard enough to leave bruises. "It will not save him, Glass."

The surrounding crowd fell into mayhem, as if the spell had been broken for them as well. The quiet murmurs turned to hysteria as people scattered, another man bumping into me as the last had. His blood splattered against the ground as Sebek tore open his throat with a swipe of his hand, the sound drowned out by the sea of screams and his dying moan. His startled gray eyes dimmed as he fell in a heap of blood and organs. The screams grew louder. Sebek's cursed and rambled words were only shadowed by the blood on my face as it cooled, and his threat that still rang in my ears going off like a siren. I reached for the wrist that he still held, suddenly struggling to breathe.

So much death, so much violence. Sebek doled it out without remorse or restraint, uncaring for anything beyond his own goal, whatever it was. Nothing would change that. Not me, not my father.

This man was a monster, and I wouldn't let Osiris be the next to fall. Sebek's words rang as he moved to step around me, letting go of my arm.

The rage from before built again, like nothing I'd ever felt, and it buried the pain of my power coming to the surface. The same that had flooded me in the safe house, the same that had been locked away like a beast in a cage. I went searching for that fury, hoping to find it in the hollow space in my chest where my heart ached.

Instead, all I found was the dark. The *Void*. And the gentle brush of assurance from the cold grip of death.

The pain from before was still there, the aching behind my ear that told me I hadn't broken through his spell that kept me locked down. That didn't stop me, as I reached for it, touching my soul against the inky black that had ripped Prince away from me the first time, that had destroyed my life in more ways than one. The power was sluggish, hesitant against the binds that Sebek had placed on me, hesitant to listen to my call after I'd abandoned it, but I pushed anyway.

I let my anger fuel me. Years, I spent *years* at the whims of this man. Under his thumb, controlled, beaten, starved, and tortured. Oddly enough, that wasn't what truly drove me, even knowing who he was.

It wasn't that he ruined my life.

It was that he'd taken *theirs*.

Fallon and Adrian were gone, and it was his fault.

There was a buzz in the air, and a brush of cold that was barely enough to bring me to my senses. Like a hand, steadying, warning me to keep my focus. It was irrational to think I could feel him, but I would have sworn I felt his touch against my cheek.

Red.

The spot behind my ear pulsed, pain flaring in my skull. I welcomed it, embraced it until it burned like a fire pulsing in my chest. Until the already-fractured seal holding me back wavered. Red helped, seeming to wrap himself around me like he had before, a warmth simmering, driving away the cold.

"I won't let you hurt him, too," I whispered, and Sebek froze, just long enough to look over his shoulder at me.

The bonds were like paper against the full weight of the Void; I gritted my teeth and pushed again. Infuriated and in pain ... lost. The voice from before, the darkness that had held me while I ripped out Crustava's soul, came back.

Just overwhelm him. It whispered as the power flared. It hurt, an all-consuming agony that would have made a normal person seize. Red danced more erratically, the bitter essence of broken fear in the air only pushing me harder. Sebek took a fighting stance, all power as his eyes went hollow and flooded red. My gift stretched across the room like a dark cloud so fast even the screaming stopped. So close, I reached out, the taste of death on my lips, and he realized it then. Sebek's eyes grew feral, and he stood up to my power, flashing the same teeth he'd sunk into my neck.

More. Don't let him get away.

I savaged him with it until the entire room was covered in a black shadow that writhed around the bodies. He let go of my wrist, hissing as though in pain. The bonds covering my magic creaked, the sound audible as the Void shot out.

More.

"Settle." Sebek's voice was cutting. "You only harm yourself."

Still, he stood.

End him, put him out of his misery. The voice demanded, a last call that ate the grief that swallowed me whole.

I screamed, and like a toy wound too tightly, I exploded, my gears and springs sparking along my skin. Blood on my lips, this time my own as darkness shadowed my vision. Something held on to me, something telling me to be careful.

We'd finally been so close to safety, even if it was just briefly. The Eternium was supposed to be our last stand, the risk that would tip our scales. I gripped my wrist, almost begging for the burning that hadn't ceased in days to roar back to life.

It felt the others in the room, their life as my power toyed with them too. Felt the bystanders that didn't have a choice in the matter. My power didn't discriminate. It lingered on them as well, ready to rip them to shreds. I should have cared ... I *did* care ...

The room danced with a faint chill as Red bounced erratically around the space.

I was too far gone, my soul in pieces that I struggled to bind back together. My chest heaved, my eyes blurring with tears, and as the power reached for life in the room, all that mattered was Sebek. His death, even if it meant the others here would follow him. The cruel voice whispered softly in my ear, telling me things it thought I wanted to hear.

It'll be quick. One flick and they die. They all die.

This time, the voice was mine. This time, my gift stretched, reaching for *Osiris.*

I choked on the power I was unable to control as it seemed to wrap itself around him, and as soon as it broke free, darkness consumed me. Consumed *us.* It swallowed me whole, stripping the room of every ounce of light. The voices faded, the life around me snuffing out, as it all went quiet.

CHAPTER 20

PRINCE

Rends were a fickle bitch that sat on me like the plague, constantly residing in the back of my mind, waiting for the right thing to tip them off. A taste, a voice, a *feeling*.

Or the stench of burning flesh that still fucking haunted me, something that was so buried in the shitty soup that was my brain that I'd never get rid of it, and my body knew that too. Pressure, a constant companion since I'd gotten to Archon's, paired again with the blood that slid over my lip and into my mouth. My body fought it, as viciously as I'd fought to get here. Only my will and the remnants of Mags's potion kept it at bay.

Not that it mattered now.

I was *useless* on this side of the door as my brothers screamed until their voices went hoarse, and Eirik stumbled into the early morning sun, trying to get to them.

Their pain was something physical in me, something that echoed in the space of long-since dried-up bonds that had just barely started to resurface in my chest. They thumped wildly, as though they'd been set on fire all over again.

Fuck, was this what they'd felt when it was me on that pyre?

"Eirik!" I reached my hand out, the sunlight hitting it, lighting up sparks of agony the moment it touched me, leaving trailing black marks along my skin. That pain lingered, soaked in until I couldn't even raise my hand to try again.

I was too late, always too fucking late.

Sebek had taken Aaliyah, Archon had strung up my brothers to burn, and *Eirik*, the fucking idiot, had dove onto the roof after them. The screaming stopped, leaving me in a dead silence, and I choked on my own as I tried to fight through my fears to rush out with them.

The little hints of bonds in my chest seized, trembling one more time, before sizzling away. When they snapped, it ripped every atom of oxygen in my lungs apart.

My hands went to my hair, a desperate laugh bubbling up as I slid to my knees. I could still hear the sizzle, the last hints of heartbeats that stuttered out.

I screamed to fill the void, clawing at the ground like it might hold some kind of answer, some reasoning why my luck was so shit. My teeth crashed together, eyes never leaving the ray of morning sun that slashed across the concrete floor.

Before a body came quite literally *flying* through that same ray of light, knocking me against the wall at my side.

Eirik.

Fucking *Eirik*.

The two bodies on his shoulders were quickly dropped in front of him. His skin trembled, wavering as a snarl slipped out, vibrating the air in the room as he kept himself standing, his body shielding the others, covering them as he slammed the door shut behind him. His breaths came out in steaming pants, his eyes flushed red, a feral mix of rage and fear as he looked over his shoulder as if to check that the sunlight hadn't found another way inside.

He crumpled to the ground, shaking and snarling, obviously fighting the beast inside of him, as he laid the bodies on the floor. Fallon and Adrian were little more than charred masses, and I pushed away my confusion at the sight of them as I searched relentlessly for heartbeats that weren't there.

I jerked back, landing on my ass. Black lines stretched under their eyes, across every visible vein on their skin. Blood slid from their noses, mouths, ears, and eyes. Their features turned into agonized mosaics.

A scream wrenched itself from my throat as I tipped forward, mimicking the keening cry that ripped itself out of Eirik.

It couldn't end like this. Not again.

"Not like this," I said, ripping the long sleeves of my shirt, exposing my wrists.

I gritted my teeth, and moved until I was next to them, tilting their heads, opening their mouths. Eirik was panting, his skin steaming but ... unharmed? He wasn't burned. Beyond the gouges he'd already gotten, and the whip marks that still covered his back, there was no damage. As if the sun hadn't touched him at all. No black singes or hints of anything beyond panic.

Nothing. Not that I had the time to think on that fact. He was seemingly healthy, and that was all I needed to know for now. Eirik was quick to follow my lead, slamming onto his knees as I moved their bodies. They were dead, unmoving and lifeless. Every part of me told me it was so, but I couldn't let it go without trying.

I didn't come this far to fucking lose them.

I tore open my wrists, sinking fangs in until I tasted my own blood, then I placed them against their still mouths, forcing their bodies to swallow. When the wounds closed, I went again, only to be replaced by Eirik as he tore a chunk out of each wrist. When he healed, I stuck to Fallon, and he to Adrian.

Over and over, we forced our blood down their throats, until even the *Rend* that had been slowly growing faded. I grew dizzy, my body strung out as I bit again. It was only when I fell back, unable to lift my wrist to my mouth, that I stopped. I choked on the tears that sank heavily to the back of my throat. Eirik kept going, shaking and stumbling as he surged forward.

Adrian and Fallon hadn't moved, their faces covered in red, eyes closed in what I hoped was peace. I might not have remembered them, but it destroyed me all the same when they didn't respond.

We were too late.

"Eirik," I said carefully as he growled, his teeth snapped together as he shoved his wrist to Adrian's mouth again.

"**Not yet,**" he said, his voice hoarse and cracking, his eyes feral blue. The next time he tore his wrist, barely any blood came forward. It grew as sluggish as his heartbeat, and when he saw it, he snarled again, ripping in until I could see bone. He swayed, keeping himself upright with a hand on the closest wall.

"*Eirik*," I grunted, struggling to move, watching as he killed himself to try to undo fate.

There was a crack of fire against my skin that bounced off the floor. Eirik bared his teeth at me. The shimmering blue of his eyes snapped to vicious seas, flushing dark as his beast swallowed him whole.

"**I said *not yet*.**" There was nothing left of Eirik behind his eyes when he growled this time, the sound straightening my spine as I jerked away on instinct.

His shift started slowly, his skin trembling as it stretched too taut, and he screamed as I heard the first bone break.

"You're killing yourself, too!" I screamed back, ripping him away from Adrian and Fallon, slamming him into the wall so he was forced to look at me.

"**Then we die with them!**" He snapped his teeth in my face, that snarl unforgiving. I shivered, snarling right fucking back.

"And what will that do? They're *gone*, Eirik," I said even as he frothed at the mouth and went to bite me again. "All this does is hurt *her* more."

The change was instant, when his wolf fell to the sidelines, the deep blues of his eyes shifting to the sky color I knew in my bones was him. It was a low blow, but it was effective. Devastation sank in as he stopped fighting, sliding to the ground. He covered his face, what started as a growl falling into a scream that had matched mine. His hand slammed down, cracking the concrete, shaking the floor. The thump continued as he did it again, taking his anger out with every hit.

Until I realized he wasn't slamming it down anymore. The thud in the air persisted, groggy and labored. We both fell silent, not even breathing ...

Until Fallon did.

I shot forward, still disoriented from the blood loss, as Adrian let out a choked gasp. They stirred, groaning as their skin slowly mended, the black streaks from the sun lingering.

But they breathed; the damned bastards *breathed*. They were alive.

Fallon was the first to come to, sitting up with a labored hiss. His chest was exposed, showing that patchwork skin and a sprawling tattoo

I hadn't seen before, the limbs of a tree across his ribs reaching up toward his heart. The white remains of his suit were marred by ash and blood, the green of his tie still wrapped around his neck, almost unrecognizable.

"Eirik?" he asked, his voice cracking as his eyes centered on our brother. He blinked a few times, coughing up a slug of what looked like wet coal dust. When he slowly turned to find me, I thought his eyes might jump right from his sockets. "*Nero*? Fuck, I must be dead."

They were a haze, one that struggled to clear as his skin peeled, and he let out a pained hiss. I should have had more restraint, given that he'd just been cooked alive, but it was past time for niceties. I fell the rest of the way forward, crashing into him as I pulled him to my chest, hugging him so tightly I heard ribs crack. He wheezed, arms circling me in an embrace that started softly and ended with his hand biting into my shoulder blade with how hard he held me.

"I know, I know. Dead looks good on me," I joked, unable to get anything else out beyond a wet laugh. There was so much I wanted to say, to do.

So many things I felt, a joy I couldn't even begin to describe. I couldn't remember them, not really ... but there wasn't a doubt in my mind who they were to me.

My family was alive. We'd made it on time.

"You really started with that, you fucking bastard?" Adrian cried, tears leaving tracks on his charred skin as he staggered to hug me as well. Then Eirik, the last, his arms encasing us like a goddamned wall. He was warm, and I breathed them in, soaking in the attention I'd been so blindly missing.

"I missed you, too, you fucking idiots." I choked, quite literally disbelieving that they breathed. I pulled back, just enough to flick Fallon and Adrian in the foreheads. Fallon's head snapped back, and he rubbed the spot with a grumble. "How did you manage to get caught up in this shit? It should have been child's play."

"You've been dead for decades, and you have the audacity to lecture *us* about getting caught?" Fallon grumbled as he clapped his hand on my back, harder than before, pulling away enough to lean against the closest wall. He looked at the door that was closed behind Eirik, and the sun that was still rising behind it. "*Asshole.*"

"*Asshole* doesn't really cut dying then coming back like the Ghost of Christmas Past as we die, Fallon. I'd say more like a dumpster cunt," Adrian said, rubbing his neck and down over his chest. On a golden mark that sat there, another price this place no doubt made them pay. "It's a long story, one that can wait if I'm completely honest. I'm with Fallon here. You're dead, or you should be. How are you here?"

There was a hesitation in the way he asked it, an obvious mistrust in his tone. I was here, physically, and even that didn't convince him. I wasn't surprised, but still, it stung. Somehow, thank our lucky stars, we all were here. Someone was looking down on us today, and from the lack of marks on Eirik, I'd bet it was Aaliyah.

Our fucking knight in shining armor, saving me even now. All over again. God, I couldn't wait to see her, *hold* her.

I'd gone willingly to save my brothers; *eagerly* even. But that didn't make it hurt any less to know that Osiris would be the one to get her back, assuming Sebek really did follow to Kri'Valta's. Every second I spent away from her side was one too many.

My nose ached, pressure pooling somewhere behind my eyes as my mind tried to convince me I smelled lavender in the air.

"Well ... it's a long story," I said, mimicking his words. I followed Fallon's lead, sinking into the wall with a hiss as I plugged my nose, tasting blood in the back of my throat.

"Good thing we have a long time then," Fallon grunted, rubbing his arms, his skin pulled taut where the burn lines stretched.

I chuckled, trying to find a place to start before realizing how badly I needed to get the words out. Everything had been bottled in, and when I started, I found I just couldn't stop.

I told them of the crypt I woke up in, the boy I'd killed. My first interaction with the incredible Mags, and every moment, disgusting and sock tasting, between. They heard of the flight to the states after I'd realized who I was to them.

And after I'd realized who I was to her.

I couldn't stop the crack in my voice when I told them of Aaliyah. How she was already gone when I got there, the mess that our home had been. I zoned out on the far wall as I spoke of the plan Osiris and I had come up with to conquer both feats, him to fight Kri'Valta alone and me to save them.

If I'd thought they'd been ready to kill Sebek before, nothing compared to now. Aaliyah suffered under Sebek, broke at his orders. He'd die for what he did to her.

I'd kill him my damned self.

I choked up a bit on the memory loss, not lingering on what little I did know since most of it had been between Aaliyah and I. It was our past, *our* secret, and I didn't want to share it without her. It felt wrong to give that piece away, even to them. I didn't tag on the little caveat of the *Rends*. It probably would have killed the mood to add on a little additional, *for now,* to my unlikely resurrection.

"I still can't believe you're here," Adrian whispered, his voice hoarse as he coughed.

"I can't believe you're Prince." Fallon laughed, the dry sound more pained than humorous. "Why didn't you try to tell us?"

Eirik chimed in with a low hum, watching me carefully from where he stood by the door leading down the stairs. He hadn't moved once since going to stand sentinel. His eyes were liquid blue fire, and I dipped my head to think. I couldn't really tell for sure, but I'd have to guess it was because I didn't want them to hurt.

"You'd lost me once; I wouldn't make you go through it again." *Not if I could help it.*

A commotion sounded down the stairs, something I'd been ignoring. Eirik huffed again as the wailing of voices grew louder. His eyes shifted, not red like I'd been expecting, instead his beast slipping to the front. It showed in his face, the twist of thin lips and the angry pull of the tattoo that curled around his eye.

Seemed the guards were done waiting for us to die.

"The rest can wait, don't you think?" I asked, dragging myself to my feet, limping to the door as I clutched my head. The damned pressure was unrelenting.

"What's the plan?" Fallon asked, grunting as he stood on trembling legs. That was a *great* question. When I didn't respond, his face went blank. "You do have a plan, right?"

"Of *course* I have a plan. Who do you think I am?" I asked, snorting as I put my ear against the door. The clanging of metal swords against that shitty armor echoed. Everything ached, and I knew without a doubt a *Rend* was creeping up. Always fucking lingering.

Like a mold.

"So what is it?" Adrian pressed, and I shrugged.

Okay, maybe I didn't have a plan. "I'm working on it."

"*Working* on it?" Fallon asked, his eyebrows hitting his fluffy blond hair.

Damned, *ungrateful*— "I didn't exactly have a lot of time to figure it out, Fallon. Storm in, kill the bad guys, save the damsels—that's you, by the way—and ride off into the sunset! That was my plan. And look, here you are! Right as rain ..." I waved my hand at them, grimacing when I looked a bit too closely at the sun ravaged skin. "Mostly."

For as sick as Fallon looked, he really pulled off angry well. He stumbled away from the wall, sweat pouring down his forehead as he sucked in a pained wheeze that made me feel *slightly* bad for instigating.

At least until the banging began at the door.

Eirik planted his shoulder into the wood beside me, leveraging his weight against it as the guards slammed into the other side.

"Just fucking perfect, saved from the sun just to get dismembered, great plan!" Fallon screamed, as I took a spot next to Eirik, barely dodging a sword as it pierced the door by my head.

I cursed, gritting my teeth. "I don't see you coming up with any better ones, you frigid bastard!"

Fallon's eyes turned red, his calm composure slipping away as he snarled. It only took a moment for him to pull the last remains of his tie off, wrapping it tightly around the knuckles of his right hand. It shielded the raw skin as he brushed his hair back, cold composure hiding the bloodlust that sparked in him.

It made my own pulse jump, a hint of a memory sneaking into my thoughts. A training room, freshly made, with sprawling windows. Fallon across from me, hands raised to fight.

His fangs may have dropped, but he had no intention of using them. He tightened the fabric until his knuckles went pale.

"Can we focus?" Eirik bit out, his words ending in a snarl.

"No!" we both said in perfect unison.

Adrian, who'd been quiet, snorted a laugh like we weren't about to be balls deep in a fight none of us could handle right now. Not like this, and definitely not when the fucking pressure went from a light announcement to a full-blown explosion behind my eyes.

Blood splattered down my chest, past my choked cry and onto the floor. The energy of the room shifted, Fallon slamming next to me as I lost my footing.

"Nero?" he asked, just as Eirik stumbled away too.

Adrian took his place, but there was no way we were going to be able to hold it back without the literal beast. Eirik snarled, viciously deep as his head snapped back. His bones cracked, his face shifting as he fought a scream and reached for his wrist.

Vertigo had me falling the rest of my way to my knees, Adrian and Fallon now alone at the door. The guards doubled down, slamming into it, bits of wood hitting the floor. Not that it mattered, as my heart sped up, and Eirik continued to descend into madness behind us.

"Aaliyah," I whispered, clutching my chest as the first *Rend* stole me, ripping me out of my body.

I crumbled to the ground, a conversation passing between the others that I couldn't hear. I snapped back just in time for Eirik to slam into the wall. His face was slick with sweat, his eyes a haze of red and deep blue as his beast fought the magic of Archon's home.

"Oh, for fuck's sake, Eirik. Now isn't the fucking time!" Fallon screamed, hiding real fear behind sharp words.

"Ever seen him look like that?" Adrian pressed, panting.

I stumbled up as Eirik went silent. The growl that had been burning in his chest died in an instant, and even the guards stopped. He turned on us, no longer looking like we were to be protected, that sentinel by the door.

He bared his teeth, and I considered taking my chances with the guards.

"You mean like we're the ones in the way?" I asked, shivering. My body begged me to pull away, to get the fuck out of his path. I was confident in my next words. "Can't say I have."

He took a step forward, just as the clanking of knuckles against wood echoed behind me. We paused and waited, listening for more chaos. Instead, there was only the soft hum of a tune in the air, one that made my head spin as I dared to look away from the frothing beast for just a second.

"Do guards knock?" Adrian asked, when it sounded again.

"You going to open up or not?" a woman's voice echoed, one that had Adrian perking up and Fallon groaning like he'd rather be out in the sun.

"I know that voice," Adrian whispered, hand already on the handle of the door. Eirik snarled before it cut off, and I looked back just in time to watch him crumble to the ground.

"Oh, fuck me," Fallon followed, rubbing his hands over his face. "This is a nightmare."

The woman snorted as she walked through the now open door. Bodies were strewn about her feet, some covered in blood, like they'd been through a good fight. Most just dropped, their heartbeats echoing in the air as two men flanked her.

"Well, good morning to you too, Fang," she whispered, as I grinned.

Well, I'll be damned, I knew this one.

"Siren," Fallon grumbled, leaning into Adrian. Looking back at Eirik the same way I had, as Eliza continued to sing a soft tune, her blue eyes glowing as a bead of sweat slid down the side of her face.

"Eliza, right? Remembered you, just a bit," I said, watching as she turned to me.

Her nose twisted like she'd smelled something rotten, and I guess that could be true, considering how dead I'd been a few weeks ago. "Great, another one."

"Please, I thought we were better friends than that," I snorted, shoving my hands in my pockets, grimacing at the dried blood. "I'll be sure to let Aaliyah know you don't like her Prince. She'll be devastated."

Eliza blinked once, then twice. Her hold on her *Siren's Call* wavered, and Eirik stirred behind us again. She was quick to force it back down, the man at her side ... Dezen? Black hair and steely eyes held her up with an arm around her waist.

"What the fuck?" she whispered, rubbing her eyes like she couldn't quite believe it. A running theme, I'd found. It'd never be not funny to see someone just 'gasp' in disbelief. "You know what? I don't want to know. Nice to meet you. Thought you'd be taller."

She shook her head as Carter, her second husband, stepped around us, taking a solid second to glare at Adrian before he hoisted Eirik onto his back.

"How'd you get here?" Adrian asked, pointedly ignoring Carter, even as he smirked.

Eliza grunted, pulling up her phone, and showing us the message on the screen.

"Because of this *very* confusing text message from I'm assuming Osiris." An amalgamation of what looked to be a singular word in *all* caps with no spacing between and several expletives, like he was trying to figure out why he couldn't delete mistyped letters. Her head tipped back, like she was trying to find some inner strength. "Reminded me of *baba*, to be honest."

"That sounds like Osiris," Adrian laughed, coughing into his hand as he leaned into the wall. Fallon followed him, grunting as he stumbled. "He stopped using spaces because I set them to auto replace with 'Adrian rules, Osiris drools' and he couldn't figure out how to turn them back."

Neither looked all here anymore, almost dead on their feet. I wasn't much better, as the lingering pressure brought the first hint of a memory forward.

Lavender eyes. I grunted. It wouldn't be long now before I was lost to whatever hell my mind decided to show me.

"I think the rest can wait. You all look about ready to topple, and Dezen can't carry you since he'll be making sure you don't roast ... at least not any more than you already have. Can you walk?" she asked, not bothering to check if we agreed as she walked down the stairs, Dezen close behind her.

Carter was quick to follow, Eirik still slung over his shoulder, teeth suspiciously close to the Dragonkin's neck ... but I wasn't going to ruin the moment for him.

"Thanks, Eliza," I mumbled, clutching my nose as the walls narrowed down the staircase. We stepped over bodies and each one had me clutching my stomach.

The *Rend* had ripped me away, and now the memory was fighting for its place.

"Don't thank me. I wouldn't be here if it wasn't for Ali," she said, unbothered by the carnage. "Wherever she is, she's probably worried about you. I wouldn't be much of a best friend if I didn't step in, would I?"

Adrian and Fallon were quiet, and I felt rather bad when the next stumble dragged me to a stop. The memory ripped away conscious thought, giving me just a breath as Fallon raised a brow. "I have some bad news."

I choked on another hit of blood, my vision fading.

"I don't think I'll be walking after all," I mumbled, grinning with bloodied teeth, almost sorry for the way Eliza's face twisted in rage. Adrian and Fallon watched me crumble, and I just had to hope they wouldn't leave me there.

Before it was lights out.

CHAPTER 21

AALIYAH

The shadows that had snuffed out the light at the ruthless beckoning of that voice in my head faded. It was barely a second before my feet touched the ground again, and I was left in a familiar room, with rolling mercury beneath me and a flickering of stars in the vast expanse of pitch-black sky above me.

My muscles tensed until they screamed, only getting worse as I wrapped my arms around myself in an attempt to stabilize my footing. My throat closed next, eyes darting from one endless stretch to another as I waited for the bite of Sebek's hand, for another growled command or the splash of more hot blood across my face.

For the deaths I was sure I'd caused.

But the Void was quiet, filled with a blistering silence I couldn't get away from. It hugged close to my skin, like the gentle embrace of a mother, careful yet insistent as it seemed to check me over. I managed two deep breaths, enough to stop the shaking in my hands and feel the ache that still lingered in the junction of my neck.

That I hurt told me I wasn't here as a ghost. So, this wasn't a memory.

I looked at my hands. The soft white of my skin was hinted with enough color to tell me I was here in the flesh. Though, I had no idea

187

how. There was a tug at my chest, like the air was testing me, trying to see if I was still alive.

Was I?

Somewhere in me, my soul stirred, and the pressure behind my eyes had me swaying on my feet. It was grueling, but it wasn't enough of a distraction to keep my mind from the lack of warmth at my wrist anymore, the bitter cold making my lips numb. Adrenaline left me in a vicious rush, sending me spiraling as I wiped away a streak of blood that slid out of my nose. Everything ached, everything burned, and all I felt was dread.

All that grief and pain just to lead to this; me alone in the Void. I'd spent so much time in survival mode since Sebek had taken me that the impact of his actions suddenly had ground to stand on. They weren't just in my head; they were *real*.

Adrian and Fallon were gone.

They. *They*—

I couldn't do this.

Not alone, not like this. Not in the silence. I *hated* the silence—

"Aaliyah?" a voice whispered, the gentle timbre a light in the endless tunnel of night that had stretched out in front of me.

Like finding water after a long drought, the weight of solitude lifted off me as I sagged and turned. "Osiris?"

He looked battered, a gouge in his side cutting through suit and flesh, his eyes sunken and dim, as lifeless as his lack of breath. And quiet ... so *quiet*. Motionless in a way that made the hair on my arms raise, meaning to caution me against a predator in the room.

I wasn't sure how he was here, in the Void with me, but I'd never in my *life* been so happy to see him.

It was as if I were watching the snowfall from the dining table, a drop of peaceful silence as he went from unbreathing to drawing in a gasping breath. He was on me in an instant, no hesitation as he pulled me into his arms, crushing me to his chest as he shook. His fingers sought out skin, tension draining from him with every spark that lit where he touched. One hand found my hair, sliding deftly through the strands, the other a strong band around my waist. I clung to him greedily. The chill of him replaced the weight of loss, and in that moment, in his arms, I fell apart.

"They're gone, Osiris. They're *gone,*" I whispered, choking on the words and the tears that burned in the back of my throat. "They *can't* be gone."

A shudder racked its way through his body, one that ended at his hands as they trembled. He didn't let me go, not even long enough for him to breathe himself.

"I know, *lux mea.* I know," he whispered, his voice hoarse. He swallowed, the sound echoing in my ear. A few seconds of silence followed as he just held me, his hands roaming, his movements unflinching. I looked up at him, his gaze far away, like I'd seen so many times before.

The numb consumed us both. The implications of the faded marks on my wrist a weight neither of us had the strength to bear.

"Archon?" I asked, even as the word caught.

Denial had me firmly by the throat, even as I said his name. Some part of me was still convinced that when we got out of this mess, the others would be waiting for us. Sitting by the fire in the library with hot chocolate and cookies, warm smiles waiting to welcome us home ... We were supposed to go home. So we could set up the Christmas tree like Adrian had promised. All of us.

"They never made it back," Osiris confirmed, his head dipping. His eyes were on the floor, the silver seeming to bubble under his feet, as if agitated by his presence. I covered my wrist, suddenly sickened just by the thought of it.

Loss warped you, broke off pieces you'd never thought you'd lose. Sebek had told me of their fate, had told me what he'd planned ... but somewhere, I'd still hoped he was lying. Begged that it had all been an elaborate ploy.

"Aaliyah—" Osiris started.

"They were in so much pain, Osiris. I can still feel it in my chest." Or maybe it was just the roaring of my heart, like a devastating wave of grief that I couldn't fight. I still didn't look down or let go of my wrist. "They were suffering, and we were there, just—"

We let them die.

"*Aaliyah.*" Osiris's words met me, dragging me kicking and screaming from my mind with his soft tenor. "Look at me, my light."

Cold hands cupped my cheeks, and the brush of age-old calluses caused me to lift my head. The press of his skin was only overshadowed by the raging melody of his heartbeat.

Outwardly, Osiris was a wave of calm, one I hadn't expected to see. There had been a volatility in him since Kali had shown up, one that left both of us off center, but this Osiris reminded me much more of the one who had saved me at the auction house. Though ... that wasn't quite right either.

He seemed free of the burdens that had drowned him. Free of the rage and the pain that came from a past you couldn't change, a past that had broken off bits and pieces of him, parts he was still trying to mend.

I hadn't realized how many of those pieces Osiris had already fit back together.

Not until now.

"Did you come for me?" was all I could manage.

"Aaliyah, there isn't a thing in this world, *living or dead*, that could keep me from your side." The Void rippled at his words like it was breathing, as if moved by them. He came to Kri'Valta's alone. Fought the Horror of the Depths while not knowing what might come for him or his brothers, to make sure we didn't lose our chance at Exilium, and based on his state, he'd won. "If I could go back, I'd choose you again without question. I have to believe that's what they would have wanted, too."

There was hesitation in the way he said it, a pain that not even his numb could hide. Osiris's arms gently came around me, and I held him as his body arched in hard breaths.

"We are Vivas," he whispered. "And above all else, my light, we are *yours*."

Mine. And what was left of my heart was theirs. The ones still there, and the ones I'd never see again. I took a deep breath, trying to settle myself against his words.

I trembled, still looking into Osiris's eyes, when one of his hands dropped, his fingers ghosting against where I gripped my wrist. The touch was soft, the spark of his skin against mine suddenly an inferno. I looked down, on instinct, dragged along by his tender touch.

"Osiris?"

He didn't look away from me. "If there is anyone to blame for this, it is me. *I* left them to die. You had no part in it."

His hand began to slip, falling away from my skin, taking that spark of warmth with it.

"They weren't just mine, Osiris. They were yours, too. You loved them, just like I did, and you can't bury your hurt because you want to shield mine. Don't let this destroy you again. That's the last thing they'd want."

The numbness broke, just for a second, just long enough for the tears that clouded his eyes to slip down his cheeks. He set his forehead against mine, shuttering when I raised my hand to cup his cheek.

"We can still save Eirik," I whispered, looking around the silver expanse.

Osiris brushed the hair out of my face. His fingertips lingered on my forehead before he looked around as well. The Void was empty, silent. "How do we get out?"

That ... I didn't know. I wasn't even sure how we got here. I held my hand over my chest, searching for the tie to the real world. It wasn't like before; I wasn't dead.

So how was I here?

"You get out by letting yourself out," another voice echoed, one that had Osiris freezing. "Preferably in short order."

My attention snapped to the man that was currently picking his fingernails, flexing his hands like a diva to inspect their color. I knew his face. It was one I still recalled in the few memories I'd had of my mother. It was one I saw in the mirror each day. His startling white hair was cut short on the sides, the long top brushed back, accepting the black streak running through it. And his eyes, a purple so light they almost seemed white, had patchwork pieces of gold shimmering inside them.

"Not that this hasn't been ... *touching*, but it's a nightmare to maintain living souls in this plane. Not that I don't appreciate that darling piece of art you pulled in there—it was a sight."

The room shook, and Osiris was standing between me and the man in an instant. He held his hand up, pinky and ring finger down in a fighting stance, head held high even as he shook. His magic was a sluggish beast, and sweat pooled on his brow, but that didn't stop the swell as his gift came crashing down on us.

The man didn't blink, looking Osiris up and down with a bored expression.

"Oh, *please.* Put it away, would you? Even if you had any juice left after that show, you wouldn't be able to fight me here." The man rolled his eyes as he spoke.

The Void, as if responding to those words, pulsed. It went from a dancing cadence to vicious energy in a blink, but it didn't move, didn't go further than that. As if it were testing our limits.

"Yet you haven't attacked me yet," Osiris said, unflinching at the display, his eyes hardening as his jaw clenched tightly. His lips pulled back to show bloodied teeth. "This may be your domain, but that doesn't make me a non-threat. I can promise that if you go for her, you will die here."

The tension rose, the Void circling harder, the pokes at my soul suddenly intentional. My wrist felt raw, my soul bruised from the loss of the others, and as quickly as it had happened before, the weight of that loss sank onto me.

I wouldn't let it happen again.

The Void bent when I stood straighter, stepping to Osiris's side. It lost its pointed edge, and in the next breath, it fell away completely. I waited for an attack, just for the man to tip his head back and laugh.

"Well, aren't you a spoilsport?" he said, brushing his hair back. "You can calm down. I'm not going to hurt him."

He looked me in the eye when he said it, not even bothering to give Osiris the time of day. The ease that he'd spit back insults at a man with centuries of power slipped away when he looked at me. His shoulders bunched tight, his face going blank like he prepped for a fight.

He didn't keep his distance because of Osiris; he kept it because of *me.*

The black faded from my eyes, and I blinked. I'd ended up completely in front of Osiris, his hand on my shoulder as he looked warily forward. The Void had listened to my call, had turned on the man that seemed to know it so well.

"You're the one from before," I started, still wary. "I saw you in the Void after Sebek took me. Who are you?"

My question must have thrown him off guard, as his confusion quickly spiraled into anger as he snarled.

"What, does the white hair and stunning eyes not give it away? Come on, use that brain of yours, darling. I know you can at least come up with a guess." His huff was met with silence. He looked between us. "And no, not our first party, though I do wish you would stop crashing my favorite getaway spot."

The white hair and violet eyes were hint enough, but it was the way he stood that would solidify it. That, and the face of my mother.

"You're an Imperial," I said.

"No, I just love the look," the man drawled, a fake laugh following his words. He smiled, like we were going to applaud him, before he rolled his eyes again. "Ding, ding, ding! We have a winner! Just call me Helia Imperial's and Kri'Valta's dirty little secret."

Bitterness leaked into his words, staining them as he flourished. Like he expected that to be enough. I searched his eyes, looking for something, and all I found was the guarded expression of someone waiting for ridicule. Anger.

Pity.

"Void," a voice whispered, a timbre that I wasn't expecting, as someone else stepped up from behind Osiris. I hadn't seen them before, I knew that with certainty, but that didn't stop the recognition that burned in my blood when their eyes landed on me.

Bog.

The whisper from before echoed in my head, a song of unknown power. It was the same feeling I'd gotten in the training room with Eirik, the one that had called me.

This was Magelav. I wasn't sure how I knew it, but I was certain I was right.

They looked around the space, flicking their short black hair out of their eyes. "Horror falls, and his spawn finds their wings. Seems we have a new friend."

Magelav kept their eyes firmly on the mystery Imperial, and I shivered. "Or foe."

The silence was endless before the man scoffed.

"Well, there's no need to be such a brute." He looked from me back to Osiris, then to Magelav. His shoulders dropped, as if losing a façade. "My name is Azer. Not that I think you'll be living long enough to remember it."

The Void flexed, as if agreeing. My head turned again, my stomach rolling as the little bits of me that were still broken sang with the pieces of the Void that poked and prodded.

I took another step forward, and Osiris followed. There was a brush of his power in the air, and I caught the look of pain as he tried to force more forward.

"I have so much to ask you—" I whispered, but was cut off when Azer shook his head and spoke right over me.

"No, no, no. There is no more time for your endless questions. You wanted out, and the Void wants you out."

As if responding to his words, the floor beneath my feet warped. The insistent touch that had been on my soul grew more insistent, and the pressure behind my eyes soared.

"Wait, we need to talk. You're a Reaper. You can help us." Osiris was the one to point it out, and the man all but snarled.

"Not my style, sorry. Too many things to deal with, places to be, freedom to enjoy, and all that. I don't have to say yes to anything. My only goal right now is to get through the Eternium intact, and honestly, you insufferable Vivas are threatening to ruin that already."

"We have other ways of making you comply," Osiris snarled.

"We'll leave," I said, and Azer looked at me. For all of his snark, he regarded me with a softness. I tipped my head in his direction. A small bow. "If he doesn't want to help, he won't. We can respect that."

Osiris grunted but didn't disagree.

Azer's eyebrow rose. "Well, aren't you a surprise?"

The floor flexed, and the ground cracked under our feet.

"Little Imperial, think of home. The Void will take you there. If you can find me again, I'll show you some tricks. Good luck!" Azer just laughed and snapped his fingers again. "Oh, and a word of advice? Time works differently here. You never really know what you'll find on the other side. Really, only *one* thing is consistent."

His face fell, and for a second, I saw pity in his eyes, like he knew whatever it was, it wasn't going to be good.

"The Void is a vicious bitch, and it *always* takes."

CHAPTER 22

ÚLFHÉÐINN

The surging of our mates' bond stitching itself to us was enough to rip me *directly* to the forefront of my shared mind. Full control tasted like freedom, something I hadn't enjoyed in centuries.

My mate, my strong *Valkyrja*. I felt her again, like the fire on my wrist that threatened to burn me to ashes in every way I'd savor. She'd been ripped away before, her presence in my mind cleared, her mark void of her touch. It tore through me again now as viciously as the snarl that came from my chest.

Something had stopped me from chasing the trail of her when I'd first felt her loss, a silent song that lingered in my head, pulsing even now. My pack, my brothers, standing between me and the door. Me and *her*.

How dared they try to stop me?

I curled in on myself, all my breath coming through my nose as I opened my mouth until the jaw cracked. My skin tightened, and a shift almost came, only to be trapped by a magic in the air I could taste ... a hint of the sea, like ruthless ocean waves on a sunken ship.

Siren.

"Oh, fuck me, not again."

I shot up from the couch I was on, turning to face the threat. My body betrayed me, staying standing on two feet even as I pushed for the freedom of our other form. Either way, I prepared for a fight, for blood I was sure to find in this fight.

I bared my teeth, watching as the woman that stood at the door, carrying a tray in her hands as another body across the room shot up with a heaving gasp.

Nero.

My other half stirred, trying to rip the reins away from me as Nero looked around, searching every crack and crevice in the room with a frantic gaze. He stumbled from the sheets and bedding he was on, hitting the floor with a thud. Sweat slicked almost instantly across his forehead as he coughed, the sound wet as blood splattered the ground.

The bond pulsed again, my mate calling for me.

"***Mate,***" I managed, barely getting it out past the crack of my bones. The shift didn't come, like it hadn't before, locked down by something barely tangible as the Siren began to sweat, a whisper from her mouth as she held up her hand. But we were breaking her down, cracking her spell.

Short red hair floated willfully around her head, a sharpness to her aqua eyes that seemed to glow. Her magic was a shackle, a breathy whisper that I could feel trying to drag me back down into unconsciousness.

Caging us.

Nero staggered to his feet, his grunt a distraction as he clutched at his chest. There was a vicious intensity in his eyes, one that didn't let up as he stared at me. There was no fear in him, and I hesitated to push.

He was our elder, the second of our pack. The need to bare my neck warred with the need to move.

"You feel it too, don't you ... Aaliyah's back," he whispered, squaring his shoulders. He took a deep breath, his head falling forward in perfect sync with the relentless pulsing of the lavender band. When his head tipped up again, it was like looking into an inferno. He brushed his hair back, adjusting his stance as he prepared to fight. Had I been in my other form, the fur at my neck would have risen. "I need to go. Can I convince you to lie back down, Eri?"

I hesitated, feeling the clawing grip of my other half as he fought me. My mate needed me, called for *me* ... I bared my teeth, hunching as I prepared to lunge forward.

I would not be caged; I would not be idle. My face sharpened enough to bare fangs. "***Mine.***"

Nero chuckled, almost drunkenly, as he wiped a line of blood out from under his nose, cracking his neck. "Eliza, get out of here."

The Siren hesitated, inconsequential as she looked between us, flinching away when I snarled again.

"You going to be okay?" she asked.

"Of course, I may not look it, but I'm pretty sure I've never lost a fight to this one," Nero said, his smile slipping away, until there was only the warrior.

He hadn't, not once in either form ... but that didn't stop us from stalking forward. My mind blended friend and foe, pack and enemy. My sweet *Valkyrja* was back somewhere, and we'd tear through anyone we needed to get to her. Nothing would stop me.

Not even Nero.

***

FALLON

"All right, look alive," Eliza called as she pushed through the door, waking me up with a start and a fucking violent headache.

Her voice held hints of a *Siren's Call*, likely the only reason it actually got me moving, as I looked around. Even Adrian opened his eyes from the bed he laid on across the room from me, his skin still a mismatched patchwork of pale and inky black lines.

I was on a little mat on the floor, covered in a few nice sheets and a comfortable, if not slightly flat, pillow. The space was in disarray, toys pushed to the soft gray walls, piles of folded blankets stacked haphazardly in the corner to accommodate us.

"Eliza, our glorious savior. Here to yell at us again for getting ashes in your carpet?" Adrian asked, snorting a laugh. "I did apologize, you know."

The breaths he pulled in were labored, a cough following that sounded like he was trying to suck in water, his lungs no doubt filled with the same blood and ash I could feel in mine. Though he seemed to take it in stride, smiling like a madman as he stretched his arms above his head. He looked a hell of a lot better than I thought he would.

Which made how destroyed I felt that much more humiliating. I grimaced and fought through the lingering tremors that even sleep couldn't stave off. *Everything* hurt. Every single inch of my skin, even my organs and my bones. There wasn't a part of me that was left untouched by the sun or Archon's sick tricks ... even my mind, haunted by the shadows I worried might jump out and bite.

Not that I was going to tell them that. I didn't want them to know how close I'd been to falling before we'd made it to Eliza's, that I wouldn't have been able to take another step if I'd tried. I'd barely had the energy to collapse onto her front porch.

Just like then, she glared my way. She was just as frustratingly pigheaded as the day she strode into our house and took Aaliyah, that same determined grit in her eyes as she tipped her chin up and looked between us. Like she was ready to go to war.

Her red hair, cut short on one side, was damp as she brushed the longer half away from her forehead before crossing her arms over her chest. "I don't have time for the sass. One of you needs to go deal with the big one. He and your friend look like they're about to rip each other apart."

Friend ... it took me a long second to realize who she was talking about. All of this seemed like a fucked-up dream, and part of me wondered if I wasn't still in Archon's lamp. Was this another ploy? Was Nero being here just another *trick*?

My mouth flooded with saliva, my head swelling as I looked at the shadows in the room, swallowing bitterly at the dark spaces that I almost swore held black eyes and the white teeth of a mischievous smile. *Aislinn's.*

As if on cue, Eirik's growl split through the air, followed by another ... deeper, more vocal in the chest and definitely not belonging to our brother. The sound of crashing came next. Eliza sighed, rubbing her temples like we weren't about to deal with a raging death machine. "And that means Carter just joined the fun. God dammit, we just fixed the tile."

Fuck.

I stumbled up, nearly puking as liquid fire swallowed my body. I managed to follow Eliza out the door, Adrian hot on my heels.

"We need to get out of here," Eirik snarled, the words cracked and clouded by harsh syllables. His furious growl filled the room as his chest heaved, barely being held against the wall by Carter.

Nero was seemingly missing, at least until I saw him pick himself up from the ground by a crumbling wall with a groan, grunting as he popped his neck and rocked his jaw from left to right.

"I thought you said you had this," Eliza said, grinding her teeth.

Nero glared at her, dusting himself off. He was slow to move as blood slid out of his nose and down over his lip. "I'm working on it."

Wonderful, so he was in over his head again. Normally—or, before he'd *died*—this matchup between him and Eirik wouldn't have even been a question. Nero could fight, and as the second eldest, that meant he could win against damned near all of us. Even Osiris struggled from time to time.

That didn't seem to be the case as he rammed his palm over his ear, grinding his teeth like it might help him see straight.

Eliza rolled her eyes, lifting her hands into the air as she began to sing that same tune she had at Archon's. Her skin glowed, hints of scales crawling up her neck, but unlike before, Eirik didn't waver. He seemed to grow even more agitated, his face lengthening to snap at Carter's throat as the Dragonkin cursed. His face pulled tight, the green of his eyes sharpening as his skin turning molten before hardening into steel. His next breath was a vapor that seemed to glow silver.

"Brilliant plan, Eirik. Biting the hand that feeds you and all that," Adrian said, laughing as he sagged into the wall. Sweat pooled on his forehead, and he covered his mouth as he gagged. Eirik's growl grew to shake the room. "I don't know if you've noticed, but none of us are currently fighting material ... you think we can calm down and talk about this instead?"

Eirik's hands shifted into claws, the scratching sound as he caught Carter's shoulder vicious. Eliza sucked in a breath beside me, her voice tapering off. I was frozen in place, like every time I was faced with the part of Eirik that was *Úlfhéðinn*.

Fuck, what would Osiris do in this situation? All I could think of was the last time Eirik's beast came out, Osiris walking up to him like a bite wouldn't be fatal. He'd put his hand on Eirik's neck, over the jagged scar across it.

And told him to *stop*.

For Osiris, that was enough ... but he was older than Eirik by several decades, had the power to subdue him if something really went wrong, and I wouldn't stand a fucking chance completely healthy.

Definitely not in my current state.

Probably not ever, as hard as that was to admit.

That didn't stop me from flexing my hands, prepping my stance as I prepared to fight. It didn't stop the adrenaline as it flooded me, opening my lungs as I pulled in a breath that even helped me stop shaking for a second.

"Something is *wrong*," Eirik snarled, his teeth clacking together as his head tipped forward. He'd gone mad, his body jolting so hard the wall behind him cracked. **"It's wrong. It's all *wrong*. We have to get to her!"**

"*This* isn't helping her!" I shouted through the chaos, like screaming at a brick fucking wall. "What would she think if you killed someone she loves? Stop being an idiot and focus!"

Every hair I had along my arms and neck stood on edge as Eirik lifted his head again. The already stormy blue of his eyes snapped nearly black, eating up my brother until there was nothing left but the beast.

Eirik grabbed Carter's shoulder, his claws sinking in until Carter howled, blood pooling past the metal that covered his skin.

In a breath, Nero was by Eirik again.

His hand on Eirik's neck, his gaze unflinching as he stared him in the eyes, exactly like Osiris had done. A smudge of blood smeared across his face, and he wiped it away as he stared Eirik down. He made it look effortless, completely in control as Eirik's growl stopped entirely.

"Easy now, brother," Nero said, his teeth gritted as Eirik's thrashing settled, just enough for Carter to get a better hold on him.

"Let's try this again, yeah? This isn't you, *muna langt fram*." Nero said the words with an ease that betrayed the cinching of his face, his head shaking as sweat pooled on his brow.

They had the intended effect, the exact words Osiris had said to Eirik before, like a call to bring him back to himself. Eirik's breaths turned ragged as he shook his head, groaning deep in his chest as he fought the change.

His skin solidified, his face softening as it lost the sharpness of his wolf.

When he spoke, it was a whisper. *"Dreyrugr."*

Bloodstained.

Nero calmed the beast, and the confused look in his eyes told me he'd done it on instinct alone.

I'd forgotten exactly how ingrained Nero had been with us. He'd been the glue that held us together, the man that had guided Adrian and I through our *Calls* a thousand times over ... a hundred years without someone would do that to you. There was no question about it now, no stray thought that made me think maybe this *wasn't* our brother.

Nero grinned, letting Eirik go before stepping away. "Not anymore, Eirik. I believe we're Vivas now."

There was a break of silence, and I tensed, letting my hands relax and rocking my head back and forth as I tried to get the blood flow back to them. It was a long second before Eirik finally responded. He grabbed his neck first, his eyes closing, before he went to his wrist, the lavender band on it dwarfed by his hand. "She's back, Nero. I can feel it."

Jealousy ripped through me, and I reached for my wrist, holding it so tightly my hand went numb. I'd been hesitant to bond myself to Aaliyah before, the idea of getting too close a fear I couldn't have overcome.

How fucking stupid I was. Now that I couldn't feel her, couldn't tell she was okay just by reaching for the mark she'd given me. The mark I didn't have anymore.

"Yeah, me, too," Nero said, rubbing his chest with a content sigh. He smiled, life flooding back into him at the thought of Aaliyah. All of us did, Adrian perking up, even Eirik calming to a standstill. The confirmation that she was okay, truly okay, was all we needed. "Don't worry, I'm going to get her."

He whispered it with such open hope, like he wasn't expecting to speak at all. The fact that he was alive was a miracle, the fact that he was Prince. *Her* Prince?

Only, Nero barely made it two steps before he was hitting the ground with an *oomph*, his entire body arching as his eyes rolled back. I staggard to his side, reaching him the same time as Eliza. He grunted, caught between a scream and a plea as he rolled onto his hands and knees, covering his mouth as it splattered with blood. He shrugged us off, and stood, looking at nowhere but the door, even as I reached out to catch him as he stumbled. I couldn't hold the weight, literally shaking under it, and I hated that Carter had to step in to help.

"Do you have a death wish? You haven't stopped—" she said, rolling her eyes when he collapsed again, this time more rag doll. "Yeah, that."

Seconds passed, the *Rend* seeming to drag on forever before Nero was gasping on a breath, slipping into a memory before he was back to us.

"Aaliyah. She's—" he grunted, managing to get to his feet again. "Whatever happened at Archon's, Eirik is right. I can *feel* her again. I'm *going* Eliza, I have to get to her."

"You can barely stand, let alone walk. Just—" she said, practically stomping her feet as he pushed forward anyway, just as Adrian butted in.

"She doesn't know about you yet, does she?" he asked, the same soft dejection I felt.

"No, she doesn't. Not unless Osiris told her," he said, still rubbing his chest, his eyes closing as he took even breaths. "I really need to fix that. I did my part, I saved you guys. Now I need to see her. So, you're not stopping me, not now. I promise, this isn't a fight you'll win."

Adrian huffed, crossing his arms and jutting his hip out, fully intending to argue. "Like hell you're going alone—"

"We wouldn't dream of it." I reached out, cutting Adrian off, grasping Nero's shoulder. He looked at me with a tilted head and a grin that I couldn't help but smile at. After so long without him, I was surprised at how natural it felt to pull him into a hug. The others went quiet as the room filled with a somber air. The same kind I used to shy away from, snarling and snapping, like it was beneath me. Nero was back. This was my brother, the man I'd buried a hundred years ago ... a man who now *lived*.

All because of her, *for* her. Ali, my trouble, the woman that got me through hell and gave me back a fire I thought I'd lost a long time ago.

Even if I did have the energy in me to move, this needed to be his. He'd saved us, left Osiris to Kri'Valta and saved us when he damned well could have left us to die for her. All with the hope we'd survive, and that Aaliyah would be there waiting for him once he got us back. "Bring her back to us, Nero."

Ever the gladiator, he laughed, his head falling as his chest shook. I couldn't remember a time I'd seen him smile harder. "Without fucking question."

He didn't even look back as he stumbled down a set of steps, cursing as he crashed into something at the bottom, before an off-tune bell accompanied the opening and closing of a door.

Eliza groaned, rubbing the space between her eyes. "Dezen, can you trail him? Make sure he doesn't get into any trouble?"

Dezen, who'd stayed mostly silent through the altercation, nodded. "Of course."

He made my skin crawl, his icy eyes as intense as the brush of his bloody magic. He and Carter shared a look before he was ambling down the stairs after Nero.

"Are you guys going to be okay here by yourselves?" Eliza said, butting in again as she started to pick things up that had fallen, glaring at the walls that had been roughed up.

"Leaving so soon?" Adrian asked, voice airy as he moved to help her.

He picked up bits of drywall, holding them in his cupped hand as he hummed lightly. It put Eliza at ease, as she rolled her eyes. "Yeah, we're all meeting *baba* at her house before we head out. Just as soon as the Selkie Eternal and his entourage get here."

"Selkie?" Eirik asked, his voice a touch past growling as he clutched his throat.

"Yeah, are you guys going to play nice?" she asked, as Adrian snorted and shook his head. He walked his handful of debris over to the garbage, tossing it away as Eliza ground her teeth. "I'm serious!"

"I can promise you, Eliza, we'll be just fine," he said, grinning genuinely for the first time in days. I honestly felt the same, a surprising feat considering I knew exactly who was coming my way. "This is just our lucky day."

The door opened downstairs again, the bell going off before footsteps echoed up the narrow hall. They started slow, before stopping entirely for a moment. A hum followed, and Eirik was already standing when Milo King burst his way into the room.

His eyes went wide, his lips still pursed going silent. All it took was one look for a hiss to rip its way out of his chest. He was typically rather carefree, even a prankster at the worst of times ... but he didn't handle those in his family being hurt well.

Losing Nero had doubled that instinct down.

"What the *fuck*. You guys look like a Demon chewed you up and shit you out," Milo said, gawking as he shot forward like a mother hen, stopping in front of Adrian. Two others flanked him, a man and a woman.

"You guys know each other?" Eliza asked, seeming somewhat stunned.

Milo didn't seem to hear, lifting Adrian's arms to check their range, as our youngest laughed.

Adrian's head tipped back. "Of course. Don't you know Milo King is an honorary Vivas?"

CHAPTER 23

AALIYAH

Our worlds shifted as the dark faded away, and we were met with familiar walls and the warmth of *home*. The library came into view, shimmering as though covered in a fine layer of dust before sharpening into the bookshelves and endless novels I'd grown used to. Our feet touched the floor, and a final whisper of Void brushed against my cheek, as if saying goodbye.

There was an eerie silence that followed as I caught my breath, my ears ringing. I traced the book-lined walls, lingering on the long-dead fireplace and the logs that sat inside of it. There were no comforting words or soft conversations. The life that had once flourished in this room felt so far away.

"At least he wasn't lying," I whispered, but there was no real joy behind it. There was no celebration that I'd finally gotten away from Sebek, no hope to hold on to. My nails bit into my palm, my throat closing as I tried to speak.

Azer had been right. We'd made it back. There was a want in me to return to the Void and see what else he might be able to show me, but his cautionary words lingered. "It takes, and it takes, *and it takes ...*"

"At least he left you alive. That man bled death." Magelav's words didn't sound so cryptic this time, though they sulked in from the shadows as they stepped into the light of the room. I flinched away when they reached for me, extending their hand for me to take. A fine layer of gold dust settled on their skin, shimmering when they flexed. "Mags. Now, come, we must go. Sebek wants blood. *Yours*. The Eternium waits for no one."

I took their hand, hesitant when they squeezed tight, thankful when they barely held on for a second before dropping it. They were different than I was expecting, with the soft wave of their black hair and the masculine appearance that felt almost like staring at a porcelain doll.

"Your words mean little right now, Magelav. Consult the fates if you must; pray if you'd like. Regardless, we will leave when we have Eirik," Osiris said, not even looking up as he turned me back to him and brushed the hair out of my face.

Mags went red, their jaw clenched tightly as aggression flooded their eyes.

"Consult the fates? As though the fates bend to the wills of petty creatures. Fickle be the fates. The fates *drag*. They use Mags. Not the other way around!" The air flashed gold, a crack like thunder sending a shiver down my spine. "We must go."

"That doesn't change our answer, Magelav." The frigid tone in his voice had me tensing as he stepped in front of me.

Mags bared their teeth and snarled. "Watch your tone, Vivas."

Osiris tensed, and he took a menacing step forward. "I'll not abandon Eirik."

The energy in the room spiraled as quickly as their words. The air, once breathable, became laden with power. Heat turned it rancid, and my eyes watered. Pressure pulsed behind my eyes.

"You wretched fang—" Mags started as I reached up and grabbed my throat.

"Stop!" I screamed, the room shaking at the sound.

Or was it the shadows that jolted on the ground like I'd been talking to them? They shuddered, flexing as though trying to get to me. My spine straightened as the decadent whisper of power came forward, like it had in the woods when I'd drained the clearing of life. It poked its head up, as if to play, testing the waters as it reached for Osiris and Magelav. The sheen on my eyes was back, and I was breathing heavily as I tried to rein it in.

They insult you, insult the men who died for you. The voice in my head called, goading. I shook it off, shuddering as a bead of sweat rolled down my neck.

Slowly, too slowly, the shadows remolded themselves to the ground.

There was silence for a moment before Mags shook their head. "Power bleeds from you. Death takes, and it takes, and it *takes.*"

Mags grunted but didn't rebut again. Instead, they turned and walked out of the game room, mumbling something I couldn't hear under their breath as they did. Red danced around me, seeming to fade in and out of thin air, his comforting chill the only thing keeping me from falling into complete hysterics.

He was still formless, little more than a puff of dust, but he managed to use every bit of that to float around me. His emotions hit me like little waves lapping against my legs. They were more intense now, varied in their nuances.

He almost felt alive, less like that speck of dust that had kept me sane after losing Prince, and more like a person. One I wanted to see more of, one I hoped would continue to get some of his life back. He'd kept me together through some of the worst moments of the last few weeks. He deserved to be known.

I glanced at the door that held Thoth's image. Behind it, I knew what I'd find. The disarray of the rest of the house from the struggle with Sebek ... and empty halls that made my stomach twist.

"What time is it?" I asked, noting the soft light that came from the skylight above, the hint of a moon I couldn't see.

Osiris looked at his watch, his face twisting in a grimace. "Nine fifteen PM, December thirty-first ... We were in the Void for *ten* days. I couldn't have expected this was what Azer meant."

Ten days since Fallon and Adrian died, then. My chest caved, my head spinning as I nodded numbly.

Was Eirik all right?

His bond was the only one of the three still standing. The faded black of the mark was like a beacon of hope. Had he felt the others when they'd died? Was he with them? "We have to—"

"Eirik is stable, *lux mea,*" Osiris whispered, soft but resolute as he kept me standing. My legs threatened to give as exhaustion settled on me. He brushed a strand of hair away from my face, thumb touching the skin under my eye. "You are not."

"We can't just leave him, Osiris. We have to *go*—" I started, stepping just enough to fall into Osiris's chest.

His arms secured around me, the weight of them somehow more binding than the grief. I didn't want to stay still, didn't want to do anything but move.

I was afraid if I didn't, then I'd only be left with myself.

My failures and the whispers that came with them.

The reminder of a loss that I didn't want to believe was true.

But Osiris didn't let me run, instead becoming a wall I found myself furious with, irrational as my knees caved and he was forced to hold my entire weight. My hands shook, my entire body demanding I scream as my mind held me silent.

Why?

"Breathe them in," Osiris whispered, his chest expanding, his breath exaggerated over the top of my head. We slipped to the floor, the cold black wood barely registering. Moving wasn't a priority; breathing was barely one as Osiris settled me in his lap, facing him. His eyes held sunken shadows. "Breathe them in ... and know that they loved you with every fiber of their beings."

I pulled in a lungful of his subtle scent, forcing it even as emotion clogged in my throat, awash with fresh coffee and mint that helped to calm some of the ache. There was an emptiness in my chest now, a void that sapped what strength I had left into it, as the fear I'd held in came barreling down. I reached for my wrist, unable to look at it, knowing that I'd find a partially blank canvas again.

Would I see their ghosts now? Would they search me out?

Would they want to move on?

My chest heaved with a broken sob, and I curled tighter around Osiris, his powerful arms radiating a chill that had me shivering.

Sebek, Azer, even the rush of death I'd felt at the Gala. It was all meaningless now. My eyes remained on the floor, tracing the intricacies of the black hardwood.

"Aaliyah?" Osiris started, louder now, his voice cracked and muddled from his own tears. "I know it hurts, *lux mea*. But you need blood."

My next breath was a wheeze. My entire body shook, my head pounding like the pressure that had welled behind my eyes. I'd ignored it and was content to continue ignoring it. I did need blood, had for days since Sebek had taken me and forced me to drink his ... but the thought of peeling myself away was borderline torturous. I didn't want to face this new reality yet, even though I knew I didn't have a choice.

My attention pulled to the stitches in Osiris's clothing, the black cloth an immaculate display. His cold hands brushed along my exposed arm, over the few marks remaining at my wrist. Even Red moved, pushing encouragement through the air in gentle waves.

My hand twitched, and I nearly reached to my bra, to see if his little piece of scarf was still there before I wheezed another hard breath and sank farther into the hold.

Any protest I had died as my head pressed against Osiris's neck, directed by a steady hand. There was a rush under his skin, a tantalizing pulse that made my fangs ache, begging to be let down. A hand brushed against my back, rubbing gentle circles as the other wound its way into my hair. My mouth watered, and the hand at the back of my head applied just enough pressure for my nose to brush the delicate cool skin. Osiris jolted when my tongue shot out against my own will. Just one bite and I'd feel better, my headache would clear ...

Thoughts of the pain that had shot through me when Adrian and Fallon had died rang in my head like a bell as a cold sweat replaced the hunger in my stomach.

"I can't," I whispered, shaking my head.

Gentle fingers, ones that belied the strength of the man they belonged to, slipped past my tangled hair, unwinding the knots with soft efficiency.

Why couldn't he just let me be? Just for a while longer ... I *couldn't* feed.

I didn't deserve to.

Adrian and Fallon were gone. I'd never get to swim with Adrian again, facing my fears in those clear waters with him by my side. Never see Fallon's lips curl into those little smiles he did when he thought no one was looking. The idea of feeding now, of feeling better when I didn't even know how they died?

I couldn't do it.

"You don't have to do anything but drink," he whispered, his hand moving to cup my cheek. He lifted my head, pushing me back enough to lean forward so he could press his forehead to mine. His eyes were marred by dark rings, the dull blues solely focused on me. "I won't make you. Your choices are always your own. Your will is a beacon I follow, but please drink. If not for yourself, then for me. I cannot stand to see you suffer like this."

My legs wound tighter around Osiris's waist, and I buried my face into his palm. His voice had cracked, his throat closing around the emotion he tried so hard to hide. I'd seen it before, after particularly bad sessions at Ascension, when Prince would do the same.

He hid his hurt. The others were gone, his brothers for centuries, and I was doing Osiris no favors. It took me longer than I would have liked, but I slowly tipped my head in a shallow nod.

Osiris lifted his free hand in an instant, his chest pulling in a shaky breath. His pinky and ring finger fell into a familiar stance as he reached up to his neck. There was a burst of air, and he didn't so much as flinch as a wound bubbled there.

A gentle pressure on the back of my head placed me face to face with the red flowing from Osiris's shoulder. It traced his olive skin, and my mouth watered, my eyes following suit.

I fell on the open wound, and my fangs dropped just as fast. They pierced the skin, and Osiris reacted, his hands tightening around my midsection. Beyond a soft grunt, he didn't make any more sound.

The richness was something I could easily get lost in, such a contrast to the dark acid taste that had been Sebek's, and the desire to devour Osiris was only overshadowed by the guilt that still sat heavy in my heart. He tasted like coffee on a chilly day, making my mouth water all over again as I took another mouthful, and he shivered under me.

I wanted to take more, to take it all, everything that he would give me. He would, too. If I didn't stop, he'd let me drink until he ran dry. I released my jaw, struggling to open it as I licked the wound until it closed. The rush of fresh blood hit me, my pupils dilating as I settled myself back into his arms.

"We need to talk about the Eternium," I rasped, the words buried in the silk of Osiris's shirt. What had felt like a lifetime away started at midnight ... We'd get Eirik, and then off we'd go. It felt like a disservice to not take the time to grieve Fallon and Adrian, something so viscerally wrong I nearly puked.

"Not now," he whispered. His head settled in the crook of my neck, his hands rubbing easy circles on my back. "Just breathe; it can wait."

Even that felt like too much, but I didn't argue. I stayed planted in Osiris's arms.

We sat in muted silence, and even mourning felt wrong. I'd lost my lovers, ones I'd known for months. Osiris lost brothers he'd loved for centuries.

"Whatever you're thinking, Aaliyah. Don't. What you're feeling is real. It's raw, and it's *yours*. Don't belittle the connection you shared just because you don't think it counts next to mine."

"We could have saved them," I whispered.

I'd run it through my head a thousand times. What if we'd left the Void earlier? Would we have made it in time, then? What if I'd fought Sebek instead of stupidly trusting his words? What if? What if? *What if?*

"There is no lesson to be learned from dwelling on the things we can't change. Feel them, *lux mea,* but do not lose yourself to them," Osiris whispered. One of his hands found my hair again, his fingers gently threading through the strands. "I know this more than most. It only leads to ruin. Lean on me. I'm not letting you go."

I clung to him at those words, silent tears staining his shirt as I lost myself in his heartbeat ... which meant I didn't recognize the footsteps that echoed up creaking stairs, or the pained groan of a man I'd never heard before. I ignored the way Osiris stiffened under me, his head lifting to look toward the door.

My mind played it off for all of a second, before I felt a chill in the air, a brush of something I couldn't place as I tried to find Red dancing across my shoulders like he did. Desolation was cleared by a wave of hope, panic starting in my chest as I questioned if I was dreaming. I *knew* this feeling.

Osiris's arms unwrapped. I was scared to look up, to be wrong.

Silver eyes. Pale, sweaty skin and a smirk that had haunted me every second since he'd died.

"Prince."

PRINCE

I'd thought about seeing Aaliyah many times since I'd woken up. In truth, she was the only thing I'd really thought about at all. I'd considered every moment ... questioning how the light would hit her face and if her smile would be as wide as it was before I'd died.

The way I'd hold her, with all the softness I knew, was reserved for only her.

The things I'd say ... the *one* thing I'd say.

Yet now that I was here, I found myself lock jawed, and shocked fucking stupid, likely looking like a crazy person as I just stared. Unable and unwilling to look away.

Were her eyes always so bright?

I couldn't move, could barely breathe as the love of my life wiggled out of a shocked Osiris's arms ... watching on like she couldn't quite believe what she was seeing.

The trek to her had been grueling, every step and attempt to *flit* as I followed the pulsing in my chest that I knew would lead me to her enough to make a weaker man curl up and die. I didn't move fast— barely moved at all if I was truthful with myself—the aching, sickly feeling a burden I couldn't shake.

Not that it would ever be able to stop me.

The red stained white dress she wore billowed out around her as she stood on shaking legs, Osiris keeping her steady by her side. She seemed thinner, skin pallid and covered in a fine layer of dried blood. The pressure behind my skull distracted me for just a second before I pushed it down.

All at once, she was here, feet from me, barely a couple of steps. My heart stuttered in my chest, my body pulsing with the need to move, and like I'd been begging since the moment I woke in my tomb; I said something.

A name that was ingrained in the fabric of my fucking soul.

"Aaliyah." A whisper, one I wasn't sure would even manifest when I

opened my mouth. I said her name like it might not even be real. Was I alive?

She didn't fade away in some cruel trick of the light, like I half expected. Everything that had been my life since I crawled out of that crypt came into focus. She was *here*, the one who'd given me meaning in death, the one who gave me life again and breathed love into my lungs.

Her eyes filled with tears, her next breath coming out on a haggard sob as she took a stumbling step forward, one I mirrored.

"Aaliyah," I said again, louder this time, my ears ringing.

I choked on the heaviness that sank to the back of my throat. I tried to say it again, the sound drowned out by the roaring in my ears. Another step, then *another*.

I caught her halfway through the room, lifting her off her feet and hauling her up so she was pressed against me. Her arms wrapped around my neck, and I anchored her to my chest. Sparks lit up under my skin where we touched, and I marveled at the warmth of her. My legs shook, giving out beneath me as I slid to the ground, hers wrapping around my waist, never letting go as we sat. I held her like I'd never get the chance to again.

Everything else faded away, and nothing, *nothing*, not even Sebek, could have pulled me from her. And I took a moment I'd waited decades for, as I breathed in that soft lavender scent I knew I'd find, the floral lightness making me dizzy in the best way. I memorized it, noting every detail I'd yearned for, the familiarity that told me she was my *home*. From the moment I'd woken up, I'd known that seeing her would fix everything I felt. Every pain, every memory that returned from the *Rends*. Every ache and every wrong within me would be better if I saw her.

I was damned proud to know I was right. The soft brush of her fingers through my hair skin was the medicine I needed to stay alive. Her breath against my shoulder was my oxygen as I continued to pull in greedy breaths. In all my memories, all of my dreams, this was all I could ever remember wanting. To hold her.

To say her fucking *name*.

"Aaliyah." This time like a prayer as she held her arms around my neck, squeezing so tight we both shook.

"Prince?" she mumbled on a wet laugh. "How are you here?"

The details around my death were still clouded by moments that didn't feel quite right ... but I had bits, emotions more than anything. Like the visceral horror that had hit me as that faceless fucker held her captive, and the worry at leaving her alone as my soul was erased and reborn ... or knowing that even with me gone, my brothers would be there for her.

"You," I whispered simply. "At the hot spring ... you didn't send me on, Aaliyah. You brought me *back*."

Her entire body jolted as her arms wound even tighter. "I thought I killed you. I thought—" She pulled back, just enough to see my face as she lifted her hand. She hesitated for a moment, flinching like she was worried what might happen if she touched me. I closed the distance between her palm and my cheek, taking that fear away as her breath caught. She ran her thumb over the skin under my eye, mapping my face like I was hers, lingering on the crooked bridge of my nose and one of the many scars I'd found myself with. "I thought I killed Nero again."

The way she whispered my old name cut me open, sounding so wrong coming from her. I was many things—Nero, one of them—but it seemed wrong coming from her lips. I was her Prince, something I wore like a badge of honor. The fact that she said it, so sure ...

She had always been the perceptive sort, and there was no way I would have told her who I was knowing there was nothing I could do to change it ... so, she learned after I was gone, and had kept it buried to stop the pain of my brothers.

Osiris startled me with a gasp, and I felt like a piece of shit for forgetting he was even here. Damned, silent bastard. He was in shambles, the remains of his familiar black suit coat now torn and tattered. Aaliyah looked up at him, her eyes softening for my eldest brother, a man with enough power to topple kingdoms and enough cruelty to smile while he did it. I didn't need my memories to recall that, a whisper in my mind more than enough.

Kingslayer.

Aaliyah stood, holding my hand for one more second, squeezing it in support before she gravitated toward the ancient, who watched her with wary eyes. It was like each step she took lessened some of their strain, and when she was finally close enough, she wrapped him in her arms. *So* close she didn't see when his expression crumbled.

Aaliyah didn't budge, just reached for my hand the same.

This story could have had a thousand endings; we could have lost another brother, lost her, but by some grace of whatever God was watching ... we'd all made it back. Some a little more busted than others, Fallon surprisingly one of them, but for the first time since I woke in that fucking crypt, I could breathe.

I felt at peace, if only for one second. It was all I allowed myself, swearing a promise on the life that Aaliyah had given back to me that we'd make it out of this. Sebek wanted a fight, Sebek had earned a fucking fight, and it was about time we gave it to him.

Aaliyah squeezed my hand, lacing our fingers together as she looked up at me with ever open eyes. The need to kiss her nearly overwhelmed me, enough that I couldn't stop myself from leaning forward and pressing a kiss to her forehead. I wasn't sure yet what she'd accept from me, and I wasn't about to steal it from her after I'd already surprised her once. The warmth that bubbled up under my lips, the spark that lit in my blood at the touch of her skin, was enough. In truth, it was everything.

"The others?" Osiris whispered, and Aaliyah looked up at him with wide eyes. A glimmer of hope she wasn't brave enough to voice burned there as she held her breath.

"They're alive. Sent me ahead to see if you'd made it back," I said, avoiding the part where I'd suggested *very* nicely that I was going, and they'd be wise to not get in my way. "Based on the fact that you're here, and with Aaliyah, I'd say you did your part too, brother."

Osiris took a breath, one that stuck in his chest as he gauged my words. He didn't confirm it, but he didn't need to. Osiris won, that much was certain in the fact that he was still standing. Instead, the first thing he did was ask about the brothers he'd feared might not be alive to see this night. "All of them? Their bonds ... only Eirik's remains."

My lips split into a grin, and for a moment, Osiris lost that razor-sharp edge. Their deaths weighed on him, the shadows in his eyes alive as his head fell back. A smile found its way to the corner of his lips.

"*All* of them," I confirmed. "There's a lot to explain, but they're at Eliza's, waiting for us now."

Aaliyah pulled out of Osiris's arms for a moment, taking a long second to look between Osiris and I. She gnawed on her bottom lip, something passing behind her eyes that I couldn't quite catch, not until she spoke. "You knew? That Prince ... Nero was alive?"

Osiris went rigid, letting out a breath that looked like it hurt. He didn't look away as he nodded once, watching the way Aaliyah jolted.

"Yes," he whispered, dipping his head and giving her his neck as a show of shame and remorse. Even then, he didn't stop speaking. "He came after you were taken."

Aaliyah took a long breath, hesitating for only a moment. "Why didn't you tell me?"

I could have answered for him, and that was without every memory I knew I was missing. It was as clear as the morning sun.

"I feared he died with them," Osiris said, shouldering what that would have meant with a calm façade that betrayed the horror of the words. "I could not place that pain on your shoulders, Aaliyah. Not again. Not so soon after you lost him the first time."

Osiris didn't seem like the type of person to back down, which was why it was rather jarring to watch him slip down to one knee. He placed his elbow on his thigh, and leaned forward, an obvious submission that went leagues past what he'd already done.

An ancient on his knees like he was born to be there, as long as it was at *her* feet.

"I apologize for keeping it from you," he said, his head down, tone low. So, he didn't see when Aaliyah walked toward him. "But I would not change my path, could I go back."

She leaned down, cupping his cheeks, and for a second I worried I was watching a show I probably shouldn't have been privy to in the moment, at least not with my shirt on. She didn't go to kiss him, though, instead pulling him to his feet. He kept his shoulders slumped, as eye level with her as he could even with their height difference.

"You took it on alone, Osiris. If I'm upset about anything, it's that," she said, clearly and with a backbone stronger than most men I knew. Osiris shivered, closing his eyes like he was waiting for the collapse of her touch. "We're in this together, remember?"

"Forgive me, my light," he whispered, reaching up to grab her hand, kissing the skin of her wrist. Taking comfort in that addictive scent.

Aaliyah smiled, nodding once. "Always, Osiris."

The moment, as sweet as it was, was interrupted by the most obnoxious sound I'd ever had the displeasure of hearing. It split the air, making Aaliyah flinch away as we looked around the room to find it. Only to realize it was coming *directly* from Osiris's pocket. Some catchy beat and a high-pitched voice that squealed above the tune.

Well, that had Adrian written all over it.

Osiris scrunched his nose, reaching into his pocket and fumbling with the little device he pulled from it, struggling in a way that almost looked like a toddler finding a new toy for the first time. A point that was further driven when he lifted it to his ear.

While it was still making that horrid fucking noise.

"Why isn't it stopping? I thought I told Adrian to get rid of this," he grumbled, pressing the button on the front of it again, and sweet silence filled the clearing.

What sounded like a voice came from it, too low for me to hear.

"It's not working," Osiris grumbled, messing with the buttons on the side, looking increasingly frustrated.

He grumbled, turning it over, touching the back, even shaking it like it was going to do anything to help him. I couldn't remember having seen the damned thing either, but sweet fucking Zeus ... it was driving me crazy to watch him struggle.

I reached for it, trying to snag it out of his hands. "Here, just let me—"

Osiris's eyes flashed red, and he swatted me away like I was reaching for his snack before he snarled at me. The only saving grace was the snort that had come from Aaliyah as she tried to hide her laugh behind her hand.

"Bring it up to your ear," she said softly, directing Osiris to move, albeit reluctantly.

Only for him to snap his head away and slam his finger against the big red button on the screen.

Ah, silence again. There was an itching in the back of my mind, a hint that this was a commonplace with Osiris. He didn't seem like the sort to just roll over and learn new tricks. Go figure.

"Why did you do that?" I groaned, rubbing my temples as Osiris shook his head.

"They were revoltingly loud."

Whatever it was began buzzing again. This time I decided to risk the consequences, reaching over to press the green circle that looked like it might do something, rolling my eyes when Osiris glowered. Aaliyah was quick to follow, hitting another spot on it that suddenly had the voice echoing much clearer.

"You're on speaker!" Aaliyah said, mirth in her tone as she bumped into Osiris's side affectionately.

For the grumpy expression he wore like a crown, he sure did look smitten there for a moment.

"Ali! It's so good to hear your voice!" The change in Eliza's voice was instant. "Oh, thank fucking *Himal*, I'm so glad you answered. I thought my *baba* was bad with new tech."

My heart skipped, and Aaliyah took the phone from Osiris's hands. She held it close to her, wetting her lips with a shaking breath. "Are they there, Eliza?"

"Yeah, Ali, they're here. Direct from Lord Fuckwad Archon himself," Eliza said softly, her voice fading away as Aaliyah hugged the phone to her chest, tears lining her eyes. "They wouldn't stop hounding me to call. Mind coming to get them before there's another firefight in my living room? *Baba* is already mad we're this late."

Aaliyah nodded to herself, her shoulders dropping, before realizing Eliza couldn't see her. "We'll be there soon, Liz. Thank you."

Eliza hummed from the other side of the phone. "You sure you're okay, Ali?"

The way she smiled was a damned miracle, and she wiped away her tears with the back of her hand. "I'm perfect, Liz. We'll see you at the Eternium, okay? Give Grigen a hug for me."

Eliza seemed to accept that, as her tone picked up the next time she spoke. "Of course, but be sure to save one for him, okay? You know he loves you more than me."

The joke was given in good fun, and Aaliyah's lips split into a quiet laugh.

"Love you, Liz," she said, and I wrapped my arms around her shoulders, giving her support as her voice cracked.

"Love you too, Ali. Be safe, sister. I'll see you soon." Eliza made a kissing sound before her voice went silent.

The chill in the air barely registered as I swept Aaliyah into my arms. Nothing had ever felt so right, even as they shook from the strain. Just holding her seemed to give me a boost, as energy amped up my blood, soaking in as I popped my neck. Pressure still lingered in my head, but I ignored it, blissfully happy to pretend I was perfectly healthy.

Nothing was going to ruin this moment.

I grinned at her, then nodded to Osiris, who watched on silently. "Well, can't very well keep those bastards waiting."

CHAPTER 24

EIRIK

Fallon gritted his teeth as the man next to him willed some kind of healing magic into him. The veins on his arms shrank, the black fading to a gray before shifting back, pulsing angrily under his skin. Both men were sweating, hearts racing so hard it was making my head hurt.

But I wouldn't leave, not now. It had taken everything I'd had to convince the others I wasn't a threat anymore, that the beast was pushed back after the fight in the living space. Not that I didn't itch for more. His presence was a constant reminder that he could rip control away if he really fought for it. He did fight, screaming at me to either go back to Archon's and make them regret caging us, or leave to follow Nero to go get Aaliyah.

He whined for her, my chest vibrating with every keening cry. I snorted, rubbing the ache away, just as desperate to see her. My *smár Valkyrja*. Though I was more inclined to be less vocal.

Still, I'd stayed. The idea of letting my brothers out of my sight was enough to make my skin crawl. Even now, the ties that made us Vivas were weak, barely detectable underneath the panic that still flooded my body with adrenaline. The shriveled remains of our bonds were acidic, like a poison in my blood trying to make me ill.

Fallon moved, his body twitching as he grunted, narrowing the space between his eyes as his next breath came out in a pained hiss. The man next to him, Will, kept his eyes closed, never losing focus in a way that was admirable. It was a dangerous game, mixing the healing magic of the living with something like a Vampire, especially one so close to death. If anyone else besides Milo himself had told me he could do it ... I wouldn't have believed them.

And Milo had stayed just to make sure, sat next to me, a worried scent washing over him as he checked over my skin, like he might find something wrong with it. I pulled away from him when he reached behind my ear to feel for a pulse, checking to see if it was irregular, glaring at him while he snickered.

"Stop moving. You're distracting me," he grumbled, swatting my hand away when I tried to rub the spot he brushed.

"I told you already. This is a waste of time," I growled back, hating the feeling of being poked and prodded. It was unnecessary. I wasn't the one who was hurt.

But Milo wouldn't hear a word of it.

"Making sure you're not *dying* is not a waste of fucking time, Eirik! I can't handle losing another one of you, so excuse me for making sure I don't." He huffed, never looking away from me. I hadn't seen him in well over two years, yet somehow he looked like a completely changed man. He still had the same auburn brown hair he'd had when we'd first met him several centuries back, but today it reached down past his ears, meeting mid neck, and he pushed it back as he leaned forward. There was a harshness that came with the fear that stained his face, his worry palpable as he bit his lip and watched Fallon's slow breaths. "You scared me half to death when I walked in, you know that? Adrian and Fallon were actively smoldering. You're not getting out of this."

"You're overreacting," I said, shaking him off again. "I'm fine, Milo."

A hint of that Selkie fire surged forward, and a mirroring of the Cheshire grin from a man I'd thought dead. It was a curse, or a gift, the fact that he looked so much like Nero when he smiled. I rolled my eyes, already starting to snarl when he opened his fucking mouth.

"Well, you're still going to sit there and take it like a good boy," he whispered, and I gritted my teeth, snarling at him. My wolf shot forward, a partial shift ending in the snapping of my teeth a few inches from his face. He gasped, like a diva, covering his chest. "Damn, that's scarier when I don't have Nero here to act as a meat shield."

Even with the fearful tone, it was half mocking, and he didn't heed it, just continued to poke, going for my mouth next as he tapped my chin for me to open.

I didn't, and he gave up, likely knowing he'd lose a finger otherwise.

"Nero's alive," I reminded him, grunting like it wasn't a fact that still floored me.

Milo laughed, hiding more than a hint of hope in it as his head tipped back.

"So you say, but I'll trust it when I see it," he mused, his lips tilted in a familiar cocky grin that did well to hide the tension there. He wasn't a Vivas, not by blood, but he was as close as someone could get. He and Nero had been brothers in every sense of the word, and his loss had hurt Milo just as much as it had us. It was a struggle sometimes to remember that. The fact that he was here had to be a twist of fate in itself, with him showing up just when we needed, like always.

Dependable asshole.

"You missed his bonfire." Was all I could manage, another grunt hiding the starting half of a growl that my beast forced up my throat.

Milo nodded, his hands clenched in front of him. He lost his smile, his eyes dimming. No jokes or poking fun, just acceptance.

"I tried to be there, but things got messy on my end. I hope it was well?" he asked quietly, rubbing the back of his neck as his eyes grew further away.

I managed a nod, leaving it at that. If it was important enough to miss our yearly celebration, it must have been unavoidable. I didn't pry, and Milo snorted. Most would have been offended by the lack of response, but he knew me better than that.

The silence was comfortable, and I soaked it in while I could.

When Fallon's eyes opened, it was with a jolt, a startled grunt that showed in the flinch of his hands. Will pulled back out of Fallon's range, as if he expected him to lash out. A reasonable fear.

Even with that, though, I breathed out a bit of the tension still clawing at me.

The moment he saw me, his shoulders dropped. I went to stand, but Milo was already moving.

"Hey, easy," he chimed in, bringing light to an unholy shitty situation, even as my beast snarled at him for patting Fallon on the back, making him grunt. "Hate to break it to you, Fally, but you are mighty fucked up."

"Milo," Fallon said, his eyes still dazed as he rocked his jaw from left to right. "I kinda thought I just dreamed you up."

Milo just smiled, a disturbing twinkle in his earthy green eyes. The fear he'd had when we first shown up had died down, now that he could see we were all mostly in one piece, but it was still there.

It showed when he lingered on the dredged-out black lines that covered Fallon's face. They stretched across his skin in crude patterns, and I'd bet it was the same with Adrian.

Fallon schooled his expression. As quickly as the pain had been there, it faded away, though that didn't stop the tremble in his hands.

"Nope, I'm here in the flesh," Milo said with a flourishing bow, the theatrics enough to make me roll my eyes. "Next time we plan a reunion, think we could do it without scaring the actual shit out of me?"

"Can't promise that," Fallon started, before quickly shifting. "What's with you and getting buddy-buddy with Ilenia?"

"My dearest Rose is a Siren, and I thought it was about time she got to meet the old Siren Eternal and company. Imagine my surprise when I got a two for one deal, and got to see you lot, too," Milo replied. That joking, singing tone hiding that unyielding curiosity that burned in his eyes, the mirthful green lighting up.

"But how do *you* know Eliza? A conquest? I wouldn't have taken you for the type to go for her. Not nowadays anyway," Milo joked, as if Fallon had been the one to indulge.

"I think you're mistaking me for you and Nero," Fallon grunted, rubbing his forehead as he rolled his eyes. He'd taken sparse few lovers, his shitty attitude more than a little of the reason, though I didn't actually think he minded. We weren't the kind to sleep around. Well ...

Nero didn't count.

He and Milo had been notorious flirts for decades and probably slept their way through every major developing city in the early eighteen hundreds. Quite the fucking feat.

Literally.

Milo shook his head, flashing a hand with two shiny rings on it. My beast perked up at the sight.

"Oh, no, I'm a changed man. Settled down, got a couple of gorgeous mates." He winked, absolutely smitten when Will blushed and looked away. It would be sickeningly sweet if I hadn't realized how close my own feelings were to my tiny warrior. "Once you're feeling up to it, you can come meet Rose, too. Until then, I'll let Adrian know you're moving again. I'm sure he'll want to see you before the fun starts."

Milo dipped his head to us as he spoke before stepping out the door. Will was quick to follow. We sat in a precious few seconds of silence before the door flew open again. Adrian's panicked and still-charred face peeked through. "Fallon!"

He dove, headfirst, without even pausing to think, onto Fallon, who had barely enough time to lift his arms as Adrian hit him. The bed groaned threateningly under the weight. The surprised looks on their faces were ridiculous, as if dragged directly out of one of Osiris's cheesy comedy movies.

Before the legs gave out from under it.

It crashed onto the old hardwood, the floor creaking and groaning. Bits of wood flew in every direction, and Fallon let out a biting curse. There was a flail of limbs that ended with Fallon's eyes going red in a rare show of outward rage.

"Let go of me, you idiot," Fallon snarled, shoving at Adrian, who just drew tighter, laughing until Fallon threw a mock blow that didn't seem so mocking.

Adrian finally moved, still smiling, as he stood. I was quick to move to his side, so he'd have me to lean on if he needed, but he barely wobbled.

"Don't be like that. I deserve a hug, you oaf. Not my fault you're too heavy and broke the bed," Adrian chided, and Fallon just rolled his eyes. "You said you loved me, remember? Was that just a lie? You just can't take that shit back, Fally. It'll break my heart!"

Fallon took a leveled breath, like the idea of strangling Adrian was crossing his mind, before he was shaking his head. "We have more important things to deal with than your heart, Adrian. I didn't think we'd be *alive* for you to joke about it."

For the first time since we'd made it back from Archon's hellhole,

Adrian dropped his jester façade. It was always jarring to see the cheerful look fall from his face, as though it had been held up by a string that had gone slack. The look behind his eyes was darker now, accented by the scorch marks. The side of him our enemies knew came to the surface, his namesake. The *Collector*.

"You're right. We should be dead. If it wasn't for Eirik and *Nero*, our long-lost dead brother, we would be." He snorted and looked back at me. He sat up with a graceful sway, setting his chin in his palm. "Fun fact, the reason we got off that roof? Eirik's immune to the sun."

So, Adrian had noticed.

I'd dived outside without a thought and covered their burning bodies with my own. I'd felt the curdle of my skin, and the blood in my veins revolting ... before it had just stopped. They bore the black lines of the sun, the same ones my skin was lacking.

"I noticed too, and not to sound ungrateful ..." Fallon prodded, coughing into his hand, rubbing his neck. "But how?"

"I wasn't immune before. Don't know why I am now," I said truthfully.

I'd only been in the rays a fraction of the time compared to them, but I still should have been marked. In all the decades I'd been a Vampire, the sun had never treated me kindly before. I'd felt it for the first time some decades after Fallon had been turned, when the idiot had gotten into trouble with the wrong crowd during one of the French Revolutions and found himself in a fight he couldn't punch his way out of. I'd had to save his ass in much a similar fashion.

I'd burned then, felt the raging touch of the sunlight, so hot even my wolf screamed for days after. It'd taken weeks to heal, and some of my nerves still went numb sometimes if I woke before the sun had fully set.

Yet they were already awake. Already moving.

"You thought you'd burn, and you came out after us, anyway?" Adrian asked.

"Wasn't about to let another brother die if I could stop it. *Never again*." It was a vow that I'd sworn the day we'd pulled Nero off the pyre. I'd die with them before I'd let them die alone. "You lasted longer than you should have; the sun was up when I got there."

Fallon grunted, shaking his head as he looked down at the dark lines that stretched across his skin. He trailed a hand over one on his arm, before landing on his empty wrist. "Ali, you think?"

My beast, curled up in my mind, purred.

Mate.

I nodded without question, reaching for that mark that made me hers. I had her blood in me, the same blood I'd given to them. The same blood that brought them back.

Why it let me stay in the sun when they burned, that I didn't know, but I had no doubt it was because of her too. Something about her blood made it possible, and it hadn't quite sunk in yet that I might be able to again.

I hadn't seen a proper sunrise in centuries. What would it be like?

What would my sweet *Valkyrja* look like bathed in its rays?

"Leave it to the little love to save her damsels without even being on that fucking roof." Adrian whistled, looking toward the door. Softness overtook him, erasing the strain cold look in his eyes. "*God*, I can't wait to see her. I wonder how her time with Osiris was? He was boring, wasn't he? Probably just stared awkwardly from the corner or something."

I snorted at that. Osiris had never been a timid man. Ruthless, calculating, and nothing if not cold, but with my *smár Valkyrja,* he fell apart at the seams, turned into a mess that not even his seemingly infinite experience could rectify.

It was refreshing to see. Just like it'd be a treat to see him finally let go. He would one day soon. Touch her, feel her. Then the world would burn at his feet before he let her away from his side.

"Maybe he tried to convince her she liked whisky?" Fallon chimed in, and Adrian chuckled.

"Or told her how he felt?" Adrian asked, with a wistful sigh.

Even I snorted at that.

Fallon grunted, coughing into his hand before responding, "We can only dream."

The room fell into an easy silence after that, Fallon rolling his shoulders to get some of the blood flowing. Adrian did much the same before he reached a hand out for Fallon to take. "Well, what do you say? You up to walk around a bit? There is a tiny Dragonkin that has been itching to talk to you."

Itching was an understatement. Grigen had been nipping at everyone's heels after he'd found out Fallon was here, only held back by his mother's promise of chocolate if he could wait until Fallon was back up and moving to talk to him. How that asshole managed to become a child's favorite person was lost to me.

"Easy does it," Adrian said, grunting as he pulled Fallon to his feet. There was a curse as sweat clung to Fallon's forehead, and he had to take several long breaths before they were able to move.

I walked behind them, watching as they hobbled along, using each other as crutches as they maneuvered the narrow hall and down a thin set of steps. We were barely hitting the ground floor when a small blur was shooting toward us.

"Fally!" Grigen cried, nearly crashing directly into Fallon's legs, before slamming to a stop as his mother called his name. Fallon, with his surprise at the tiny Dragonkin, simply watched. "You're okay!"

Grigen was barely up to Fallon's waist, his hair a matching brown to his father's. His nose flared, a hint of smoke puffing out in front of him as he shoved a hand in to his pocket, searching for something. After a few moments, he finally fished out his prize, holding his hand out, happily smiling when Fallon followed his instruction to do the same. Grigen set something in his palm, his tiny hands closing it for him. "Momma said I had to wait before I gave this to you. Said you needed to rest. Can you have it now?"

Fallon unraveled his fingers, his eyes going wide for a moment as he rolled whatever it was in his palm. It was only a second later when a rare smile came to his lips.

"I think I can manage, thanks," Fallon said, as the scent of chocolate reached me. He put the golden foil in his pocket, folded neatly, before popping the small treat into his mouth.

"I have more!" Grigen was giddy as he went digging again, taking far longer to sort through his pockets this time around, pulling out what looked like several rocks in the process.

He set another chocolate in Fallon's hand, one wrapped in similar golden foil and looking a little coin. "This one's for Aunty Ali. You can't eat it."

"*Grigen*," Eliza warned with a hiss.

Grigen gave her a look over his shoulder, wringing his hands in front of him as he swayed. "Momma said Aunty won't be here in time for me to see her. You have to give it to her," he said, showing an impressively stern glare that had Fallon snorting.

Eliza shot Grigen another withering look that had him shuffling sheepishly. "*Please.*"

"Of course," Fallon swore, dipping his head as he tucked the chocolate in his pocket, keeping his hand there for a few moments.

"All right, you got to see him, G. Time to go," Carter said, grunting as he picked Grigen up.

Grigen folded around his father, sagging into his shoulder.

"I don't wanna go yet, daddy." His protests landed on deaf ears, as he rubbed his eyes with the back of his hand, yawning in the same breath.

"I'll make sure Aunty Ali is with me the next time you see us," Fallon assured, in a soft tone.

Grigen mulled over the words, considering them carefully before he nodded once. "Promise?"

Fallon's expression softened, his eyes crinkling at the corners as he smiled again. He put the chocolate in his pocket, reaching out a hand with his pinky finger out for Grigen to take. "Promise."

Grigen crossed his pinky over Fallon's, returning what was supposed to be a stoic nod before he leaned back into Carter. He waved as Carter gave Eliza a kiss, whispering that he'd be waiting in the car, before they were walking through the door.

"Thanks for humoring him. He's been talking about you all day. Though, I can't really imagine why." Eliza sighed, eyeing Fallon warily, not bothering to hide her at least slightly lessened resentment. "But at least you talk more than Osiris. He spent more time trying to figure out how to answer the phone than he did talking on it. It was like walking my *baba* through how to set up her printer, I swear. Just shoot me next time instead."

"You're being suspiciously cordial," Adrian said, as he stretched, clothed in baggy pants and a loose dress shirt that I'd guess came from Dezen. "Don't tell me you've grown a soft spot for us."

Eliza laughed, the sound dry. "You're Ali's. That's enough for me." She lifted her pointer finger to her chin before amending. "Even if you're Vampires."

That got a chuckle out of Fallon, before he rolled his eyes. "Thanks, *Siren.*"

Tension filled the room, and the clock seemed to count down in slow motion as it clicked from somewhere across the room. Osiris had been called. They'd be here soon. My beast paced behind my eyes, my skin shifting, growing tight against my bones as he pushed me to move.

"Rose and her boys are still upstairs, if you need anything. Milo mentioned something about wanting to see Nero, so I imagine they won't leave until you do," Eliza said, rubbing the bridge of her nose. "Try not to break anything, yeah?"

"Wouldn't dream of it," Adrian said, marking an X over his heart with the tip of his finger as she hauled a backpack onto her shoulder, one that looked like it had several of Grigen's toys and I'd imagine all the necessities for a toddler inside. She was already half out the door, when he added. "And thank you for the rescue. We owe you."

She snorted over her shoulder, rolling her eyes. "Just make sure you bring Ali by more often once this is all over, yeah?"

She paused, before sighing. "You're welcome."

Eliza slipped out, the door closing softly behind her. Then it was silent, and I paced the floor as I waited. Each second was torture, each breath having me reaching for my neck again. Aaliyah would be here *soon.*

Not that it would be soon enough.

Chapter 25

Aaliyah

Every broken piece of me that had been strung so tight for the last couple of days fell away, dissolving like the pressure in my head as Prince set me down in front of the little herb shop I'd once called home. I grabbed my wrist, holding the blank spaces that still ached. Sour thoughts gave voice to the scars I ran my fingers across, the pieces of my soul that hadn't quite mended unsteady.

Now that I was here, doubts began to creep into my mind.

I struggled to move, to make the decision to walk toward the door that seemed so daunting. Fear was an ugly thing, especially now that I'd had a moment to hope. Hope that this wasn't just a dream.

Prince was by my side.

Osiris had beaten Kri'Valta.

Eirik, Fallon, Adrian ... were they really here? *Alive*?

A soft hand settled on my arm, a brief hint of cold being washed away by the spark of Osiris's touch. I looked up as he cupped my cheek, and his thumb ran under my eye, wiping away a tear I hadn't realized had formed there.

The way he looked at me, with such sweet reverence, had my heart fluttering, and I didn't think before slowly wrapping him in a hug. There was a hint of hesitation evident in the shake of his hands as he held me close, but he didn't let me go.

I wasn't sure what started it, this need to have him touching me, to embrace the man that had once embodied my fears, but I *couldn't* stop now. Not when every time I pulled him close ... *he pulled me closer.*

I fell into his rich dark coffee scent, soothed by the hints of mint it held. The worries slipped away, buried by the strength he gave me just standing by my side.

"Thank you," I whispered, needing to say it to him.

The press of Osiris's lips against the top of my head told me more than words could. He held on tightly for a second longer, lingering even as his arms unwound, his expression steady and calm like the tilt to his lips. "Go to them, *lux mea.*"

His words were barely out before I was being hauled into a warm set of arms, the characteristic sound of an off-tune bell my only inclination that the door had opened. All at once, the aching that had come from being separated from the other Vivas brothers stopped. My body knew before I did that I was *home* as Eirik's musky sea scent invaded my nose, and I found myself curled into him in an instant. I reached for his hair, running my fingers through the strands that weren't pulled into a braid, tearing a purr from his chest as his arms tightened around me. I skimmed his jaw, searching for his eyes, memorizing that open-sky blue that jolted to near black, before shifting clear again.

Our brave, beautiful *Valkyrja*," he whispered, a mix of him and his beast. His voice had always held a deep guttural tone, the vibrations of it knocking me off center. Now, there was vulnerability there, a crack as he held me close to him. He looked at me like I'd looked at the sun when I first crawled from my grave, with a mix of awe and elation, and an understanding that everything had been worth it.

Something came over me, something that pushed me to move as I leaned in, pressing my lips softly to his. We lingered, a heated breath accompanying a shiver that went through him, ending where his hands gripped my hips.

He was slow to set me on my feet, brushing his nose against mine as he did. No words were needed to explain why as cool hands reached for me, touching my sides, my hair ... anywhere they could, as if making sure I was really here. I pulled away enough to see Adrian and Fallon, flinching at the darkness in their eyes and the shaking hands they tried to play off as exhaustion. They looked like hell, covered in the same shadowy lines that I'd seen on Osiris's hand in the game room the night Eirik had gone missing. Only they didn't stop at a wrist, instead extending over every inch of skin I could see.

I knew torture, had been faced with it for years ...

Rage built in my stomach, becoming an anger so fierce that the power inside of me came crashing forward as if to answer the call. The space behind my ear stung, a reminder of the spell that had locked my powers down, that now screamed when my thoughts spiraled. All this pain, this hurt, was because of *him*, because of a man who should have protected me. Who should have loved me when my father died, not resorted to locking me up and allowing his doctors to play.

He should have loved them. The men he'd Turned.

"I'm sorry," I choked out, my throat aching as I held back tears. I let Fallon and Adrian guide me, encouraging them to show me how they needed me with soft brushes against their cold skin. The last thing I wanted to do was hurt them ... or trigger them. "I'm so sorry—"

"None of that, Ali." Adrian's voice cracked, cutting me off as he grabbed my hand, lifting it so he could kiss my wrist. His eyes were shadowed and marked by deep sunken pits underneath them, red rims lining the copper hue I loved so much. "We're safe; we're here."

They didn't hesitate to pull me in, wrapping me in a hug between the two of them. Relief stripped away the panic, the cold it brought making me realize how tired I was. I'd been moving, terrified, and in a state of survival for days. Now, it felt like I could finally breathe.

"And we're not going anywhere, Ali," Fallon chimed in, clinging to me just as tightly, the sound of their hearts beating sporadically in their chests soothing.

Adrian and Fallon were right ... they were alive. They were *safe*.

That was all that mattered in the end.

No one else moved, and I appreciated the space ... the moment to breathe. Even Red had been primarily quiet, his listless emotions in the air dulled. The silence, normally a bane, helped to calm me.

"What happened here, love?" Adrian murmured, his hand brushing against the bloodied expanse of my neck, though now dried and peeling from my skin. He moved to my cheek over my ear, stumbling on the small scar that now resided there, frowning when I flinched at the abrupt sting.

I reached up, instinctually searching for comfort in the lavender gem that used to sit around my neck, only to find an empty chain.

The following conversation was ... harrowing.

I told them about Ascension and the man that Sebek had killed with my blood, skimming over the way Sebek had forced me inside. I talked about his safe house and the crazed way he'd spoken, his manic thoughts on my father. I told them about Kri'Valta's, and the mistake that I'd almost made, flinching when I looked at Osiris, knowing how close I'd come to hurting him. That was the part I struggled with most, the reminder of the dark voice that still lingered in the back of my mind, tempting me with whispered words. I told them of Azer, the Imperial we'd met in the Void, the one that had saved us from Sebek by pulling us away from the Gala.

I skimmed what I could, leaving out the bits that would haunt me to save them from it, but it didn't stop the wounded looks on their faces, the pain that mingled with dark lines against pale skin. The pain that sat in eyes that had already held enough weight.

"I'm going to fucking **kill him**." Was all Eirik could manage, running his hands through his hair, unraveling the braids one strand at a time. The veins on his arms popped like the crack of his teeth as he ground them together.

I was used to seeing his beast come forward, but the others still warily looked on as Eirik's eyes flushed a deep blue. A crack echoed as his head snapped to the side, the shift starting in his jaw as he began to pace. I watched him quietly, fiddling with my hands as I struggled with what to do.

I wasn't scared of him, not anymore, but the stress in the air made me sick, and I had no idea how to deal with it. Minutes drew on, until I shivered, and that was enough to break the tension. Eirik sighed, his shoulders dropping before his warm hand was at my back.

He ushered us inside, covering me with his body to try and keep me warm. He held me with a love I felt in every gentle touch that was given with hands I knew would always protect me.

I glanced around the room, quickly, making sure that all of us had made it inside, needing to check that we were all accounted for. Even Red, as he bounced about, lingering on each of the Vivas brothers that had been at Archon's as if checking them, too. His last stop was Prince, who scrunched his face and tried to brush away the feeling, unaware of the amusement that flooded the air as Red danced in the strands of his hair.

I'd seen Prince in this room more times than I could count, standing by the window where he liked to watch the setting sun ... now was no different. His leg was perched up, his foot against the wall with his arms crossed over his chest. That soft look in his eyes was there now as he glanced at Eirik and I, but I didn't have to guess what color they were anymore. *Silver*. He flashed that crooked grin when I didn't look away, giving me the same wave of his hand that he'd done to get my attention before, to refocus me back on Grigen as he'd tried to guess which hand I'd had chocolate in.

"You've made us whole again," Eirik whispered, his breath skimming against my neck as he pulled me tightly to him, my back to his chest. I knew his eyes were on Prince when I watched my knight in astral armor tip his head in our direction. "*Elskan*, it's a debt we'll never be able to repay."

"I don't know how I did it—" I started, stumbling over the words as I dropped my chin.

Soft fingers directed me to look up, and I found myself staring into those silver eyes. "The how doesn't matter. The only thing that matters is that you did, Aaliyah. You brought me back."

Someone scoffed, the sound lingering in the room like the echo of broken glass as one of the herb jars hit the ground. "She brought *trouble*, just like wet brings the mold," a voice chimed, disgusted and cracked. "You Vivas are so prone to decay. I recommend ground blue puya."

Magelav stepped into the light from where they'd been by the wall, directly over the glass they'd just shattered across it. Each step echoed with a crunch, but when they lifted their feet, the glass was *gone*, the jar they'd broken piecing itself back together on the shelf. Their eyes, a shallow swirling gray, landed on me. "Or consider less dying."

Magelav moved like they hadn't thrown the rest of us into a panic, constantly mumbling, hunching in a way that didn't match the seemingly young physique they had. The hairs on my arms stood on end, and my body prepared itself to run as my heart sped up in my chest, my focus narrowing on the threat.

It took all of a beat for Adrian to force a smile, chipping in to ease the tension, stepping quickly between Magelav and I as the Sorceri fiddled with another container of herbs on a low shelf in the middle of the room. "My, such an interesting character. Someone mind introducing us?"

Prince grumbled, rubbing his temples as he looked at the person who had helped bring him here. There was respect in his eyes, and no small amount of annoyance. "I guess I should do a little explaining myself. After I woke up in the crypt in Rome—and had a little midnight snack—I ended up running face first into a skillet. The person holding it happened to be this completely stable and not at all bat-shit crazy ... uh, friend of mine?"

He scrunched his nose, the sight making me smile. It was an expression I had seen so often it almost took my breath away to see it now. It was cute, in a way, the way he grunted when Mags clapped him on the back.

"Mags. Just Mags. *Always* Mags. Magelav ... " Mags trailed off, like they were contemplating something, crossing their hands over their chest with a huff. The air in the room pulsed, almost like it was standing still for them. "*Magelav* is also fine."

Then they stopped talking, leaving the room in silence again as Prince groaned.

Magelav gave off a feral energy that didn't mesh with the power they held. So much so that even Red kept his distance, sticking close to me, the little red cloth that I'd snuck into the bra I was wearing heating against my skin.

Time seemed like something that was about control, and Magelav toed that boundary with every step they took. I wasn't sure what to think of them, not in any way I could vocalize, but I didn't get *violence* from them.

"Damn, shit really did go to hell while we were gone, huh? At least that ticks the Bog Sorceri off our list, right?" Adrian asked, whistling for but a moment before Mags was suddenly by his side. Tension exploded in the room as everyone watched on in horror.

The move was so fast no one had seen it until they were already there, the scent of rotten mulch flooding the air, mixing with an acidic hint of burned sand. They flicked Adrian in the forehead, catching him and me off guard as a shiver shot down my spine, pairing with the rising of that voice in my head.

Remove them.

"*Mags*," they chided, wagging their finger as they clicked their tongue. "*Just* Mags. Do you need a lesson to remember it?"

They waited patiently for Adrian to answer, huffing when he paled but nodded. "Noted. No, I don't believe I prefer that. Sorry, Mags."

They ambled away, going back to that shelf they'd found, picking up one of the shells I hadn't realized had been tucked away on it. Everyone let out a collective breath, and I forced the voice down as it tried to surge forward again. Fallon, still rubbing his arms, broke the silence with a cough that he hid behind a closed hand. He wobbled before stabilizing himself against the wall.

"What's the plan, Osiris?" he asked, glaring as Adrian moved to help him. The black lines that traced them made my stomach lurch.

Eirik's growl started low, and Osiris ignored it as he contemplated the question.

"With Kri'Valta out of the way, we've fulfilled our part in the contract with Drakon. Only the Eternium is left," he said.

"And now we even have some aces on our side. After all, who would expect a Vampire that can walk in the sun and a long-lost Gladiator baddie?" Adrian joked, snorting as he shook his head in obvious disbelief, one I shared as I jolted to look up at Eirik from where he still stood at my back. "Eirik here pulled quite the party trick to get us off that roof."

His chest vibrated against me, his cheek running across the top of my head. I almost didn't believe it. Eirik wasn't covered in the streaking black veins that lined Adrian and Fallon, and I had assumed that he hadn't burned with them. He was healthy and seemingly stable.

"How?" Osiris pressed as his eyes drew tightly together.

Eirik grunted, shrugging his shoulders. "I think it was Aaliyah's blood, the *Hallen Bond*."

"Do you think it's permanent?" Prince asked this time.

Eirik looked to the open windows that now were flooded with the soft light of the moon. Longing was an easy emotion to read as he tipped his head to the side. "No idea. I'd like to test it, though."

Soft puffs of breath tickled my temple with the promise of something I hadn't expected. I might get to see the sun with him someday.

"There is one other elephant we should probably address ... as we're going to need some good press," Prince added, sharing a quick glance with Osiris. Something passed between them that didn't need words, and Prince only continued when Osiris nodded. "Kali got Sebek through the wards, thinking he'd kill Aaliyah. Osiris took offense to that and turned Kali into a pile of goop."

"Wait, as in the boiler of blood, Kali?" Adrian asked, blinking several times, and leaning in as if to hear it again.

I'd seen how Osiris was after Kali had shown up the first time. Frozen with fear. Even with all his strength, he'd been broken down by her. It was a feeling I remembered as I thought about looking at Castillion's skull.

Hunting for his ghost like it might jump out to bite me.

"Yes. It was a moment of weakness," Osiris whispered, and stepped out of Eirik's arms, moving toward me.

I expected the numb to be back, lingering in his eyes like I'd seen so many times before, but there was something else there now. A determination that had me smiling as I reached out and took his hand.

"Oh, no, weakness it was not. *Deranged*, I'd give you that, but that conniving bitch had it coming," Prince said, snorting as he crossed his arms. "If you hadn't, then I would have. She nearly got Aaliyah killed."

"Still, it could hinder things on our front. I don't know how much it will affect our chances with the Exilium vote," Osiris whispered, and the others scoffed.

"We'll deal with it when we get there," I said, unable to find any remorse in me for the woman who'd hurt him. I didn't care if it was cruel, or that it made the dark voice purr. I was glad she was gone. "I'm proud of you, Osiris. She's had you by the throat for too long."

His eyes grew clouded, and he brought his hand up to cup his branded wrist. "With her out of the way, Darius will be destabilized. He'll look for Retaliation, but his allies will look for alternatives. We might be able to use that."

Eirik grunted, shaking his head.

"How very *Kingslayer* of you. If I didn't know any better, I'd say—"

His words were cut off by the sound of a door slamming open, hitting the wall with a resounding thud.

A man I didn't recognize came barreling down the stairs two at a time. His brown hair was wet, fresh from a shower, his green eyes homing in on Prince. "Holy *fuck?*"

I tensed, not sure what the stranger was going to do. Prince did the same, squinting at the man as he strode toward us, and before I could even question whom he was ... he slammed his lips down onto Prince's, claiming a kiss that looked like fire. Stunned to silence, I watched with my own mouth open, blushing red as Prince's eyes went wide. The man pulled back, tears falling freely down his cheeks, still cupping Prince's face.

"Yep, that's Nero all right. Guess I owe you that drink after all, Eirik," he said with a wet laugh before he pulled Prince into a hug that had him grunting at the force of it.

There was more commotion, and the sound of a sigh from the staircase. "Milo, want to tell the class why you've decided to kiss a random man in the middle of Eliza's living room?" A woman asked, stepping down from the stairs with another man by her side, moving with a grace that caught me immediately. She smiled adoringly, flicking rich brown hair over her shoulder, and the first man, Milo, gave her a sheepish one back.

"Sorry," she said softly, taking my hands in hers with the gentleness of a sister. "He gets excited."

At the same time, the man by her side grunted. "We're working on house training him."

I recalled the name Eirik had told me of before ... Milo. Nero's, or Prince's, closest friend. The man who'd stayed by their side through the last hundred years. He felt different, like some Naturals did, giving them away before they could flash teeth or wicked words. I knew before he'd even stepped down to this floor that he hadn't been human. He oozed a power that felt like the ocean, raw and unyielding, yet endlessly patient.

With a beast behind his eyes that watched every single person in the room, as if sizing up the threats.

"Only Nero can kiss like that. I had to be sure it was him," Milo joked, tipping his head as he flashed a brilliant smile. He turned back fully to Prince, throwing an arm over his shoulder. "Jesus, next time you plan to fake your death, at least let me in on the joke. I thought you were dead."

Prince huffed a laugh, falling into an easy comradery as he laid his arm over Milo's shoulders in the same way. They stood about the same height, eye level, and he beamed. "Oh, I was dead. I just got better."

He looked Milo up and down, a spark of recognition buried in the confusion in his eyes. It only took that one look for Milo to balk before he staggered back, suddenly losing his smile.

"Milo?" Prince pressed carefully, and Milo stepped back like he'd been struck.

"Who the fuck else would I be? Don't tell me you forgot about me? I'd like to think I'm more memorable than that," Milo said, playing it like a joke, but I saw the way his hands trembled, the pain that had seized his voice as it cracked. "I'm offended. You don't forget your best friend, *ever*. Pretty sure that's a rule somewhere."

The woman was suddenly by his side, taking Milo's hand. He squeezed it carefully, looking at her like I did at my guys. The love in his eyes helped to break up the grief that had crawled back over him.

"It's not his fault. Dying messes with your memories. He's still getting them back," I whispered.

Milo's smile cracked, his expression falling as he looked to the ground with conflicted anguish, covering his face with his hands.

"You really don't remember me," he whispered, the emotion in his voice a volley of raw grief. He shook his head, and just as quickly, he looked up with a stare that bled determination. He stepped forward, like he wasn't sure if he could, before he wrapped an arm around Prince's shoulder again. "Well, that just means I can recycle some of our best pranks. Fallon's going to *love* it."

I'd never seen Fallon afraid before, but I would have sworn he grew pale. There was something to be said about that when Prince snickered, and Fallon snarled at them both. "Don't you fucking—"

They paid him no mind as Milo moved to stand in front of me. He smiled, an almost goofy air about him as he extended his hand out for me to shake. "And you must be the lovely Aaliyah. I've heard a lot about you, you know. These boys wouldn't stop talking about you."

I reached out and carefully took his hand, shaking it. He exuded warmth that put me at ease. "Likewise, Milo."

"Only the best parts I hope?" he asked, and I smiled.

"You're a great friend to them. That's all I need to know," I said, smiling as a light blush dusted his cheeks.

With a sheepish grin, he rubbed the back of his neck, before he wrapped his arms around the two people at his sides, lovingly kissing the tops of their heads. The woman smiled, leaning into him, while the man blushed as red as an apple and tried to look away.

"Well, these are my motley crew. My mates, the stunning Rose and dashing Will," Milo said with no small amount of pride. Even as Will grumbled next to him, hunching as he tried to brush Milo away. He reminded me of Fallon, grumpy in a way. "Ignore Will. He's got a stick firmly lodged up his ass, like a certain Aussie—"

He didn't get a chance to finish, as Fallon clapped him on the shoulder, standing behind him with a smoldering rage in his eyes that made Milo smirk.

"*Thank you*, Milo. You're always a joy to be around," Fallon snarled, pulling Milo backward, taking Rose and Will with him.

"Only for you, Fally," Milo joked with a bow. "Well, this has been quite a shock, and right before the Eternium, too. Of course, I'll back you, you know that. Just say the word and I'll fuck up whoever you send my way."

Osiris nodded. "Thank you, Milo."

Milo's eyes softened, tears brimming in them again as he looked between those of the Vivas house. "*Always*. You're my family. It's the least I could do."

He shook his head, wiping his face with the palm of his hand. "But enough about that. We're already late, and I stood up our plans longer than I should have to try and see if Eirik was hallucinating. We need to go meet Eternal Ilenia and get to Eternium grounds."

A somber tone took over the room, and the exhaustion suddenly felt all too real. Adrian and Fallon were still clutching wounds, physical and otherwise, and the others looked around with wary hesitance.

Kri'Valta was gone, our part of the deal was finished, and now all that was left was the Eternium. It was a daunting thought that, after all this time, it was finally happening.

"Yes, we should," Osiris agreed, and Magelav came hobbling out into the middle of us.

As usual, their presence came with a soft wave, one that had faded into the background of the conversation. They tilted their head before slowly pressing their hands together. Pressure filled the air with the scent of boggy water, and their magic grew. It started off invisible, their fingers weaving a spell I couldn't see before it shifted into a gold arch that looked like flowing sand. It swirled around their hands.

"Now that Mags can help with," they whispered, showing their palms that suddenly leaked a black ooze. "The Eternium awaits."

Nero groaned to my right. "I think I'm sick of teleporting."

He didn't hesitate to slide his hand in mine before reaching for Osiris. The touch was electric, a reminder that we were alive. That we were so close to freedom.

One by one, we laced our fingers together. Magelav stepped forward and reached out to me. "Come. Best not to linger."

I looked at everyone, my family. Adrian. Fallon. Osiris. Eirik. *Prince.* Even Red, who swirled softly around the room, his presence settling over my chest like a part of my heart. His scarf burned in my pocket.

Milo, Rose and Will gave one final wave, and I let out a breath as we were left completely alone in the herb shop.

"We're ready," I said, hesitating for only a moment.

The room grew quiet, everyone taking a moment to settle themselves. My mind was abuzz with worry, with the fear of what could go wrong. I stared at Magelav's extended hand.

"Forever, Aaliyah?" Prince asked, squeezing my hand, the gentle question enough to bring me out of my own head.

I memorized the soft lines of his face, the twist to his lips that I would fight to the death to keep this time. I smiled, squeezing his hand back, as I set my other in Magelav's open palm.

The power was immediate, the flush of teleportation magic making my stomach cramp.

"Always, Prince," I whispered as the room around us disappeared.

CHAPTER 26

FALLON

I *hated* magic.

The way it crawled along my skin and into my lungs whenever it was cast, like little ants marching in your veins. Even before all this mess, Kali had cemented that hatred when she'd made my blood literally boil—God, I was happy the bitch was dead.

Archon's lamp had been the final straw.

This spell was no different, even when cast by someone as skilled as Magelav, the Bog Sorceri themself. I could taste the hints of their power, almost like the grit of sand on my tongue, my eyes watering as I rubbed away the remains. The room that we'd been in inside of Eliza's herb shop melted away to reveal snow-capped trees and a lush forest that was deep in the throes of winter.

It was an eerie night, with the ominous glow of the moon and the crashing of waves against the weathered rock just below the sheer cliffs at our backs. Adrian grumbled something before he slung his arm over my shoulders, pointedly laughing at my sour expression. The dramatic flair was expected, even after everything that had happened.

I wasn't expecting to crumble under his weight, my legs seizing as pain shot down them. I grunted, my vision blotting as black spots danced in my peripherals. Adrian pulled his weight off me, faster than I was able to push him off, a sheepish smile seeming forced on his face. We mirrored each other, a patchwork of black veins and scorched skin.

I didn't understand how I was so fucked up, while he walked it off like it was nothing.

"You look sick, Taz." A sweet voice hummed in the air, and I shivered on instinct, looking over my shoulder to find Aislinn leaning against one of the trees at the edge of the clearing.

I didn't have to look around to see if the others saw her, shaking my head as I turned back to center. She clicked her tongue, and I was hit with a cold sweat.

"It's rude to ignore someone when they're talking to you, you know," she said through a laugh.

No one else spoke, lost in their own thoughts. I clenched my fist, searching for pain, letting it ground me as I stood tall. Aislinn's laughing continued, crossing the lines of real and what was just in my head. I reached for my chest, for the mark of the Fae Bargain. Hadlie got me out of the lamp ...

Unless it was just another trick. Archon was conniving, and his illusions were stronger than I'd given him credit for when we'd first come to his door.

I looked at my brothers, the men I'd lived with and fought with for two hundred years, and I couldn't stop myself from questioning the way they moved. The way Adrian's smile dipped, his face going blank. Osiris's numb stare replaced with a resolve that clashed with the power of his stance. Eirik's beast, and the way he hovered over Aaliyah, eyes a vicious blue that seemed almost *too* dark.

Nero being *alive.*

Was it normal? Was this really happening?

"Fallon?" a voice whispered again, warped and clouded as I flinched away from warm fingers that brushed against my knuckles.

I looked down just in time to see Aaliyah looking up at me with a tilted head and narrowed eyes. Aislinn whispered something mocking I was thankful not to hear as I took Aaliyah's hand. She shivered, her breath fogging in front of her as she looked around the clearing with the same confusion I did. The unnerved feeling that came with the unknown was so much worse when I realized I was just as blind here as she was. I'd never been to an Eternium before, and beyond stories, this was new to me, too.

And now she was cold on top of it.

I wasn't wearing my normal suit, instead dressed in some horrendous amalgamation of color that Dezen had given me, and I hoped it had some bearing in fashion. From the smugness in his eyes, though, I'd assume it was deliberate. But he did give me a jacket, which was going to find some use.

I shrugged it off, then wrapped it around Aaliyah's shoulders until she was bundled tightly. Her cheeks were flushed, her nose dusted red in a way that made it hard to look away. I grabbed her hands, warming them with my breath, focused on the way hers hitched when I got close enough to kiss the skin of her wrist.

"This is the Eternium?" Aaliyah asked, cutting into my thoughts as Eirik came to her side.

The wolf behind his eyes kept close to the surface, the light blue going nearly black in an instant as his nostrils flared, and he leaned down and ran his nose over her forehead. "It is."

I avoided looking too far into the way she moved as she pulled away from me, afraid of what I might find. I spent two years waking up to her, her touch and her caring smiles. It had to be her now, the *real* her.

"Real is subjective, don't you think?" Aislinn whispered, her voice echoing behind me.

I shivered, refusing to answer.

"It will be," Osiris clarified, a low tone in his voice as he turned to stare over the cliff. The ocean surged violently, the waves seeming to grow as he lifted his hands, before splitting one open with a slash of a fingernail against his palm, slicing deep enough for a well of blood to gush out.

Aaliyah made a shocked noise as he tightened his hand into a fist, drops of red hitting the snow-packed ground before the wound sealed shut. The moment it hit, it branched out, scattering under our feet in large winding roots that dragged all the way to the edge of the cliff, pulsing, as though following the beat of his heart.

Adrian grunted at my side again as the ground trembled under us. I stumbled, held up on my other side by Nero as we both braced for a fight, hair standing on end as a fine mist filled the air.

Osiris's blood lifted from the ground, floating around us, and I waited for the cocky call of his magic as Aaliyah checked his wound. But whatever this was, *wasn't* Osiris.

It didn't seem like much at first, like dust falling from the crumbling rocks, caught in the light of the moon, but eventually, that dust moved, taking shape. What it became was short, round, and lacking any defined features. It had no mouth, nose or eyes, like a store mannequin that was waiting to be placed on display. Instead, it had several smooth, almost tentacle-like waving appendages for limbs that stuck out from seemingly random places on its body. A plain white robe hung loosely off it, a contrast to its ashen skin.

It was a tense few seconds of waiting to see if anyone else rushed it before its skin rippled.

"Vivas," it whispered, its voice everywhere, bouncing around in my head, making my teeth chatter. Osiris didn't seem surprised as he moved to step in front of Aaliyah, a shield that seemed unwavering in the face of the creature.

"Ra." I clenched my jaw so tightly I would have sworn I cracked a tooth. Ali went rigid, but the creature didn't linger.

"Rourovic." Magelav stepped forward as it called their last name, nodding their head in deferment, for once startlingly silent.

The thing bowed, its head tipping low, before angling toward us again.

"Sage, Guardian of the Eternium," Osiris said, the stiff words echoing around us. The *Flame* lit on his skin, his blood pulsing in the air as the ember danced over him with a control that made it seem effortless.

I sagged, forcing myself to stay standing, even if that meant turning into a sweating, panting mess, every ounce of spare energy used up.

"What is your purpose?" The Sage moved as if dragged along by a stray wind, its form disintegrating before reappearing just inches from Osiris's side. It reached out, touching his shoulder with one of the many tendrils that extended from it, the spot glowing a faint blue.

"Osiris, head of the Vivas Crypt, Vampire *Challe*. Requesting entrance to the Eternium as Secondaries to Vampire Eternal Sebek Ra," Osiris said, shuddering as the Sage touched his face before pulling away.

It was almost a fever dream to hear Osiris say his title out loud, his hatred of it sticking to the word. *Challe,* a person with the right to Challenge. In stating it now, officially, to the Sage, he'd made it clear that he was able to Challenge Sebek.

It was a declaration, an insult, and just saying it was threat enough. It was damned well war on our Maker.

One by one, the Sage's head turned as if to look at us. It gave the stomach-cramping anxiety you got when you were being hunted by something stronger than you, *older* than you. It was as if it were sifting through the remains of my soul, examining me.

It stayed pointed toward me for longer than it had any reason to before its head tipped in another soft nod. "Thank you, Secondaries of Vampire Eternal Sebek Ra."

That was the only warning we got before the ground disappeared. The red roots Osiris's blood made dashed away from me as we were ripped back from the Sage ... and directly over the lip of the cliff.

I didn't have time to scream, or question if this was really the outfit I wanted to die in, a hand-me-down sweater vest that was three sizes too big, before my feet touched solid ground.

"At least the view was worth it," Adrian grumbled at my side, rubbing his arms as though the chill lingered, and I followed his gaze.

The air between us and the gaping mouth of the cave wobbled like liquid glass, as though dancing to the soft keys of the piano that played dimly behind us. The sea that I'd heard stretched on for miles. Adrian gagged, covering his mouth and looking over his shoulder to escape the rush of endless water. I did the same, freezing at what I saw.

The large room was filled with all manner of people. Eternals, *Challe,* Secondaries. The power was enough to strangle me.

They were dressed as I'd expected of their status, and they glowered down on us, taking in the rags we'd shown up in. We were mud on their boots, dirt to sully the polished floor they danced on, in their shining palace made of marble and gold. Tall pillars stretched from floor to ceiling, and shards of glass were draped like suspended rain, glowing with enough light to illuminate the room.

"Can you believe this?" I asked, keeping my voice low as Adrian looked over the crowd.

"Not in the slightest," he whispered back.

Nero tensed, keeping his head low as some drew close, curious or just wanting to see if they were really seeing the Vivas Crypt looking so ... poor.

"It's a lot to take in," Osiris said, suddenly by my side.

"Just another party full of stuck-up assholes," I said, shrugging it off, glaring at a Hydra as he sneered at us. The hint of frill webbing popped up on his head, almost like the fur on the neck of a pissed-off cat. "The Three really know how to get the people going."

A hint of their power seemed to finally sink in, more than I could ever get from stories and secondhand whispers. They were the boogeymen, the monster under the bed that Naturals tried to pretend weren't real, the personification of a very real fear, the only one people like them tended to have.

Death. Time. Space. Everything that could spell doom for someone with seemingly endless lives to live.

"To put it lightly," Osiris affirmed, glancing around the room one more time, before he began to move.

Like a happy little family, we scurried off after him, gazing in wide wonder at the absolute cluster that was going to be our lives for the next few days.

I homed in on the people I knew, nodding to Avedal as he raised a glass in our direction, his long black hair pinned behind him in an intricate tie. Hillam, his mate, was to his side, a rare appearance and more of a show of strength than we could have hoped for. A Kraken Mythic, one of the last, the six eyes on his face a display of age and power. His black hair seemed inky, the same way most water-faring Naturals did, floating in midair as if suspended in water.

We were only about halfway through the crowd when I realized something was wrong. It started with the whispers, the mocking looks that shifted slowly into anticipation.

Adrian noticed, too, freezing, leaving the two of us standing stalk still as the others meandered on their way, parting the crowd that had gathered.

A scent filled the air, bitter and fake, the scent of a man I'd promised to *kill*.

Fool's gold.

ADRIAN

A familiar and instinctual need to flee made me shiver. I reached for my wrists, the gouges from the shackles long since healed. My lungs constricted, and I couldn't seem to force myself to breathe as my ears strained and the noise of the crowd melted away ... into the clink of boots, deliberately slow on marble floors, as if to draw out the torment.

"So, you made it off the roof after all," a familiar voice gloated at my back. The dark veins on my skin mocked me as he clicked his tongue. "I must admit, I have to admire your resilience."

I couldn't even turn around as my breath caught. My mind seemed to know enough to stop the pesky bodily function, to hold it in as though my lungs might collapse if I took another breath. I rubbed my arms, hating that the frigid air didn't make me shiver. I'd never liked winter. The only thing it was good for was a hearty soup, but I'd take even the cold now.

The cold hurt, and I hated that I missed that.

"Archon," Osiris, now behind me, said, his voice steady and unbothered.

I looked over my shoulder, catching Archon's eyes. He was looking directly at me, only at me. He didn't waver for even a second as he smirked. "Vivas."

"What do you want?" Eirik bit out, taking a stance next to Osiris, his voice a medley of furious growls as his eyes shifted to a deep blue.

Aaliyah, still by his side, grabbed his hand, calming the beast that raged inside as Archon laughed. All of them together formed a wall, though that didn't stop the words. Or the stare. "Don't look so glum. I was just being polite and saying my greetings to my new acquaintances. It doesn't hurt to see who might be calling for Challenge."

His teeth showed as his grin grew. Our deal flickered in the back of my mind, ending at the sigil on my chest that pulsed with him so nearby. I reached up, rubbing the flesh that was no doubt still raw.

"Or *Exilium*," he said, loud enough for the crowd to hear. The whispers started a breath later, the eyes that had been on us growing until the room had only two sides. Us and them. Exactly as Archon wanted. "Ah, my apologies. Adrian let it slip in one of our chats. That wasn't meant to be a secret, was it?"

Worthless. I crumbled under the pointed stare that came from Fallon, his head snapping to the side. His face scrunched, his nose flaring as a fire lit behind his eyes that promised the kind of retribution he'd used to save for our enemies.

I was no better. I'd sold us out for nothing.

I *was nothing.*

I sank into myself, my hearing dulling until the whispers were barely static, and I half waited for my brothers to explode. My failure exposed and oozing.

Osiris didn't even breathe as he took a step forward, then another ... until Archon finally looked away from me. He homed in on the threat that drew close, on the way Osiris's expression remained carefully neutral.

The switch in the room was slow, the outraged cries turning to fearful whispers. There was a hush that came over, a hesitance that came with experience. *Osiris.*

The eldest living Turned of Sebek Ra.

Rex interfectorem. The *Kingslayer.*

I tended to forget sometimes that the short few hundred years I'd known Osiris were barely a fraction of his life. That the man that I teased and goaded was one of the most feared Naturals to walk this earth.

The others in this room didn't forget, the ones with power of their own shrinking back.

"Nearly six hundred years you spent in that lamp, and it seems you still don't have the good sense to learn your place," Osiris said, not moving when Archon's face turned red, his lips pulling back to expose his teeth again.

Gold dust filled the air, spiraling around Archon's head in a flashy show as Osiris turned away, facing the crowd. Giving the Djinn his back, as though he weren't even worth the effort of guarding against.

"If I might have your attention," Osiris said, and attention he had, as everyone grew quiet, waiting eagerly for what he might have to say about the accusation. I wasn't even sure what I expected as he adjusted the cuffs of his tattered dress shirt. "Archon speaks the truth. Crypt Vivas intends to impose *Exilium* upon Vampire Eternal Sebek Ra. *The Honored Death* for Death's Butcher himself."

A silence stretched over the room, for once music to my ears, as Osiris's declaration stole every single person's words. The confidence in how he said it, the power ... the look he gave over his shoulder pointed at me; the same one he'd had when he extended his hand out to help me from the ground after they'd found me in the pits of London. Covered in enough innocent blood that I knew I'd never wash myself clean of it.

"If you are going to expose something like it's some kind of sick secret, the least you can do is make a better show out of it." Osiris sneered at the gaping Archon before turning away entirely. "*That* was pathetic. Even for you."

"I—"Archon started, the babble in his words buried by Osiris's steps as he moved to Aaliyah, wrapping his arm carefully around her shoulders.

The whispers began again as he directed us through the throngs of people. "We're done here."

The move from the main hall to one of the conjoining doors was a rush, as we flashed by the stunned guests of the Eternium. I smiled as I always had, waving like this was all part of some grand plan, but it had never felt like such a mask before. The man that I was and the man that I played seemed to blend into one being that I couldn't distinguish between.

Which one was even real anymore?

Keep the mask on. *Hide the weakness* ... but the mask was fractured. Archon had revealed our plans, had told my brothers what I'd done. Osiris had covered well ... but it didn't change a damned thing.

I'd betrayed us. I broke.

"Adrian, look at me," Aaliyah whispered, cupping my cheeks, her hands so reminiscent of what had almost been a rescue from the lamp that I nearly pushed her away. "You're okay. It's going to be okay."

"Osiris, you know where to go?" Nero asked, his voice low enough that only our group could hear, as the mumbled voices around us grew. Aaliyah didn't let me go, instead taking my hand in hers, so she could help to guide me forward.

I ran a thumb over her wrist, searching for her heartbeat with my ears, proving that she was here the only way I could manage.

"Follow me," Osiris said, dragging us down a hall that seemed to go on forever, the same white and gold lining it, even as we passed through a solitary door.

The inside was quaint, brightly colored like the rest of the cavern. Though it was startlingly barren of anything else of comfort. There was a couch that looked a little too stiff and an attached kitchen that was missing a fridge. Along with a single door at the back of the room.

The door behind me closed, and the mask fell the rest of the way off.

Every bit of loathing and panic that I'd bottled up came roaring to the surface as I felt my smile slip. I lost myself again to every swipe of a bloodied knife and jam of fingers in open wounds. Every worthless beg for the pain to stop and every second after that I had to spend realizing what I'd exchanged that lack of pain for ...

They won't come, not soon enough.

"He's right. He wasn't lying," I spewed the words, gripping my hair and begging for pain, for what I deserved. Aaliyah wrapped herself around me, her chest to mine, her head over the mark that I'd gotten for this. For nothing. "I gave it up, Ali. I—I couldn't handle the torture, and I gave it up. I was stupid, so fucking *stupid*. I made a deal with Archon, and he took it away."

She didn't let me go, clinging to me tighter. Enough that I should have felt it in my ribs.

I held her, soaking in every bit of the touch she was willing to give me, every bit of proof to show that she was real.

When her eyes landed on me, with all that softness, I couldn't hold her gaze. I dropped it to the floor, staring at a rug that suddenly seemed very interesting. It felt dirty of me, to hold her trusting look after what I'd done.

I'd risked our safety.

Ali had gone back to her hell, the place that had given her those scars that still made my blood boil. Had walked through the doors with her head held high for us.

And I'd lasted *three fucking hours.*

"What do you mean, he took it away?" she asked, endlessly patient, even when I didn't deserve it.

There was a moment of hesitation, one that locked the truth of what had happened inside of me. I didn't want them to know, didn't want them to realize how much I'd lost. I was weak enough as it was—the youngest of our Crypt—I didn't need to add this burden to them, too.

But Aaliyah didn't let me go, didn't pull away as she traced one of those torched veins on my face. I knew how much she worried, how much she'd sacrificed to try to *save* us.

I couldn't lie. Not to her.

"I needed the torture to stop," I choked, my head dipping, looking at the ground as my vision clouded, tears falling freely to the floor. I laughed, the sound still gravelly from my hours spent screaming. "He took away my pain. All of it. Even now."

"You told him our plan?" Osiris asked, still as calm as he had been when he'd ripped Archon apart earlier.

His eyes were observant in a way they shouldn't have been, or rather, a way I hadn't seen in ages. The haze of numb was there, like always, but underneath was the man who'd saved me after my turn. He watched carefully, examining the same marks the others had.

Where the sun had scorched me, a match to the lines that still lingered on his hand.

I nodded, grabbing Aaliyah's hand in mine, searching for the warmth of her.

"Just Exilium. It was all he got." *It was all he needed.*

I didn't know someone was behind me until I was turned, the unexpected pull making me stumble.

"What—" I said, catching Fallon's face just in time for his forehead to crack against my nose. He grunted at the headbutt, pulling back worse for wear, obviously. I scowled, reaching up to catch the blood as it spilled down my face. "What the fuck was that for?"

He grunted, baring his teeth as he rubbed his forehead. Ali went to his side, maneuvering to take some of his weight even as he grumbled. "You beating yourself up over breaking to literal fucking torture is helping no one. We don't blame you. If anything, it was the highlight of my night seeing Archon look like an overripe tomato."

"You did well," Eirik added, clapping me on the shoulder. "You saved yourself, kept yourself alive while giving him the barest amount. That's worth praise, not mockery."

"Besides, you weren't the only one Archon got the slip on, Adrian,"

Fallon said, lifting his shirt, showing a mark that was much different from the black streaks that crawled along his veins. I'd seen hints of it before but had been too lost in my own head to really look at it. A tree littered with green petals stretched up his side, a long winding branch landing directly over his heart. "He's a tricky fucker. I'll give him that."

The design seemed to move on his skin, as a leaf fell from it. It tumbled down his side, landing on one of his ribs.

"A Fae Bargain?" Osiris asked, moving to get a better look. He ghosted his hand over the mark, never quite touching Fallon as he studied the intricate moving ink.

"Yeah, unfortunately, can't say anything about it," Fallon grunted, like he went to try, but was stopped. "I have to take care of it before the end of the Eternium. Plus side, pretty sure I need to go to the Fae Eternal, which means either he's going to be on our side—"

"Or we put someone in who is," Osiris filled in.

Fallon nodded, letting his shirt fall, curling around Aaliyah again. "Exactly."

Osiris tapped his chin, looking around the room at each of us. "Sebek very likely already anticipated Exilium. I never expected it to stay a secret for long. The only question that matters is what we do next."

"None of this has gone to plan. Everything is exactly how he would want it. With one exception," Aaliyah cut in, still holding Fallon's weight, even as Nero came by to help her. "He wants us fighting. He wants us torn. We can't give that to him, or we lose. But we have another way to throw him off. *All* of them off."

She looked at Nero, and he raised a brow with a smirk. She smiled at him, her face softening as she admired her Prince.

"They don't know I'm alive. *Yet.*"

Aaliyah nodded, humming softly. "Sebek ... holds sentiment in weird ways. My father is a sore point, so are all of you. Seeing Nero will throw him off. We may not be able to surprise him with Exilium, but we can give us an edge before we call it."

If I'd learned anything about Sebek, it was that he was odd. He cared for us, in his own messed up way, but I hadn't thought that was something we could use. It seemed almost silly to think he could be swayed by something so trivial as emotions.

But Aaliyah looked sure, and I wasn't about to doubt her ability to read people. She had a knack for it, one I remembered all too well from our visit to The Weathered Needle.

"Head up, *lux mea*," Osiris whispered, his fingers gripping her chin when she glanced at the ground, looking almost embarrassed, lifting it so she'd looked straight ahead again. There was a soft command in his voice, one that spoke of his influence as much as it did our precarious situation. "Your words hold power."

She smiled at him, kissing the tip of his thumb as it ran over her bottom lip. The nonchalant touch messed with my head, and I had to do a double take to make sure it was really Osiris and not some body double that had replaced my brother.

Damn, maybe he had told her how he felt when we'd left them alone to go to Archon's ...

He pulled back like it was nothing and looked at the rest of us. "What else?"

Eirik grunted. "Brazen was there, too."

Like usual, the words were short, grunted like they held no real meaning. He said it with his head high, the eyes of a beast staring us down.

Osiris went stock still, Nero's face going blank as he tried to register the name, one I had no doubt he knew somewhere in that head of his. Even if it was held back now.

"Brazen?" Osiris asked, a spark flying across his skin.

Eirik grunted again, shaking his head, his eyes surprisingly a steady sky blue. As if the wolf was dragged to heel. "Don't, Osiris. I'll handle it."

It was a tense few seconds of silence before Osiris nodded.

"Well, if we're spilling our guts. Mags craves a *deeply* intimate rela-tionship and has been stalking me for the better part of the last several weeks trying to get me to agree to it," Nero included, looking at his nails as the Chronomancer balked. "Rather desperate, if you ask me."

I hadn't even realized they were here, but they sure made proof of their presence when they sputtered.

"Mags is owed a favor! Nothing of physical gratification. You sing falsities!" Magelav hissed, face shifting around like they might transform into some beast when Nero shrugged his shoulders.

"Potato, *potahto*, same fucking thing, Mags," he said, rolling his eyes and leaning back into Ali. He switched so quickly from joking to serious as he ran a hand over the front of her forehead. "I think that's about enough for today, don't you? You need some rest, Aaliyah."

That I could get behind. Sleep sounded like a dream. True sleep, the kind where I could fall into her arms and forget that this was happening.

I hesitated again, struggling to find the will to go to her, when Fallon bumped his shoulder into mine, pushing me forward. Aaliyah smiled at me, and I couldn't hold it back anymore as I pulled her into my arms again.

I waited for this all to fade away, for this to be another trick that Archon was playing with my head. Aaliyah's arms wrapped around me, her head tucked securely under my chin. "This family can only take so much soul searching. Trust me, it'll start to get weird. Fallon might cry, then he'd have to kill us."

Fallon grumbled behind us, but Aaliyah laughed against my chest.

"Then ... at least let me help you first?" she asked, tracing the black lines that stretched across one of my arms.

They were jagged, deep marks, almost like scars, and they covered the vast majority of my skin. Fallon grunted, moving over to us to press a kiss to her forehead.

"I'll get some glasses," Fallon whispered, and she shook her head.

"No, that won't be enough," she whispered, taking Fallon's face when he tried to protest. "I need to know you're all right."

It wasn't hard to notice that her eyes lingered on our wrists, on the place where her marks used to be. Fallon and I had lost ours, and it wasn't just us that were taking that toll. The intricate black designs that had traced her own wrist were missing now, too. Only Osiris's and Eirik's remained.

All it took was one look to know we weren't winning this fight.

"Aaliyah ..." I whispered, burying my face in my hands. I hated the idea of adding any more stress to her. "You're stubborn, you know that?"

She hummed, brushing her finger over my nose. Along another mark, another scar. Another patchwork of misdeeds that I needed to pay Archon back for tenfold. "Maybe, but you're not going to change my mind."

She wasn't going to back down, not on this, and Osiris seemed to get that as he sighed. "Just Adrian and Fallon tonight, then. The rest of us will be fine."

The others looked on, worry still clouding their eyes. There were more weak protests, but they fell away as she pulled Fallon and I to the couch. I was glad she at least didn't push further, because I knew given even an inkling of a chance ... she would have. Even to the detriment of herself. The rest of them were standing well enough. Breathing easily.

And she might have won the fight to give us blood, but Osiris would have pushed back against any more.

She sat down in the middle of the couch, grimacing as she tried to get comfortable. I struggled, too, the damn thing like a brick. She held out her hands to both of us. I was quick to set mine in hers, rubbing a thumb over her wrist.

"If you think you're not taking from us, too, you're crazy," I said, brushing the hair out of her eyes.

"That, *I* can help with," Nero said, stepping behind me, leaning over the couch. Another wrist appeared in front of Aaliyah's face. He leaned close, dragging his lips along the back of her neck, not so subtly whispering, "I've been dying to see what my mark looks like on your skin."

I looked to my own wrist, where the mark had disappeared from when Archon's deal had sealed. I hoped that this would fix it, but at this point, I wasn't holding my breath.

I pressed a kiss to her wrist just as she leaned forward and sank her teeth into Nero. It was hard not to notice the way he jolted, groaning deep as he leaned in, holding her closer, tighter.

I extended my tongue, licking the thin skin, listening for the pulse of blood under it. My body picked up the slight iron in the air and my mouth watered. I bit her slowly, making sure I didn't sink too deep.

She gasped at the feeling, her eyes rolling back as she muffled a moan around Nero's wrist.

We stayed glued to each other, taking steady mouthfuls that rejuvenated me like nothing else could. My vision sharpened, my mouth opening to take her deeper. When we pulled back, not one of us wasn't panting, licking the wounds we'd made.

My wrist remained unmarked. As had Fallon's. Aaliyah brushed her thumb against the blank skin, eyebrows furrowing as she pressed a kiss to it. I wasn't surprised that it hadn't come back.

But it hurt to see, regardless.

"Thank you, love," I whispered, my arms wrapping around her again. "Now it's time to sleep."

Aaliyah must have felt the same as she sagged into me. The move from the couch to the back door was a blur, and I was half expecting a hallway with multiple other doors behind. Instead, there was a single bed, a *large* one, but only one, regardless.

We'd have to get comfortable.

"Just promise to keep your hands to yourself, eh Eirik?" Fallon asked, already shedding his clothes. "I do *not* want to cuddle with you again."

I was exhausted, drained to the point that even a shower sounded like too much work. I set Ali on the satin sheets, asking her quickly if we could get her comfortable.

She rubbed her eyes with the back of her hands as she nodded. We got her into just a bra and underwear, then fell into place.

Fallon was to one side of her, Eirik to another, and I found a place wedged between her legs. Nero crawled behind Eirik, snorting and making a joke that I was too tired to listen to but made Eirik snarl.

Osiris stayed to the side, something I expected. He pulled up a chair and offered her a hand that she happily took.

My eyes were already sliding close when Eirik's purr surrounded us.

"Goodnight," I whispered, making sure I was touching her skin, trying to find comfort in the way she brushed against me. Then I slept, and for the first time in days, it was in peace.

CHAPTER 27

AALIYAH

It took a moment for my eyes to adjust to the dark, my entire body easing into a dull ache as I stretched carefully. Fallon was unmoving behind me, his soft snores the only sound coming from him. Eirik and Adrian were much the same, with Adrian curled around Eirik's back and Eirik laying a loose arm over my body, holding me to him.

It was comfortable, safe, but the hair on the back of my neck stood on end, a cold sweat pooling as my sleep haze slowly cleared.

Prince was nowhere to be found.

I jolted, trying desperately to stop myself from waking the others, as my heart rate skyrocketed. My breath hitched as I searched the room, hunting for him like I had the night after the incident at the hot spring. The night I'd lost him.

Please.

"He's out in the living room. He was having trouble sleeping," a voice whispered, a point of calm in my steadily increasing anxiety.

Osiris sat by the side of the bed, my hand still tucked carefully in his.

He watched me with a hooded gaze, his shoulders tense as he looked me up and down. The heat that I'd grown so used to finding in the depths of his mismatched blues was there, hiding behind the worry that glazed them over. His shoulders stayed tense as he let out a shaking breath.

I'd seen him every way I'd thought possible, from facing Kali to grappling with the loss of his brothers ... reading to me in our warmly lit library, holding me as I cried over the loss of Prince. But this was different, something I couldn't place.

I crawled my way out of the pile of bodies until I was standing in front of him.

"Osiris?" I pressed gently, and he swallowed. "Is everything all right?"

He reached for my hand again, rubbing a shaking thumb against the back of it.

"What will you do now, *lux mea*?" he asked, placing a gentle kiss where he'd touched. His cold lips sent a shiver down my spine, one that raced directly into the muscles of my heart and the flush of my cheeks. "Prince has returned to you. Would you still have us?"

My words caught as he leaned forward and took a deep breath. It was strange for him to do so, the action almost foreign to me now.

"Would you still have me?" He whispered it so low I could barely hear it.

Like he'd expected me to turn him away, as if that were the only option he could see. It had never even been considered, not now, not after everything we'd been through.

Osiris was a piece of me I'd never be rid of. I loved Prince, for everything that he'd been for me, for being my rock and my best friend. Just like I loved the rest of them, each filling a gap in my soul that had been carved open like they were made to fill the slot.

"Always, Osiris," I whispered as his fangs dropped, and he shivered. His power pulsed in the room, reminding me of the man I was in front of. He'd lived far more lifetimes than I could imagine and had brought my demons to their knees. He'd fought for me, killed for me ... He was *mine*. "As long as you'd have me, too."

I waited for him to pull back, for the drag of his kiss against my forehead, the intimacy that I knew he was comfortable with. The moment his lips molded to mine, a delicate dance of fire and ice, I melted. I'd been without him for so long, wondering if this was what he'd even wanted, and finally getting to taste him again after what had happened soothed me.

He pulled back too soon, setting his forehead against mine as his huffed breaths cooled against my wet lips.

"You are my light, Aaliyah. I never want to face a night alone without you again," he whispered. "And you are Nero's queen. He needs you right now."

His eyes trained on the door, and he let go of my hand.

I hummed, cupping his cheeks like he'd done to me so many times. I kissed his forehead, not wanting to let go of him just yet. He relaxed into the hold. "Thank you, Osiris."

His lips tilted, the small adoring smile never leaving as he gently ushered me to move. I walked carefully out of the room, glancing back just once to catch Osiris's sure gaze.

The floors were cold, much like the day I'd first woken in their home. It seemed like a lifetime ago.

I trailed my hand along the door as I slid it closed, smiling when Red stretched out next to me, moving slowly around me, as though he were waking up as well. I turned, facing the living room and expecting to find it as I had before we'd gone to sleep, but it looked ... wrong. The kitchen was bigger now; the cabinets seemed to stretch an extra couple feet high, with new appliances that I would have sworn hadn't been there before. The entire area was more spaced out, more comforts strewn through the previously desolate room, with a couple extra doors added on. Like it had changed to match us.

"Odd, isn't it?" Prince asked.

I'd never get used to the sound of his voice. It was rugged, lit with a husky tinge and a masculine grunt as he thrust the heavy sword in his hand forward, before bringing it down in a sure arch. He was shirtless, and the well-defined muscles that splayed across his chest and abdomen that I'd only dreamed of seeing were suddenly *all* I could see. They were a masterpiece etched into his skin, like the scars that matched the very sword he wielded. His hair whipped around his head, his eyes focused like wells of molten silver, his mouth open in exertion as he swung again in a move so practiced it looked like the blade was an extension of himself.

My jaw dropped, and I couldn't have looked away if I'd wanted to.

He said something, taking a step toward me, twirling the sword up so the blunt face of it sat against his shoulder.

"Aaliyah?" He was in front of me now, close enough that I could see the heaving of his chest. I reached up, pressing my hand to the skin on instinct rather than replying to my name. That was only fueled by the spark that lit under my palm, a heat that traveled lazily over my skin before ending in my core.

Prince chuckled, pressing his hand over mine when I stayed silent.

"Sorry, what did you say?" I mumbled, my cheeks heating as I shook my head.

Lust wasn't new to me, not anymore, but I was off center with Prince. I'd spent most of my life loving him, at least the life I could remember, and now that he was here, I wasn't able to separate those feelings from then to the man that was in front of me now.

He was *alive* ... but he was also missing his memories. There was a chance this wasn't what he wanted. A chance that *I* wasn't what he wanted.

"Now, I know I'm quite the looker, but at least pretend you like me for more than just my body." Prince's smile turned sinful as he washed that worry clean away. His fingers grabbed my chin, tipping my head up so I was looking him in his silver eyes. "Not that I mind you liking that, too."

Right, Prince could *talk* now, and I had to remember that meant he could say things that made my thighs clench. That didn't unscramble my brain like I wished it might have. I was still too focused on the mischievous curl to his lips and the little beads of sweat that painted his skin.

What had he said? Something about the room?

"It is odd," I mumbled, suddenly needing to look away from him, embarrassed by the unapologetic ogling. "Just another one of those things the Eternium does?"

"Something like that, I think," he said, whispering something else as I kept my head down.

Prince's sigh drew my attention back up to him, and he took a step back, my hand dropping away from his chest. The distance, the lack of contact, squeezed my heart.

"Shit, I'm sorry. I swear, it's like my words have a mind of their own." He ran a hand through his unruly hair.

"Prince?" I asked as his head tipped back, and he swallowed. His Adam's apple bobbed, his eyes closing as he swung the sword down, planting the tip into the floor.

"I love you," he blurted out, without any warning. My stomach erupted into a sea of jitters, butterflies alive and well as my jaw dropped. Prince's eyes opened again, all fire. "*That's* what I meant to say. What I've wanted to say for as long as I've been back, and I'm sure for decades before that. I *love* you, Aaliyah. More than any life I've ever had, and that I can promise."

He raised a fist, thumping it on his chest like a solemn vow. I tried to get something out, to break in, but he kept going.

"I understand if you don't feel the same, if now that I'm alive you don't want me, that's fine. I'll always be by your side, forever. Your knight in astral armor, okay?" His voice cracked.

There was a fragility in the sudden slouch of his shoulders. I'd always struggled with words, fought them with every whisper of a mantra that still burned in the back of my mind, telling me to stay quiet ... all I wanted to do now was to speak, but I couldn't seem to get anything out.

"I just—" he said, and something about how he stood, looking almost defeated, got me moving.

I couldn't speak ... but words had never been needed between us.

I was on him then, literally diving into his arms. The sword clattered to the ground, and my legs wrapped around his waist, my hands going around his neck as I took his lips like I'd imagined for so long. There were few things in this world I loved more than the man that moved to catch me.

I dragged my hand back, touching every inch of skin I could before I settled on his chest, above the heavy beat of his heart, my ring and pinky finger tucked in. I kissed him that way, hung in his arms like I was a gift, the symbol of our love trapped between us.

The taste of him, the smell, the beat of his heart under my palm, it was so overwhelming that tears came to my eyes.

Prince was here. He was *alive*.

"I love you, too," I finally managed, the words choked and anything but perfect, but they were real, and they were mine. I spent so many years trapped in the silence of my cell, in my own head, and I wouldn't let it steal my voice from me again. I pulled back, just to go back in for another kiss. This one slower, giving me more time to enjoy the softness of it. His hands tightened where he held me, fingers digging into my hips. "I love you, Prince."

"You have no idea how badly I've wanted to hear that," he whispered against my lips. "*My* Aaliyah."

I was obsessed with the way he said my name.

"Say it again?" I begged, leaning in so my head was tucked into his shoulder, against his neck.

"Say what?" His question vibrated me, and I tightened my legs around him, suddenly aware of how close he was. Of the press of his hands and the hot fan of his breath against my neck. His skin was cold, but the little sparks that I'd gotten so used to at his touch had lit me ablaze. My cheeks flushed with it.

When I didn't respond, he kissed that spot, murmuring something that sent a shiver of desire down my spine.

"My name. Say it again," I managed, and his chuckle echoed.

One of his arms stayed bracketed around my hips, holding me up as the other came to my hair. His fingers threaded through it, his tanned skin contrasted against the white strands as he pulled back and molded our mouths together in a savage dance.

He had me gasping, grinding against him as his tongue worked me into a frenzy, dipping and teasing my mouth until my head was spinning. He tasted like a fire meant to mold steel, sharp and addictive, and he burned like it too. No matter what happened, my life would be forever changed by this moment.

When he pulled back, I fought to follow him. He stopped me with the hand in my hair, keeping me steady as he looked me in the eye. His expression softened into one I'd seen so many times, the loving look he used to have when he thought I wasn't watching. The kind that he'd give me when I knew he was letting me win a game, or when he was telling me a story with the wild flicks of his hands in our makeshift language. Now, he gave me that look openly, letting me bask in every second of it.

"Aaliyah," he whispered finally, leaning in and adoringly kissing one of my cheeks, his soft lips lingering.

I tightened around his waist, trying to get closer.

"Aaliyah," he breathed, like it was the only word he ever needed again, as those lips traveled along my jaw.

He met my growing need with his own, taking my movements in stride as he helped to anchor me to him.

"Aaliyah," he praised, a purr in my ear, and I melted, losing what I was to him.

All the lust and love blended into one. I was touching him; I was kissing him, and he met me every step of the way.

"Prince," I whispered, shuddering as his hips flexed at the sound of his name, my name for him. The name *I* gave him.

"Yes, my queen?" he asked, reverence in his words, a devotion that showed in how he came back to me.

"You know how I feel about the others?" I asked, glancing over my shoulder at the door that separated us from them. The other Vivas brothers, the other men who held my heart. Prince didn't push me away, like my brain was telling me he might, instead using the moment to pull us closer. His nose rubbed against mine, and I sighed into his touch. "You still want me, even though I love them too? I can't let them go, Prince. I can't—"

"Aaliyah, I'd never take you away from them. I'd kill anyone that tries," he said, a breath of fierceness with the promise. "We're Vivas, and those bastards are as much mine as they are yours."

His words warmed me like his hands still tracing my sides, setting me at ease. I hummed, focusing on the way he'd said my name. The breathy whisper, the little sharp intonation at the end of it that spoke to an accent I couldn't dream to place.

In that moment, I knew he'd do whatever I asked. He'd let me down, come back with me so we could sleep with the others, who were only a door away. He'd kiss me silly until the only thing I could think of was his name. He'd dance. He'd fight. He'd kill.

Tonight, I just wanted him.

"Prince, I need you," I whispered into the crevice of his neck, before peeking up to see his face again.

I didn't think his eyes could get any more savage, but the way the silver deepened, his pupils blowing out, told me I was wrong. His hips flexed again, this time seemingly involuntarily as he groaned. His head tipped back, his Adam's apple bobbing as he swallowed hard. I felt his restraint in the way his hands shook, the one still in my hair tightening enough that a burst of pleasure-lined pain had me whimpering.

"You have me, always. Just tell me what you want me to do," he said, giving me an out, a path to something different, but I wanted this with him. He was my first love, and I loved the others with as much ferocity, but I needed this with him, this moment, this feeling. I'd spent so many sleepless nights by his side, begging for just one touch.

Now he was here, and I almost couldn't believe it.

"Make me yours," I whispered. "I need you to prove that this is real."

We were moving then, his long strides taking us to one of the doors that had appeared while we'd slept. It was another room, this one filled with books and swords I was sure I'd take the time to admire later. The rustic charm and earthy tones lit it up, like it had been handcrafted for Prince.

He walked me carefully over to the bed, laying me down on the silken black sheets. He was already shirtless, flexing as I reached my hand out to touch him, skimming his taut abdomen. His head tipped back again, his jaw clenching as the strain in his pants jumped where he was pressed flush to my core. The length of him was intimidating, the heat of it making me gasp.

"How far have you gone?" he asked, breathlessly.

He hovered over me, his hands planted on either side of my head, encasing me with him. Surprisingly, it didn't scare me. Maybe it was because it was Prince, or maybe because I was so worked up, my brain didn't have the time to question why I should be scared.

"Just touching," I said, blushing at the words.

Milo had kissed Nero today, and it didn't take a lot to guess that Nero had been experienced before he'd died, before he became *my* Prince. I almost felt inadequate at the thought, unsure what to do with myself, but that was washed away as Prince leaned forward, pressing a tender kiss to my lips again. He released a desperate groan that made his entire body shake as he slid a hand down my bare stomach.

"I'll take care of you, Aaliyah," he whispered, leaning down to kiss the feverish flesh right above my belly button. "Forever."

He followed his hands with his lips, trailing down my stomach, but he never let his eyes fall away from mine, keeping me entranced by him until he was kissing the black satin of my panties, grazing his teeth along the top.

He dipped his fingers into the sides, easing the soft silk off me as I lifted my hips for him. He mumbled something, sounding like a prayer as he dipped his head away from my eyes for the first time. Liquid fire suddenly burned there, as he teased a finger from my thigh, up, and up ...

It was delicious torture when he finally reached my core. The tip of his finger slid over the sensitive skin of my entrance, dipping in just a touch. His eyes closed, and he groaned when he realized how wet I already was. Suddenly, he was moving back, sliding over the edge of the bed and dragging me with him. His knees hit the floor with a thud, and I was pulled until his face was level with my sex.

The position allowed him to put my legs firmly over his shoulders, with him bending so my heels could dig into his back. The position felt startlingly vulnerable, and I nearly jumped off the bed when his tongue dipped inside of me. It was so fast I didn't even have the time to be nervous about it. There was no careful exploration as his hands gripped my hips and kept me anchored to him, his touch like worship, his tongue offering a sacrifice that I was all too eager to accept. It didn't take long for the pleasurable hint of climax to build in me, sending me soaring toward the edge of rapture before I could even begin to comprehend how close I was.

The orgasm had me writhing and whimpering in his sure hold. Still, he didn't let up, pulling his mouth away just to attach to my clit, toying with the bud as he slid a finger into me, not moving, just applying a gentle pressure to a spot inside of me that made me see stars. I was still in shock, trembling from the last orgasm, as he dragged me through it, almost into another one.

"Prince," I whimpered, and the sound he made was somewhere between a groan and a growl as he doubled down. He added another finger, stretching me even more, a light pressure building as his tongue worked its magic.

"Don't stop, say it again," he groaned, out of breath. "Say my name, Aaliyah."

I reached for his hair, digging my hands into the unruly, red-tinted locks, desperate to keep him on me and push him away all at the same time as his name spilled from my lips with a cry. Another wave of pleasure, and I was left crumpled on the bed, breathing so hard I swore I was going to pass out.

Prince just looked up from between my legs, looking pleased with himself as he licked his lips.

"You're so fucking beautiful," he whispered as he sank his finger deeper at the same time, making me twitch and groan again.

Even with the smug look on his face ... God, I'd never get tired of hearing him speak.

He slid his hand away before he stood slowly, carefully removing my legs from his shoulders. I inched back up the bed, and that shine of brutal silver in his eyes grew languid, soft, as he looked me up and down.

He was heaving breaths, the pupils in his eyes nearly fully blown, and I didn't miss the fangs that had dropped. He shook, flexing one hand, running the other through his hair. His entire body tensed as he did, the muscles at his side trembling as he tried to level his breathing.

He strained against the front of his pants, a small wet spot there making my mouth water. He looked rabid, like he might descend into madness and devour me. I wanted him to, so he might get as lost in me as I was in him.

He still paused to ask, "You sure?"

I didn't say anything, sitting up. I reached behind me and unclasped the bra, baring myself entirely, before I crawled my way over to him. It was embarrassing, and I knew I was blushing when I finally reached him, close enough that I could set my hand on his chest. He didn't move, his breath hitching as his head tipped back. I traced my way down his smooth skin, lingering on the hints of scars that stood against strong muscle. When I reached the divots at his hips, I toyed with them, engrossed in the noises he made when I touched him. Groans that started in his chest and ended in cries so full they were almost pleading.

When I reached the waist of his pants, I looked up, catching his eyes, which were already back on me. He cursed behind clenched teeth when I ran my palm against his clothed length, urging me to move as I unbuttoned and slipped them slowly over his hips, taking his underwear down with it. He helped me, shrugging them the rest of the way off until I was face to face with him.

He was built like the Roman warrior I now knew he was. Savage, strong, and viciously breathtaking. I hadn't expected him to be so ... *large*. In every way. His legs were well defined, solid muscle that flexed when I brushed my hand across his thigh. When I let myself look at the length that I'd been pressed against, I shivered.

He was long and slightly curved. A bead of pre-cum leaked from the tip, and when I reached out to wrap my fingers around him, he choked out a strangled gasp. He didn't move, letting me explore to my heart's content. I trailed my finger up the bottom of his shaft, flinching as it twitched, and his balls pulled up.

"Aaliyah," he whispered, more groan than a word. "Gods, you're killing me."

I shivered at the desperation in his voice before I leaned forward and licked the mushroom head, hoping to hear it again.

A salty sweetness had me humming, my eyes rolling back. I wanted to make him feel good, too, but as I went to take him into my mouth, he pulled me back. "You're going to make me come if you do that, and as heavenly as your mouth sounds, I *need* you, Aaliyah."

I wanted to protest, but the way he'd said it had an entirely fresh wave of arousal sinking into my core. He was already crawling onto the bed with me again. This time, he didn't curl over me, instead sitting in a crossed legged position. I paused, unsure what to do, until he held a hand out to me.

I took it without hesitation, letting him guide me until I was seated in his lap. I was pressed flush against him, my clit dragging along the bottom of his shaft. I pressed my hand over his chest, where I felt his heart beating one soft pulse at a time, something that I'd never take for granted. When I rolled my ring and pinky finger down, he let out a shaky breath.

He brought his hand up, doing the same over my heart. We sat like that for a moment, just taking it in, every breath, and every touch. I tried to memorize every place where my skin hit his. I never wanted to forget it.

I didn't dare to move or blink. I wanted to see him, feel all of him, and it seemed he felt the same as he slowly licked his hand, getting it wet, I realized, as he reached down to rub it over his aching length.

I shivered again, using him to support me as I took a few more breaths.

He was big, something I knew already, but the sight of it so close to where he was supposed to fit suddenly made my nerves second guess themselves. I tried to pull the thoughts in, to keep them away from my hell, but I *hated* pain, hated the thought of it souring this.

Prince lifted my chin, looking into my eyes, asking again without words. When I didn't respond, he kissed me.

"You're in control, Aaliyah," he said as he lifted me gently and lined me up with him. I felt the head of his cock press against my entrance, straining against it. He didn't move farther than that, one of his hands supporting me, so I didn't sink down. "You can lower yourself, as slow as you want. We can stop. You can tell me to go run the bath, and we can cuddle in the warm water instead. *Your* pace."

His hand at my hips kept me steady, the other still pressed over my heart, his ring and pinky finger trapped between us. I could feel his heartbeat through it, the raging sound like a soothing storm.

"I'm yours, all yours." His voice cracked, and his eyes glazed. "Every heartbeat, every breath, and every word I have is yours, *Aaliyah*."

This moment, as monumental as it was to me, was the same for him, and he still held back, still waited, still *loved* me.

I braced my hands on his shoulders, pressing as close to him as I could. I needed the comfort of his touch, and when his hand tightened, I let myself fall that first inch, the initial resistance making my nose scrunch as I tensed up.

"Easy, you've got this. You can take me," Prince whispered, kissing my left wrist, shuffling just a touch. "I was made for you."

I shook, his words shocking me as the head made its way inside.

Prince's hand was a steady anchor on my hip, his thumb rubbing small circles as I breathed into the feeling of him, the unfamiliar stretch curling in my core as my brain muddled the pleasure of the previous orgasms with the dull throb of unfamiliar pain.

It wasn't as bad as I was expecting. The ache was there, but it was manageable and quickly fading away as the stretch coiled deeper inside of me. Hinting at something that he hadn't quite hit yet.

Something that left me reeling, searching for the fullness I knew he'd be able to give me.

"That's it," Prince whispered, not moving an inch. His hand against my chest trembled as he let out a breathy, *"Fuck."*

With how we were currently, I was just about eye level with him and I shuddered as I leaned forward and brought our lips together. He tasted like he smelled; molten fire and brimstone mixed with the most deliciously masculine hint of cedar.

Prince, refusing to be idle, moved his hand lower, toying with my clit, taking the edge off as I sagged into his chest. My head found the crook on his shoulder, my arms wrapping around him. My legs relaxed, my core flexing as I slid down.

Prince pulled back enough to watch, his eyes rolling back as he swallowed. He moved back to my neck, kissing the skin there, sending jolts of pleasure down my spine until I felt almost lucid. "You are so fucking beautiful, taking me like that."

His words were a balm that I tried to focus on as I heaved heavy breaths, shaking in his sure arms. I couldn't do the last few inches, not on my own. Frustration came bubbling up, the fear of inadequacy threatening to squash me. I tensed, trying and failing to gain any more ground.

Worry came flooding, my legs beginning to shake as I strained further but took no more. Fear came next, like a wave, telling me that this wasn't enough, that *I* wasn't enough. What if I couldn't take him? What if he got mad and left?

What if? What if? *What if?*

"Breathe," Prince whispered in my ear, as if he knew exactly what I was thinking, his free hand becoming liquid as it ran up and down my side, across my back in gentle caresses. His reassuring touch had me relaxing enough to slide down a bit more. "I'm not going anywhere, Aaliyah. It's just you and me. There's no need to rush or force it. This moment, every bit of it, is perfect."

Prince groaned, the sound deep in his chest as he leaned forward enough to place a tender kiss on my collarbone.

"I need you. *Please*," I whispered, not sure what else to say.

"You have me, always." He looked tortured himself, sweat curling on his brow, and it was only now I realized he was trembling. His arms and shoulders were so tense he looked like he might combust. "But I won't hurt you, Aaliyah. Not a goddamned second if I can help it. You're worth the wait. This is worth the wait. Trust me."

His finger sped up on my clit, and he leaned in to lick a trail across my neck. When he reached my jaw, he left little nips there. "Breathe into it. Let me show you how good it can feel."

His spare hand lifted to my chest, where he'd kept it holding our little symbol. I gasped as he began to rock my hips in time with his moves, slowly helping me down his thick shaft, keeping my thoughts on the bits of pleasure he brought. It was still slower than I wanted, but the pace was steady now.

When he pulled me down the final inch, there was a sharper hint of pain, one that was wiped away by the utter fullness and pride I felt. My shaking legs brushed the top of his thighs, his hands running over my back as his breath fanned over my neck. He groaned, twitching as I adjusted to get closer to him.

I didn't want to pull away as he braced one hand behind him and began to rock again. It was a movement that kept him buried deep, his hips molding with mine with every rolling thrust that ended in a delicious grind. It was gentle, a building pleasure that grew with every drag of my clit over the hot flush of his abdomen.

The pain grew into nothing more than a memory as I clung to Prince's broad shoulders. He worshiped my neck, licking and nipping as he continued his leisurely command of my body, sparing a few seconds to whisper sinfully sweet nothings into my ear. Every time he hit somewhere new inside of me, I saw stars, and when his hands went to my hips again, and he gave a harder thrust up, I cried out.

The deepness of his chuckle had me in a fit of trembles, my climax shimmering just beyond reach, starting as a vicious heat deep within my core.

"Prince," I whimpered, and he stole the breath from my lungs with a ferocious kiss, one of his hands moving to my clit again as the other found my hair, keeping me molded to him as he masterfully wove pleasure with me, wave after wave.

"Don't worry. I've got you," he whispered, panting as his head fell back, a deep groan getting lost in my lust-riddled mind. "Come for me, Aaliyah. Fucking claim me with it."

I came with him deep inside me, the rhythmic thrusting addictive as I tightened on him, his own guttural groan nearly making me come again. The heat from his release filled me with pleasant warmth.

He didn't let me go, still holding me firmly to him, brushing his hands over my skin as our breathing settled.

He slipped out of me, and a rush of liquid slid down my thighs. I wasn't ready for the empty feeling to persist, and I blushed, embarrassed until I saw Prince's face, his eyes narrowed on that combined release. He brushed his hands through it, his fingers delicate on my inner thighs. The shift in his eyes was slow, the color slipping from that silver to an all-consuming red as he pulled them back up to my core. I was sensitive enough to jolt when he pushed his fingers, still covered in cum, back up into me.

"Fuck, that's so much sexier than it should be." He groaned again, closing his eyes, his dick twitching against my leg.

"Still up for that bath you mentioned?" I panted, when he opened his eyes again, my breaths still hard as I grinned.

Prince laughed, kissing my cheek before he maneuvered us up. I was in his arms in the next second, and he walked us toward another door. "Are you kidding? This is going to be a treat. Let me show you what a *real* pamper session looks like."

PRINCE

I sat comfortably behind Aaliyah in the hot bath, toying gently with the soft strands of her hair. She sighed, sinking farther into the water.

I wasn't sure if there was a heaven, but if there was, I'd imagine it *wished* it could be this. It was like everything had fallen exactly as I needed it to, every moment, every hardship. Every tear and ache were worth it if it led to this.

Even that fucking sock potion.

I pressed a kiss to the back of Aaliyah's head, and she hummed. It was perfect ... but it was only here because Aaliyah had been through hell. Had been strapped down by the same man that had turned me.

By her own fucking blood.

"I'm sorry, Aaliyah," I suddenly whispered, the release of it something like gauze on an open wound. My pathetic apology would never be enough, not after what I'd remembered. Not after having watched what had been done to her and being able to do jack about it. "I'm sorry I wasn't able to save you."

It would haunt me forever. I hadn't remembered much beyond her, everything narrowing in on my years by her side, the good and the bad. The laughs and the unending screams.

Prince.

"None of it was your fault, Prince," Aaliyah whispered as she looked at me. Her cheeks were softly flushed, going even more red when I looked down at her. She was naked in my arms, and she still shimmied to cover herself. It was adorable. "You kept me sane when we both know I would have gone crazy alone. Please don't discount that. I wouldn't have survived without you. I wouldn't have wanted to."

I gritted my teeth, wrapping my arms around her as I set my head on her shoulder.

"I should have kept you safe," I whispered.

I should have been able to save her, to keep her from the monster that paraded himself as her blood. I never should have died ... but then, had I not, I wouldn't have found her.

I hated that thought even more.

"You can do that now," she said, so easily, but she'd always been like that, able to look ahead when everything else was crumbling. That will, that vibrancy in her, was everything. God, I didn't deserve her, didn't deserve this love or the joy of being hers, but fuck me if I wasn't going to soak it all in and earn it. "Just like I'm going to keep you safe. All of you."

Of course she would. She was a powerhouse, a literal walking bomb, but she was caring, as well, too good for the world she'd been thrown into.

I chuckled, kissing her neck, my fangs aching with how close she was. All warmth to the cool chill of my skin, sparks of heat igniting where she touched.

"I love you, Aaliyah," I whispered, needing to say it again.

I needed to say it every day, every spare second I had that wasn't spent worshiping her between her thighs like the good Prince I was. Every moment I had was hers now.

"Do you mind that I call you Prince? Or would you prefer Nero?" she asked, trailing a finger down my arm.

I hadn't really thought about it, not in the way she was thinking. I was Nero, would always be, I'd bet, but Prince was a name that I clung to. A name I treasured above all else.

"Prince is who I was when I met the love of my life. Prince is the man that fought to come back to you, that conquered death. I couldn't ask for a better name," I said simply. "The others will call me Nero, but I'll *always* be your Prince."

Because Prince was the name that made me hers.

Aaliyah swiveled in my lap, suddenly pressing against me in all the right ways. I forced a few breaths, cursing when I hardened between us against my best effort. The tender give of her under my hands was more than enough to wake the damned spry bastard between my legs, and he was more than happy to poke up and say hello. I tried to will my erection down, but it wasn't effective at all when she leaned close, her wet chest sliding against me. Her lips brushed mine with the softness of a dream. I groaned, my head tipping back as I adjusted forward, trying to give her the space to move without grinding her down on me.

Because good fucking hell did I *want* to.

"I love you, too, *my Prince*," she said, with a dashing smile and a glint of mischief in her eyes.

She didn't pull away, her legs instead sinking deeper into the warm water, her knees firmly beside my hips as she bared down and slid against the underside of my shaft. I damned near fucking choked.

I jolted, my hands gripping her sides as I hissed. My entire body tensed, lust a living thing in my veins as it stole my rational ability to think. This was supposed to be a nice bath after a passionate night.

Now all I could think about was flipping her over and fucking her again, anything to hear those sweet whimpers and feel her thrust back against me, maddened by her own lust. One thought took over, one focus on the woman who was destroying my will to be a gentleman.

She ground again, moaning in my ear.

Oh, fucking hell, I was just a man.

"If you keep doing that—" I managed, cut off by my own grunt as she did it again.

My mind blanked entirely, the hands at her hips lifting her so I could slide her back down again. My eyes focused, senses sharpening as my fangs dropped. Blood flooded my mouth where they pierced my lip, and I jerked again when Aaliyah saw it, licking her pouty lips.

"What? You'll have your way with me again?" she whispered, stumbling slightly on the words as she blushed. She brushed her hair behind her ear, fidgeting in the most adorably sexy way. "What if I wanted you to?"

The quiet confession, like everything she said, was a code I'd live by. She wanted me, and I was hers. She wanted to come again? I'd get comfortable with her legs on my shoulders and make sure it happened if it was the last thing I ever got the pleasure of fucking doing.

"You're going to be the death of me." I leaned in to lick her throat.

The water sloshed around us, hitting the floor as I easily lifted her, stealing a second to grab one of the towels I'd laid out and place it on the side of the tub, so she'd have something soft to lean against.

"A good way to die, then?" she whispered, the dark joke wily in her eyes. The pupils were blown, slits of lavender surrounding the black void.

She rolled her hips tentatively, as though she were testing her own reaction as much as my own. I gripped the sides of the bath, my fingers digging into the porcelain until it cracked as I grunted at the feel of her.

"I'd have it no other way. *Fuck*, I love you," I growled, snagging her legs to wrap around my hips. I slid my hand under the water, finding her core still soaked with arousal and my cum, something that had me leaning over her, groaning into her neck. It didn't take much for me to admit that it had me nearly savage to get inside of her again. The idea of her full of me, pumped to the brim, was enough to drive a man crazy. She cried out when I slid two fingers in, deep.

"Look at you, all spread out for me. A little treat all to myself while the others sleep the day away," I whispered, chuckling when she jolted, my fingers finding the place that made her moan so deep I felt it against my skin. Gentle pressure was all I used, keeping my palm on her clit as I rubbed back and forth against it. "Just imagine the looks on their faces if they were here."

They'd be feral, sitting ever so patiently as they waited for her to let them come to her as well. They'd stand in their own want, grinding into their palms, waiting for her to let them in ... and she would. I knew she would. She held power over monsters, over the beasts that stalked the night, and over every one of my bastard brothers.

They'd wait, then they'd feast on everything she'd give them.

"I need you," she whimpered, her head tipping back, white hair splayed around her like a shimmering halo. A bright red blush spread across her cheeks and down her slender neck, highlighting the dusting of freckles there. Tears brimmed in her eyes as her walls contracted around my fingers again. She was close, so close I could taste it.

I slowed my moves before pulling away entirely. Aaliyah protested, trying to follow me as I placed a hand on her chest, holding her in place. I lined up with her, notching at her entrance as she went completely still.

"You deserve everything, Aaliyah. All the pleasure you can handle, and we'll give it to you until you're begging for us to stop." She opened her mouth to speak before the words were ripped away by the moan that tore from her chest as I sank inside of her in one smooth thrust. "Or begging for more."

It was like coming home, finding the place where I was always meant to be. She wrapped me like a vise, and I grunted as I tried to dig deeper, finding it difficult in the slippery tub. She shook against me, her legs turning to putty as I wrapped my hands around her calves. Words weren't needed after that, as I pulled out, watching my length slide out of her, before I dove back in with another sharp thrust.

I kept that pace, slow out, fast in, grinding each time to savor the way she'd moan, until she was riding the line to her peak again. Each gasp was a symphony, each cry another memory I locked away to remember later.

She clawed my arms and chest, until I hoisted us both out of the water, keeping her impaled before her back hit the wall. The new position had her sinking down just a *hair* further. The added depth was exactly what I'd been looking for, and the way she moaned was nearly what did me in. My hips stuttered, and I had to breathe, counting back from ten as I rotated my hips. Even then, I was holding back, keeping things soft for her because after everything that had happened, she had to be sore.

Until her little fangs sank into my fucking neck.

It was like a jolt of adrenaline found its way directly into my dick, the pleasure overwhelming as my hand slammed into the wall, my eyes flushing red. A grunt forced out of me as the tile cracked under my palm, and my thrusts became little more than erratic desire. She drank from me, savoring it with little sips until my own mouth watered.

I struck before I could ask, before I could think about it, my fangs finding her throat. A sharp jolt went down my spine, as if the Eternium warned me not to push it too far, an act done in pleasure riding the line of what it would accept. If I thought her feeding from me was a new level of satisfaction, the feeling of being inside of her while we swapped blood was enough to send me to heaven.

Any gentleness fled as I fucked her with sharp thrusts that left her reeling. She released my neck at the same time she clamped down on me, her head thrown back in a choked cry that I had to see.

I licked bloodied lips, my hips stuttering before I came, too, deep inside of her again. Exactly where I was meant to be. I ground my hips, twitching and writhing at the thought of filling her again.

Fuck me, did I have a breeding kink?

Our breathing was heavy, the room smelling of sex and steam as she leaned forward and licked the wound on my neck that had already started healing. I did the same, clearing the blood from her shoulder with sure licks that had her shaking against me, clenching on my shaft and keeping me hard inside of her.

I placed both hands beside her head, brushing my nose against hers, before ink caught my eye.

"Guess that cleared that up," I said, humming as I admired the lavender band that now wrapped around my wrist. Aaliyah eyed it with wonder before looking at her own. My mark on her was a deep black that matched the others, sharp points and the appearance of feathers reminding me of Rome. "Told you I'd look amazing with your ink on my arm."

She smiled at me, pressing her hand to my chest. "I'm glad."

"I never doubted I was yours, Aaliyah. This just proves it." The worry she'd felt about it was gone. Something I'd known was going to be an issue, anyway. At least this we could be sure about. I looked between us, at the mess we'd made of ourselves and the once-quaint little washroom. "Now, you need another bath."

She blushed, shaking her head with a laugh. "Whose fault is that?"

"Surprisingly, not mine. Well, not *entirely* mine. I say I'm at least twenty percent innocent," I mused, smiling broadly when Aaliyah's laughs grew belly deep.

I placed her on the counter, not wanting to make her try to stand after that, and moved back to the bath, emptying it before refilling it with fresh, steaming water. I added some more scent and hid where my hand marks had dug into the shiny white porcelain with some spare towels.

Like it had never happened, and if Osiris asked, I was going to blame Fallon.

"I love you," she whispered from behind me.

I shivered at the words, looking over my shoulder at her. She sat so regally, her hair falling over her pale shoulders in stunning waves, framing where her hand was placed over her chest, with the ring and pinky finger down.

There wasn't anything I wouldn't do for her.

"I love you, too. Aaliyah," I whispered, my fingers already falling to the language we'd made. "*Forever.*"

Chapter 28

Aaliyah

Prince was curled around me, his chest to my back, his fingers intertwined with mine, the same way they'd been last night when we finally went back to sleep. The steady thrum of his heartbeat was a mantra I leaned into, cherishing it as the lull of sleep faded away, just like the chill in front of me that slowly registered as another person.

I blinked once, twice, before smiling.

Dark sooty lashes fanned over pale cheeks, and Adrian snored softly. His hair was disheveled, his upper body exposed where he'd shoved off the blankets from last night when he must have crept in. He still slept blissfully, one of his hands draped over my hip, one of his legs wedged between mine, and his face so close I could see the flutter of his eyes behind his closed lids ... and where the gentle slope of his high cheekbones were marked with vicious black lines that stretched from his eyes along the veins on his face. They reached down his neck, covering his skin in savage patterns that looked raw. I'd hoped that my blood would help them heal from their encounter with Archon.

It hurt to know it hadn't.

I settled farther into Prince's arms as I reached up to Adrian's face. I pressed my fingertips against those lines, achingly careful as I traced them out, willing them to fade away. He looked so sweet, the softness in the rise and fall of his chest settling like a warmth in my belly that contrasted with the ache I still felt for him.

I hummed, continuing to trail as Adrian's face scrunched up.

"Having fun, love?" he grumbled, peeking one eye open, smiling lazily at me as I moved to twirl a piece of his hair around my finger. "Did you mind me joining you? I ... I really needed to hold you."

A surge of protectiveness grabbed hold of me at the vulnerability in his cracked words, one that pushed me to move. Adrian swallowed as I leaned forward to claim his lips. It should have been odd, kissing him while Prince cuddled against my back, but it felt as natural as breathing. I needed it, too, the reassurance of his presence. The last few days had been a hurricane of the worst kind. Having him here was all I'd wanted. The only thing that would make it better would be having the rest of my men here, too.

It would take nothing short of the Hallowed Themselves to pull me away from them now that I got them back.

The kiss ended as quickly as it started, a brush that left my body on fire and both of us pulling in shortened breaths. He'd gotten closer, until he was chest to chest with me, erasing the last of the space between us as I laid my forehead on his bare skin.

"I'm glad you came. I love waking up to you," I whispered, blushing when Adrian groaned and turned his face into the pillow before whispering something I couldn't hear.

"God, I'm lucky I can't blush," he mumbled, and I laughed, trying not to wake up Prince.

An act that failed, as the body at my back grunted, soft lips finding the curve of my neck as he nibbled at the space there. A pleasurable, full body shiver racked its way down my spine as I felt the imprint of fangs. "Five more minutes."

"I see you're still not a morning person," Adrian hummed, laughing again when Prince grumbled.

"I'm about this close to making you bleed if you don't go back to sleep, Adrian." His voice was gruff, clouded with irritation as he pulled me closer to him, curling around me so he was touching every bit of me he could. "I said five more minutes."

He was already snoring again when Adrian's head tipped back in a hearty laugh.

"Now, none of that. There's breakfast to be made, and I have a feeling our girl is rather famished." Adrian wiggled his eyebrows as I ducked my head.

I wasn't ashamed of what I'd done with Prince, but that look always had the tendency to make me blush. Memories of the night prior had me shuffling, trying not to accidentally grind on Adrian's leg as Prince chuckled. His arms tightened around me before he was standing. The abrupt loss was a daze, and I looked over my shoulder just as he stretched out his arms, raising them above his head, and giving me a wonderful view of a toned back.

He was a piece of art, every dip and curve on him something I wanted to savor, and touch again. Suddenly, I was hungry for something a little different from the food Adrian promised. My thighs clenched, and the delicious soreness between my legs made itself apparent. I shouldn't have wanted another round, not after the *three* we'd had —the third catching me by surprise after we'd lain down, Prince at my back, sliding in without resistance, making love to me slowly as he'd whispered to me. Never anything too heavy, or sinful ... just my name. The way he said it was somehow the sexiest thing I'd ever heard. I should be too worn out for more.

But that didn't mean seeing him like that didn't make my mouth water all over again.

He must have known I was staring, that little piece of him that was attuned to me letting him know as he looked over his shoulder. The twist of Cheshire lips was deepened by a look that promised everything I wanted would come true ... if I just said so.

Until my stomach grumbled, and both he and Adrian chuckled at the sound.

"Food it is. Everything else can wait," Prince said, smirking as he shrugged on a shirt.

Adrian sat up next, bare from the waist up, every inch of skin flexing as he rolled his shoulders and stretched away the lingering effects of sleep, begging for me to reach out and touch. I hesitated for only a moment until his hand grabbed mine, and he pushed it flush against the skin of his abdomen.

The shock from his touch was enough to make me gasp, the

muscles there rippling as he chuckled and leaned in. His fingers trembled around my wrist.

"Food first, Ali. We can play later," he whispered, his lips suddenly flush against mine.

His kiss demanded my attention, and I savored every second of it before he pulled back. The part of my brain that wasn't muddled with lust tried to come to the forefront. The need in me was overwhelming, something I'd never experienced so acutely before.

Control was something I'd grown very used to having, but this felt ... feral.

"It's the blood exchange. It's got you both wired. That's why you're still feeling so feverish," Adrian filled in, without me having to ask. The lust had faded to the background of his voice, a gentleness to it that followed in the brush of his fingers against my heated skin. "It'll fade. Though ... there are some activities that can help with it."

One suggestive tone, and a trail of his finger over my jaw, and I was lost again. His words dug in, my mouth watering as the fangs there itched to find a place in his skin.

"Can you guys stop teasing? I'm really not going to be leaving this room if you don't." Prince's husky words got me moving sluggishly, because as much as I did want to do exactly what he'd said, I *was* starving.

Adrian helped me find my clothes—and "helped" me put them on, almost derailing us again—before we all headed out to the main living room. He didn't let me go, keeping his hand tucked firmly in mine, brushing his lips against the back with an indulgent smile. Just like last night, it had changed again, though this time the differences were much less noticeable.

The wallpaper was a couple of shades darker, the furniture more toward the tastes that I had seen at the Vivas house in smaller ways, like the table that was now reminiscent of the old oak that I'd grown so used to sitting at. Even the décor on the walls had changed, small paintings and flashes of color to break up the blank space.

It breathed homey, like things had been placed with care and not spawned by an ever-shifting Eternium.

"When will it stop changing?" I asked, looking around as Prince wrapped his arm over my shoulders, and Adrian's hand settled on my back.

"When it's found all that it's looking for," a cryptic voice said.

Had the gnarled tone not given them away, the taste of boggy water that suddenly flooded my mouth would have. Magelav had an air about them, a power that crept up on you and hid behind the crazed shadows in their eyes. I had a feeling they rivaled Osiris's, even Sebek's, and the way they spoke, the echoing tone of their voice ...

Bog. That had been their word, their warning that I hadn't been able to see coming for what it was.

I turned to see them standing in the doorway, the hall empty behind them. They picked at their talon-like nails, flicking the grime onto the floor with disinterest. Their eyes had changed again, shifting to a vicious rouge that popped against ivory skin and ink-like hair. It was the feral gleam in them that got me, that froze me to the spot.

"Ah, good morning, Mags. Haunting as always," Prince said, kissing the top of my head before walking over to the kitchen. He barely even blinked at the odd behavior, not seeing how Magelav turned a sour glare his way. "Any other words of wisdom, or can I drink some coffee in peace?"

Adrian and I followed, watching the Sorceri warily as we walked. The kitchen was broken into two main parts, with a dining table and a set of counters that wrapped around the space in a *C*. There were several stools next to the counter, facing the living room, and I took a seat just in time for a chill to spread down my spine.

Red danced among us, and I took a second to settle in his presence. Ghosts weren't new to me, but that didn't stop me from shivering even as I smiled at the lazy way Red prodded against me. It was so different from how Prince had behaved, from how he'd felt. There was character to the way Red almost joked, his emotions closer to the surface. More savage, more raw, like it was all that was left of him.

"Aaliyah, is there a ghost here?" Prince asked, suddenly brushing the back of his head like he felt something lying there.

His face scrunched, and Red hovered over him, almost teasing until Prince was swatting again.

"Yes. Red," I said, grinning and trying not to laugh as Prince scowled and flipped around like he might find Red standing there. "You can see him?"

Prince shook his head, now holding up his coffee mug in front of him like it might ward off a mischievous spirit. It didn't, as Red took the challenge in stride, moving to Prince's back to prod again.

This was probably the most physical I'd ever seen him, an outline of a body, even the smooth features that could almost be distinguished as a face.

"No ... just. I can *feel* him, all cold and dead like. Have since I found you," Prince grumbled, rubbing his eyes. "Not to mention the brushes I'm getting off of him. The bastard."

Red seemed to light up at that, agitation suddenly bubbling up from him as he pressed more incessantly on Prince. For a second ... it even looked like Prince's hair moved, and Prince snarled as he ruffled it back out.

"Like what?" I asked, curious as to what he meant.

Red swayed away, swirling around me once again, his form dusting the air in front of me. Almost a caress, like an apology. I couldn't very well be mad at him, and he seemed to know that as he settled comfortably around me, almost like a shawl on my shoulders.

Or a cat on my lap.

Prince just grumbled again, sipping his coffee, before Red dashed at that, too, causing Prince's hand to slip, sloshing the drink onto his fingers.

I had to physically hold in the laugh as Prince's face grew taut, and a vein showed on his forehead. "Nothing. I'm just glad he's dead. We have enough competition as it is for your attention."

The door I'd been sleeping behind before going to find Prince slid deftly open, and Fallon stepped through, rubbing his hazy eyes. The rich green was clouded, his nose scrunching as the lights in the kitchen beamed down at him. He covered his face, swatting as if trying to brush the rays away. His hair was ruffled, and even with a scowl, he looked adorably sleepy, a fact I would stow away so he might never get wiser about it. It was like watching a switch flip when he looked up, finding me. His eyes lightened, the green softening as his shoulders lost some of their rigid tension. He crossed the room in a few long strides.

I leaned into him without hesitation, kissing him softly when he reached me. His lips were icy, and he held me there for a few brief seconds, short and sweet, just like the lazy smile that lit up his lips as he brushed his thumb over my cheek. "Good morning, Ali."

The black lines that had graced his skin were mostly faded now, a bit more than Adrian's, though the ones that had been more prominent shone through. He didn't limp, per se, not in any way that anyone beyond me would recognize, but there was an ache to his step, a pain that was hidden in the tremor of muscles as he tried to hide it behind a stoic facade.

I reached up to trace one of the lines, preening as he leaned into the touch. I'd have to see about giving them another dose of blood.

"Good morning, Fallon," I whispered back.

Prince hummed happily from the kitchen, bickering with Adrian as our resident chef mumbled something about making the food. I was more than content to stay like this until Fallon told me to pull away, and from the look on his face, that wouldn't be anytime soon.

But suddenly, and with basically no warning, I was out of my chair, gasping as I was settled into another set of arms. The initial shock and burst of fear faded as I caught the scent of the sea and saw Eirik's ink-covered skin. I laughed as I was pulled to his chest, a bubbling purr bursting under my ear. "Eirik, put me down!"

His nose ran along my jaw, and I could feel the smile that graced his lips as he doubled down, his nose trailing along my neck before burying in my hair.

"What's with you and holding me recently?"

There was a distinct playfulness to him, a wildness that told me it wasn't him in control. That was only confirmed when his voice lit the air. "**I hold you because you're *mine*.**"

His beast nipped at my neck, as if pushing me to join in and do the same. The want to do just that was buried by only one thing, the pain that split down my neck, from behind my ear where Eirik had moved.

The blocker that Sebek had placed there, to keep me from using my gifts ... I'd forgotten about it. With everything else that happened, the remains of the spell just hadn't been at the forefront of my mind. It pulsed beneath the skin as my mouth flooded with saliva and I grew dizzy, held up only by Eirik as the room swayed around me.

"*Elskan?*" Eirik said gruffly, his voice a blend of him and the beast.

His nose touched the mark, and I jolted away with a gasp. A strangled noise worked its way up Eirik's throat before I was suddenly on a couch. "What happened?"

Firm hands tilted my head, and I struggled to stay still under Eirik's sharp gaze as he inspected the mark there. I hadn't had a chance to look at him yet, really look. The others showed their experience in the marks on their skin, but Eirik seemed startlingly calm about his time at Archon's. His body was healed, his demeanor unchanged ... but I didn't like the shadows under his eyes or the tension that didn't seem right in the clench of his jaw.

He didn't give me time to ask as he got too close, a spark of residual power arcing off and singeing his skin. His curse was pointed as he jerked his hand away.

"Sebek put something in to stop me from fighting," I said, as I reached up, pressing my fingers against the tender mark. It pulsed under my hand, and I shivered. "I thought I broke it."

I kept the fact that it had been the severing of their bonds, the fading of the ink from my wrist, that had been the final straw that had cracked through, breaking it. It was a pain I held too close to my chest, one I didn't want to burden them with after their own ordeal.

A clicked tongue sounded before Magelav had taken the space of Eirik. "Curious. A block. Still active, if not cracked."

It wasn't as if the Sorceri had pushed him; they hadn't even moved, but Eirik faded away, replaced with Magelav as they tilted my head. They used more force, were more vicious with their prod as the magic reacted to how close they were.

"Needs to come out. There is no Reaper without its claws." The pain was instant as their fingers brushed against the raw skin, and I grit my teeth as I tried to jerk away from their hold.

Tension built, fangs falling as I was surrounded by blood-red eyes. The others snarled out threats, and my head throbbed. I lost their words to Magelav's as they glared at each one of them, not letting me go. "She leaks magic, the *killing* kind. I thought you liked her alive?"

Fallon was the one who stepped forward, a vein popping on his forehead, the dark black marks on his face growing more vicious. The rage there simmered openly, not hidden by a mask of ice, his eyes a frantic gleam. A spark danced along his skin, the *Flame* crisping his shirt. He bared his fangs, his entire body tense as he stood toe to toe with Magelav, snarling. "Get the fuck away from her."

A pin could have dropped, and tensions grew in the room as Magelav's hand tightened on my chin. The spark of a response started in their eyes, their mouth opening to spew what had to be venom.

One look told me they would fight; one look told me we couldn't afford for them too.

"What do we need to do to get it out? The right way?" I asked, breaking the tension as I reached for Fallon.

His jaw tensed, hesitation a visible war on his face as he ground his teeth, before he jerked his head away from Magelav's wicked stare and walked to me. I relaxed when his palm fell onto mine, trembling as he rubbed his thumb over the back of my hand.

Magelav grunted, pulling back and shaking their head.

"A block to stop it from spreading further, a knife for the skin. A sever for the broken magic," Magelav counted off, sounding bored as they turned away. They mulled over the words for a moment more before looking at me curiously. "Something to bite so you don't squirm."

Their hands opened, something like leather appearing there. It was a thin strip, a black bind that I would have sworn I saw the wary groves of teeth marks in, carved in the material like a remembrance of the past.

Pressure found a place behind my eyes, toying with the sight in front of me, shifting it, warping the hands that held it into that of a monster. Castillion replaced Magelav as I stumbled back, his face lined with a sickening sweetness.

Never make noise.

The room dulled, color becoming shades of gray, coiling around me until I couldn't breathe. There was a brush against my face, like cold fingers or the bite of metal on my cheeks.

They get more violent if I make noise.

"Look at me, Aaliyah," a voice whispered, cracking from Castillion's lips, which didn't move with the words, before he was blocked from me entirely. A face that had dragged me back from hell itself a thousand times more than I could count took his place as sharp silver eyes and unruly brown hair filled my vision. "You're not there. You're *not* there."

I blinked slowly, looking around with shaky breaths. I'd managed to back myself off the couch, and I choked on the words that I tried to get out. I could disassociate before, remove myself from the memories that didn't quite feel real. That wasn't the case anymore, not now that I'd felt the steel table under my back and stared into the harsh lights that had burned my eyes day in and day out.

A brush of cold sent a chill down my spine, and Red helped me to swallow as he pressed against me. There was a comfort to be found in his presence. His encouragement kept me moving. "It's all I can see, Prince."

When I closed my eyes, I felt Sebek's hand on my wrist, dragging me forward as he pulled me through the doors I'd agreed to walk through.

I thought I'd be fine, that I'd pushed away the memories like I'd done so many times before. Still, they lingered, and still they haunted me.

Never make noise.

"It's gone now. Burned to ashes with everything inside of it, Aaliyah. I promise," he swore, clearing some of the panic, but I couldn't fight off the inkling in the back of my head, the worry that it'd find a way back.

It didn't have to be around in a physical sense; it lived in me now, was a part of me in ways I wasn't sure I would be able to get rid of.

But Prince's sure face made me trust him, and I hoped that step by step, one day I might be free of Ascension. The physical bonds, and the ones that trapped my mind.

"Mags has not the time for drivel," Magelav drawled, and I looked up at them.

Prince had taken their place in front of me, and it was like watching him grasp for patience as he swallowed, his nose flaring as he looked at Magelav over his shoulder. "Mags, have you ever—in your *many* years of life—considered learning how to read a room?"

Mags didn't have a response for that, just scowled.

A moment later, Adrian was by my side, his gentle fingers pulling back my ear to inspect the wound. I let him, not hesitating to move as he adjusted me to see it better. "It looks ... infected."

"Magic doesn't like bonds," Magelav replied.

Adrian hummed, gently letting my ear go. "Tell me what to do. I'll get it out."

He rolled up his sleeves, showing the softly defined muscle along his arms as he did. He tapped his wrist twice before he went back to inspecting the mark.

Magelav's laugh was bitter. "*You*? She's better off leaving it."

"You seem to be under the assumption I was asking." Adrian's voice was forcefully bright, his stance protective as he joined Prince to block me from Magelav's view. "I was training to be a doctor before I was turned. I'm the *only* one I trust to get it out. Fallon, pain meds and a knife, one that's been boiled?"

Fallon nodded once before he was gone. Seconds later, he was back with a box in hand, a soft scent of gas lingering on him. Adrian searched through it, grumbling before pulling out a bottle of pills. He counted them out, looking worried before he handed me three.

I knew this was going to hurt, regardless of the medicine he gave me, but I took them anyway, to make him feel better. I still traced the lines on his face, the worry that crept into his smile as he tried to hide his own fear. "You won't hurt me."

I could take the pain, mine and his. The dark marks on his face stretched when he grimaced. "Never, love. I'll do all I can to make it quick."

I nodded, smiling at him as I took his hand. I brought it to my lips, kissing the back of his knuckles while we waited.

"I know," I whispered, sitting up so he could have better access. It was a tense few moments before Fallon returned once again with a hot knife. I nodded to them both, doing my best to smile. "I'm ready."

Magelav grunted from somewhere on the other side of the room. "Wow, so sophisticated. Should Mags get a plague mask?"

Adrian didn't respond, just looked to Magelav to begin their part, before I felt a weight settle in the air. Their magic spread through the room, the heavy scent of boggy water making my eyes water. It seemed slower to come forward than their other spells, almost reluctantly.

"You can't move. Understand?" Magelav whispered, the strain in their voice emphasized by the grunt they gave as a bead of sweat formed on their forehead. "Spell is ready. I'll hold the binding together as long as I can. It will fight you."

Adrian nodded, and I noted the glove on his hands, the knife that he clutched gently in his deft fingers. I had to close my eyes, block away the image that it dragged to the forefront of my mind.

This was Adrian. A man I loved. A man I trusted.

I took a steadying breath that cinched my lungs before a warm body settled at my back.

"Eirik?" I whispered as one of his hands settled on my hip, the other laying palm down over my mouth. It kept him out of Adrian's way, while still holding me.

"You're not fighting this alone. Take what you need, give me the pain," he said, his thumb brushing over my nose. "We're here."

I let out a breath, ready to fight the suggestion, when his wrist touched my mouth. His pulse was a steady beat under his skin, unhurried, as he settled firmly against my back. His breath hitched, a steady thrum starting in his chest as his purr soothed the remaining anxiety I held.

Fallon squeezed my hand, never having let go.

I nodded softly, my mouth watering as I ran my tongue over the thin skin. I bit Eirik carefully, slowly sinking fangs deep as the taste of him lit up inside of me, stars blinking behind my eyes. There was a question of starting, and I nodded, still attached to Eirik's wrist.

The first cut of the blade was enough to drag me out of the euphoria, freezing me as the pain turned sharp.

"Almost got it," Adrian whispered.

I held on, staying completely still as Magelav chanted in the background. Sweat pooled on my neck, a clammy chill making my hands shake as my fangs slid back into my gums.

"Hold on, trouble," Fallon said, as I clenched onto Eirik's wrist, using him as a weight to keep myself steady.

Several seconds later, Adrian's cry of triumph had me sagging into Eirik's chest. He vibrated beneath me, his beast soothing me without words.

"This was what was inside her? It's so tiny," Adrian said before Magelav took it from his hand.

It was just a small thing, barely a few centimeters long. Magelav was much more careful with their handling of it, watching as the blood dried. Their magic came forward, and the bead grew red hot as my blood burned off it, until only the strange seed was left.

"Kali was crafty. Her magic, her power, her greed," Magelav explained.

Before promptly popping it into their mouth and chewing. I heard the crunch, saw the burst of magic from the seams of their mouth as they swallowed the remains whole.

Silence was a friend as we all stared-slack jawed.

"Mags, I thought we talked about eating random shit." Prince groaned as he rubbed his temples, breaking the silence as Magelav showed a dangerous smile lined with razor-sharp teeth. "You're going to get sick one of these days, and I don't think there's a doctor alive that'd be able to help."

The wound behind my ear began to close, the skin stitching together as my body registered the lack of foreign magic.

It was almost numbing, as though there had been an ache I was ignoring, something I'd pushed out of my mind. Now that it was gone, I felt it. Persistent, irritating.

One of the marks on my wrist began to itch, the ancient font woven with archaic swirls. I squeezed Fallon's hand as I closed my eyes, leaning my cheek into Eirik's palm. "Where's Osiris?"

"He went to go get Drakon," Eirik whispered, silencing the rest of the room.

"The Eternium starts tonight, right? Officially?" I asked, and each of them nodded.

I pulled in a shallow breath. This was it. The start of the last fight. The beginning of what I could only hope was the end. Ascension Rising had started this, *Sebek* had started this.

Now we had to end it.

I hated the part of me that still saw Sebek as the man who lived in the stories my father used to whisper fondly to get me to sleep. That wasn't the man who had made these men. That wasn't the man who had locked me up and saw me tortured.

"When the clock strikes midnight, the devils make their deals," Mags whispered, their eyes hazing over, a shadowed look in them.

"That means yes, I think," Prince whispered, as he crossed the small distance to me, taking the seat by my side.

"Tonight's mostly an informal declaration and a lovely little masquerade ball. The First Rights, when everyone is allowed to officially call for Challenges and Retaliations, starts in three days' time," Adrian chimed in, placing a plate in my lap. The pasta was slightly cold now, covered in a white sauce with bits of green sprinkled throughout. "Come on, love, nothing to be done about it now. Eat something. You need it," he whispered, kissing the top of my head.

At the end of the day, whatever happened tonight would lead the way into the rest of the Eternium. Our lives were on the line, heads already hanging over the block under the executioner's ax.

There was still so much I didn't know, so much that hung in the balance. There was a very real possibility that if we failed here, we'd end up dead. Or worse.

Those black lines on his skin sank home for me, and I picked at my food in silence.

CHAPTER 29

OSIRIS

Quiet halls were a guilty pleasure in a place like this.

I trailed my hand along the wall, testing the give of the magic that held it together. I'd never thought to assess the limits of the Eternium before, to see if I could feel what bound each brick together. Unsurprisingly, it was hardy, a power well so deep no amount of searching would find the end to it, which meant there were no cracks to dig into, no pieces that I might exploit and no way into The Pits that didn't involve me being sent there.

I struggled to keep my hand up, to dig into the magic I'd kept locked down for so long. It was like reaching out for something that was no longer mine, for a gift that had long ago been stolen from me. It made me sick, still squeezing my lungs, stealing my ability to breathe.

I let my hand fall, the hall morphing in minute shifts that I could hear in the air and feel in the magic of the mountain. The Eternium was an astonishing piece of architecture and art, one that glowed like the finest of gems as it walked me to where I needed to be. I didn't move with any destination in mind, only intent on getting Drakon before heading back to the others.

"Osiris."

The voice broke me free from my thoughts, sealing the air in my lungs as my breath stopped. All semblances of life fled from me, my eyes narrowing, my hands shaking at my sides. I knew it, ingrained in every part of me he'd molded to his liking. I knew that voice like I knew the darkest parts of myself. The same parts that had killed Kali, that were still strapped to his bed, begging him to leave me be as another hand trailed across unwilling skin.

I turned slowly, not sure if I'd actually heard him speak, but when he came into view, I nearly puked.

Darius the Great, in all his glory. Seeing him was bound to happen. Even at the other Eterniums, it had been a surety. I'd hoped it'd be later, in a place where others were, when I had time to prepare. Instead, it was in the middle of an empty hall, with only air between us.

He wasn't flashy or larger than life ... he wasn't different from any other man I might see in these halls or walking down a dreary city street. From dark black hair that seemed dull in the lighting to his soulless brown eyes that leered at me, touching like his hands used to. A powerful build hid behind the glamor of the gem-lined and billowing golden robe he'd worn religiously for as long as I'd known him. He stood several inches shorter than me, and even with the heels he had tucked in his boots, he wasn't able to look eye to eye. It was enraging how startlingly *boring* he was.

And it was an embarrassment that I still felt small under his furious gaze.

"Don't just stand there. Explain yourself. You were supposed to be here ages ago with Kali. Where is she?" he demanded, his voice a curse.

My heart thundered, my ears suddenly ringing as I turned to face him entirely.

Suddenly, I wasn't me again, like when I'd first come face to face with Kali. He'd always been worse. His hands, his voice, his *touch*. The way he moved.

The brand on my wrist burned, and I covered it on instinct, recoiling when he glowered at my hiding of his mark.

"I don't know where your wretched witch is," I whispered.

His face burned red, and I saw the flash of the Griffon beneath his skin. Darius had been the Mythic Eternal for eons, longer than I'd been alive, and seeing the flash of the beast that had shredded the skin off my bones more than once was enough to send me spiraling into fight-or-flight. Long ago, I would have turned tail and run, exactly like he wanted, so he could let his beast out to play.

"She came to collect me. I turned her down. I haven't seen her since."

I wasn't the same man that had cowered under his and Kali's palm like a little ant, dancing in hopes it would please him enough to be lenient. I was more. I had more, and I'd never take that for granted again. I might not be the perfect protector I'd fought so hard to be, but I'd do anything I could to keep my family safe. I might drop, but I would do it fighting.

"Tell me where she is, Osiris. I won't ask again." Chilled words and the thick push of a rageful aura would have been enough to make a weaker me bow, but I wasn't the same as I was the last time we'd met. A part of me was rebuilt now, stronger, *loved*. He couldn't hurt me here, and that I could use. "You know better than to cross me like this. I've been lenient. Do you intend to make me regret that?"

A shiver followed the *Flame* across my skin as my eyes went red, and my fangs ached to drop. It flashed against my skin, burning into me like an open flame over paper.

"You do *not* own me, not anymore, Darius," I said, searing every word into him. I wanted to rush forward, my body begging for his blood, but the Eternium stopped me, literally holding me in place as it felt my murderous intent. I pushed it so hard the veins on my forehead popped, but still, I didn't move. "You should do better keeping your hounds in check. They're not my problem."

There was no give, and I didn't want to see his sickening face anymore. Every time I looked at it, I just remembered that room, remembered the hands and the words that had stolen my soul for centuries.

I flipped around, Darius talking after me but not following, quiet, calm. "You may be safe here, but the Eternium only lasts so long. This will not stand."

Kali wouldn't be there, and there was a steady calm to Darius's voice telling me he already knew that, too. I couldn't find it in me to be remorseful. Kali was gone, and I'd never felt lighter. The only thing that would free me, truly free me, was if Darius joined her.

I walked in a haze after that, coming up on a door that I knew held what I was looking for. I walked in without knocking, and I only realized I was still leaking power when everyone in the room gasped, stepping away from me.

Whatever conversation they'd been having fell off, the room suddenly silent, the faces going pallid. More than I would expect from just my appearance. A few I knew, those of the Alderi Demon Horde were here, Vidius passing me a nod of his head. Adathan, the Angel Eternal, a man who beat most of the Eternium in age, looked on with vivid curiosity and a begrudging respect I'd long ago earned.

Though most I ignored, looking to Drakon.

It was time, and I wasn't in the mood to dawdle.

"Osiris, ever heard of knocking?" Drakon asked, the brash Dragonkin crossing his arms as he stepped forward. "Or is that beneath you, oh *mighty Kingslayer*?"

It was a dominant display that rattled my instincts, and after the run in with Darius, I found I couldn't hold them back as I let the bonds on my gifts loosen.

A spark of lightning flashed across the room, shattering the lights one by one as I stepped up to him, face to face. "Am I interrupting something, Drakon?"

His bravado wavered, but he didn't back down, a trait I was slowly growing to despise as he sneered. I could practically see the tail behind him swinging as one of the members of his Clutch walked to his side.

He wasn't one I knew, with long black hair and steely black eyes that watched my every move. His face was strong, with the broad characteristics of early Arabic descent, likely around the same age as Eirik and easily just as large. He stood silently, a quiet guardian here to add some consequence.

The Enforcer, no doubt.

It didn't spark fear in me, not in the way he was hoping, but I respected the attempt, nonetheless. It cooled my blood, in a way.

"Nothing that pertains to our deal," Drakon added resolutely.

I didn't have the patience to deal with an uprising, not after we'd already done his dirty work. We'd made it too far for that.

"I would hope not. The last thing either of us wants after the death of Kri'Valta, is another enemy," I said, waving toward the door, keeping a tight leash on the *Flame* as he nodded.

The clench in his jaw told me he wanted to do more, to bite back with an insult of his own, but we both knew who would win that fight.

He was smart enough to hold his tongue.

"Come, we have business," I said, turning around, knowing he'd follow.

"And I'm in the middle of something," he snorted, but still obeyed my order, the one he'd called Aldric close behind, with the black-haired Enforcer right on his heels.

"I wasn't asking, Drakon," I added, as I checked my watch, reading the time. An hour before midnight. "If I call, you *follow.*"

"Jesus, you need to let off some steam or something," he retorted, the sound of a door closing behind us. "Anyone ever told you that you're fucking insufferable?"

I didn't give him anything else, eyes on the time as it glared back at me from my wrist.

One hour to hell.

CHAPTER 30

AALIYAH

Our once-quiet room had grown into something that breathed chaos, filled with panicked chatter and seemingly endless tension. Others had found their way in, people I hadn't expected to see, some I didn't know. One of them got too close—a man that towered over most of the room, with tall colorful frills that flared over the top of his head—and I flinched away, deeper into Eirik's arms as he snapped his teeth.

I waited for bloodshed, for a body to hit the ground as it had at Kri'-Valta's Gala. My lungs froze, fighting to take in oxygen as the room spun around me. It took far too long for my heart to calm down, and for the fight-or-flight response to settle.

There were barely enough people here now to be considered a group. A crowd was going to kill me. The thought of it made me sick.

Eirik's cheek brushed against the back of my head, his purr a steady cadence that I focused on as a snarl ripped through the air. It wasn't one I knew, the sound feral in its tone, and the hair on the back of my neck stood.

"Magelav, you beautiful fool, I've missed you," Xander cooed, standing in front of the one making the sound. He half leaned in as if to hug Magelav. "I do love the new look. It's dashing."

The surly Chronomancer for once looked something other than crazy as their face contorted, splattering with red as their teeth gritted.

Followed directly by them *spitting* in Xander's face.

"Dryad. Why are you here? You are never here," Magelav hissed without any break, and Xander just laughed, brushing off his face without a care, licking his lips with a pleased smile.

Xander was an image I remembered all too well, the glaring white of his suit a contrast to the forest green accents that lined it, matching his eyes down to the hue. There was a mischievous glint to them as he stared down Magelav, an unmistakable softness there, too, as his lips tilted into a lazy smile, and he tucked his hands into his pockets. His lips pursed, his shoulders shrugging up as he leaned in to whisper. "Neither are you, my love. Yet here *we* are."

The room suddenly tasted metallic as Magelav's eyes flashed gold.

"They know each other?" Adrian asked, apparently too loud, as Xander's head tipped back, and he laughed.

It was a rich sound, one that reminded me of the forest around the Vivas house, an endless and dangerous mix of dark shadows and tempting light. Even that sound, so natural, held a weight that I couldn't describe.

Power wasn't new to me, but I'd never seen this much in one room, this many individuals with their own feats and victories. This many that could build something new.

This many that could destroy the hope we held for this Eternium.

"Oh, quite well," Xander said, responding to Adrian's question without even looking at him.

"Barely at all. Nothing more than passing time," Mags added with a scoff, never losing the grit to their teeth or the vein that popped along their jaw.

Xander shook his head with a 'tsk'. "I've known you mentally, physically, and biblically. There's not a person alive or dead that knows you better than me, Magelav," Xander pressed again, the smile slipping away for the briefest of seconds, a flash of history that could have been missed with little more than a blink. "Not even yourself."

Something told me he liked to cause chaos, especially where Mags was concerned. I thought they might pop a vein when they turned to face Xander fully. They were shorter than the Dryad by a couple of inches and were almost reminiscent of an angry kitten as their lips pulled back into another snarl. Their look was much like a wolf in sheep's clothing, hiding the power that I knew hid just below the surface of their skin.

"Then forget, you daft *cumberworld*!" Mags screamed.

The silence was almost deafening in the absence of words as Magelav heaved heavy breaths. Their hands were bunched into tight fists, years of conflict stored in the malice in their eyes.

Eirik's arm wrapped around my shoulder as magic flooded the room. It felt different from any other I'd sensed before. It sang, humming softly like the flap of bees' wings. It was like a stream of water that kept moving, never staying in one place for too long.

It even got the attention of Red as he fluttered. For a moment, I even thought I could see him. It was enough to draw all my attention to every fine detail. Strong jaw, a narrow waist, the ruffle of long hair on the top of his head.

Then he was gone again.

"Well, that was uncalled for. I can take up plenty of space. Need I remind you—" Xander didn't get to finish, as Mags cut him off.

"*Why* are you here, Axandre? You do not belong; the fates do not wish it."

Xander crossed his arms, tapping his chin with a long middle finger. The pointed nail on the end glimmered green, as though an emerald instead of shimmering paint. "You and I both know the fates do what they will. You just see the strings. I'm here, because you're here, Mags. You've been ignoring me."

"Is this really a lovers' quarrel? Can we do this some other time?" Prince asked, and both snapped their heads toward him.

He raised his arms in mock defeat as Xander snorted. I expected him to say something about Prince, to mention the fact that he was here, but his lips just tilted in a knowing grin. Though I didn't like the look in his eyes as he stared.

"Oh, don't worry. My being here is worth your precious time. After all, contrary to Magelav's words, I'm not useless. Heidel is only Nymph Eternal because I don't Challenge him for it. He'll listen to me, or he'll die. Fair enough?" Xander asked, a bit of what I'd seen at the meeting at his home sneaking through.

He stood confident, with his shoulders back like a proud statue that had weathered every storm that had come at it, and this was just another bout of wind. I wasn't going to be the one to say anything else about it. He was a brash man who pushed a little too hard. He felt like a snake, like someone we probably shouldn't trust, but in the grand scheme of things, he wasn't bad in the sense that those at Ascension were. Not like Sebek.

Though, that didn't mean I trusted him.

Soft footsteps followed the creak of a door opening. There was something familiar about them, light and steady, that had my shoulders relaxing as the room fell into an uneasy silence.

"Xander, what are you doing here?" Osiris's voice was a delicate mix of control and authority. After my ordeal with Sebek, the need to have them close was nearly unbearable to ignore. I turned and caught Osiris's curious eye as he watched Magelav and Xander with an unreadable expression and a tense jaw, one that was accented by his lack of breath, his eyes set heavy as though bored. Something was wrong.

"Osiris, so nice to see you again as well. I'm doing excellently. Thank you for asking. Can't I stop by and see an old friend?" Xander asked.

Magelav made a disgusted noise in the back of their throat, the protest getting lost in the static of the background as I stood and walked over to Osiris. He watched me with a tilt to his head, his hands flexing at his sides, the muscles in his arms trembling as I reached up. I waited a moment, giving him time to pull away, before slowly curling myself around him. He was tense for a moment longer, his lungs holding the air in them before they released like a deflated balloon on the first breath he'd made since he'd walked through the door. His entire body sagged as he hugged me to him, and I sank into the hands that brushed my back with a gentle care.

I wasn't sure what happened, and I didn't need to ask. Now wasn't the time, and even this might be seen as a weakness, but it let him know he wasn't alone, that when he was ready to talk about it?

I was here.

Cold lips pressed against my forehead, a spark following them that had once been so overwhelming I thought it might consume me. Now it warmed the cold parts of me I'd sworn Sebek had broken when he'd brought me back to Ascension. The parts that were still stuck to that silver table.

He was like a wall, a barrier against everything that threatened to hurt me. His arms were the supports I needed to breathe, his heartbeat a steady drum.

"My God," a voice whispered, partially a grumble, and I realized it was Xander only when I looked up and found him staring. His shock washed away with his next blink. "I never thought I'd see the day."

Osiris didn't respond, just held me tighter.

"Well, this is the shittiest party I've ever been to." A husky, gravelly voice echoed as a beast of a man stepped past Osiris, one I'd never seen before. His presence broke the spell, shattering the silence that had fallen over the room. "Where the fuck is the booze?"

He had brown hair and a smell like welded metal, making my nose scrunch. A peek of red scales stretched up his neck, and when sharp cedar-colored eyes scanned the occupants of the room, it wasn't just him that was watching. There was a brashness to him, a confidence that screamed fighter. He was large, not just the size of him, but the energy he brought, the aura of confidence that bled from him.

An attitude that *screamed* Dragonkin and a beast behind his eyes that unfurled at the sight of so many powerful people in one place.

This must be Drakon.

"I second that," Prince said with a raised hand before moving toward the kitchenette at a leisurely pace. He stopped at a cabinet, not even looking as he reached in and pulled out a bottle of a deep brown liquid. It swirled as he poured several glasses, and slowly each person in the room took one. Osiris pulled back, tipping my chin up so he could look me in the eye. When he was happy with what he saw, he moved as well, grabbing a glass. "Nothing quite like talking life and death over a drink."

I didn't do the same, my nerves already a little too frazzled and raw. The nagging at the back of my head, the voice I knew wasn't mine but whispered vengeful nothings, pushed me to go to it. I didn't want to make it worse, so instead, I moved back to my seat as Drakon sighed.

"Who the fuck are you?" Drakon grunted, lifting his drink toward Prince, who jolted with a surprised laugh.

He crossed one of his arms over his chest, resting his hand in the crook of his elbow as he leaned back against the island with a smirk that failed to highlight the fire in his eyes as he swirled his drink. "I could ask the same thing, considering you're the one in *my* space right now. You always this rude to your betters?"

The fight was picked in an instant, and Prince did it with a confident swagger and a swig from his glass as he tossed a shit-eating grin toward Drakon.

The room was silent. Even Drakon was too stunned to move, before a growl started in his chest. There was a flash in his eyes, like Eirik often had, as his Dragon came tumbling forward.

"Nero," Osiris chastised, and Prince rolled his eyes, downing the rest of his drink as he turned his back to Drakon to look fully at Osiris.

"What?" Prince asked, still grinning even as his jaw twitched. He didn't even look over his shoulder as he tossed more words over it. "Should just count yourself lucky I can't hurt you, kid. I've fucked up stronger men than you for much less than that."

Another beat of silence before another in the room hummed.

A man stepped up beside Drakon, and the way he carried himself reminded me of Fallon, with cool black eyes and brushed-back black hair that screamed of perfection. Even his attire, a suit with a charcoal tint to it that molded to his body, was flawless.

"Nero?" His voice was hoarse, cracking on the name as the brittle sound rattled in his throat.

Prince smiled, turning back around with a tip of his empty cup. "The one and only."

Drakon grunted again, looking like he was about to argue. I wasn't surprised; Nero being alive was a shock, and that was what we'd hoped for.

What we were betting on.

"How—" Drakon started, before Osiris cut him off.

"It doesn't matter how. He's alive, and that's all you need to know. The rest of the Eternium will learn today, too." Osiris's words held a finality, and Drakon held his ground for a second, his teeth baring as he struggled with the beast in his head before his eyes cleared again.

Eirik curled around my back, a protective force as Drakon grumbled.

"Well, since we're all here, I'll give you a breakdown. Then you can go pretty up for the party," Drakon said, sipping his drink. "We're riding the line for Exilium. I've talked to everyone I can, everyone that has even considered turning on Sebek. If *everything* goes right, and I do mean everything. Every Challenge, every promised word, every goddamned miracle, it'll pass."

"Who are our worries?" Osiris asked.

Drakon grunted, shrugging his shoulder at the man at his side again, who was quick to speak up. "There are several. Axius could lose Gargoyle to his brother Hyland, who's already on the chair. Assuming he even fights for it. Alderi'Vidius could be Challenged by someone more experienced, someone older. There are several Demons that came flocking the moment they heard of Kri'Valta's fall, some older than even the Horror of the Depths. There's no limit to what could go wrong."

"Tonight needs to be about observing, getting our enemies to play their hands," Osiris said. "We need them to make the first move. We need them *scared*, so we can counter appropriately. They won't take the threats to their reign lying down, but they also won't know what rumors are true. That is our biggest advantage."

I looked up, instinctively searching for a clock. I found my answer on the far side of the wall.

Eleven fifteen.

The first night of the Eternium started exactly at midnight, on the eve of the first of the year, and we had just forty-five minutes until it started.

"I'll make sure Axius Challenges. If there are any others that I might be able to push in the right direction, send them my way," Adrian chimed in. "I'll also spread some rumors. Get the mill going to push along the more ... jumpy Eternals."

Drakon nodded, his shoulders tensing as he looked at everyone in the room before his eyes stopped on me. Eirik grew tense at my back, his chest vibrating as a growl crept up.

"You must be Aaliyah, the Reaper," Drakon asked, non-threatening, as he showed his palms. I lifted my head slowly, nodding when the words escaped me. "I'm Drakon. This is my Second, Aldric, and my Enforcer, Cassius."

The reserved man with inky-black hair nodded once, his eyes just as sharp as Drakon's. Dragonkin as well, it seemed. His fire was hidden deeper, less noticeable, like the pale scales that hid beneath his shirt collar, but as I looked closer, I knew he was no less dangerous.

The third was one I'd missed. The way he slid into the background was almost comical for his size, his body and stature almost matching Eirik's. Steely-gray eyes held the same fire I saw in Prince, the same brashness that told of age and a want for blood.

His Dragon seemed to think the same, though I couldn't pick anything else out about him, as he dipped his head once, and stepped back into the shadows.

"Just Aaliyah," I whispered, and he nodded his head as Aldric's lip twitched.

"You plan to keep that a secret, right?" he asked, referring to what I was.

Of course I had, and even if I hadn't, I wouldn't want others to know. Not like this. Not when I knew what my blood could do, the reminder as clear as the soulless body of the Gargoyle that Sebek had killed. The chance of a riot or of full-scale anarchy was too high.

No one would side with a Reaper, not now. My hands grew clammy, my breath suddenly catching as I remembered the feeling of power sliding through my veins.

"Pretty sure that about sums it up, yeah?" Drakon mumbled with a huff.

I froze for a second, wondering how I'd managed to say that out loud, when Drakon laughed. "You didn't. I try not to listen in on people, gives me a headache, but you're thinking real loud right now."

Heard it. I'd forgotten that Dragonkin could hear thoughts. The memory threatened to shoot me back to a dark alley, to sinister streets and Fellow Manor hanging just out of reach. Suddenly it was cold, and a weight settled on me as ash from a lit cigarette fell to the ground.

Red hesitated near me, dancing in the air and giving me enough strength to shake the memory from my head.

I hesitated to lift my eyes, to see the man that I knew looked familiar. Drakon was a son of Teviticus, the old Dragonkin Eternal, one of many sons, which meant that Curtis had been his brother, too.

"Oh, I couldn't give any less fucks about Curtis, trust me. I'm not mad he's dead, just wish I'd had the chance to put him out of my misery first." When Drakon huffed this time, a burst of smoke fell from his nose, and fires lit behind his eyes as the Dragon there paced. "Heard it was your blood that did him in. That true?"

I hesitated, leaning farther into Eirik, who grunted against the top of my head. I could only nod and grit my teeth.

"If the Eternals find out what Aaliyah is, there will be nothing short of a riot. The only thing they're missing is true immortality. She's a threat to that," Osiris added, a lethal meaning hiding behind his words as he looked among each person in the room. One by one, as if assessing threats in them. "We keep it to ourselves until it's time to expose Sebek's plan."

It wasn't a question, not one they could push. There was a *Charm* in those words, a power that promised pain if they went against them. That darkness should have scared me senseless, but the idea that Osiris would protect me, even from them?

It calmed the racing of my heart.

Murmured acceptance filled the room, soft assurances that what we spoke of would not leave this conversation.

"Any more on that?" Drakon pushed. "What does the Butcher plan to do?"

The change in how Osiris stood was minuscule but enough to catch my attention. He tensed, his eyes clouding with that faraway look.

"We found a body at Ascension Rising, where Sebek had kept Aaliyah," he whispered, and I froze. "Sebek used Aaliyah's blood to kill him. I think he plans to do the same to those that oppose him, a way to instill order in the Eternals."

I'd wondered if they'd found him, the man that had been left to rot in that horrible building. We hadn't had much time to talk about what had happened. About the way Osiris had been left, broken on the grounds of our home, about Sebek stealing me away. Or about having to again sit in my glass cell.

I'd pushed it to the back of my mind, buried it so deep I'd almost willed it into not being real. There was a brush of something against me, like a hand on my shoulder, and I smiled as Red's encouragement filled the air, just seconds before Prince was by my side.

Like every time I needed him, he was always right there. He'd always known and now was no different.

I looked up at him, catching his worried silver eyes. I let myself fall into the feeling of his hand on my shoulder and the ache that still sat between my legs.

"How? He can't kill people here," Drakon grunted.

Osiris shook his head, dark shadows claiming the lines of his face.

"It's Sebek. It's best to assume he has a way," Eirik added, his voice a teetering growl.

There was a flash of deep blue in his eyes, the pupils slipping into slits as his nose flared. As if sensing my eyes, he turned to look at me, the raging storms in them making me shiver.

"First Rights is when we make our move on him. We use the Distilled High Fae Mana to prove his intent to destroy the Eternals. Any votes that were bordering Exilium should turn," Osiris finished.

I wanted to believe this was all we needed, that Sebek wasn't going to go down in a ball of fire that would threaten to take us all out, but it was *too* easy. He'd been too calm when he'd spoken of it before, too sure of himself.

Sebek was a monster with my father's face. He was crazy, but he wasn't stupid.

"There's something else," I mumbled, looking up.

The room turned its attention to me, and I swallowed hard as I flexed my hands, tracing the ink on my wrist as I tried to center myself.

"When we were at Ascension, Sebek didn't just kill that man," I whispered. The moment he'd died still haunted me, the scream he'd released, the way he'd writhed against his restraints ... and the cold way Sebek had regarded him, like he was nothing more than a puppet. "Whatever Sebek did with my blood, it destroyed his soul. I never saw it."

"Saw it?" Aldric asked.

Prince's hand tightened on my shoulder. A show of support. I didn't have to speak if I didn't want to. He even moved to stand slightly in front of me, blocking their gazes as I shivered, but they needed to hear it. They already knew what I was. This was nothing.

"I know my blood's the part you're worrying about, but I can do more. Reapers can see ghosts; they send their souls on after they've died, but whatever he did to my blood destroyed the soul before I could see it. He's not just going to kill the other Eternals; he's going to make sure there's no chance of them ever being sent on." At least, that was my theory, the only thing that made sense. Sebek wanted a world he could never lose in. "He wants to stop them from ever coming back."

He didn't want to just kill them. He wanted to make sure there was no way for redemption. A true death, and for people who lived forever ... what more could they fear than that?

"Fuck. Nice to know what we're up against," Drakon grumbled, his teeth flashing as he tipped his head back with a groan.

The room fell silent, beyond the ticking of the clock.

"If worse comes to worst, I'll Challenge," Osiris added, and I all but jolted out of my seat, Prince's hand staying steadfast on my shoulder.

"Blood knows blood," Magelav grumbled. "One will pay for their sins before the end."

The words meant something, a piece we were missing, but I had no idea how to put them together. Magelav turned their head up and glared at Osiris.

Osiris's cold whisper followed. "We have already settled this score, Magelav."

"Maybe, but fickle *be*. You're forgetting something, Vivas." Magelav took a steady step toward him, soulless eyes glancing curiously between Osiris and I with a pity that worried me. I tensed, nearly lifting to go to him, when Magelav whispered, "What of Kali? Or have you forgotten her death so soon?"

The air fled from the room, Osiris's power snapping against his skin as a spark flashed across it.

"Eternal Kali?" Drakon asked, breaking the silence.

Magelav grunted, nodding their head but never looking away from Osiris.

"Blood has been spilled, staining the ground, staining the hands. *Haunted* again." Magelav could have left it there as their eyes lost the haze that had covered them. Instead, they clicked their tongue. "Fickle *be*."

Smoke poured from Drakon's nose, his lips pulling back in a snarl. "That wasn't part of the plan, Osiris. We don't have the force to deal with Darius breathing down our neck."

It was silent for a moment. Osiris reached for his wrist as he covered the ink with a tight grip, and a shudder of disgust rolled through him.

"I'm aware. You can hold your tongue, Drakon. No words you say will take back her death. If it comes to it, I will Challenge."

"Fucking typical," Drakon spit, looking like he might combust as embers joined the smoke. Aldric put a hand on his shoulder; one Drakon brushed off with an irritated swat. "You're forgetting that Darius'll call for Retaliation. You won't make it to Challenge, if you even get to the fight! He'll throw you in the Pits and leave you there to rot."

Osiris's face stayed a sheen of calm as he took a step toward Drakon. Electricity filled the air, shining behind Osiris's eyes as he homed in on Drakon's furious complexion. "I will not lose to Darius or his whims."

"Retaliation isn't meant to be beaten. It's meant to be a mockery. A show to appease the scorned." Drakon snorted, throwing his hands in the air. "You've fucked us!"

Magelav clicked their tongue again, my blood boiling at the sight of pride in their eyes. "Death comes for us all, even you, Vivas—"

"Stop with the *fighting*," I said, looking over my shoulder. There was a grunge in my voice, one I didn't push away as the shadows pulsed. "It's not useful; it's not helpful. All it's doing is causing rifts we don't need. If that's all you have to say, then leave. We need to get ready."

"Pull it in, trouble. You're scaring the extras," Fallon whispered in my ear, and the haze over my eyes cleared enough to see the shadows that lurched along the ground.

It had gone silent, the argument dying down with a finality that only furthered to weigh my shoulders down. I nodded, looking away.

I didn't have the energy to deal with it, or to think on it.

"Death always wins, Reaper. Best remember that," Magelav whispered. The door slammed shut seconds later, and I worked my way through the fire that still raced in my blood.

Drakon grunted, reminding me we weren't exactly alone. "Fucking hell. Well, this was fun. Let's hope tonight goes well, yeah? I'd really like to live."

He didn't linger, moving toward the door, Aldric and Cassius following. The others that had come swarmed after him, filing out until we were alone in the room.

I looked at the clock again.

Eleven thirty.

I wanted to stall a bit longer, to pretend we weren't about to walk into the fire. We had to get ready; we had to steel ourselves for what was going to happen, but everything collapsed, and I struggled to breathe.

Cold arms surrounded me, and I breathed in the scent of Adrian. I'd never been in a bakery, but I imagined this was what one smelled like. "One step at a time, Ali."

I tried to hold on to that. One step.

"Ready, *smár Valkyrja*?" Eirik asked, and I lifted my head.

It was a silly question, one I knew he meant as deeper than just for tonight. My answer was just as silly, just as scared as I'd ever been. I may be free now, but that didn't mean I felt any more in control than that girl in a glass cell.

I'd never be ready. Not for what this could bring us.

But one way or another, it was here, and I was tired of running.

I nodded, regardless of the fear that still tried to hold me down. Regardless of everything that threatened us. I was Aaliyah. I was more than the torture that led me to this moment. I survived Ascension Rising. I had the blood of Arvand Ra and Iris Imperial in my veins, and I would not be quiet anymore. My mantra died down, nothing more than a whisper that passed through my mind as I took Adrian's hand. The one that was still marked with the scars of the sun, and I moved.

Because I would not be afraid, not anymore.

When we made it into the back room, where the bed had been the night before, it had changed again. The bed remained, still covered in tangled sheets, but the space was larger, more open, with a few things added to the fray.

An end table that seemed slightly tilted to one side. A mirror that was cracked on the bottom left that stretched from the floor to the ceiling. An encompassing closet that held rows and rows of clothes, none of which had been there before.

They beckoned us closer, each of us already weary as the weight of the night bore down. I didn't have the energy to question it, and I picked out a dress in silence, fingers running over each of them until I stopped on one that didn't make my skin crawl. The gentle lavender fabric was smooth under my fingers but not the silky finish that Sebek's had been, and it would cover most everything but my arms.

It was long, trailing down behind me, shifting from silk to a see-through lace. Even then, I felt more vulnerable in it than I did without any clothes on. It accentuated my waist and brought attention to the scars that lined my exposed skin, but it also brightened the intricate black designs that ebbed and flowed on my wrist. I trailed a finger over them, humming as a chill filled the air, and joy filtered in. Red's amusing flit of emotions calmed me as he fluttered around before landing on the final piece.

A mask.

It was intricately designed, a white lacy material that would cling tightly to my face, small lavender gems across the surface. They glittered in the low light, warm to the touch, like the one that used to hang around my neck.

I never did get to pick up the pieces of the one that had been stolen from me. Broken. Shattered. The loss of it suddenly made me sick.

"*Lux mea?*" Osiris called from behind me, his voice a balm.

That night by the fire had been when I'd really taken a step back and recognized these men for what they were. It was when I'd first trusted them, truly trusted them, and I'd lost the piece that had sealed that for me. Lost something that I knew Osiris had used a part of himself to make.

I turned to him, struggling to find words as I took in his tense form. He stood straight, only partially dressed in tight deep-blue suit pants and a black undershirt that was still undone on the top few buttons. His chest was unmoving, his eyes only partially focused as he looked me up and down with worried, narrow eyes.

"Sebek destroyed your gem," I whispered, my lips trembling. Osiris's eyes went there, to the empty chain on my neck. "I'm sorry, Osiris. I know how long you spent on it—"

I didn't get the rest of the words out, Osiris moving too quickly for me to catch, his hands suddenly cupping my cheeks before his cold lips were brushing against my forehead. He was still so cautious, his hands shaking, but that didn't matter to me. The feeling of him, in whatever way he could give to me, would always be enough.

"I'll make you a new one as soon as I'm able," he whispered, setting his forehead against mine. "I'll make you a thousand necklaces and a thousand more after, however many you want. They're yours, my dear."

His next kiss was a promise, softness against my lips, a caress. Slower, more deliberate. As if he were savoring it, not questioning if he should back away. When he pulled back, he pushed my hair behind my ear before setting the mask on my face. He tied the delicate strings with expert hands, and I watched every move he made, eyes catching on the slivers of black that still clung to the veins on his wrist.

Eirik was next, the door closing behind him, taking Osiris's spot with a smooth grace. He was already dressed, a simple black suit seeming out of place on his large form, like he might bust through the seams of it at any moment. The mask, though, curled around his face, sticking out above his nose like a skull. The shape was distinctly canine, the color the same almond hue as the fur of his wolf.

He tipped my head, working quickly to tie my hair into an intricate braid that hugged the side of my head like armor, just like he had before.

I held my head a little higher when he finished, blushing at the fierce heat in his gaze that warred with a pride that leveled me. It was like watching his beast take the reins as his eyes fell into dark seas, as if he could read my thoughts. His palm centered on my cheek, and no words were needed beyond that look of promise that had me leaning farther into his touch.

"You ready, love?" Adrian asked, breaking the moment, and I took a steadying breath.

I should have expected him to have more color, his suit a coppery red that complemented his hair. His bowtie was tied intricately on his neck, tucked tightly against him as he slid one hand into his pocket, the other toying with a golden pocket watch that dangled from his chest.

His mask was silver, little cogs tracing it that seemed to rotate when I wasn't looking. Flecks of gold littered it, out of place.

Each piece, from the suits to the masks, seemed like they were designed with us in mind. It went further than I would have expected, more personal, less detached. Like the Eternium wasn't just a guide, but rather something that was learning us.

One day at a time.

I stood, giving Eirik one more glance, stealing a kiss when he wasn't expecting it, and pulling away far too soon for either of our liking. We both followed Adrian back to the main room.

Osiris was dressed fully now, wearing a simple deep blue suit, his hair slicked back, his hands tugging warily at the sleeves of his black dress shirt. His mask was almost like Eirik's, with canine features embroidered with rich blue stones. But it was different, sharper, clinging more to his deep olive skin, and the more defined angles of his face. It made him look ethereal, godly.

Prince, to his side, held his danger in a much different way. Osiris seemed like an omen of death, but Prince dressed like he was the guide meant to bring him those lost souls. His suit was a burgundy red, black accents drawing to the silver of his eyes. Devilish, with a sinful smile that had my insides melting all over again. The mask he wore resembled something I'd seen before, the helmet in the basement of the Vivas house, the brutal gold with angelic Roman architecture that seemed dirtied and crumbling.

I dragged my eyes over each of them again, all fully dressed besides Fallon, who was still tightening the straps on his outfit. His hands were on the strings at his back, his eyebrows drawn close as he pulled them tight. It took me a second to realize what it was, the fabric stiffer than a waistcoat.

He was wearing a corset.

My mouth watered, and I had to swallow as my body lit an inferno inside of me.

It was a light green that complemented his eyes and the white dress pants he already had on. It accentuated his slim waist, bringing attention to his back and strong arms as he grunted and tried to get the last few strings tied. The green material stretched, and his golden hair bounced over his heated eyes.

"I may not swing that way, but even I can say he's looking sinful," Adrian whispered in my ear, and I jolted when I realized how close he was. His laugh was addictive, reminding me of the way his hands had felt against my skin as he reached for the zipper on the back of my dress. He pulled it up the rest of the way, making sure it fit snug as he lingered on my sides. "Why don't you go help him? He looks like he needs it."

I didn't need to be told twice, walking over to Fallon on autopilot, then stopping in front of him with a dazed look on my face. His eyes were confused for only a second, before they trailed down me, his hands twitching as they fell away from his back. Watching his hands pull into fists nearly did me in. When he leaned forward and pressed his lips to mine, I considered just staying here.

We didn't need to go. This whole Eternium thing was a waste of time.

"What did I say about looking at me like that, trouble?" he asked, and I melted as he turned around, crouching so I could grab the strings that had been giving him trouble.

My fingers shook, and it took me a lot longer than it should have to thread them through the little holes in the back. When I managed that, I pulled them tight and started to tie the knot when Fallon reached back to stop me.

"Tighter, Ali," he whispered. There was a challenge there, excitement in his husky voice, and I yanked the strings, causing him to hiss as his head tipped back. His dark chuckle as I finished tying the knot would stick with me for the rest of the night. He stood and fixed his tie before throwing on his overcoat. "I'll remember that."

His mask was the last to go on. It was white, a simple straight color, beyond the cracks that lined it. They dug into the heavy material, splintering as though put under tremendous force. He tied it, a cold expression slipping firmly into place.

His smile dropped completely. The man I knew before taking over, shrouding his face in an armor of frost. The others surrounded us as Fallon offered me his arm.

I took it, clinging to him, and we moved. One unit, one family.

The clock chimed, signaling the start of the masquerade. The opening ceremony.

Let the Eternium begin.

Chapter 31

Aaliyah

The halls were barren, creaking and groaning around us in an eerie symphony, tiles shifting as though pulled around by tiny magic as they took us to where we wanted to go. Or, in this case, where *it* wanted us.

"I really think if we try hard enough, we can get the Eternium to conjure us up a Christmas tree," Adrian mused, breaking up the silence as he appeared by my side.

He stretched his arms up, hands tucked behind his head as he tilted it to look at me with that silly open grin. There was a twinkle in his eye, one that seemed to have been lost, one I grabbed onto as Fallon bumped into his other side.

"There's no way," he grunted, shaking his head as Adrian pouted.

"Look, it can take us anywhere, and if my absolute desire is to *cut down a tree* like a rugged mountain man, you'd think it'd let me do that. Who knows, it might even give me some overalls." He sighed wistfully, and Fallon rolled his eyes again as I laughed into my palm, an act that had his smile growing. "I'm just saying we should try it once tonight's over. I promised love that we'd get her one and I'm not one to break promises."

I hummed, thinking of the idea. I couldn't remember the last time

I'd had a real tree, and a few months ago, I might have preened at the thought of one. A piece of my childhood I could steal back.

Now, it wasn't so much the tree that I wanted. It wasn't the grand idea, or the flash and pomp. We were all together, and at the end of the day, I couldn't have asked for anything more. But Adrian saw it differently, wanted the tree for what it represented. For what it meant. A promise.

"Does it have to be a tree?" I asked, humming softly as I contemplated what else we might be able to do. "We could put something up. Maybe make a fort that looks like one or draw one on the walls." Then we wouldn't have to rely on the Eternium at all.

Adrian snapped his fingers, a plan already forming as he nodded his head. "I like the way you think, love. I hadn't thought about that. Oh! What about lights? We could string them in the shape of one, like I saw on a little video a while ago. I think that'd be fun!" Adrian rubbed his hands together in a way that was both enduring and looking a little like a mad scientist. "Yes, that should do. What do you think of that, Fally?"

Except Fallon didn't answer.

"Fallon?" Adrian asked, looking over his shoulder at the same time I did, just as Fallon's face registered. He'd gone an ashen pale, sweat lining his forehead as he swayed. "Whoa, easy!"

Adrian caught him before he hit the wall, the others circling at the commotion as I rushed to support his other side. His weight bore down on me, and I felt the shake in his legs as he tried to keep as much weight off me as he could.

The fact that he struggled, that he still leaned on me, told me enough.

"I'm all right," he grunted, but didn't try to get out of our hold.

"No, all right is someone who hasn't been cooked in the sun. You, brother, are not all right," Prince whispered, moving like a mother hen, checking Fallon's face and pressing his hand to his forehead like Fallon might be something other than cold. He gave me a soft smile as he slid Fallon's arm over his shoulder, taking my place so I could move in front. "It's okay to lean on me. Don't worry, I'm told I'm quite strong. I probably won't even drop you."

Fallon looked at me with glassy eyes as I reached up to cup his cheek. His nose ran along my wrist, and I heard his fangs fall as he drew in even breaths. There was a hesitation there as I pulled him closer, like he didn't want to take anymore.

But I wasn't going to let him get away from it.

"You bite, or I will," I whispered, a partial threat. He knew how to go gently, how to aim for the right place. I'd tear into the skin, hit muscle, hurt *more.*

Either way, he'd feed.

Fallon sighed, his jaw clenching, a rogue vein popping on it before he took my wrist in his hand. His breath was warm, contrasting with his cool touch and the heated spark that came with it. Lips brushed skin, and my pulse stuttered as his tongue traced a path along my vein. I blushed, unable to look away as he caught my eye, sinking fangs in a shallow bite. I sucked in a breath, the penetration stinging for a second, making me jolt as the pain was replaced with a warmth that settled low in my stomach.

When he lifted his head again, licking his lips, he looked less dead on his feet. His eyes cleared, and he stood, Adrian and Prince stepping away cautiously.

The marks that littered his skin faded more, the ones on his face pretty much gone all together, the trace reminders still crawling up his neck.

"Thank you, Ali," he whispered, gently brushing a thumb against my cheek as he reached up to cup my face before he looked at Adrian. "You holding up okay?"

Adrian's smile slipped, just enough to catch the fall in it, before it was swept away with a goading, narrowed grin. His eyes squinted, and he tipped forward slightly, as if to imitate looking down on Fallon.

"Me? Oh, yeah. You know, I guess there was something good to come out of Archon's mess." He shrugged it off, exaggerating his nonchalance by brushing his hair back with a tilted swagger. "What can I say? I knew I had the higher pain tolerance. Fally, are you going *soft*?"

Fallon's eye twitched, his nose flaring as he bared his teeth. The worry he'd held for Adrian was lost behind the clench of his fists. "Fuck off, Adrian."

He stalked forward, shoulder checking Adrian, who laughed again. "I probably just got more healing. Will about ran out of the room like you lit his ass on fire. You really only have your sunny disposition to blame."

Adrian snickered, lifting his hands and placing them behind his head again, a mischievous pride clinging to his smile as Prince rolled his eyes, laughing as though sharing a joke.

The shifting halls split then, opening up to a loft room and a door, one that others lined up for. Most I didn't know, hidden behind their masks, but I knew the looks they gave, the glowers and the stares. Like they were waiting for us to fall.

I lifted my chin as Fallon slowed, coming to my side again, sliding his hand into mine.

"Let's give them hell, trouble," he whispered, and a hearty chuckle went off behind us.

"Now that's an idea I can get behind," Prince called, his arm lying over my shoulder.

Our time came, and the same creature that had let us into the Eternium looked us up and down. Its featureless face seemed to bore into us, calculating, before the doors at its back slid open.

Bright lights blinded me, and for a moment, I was back on stage at the Devil's Details. The sound of people conversing was familiar, drowning out my own thoughts. I was exposed under the endless stares, trying to hold my head high as Osiris had said, keeping myself from hiding the scars I knew they could see. Except this time, it wasn't Curtis by my side.

The men I trusted, the men I loved, were with me now as we stepped forward into the room.

"Now announcing, the Vivas Crypt, Secondaries of Vampire Eternal Sebek Ra."

CHAPTER 32

EIRIK

Crowds made my head hurt, and my feral side hungry.

They'd been on us since the moment we'd walked down the stairs, watching on with a mix of glee and disgust, hatred and envy. Normally, it was Osiris who was focused on, the esteemed eldest of the Crypt.

Today, their eyes landed on the one person who might throw them off. The one who shouldn't be here.

Nero.

He stood proudly, as he always had, overlooking the crowd with an air of superiority that screamed Roman Gladiator. He was here, and he was alive. Something that not one of them could have expected, and that was exactly how we'd wanted it.

Nero soaked it all in, letting out a breath as his head tipped back. He'd always loved the spotlight, and he was preening at the attention now. I didn't have any doubt that he was struggling with keeping himself hidden up to this point.

It was good to see him smile again.

"We know how to make an entrance, don't we?" he asked, winking at a passing Titan that looked at him like he'd grown a second head.

I wasn't sure who it was, with long gray hair flowing untamed over his shoulders. He was no different from the rest, face covered in an intricate mask that looked like the rugged side of a rocky mountain.

"They're looking at you," I grumbled, an itch starting at the base of my neck, my skin too tight as I fought the growl that came forward. I didn't like the way they looked on, some with fear, some with surprise.

Others with hate.

"What, do I have something on my face?" Nero asked, snorting. "That has to be it. You couldn't be glaring like you're worried I'd lose to one of these schmucks?"

It diffused me, in an instant, as I rolled my eyes and then my shoulders. Typical Nero, with that cocky smile and "take on the world" attitude. It centered me, and my wolf calmed. We fell into an easy silence, keeping track of the room. I snapped easily between my brothers and my *Elskan*, always keeping them in my sights.

Fallon didn't try to hide his disdain, all but snarling at everyone who approached him. That haughty attitude was hidden behind his ice, only falling when he tipped his head to make sure Aaliyah was still close by. Adrian was by their side, chatting with a man I knew, one that had stormed into our home some weeks ago.

Avedal nodded to whatever our youngest was saying. His head was held high, looking far more imposing than he had the day he'd stumbled into our house, like the demons of hell were on his tail. He smiled brightly, nodding fondly at Aaliyah when she whispered something I couldn't make out, his head tipping toward Hillam as he introduced his mate.

The only one I couldn't see was Osiris, lost somewhere in the crowd.

"Was it always like this? So ..." Nero said softly with a breath, pausing to search for the right word.

There was a peace that came with having him by my side again, one that didn't need words. Nero's face scrunched, his missing memories showing blatantly in his confusion. There were few people that could bear the weight of my silence. He'd always been one of them.

"Easy?" I asked, and he hummed.

"Yes, *easy*. I have a feeling I wasn't the silent type, but with you, that doesn't seem to be a problem."

I snorted, finding it hard to remember a time when Nero wasn't speaking. Or bitching or *screaming*. Gods, his fucking screaming. "Not at first. You and I fought a lot the first few centuries, like bickering children."

It had driven Osiris mad, and he'd had to break up more than his fair share of fights. I'd have sworn I'd kill the egotistical bastard one day, only for him to end up my closest confidant. One I'd trust with my life.

Nero chuckled quietly. "And Osiris was the single mom at his wits' end?"

My wolf settled further as the conversation drew on, the most I'd seen since we'd escaped Archon's. His exhaustion bled into me, the same that lingered when I rubbed my eyes, finally catching sight of our eldest as Osiris prowled through the people in the room. No one approached him for a very different reason than Fallon. Power pulsed from him in endless, sure waves. "An understatement."

Nero was silent for longer than I expected, and I turned to find him still looking at my face. His eyes were narrowed bits of pointed steel, expression serious as he looked me up and down.

"You good?" was all he asked, gruffly, with all the subtlety of a boar.

I grunted, nodding my head once, not offering any words. Nero didn't look away, that contemplative look in his eyes so starkly familiar, like he knew I was talking out of my ass.

"Then why do you look so tired, brother?" he said, unwilling to look away, like he'd meant anything beyond exactly what he'd said. That directive shook me, and I shuddered. "You can't fool me, you know. You haven't slept."

I snorted, quick to rebuke him. "Of course I have."

It was a lie, one I'd held on to for days, and one I'd thought I'd gotten away with. Sleep was *useless* right now. I searched the crowd for Archon, for Sebek, Darius. *Brazen*. They were threats, and I couldn't afford to let my guard down. I could go weeks without it anyway, and I couldn't very well protect them if I slept ... not even by Aaliyah's side, knowing that Osiris was awake.

I'd lain there, listening to her heartbeat, making sure my brothers continued to breathe.

"No, you haven't," he said again, fire lingering in his words like the finality of a gavel. He stood several inches shorter than me, yet somehow made me feel like the small one as he scolded me like a mother might a child. "You're so intent on protecting us, you haven't taken care of your-self. It's not good for you, Eirik."

"I can sleep when we're home." *When we're safe.*

I itched the skin at my neck, the scar there burning without the medallion to cover it. My ears homed in on the crowd, the bustle of people that I struggled to separate. I searched for a heartbeat I shouldn't have, for the hints of oak in a sea of people that suddenly made my skin crawl.

I scratched at the scar until it hurt, taking my mind off the wandering thoughts.

"It's not your fault you didn't burn, brother," Nero said, and I jerked my head back to him. The remorse of that day had weighed on me, locked away with the rest. He shouldn't have seen it. "You need to let go of this guilt. You protected them. That's what matters."

Adrian caught my eye from across the room, his head tilting as he shot me a confused look, the black marks of the sun stretching savagely up his neck. Even now, he felt different. It was like a mask fell into place, one that hid our brother behind it. Hid the pain of what a monster did to him. I'd saved them from the sun.

But I didn't save them from the rest.

His face shifted into a practiced smile when a laugh filled the air. It dragged my attention to where Aaliyah stood next to him and Fallon.

"Did I?" I asked, brushing the topic off, snorting when Nero went to butt in again. I wasn't in the mood to hear it, and a growl built behind my teeth as my wolf thought the same.

I turned all my attention to what it should have been on, my sweet *Elskan.* Aaliyah rubbed her arms, chewing on her bottom lip as she tried desperately to cover the scars that traced up and down the smooth skin.

"She's worrying again," Nero whispered, solemn. But at least he'd changed his course of conversation. "God, I wish we didn't have to deal with this right now."

Her violet eyes lit beautifully under the soft lighting. The small narrow of her waist, her thin neck and skin alight. The way her lavender dress clung to her, and her pearlescent masquerade mask seemed to emphasize her eyes. She was the most stunning person in the room.

And I wasn't the only person to notice.

Everyone, male and female, couldn't take their eyes off her. Her looks were one thing, but the fact that she'd come with *us* was another. It filled the crowd with varying mixtures of fear and awe.

"Where are you going?" he asked as I moved my way through the crowd.

I didn't answer but knew he followed when I heard him curse, the sound of a drink grinding against a metal serving platter as it was lifted before being set back down echoing behind me.

I walked directly to her, nodding to Fallon and Adrian, a conversation passing without words as I glanced between them, checking that they were okay. They nodded, and I looked back to Aaliyah.

She stared at me with curious eyes, her shoulders softening as she took a deep breath, taking a step closer to me as my chest expanded in a purr. Why had I come over here? There wasn't a reason, not one I could say.

I needed to be near her, and my beast agreed. I needed her in my arms, in my presence, so I'd never lose the touch of her hands and the breath of her scent.

"Elskan," I said gently as I held out my hand. She took it like she'd done that night under the stars, and I threaded my fingers through hers. They were small, delicate, and I ran my nose over the back of them before placing a kiss on her knuckles. "Dance with me?"

I hadn't been lying when I'd told her dancing wasn't my strong suit, but the way her eyes lit up was worth whatever humiliation was coming my way.

"Of course," she said, giving a small curtsey before I pulled her to my chest. Adrian snickered, and I glared at him over her shoulder as I directed her to the dance floor that sat mostly empty in the middle of the room. "I thought you didn't know how?"

I grunted, spinning her so she was facing me, adding a bit of flair when I brought her back into a shallow dip. I ignored the stares as I lifted her hands so they sat against my chest, bending so I could hold her hips. I stuck to something easy, swaying to the soft keys of the piano music that filled the air.

"I don't," I said, giving her a small twirl that swirled her dress around her.

I had two left feet ... but that hadn't stopped Nero from getting us dancing lessons one of the several years we'd spent in France. I'd hated it then, but I had to admit the bastard did some good. I wouldn't be here like this if he hadn't.

We continued to sway easily, the others around us keeping their distance. The room faded away, just me and her ... until Adrian and Nero dashed past.

I barely caught it, looking up as they twirled, one set of hands clasped together, the other at each other's hips as they stared stoically ahead. They whirled around us, Nero going as far as to put Adrian into a dip, breaking both of their expressions as they snickered, before falling back into the swing.

"I'm going to kill them," I grunted, rolling my eyes as Aaliyah laughed at their antics.

She leaned into my chest a little farther, watching them with an ease I hadn't seen in days. "How can you do that when you're dancing with me?"

Well, it could always wait until later.

I ran my nose over the top of her head, purring low in my chest as we continued to sway. She trailed a delicate finger over my arm, and I ground my teeth as my wolf shot forward, furious at the barrier between her skin and ours. It made my mouth ache, watering as her hand came to my cheek, tilting my face until I was looking at her.

Sweet, calming lavender flooded my nose, gracing me with her as I kissed her wrist.

"Are you okay?" she asked, the same way Nero had. Her eyes lingered on mine, her hand stretching up to cup my cheek.

I nodded.

I was tired, my body worn and my head pounding from the lack of sleep ... but I'd never been anything but perfect in her arms. Her worry was a relief, one I wouldn't add to. My strength came in my endurance, and I was more than capable of watching them as I was.

Aaliyah pulled back suddenly, and the loss of her heat made my wolf jolt, suddenly back to the front of my mind as he snarled. She reached up, not even noticing as my eyes shifted. I swallowed, the loss forgotten as I felt her hand brushing against my collar.

"Eirik, your necklace?" she asked, and I nodded again.

I found myself reaching for it, even though it was no longer there.

The heavy medallion was as much a source of peace as it was remembrance. I intended to get it back. Later, when this was over and we could afford a distraction. Until then, I'd bear the weight of its loss.

"Brazen took it," I said, shaking it off, forcing my wolf back down as saliva pooled in my mouth, and the first shift of a change came over my face. Aaliyah froze, and I pulled her back to me. "He doesn't even deserve your hate."

He didn't deserve a single ounce of her time or thoughts. He was worthless to her, to anyone. I wouldn't let him be a stain on her mind, not even in passing.

I gripped her chin, tipping it up so I could see her eyes. There was a fire there, the one that had given her that name I treasured so much. My Valkyrie, like an avenging angel, looked at the scar that cut across my throat.

A growl slipped past my lips, one led by my beast as heat soared in my chest, silenced by her lips as I kissed her. For a blissful moment, everything went quiet, even my wolf calming at the touch of her.

She sighed into my lips before she sank back into my chest.

"Dance with me," she whispered, closing her eyes. "Just for a while longer."

Like I'd ever be able to deny her.

Chapter 33

Prince

Damn, and I thought *I* was self-centered.

"Well, leave it to the Hallowed to be even more pretentious than Fallon," I muttered, looking at the obnoxiously grand ballroom we found ourselves standing in the middle of. Bodies moved around us, like little dolls pulled by marionette strings. Everyone's faces were covered, but I'd never needed them to pick out people in a crowd. "You think we'd be able to snag one of those paintings? I think it'd make a great souvenir."

I grabbed a glass off a passing server's tray, bringing it to my nose, and enjoying the soft scent of white wine as Osiris continued his search of the room to my right. He looked down at the same paintings I'd been eyeing, the ones Fallon was doing his best not to drool over from across the room. "Not on our lives. Stay focused. We have to keep our guard up."

He'd switched languages so quickly it could have given me whiplash, Latin flowing easily off his tongue.

I chuckled at that, focusing on the chaos around us as everyone either gave us a wide berth or openly glowered. I'd expected surprise, the shocked looks at my fortunate resurrection, but seeing it up close was something else. People looked at me like I was the bringer of the end times, Nero, *fifth turned of Sebek Ra,* back from the dead.

It was kind of comical, in all honesty. I wondered what they might say, if any got brave enough to come up and talk to me. Osiris's gift touched the air, a hint of fire lighting the space between us.

Which meant the idea of a conversation was little more than a pipe dream.

"Have I ever been one to let my guard fall?" I said, draining the rest of my drink. I rethought my words as Osiris's eyebrow rose. "Actually, don't answer that. Just calm down, will you?"

Osiris rolled his eyes, before taking a few settling breaths, clenching his hands, shaking a little as he adjusted his tie. I didn't know exactly why he did it, didn't need to. Something inside me told me what I needed to do, so I reached out and set a hand on his shoulder.

"We've got this. I'm just saying ... this place could use a bit of fun."

It was a brief moment of silence before Osiris scoffed next to me. He didn't move to shrug me off, like I half expected him to, instead going back to searching the room. His eyes, did enough to keep most of the passersby away now, but it was his aura that sealed their fear.

The flash of magic he couldn't hold back threatened to burst forward. It was tastable, a living thing that bled from him.

"They can be plenty chaotic, I assure you," he said, tugging on the sleeves of his undershirt. "During the last Titan Challenge, they'd nearly ripped the entire fighting ring to shreds, and you'd been star struck, wondering if Roderick would be up to fight you after. If I recall right, he'd said 'I'd rather lose the title I just won than have to fight you, *Emperor*.' It was quite a scene."

The way he'd said it, his lips tilting like it was a shared memory, made my stomach ache. I wanted to reminisce with him because fuck me if that didn't sound like something I'd have loved.

It was strange, knowing he was right but *feeling* like he wasn't. My body was convinced he was my brother, moving in a way that I couldn't explain. My mind wasn't as sure, and Osiris could tell, his head tipping down. "You don't recall, do you?"

"Not a lick. It's a bowl of really shitty spaghetti up there right now. But it's coming back, slowly but surely," I said, trying to bleed some humor into the words. Osiris's sullen look didn't fade, and I wrapped my arm around his shoulder. "Tell me about this fight, would you? It sounds like something right up my alley."

He was quiet for a second, seeming to think through if he really wanted to, before he was grinning.

"It was a haughty affair. There weren't supposed to be any Challenges, and we were only there trying to gain information. Though you had other plans; you always did. You, Milo, and Eirik decided you were going to try and drink the entire room under the table. I had to give away more than a few of my favorite treasures to soothe several Eternals' rotten moods. Then there was the incident with Frileti. You had always wanted to sleep with the Fae royalty. I just wish you would have tried before her betrothal." He scoffed then, shaking his head before his face settled back into a stoic lull. " It was a night I'll never forget. I ... I wish you remembered it."

The whispered confession took me aback, and Osiris continued on like he hadn't said anything, surveying the room, but something in my chest, in the pits of my soul, told me that was important.

"I will, one day," I whispered, more distraught than I thought I'd be as I sighed. "I can feel it. The memories, they're there ... I just need to get them out."

There was a moment of hesitation before Osiris nodded back. A few seconds of peaceful silence followed.

"It's strange. You're him, the brother I lost all those years ago ... the one I'd begged I'd get a second chance to see, to speak to. You have his face, his smirk, even his scars. Yet you're so different. Someone else, in some ways."

I snorted as I sought out Aaliyah, like I always did, finding her with my brothers and still flushed from her dance with Eirik. Safe, looking worried around the room as she pushed her hair over her shoulder. She reached for Adrian's hand, whispering something that had him turning to her.

It warmed my heart when Fallon brushed the hair behind her ear, shielding her back from any attacks, even if that wasn't something we had to worry about here. I wasn't seeking a drink, or a lay for the evening. I wasn't hard set on a fight like I had been all those years ago that barely felt like a dream.

I looked again at Osiris, finding him scanning the room, holding up our defense while my focus had been elsewhere. Always watching. My brother, regardless of what else had happened. I *was* different now, and

I couldn't find it in me to be mad about it. His Nero might have been Vivas, and I knew I still was, but the Prince I was now was Aaliyah's too.

I didn't see a reason why I couldn't be both.

"You're right. I am different. I don't remember things I know I should, and I'm sorry I can't share in those memories with you yet." *No matter how much I want to.* "But I *see* you, Osiris. I remember how it feels to be by your side, and I know I don't have to look over my shoulder when you're here with me. The memories aren't there, but the emotions I feel are plenty enough. There's no strain in that for me, Osiris. I don't need to remember you or the others."

I stopped us in the middle of the masked-filled room, banging a clenched fist against my chest. "You're as much a part of me as Aaliyah is. Always. We're family, brothers, and not even death would make me forget that."

The room died away, and it was only us in it for a moment. I saw a man who'd spent centuries by my side. I felt his presence, his love like an extension of myself.

"I'm glad you're back, *frater*," Osiris said, dipping his head.

I couldn't help but smile at that, suddenly speaking before I could even question the words. "We are Vivas. When one fights—"

I didn't have to finish it, whatever it would have been, as Osiris smiled and responded. "We fight with him."

No words had ever felt so right. It wasn't the first time I'd said them, but I still didn't know why they struck such a cord. Somewhere in my memories, they were important, and even though I couldn't remember why, I still held them close.

"Speaking of fights, what *is* the plan?" I asked, shoving my hands into my pockets, needing to clear the heavy feeling in my chest.

There would be time for reminiscing later, when we didn't have the entirety of the Eternium ready to jump down our throats. Osiris's eyes grew clouded with the weight of time lost before they zeroed in with a focus that startled me. The numbness there deepened, sharpened into points.

"Making the first move here would be a mistake. Someone will come forward, planting the seeds for Challenge, or a Retaliation. Either way, we wait," he said casually.

The words finished off, and no more were needed. We moved like we'd never been apart, Osiris scanning the left, I the right. Then I saw him, a man that my mind recognized but couldn't place. A visceral hatred told me all I needed to know.

Osiris froze next to me, a picturesque statue, as he saw the man I'd caught foaming at the mouth in our direction.

"It seems we don't have to wait long," he whispered hoarsely.

He clutched his wrist, his hand over the mark that Aaliyah had left there, the one that blended with the brand that dug into the skin. His eyes bled red.

I didn't know the man's face, didn't even know his name, but I flipped us away from him all the same, grabbing Osiris's shoulders, forcing his gaze on mine. Every move I made felt like instinct, as my hands went to his ears and I covered them. He struggled against my hold, enough that I had to more or less slap him upside his fucking head to get him to focus. "Look at me, *now,* Osiris! What do you see?"

I wasn't sure where the question came from, but Osiris startled, his eyes flashing back to a familiar mismatch of blue for about a second, before they were red again. He opened his mouth, gasping for air.

"The room, a chandelier, white walls." He paused, pulling in a hard breath this time, seeming to force it. His eyes gave again, staying blue for longer this time. "I see bodies."

Good, that was good, probably?

"There you go. Who do you see?" I asked, more confidently this time as the words slipped out, and I took a settling, exaggerated breath, watching as he did the same.

His eyes glazed as he swallowed, but I didn't let him turn his head. Sparks flew across his skin, singeing me, and I flinched. Electricity filled the air, like raw ozone flooding my veins. "You. I see you, Nero."

"More," I pushed, as the click of boots grew louder. Osiris flinched, his hands digging into my wrists. "*More, Osiris.*"

His eyes opened, showing fire in the depths. "My brother."

"Good, deep breaths. You losing it here will do no one any favors," I whispered, and Osiris shook his head.

"But—"

"I know. He's a fucking bastard, and he has no hold over you now." I pressed my hand to my chest. I didn't know the man that walked our way, couldn't place his name if my life depended on it ... but fuck if I didn't want to lay him out for the way he was looking at Osiris. "You're not alone."

Osiris nodded, unable to speak, and just as quickly, another voice cut into our conversation.

"*Nero* Vivas. You're supposed to be dead."

Pressure built in my skull like an avalanche that I was directly in the way of. I turned my full attention to the man in front of me.

He was short, stubby, like an overwatered cactus with all the prickly bits on display. His black hair was styled around his head, shit brown eyes staring at us, as though we should be kneeling. His mask was something of an extravagant frilly beast, over the top and obnoxiously jeweled.

"I always have been one for explosive entrances," I said, giving him a haughty smirk.

The man didn't respond to my quip, instead raising an eyebrow, fully intending to blow our plan to shit.

Watch. Wait.

"No matter, it's better that you're both here for this." His words flooded the room, silence falling. I held my breath. "Osiris, Turned of Vampire Eternal Sebek Ra, has killed Sorceri Eternal Kali in cold blood, and as her closest confidant, I, Mythic Eternal Darius the Great ... request vengeance for her death, blood for blood. I call *Retaliation*."

Darius's decree fell across the room, exactly as Osiris said it would.

Fuck.

Well, plan. Meet a vicious fucking end.

Chapter 34

Eirik

Claustrophobia had me feeling like my suit was closing in on me, scratching along my skin, needling right into my nerves and making me twitch. Darius's words had done exactly what he'd wanted. I'd heard them even from here, across the room, and I wasn't the only one to notice.

Murmurs began low before they picked up in vicious cadence. The first vote to be called, the first grievance to air. The only thing that kept me from questioning how this became such a fucking disaster was the way that Osiris reacted. His head was high, even as he stared down his worst nightmare. Calm, understanding, like this was exactly what he'd expected.

Nero, still firmly planted by Osiris's side, tensed. I moved swiftly through the room until I was next to him. The formation the three of us fell into, like an unshakable unit, was as easy to slip into as breathing.

My hands clenched and unclenched, a narrowed focus on the heartbeats and voices around us. My beast writhed behind my eyes, a feral thing that only had one goal as I scanned the room, searching for white against the flow of hair and masks. Everything in me screamed to find her, to sift through the crowd until she came into view. She was still by Fallon's and Adrian's sides, watching on with a worried expression as Darius pranced and postured.

They did their best to keep her calm, but even I could see their struggle. The pain from the sun still clung to them, the marks faded now but still there, still raw. The anxiety that came with the unknown just stacked on it as they were surrounded on all sides.

They were Vampires, turned of Sebek Ra and members of the Vivas Crypt. It was hard sometimes to remember how young they were, how few years they'd really had to understand what came with this name of ours.

This was their *first* Eternium.

Darius reached his hand out, and I held my breath as Osiris flinched away. Light glowed behind his eyes, and the only thing stopping him from attacking Darius was the magic that held those at the Eternium in check.

Osiris hated touch, despised it.

Power pulsed off of him in endless, sure waves. He had hidden his rage and his guilt behind his power, as he had always done. Kept it caged so no one else would have to deal with it. My biggest hope for him was that he would learn to confide in someone. If it wasn't me, or any of our brothers, I hoped it would be her.

My Valkyrie. The one who took a step forward, moving to walk toward the beast that was Osiris, toward the *Kingslayer*. Only Adrian and Fallon held her back.

The room devolved into discussion. Some were about Darius's words, others calling out their own thoughts on Challenges, unwilling to be outshined. Mayhem grew so quickly everything else dissolved into furious discussion.

Darius made another outraged cry, and I barely even heard it as the door slammed open.

"Ladies and gentlemen. Eternals and Secondaries," a loud voice echoed in the air, coming from one of the Sages that still stood at the top of the ornate stairs. They overlooked the steadily quieting crowd as a vicious light shined through the door, blotting out the figure that walked through it. The Sage bowed its head, shuffling to the side as Sebek stepped forward.

"May I introduce Vampire Eternal Sebek Ra."

I pulled closer to Nero's side, snarling at Darius when he got too close. His Griffon was behind his eyes, staring me down with the same vigor as the man. My wolf took the challenge, coming to the surface with a fierce moment that had my skin shifting tightly against bones that suddenly didn't feel like my own.

I rolled my neck, feeling the pop there and preparing to face off with the Mythic.

"Your *Retaliation* has been heard, Mythic Eternal," Osiris said, sickeningly sweet, his head tipping before he looked away entirely, toward the one monster more devastating.

Darius protested, but it was lost, fading out as even he took a step back. Sebek made his first move down the stairs, and it was like watching a crowd realize a king had just appeared. The voices stopped, the heads dipping low as even the Eternals hesitated to move.

Adrian and Fallon found their way to us, treading carefully as we regrouped. Everyone waited with held tongues and bated breath. For famine or feast. I only managed to calm when Aaliyah's hand found mine, shaking and cold.

"I have an announcement," Sebek said, and it sent an involuntary shiver down my spine, even my beast stilling as he listened for the rest.

For the bloodshed that a man like *Death's Butcher* could bring.

"This isn't going to be good." Nero was just as dumbstruck as I was, tension keeping his spine straight as he flexed his hands, popping the knuckles. "What could he have to say?"

Sebek scanned the crowd, and I wasn't stupid enough to think he wasn't looking for us. His head stopped, his eyes narrowing behind his mask.

"Have you met him? Something fucking unhinged," Adrian whispered.

"There was a discrepancy, one I cannot allow to slide. The Vivas Crypt houses one of higher status than their name," he said, looking directly at Aaliyah. Osiris froze, his eyes going wide in a way that told me enough. This wasn't part of the plan, and it damned well shouldn't have been. "It's only fitting to give them the recognition they deserve, as another member of house Ra."

Sebek wouldn't do something that would risk Aaliyah, his trump card. *He wouldn't sacrifice his plan.*

Sebek had always been a standing epitome of power, and now, with a stone expression and dead eyes that even my beast cowered at, I realized just how outmatched I was. How little I knew of the monster that he'd become, that he'd always been. Without hesitation, without looking away, he played his ace. "Allow me the pleasure of introducing you to my kin. Daughter to my brother, Arvand."

The breath was pulled from my lungs as gasps and murmurs filled the room; I was already moving, keeping my chest facing the threats I knew couldn't harm us here, but worried about anyway.

Nearly all seemed to know the name, likely knew the story of how Sebek had fallen from grace during the Natural War, and knew he *never* spoke his brother's name. It was a curse, a death sentence, and the one thing that even he evaded. Unless it suited him.

Unless it proved his fucking point.

His lip tilted, his stance one of victory, but he wasn't looking over a bloody battlefield, not yet.

"Aaliyah Ra *Imperial*." It was quiet, for just long enough for the elders to really understand what he'd said. Some of the new faces looked on with confusion and distaste. Then the whispers started, the frantic move of Eternals as they struggled to get farther away from us. I ripped my lips back, snarling as some bared their teeth. Her name alone caused an uproar, people's eyes searching for her, having seen her come in with us. Sebek's expression gave nothing away. "The last Reaper."

Chaos, vicious and cruel, swallowed those pretending to be civilized. The crowd closed in on us, reaching for Aaliyah, faces muddled with rage and fear. All while Sebek watched on, like a king admiring his pawns. His thoughts were as clear as the way he dipped his head, as if to tell us to make our move.

He'd made his, placed his next piece, and drawn us into a corner. Called checkmate before the game even fucking began.

We'd never stood a chance.

CHAPTER 35

AALIYAH

Pandemonium.

The room erupted into chaos like I'd never seen. The snarls, crashes, and overall panic.

The eyes that were all pointed at us. At *me*.

Between Sebek's declaration and Darius's accusation, we were cornered. Other Challenges were called over the ensuing mayhem. I heard the likes of Milo and Drakon cutting through the fog in a lawless blend of fire. Yet, nothing drowned out the cries of the Eternals going rabid at the idea of being shown up. Other issues were screamed, but I blotted every single one of them out, my mind focused solely on the pounding beat of my own heart.

Of the flex of the shadows that surrounded us.

I didn't want the call of my power, not now, not when everyone was already in a frenzy. They were *terrified,* and my power reveled in it, that dark voice brushing along my skin like a rabid beast, sinking into me with furious intent.

Get rid of them.

I held in a startled gasp, stepping back directly into Prince's arms. I tried to keep myself stable, to keep my eyes open. The shadows flexed again, but there wasn't the give they should have had, not the swirling ease that had come before. The Eternium's lock on intentional violence toward others was absolute. Even still, I struggled to pull it in; I struggled to let it go, as sweat pooled on my brow. It was right there, pushing at me to move.

Yet staying locked inside of me, like it couldn't break out.

The air grew cold a breath later as Red's energy came barreling toward me, his fear so thick it nearly took me off my feet. The hair on the back of my neck stood, my mind narrowing on the instincts of prey about to be mauled by a predator. Fight-or-flight.

Attack-or-run.

The others felt it, too, freezing as steps sounded behind us, like warning bells that none of us could avoid.

"I half expected you to run," a familiar voice said, the frigid calculation pointed. "You should have run. Would have saved me the trouble."

Varying degrees of fear lined each of my men's faces, hidden only partially by the masks that sat there. Hands that had found mine tightened, and they circled me as ice took root in my veins.

The voice of a man I'd never forget. I hated the way it made my stomach spasm now, the same voice that had read my bedtime stories and used to sing me to sleep.

My ab.

"Sebek," Osiris said, a spark traveling along his skin, lighting up his eyes. "Do you really think that was the best move? Think of how many will want her head now."

He was the first to look back, the first to turn around as he placed himself between us and the monster, like a shield. Power flooded the air, ancient and cruel, fire dancing over Sebek's arms the same way it was Osiris's. It buried everything else, snuffing out Osiris's spark.

"Of course, they'd have to get through me first." Sebek took a step forward, his hands in his pockets, black hair slicked against his head, his red eyes beaming behind the blood red mask he wore. It was split down the middle, showing half of his face, intricate details lost in the fear I couldn't hide as he smirked, like he was proud to see what Osiris could do. "Usire."

"We have no words for you," Osiris said, but Sebek paid him no mind.

His eyes landed on me, and even behind the bodies of Eirik and Fallon, I still felt that gaze. It burned me, singed the hair on my arms as I took an unwilling step back. He tracked me, his head tilting like a beast getting ready to strike.

The others were silent, tension sitting so heavily I could feel it in the heaves of their breaths. Sebek watched on, endless power, endless greed, and rage.

We couldn't win.

"I will not ask again, Glass," he said, the others looking between themselves in confusion.

But I knew what he meant, understood it with a clarity that ripped me to shreds, the same way it had when I'd woken with his blood in my mouth. A pin could have dropped, and he didn't even need to look at them. Each of the men that I knew would give their lives for me ... Suddenly, I wasn't here anymore. I was standing with Sebek in front of Ascension Rising.

Asking myself if I could walk into it again.

He extended his hand.

The answer was and would always be, yes.

My men flew into action, fangs dropping, eyes bursting red as they snarled and snapped. But none of them moved closer to him, caught by the magic of the Eternium. I was glad, the runaway panic in my body nearly sending me into a spiral.

For a moment I considered his offer, thought of what would happen if we failed.

"I think the fuck not," Prince said, his voice nothing of the carefree one I'd been soaking in. It was deep, dipped in a fire like a warrior preparing to fight as he stepped forward. "Back the fuck up, you prick bastard."

There was a moment of confusion as Sebek's eyes narrowed before they blew wide. It was like the breath was sucked from the hall, a chill in the air as Sebek took a step forward.

"Nero?" he asked, shock a look that was quickly washed away by feral intensity.

"In the flesh. Now, if you don't mind, we have a shit show to get out of," he said, the prettied words hitting like a bat, no kindness behind them as he sneered.

Sebek didn't move for a second, making me nervous. The cold efficiency ate the crazy behind his eyes, and this Sebek, the one with a plan, was infinitely more terrifying than the one that rambled and killed seemingly without reason.

His head tipped as his lips tilted up. "I can't harm you here. You know that. Even a *Charm* would push the limits."

His eyes danced between us, for the first time looking at the men he'd Turned, as if picking out a piece of fruit to bite into. Red eyes, like hollow rubies, played with us. His dance stopped on Adrian, whose hand tightened, growing shaky in mine. I sucked in a breath.

"But ... reiterating one?" Sebek whispered, just as I turned, Fallon's hand landing on Adrian's shoulder. "Where's the harm in that?"

Osiris flung forward, tension bursting in the air, but nothing could have stopped his next words.

"After all, a live command is still a command."

The scene that unfolded seemed to happen in slow motion. Adrian's face grew pale, sweat slicking it as he ripped his hand out of mine, stumbling away as his eyes rolled back in his head. He let out a strangled gasp, reaching for his throat like someone had taken hold of it. He nearly collapsed as Eirik grabbed him, keeping him standing.

Fallon was next, with a grunt and a flash of red eyes. Pain laced the cry that slid past his lips as Prince had to lean into his side to keep him standing.

Sebek clicked his tongue, and I was frozen in place as he took a step forward. So close now he could nearly reach out and grab me. "I can't hurt you, and unfortunately for you, you can't hurt me or anyone else, either."

The wall of men in front of me was the only thing stopping him. I brushed past them, planting myself between them and him as they panicked and thrashed, trying to help as Adrian and Fallon cried out.

"Let them go!" I screamed, choking on the pained noises coming from behind me.

Sebek ignored me like I was little more than filth. He lifted his arm, pointing back in the direction we were going. "Well, what are you waiting for? *Feed.*"

The sound of cracking bones as Adrian thrashed against Eirik's grip haunted me. He couldn't feel it. I knew that, which made the snaps hit me that much harder. Fallon wrestled in Osiris's and Prince's hold, blood pooling in his mouth as his entire body twitched.

I took the last steps forward until I was right in front of Sebek. His red eyes focused on me, his power a dangerous brush that warned me to be wary.

"Aaliyah—" Prince managed.

"I said let them go!" I gritted out again, my head starting to ache as a pounding sear started behind my eyes. A gray sheen covered them, darkening the room and stealing the colors around me, searching for an outlet ... but with nothing else to target, it settled in me, slowly turning me to ash one pained groan at a time. It was cold, viciously so, circling in my veins and ending as sparks of pain that turned my hands numb. That cold found a place in the air as Red became my grounding force, an anchor to hold on to as I stared Sebek down.

"You've had your chance to come nicely, Glass. They suffer from your selfishness," Sebek said finally. Not even bothering to look at the others.

My heart sank, and I recoiled. A creeping feeling that had no place in my mind spread, touching every thought, corrupting every breath I had.

My fault. *My fault.*

"Your lies have no home here," Eirik shot in, moving so fast I felt the brush of wind against my face. He stood by my side, a shield and a sword with his teeth bared and arms held high. The tattoo on his face seemed to move, like it was joining in on the fight.

"The only person to blame for this is you, *Butcher.* Like a child throwing a tantrum," another voice bit in, coated in a pain that I felt in my soul. Fallon stumbled to my side, and I moved just in time to catch him, supporting his weight as he trembled.

Sebek watched with a blank expression before his lips curled in disgust. "We'll see if you still feel that way after a few days, won't we?"

Then he simply walked past, his back to us, his head high as he faded from view, blending into the crowd that rioted around us. Destruction left in his wake.

I shook his words out of my head as I turned my attention entirely to Adrian and Fallon, as the two writhed from the ache of the *Maker's Call.*

"Don't worry, love. We've dealt with worse," Adrian grunted as he spoke, the red in his eyes finally wavering. He panted, sweat sliding down his face.

"We need to get them out of here," Osiris called, looking to Eirik and Prince, who held Adrian and Fallon up, straining as they writhed against them.

More bones snapped, more screaming cries echoing as the whispers of the other Eternals grew again.

Until all focus was on us.

The room, already in a mockery of shambles, blew up again. The guys paid no mind, shuffling up the stairs, away from the mob that'd formed. I was heaving hard breaths by the time Osiris got me there, too, tears stinging in my eyes as we hit a hallway.

"Breathe, *lux mea*, breathe." It took me a second to recognize Osiris's voice. But I knew what he meant.

I could feel it. The dark inside of me trying to tear me apart from the inside, desperate to get out. The voice was a cadence now, a mocking scream that wiped away the sound of the Eternium.

I let out a cry, grabbing my chest as I pitched forward. It pressed again, and hands desperately tried to hold me up.

"*My light*." Osiris's face was a shaded view, hazed over in a black and white sheen. "Focus on me."

His power was like a summer rain, gentle on my skin as his hands ran up and down my exposed arms. It pushed mine down, covered it as he forced my eyes on his.

The darkness wavered.

I pulled in a breath, then another, following his exaggerated movements. It helped; it settled the dark, pushing it down until it was less of an inferno in my chest, and more of a simmering ember. It didn't stay that way. The Void had never liked being ignored, and the moment I let my guard fall, it came crashing down full force.

I didn't have the time to worry about what it would do, my entire body wrenching away from the hands that held me stable, the world falling away. Mismatched blue eyes watched in shock as I was ripped away. Then there was only *nothing*.

Obsidian sky.

A Mercury floor.

The bitter cold of Red as he bounced nervously around me,

pushing me to turn around and face the danger that I could feel as the hair raised on the back of my neck, and wisps of the Void circled me just like they circled *him*. Azer. The Imperial, my uncle. He looked the exact same as he had before, though with a better pep in his step as he moved toward me.

He was dressed in a tightly fitted suit, his hands tucked into his pockets as he took sure steps toward me, the Void opening up for him, as though singing for each move he made.

"Well, isn't this a surprise, little Imperial," he said, reaching me, squatting down to see me at eye level, that lavender tinted with gold so gripping it was all I could focus on. It was strange, seeing him in color here. "I was wondering when I'd see you again. I've been dreadfully bored."

CHAPTER 36

ADRIAN

*F*eed.

The need strangled every thought that I had, changed my mind into something that was barely more than instincts. Sebek's reinforcement did its work, the *Call* just as vicious as it was the day he'd turned me.

It devoured me. Faces blurred, bodies becoming nothing more than flesh and blood that I snapped and snarled at as I was dragged through a mocking crowd that was still in shambles.

Their faces shifted, molting into those whose throats I'd already ripped out once. The picturesque gold and marble of the ballroom was replaced with the gritty underbelly of old London, dreary brick splattered with red. I arched in the arms that held me, fighting them and the will of the Eternium until I heard a bone snap, and my arm went limp.

The taste of blood on my tongue.

Blood that flooded my mouth. My own. I hadn't realized I'd sliced into my tongue as my fangs fell, until I choked on it. My body revolted, seizing as my eyes rolled back, straightening to a taut line as I nearly ripped myself out of Eirik's arms, accidentally slamming an open palm into his cheek as he grunted.

There was no pain, not like normal. I was used to tackling the feeling of my stomach trying to twist its way inside out, and the body

343

aches that followed. Even the constant pulse in my gums that drove saliva to flood my mouth. But right now, the gnawing ache to feed wasn't physical as much as it was mental, tormenting me with visions of blood-soaked streets, my ears straining, searching for the pulse of a fearful heart.

And me begging that I wouldn't find one.

A scream filled the air that wrenched me aware for long enough to see Nero drop Fallon, cursing as my brother screamed until his vocal cords gave. Tears in his eyes, his entire body living agony as the *Call* pushed for something we couldn't give.

Blood. It wanted blood. Craved it. My mouth watered as Nero hauled Fal up again.

Wide eyes. I took another step forward, toward the girl whose fear sat heavy in the air. I was sticky, licking the blood off my lips as I screamed to stop in my own head, begged my legs to break and for me to fall.

The *Call* was everything I needed it not to be as it whispered heinous acts into my head. It was never what it should have been, Sebek's words mocking me, until the voice was my own, the devil on my shoulder.

But I didn't stop. Couldn't. Another body at my feet.

It brought up every memory I tried to push to the back of my broken mind. Every kill I fought so hard to hide behind a mask of a smile. The pressure of hands in my stomach, twisting organs, the blare of a digital clock counting down the moment until my failure. Even as that push drove me, I couldn't move, the force of the Eternium keeping me locked into place.

Three hours.

The reminder of those wretched hours strapped to that cold steel table was enough to drive me mad with rage.

Thirty-six minutes.

Emotion ran wild, my control tumbling down and down ... until my vision darkened, splattered with red.

The halls quieted, the rush of people fading away.

My hands went to my head, fingers digging into skin, and I cried out as another wave crashed through me, my teeth gritting just as hands gripped my face. They pulled away my own, showing bloodied digits I couldn't feel.

I expected it to be Fallon, as it usually was. Cold hands and frigid green eyes that somehow calmed me down. Even with as insufferable as he could be. Instead, I was met with *Nero*.

Everything in me froze, and I was stunned to see him for a moment. I'd grown almost used to his absence. It felt too real to see him grimace at the no doubt abysmal state of me.

I'd been drifting along since we found out he was alive, my mind never really trusting that it was him. A few times I'd touched him just to see if he'd fade away, or looked a little quicker than I should have to make sure I hadn't just seen him out of the corner of my eye.

Even then, I couldn't be sure he wasn't a figment of my imagination, or another sick toy in Archon's lamp.

I searched my chest for the bonds that Archon's deal had severed, hunting for the one that felt like a steel thread, that held my soul to his in a tie that had been breakable only by death. It wasn't there, the pulsing mark over my chest a reminder of that even if I couldn't feel it.

Nero pulled in an exaggerated breath, dragging me to the floor in a practiced move. So I was sitting in front of him. Fallon was already there, and I was forced to lean on his shoulder to keep myself from tipping over.

Nero sat, crossed legged, before he grabbed my face again. "One breath in, settle the mind."

I was already breathing before he'd even said the familiar words that had gotten me through the worst of my *Calls*. Words I used to try to remember when we'd fought them after he was gone. I'd forgotten how much calmer he'd sounded, the steady way he breathed like nothing could shake him.

"One breath out, bring peace to the body," Fallon added, and his exhale forced its way past clenched teeth.

He grimaced, shaking as he snarled, losing focus enough for the red to completely swallow his eyes again. His breath caught, ending in a tortured scream as he bowed over. Nero was patient, more than we'd ever been with ourselves, as he took another breath, focusing on Fallon, watching as he struggled to follow.

Keeping at it until he did.

There was a waver in the hunger, a slight dimming to the red of my eyes as my vision cleared for a second. I breathed in deeper, easier.

"That's it." Nero's voice was a steady cadence, the hint of his Roman accent all sharp poise and haughty arrogance. For the first time since Sebek slammed the *Call* back down on me, I saw clearly.

Our room came into view, the concerned shuffling and whispers of everyone around us. It'd been a long time since the *Call* had been this bad.

I rubbed my temples, more out of habit than anything else, looking at Fallon as he still shook between flashes of red in his eyes.

"She's gone," someone whispered, slipping past the lull in the *Call*, and I lifted my head to catch Osiris's eyes, almost too groggy to understand his words.

Gone? *She's* gone?

"Aaliyah," I whispered, clenching my fists as I staggered to my feet, grunting when Eirik shot forward to keep me from absolutely eating the floor. The lack of Aaliyah's hands suddenly made sense, the missing heartbeat and the tender words leaving me hollow. I'd been so lost in the *Call* I hadn't even thought to look for her.

I made myself sick just thinking about it, covering my mouth as all that work we'd done flew out the window. A small, horrible part of me was glad she wasn't here to see this. To see *me* like this. My fangs caught my tongue again as I wet my lips at the idea of her blood sliding down my throat. It was washed away by the fear, the disgust that permeated my mind.

"Where is she?" I asked, the bitter bite to my words as much a surprise to me as it was to Osiris as his eyes widened. I didn't have an apology, too wrapped up in the fear that came with the lack of her presence to try to force one behind an easygoing smile.

"Did he get her?" Fallon asked, the rage in his voice added to mine, bouncing off me and clouding the room. "Did Sebek take her?"

The tension grew like wildfire before Nero was standing between us. He raised his arms as though we were two bulls about to go tearing through the room.

"No," he said firmly as he looked between us. "She disappeared after Sebek's bombshell ... this is the same feeling I got at Archon's."

Eirik grunted, his face still beyond the cracking of his jaw as the skin on it pulled taut.

He rolled his head, fighting the snarl on his lips as his hand landed on the scar at his neck. His beast fought to get out, the frothing menace behind his eyes jolting, surging forward, but he looked to be at least *mostly* in control for now. "Same here."

Nero snorted, shaking his head. "At least you don't look like you're going to fully wolf out on us this time."

"Perhaps she's in the Void again," Osiris added, seeming as lost as I felt.

The Void. I pulled my hands through my hair, looking at the wrist that used to hold her mark. Had this happened before, I probably wouldn't have even worried. I'd never struggled to feel her, but now ...

Was this even *real*?

My breathing spiraled again, my eyes blotting as I backed up until I hit a wall. Nero followed me, trapping me there, and I felt rabid at the idea of him getting close enough to touch. The lights glared brighter than they were a few seconds ago, and I waited for the walls to fade away, to crumble into golden dust. I waited for the clock to tell me how much further I'd gotten. "That's not good enough, Nero. She could be in danger—"

Nero didn't stop, like he could tell exactly what I was thinking. His hands landed on my shoulders, his eyes never leaving mine. I couldn't feel it, but it was grounding, even as my ears continued to ring, and my chest heaved.

"Trust me, if she was in danger, we'd know," he said, tapping his chest and showing the lavender mark on his wrist.

Jealousy fired hot in my chest at the sight of it, anger stealing my voice. I shrugged out of his hold. Emotions weren't something I avoided, not like this, yet I couldn't seem to get past how raw they felt.

I reached for my chest, for the golden mark that sat over my heart like a mocking bow. It was easy to move the blame, to take the panic I felt and tie it to Archon.

Archon wanted to destroy Osiris. He wanted us broken to do so.

"Would we? I've already had to deal with the feeling of her dying on me before, Nero. And now I can't feel her. She isn't there for me!" Fallon snarled, cutting into my thoughts. Nero stepped away, turning to face Fallon fully. He stood eye to eye with him, looking ready to finish a fight if it came to it. If Fallon didn't also look so pallid and sick, he probably would have already been throwing blows. "So, I'm going to need a better answer than *we'll know.*"

There was no hesitation in Nero's stance, no worry that leaked out of his words. "I don't have any better, Fallon. You have to trust me."

Trust was something I had in abundance a few weeks ago. Trust was something that didn't hide behind the smile. It lived and breathed in the bond I had with these men. Trust lived in the bonds I'd *lost.*

After I'd burned.

After I'd been tortured and ripped apart and turned into something I couldn't recognize. Eirik and Nero had saved us.

But they'd been too fucking late.

"I'm with Fallon. We can't just go off your instincts here. Not with this," I said, gritting my teeth when Nero's eyes narrowed at me over his shoulder, a look of disbelief flashing over his face. "The only thing I'll trust is seeing her in person."

Another wave of the *Call* had me tipping over, holding my hands over my stomach as I heaved. Fallon did the same to my side, alone in this struggle like me, in the emptiness that we felt. The bonds were gone, the mark that tied me to my little love ...

Gone.

"I wasn't on time, and I didn't save you. Eirik did. He went on that roof expecting to burn, and I froze. That's on me." Arms wrapped around me, pulling me into a strong, familiar hug. Nero had always been touchy, he liked knowing that you were close. Part of me wanted to push him away in my righteous anger. The other had forgotten just how much I'd missed it. "I'm sorry, brother."

He pulled back, that Roman fire in his eyes a strength beyond what I could even imagine. I let out a breath, looking to the floor, desperately stomping down my rage. I had to shake it off, the way my vision narrowed and my eyes lingered on my bare wrist.

I'd pictured him before, like this, in my memories. Head strong and unrelenting.

Not once had it ever been so clear as it was now, with my brother in front of me, his voice not lost on the end of a scream.

Fuck, Nero was alive. I'd never have questioned him on this before, never would have even dreamed to. If Nero said something, then it was true.

He'd make it so.

The *Call* was barely a thought when I flung myself at him again, hugging him as tightly as I dared. His arms wrapped around me, and he grunted at the impact. His hand clapped on my back, but he didn't pull away, sinking into the affection like he always had.

Nero was alive, my *brother* was alive, and I had to trust that. He'd always protected us, guided us. Been the light that pulled me through the *Call*.

What on earth was I thinking?

"But if you think for even a second that I would let Aaliyah fall into harm, you don't know me as well as I thought you did," he said, as if he hadn't beaten death. It was all so very Nero, yet so different, too.

"How do you know she's all right?" Fallon whispered.

"I can feel it, here." Nero tapped his chest as he pulled back, humming as he looked around. "She'll be back when she's done doing whatever called her there. She's fine, I promise you this."

An awkward tension filled the air as Nero looked around. He checked each one of us carefully, grunting when he was done. "We good?"

There was a bit of silence before Fallon nodded. "Yeah, we're good."

Nero laughed at the back of his throat, shaking his head. "Wonderful, because I'm going to be honest. You really pissed me off right there, and if I was in a less giving mood, I'd probably have punched you in the fucking throat." The way he said it was filled with joking mirth, though I wouldn't have doubted it. Nero liked to solve problems with violence, and Fallon wouldn't have turned it down. Nero's face grew serious again, dipping his head solemnly. "But I did let you guys down, so I suppose I deserve that."

I shook my head, trying to clear the demons that Archon had planted there in his stupid fucking lamp. I stepped forward and set a hand on Nero's shoulder, like he had for me. His silver eyes gleamed when he looked up. "We're in this together. Come hell or high water, Nero."

Three hours.

Another wave came crashing down in my head. *Feed.* It whispered, taunted, and cried.

Thirty-six minutes.

I hoped to God I could last longer than that this time.

Chapter 37

Aaliyah

Silver. Rippling silver.

The unholy pressure that had flooded me vanished, and in its place was the Void. It touched me like it had before, cooing softly like a worried mother hen.

"We really do need to stop meeting like this. Can't you pick somewhere normal, like a coffee shop?" Azer asked, picking his nails.

The blinding white of his hair was pulled back today, only the streak of black left out, hanging loosely over his face. He sat cross-legged on the ground, watching me curiously as he had been since I'd found myself here again.

I was still heaving hard breaths, searching the Void like it would take me back. I rubbed my face, trying to soothe the adrenaline that was still hot in my blood.

"Why did you bring me here?" I asked.

I didn't have the time for this. The night was in shambles, and the guys needed me. I needed them. Fallon and Adrian were facing the *Call*, and I wasn't there. I was falling apart, and I couldn't deal with whatever this was right now.

"Me bring you? Oh, *no*, baby Imperial. This was all you this time. Not sure how you managed to get me here, too, considering I am nowhere near the Eternium, but here we are," he said, and I flipped my head up to look at him.

Me?

"I wasn't trying to come to the Void," I said, and Azer's eyebrow rose.

"No? Well, you sure made it think you were, and me, right along with it. That takes power—a kind *I've* never seen—not even from mother dearest," he said, for the first time actually looking at me. His expression soured. "Regardless of what you believe, you did it."

"I didn't mean to," I said, flipping away from Azer as I closed my eyes, searching for home like I had the last time.

Except the Void didn't give like it had before. It held on tightly, binding even the soul in my chest as my breaths turned to pants. I opened my eyes, my hands going to my hair.

"Tell the Void that. It doesn't seem to believe you," Azer huffed, falling backward as I looked over my shoulder at him. He looked up at the sky with a bored sneer. "And it doesn't seem to want either of us to leave yet. So, you better get comfy."

Like it heard him, it responded. The floor under my feet pulsed, sending a shiver down my spine as the energy around me rolled over my skin. Testing. It was different when I was alive, in a way I still wasn't used to. It wasn't toying with my soul, trying to send me on.

It was talking to me, holding me close. As if it might not get the chance to again for a while. Like the shadows in my cell used to, before Prince had shown up. The Void felt like a living thing for a moment, and it was like coming home, my entire body leaning into it.

Like a mother's hug. Like I'd spent lifetimes here, and it was trying to make sure I was okay. The memory from before, the one of my mother in the Void with me, made it seem like it very well might be trying to do just that.

It was comforting, in a way.

"How did this happen?" I asked, and Azer hummed.

He didn't sit up, just flashed his hand in the air with a loud sigh. "Couldn't tell you. *But* I did agree to teach you some things if I saw you again. So, why don't we start with a lesson?" he mumbled, sighing as he rubbed his hands over his face. "Where are we?"

The silver floor wobbled. "The Void?"

He hummed, closing his eyes as he breathed deeply. He twirled a few strands of black hair around his finger, rubbing the bridge of his nose like this was all some big chore.

"You call it the Void. Others have called it the Asphodel Meadows. Bardo. Purgatory. It's kind of like a bridge. It connects everyone to their eventual deaths. It's the in between, the border between time and space, life and death. It's everything, and it's nothing."

I scooted toward him, stopping when he tensed. His hands were what gave him away, as they clenched on the material of his pants, the fitted suit bundling under the pressure. When I didn't move any closer, he relaxed. Only then did he sit up. He motioned for me to move forward, and I did, eventually sitting in front of him.

"Everyone?" I pressed.

Being so close, I really had a moment to trace his face. He looked so familiar, my mother shining in his eyes, in the tilt to his nose. It put me at ease, even as he brushed the black patch of hair back and glared.

"That is what I said, yes," he grumbled. "Reapers, though, get a little more in tune with it, a little more leeway. That's why you can talk to me here, why your physical body can sit here without fading away."

The Void pressed again, and I let my hand settle on the silver. It slid over my fingers, pressing against my palm as if a living liquid, even stretching as high as the markings on my wrists. Power flared in them as well.

"But you had Osiris here, too, before," I said, and Azer nodded.

"And it costs a lot of energy to keep him here without him, you know, dying. Reapers are different. Our souls are built for this. Others, not so much." His words sank in, and for the first time in what seemed like forever, my gifts didn't feel like demons on my heels.

I recalled my time with Osiris, when I'd destroyed the forest and nearly taken him with it, when I'd been at my lowest after Prince had faded.

I was a monster. Or that was what it had felt like, but this curious, playful Void felt like something different. There was life in it, a toying thing that had a purpose. It wasn't evil.

Maybe I wasn't either?

"Azer ... Did you know my mother, Iris?" I asked, quietly.

I didn't think he'd answer me at first, as he rolled his eyes like it was a chore to even speak to me. Then he sighed. "Not even a lick. The other Imperials weren't exactly fond of bastards." My breath caught, and I opened my mouth to ask something else when Azer raised his hand. "Don't look at me like that. I didn't do this out of some familial love. I did it because you freed me, or rather, that lovely hunk of man you were in here with did."

The Void rippled again, but this time, a sound rang out with it, like the banging of a gong. It shattered my thoughts, even the ground below trembling.

"What was that?" I asked.

Azer's face sparked with joy for the first time since we'd gotten here, and he shook his head like he couldn't believe he had to explain this. He stood, stretching his neck.

"That was the sign for times up, and not a moment too soon. I'm not a fan of long, intimate conversations. They give me hives."

The Void rippled again, more urgently this time.

"I thought you said we could stay here," I whispered. The ache I'd felt before, the one that pushed me to go, seemed lost. Why would I want to leave? The Void cooed again, crawling up my feet and over my ankles. "I thought you were going to teach me."

This moment felt like it could go on forever, and each second I spent here, the more I wanted to stay. I wanted to learn, to understand what I was. Azer was my key to that. Hopefully, he'd be the key to figuring out what I could do, and maybe that could save us.

Azer shook his head, a dry laugh slipping out as he ran a hand through his hair. "And I thought you wanted to leave? Forgot all about that, didn't you?"

Adrian and Fallon, the disaster that was the opening masquerade. It was like it had slipped my mind entirely, lost to the Void. Lost to me.

"Reapers can last a few minutes here, hours at most. This place will eat you up and spit out the bones if you linger too long," he said, the joking tone lost behind the shadows in his lavender eyes. Runes crawled up his skin, horns poking out of his skull, golden like the hints of ruins that cut across his face, over his high cheekbones and down into the collar of his suit. "Aaliyah, never forget this place takes. One way or another, if you stay here, it will have you. If not your life, then your memories, of which you seem to have startlingly few. The Void is great for visiting, for getting around from one place to another, but staying here is a death sentence."

I wanted to deny it, but the Void still moved, still "plucked" curiously at me. Toying. Playing. I nearly opened my mouth to protest again, but managed to keep it shut as I took a deep breath. The moment I decided to leave, it was like the Void realized it, too, sadness seeping into my bones.

"As for teaching ... you need some practice understanding what you are first. You need to come to terms with the fact that you're a Reaper." There was no give to his words, no softening the blow. Or the fact that he was right. I'd fought what I was every step of the way, and the idea of digging into those gifts still terrified me. "Otherwise, no training is going to help you. So, take time, really think about it, and decide if you want to know the ins and outs of us. Decide if you're ready to fight. To *kill*."

Silence fell between us, and I nodded, understanding. The voice in my head preened, and I kept my head low. "How do I get back?"

Azer moved, putting his hands together, before pulling them apart, keeping his fingertips joined. When he didn't move, I did the same. "The same way you did last time. Think about where you want to be, and picture yourself landing there. *Softly*. Made that mistake more than once."

Home was my immediate thought. Just not the home I recalled in my memories.

Not the Vivas house, or Eliza's.

Home was between them, the men that had made me realize life was worth fighting for again. The men that Sebek had just rained hell down on. They needed me, and they were where I wanted to be, always. "Thank you, Azer."

His face shifted into a flamboyant smile as he dipped in a bow. The sky melted, raining over us like black paint on a silver canvas, covering Azer in a flash, his last words following me.

"Sure, sure. Come back soon, yeah?"

If going into the Void felt like a tear on my soul, coming back felt like the warmth of an easy summer day.

It was gentle as my feet touched the mostly unfamiliar ground of our room at the Eternium. I still wasn't used to the space, the one that changed every time I set foot in it. It was strange, even the colors now matching that of the Vivas house, down to the stone accents along the gray walls.

I didn't fight for breath, or choke on my own blood, like I had before when coming out of a *Rend*.

I could get used to this.

I looked around, expecting to find someone waiting for me. The time jump made me nervous as I rubbed at my wrist, a sudden ache in the marks there, silence my only answer.

A chill filled the air, the dancing of joy as Red came to my rescue, trying to clear the unease. His emotions were all over the place, a mix I couldn't nail down as he curled his way around my shoulders.

"Where are they?" I asked aloud, I realized, as Red's chill became intense.

Reading a spirit was an odd experience. It was never exact, and most of the time, I had to guess at least to some degree. With Prince it was easy because I could see him, watch his face and gage his reactions if what I was feeling wasn't complete. Even then, we had our own language to make up for the parts I couldn't read. With Red, it was harder, and I guessed a lot more. But right now, I knew exactly what he was feeling because it mirrored my own thoughts.

Worry.

His chill danced away from me, and I followed, trying to stop the hope I'd found in the Void from withering away. We came to one of only two doors in the room, and I stepped up gingerly, my hand falling on the wood. The instinct to keep quiet was a constant presence in my mind, even when the mantra that destroyed me didn't ring out loud. I pressed my ear to the door, when the sound on the other side had me snapping back and pulling it open.

It was agony, the groan of someone that had been flayed open. I knew it, felt it inside.

The room was dark, and Red bound away from me as I took in the sight. Adrian and Fallon.

Adrian was sitting in the corner, his knees clutched close to his chest, head buried there. He flexed, another ripping sound echoing from him as he burrowed deeper into himself.

Fallon wasn't better, with his legs stretched out in front of him. His eyes were a blood red, with narrow gashes on his chest where his nails had dug in. His suit, that beautiful green corset, ripped open and stained, tie strewn on the ground next to where he was sitting.

A breath of fear surged in me, ending in my mouth as sour bile flooded it. My muscles tensed, my head suddenly pulsing with a need to flee. Like an instinct I couldn't quite shake, the sight of his red eyes almost too much. Fallon gritted his teeth, tears lingering in the corners of his red eyes.

Another agonized cry came pouring out of him, his head tipped back in a look I'd never seen.

I couldn't abandon them, not now. He didn't move even when I stepped into the room, closing the door. The floor creaked under my feet, exploding in my ears.

I cautiously reached out to him as I kneeled, gently wiping away the sweat that had pooled on his brow, sticking his sunshine hair to his forehead.

Fallon's hand shot up, grabbing my wrist as I fought a strangled gasp. His fingers dug into the skin, his red eyes suddenly flaring as he dragged his nose on the thin skin there. I didn't dare move, trapped by the intensity, by the feral need I saw, and the short breaths that came from him, each ending on a tormented moan. When his fangs dragged over my skin, I shivered.

I waited for the biting pain of them, but he didn't move, his breath growing haggard as he breathed me in. The Eternium likely wouldn't even stop him, because I wanted him to do it, to sink into me and take what he needed. I wanted him to feed.

If he couldn't bite, then I would for him.

"Fallon?" I asked.

His eyes drifted to mine again, fire burning in them. Hunger, confusion, lust. They blended, morphing until he pulled back, still panting.

"*Aaliyah,*" he managed, his head tipping back, his throat exposed as his fangs tore open his lip. A deep, keening cry ripped from his chest as he contorted. "It's not safe— You ... You need to leave."

The fear I'd had for myself was gone, washed away by this man on the floor who tried so hard to keep himself together when the commands of a madman fought inside of him. I found it almost silly that he'd ask that.

I couldn't leave him—them—not like this. Never like this.

"No, Fallon. I won't leave you to suffer alone."

<hr>

FALLON

Everything ached.

My bones, my blood, my fangs. The skin on my body, which felt like it was trying to flay itself open. It was internal, a feeling that seemed ingrained in me, down to the fucking marrow.

It'd been years since the *Call* had been so violent it shook me physically. I didn't want to admit how bad it was.

I jolted again, trying to follow Sebek's command, and the Eternium held me in place. I was both thankful and endlessly pissed that it kept me from what I needed. From the feed. Heat had taken hold, my skin feeling as though it were on fire.

Adrian wasn't any better, pressed into a corner, surprisingly silent as he trembled. The same position he'd been in since the others had dragged us in here.

They'd left us, reluctantly, to fend for ourselves. Our time was short enough as it was, and someone needed to play damage control after the shit show that went down.

We should be there, too, but there was no fucking way we'd be moving like this. Our only option had been to wait and hope that Nero hadn't been lying when he said Aaliyah would be back. Based on the warmth that seeped into my skin from where a hand touched my face, I'd guess the asshole was right. There wasn't anyone else with a pulse that would be brave enough to get close to us right now, to open the door when they no doubt heard us.

Aaliyah, my fucking troublemaker, wasn't one to turn away from something like that.

Lavender flooded my lungs, and my mouth watered. I nearly moaned, the scent of her driving me crazy, and I almost didn't believe it was real until the sound of her heartbeat burrowed into my mind as saliva flooded my mouth. My tongue shot out, licking the sweat from her wrist. I wanted everything she'd give me, and that seemed to be the only thing that could get through to the *Call*. Her soft looks and the way she touched me. Her heart. Her mind.

Her *blood*.

I hardened in my pants, aching as the Eternium kept me from biting down.

All at once, I realized how much of a mistake that could have been. Aaliyah was the only person I wanted my fangs in, and the *Call* registered that. If I got her permission, the Eternium wouldn't even get in the way.

I bit my own tongue to stop from asking, from begging her to let me have just a taste.

Another eternity passed when her hand pulled away, and I loathed to admit my own fucking weakness as a beg caught behind my clenched teeth.

"What can I do?" Ali asked, allowing me to breathe again.

Her hair was a halo of white around her head, framing her face as she looked down at me, her hands hesitating above my skin like she was worried she might burn me. She was an angel, one that I reached out for, aching for her touch as the *Call* quieted in my head. It was still there, demanding sacrifice, demanding things that tore me apart to even think, but at least it gave me enough room to speak.

"Run," I whispered, my voice hoarse. "Get out of here, Ali. It's not safe."

Blood against a barren ground.

I hated to think of the moment that had been my deepest regret. The moment that I tucked away, a moment that had been so close to the surface even before Sebek forced the Call to come barreling back into me.

I'd killed Aislinn, and I'd seen her face in everyone since the moment I was pulled off Archon's roof. Felt the fear in my chest every time Aaliyah got a little too far away. Felt that fear everywhere when she got too close.

It hurt even to speak, and she hummed, setting her hand in mine again. I fought a whine that tried to force its way out when she pulled. I shook, screaming at myself to let her go, even as my body warred with the idea.

"Not a chance, Fallon," she whispered.

Had I not felt like dying, I would have laughed.

I frothed at the mouth like a freshly Turned Vampire. Eyes red, fangs down and dripping. And she still told me no. Still looked at me so tenderly, and I couldn't for the life of me figure out what I did to deserve a look so adoring.

"You can't save her, you know," Aislinn whispered, sending a tremor down my spine as her face took over Ali's, snarling like a rabid dog as her eyes rolled back.

A streak of red slid out of her nose, across her mouth. Her neck, like always, was ripped apart, blood sliding down the front of her, pooling on the ground beneath her.

I jerked away, crumpling farther against the wall with a haggard breath. I slammed my head back against it, trying to clear the mirage, some wrecked part of my head whispering my worst fears when it stayed where it was.

Was this just another trick?

"Look at me," Aislinn whispered, her voice calmer than it should have been with the way her face contorted, painted with rage. "Fallon. Look. At. *Me*."

Ali was there, just for a second, enough to grab onto. All at once, she was all I could see, Aislinn washed away to the background, standing against the wall as I gasped for breath.

Ali looked over her shoulder until Aislinn faded away. Only then did Ali look back.

"Can you see her?" I asked, partially broken by the thought that this was more than just my imagination.

Was Aislinn really back? Here to pay me back for her death?

I'd deserve it.

"No," Ali whispered, brushing the hair out of my face. She cupped my cheek, and I pressed my nose into the thin skin at her wrist. Where my mark no longer sat. I'd done everything I could in the past to deal with the *Call*, but nothing soothed it like her touch. "But I know what it feels like to look at someone who no one else thinks is real."

"She's a smart one," Aislinn hummed, materializing next to me with a grin. She wore the same hide skirt and covering she did in my memories, making it that much harder to ignore her when the *Call* came raging again. It was like watching dominos fall when I lurched toward her, not able to stop the reaction as my body pushed for blood I wasn't giving it. "Then again, so was I. And look where it got me."

She flashed her nails, raising an eyebrow when I looked away.

"What's she saying?" Aaliyah asked, all kindness in the way she held my hand while Aislinn sneered next to me.

"You can't save her," Aislinn whispered again as the *Call* sent another shiver down my spine. My fangs ached, and again the Eternium held me back. I jolted forward, snapping my teeth together. "You can't even save yourself."

What about once the Eternium was over? What if we didn't kill Sebek, and none of this was worth it? I'd fought the *Call* for decades, and I'd never feared it more than when Aaliyah was nearby.

Aislinn was right. I was the threat, the monster. Just like I'd told Ali after she'd barreled into our lives; I hadn't been lying then, and I couldn't lie to myself now.

Aislinn's smile was venomous, victorious, as clear as the bloodlust.

"You aren't alone, Fallon," Ali said with a breathy whisper as she shook her head. "I'll take care of you."

She managed to get me to my feet, half dragging me the few steps to the bed. I followed, willingly. She got me laid down, making sure I was comfortable, before she left.

The moments she was gone were agony, the *Call* coming back full force. She walked by a few moments later, Adrian on her shoulder. He was doing his best to support his weight, lacking a smile as she finally got him here, too.

She crawled her way between us, Adrian pressed to her front and me to her back. My arms went around her instantly, even as I fought it. Her skin was a balm, her touch like the first sip of water after days in a wasteland. The *Call* dulled again, enough to breathe, to register the room.

The voice in my head screamed at me, told me to snap and bite and kill. I saw every person that had died at my hand. Aaliyah's veins pulsed under her skin, and the fear of the *Call* lingered.

"I'm *not* leaving you." Aaliyah said, resolve settling in the stubborn tilt of her nose, and I looked down at her. "You won't hurt me, Fallon. You can't."

Her hand was brushing against my wrist, the one that encased her against me, her fingers toying with the blank space where her mark had been. The mark that had made me hers. She scooted back, molding to me, and I wrapped my arms around her.

I was obsessed with the heated touch of her hands and her sweet lavender scent. The blood lust grew out of control, and arousal was quick to follow. She flushed where my lips brushed her neck, but she didn't back away. I shook out of my mind as the *Call* blended with desire.

I pressed a hand into her abdomen, fingers shaking against her taut stomach as I held her still, not able to stop myself from rolling my hips and grinding into her as she wiggled.

"I'm not in control right now, Ali," I whispered, my lack of it hurting nearly as bad as the unfulfilled *Call*. It soured my mouth, making my tongue numb, like I'd failed her. "Stop moving."

It was silent for a moment, when Ali rotated just enough to look me in the eye. I was surprised to see the haze in hers, the heat that had coiled and smoldered. The slight arousal I'd felt suddenly slammed into me, my cock like stone in an instant.

The haze of the *Call* faded more, and I stifled a moan when she pressed into me, shivering slightly.

I tried to open my mouth, to warn her again, but all I could get out was a groan that I buried in the silk of her hair. Adrian shuffled in front of her, his own panting slowing.

"Will it help?" Ali asked, blushing. The concern in her eyes was like a bucket of cold water, cooling me down, but not enough to drench the heat completely.

"I don't know," I answered.

I'd never fought the *Call* with sex before. Of all options, this was the last thing I wanted for Ali. She deserved to be treated with care and love that I couldn't give her right now.

It'd destroy me if I hurt her. I was already shaking my head when she grunted, stopping me.

"Fallon, I can't just sit and watch as you both suffer," she whispered.

When she moved again, it was to mold herself entirely to my front. Her hand came to mine, interlacing our fingers and bringing them up so she could kiss the back of my hand. "You won't let me feed you. I won't even ask. Let me try this, please."

Fuck.

She wasn't wrong. There was no way I would be biting her, not right now, but the idea of having her ...

Every moment of those two years in the lamp with her, every touch and breathy moan came rushing back. It was strong enough to knock some of the haze away, clearing my mind and my eyes as the red bled away.

I held her until my hands shook, grinding my teeth as each shift of her body had me searching for more.

It was tempting, to the point that I had to physically stop myself from pulling her closer.

"I can't give you soft right now, Ali," I managed, my breaths coming out in between grunts. My hips jolted, and I gritted my teeth. "You being here is enough."

This wouldn't be like the training room, where I could work her down and be in control of the situation. There was only the drive to feed, and if it wasn't going to be on blood, then the sex would fill the gap just as viciously. Soft words were all I'd have, and even then, I questioned my ability to give her that.

Blood on a barren ground.

"Fallon, I don't need you to be gentle," she whispered, and fuck me if the absolute certainty in her eyes didn't make me groan. "Let me help you."

Denial was a sharp word on the tip of my tongue that I couldn't quite get out. I wanted to push her away, to get through this fucking *Call* so I could track her down later, when the time was better.

When I could treat her like a queen, not fuck her like a beast.

"For what it's worth, I'm in," Adrian chimed in, breaking the last of my control. He seemed to recover quicker than I could, his eyes clear, though still red. He brushed his lips over Ali's neck, toying as she threw her head back in a throaty moan. " I'll make sure things don't get too out of hand. Though ... I'll be abstaining from the main event. I don't want my first time to be within eye shot of Fallon's dick."

Aaliyah turned, wrapping her arms around my neck. Adrian took up the spot at her back, before groaning as her scent flooded his nose.

"I trust you," she whispered, and I struggled to keep my grip on my control.

Then her lips hit mine, and she tasted like fine strawberries and the sweetness of Aldovin Chocolate. Any fight I had fled, and I was lost to her.

I flipped us, putting her back flush against the bed, swallowing her startled breath as I claimed her lips fully, intent on devouring her. The *Call* was a nagging in my mind that dulled, and every touch of her skin was solace. Each gasp was another second of clarity.

"You can't be having all the fun," Adrian whispered, his voice cracking.

I had to physically pull myself back, my head tipping as my throat closed up, my fangs biting into my lip.

Adrian was quick to capitalize, finding Aaliyah's mouth. Her eyes were still closed, but the sweet little moan she made was as captivating as kissing her myself.

Aaliyah was still wearing the dress that she had worn earlier tonight, a flushing purple that clung to her like a second skin. On a more rational night, I would have taken it off properly and worshiped every inch of skin I was eager to unveil.

But as soon as my hands touched it, I was tearing it in half, ripping it away from her with a guttural groan. Aaliyah's startled gasp spurred me on, the sound swallowed by Adrian's kiss as my lips sought out skin. I started at her neck, fangs aching to sink in, traveling down her chest and lower until I was pressing my nose into her cloth-covered core. I breathed her in deep, laving my tongue over the fabric, her flavor exploding on my tongue. I moved again, licking, toying, my fingers digging into her hips.

"You have to give her more than that, Fal. Our girl's begging," Adrian whispered, his voice bringing me back to the noises that Ali was still making.

Her eyes were completely blown, tiny gasps mixing with the

softest begs as I pulled away enough to look at her. I thought she might cry when I didn't immediately dive back in. I was starstruck by her face, the expression on it something I wanted to burn into my mind.

"I don't think he can hear you, sweetheart," Adrian whispered into her ear, his hand sliding over her exposed nipple, toying with it until the peak was hard, and she was straining to get closer to his palm. "You can do it. *Beg him again.*"

She looked at him, her eyes tearing up as she arched again. My mouth watered as some twisted part of me watched her suck in a harsh breath, craving the way she whimpered when she did.

"P-Please, Fallon. I need you," she cried out, her head tipping back.

Her legs trembled around my head, her thighs brushing my ears.

"Did you hear it that time, Fal?" Adrian asked, watching Ali with an adoration that had blown away any trace of the *Call* on his face. "Our girl needs to come. She asked so sweetly."

I grabbed her underwear, tearing them off like the dress, the fabric snapping. I was sure it stung as Ali cried out, but as soon as it was out of my way, I fell on her.

Thumb on her clit, tongue buried inside her. She was ambrosia, and I hoarded it as Adrian brushed her hair back, whispering sweet things in her ear until we had her entire body shaking. I didn't let up until I felt her tense around me, her walls pulsing as she came.

I should have pulled back, my tongue trailing another line over her slit that had her sobbing. My remaining grip on my control wavered, and I craved it again. The sight of her flushed with a pleasure that I gave her. I slid one finger inside, curling it upward until she choked on a moan. I pulled another climax from her, just as ruthlessly as the first, my eyes never leaving her face as her flush went all the way down her chest. My dick was iron in my pants, weeping as I ground my hips into the bed.

By the time the third orgasm hit, she was a panting mess. Sweat stuck her hair to her skin, her teeth leaving an imprint on her bottom lip.

On the fourth, her begs had turned into whimpers, tears streaming freely down her face as she shook. Adrian was quick to dive in, dragging his tongue over the salty trail, licking them away with a groan. Her walls fluttered around my fingers, her stomach quivering as I ran my tongue over her sensitive clit.

Adrian cooed, running his hands through her hair, giving her his hand so she'd have something to squeeze. Through it all, she never said to stop, never losing that beautiful lust-drunk face.

"You're gorgeous, love. You can give us one more, can't you?" he purred, as lost as I was as he traced her neck with his tongue.

I groaned, grinding again into the bed. I needed inside of her like I needed to feed. There was nothing I craved more.

"I can't, I *can't*. Please, I need you, Fallon," she cried, arching her back as I curled the two fingers I had inside of her, making sure she was warmed up enough.

The part of me that was hesitant had long since died, and I was already crawling up her body, shedding what was left of my clothes in jerky movements. I kissed her, letting her taste herself on my tongue.

"You have me," I whispered, pulling her away from a hesitant Adrian, flipping her onto her knees.

She dropped forward immediately, ass in the air, moaning loudly when I ran a hand over her sensitive nipples.

"That's it. You're ready for him," Adrian said, with such a careful tone that I wouldn't have known he was as feral as I was if I couldn't see the red in his eyes.

The *Call* was still riding me, shifted from blood to lust like a switch. I was a mess, and I knew I'd likely kick myself for this later. I'd thought of this moment so much over the last few weeks. I didn't want it to be like this, so rough, so carnal. I'd wanted to show her what she meant.

I couldn't this time. So, I vowed the next would be different.

"Ready?" I asked, trailing my hand over her back, soothing the bunched muscles as she relaxed in my hold. She looked back at me, her face pressed into the sheets, stained a red that had my hips jolting against her, the top of my shaft sliding over her clit. Lust simmered in the lavender of her eyes as she pressed back against me.

"Yes." Was all she got out before I lined up and sank deep.

I grunted, bottoming out with a breath, Aaliyah's high-pitched moan music to my ears. Her fingers dug into the comforter, the silken red making her look like a meal placed out in front of me. I held still as long as I could, running a hand down her sweat-lined back, until I physically couldn't stop the need to move. I pulled out with as much gentleness as I could muster before my hips snapped forward. Her moan was all I needed.

Adrian crawled onto his hands and knees in front of her, claiming her mouth with a kiss that dominated, and she squeezed around me so tight my eyes rolled back.

"Look at you, taking him so fucking well," he purred, all gentleness to the brutal pace I set, one I had no chance of controlling. My fingers bit into her hips, my body slinging over hers as I reached around, toying with her clit. She spasmed around me, her body exhausted. "That's it, breathe through it, love. You're doing beautifully."

"I can't come again. I *can't*." She arched, Adrian catching her face, kissing away the tears again.

"One more, Ali," he whispered, his hand sinking into her hair as he traced his tongue over her lips. He kissed her gently, toying with her as I sought to drive myself deeper. She gasped, squeezing tight enough that my pace stuttered, and my eyes rolled back. "Give us one more, beautiful. You can do it; you're doing so good."

Her back tensed, her legs trembling as she sobbed. Had she not nodded, I would have stopped. Done anything in my power to make sure I pulled away, but she pushed back against me, powering into my thrusts as she fumbled for Adrian again. He held her arms, being the anchor she needed as the bed creaked loudly under us.

A normal human would have broken under my next thrust. It was a mess of sweaty limbs, grunts, and groans. When she shattered, I was right behind her. I came, burying as deep inside her as I could go.

The need to bite down was there, so strong I nearly blacked out. My heart raged against my mind, my fangs sinking into flesh as Adrian jammed his wrist at my mouth. I grunted, glaring at him as he snickered.

I bit down a bit harder for that, pissed he couldn't feel the pain of it.

We stayed like that, panting as the world came back to us. Each breath brought a moment of clarity, a moment without the ever present need to feed. I didn't have blood on my mind as I slipped out of Ali; her moan cracking as she sagged to the bed. The only thing I could think as I stared down at the woman I loved was that, *fuck*, we were *sticky*.

The *Call* had receded, buried again for the time being.

"Did it help?" she asked, panting as she checked me over.

Even if she had made it worse, I'd have told her yes.

"Absolutely, love," Adrian whispered, his eyes clearing, the amber dulling as the *Call* faded. He stood, pulling her bridal style into his arms. He walked toward the bathroom, and I followed.

I ran her a bath, but she was already out by the time it was full for her. We cleaned her up, gently washing and checking the marks that had been left on her skin. I glowered at the bruises I'd left, promising to her and myself that next time I'd be more careful. We pulled one of my shirts on her before sliding back into bed.

We should have followed the others out, should have gone to deal with the crowd of frothing Eternals ... but we didn't.

When we slept, it was easy. The *Call* gone.

Only lavender remained.

CHAPTER 38

EIRIK

I didn't like leaving the others.

My beast had been a nuisance ever since Archon's. Hell, since my *Valkyrja* had come to stay with us, but this was a whole different kind of feral.

I knew Aaliyah was safe, felt it in my bones in a way I couldn't describe. Felt her under my skin like the ink that branded me to her, but that didn't mean my beast didn't want to be there when she came back. That he didn't want to search for her, that he didn't want to chase her down and make her his.

Which was exactly why we'd left Adrian and Fallon. They couldn't help right now anyway, and maybe her being around them would settle the *Call*. That was the hope, at least. At the end of the day, they wouldn't hurt her. That much, even my beast knew.

"Look at us, the trio back together again. Just like old times," Nero hummed, bumping into my side before throwing his arm over Osiris's shoulder.

The sight of them together again, Nero's tilted smile and Osiris's raised eyebrow, was like a dream. This had been our life for hundreds of years. Just the three of us, before Fallon and Adrian were turned. We'd been a family, the only one we had.

When we'd lost him, Osiris had fallen away from us, trapped in a regret that still ate him alive. I'd locked the emotion down, shoved it so deep I couldn't feel it ... like it never existed to begin with.

It boiled up now, shining in my throat as I grunted and reached for the scar there. "You don't remember the old times, Nero."

He snorted, pushing his red-tinged brown hair away from his eyes, the silver sparkling with mirth.

"Not true. I remember some of the fun ones," he mused, his grin turning wild as he tipped his head back and laughed. "Why don't we talk about our month-long trip to India, fourteen fifty-six, wasn't it?"

We stopped in the middle of the fucking hall, Osiris and I sharing a look that passed like a war story between the two of us. Because of course, of all the times he could have remembered, it had to be that horrific fucking month. Getting locked in jail and spending the entire time organizing a riot to get out, only to end up in the worlds worst game of cat and mouse?

"Of all the things to remember, *that's* it? Why am I not surprised?" Osiris groaned.

He rubbed the space between his eyes, and Nero just laughed harder. "Oh, Osiris. It almost sounds like you didn't miss me."

It was a joke, the way he said it, and the way he poked Osiris in the face while the ancient grumbled. Even so, I didn't like it.

"You were missed, Nero. Every day, you were missed. You might not remember it yet, but this family loved you more than anything." I grunted, shaking my head. "Even the annoying parts."

Nero's eyes cleared, a silly pride shining there. He went to speak, probably to say something fucking grating all over again, when another snarl ripped through the air.

"Someone want to explain what the *fuck* happened out there?" a voice boomed, the sound of a door slamming against the wall. Nero was already raising a brow as a man stormed toward us. The hall shuffled, seeming to tremor under the rage, the sound of panic still ringing in the air from where he came as the door slid closed.

Dragonkin. Strong golden-brown eyes, smoke that danced from his nose as he snarled. He was power, his beast straining, so feral it didn't even flinch when my wolf shot forward.

"Drakon," I said as the male stormed toward us.

His eyes were liquid fire, rage incarnate. He ran a hand through his hair, and I couldn't blame him.

This was a nightmare. Everything we'd thought had been thrown into chaos, and our chances at Exilium had damned well hit the dirt. The last thing I'd expected was for Sebek to expose my *Elskan*. It would ruin him as much as it would us.

He was nothing if not calculating, if not a monster. We'd forgot that. Didn't think he'd be crazy enough to show his hand, too. He was.

We'd pay for our oversight.

"This is a disaster!" Drakon screamed, and it was Osiris who stood up to him.

"We knew something like this could happen," Osiris said, a cruelty to his words. I looked at him, expecting the numb, but that was the furthest thing from Osiris's eyes. No, there was fire, rage, and fury like nothing I'd ever seen there. "Take a deep breath. Plans have not changed."

"Not changed? Half of the Eternals are calling for the Eternium to end early. The other half are suggesting we kill her before she can be a threat," he hissed, and I growled back in response. "Sebek holds all the power here. They fear him, and some of the ones that had been on our side for Exilium are reconsidering."

Drakon opened his mouth to speak when the hall wobbled. Osiris's gifts flooded the narrow space, choking the breath out of Drakon before he could so much as move. One tip in the wrong direction, and Osiris would lose it. "It will be dealt with."

He couldn't kill Drakon, not here, but he would do everything in his power to try. "*Leave us.*"

Drakon was smart enough to recognize the rage that poured from Osiris. It was enough to make my wolf cower behind my eyes.

"Fine," Drakon spit, flipping around, tossing his middle finger up as he stalked away. "If this ends up on our heads, it's on you, *Kingslayer.*"

He left with a trail of self-righteous fire and two of his Clutch at his back. The hall went quiet after he left, the walls stretching, almost goading us to continue moving. The impatience of the Eternium only grew, the air heating.

"Well, isn't he just a ball of fun," Nero mused, before shaking his head. We followed the will of the hall, the Eternium leading us forward like little dolls, through an unfamiliar door. The masquerade was beyond it, bypassing the stairs as it opened to a vast sea of people. "So, who's the first person we need to see?"

I grunted, already knowing at least one. Valen had warned me before, and I wasn't going to ignore that. The spot of Gargoyle Eternal was one of the ones hanging in the air. Axius and Hyland were at odds, and Hyland wasn't currently on our side of the deal.

My wolf snarled, my eyes deepening as my face started to shift. Adrian was out, and I had no idea when he'd be back in shape to go scouting, which meant it was on us.

"We need to talk to Axius, *Challe* for the Gargoyle seat," I said, scratching at my arm, the skin there tense as my wolf continued to push.

We'd need to get Axius on board with a Challenge, if he was even going to be a good fit for what we wanted. Someone that wanted Sebek gone, that didn't see Ali as a pet project.

Osiris was quick to chime in, shoulders back as he surveyed the crowd that seemed to realize all at once that we'd returned. "Emery for the Fae. She would be a good start for unseating Koldan now that he's taken the spot from Frileti. He doesn't share her kinder views, from my understanding."

That was two. We hadn't bothered with the ones that Drakon said he would handle, but at least there were a few we could talk to. With the shit show that was the ball, we didn't have a choice but to sway.

People milled about, talking, whispering. Tables replaced the dance floor with little booths of food and drink. The decor was largely unchanged, with the marble structures still being the highlight.

Motion caught my eye, blonde hair and steadfast fiery eyes. I jolted to a stop, my wolf seizing the weakness to force a sound from my chest, somewhere between a growl and a snarl.

It couldn't be. There was no fucking way.

"Eirik?" Nero asked, looking to where I was.

I was already moving, pushing through a crowd of outraged Eternals.

"Can you handle them?" I asked over my shoulder, and Osiris nodded.

His head was tilted to the side, the harsh black of his suit coat ruffled as he brushed it off, ensuring it was pristine. I didn't doubt him. Osiris was exactly what we needed right now. His silver tongue.

The Kingslayer.

I lost myself in the crowd. The figure had been what caught me first, but the smell, like summer lilies and roasting pies, solidified it just as a hand grabbed my wrist,

I was ripped into an adjoining hall, away from the noise and bustle of the ball. The snarl died on my lips as familiar eyes bore into me. Steadfast sky blue, like the winters that used to grip my family home. Eyes I *knew*.

Because they were mine.

"Who the *fuck* are you?" Yrsa, my eldest sister, snarled in my face, her beast like an avenging angel behind her eyes.

Even my own wolf quieted, quelled by an elder of our family, by an elder *Úlfhéðinn*.

She hadn't changed a day since the last time I remembered her. The same spitfire rage she'd always had, though now she held the dagger my father had made for her the night of her quarter celebration to my throat.

Yrsa was two decades my senior, the eldest of my parents' children. I recalled the last time I'd seen her. After a gathering to celebrate a successful voyage that my father and his men had pulled off. She'd been fighting a man twice her size who'd thought to ask my father for her hand in marriage, without even glancing at her first. I'd been enthralled by the way she'd pulled him into the ring without a second thought and spent the better part of the night ripping him apart, piece by broken piece. She'd smiled at me then, after she'd laid him out for the last time, bloodied teeth matching the fire in her eyes.

That had been *centuries* ago. Lifetimes between now and then suddenly feeling like lead on my shoulders. I'd been in her life for barely a thought, twenty years of the more than a thousand that she'd been alive. Did she even recognize me?

I wasn't sure I recognized myself.

"Yrsa," I whispered, her knife digging into the skin at my neck at the sound of her name. The noise that came from her coiled into a keening snarl, one that braced the tears in her eyes. My wolf snapped and howled in my chest as the blade pressed into the scar that stole me from the rest of my family. "Blood of my blood—"

Yrsa bared her teeth, her face sharpening as the dagger drew across my skin, digging a gash that bled. Her wolf came forward in force, a dominant presence that shifted the bones on her face and bared its teeth. "Do not lie to me with the words of our oath, Changeling! How dare you steal my brother's face!"

The crack in her voice was broken only by the snarl that continued to build in her chest.

I hadn't wanted to find them like this. My family had been safe. Osiris had made sure of it. Yrsa wasn't supposed to be here. Now she was another point of weakness, another exploit Sebek could use, but even knowing that, seeing her now settled something in me. I'd missed her. Missed them all.

"It's me, Yrsa," I said again, swallowing against her blade, pushing into it, willing her to look me in the eyes that she shared with me. "Eirik"

She had her hair tied up, pulled into a high ponytail, her defiant cheekbones splattered with red. She did as I said, looking over my face ... from the scar that she'd seen made to the tattoos she'd helped me get.

And the braids she'd taught me how to do. The same I'd done for Aaliyah, time and time again.

"No, this is a lie. If you were Eirik, I wouldn't be learning of your existence at my first Eternium," she cried, and my gut soured as tears formed in her eyes. The knife at my neck shook. "And you smell like *them.*"

She hissed it, her eyes flashing ocean blue.

"I'm a Vampire, Yrsa. Have been for centuries," I whispered, and she snapped at me, like she might follow through. Her knife bit deep, almost cutting flesh again, before she pulled away, sheathing her blade.

She wasn't as tall as I was but still held a height greater than most women, and she carried herself well, confident in the way she crossed her arms. Hesitance bled from her eyes, and I straightened my spine, more than ready to fight her to prove who I was.

It was in my blood, my wolf already baring his fangs.

"Yrsa—" I started, and she raised her hand.

She closed her eyes, taking a deep breath. When she opened them again, they were a bright sky blue. The tears were still there.

Then I was in her arms.

She pulled me down to her level, hugging me to her chest. The rumble of her purr like mother's had been when I used to have night-mares leading up to my first shift. She held me close, running her hands over my hair, and I pulled in her familiar scent.

"You have so much explaining to do, little *bróðir*," she whispered. When she pulled back, she really examined me.

She tugged at my hair, pulling it from the braids as she ran her hands through it, grunting at the new scars I'd gained, and trailing gentle fingers over them. There was plenty for her to see, plenty she hesi-tated on, but it was my neck that she really paused at, her thumb hovering over the jagged mark there.

"It happened after I was taken," I whispered, not able to get any more out.

I hadn't even told Aaliyah, not really, and saying it now seemed wrong, after I'd kept it inside for so long.

"Who stole you? Tell me who it was that spited my kin," she grunted, and I shook my head.

The night I was taken was a curse. They'd dragged me out my window just hours after my first turn, still sore and broken from it, waiting to heal, my mother having just left to get me more tea to help me recover.

It was supposed to be a night of joy.

"Doesn't matter," I grunted, shaking my head, trying to dislodge the memory.

Her eyes flashed between sky and ocean blue as her face went red. I'd seen her destroy men like nothing more than babes with her silver tongue, and I braced for the verbal lashing that was coming my way. Only for her mouth to slam closed when she looked at the scar at my neck again.

"Why didn't you come home?" she asked instead.

It was a loaded question, one I hadn't prepared an answer for. There were so many reasons, and all of them seemed so fucking stupid now.

"It wasn't safe," I said, and Yrsa saw through it immediately.

Her eyes spiked, going dark as she growled. "Oh, cut the shit, you overgrown *geit*. We may be wolves, but you of all people know that safety comes in numbers. *Why* didn't you come home?"

I held back the snarl at being called a coward before I let out a breath, reaching for the medallion that no longer hung at my neck. Those months after I'd been taken, all I'd wanted was to be back home. I craved the safety of my pack and of my family. The laughter of my sisters and the strength of my father. Months turned to years in the blink of an eye, and my scars stretched, molding me, breaking me.

Then I'd died, and it hadn't felt right to take what I was back to them. A husk that was no longer fit to be a man, let alone a *Úlfhéðinn*. It would have been a risk to them all for a man that wasn't even the same Eirik they'd known anymore. It felt wrong, fake.

Like I was a fucking monster.

"I feared you'd reject me. What I was. *Who* I was tied to," I whispered, voice cracking. "I was worried you'd turn me away, knowing what I'd become. Or worse, that you'd die because of it. Sebek doesn't like his toys having weaknesses."

Yrsa shook her head, the wolf in her shining behind her eyes as she banged her fist against her chest twice. Something I'd seen father do to rally his men.

"You are *not* his, Eirik. You are ours, always. Scars or no scars, fangs or claws. My *bróðir*, always. Your family is our family," she whispered, like I was a little boy again, learning how to wield a blade for the first time.

Yrsa never said something she didn't mean. In one breath, she'd cleared all the worries I'd held around seeing them again. Every fear that had kept me from reaching out. "Even if it is the Vivas Crypt I've heard so much about. I'll admit, it is like a nightmare come true, though."

I chuckled at that, and Yrsa followed, before her eyes narrowed. Her nose twitched, and she leaned in, smelling me. If it were anyone else, I might snap at them to back off, but Yrsa meant no harm.

My wolf knew that.

"What's that smell?" she asked, her brows turning up in confusion. "Almost ... sweet. Lavender?"

I reached for my wrist, instinctively searching for the tie that held me to Aaliyah. The mark still glowed brightly, my soul at ease even if she wasn't by my side. My *smár Valkyrja*. Pride swelled like fire in my chest.

"My mate," I whispered, and the mark on my wrist calmed.

I touched the lavender line that coiled there, soothing me as it warmed like her touch against my hand. It felt like Aaliyah was here with me for a moment, providing strength as I stared at a woman I thought I'd never have the chance to speak to again.

Mate. My beast called again, almost like a coo, as if he were willing her to appear. Now, *soon*, I'd make that thought a reality. I didn't know how much longer I could wait, my teeth aching to sink into her skin for more than just blood.

"You have a *mate*?" Yrsa hissed, looking around like others might have heard, but I didn't miss the pride in her eyes. Her hand landed sharply on my shoulder, with enough force to make me grunt. "You need to stop dropping these things on me, Eirik! Trying to give me a heart attack, I swear!"

I snorted, shaking my head. Though, now that I thought about it, Yrsa might be the exact person I needed for this. I'd been running blind, going off instincts and what I'd remembered from father's teachings.

She might know more about what to expect.

"It's not official yet. Offered her the courting blade," I said, and Yrsa nodded.

She pulled back, her hand going to her own, the one that sat at her side, from a man I'd never met. From the look in her eyes, though, he was everything she needed him to be.

"She accepted?" she asked, almost incredulous. I glared at her when she laughed, then nodded my head.

Yrsa's face split into a smile, and she reached up, fucking patting my head as if I were a pup. I hated that I blushed like I was one.

It was strange, a touch so gentle, a smile so warming.

"Good job, Eirik," she whispered.

I huffed, running my hands over my flushed cheeks. Hail fucking Odin, I was glad no one else was here to see this.

"You have been through first Marking then? I do not *see* a mark," Yrsa said it nonchalantly in a way that told me it was something I should know.

"First Marking?" I asked, and my beast perked up.

I knew about the bite, could feel my wolf constantly pushing toward it, but the intricacy failed me. Instincts would get it done, but

I'd like to know what I was getting into. What Aaliyah was getting into.

"Just because I haven't seen you in literal centuries doesn't mean I want to have the sex talk with you, Eirik," she joked, like I hadn't seen her and the entire pack fucking at some point or another. Wolves were sexual creatures by nature, and it was as normal as breathing. She lifted her hand off my head, holding up a finger. "The first Marking is the most important milestone you have. It's the first sexual joining, and the binding. It ties you and your other half to her, a true start of your pack. It's typically done in the woods, where your mate can run. And you can chase, claiming them."

Heat spiked in my chest at that, the thought of Ali running, of chasing her. I sucked in a breath, searching for her scent at just the thought of it. It excited as much as it worried me. Ali wasn't the fragile type. She never had been, and I wouldn't insult her by even thinking as much, but triggers came in many forms, and I worried that would be too much. I'd have to talk to her about it before we sealed the bond.

"You had no idea," she said, audibly gasping before she flicked my forehead. "Eirik, you must! It's no wonder you look so drained. Your wolf is feral."

I grunted, unable to dispute that. "What else can you tell me?"

She ran her hand over her hair, the flush of her eyes going dark as the wolf swirled behind them. I traced her neck, over the silvery scar that bit into her shoulder as she reached up to touch it. A tender smile crossed her lips, as if she were remembering the moment she'd gotten it.

"The bite will hurt—at first, at least—the binding of souls isn't easy on people, you know. It's carnal, violent, and it's in our blood," she said, laughing again when I snarled. "It's a good kind of hurt. Just tell her beforehand, and if she loves you like I bet she does, she'll understand. I promise, it's worth it. It will calm your beast and make sure she's never without your protection."

I hoped so. I wanted it with her, wanted to tie her to me for eternity in a way that even the mark on my wrist couldn't replicate. I wanted to remember the moment I'd first seen her forever, remember the fire in her eyes when she'd struck me in the kitchen.

I wanted her in my soul, a permanent fixture.

"I take it she was the one that caused all the fuss earlier?" Yrsa asked, and I nodded. "She suits you. Looked ready to fight the whole room when they turned their eyes. I really must meet her now, you know?"

I nodded once, warmed by the thought of my families melding together.

"Will you side with us?" I asked, quietly. "Against Sebek. Push for Exilium?"

For a terrifying second, I wondered what I'd do if she said no. The answer came just as quickly.

I'd kill my sister without hesitation if she planned to stand against us, against Ali. I'd end her life myself and walk away. My *smár Valkyrja* was worth it, but Yrsa didn't say that, scoffing like I'd insulted her.

"Is that even a question? Of course I will. I'll talk with my partner, and make sure he's aware it's non-negotiable," she said, knocking her palm against my forehead. So much like mother. What I wouldn't give to take the rest of the night to speak with her about them. Had they had more children? Did I have more siblings? How were hers? "Now get that look off your face. There will be plenty of time to talk once this is over, and you better be ready to, because ma is going to lose her shit."

Oh, Odin, preserve me.

I'd been so filled with hope, and the thought of my mother's scolding suddenly had me questioning if going back was the right choice. I wasn't the boy she'd lost all those years ago. Yrsa must have seen it, snorting as she shook her head.

"She wants you back, little Eri. More than anything. Don't keep yourself from her because of this fear," Yrsa said.

I filed it away, steeling myself with a nod. I'd see her after we got out of this. After we survived the Eternium, and Sebek was no longer a threat.

"After," I said, and Yrsa's face hardened.

I saw our father in her eyes when she nodded. All power.

"After," she agreed. "Now go. This whole thing is giving me a headache, and it looks like you have company."

She didn't give me any time to introduce her to Osiris and Nero, as she marched into the hall, looking between us with curious gazes. She was gone by the time I glanced back.

"Who was that?" Nero asked, an eyebrow raised.

"My sister Yrsa," I said, and Nero made a strangled sound.

"Well, sugar me impressed. I didn't remember you having a sister. She looks just like you, down to the eyes. Crazy," he said with a whistle.

Osiris didn't say anything, just looked at where she disappeared with a calculating intent.

"How did it look?" I asked.

"I was hoping we'd be enough to get through to Axius, but he was more bull-headed than I expected. We'll need to get Adrian with him. Avedal stands with us, and he confirmed his support tonight. Romulous is weighing both sides, but seems to be with us," he said, coldly efficient. "If he doesn't follow through, then I've informed him that our support in his endeavors up north, with the Cryptid culling, ends."

I grunted. Cruel, but one way to get the point across. The Cryptid culling was a movement that started some forty years ago, one that saw the newest race of Natural's shunned at best. Hunted at worst. Osiris knew more than his fair share about being the outcasts, even to those like us.

It had been easy to side with them, and Osiris's word in the matter gave them a layer of protection that would be detrimental to lose. There was no doubt he would follow through with the threat, though. His eyes were hardened, bitter like a harsh winter. Empty like the Void.

Like Sebek.

"Yrsa, the new Lycan Eternal? I'd heard the old one stepped down, just days before the Eternium. Is she on our side?" Osiris asked, pushing away the look, and I nodded. That was enough for him.

I didn't feel like spilling my guts here, not again. Not that I had time, as Nero let out the most ungodly, agonizing sound, and pitched forward, holding his nose as blood gushed from it and his mouth.

Osiris moved just fractions faster than I did, catching Nero before he hit the ground. Panic replaced the hope so quickly in my chest it was like my heart had tried to rip itself out.

"Fuck," Nero whispered, hacking up another volley of rich red blood that painted Osiris's shirt and the floor a red that molted black.

I grabbed Osiris's arm, dragging him and Nero deeper into the hall, willing the Eternium to take us back to our room.

"What's happening?" Osiris asked, his voice cracking as Nero cried out again.

"Feels like my head is splitting the fuck open," he said, no longer even able to support his legs under him.

The sickly look, the lack of shine in his eyes, and I was picking him up. He flailed, a bit like a fish, grunting as his head shot back, and his body went taut.

"We need to get him back," I grunted, *flitting* down the hall.

"Get Mags," he said, covering his nose as he choked on his own blood. "And for the love of God, set me down before we get to the room? This is by far the most embarrassing thing I've ever done."

I grunted, a shocked bark of a laugh expelling from me just as a door came to us. There was always something about the Eternium that told you that you were in the right place, and I knew this was our room without any markers to confirm it. "Not the time."

Nero laughed, ending on a cough and more blood. It covered me, staining my shirt.

"Eirik, you're carrying me like a blushing bride on my wedding day," he mumbled, but made no move to get down. This was serious, whatever it was. The fear in his eyes told me that. "Now is *exactly* the time."

Then his eyes rolled back, and I was slamming the door open as Osiris darted down the hall with a final breath.

"I'll get Magelav."

CHAPTER 39

ADRIAN

My skin *itched* where the black marks of the sun stretched across it. I swore on it, even if I couldn't feel the irritating sensation. The marks should hurt, and it only confused my poor brain when they didn't. I scratched and prodded until blood welled, and I had to pull away to stop the risk of making the new wound worse.

They sealed closed a few seconds later, slower than I ever remembered them taking before.

I lay in bed, awake as the others slept, staring at the ceiling with endless thoughts running along in my head. Bodies were strewn about around me, the comforting sound of easy sleep almost enough to drag me back under myself. The *Call* was still there, though much less now, not quite as sated as Fallon's had been. Not that I would ever complain about it.

Aaliyah had been perfect, everything that I could ever have dreamed of. I ran my hand up and down her side, her shirt having ridden up enough for me to touch skin. A reminder to myself that she was here, *real*.

She was every ounce of love that I'd wanted for so long.

I ran a hand over her hair next, the white silky tresses flowing under my fingers. I went to her cheek, brushing against the skin, needing just a second more to touch her.

I'd done it a lot the last few days. Sought out her affection, even if I didn't deserve it after Archon cracked me open. I searched for the warmth I knew she carried, hunted down every second I could to try to plant myself in the present.

To convince myself I wasn't in the lamp.

But with every touch, every kiss, and every moment I had, the more I worried. Archon took away my pain, stole a part of me when he'd ripped the bonds out of my chest and off my arm. I could have lived with that, had it been *just* that.

The days seemed darker, colors less vivid even in the places I'd known them to shine most brightly. My kinder emotions felt brittle, pushed aside for a rage that came in waves and threatened to swallow me whole.

I could have lived with that.

I ran a shaking finger across her eyelash, my nose touching hers as she huffed out a sleepy breath. One I only knew happened because I'd seen it. The flush of her skin was the only indication she could feel me.

Because I couldn't feel the warmth.

It wasn't a fact that I'd really considered after being pulled from the roof. It'd been too chaotic to think about anything else, and all my focus had been on the pain. The *lack* of pain. I hadn't even considered that it was worse than that.

I ran a shaking thumb over her lip again. No matter how many times I looked, how many times I touched ... I hadn't *felt* since Archon's, since my deal. Not pain, not touch, not *pleasure.*

I'd hoped I was wrong, that the shock had stripped it away, that I hadn't destroyed something integral to myself by taking that deal. A deal that I'd been too weak to resist. A deal that had broken me in not even four hours ... and it had given us nothing, and Archon *everything.*

I hadn't felt Aaliyah last night, even with all that passion and lust. Even when I felt it in my head and in my chest, and my body told me I should be reacting. I could see it in every move she made, and every moan I had the good luck to hear. I hadn't even been able to get hard or feel the sparks that had once bubbled up when I touched her. Those hints of fire no longer even embers.

I pressed a final kiss to her cheek, savoring the flush on her cheeks that came from it, wishing I could feel the spark that used to burst under the touch of her skin. Her eyes slid open, dazed from sleep as she looked over her shoulder at me.

"Adrian?" she asked, her voice husky after the rather rigorous night Fallon had put her through. She rolled in Fallon's arms, and he grumbled at her back, pulling her close again once she was situated with her front facing me.

"Go back to sleep, love," I whispered as I sat up, rubbing my eyes with shaking palms.

"Are you going out?" she asked, and I nodded.

I took her hand, searching for a feeling that wasn't there.

"Yeah, I'll be back soon, though," I promised.

She hummed, rubbing her thumb along my palm. Her fingers traveled up, landing on the blank space on my wrist.

"I can come with you, if you need me," she said, and I shook my head.

I kissed her wrist before I tucked her back in against Fal. I couldn't help but lean in, stealing a kiss from her pursed lips. My fangs fell, my eyes flashing red for a moment. The *Call* came like a flash, ending in a shiver down my spine as I pulled fully away.

"Stay with Fally," I whispered, standing and backing away. It hurt, almost like a physical ache I knew was there but couldn't feel, to move away from her. Her eyebrows furrowed before her head dipped back down to the pillow. "I'll be back before you know it."

I threw on a fresh set of clothes, crept out the door, and closed it with a soft click. I was careful to move, sneaking out without a sound.

Archon had won one round, and I only had so much time before the next. I needed to find someone that could remove the deal, get him to go back on it, or break the terms ...

Or I could just fucking kill him and be done with it. That would be *nice*.

Whichever way I went, I'd need a bridge, most likely a person that had been slighted by Archon before, and who wouldn't mind putting the Djinn in his place.

The room I was met with had adjusted again, more minute details taking up the walls. Even the step of my foot, and the creak on wooden floors, was familiar now. I moved to the kitchen, more or less on autopilot as I pulled varying ingredients from the fridge. The Eternium had mostly stopped changing our room at this point, the kitchen a near replica of the one at home. I reached for the milk, and it was exactly where it should have been.

It was honestly kind of creepy.

The Collector came forward, and a plan began in the roots of my brain. I could find a way to corner him for a fight ... a Retaliation. What happened to me wasn't grounds, but I knew people with enough anger toward him to go hunting. There had to be someone that Archon had scorned enough to warrant one.

I cut up vegetables and some ham, whisked a few eggs, and was well on the way to an omelet, when a door cracked open. I tensed, waiting for the sour scent of gold to fill the air. The soft trail of footsteps startled me enough for my grip to slip as I flipped around.

Fallon leaned over the island.

I let out a shaking breath, squinting when he huffed and looked at my hand. Blood gushed out of a slice that had cut clean into my palm, deep enough I could see the white of bone and tendon. I cursed, grabbing one of the kitchen towels to stop the bleeding. I glared at the floor, and the unfortunate puddle that now sat at my feet. I'd have to mop that up before Osiris got back.

This wasn't technically our home, but I wasn't going to risk pissing him off today by getting blood on his *precious* floors.

"You okay?" Fallon asked, face carefully neutral when I hummed. I *flitted* to the sink, putting my hand under the water, grimacing as it took precious more seconds for the blood to stop.

"Just peachy, Fal. You need to learn to not sneak up on people," I grumbled as Fallon pushed away from the island and walked over to me. "I could have lost a finger, and I do *not* want to see the process for regrowing one of those."

He stood, all macho energy mixed with a pissed-off expression that didn't exactly scream "open for conversation." He crossed his arms, dipping his head toward me. "What's going on, Adrian?"

I raised a brow, pointing to the bowl I'd been prepping, making sure to speak nice and slow so he'd hear me. And because I would never slip on a chance to piss him off. "I'm making an *omelet*. It's not rocket science."

I pulled my hand back to my chest, drying it, before tossing the towel into the sink so I could deal with it later. Fallon might be slick, but I wasn't in the mood to spill my soul to him.

This was my mistake, my burden, and I'd bear it. Regret closed my throat and made me sick.

"Cut the bullshit. Don't act like you haven't been anywhere but in your own head. It's insulting," Fallon said, surprisingly level-headed for a man that was pretty much always one mocking comment away from a fistfight. "Archon still fucking you up?"

How eloquent.

"Yeah, that's it," I said with a wave of my hand, taking great care to hold the cracked pieces of my mask in place, grinning at him cheekily, as I picked up the bowl again. I whisked the contents, staring into them as I took a steadying breath. "He's a tricky bastard, isn't he? As I'm sure you know."

I looked at him, eyeing the side where I knew his mark to be, the one that had been his curse to bear. He'd only shown it once, and I was curious if it'd gotten any worse.

If the thorns had grown any closer to his heart.

"You're deflecting," he said, not taking the bait.

"And you're a buzzkill," I pushed, slightly more aggressive than I should have been, gritting my teeth when Fallon's eyes narrowed further. Why did he have to choose now to learn how to hold a conversation? I set the bowl on the counter. "If you'll excuse me, I've lost my appetite. Finish this for me? Ali likes her omelets with bits of red onion on top. Don't forget it. Ketchup's in the fridge."

When I moved, Fallon mirrored me. When I went to walk around the island, he was there, too, and I couldn't help the dry laugh that came barreling out of my chest.

Damned frigid asshole.

"No," he said, still crossing his arms, still acting all high and mighty.

"No?" I asked, raising a brow.

"Tell me what's wrong, Adrian," he pushed.

Fallon grunted when I slammed into him, harder than I should have, forcing my way past in a bold attempt that was likely to get me leveled. A good way to piss him off and get him off my back.

Sure, I'd probably have a few bruises to show for afterward, but today, I might actually stand a chance.

"No," I said, overly cheerful, taking a bit too much joy in how nice it sounded. "My, that was fun. I should say it more often."

He straightened, and for a moment I saw all the ticks. The clench of his jaw, the popping of a vein on his forehead as he tried and failed to find a calming breath.

"You know, Fally, I can't feel pain right now. This might just be a fight I win. That sounds lovely actually. Let's do it!" I said, laughing as I raised my arms in a mock boxing stance.

Just one little fight, and I'd be out of here. He was never one to back down from one. Then I'd be free to fix my mess.

He took a deep breath, and the hit I was expecting, the one I tried to tell myself would be worth it, never came.

"A fight may have worked with me, but you've never been the fighting type," he said, the words mirroring the ones that I'd thought the entire time I'd been in the lamp. The words that had led to my failure, my fuck-up. The words that still fucking *haunted* me. "You're not leaving like this, Adrian. Not alone."

He was trying to be my brother, to be the one to lean on like I'd said we should be. Yet, I couldn't let him. Not knowing how right he was.

I wasn't a fighter.

And that fact had damned near killed us.

"Fun chat, Fally," I said, losing the smile, *flitting* around him, nearly reaching the door when he was standing there, too.

His face paled, his skin still riddled with the black scorch marks of the sun. He wasn't taking the healing as well as I was, crippled by pain every time he so much as breathed.

"You're scared. Archon fucked with your head. That lamp was a nightmare, and you broke," he said through gritted teeth, shaking his head like he might pass out if he moved the wrong way. "You aren't the only one, Adrian. I did, too. After I had to watch Aislinn die, again and again, and when that stopped working, he switched to Ali."

His eyes closed, as if reliving it again. "He didn't put us in situations that we would have been able to get out of. That's not your fault."

Not my *fault*?

That wasn't an excuse I could use, not when our lives were at risk because of what I had done. No amount of sugar-coated words would change the fact that I did exactly what Archon wanted.

My chest ached. Even if I couldn't feel it, I knew my heart was breaking. My resolve crushed to dust.

"What do you know of what he did? Hm?" I asked quietly, looking at the black scars that traced my skin. "It wasn't even what was in the lamp that got me, Fallon. It was what came after. I was tied down and tortured for less than *four hours*."

I choked on the truth, the undeniable fact that I was weak.

"Before I broke. Before I put everything at risk, before I put *Aaliyah* at risk!" I could have damned well been drinking acid, and it would have hurt less than admitting that out loud. I'd threatened the safety of my love over four hours of pain. Thrown away our chance at surprising Sebek with Exilium, gave Archon a leg up on us and leverage to make sure he stayed Eternal. "How long were you in your hell?"

I didn't need him to answer to know it was ages longer than anything I'd dealt with. Fallon might have broken in his own way, but he didn't betray us.

He got out, at the detriment to himself, the mark on his chest proving that. I got out at the detriment of Ali.

"Four years, twelve days," he eventually whispered, looking away. His eyes clouded, focusing on the blank spaces in the room. Lingering there, as though looking for someone. "I started counting when I realized the days kept coming."

Four years he watched the people he loved die. Four years he was stuck in his own head. The perfect trap for a man like Fallon, who solved every problem with a fight.

"See?" I said, letting out a breath, deflating like a popped balloon. "This was my fault. I have to fix it ... I *need* to fix it."

Fallon didn't budge, and I expected to see rage in his eyes again, like he had when Archon first told them about my blunder. Instead, he stood firm, like an obnoxious tree that somehow planted itself in the middle of the damned living room. "I'm not letting you go, Adrian. Not with that look in your eye. So, you can either sit the fuck down and talk to me, or you'll have to get fucking through me."

Tempting offer, but even without pain, the idea of trying to fight Fallon made the back of my mind ... pause. I glared at his scarred knuckles and cursed every bit of albeit good instinct that made me wary.

"Wonderful, you're serious. Fallon, I really have somewhere to be," I sighed, rubbing the bridge of my nose. The mask slipped on, as easy as it always had, crack and all, as I smiled wily. "Fine, I'll bite. What look?"

I smirked, expecting him to say something standoffish or crude. Instead, he paused, as if considering his words. He looked at his wrist, tracing the spot where his mark had been with the delicacy of a painter and not a brute.

"Do you remember our fight in the training room?" he asked suddenly, grunting as he covered the bare skin. "After Ali almost died at the hot spring?"

The memory *tore* through me. I'd never forget the fight, the raw emotion that had built up in me and came spilling out like the blood we'd shed. How I'd begged for him to understand where I was coming from, the emptiness I'd felt trying to help Ali stand again after her loss.

I'd never felt more alone than in that moment.

"Of course. How could I forget?" I whispered, remembering almost fondly how Fallon had snarled.

"I loved her, Adrian. I loved her, and she died."

It had taken a fight to drag it out of him, a fight I knew I wouldn't win but went into, anyway. I hated pain, hated the idea of hurting, but the thought of being alone had outweighed it.

"*That* look," Fallon grunted. "Like we left you behind. Like you don't know where to go or who to turn to. Whatever it is, you don't need to fight it alone, brother. Please."

All he was missing were the crocodile tears. Fallon seemed to be picking up some tricks. I whistled, really looking at the man I'd spent my entire immortal life with. Fallon was many things—asshole being right at the top of the list—but I trusted every word he said, more than anything else. I took that plea and held it close to my chest, knowing how hard it'd been for him to even ask. I'd been the same, once, staring him down in the middle of the training room, begging him to come to terms with what had happened.

To admit how much he might lose if he didn't.

Now I was in the same spot, blinded by emotion, dragged down by a curse and too prideful to ask for help. I'd done the only thing I could think to get him out of it.

A fight.

He was doing the only thing he thought he could to get me out of mine. Fallon, my brawler of a brother, a man of few words and a shorter fuse, *talked* to me.

"You're quite the asshole, you know?" I said, brushing my hands over my face. "Never would have guessed you would be the one to step into the caring role. Why can't you let me mope in peace?"

Fallon huffed his response lightning fast. "When you mope, it makes the food taste bad. Pretty sure you add extra salt out of spite. Can't have that. Ali likes it too much."

That she did. Every drawn-out bite, like it might be the last time she'd get to eat it. I reached for my wrist, where the vivid lavender mark used to sit. I listened closely for the subtle sound of her heartbeat, so slow and steady compared to the night before.

"I can't feel anything," I said, practically spitting it out before I could change my mind.

Fallon just nodded. "I know."

I shook my head, running a hand through my hair. "I don't mean just the pain, Fallon. *Anything*. Pain, pleasure, joy. Last night just proved it. It's like Archon took it away entirely."

It was like the only thing left in me was anger and hate. I was sure he had something to do with that, too.

Fallon held his composure surprisingly well, his jaw clenching. "What do we need to do?"

The age-old question. I hummed, tipping my head back. "I have an idea, I think. I figure I can be the spear for someone's Retaliation, if I can find the right person." There were plenty that had been on the wrong side of Archon's ire. It just took one that had reason to retaliate, but not the strength to do so. "I just don't know who yet. Still figuring that part out."

"Okay, we can—" He didn't get the rest out, as the door behind him flew open, and the bodies that tumbled in nearly bowled us both over.

Eirik cursed, Nero dangling from his arms like a besotted bride.

Though, you didn't typically see brides covered in their own blood and built like a linebacker.

The shock wore off fast, Nero's state clicking as I rushed forward. "Holy fuck, *Nero.*"

He looked like a ghost, and that was saying something. He was sweating, his complexion almost gray as his eyes rolled back, and he seized. It was a tense few seconds for him to breathe again.

"Please, please. Don't let me stop breakfast," he groaned, dragging himself out of Eirik's arms, not exactly standing on his own two feet as he puked up a mix of blood and vomit. He laughed dryly. "*Not it* on cleaning that up. Fallon, I hate to tell you this, brother, but I'm going to blame that on you if Osiris asks."

He wobbled, nearly falling, when Eirik grunted and held him steady. "He's delirious. Been in and out of consciousness the entire way back."

Nero convulsed again, this time, his knees giving out entirely. We took him to the floor, his head twitching as I tried to stop him from bashing it into the wood.

"Osiris is getting Magelav," Eirik said, holding Nero steady.

"Get him on his side," I whispered when more bile came up his throat. I sought out his heartbeat, hand on his pulse for a few seconds before I realized I wouldn't be able to feel it. I listened next, almost missing it by how quickly it stuttered in his chest. "Jesus, his heart sounds like it's trying to win a marathon."

"What do we do?" Fallon asked, weathering the next wave as Nero thrashed.

I was out of my element, and I knew no matter what I did, it would be temporary. This wasn't a normal sickness; this wasn't something I could fix. "Keep him as comfortable as we can and wait for Mags."

I hated that it was all I had, that I didn't have some miracle stowed away in my pockets. Nero coughed again, splattering blood across our shirts ... his heart stuttering to a stop again.

And we waited, frozen and terrified.

Because it was all we could do.

Chapter 40

Aaliyah

The bashing sound of a door cracking open against a wall shot me awake.

I was in a daze, my entire body freezing as I fought to understand what was happening. The first thing that came to mind was Ascension, and I looked around as I searched the room for Castillion. I would have sworn I heard his laugh, seen his eyes hiding in the dark corners of the room, but as consciousness came, and the glass walls of my cell faded, I realized where I was.

I got off the bed, darting into the living room. My eyes clouded, my body still lumbering from sleep, but I'd never forget what I saw in that moment.

The blood that covered Eirik and the black hardwood, the copper-tinted hair of Prince as his eyes rolled back, and he went limp. Eirik barely caught him before lowering him to the floor, screaming something I couldn't hear.

I spent several long seconds wondering if he was breathing, waiting for his chest to rise ... only it never did.

I took a hesitant step forward as Fallon and Adrian rushed by me, their voices a blur of screams and panic. I could only see Prince. Copper hair muddied by white, silver eyes lost to the Void. The flash of cold and the transparent skin of his ghost. I used to find such comfort in it, would seek it out, but now that he was alive, seeing him dead again made me sick. Another brush, another emotion in the air as my mind swore it was Prince.

He was gone again. Dead.

His ghost stared back at me, shocked eyes enough to rip my heart into shreds. I turned to the side, retching, vomiting on the floor as true hysteria had me bowing over, cold hands barely keeping me up as I sobbed. What the fuck was happening?

Prince flashed once, twice, forcing me to look at him as he desperately tried to show me something I was too lost in my own head to see. His hands came up, palms against one another, before he gently pulled them apart. It took longer than it should have for me to recognize the sign.

Rend.

Prince was *Rending.*

I sobbed as I moved to his body, landing on my knees by his side. I didn't touch him, didn't dare to, just watched his ghost, counting the seconds on the clock.

Well over five minutes passed before his soul snapped back, hitting his body with a jolt. I was already moving, pulling his head into my lap as he shot up, gasping and coughing, blood splattering his shirt before his eyes rolled back again. He didn't breathe, but I felt his heartbeat as I reached out, pressing my hand to his chest.

Was this what he'd seen? What Eliza had dealt with for six months? It was terrifying.

"He's *Rending*," I whispered, so the others would know, too.

It wasn't much, but they relaxed, enough to take a breath.

Adrian and Fallon were haggard, still in the clothes they'd fallen asleep in, hair matted with sleep and sex. Eirik looked like he'd seen a ghost, and I wondered where Osiris was for only a moment before the door flew open again. He shot inside, dragging behind him a snarling Magelav, who snapped and lashed out.

"What's happening to him?" Osiris asked, letting go of the Sorceri's arm, practically throwing them at Nero as he turned a furious glare on them. They grumbled but still crouched on Prince's other side with a seething hiss.

But they didn't turn away, just grunted as they studied him, brushing a hand against his face, then down to the mark at his wrist. Burning sand filled the air, mixing with boggy water.

"Out of time," Mags whispered, shaking their head. "The bandage is gone, the wound reopened."

Their hands unfolded, a brush of their power filling the air. It was like a fog, broken in the way it crawled through the room. My breath slowed, my heartbeat following it as time seemed to drag.

"Mags, how many times do I have to tell you? Don't talk in fucking riddles," Prince said, his voice hoarse. He was sprawled across my lap, leaning his nose into my stomach as he took a settling breath. He tensed, grunting as he tried to shift, but the pain of the *Rend* kept him still as his muscles contracted. "People are going to think you're weird."

He tried again, this time with my help as he moved to a seated position. He shook, his breathing becoming more labored. His eyes rolled back, his body tensing as he released a strangled cry, only for his soul to be ripped out again. He looked at me, in shock the same as I was, that transparent frame that used to be such a point of comfort now only bringing dread. He lifted his hand, bumping it against his chest two times, his ring and pinky finger down.

"Are the *Rends* going to kill him?" I asked, unable to look away as he grimaced.

Mags didn't move for a moment, looking between us with an empty gaze that spoke to the ties they had to us, to Prince.

"I only fixed him for a time. Temporary. His soul is fragmented. Not *meant* to break. To be *reformed*. Too many memories holding him together, not enough time to bring them all back," Mags said finally. They tipped their head up and sniffed, their face twisting in disgust. "Not much longer now."

It felt like the air drained out of the room, as I curled over Prince. I just got him back, and now he was dying. Of all the things that were happening, this needed to be wrong. Prince was fine. I brought him back.

You brought him back broken.

My body snapped taut at the thought.

"Worry about yourself, Reaper girl. Even those of royal blood can't escape *Mortui carmen*," Mags mused, laying their focus entirely on me.

I'd gone pale, my lips suddenly cold, my hands numb where I still touched Prince.

I hadn't saved Prince. I'd done something wrong when I'd first touched him. I knew it. I didn't know how to Reaper, and Prince was paying the price for it now. His soul snapped back, a wrecked breath freeing itself from his lungs as his eyes shot open. I held his head, shaking.

I gritted my teeth, not letting go of Prince as I looked Magelav in the eye. "How can we fix it?"

A body was suddenly on my other side, one I recognized as Eirik as his heat seeped into my skin, and the rumble in his chest helped to soothe me. I hadn't realized I was crying, not until his hands cupped my face, gentle fingers wiping away the tears.

"Same way it begins," Mags said. "With a memory."

For a second, I was back in my grave, crawling my way out of the dirt, gasping for breath, unsure of even my name. That was what I'd been hunting for this entire time. Wasn't it? A past that clung to me like a mold, a life that should never have happened.

To live, we had to remember, and the thought of reliving those moments ... haunted me. But if this was what it took for us to survive, then I'd do it.

"And you can make us remember it? All of it?" I asked.

Fallon was the one who broke in, sucking in a hard breath that seemed to steal the warmth of the room.

Mags shrugged, pushing the black hair away from their clouded eyes. "Mags knows many things, but it's too soon. Everything tips the scales. You must wait, the both of you."

Prince shivered, blood sliding down from his nose as he opened his eyes again. That startling silver was clouded with pain as he reached up to brush it away. He wasn't even looking at me, as much as through me, when he shuddered again.

Another pull.

"How much longer does he have?" I asked, counting down the seconds as he stayed outside his body.

I couldn't see as much as feel the tether that was tying him to his spirit. Like it was ingrained, the same one that kept me tied to myself when I *Rended.* Even Red took notice, fluttering around Prince's monochrome head, as if checking on him.

"Depends on the soul. Hours ... no more than days," Magelav whispered. "Must make it to the night post First Rights."

They didn't need to say anything else.

"That's it. That's all you have?" Fallon asked. "What fucking use are you if you can't fix him?"

"I will fix him if he survives," Mags said, the noncommittal shrug they finished with like a nail in the coffin. They turned, leaving us to whatever fate would follow. "Until then, it's up to him."

CHAPTER 41

AALIYAH

I dabbed the back of the wet towel against Prince's sweat-slicked forehead as he pulled in another horrid, broken breath. His eyes were vacant, his body a continual mess of trembles as his eyes rolled back, and another memory took hold.

It was agonizing, every second of him fighting this, every *Rend* we were forced to watch. They hadn't stopped again since Mags had left, as if suddenly on repeat. The pull, the *Rend*, the memory.

A few brief seconds of peace before it began all over again.

"Please, sweetheart. You need to rest," Adrian pleaded, his voice hoarse. He was the latest that tried to pull me away.

They'd all given it their best, but I wasn't leaving his side. I refused because I knew he wouldn't leave mine. I held Prince's hand tightly, unwilling to let go or look away until he pulled in his next breath.

Sleep had been a luxury, and I'd been spoiled by it since we'd gotten to the Eternium. Even then, the few sporadic hours in the arms of my men weren't enough to stop the press of exhaustion now. The idea of letting Prince out of my sight, for even a second, made me ill. What if he didn't come back on one of the *Rends*? I rubbed my eyes, hand shaking as I ran a thumb over the back of Prince's hand.

What if this was the last time I'd get to see him whole?

"I can't, Adrian," I whispered, looking at him, filled with remorse at the way his face crumbled. "I can't leave him."

Prince's cool body was enough to ground me again, but the memory of his ghost still stuck to me. Eirik was the only other one in the room, perched against the door, watching over us like he had been since we'd moved Prince into the bedroom.

He'd been silent, but his presence helped, kept me sane for each and every *Rend*. He looked on now, a stark hope in the way his purr hitched when Adrian grabbed my free hand.

"He wouldn't want you to do this to yourself. The last thing he wants is for you to fall over sick." His voice cracked as he spoke, bringing my hand to his forehead in a plea that had me sagging forward. "Please, love. Just a break, a small one, then."

I ran a hand over Prince's knuckles, looking up to catch the eyes of his ghost. He watched on with worry, a dread that I'd learned to catch in his eyes. The expression he made was only amplified when he raised his hands, as if going to speak to me in the language we'd made.

He hesitated, as if trying to find the words in a voiceless place, before he brought his hand up, pointer and middle finger directed at his eyes ... *All clear.*

Prince was back in his body just as quickly, another gasping breath as he bowed off the bed. I dabbed his forehead again, pulling away from Adrian with a slow shake of my head. I hated the way his face fell.

Prince coughed, reaching up to grab my hand, pulling it down to his chest as he opened his eyes. He swallowed, a fight clear in the way he gritted his teeth before he spoke. "Do it— Aaliyah—"

"Prince," I whispered. I held on to the touch of his skin, the feeling of him because I knew what it was like to be without it. I couldn't do it again.

He groaned, a tremor working its way through him.

"Don't worry about me. It takes more than a few shitty out-of-body experiences to keep me down," he whispered, pulling me softly into his arms, until my head was seated in his lap, just like I'd done with him yesterday. His hand ran over my hair, plucking through the tangled strands. Exhaustion hit like a wave, and I breathed into the feeling of him while he was lucid for a moment, fighting the next part of the

Rend. "Please, he's right. You need rest, as much as you can get. The First Rights are tomorrow. We need everyone at their best."

Prince pulled away, enough to look me in the eye, the silver burning fiercely. He pulled up his hand, pressing it to my chest. Ring and pinky finger tucked in.

It wasn't just my gasp that echoed in the room as Prince's solemn vow echoed. "Forever."

I nodded, lifting my own hand against his chest.

"Forever, Prince."

There was silence around us before the creaking of floorboards alerted us to Osiris moving closer. I hadn't even realized he'd walked in until he was kneeling next to my side. He examined us, eyes focused on our hands. His own twitched before he reached for the dark ink on his wrist.

"That's my caster hand," he whispered.

The flashes of his spell-casting were quick to find me, each moment a mantra of their own. I recalled the specific one that had tied the connection together before. When he'd wanted to show me what my power was capable of.

When I'd leveled the forest around him.

It was how he'd cast spells, a tie that had undeniably been in Prince's mind when the first press of his hand against his chest came. *Forever.* An ode to his brother, to his last life.

"That, I do remember. It is, brother," Prince responded, with a wry smile lighting up his face. He shivered again, a bead of sweat sliding down his face, over his top lip. "A reminder of you guys."

Osiris's eyes widened, the calculated numb fading away enough for the blues to lighten, and a smile to slip onto his face.

The memory pulled Prince under, his eyes rolling back. I couldn't leave him ... not like this. I tucked low, keeping his hand in mine when I was pulled away. The protest was hot in my throat, my arms shaking as I stood.

"Fallon and Adrian will watch over him," Osiris started softly, brushing the hair away from my face.

One look told me I wouldn't be getting a better deal. There was a firm warning to his expression, the sureness in his words enough to make me sigh. I ran my hands over my face, looking at Prince one more time as he opened his eyes again.

His smile was bright, stretching over his lips in a cocky grin that screamed *I've got this.*

Did *I?*

The room seemed to collectively take a breath as I nodded, hesitantly. Osiris led me out before I could change my mind, Eirik close behind. Adrian and Fallon stayed right by Prince's side, exactly like Osiris had said. Fallon took up the wet rag, dabbing Prince's face, and Adrian kept close, looking at the wristwatch on his hand, counting under his breath.

They'd take care of him.

Not that it made it any easier to leave.

CHAPTER 42

OSIRIS

The Eternium always knew where to take you. Knew what you needed, what you wanted, often before you did. So, when we walked back out to the living area and found a mound of blankets and pillows plastered on a now-plush floor in front of a roaring fireplace, I wasn't surprised.

It had always been particular, like a puppet master toying with taut strings. It made the furthest recesses of my mind curl, and I popped my neck, waiting for the ominous dread to fade.

The carpet was soft, warm even in the early cusps of winter. Much more comfortable than the black hardwood. Aaliyah practically sagged at the sight of it, moving forward as she rubbed her eyes. She walked slowly, gait slightly limped as she mumbled, "Just a few minutes."

When she hit the pillows, she sank into them, easing into the warmth with a sigh. It helped us breathe a little easier when her eyes fluttered closed.

Eirik grunted, moving toward the kitchen with purpose. His eyes were sunken, and he seemed to almost stumble over his feet as he pulled out a pot to boil some water. There was no grace in the way he brushed his hand through the remains of his intricate braids that had been mostly unwound already. He dipped his head toward her, and as much as I wanted to probe his odd behavior, I understood what he wanted.

I walked over to her, watching carefully as she peeked at me from her fort, smiling tenderly at me from the floor. She lifted the blanket, giving me ample room to sink in. The idea tempted me so much I fell to my knees at her side, but I couldn't make the final move in as I pulled her hand into my own.

She watched me for a long moment, not commenting on it as she warmed me with the spark of her touch, the gentle brush of her delicate fingers against my wrist. A touch would have sent me into a spiral if she were anyone else, but she was Aaliyah, my *lux mea*. My light.

She made my soul dance in my chest. I didn't put distance between us, and I didn't seek to cover my hands or the skin that touched hers. It was freeing, in a way, understanding how badly I wanted it.

"Do you wish to speak of it, my dear?" I asked, knowing full well how heavy the days had been on her, and if she needed the space to say it, I'd give it to her. It had been a harrowing night, a harrowing few weeks.

She let out a breath as Eirik appeared, a cup of tea in his hands. He set it next to her, on one of the few tables close enough for her to reach. Aaliyah hummed, watching the steam as it fluttered up from the cup.

"The Eternium, Exilium, the *Rends* ... It's all so much. I'm not sure how to deal with it," she admitted in a whisper, again showing her strength. Her ability to just speak sometimes astounded me. "I feel lost. I don't know what I'll do if we lose. Or ..." She swallowed, closing her eyes. "If I were to lose one of you."

I hummed, twirling a piece of her hair around my finger, tucking my nose against the top of her head, filling my lungs with her, leaving a steady ache in my fangs. I reached for the numbness inside of me that had shriveled up, the one I'd been drawing on to fight our way to this point. Though this time, it wasn't to reach out to the magic that haunted me, or to cover the deeds I'd done, the monster I'd made myself into. Not to hold on to it, to let it drag me through the next day, but to consider her fears and her worries.

I ran a gentle finger over her cheek, the flush of her skin an addictive warmth.

"What do you wish to do when we are free from this?" I asked softly, providing a distraction.

Her eyes had caught me from the moment I'd seen them, the fierce-

ness in them still to this day taking my breath away. The fear was there
—it always had been—but Aaliyah had a distinct knack for moving
forward, anyway.

She persevered like no other I'd ever seen. She'd pivoted since she'd
met us, giving us some of that burden, some of the trust she held so
close to her chest. I'd protect her and it with my life.

"If we make it out, you mean?" she asked, running a finger over
my arm.

She focused on her mark, on the brand that it sat over, tracing the
lavender as though it might wash away the inky black. Each swipe of her
sure fingers erased the pain that had come from when Darius had
placed it.

"*When* we make it out," I corrected. "What would you like to do?"

She didn't answer me for a time, just looked off into the distance
before she grabbed her drink. I didn't stop her when she sat up, still
clinging to the blankets, blowing softly on the tea that Eirik had made.

A rumble that felt commonplace now started in his chest as she
took a tentative sip.

"I want ..." she started, biting her lip. Her eyes glazed a touch as she
reached up to toy with a strand of her hair, her other hand tucking her
mug close to her chest. "I want to have a picnic again. With all of us
there. Adrian and I can bake cupcakes."

Her lips tilted as she looked up at the ceiling, as if hunting for the
stars that lay above the mountain peak we were in, before she closed her
eyes, as if imagining the moment.

That moment came spiraling back to me. I hadn't been there with
them then; under those stars I'd stopped finding wonder in decades ago
... I'd been too afraid of the organ in my chest and the implications of
the warmth it held for Aaliyah to join them.

I'd been a scared man, a broken one. I still was, but at least now I
saw that. I knew it was no longer something I could live with, not when
she needed more. Next time, I would be right there with them, gazing at
the stars, enjoying my brothers' company.

Caring for the woman I had grown so fond of.

"Then you'll have it," I whispered.

She swallowed, the sound grating as she closed her eyes. "You can't
promise that, Osiris."

I'd done many things in my life. Some I regretted, some I savored, some I loved, but I'd never known with more certainty that we'd be coming out on top of this. One way or another.

I didn't care if I had to fight Darius a thousand times or find myself in his bed again at his mercy. It didn't matter if Sebek himself stood opposing me, and a Challenge was called.

We would not lose.

"Do not discount my words. You will have your night under the stars." I vowed it, the words sinking into my soul, marking me with them. My magic swelled with the promise, fire burning in my veins. "You saved me when I swore there was nothing left to save. You convinced me that finding myself in a world without Nero was something I could do. Then you gave him back to me, too."

There were parts of him I remembered in those silver eyes, parts that I knew would never fade. Then there were the bits that had been reborn with Aaliyah, the new hints of him that I had the joy of uncovering each day.

It was a gift.

"If it is in my power to give, it is yours, and if it isn't, I'll find a way to make it happen regardless," I finished.

She still didn't look convinced, that doubt in her eyes. She'd been through hell these past few days, and the months before it. Which was why I reached into my coat pocket, hand on a warm stone that pulsed at my touch. My magic responded to it, coaxing the stone to glow.

It wasn't the same lavender gem it had been when I'd first given Aaliyah the protection from us, but the blue sapphire was just as stunning, and it would work in a pinch until I could replace her other one fully.

Aaliyah saw it as I raised it, clipping it to the remnants of the silver chain around her neck. "It's spelled the same as before, with stronger bonds. Not even Sebek should be able to get through now."

It had a few other perks, but they were mostly benign, and I didn't get a chance to explain them as Aaliyah set down her cup, then wrapped her arms around me in a tight embrace. It was an awkward angle, but I savored every second she gave me. "Thank you, Osiris. It's beautiful."

Her tears were bittersweet, something I never wanted to see but understood they came from a place of joy. She'd been so distraught after the loss of her other one, I knew that the first thing I wanted for her was to replace that pain.

I was glad to see it worked.

Aaliyah's eyes sparked with a warm light, and her lips tilted into a hesitant smile. The scar above her lip, soft and white, flexed with the move. She sank back into the depths of her pillow haven, closing her eyes again.

"You'll wake me up if something changes?" she asked quietly, her voice cracking.

I settled my hand on her head, keeping contact with her until I felt her breath steady. Everything about her called to me, every inch of her skin and every spare piece of her endless soul.

I'd never grow tired of her touch. One day soon, I hoped to explore more, to search her body for the curves I knew I'd spend eons memorizing. It was a thought that pushed me forward, that kept me going as I sorted out my own feelings enough to take that step.

To feel another against my skin so entirely. The thought still made me sick to my stomach, so I held back, until I was sure there wasn't a shadow of a doubt that Darius would not ruin it for me.

"Always," I whispered, leaning down and placing a kiss on her forehead. One that burned the same way it set me free. Like each one I'd ever had the pleasure of experiencing. "Sleep, *lux mea.*"

She was quick to listen, faster than I ever could have expected one to fall asleep at my hand. Her heartbeat settled, her breathing falling into a steady rhythm. The moment it shifted, Eirik turned to me.

"What are you planning?" Eirik asked quietly under his breath as he watched Aaliyah with the same fascination I did. His eyes swirled with his beast, the flexing pull of the ink on his skin rolling as he crossed his arms.

I guessed he'd noticed something was wrong from the moment he'd followed me out of Nero's room. He stalked like a beast, his instincts so rarely leading him astray, that they had almost become a code to live by.

I looked him in the eye, the jagged nature of the scar over it seeming harsher in the low blue light.

"Darius won't stay quiet for much longer. I'll be detained for holding until they can verify the validity of his claims," I said. He was too proud not to lock me up, needing to make a show of it so he could prattle and weep and garner sympathy. It wasn't in his blood to back down when he'd been slighted. If nothing else, I could guarantee that, and that single flaw would lead us to our greatest gain. "He'll send me to the Pits until First Rights, an insult and an advantage. He wants to bring me low, and what better way than to cage me like he did before?"

Eirik stiffened, protest already firm on his face, but this was the right choice, the *only* choice. Drakon's allies were not foolproof, and they weren't ours. I needed to fix that if we had a chance at winning an Exilium vote, which meant rallying.

Tearing down a beast like Darius was one way to do that.

"So, you accept his Retaliation claim, then?" Eirik asked instead. "Knowing that he'll pick your fight?"

Retaliation was a tricky subject, one that very few survived. It wasn't meant to be a Challenge; it was meant to be a slaughter. A fight for some, a show for others. Revenge in its purest form.

Some had pitted their enemy against beasts of mythical nature, some had decided on a simple beheading, others a fight to the death. The rules were picked by the one that called Retaliation, and Darius would want the most humiliating of them all. He'd choose to fight, knowing he couldn't lose, intent on making me submit, and on giving him my will like I had all those years ago.

"I'll remove him during our bout, but I must get to the Pits first," I said.

Flashes of Kri'Valta's words pushed me to it, and if I could not force my way into the prison of the Eternium, then I had to be invited in.

"Why?" Eirik grumbled.

I'd been planning this since the moment Kali had died at my hands. I knew Darius far better than I'd like, and I knew what he'd do. Kri'Valta's words echoed, and even with his slimy nature, I trusted them. The key to Darius's fall lay in the Pits. I just had to find it.

Destroy it.

But the others didn't need to know yet exactly my plans. Darius was crafty, and they didn't need to be tied up in this mess in any way that could fall back on them.

I didn't have to speak for Eirik to know what I was thinking, his head dipping in a resigned nod.

"And you're confident you'll win?" Eirik asked, that spark of fight in his eyes enough to get me to nod.

Fighting Darius was my worst nightmare. Being in his presence was horrid enough, and having to see his tricks all over again was going to test my limits ... but I *would* win. If I had learned anything from my fight with Kri'Valta, it was that. *Lie, cheat, steal.* Whatever the cost, I would not lose to him.

"Without question," I whispered, staring into the fire as Eirik grunted at my back.

Silence followed, Aaliyah's soft breaths calming me, allowing me to breathe. I accepted every one of them, took them in like they were the last I'd have, and if I was right, they might be.

Darius was coming. It was only a matter of time.

And may the gods help the poor unfortunate souls that got in his way.

***

When I'd made my guess on when Darius would make his move, I hadn't thought I'd be proven right so soon. But the moment a knock rang in the air, I knew we were out of time.

Eirik looked on, his face pulling tight, his nose lifting as he scented the air before he snarled. Aaliyah jolted up, rubbing her eyes as Adrian and Fallon peeked their heads out from the bedroom.

"What is it?" Aaliyah asked, as another knock sounded.

I ran my hand over her hair, touching her again, savoring the last breaths of her in my presence.

"Darius comes to collect me for the Pits," I whispered, and her eyes went wide.

She shot up, desperation and panic clinging to her as she tried to hold on to me. The door opened, and I looked over my shoulder just as three walked in. Darius was the first I saw, a smug pride etched into his features, like everything was going to plan.

I was already standing by the time he and his entourage turned to us fully. He crossed onto the rug, dragging what looked like dirt onto it, his steps sure and heavy. My jaw popped at the sight, teeth grinding as I held my tongue.

"There he is," he called, his arms crossed over his chest. The beast behind his eyes shriveled when Eirik growled. "The man that killed the Sorceri Eternal."

His bolstering faltered, and I took a step toward him, even as Aaliyah's sound of protest rang from behind me. I had to do this; it was imperative, but that didn't make it any easier to move. It didn't remove the weight that settled on my chest and told me to turn back into her arms.

"Osiris Vivas, you've been accused of the murder of Sorceri Eternal Kali Rourovic. Plea?" the creature to the left of Darius said.

It was another Sage, the faceless mirage digging into my soul. This one differed from the last, with two hands pressed together in front of it, as though it were praying, head dipped low as it waited for me to respond. Its robes stretched over its head, its body the same ashen gray.

"I will not comment on the accusation," I said, head held high, even as Darius's eyes flared with rage.

His face molted, shimmering with gold flecks as his Griffon fought its way to the surface. The power of his shift flooded the room, ancient and potent.

"Acknowledged," the Sage whispered, and it was barely seconds before I felt the bindings settle on me. They were the same magic that the rest of the Eternium held, unbending as they silenced my own. It was like losing all power, my human magic shriveling up, the *Flame* dying in my chest. "Holding has been requested until Retaliation can be proven. Please do not resist."

I was to be held until voting could be called and Darius's claim for vengeance could be carried out. So I couldn't run from it.

Most didn't bother. The Eternium held us here, regardless, but the move to the dungeons added insult to injury. It was a curse for most, as many didn't return. Today, it was an opportunity for me.

"You'll regret this, Osiris," Darius gritted out, his hand landing on my suit covered arm. "I'll teach you why you should learn to stay in my good graces."

Even then, I jolted at his touch, growing sick from it. A cold sweat pooled down my neck, and I struggled to swallow the dread.

Just as quickly, the hand was removed, and a startled gasp was followed by growls and shouts.

White hair, the kind that lived in my dreams. I wanted to reach out to it, to touch it, to gaze forever into the furious lavender eyes that flashed my way before settling back on my demons.

"You don't touch him," Aaliyah hissed, as the shadows around us snapped up from the floor. The one at her feet grew, expanding to swallow most of the space between us and Darius. "Never again, do you hear me? *You don't fucking touch him.*"

The voice that had called to her at the hot spring slipped forward, the one promising a nightmare beyond Darius's worst thoughts, causing even the Sage to shudder. Her power was alive in the air, reaching for Darius even as the Eternium broke it up, keeping it from him. His face was a sheet of white, his eyes wide with a horror that I relished.

"You're an abomination, Reaper," Darius mocked, jerking away from her.

I saw the flinch, and the dread that bundled in her shoulders at his callous assessment. She was everything we weren't, the light, the joy in the world. She was what gave me the strength to do this, to face Darius like he hadn't been my hell.

I pressed against the Sage's power, fighting it as it tore against my skin, and my blood leaked out of me like my magic. The *Flame* burst, skittering across the floor and into the air. Darius was forced a step back or risk getting burned.

His face filled with fear. The same fear I'd felt with him for decades. The same *fear* that had destroyed me, broken me down, and left me in pieces.

Now it was his turn.

"You don't talk to her like that, friend," Nero butted in, from where he sagged against the far door, looking like he'd managed to stumble his way through a *Rend* as he shook his head. Not a thing could have stopped him, seething with rage as he stepped up to my side, putting an arm around Aaliyah's shoulders. "I promise you'll regret it."

"Nero," Darius sneered. Nero might not remember their last true meeting, but it was one I thought on fondly. When Nero had bested Darius's highest-ranking soldier in a Retaliation, a few Eterniums' back, and had paraded around the ring with his head on a spike. It seemed old wounds still festered. "You should have done us all a favor and stayed dead."

Nero laughed, grinning like a madman as Darius's ire grew. "Ah, and we seemed like such good pals."

The others moved, as well, standing like a wall, enough to make Darius nervous as he swallowed hard. "I don't know how you managed this affront against the Hallowed of Death, but you can't expect it to stand."

Darius kept his head high, even now. That pride would be his downfall, even if he didn't see it yet. He was strong, more so than most I knew. Even Kri'Valta was nothing compared to him, but I'd never in my life needed to win a fight more. For myself and for Ali.

Because no one was allowed to talk to her like that and live.

"You called your Retaliation, Darius," I whispered, tilting my head to the side. I stared him down until his lips pulled back, and the Griffon behind his eyes took offense to my lack of submission. The disrespect wouldn't stand, and the embarrassment he felt showed in the red on his cheeks as he looked around the room. "If that's all. Then get out of my sight."

I stood tall, looking down at Ali, who'd placed herself between us. She had her arms spread out, guarding me like she'd guarded Eirik at Xander's the day we'd learned who she was. I knew, without a fraction of a doubt, that she'd do the same thing for me, even if she was completely powerless.

But she wasn't, not my light. She *was* power, violently destructive and endlessly compassionate power.

"Please proceed. The Pits will hold you until the vote," the Sage said, the power of the Eternium forcing me to walk. Darius flipped around, his black hair waving, his shoulders humped.

He would fight to make me regret this, the way we'd debased him today. I couldn't care about that now, not as Aaliyah's hand found mine. Her fingers brushed the marks on my wrist.

The mark of a demon, and the mark of the love of my life.

"See you soon, Osiris," she whispered.

I was Darius's *no longer*. I was hers, and the mark on my arm proved it.

I turned, losing the warmth, the spark of her touch. I already missed her. I let that emotion swell in me, mixing with the rage, with the numb. With the power that cradled me and made me what I was.

I let it fester and rot when I should have buried it. When I should have thrown it away and lost the key.

"Not soon enough, *lux mea.*"

I was to be her monster, and I would do whatever it took to get us through this.

Even if I lost myself in the process.

Chapter 43

Aaliyah

Osiris was gone in a blink, fading away as the Sage at his side took him through the door. There was a sharp burst of power, a wave that washed over us before the dust settled. Osiris was *gone*, and he took a piece of my heart with him.

To the dungeons, the *Pits*, wherever that was.

I'd wanted to protest, to do whatever I could to keep him here, but something in his eyes told me that this was exactly what Osiris wanted. And if he thought he needed to be there ... then I trusted that. My heart ached at the thought of him alone, though, just like it had when Darius had looked at him. Had licked his lips like he might reach out for a taste.

Eirik's arms wrapped around me, holding me to a warm chest as his cheek rubbed against mine. The slight bristle of his beard tickled my neck, and I let my shoulders drop. There was a low rumble in his chest, onc that vibrated up my spine, and washed away some of the tension of the moment.

"Let me guess, don't do that again?" I whispered, looking up to find Eirik's eyes crinkling at the corners.

"Oh, no, please do it as many times as you'd like, love. Darius looked ready to piss himself," Adrian butted in, shaking his head.

"I didn't expect Osiris's prediction to come true so soon," Eirik said, grunting as he dipped his head to my neck again, seeming far more interested in the little divot there than wherever Osiris had been dragged to.

"Will he be all right?" I asked, unable to look away from where he'd disappeared.

"He can't die down there, though I couldn't begin to tell you what it's like," Adrian said, looking confident. "Trust me, Osiris can handle himself."

The room around us grew quiet, everyone a mangled mix of emotions. It was exhausting, my head throbbing as my body seemed to riot at the fact that we were awake again. The others seemed to follow, varying mixes of dread making it hard to even breathe.

Prince grunted, holding his head, shivering as Fallon went to his side and held him up. His face went pale, his body somehow seeming thinner, the muscle mass that had made it up just yesterday seeming to have faded away. There was a gauntness to his cheeks, a sickness that only got worse on his next *Rend*.

He was ripped out, his entire weight dropping onto Fallon's shoulder as he sucked in a breath.

I couldn't watch him suffer like this. I wouldn't lose him; I wouldn't lose any of them. Osiris leaving ... just solidified that. I knew what I needed to do, even if it scared the *shit* out of me.

"I want to go to the Void," I whispered, pulling out of Eirik's arms like it might distance me from their shocked expressions and quickly building protests.

Silence for one beat, then two.

"Please, for the love of all things holy, tell me you're joking, trouble," Fallon bit out through gritted teeth as he shuffled Nero's arm over his shoulders. It came heavy with a sharply pointed stare, the disappointment behind his words so blatant I almost broke under them.

They all tensed around me, stress bleeding from them one forced breath at a time, but this had to happen.

I'd thought about it a lot while watching Prince *Rend* ... whatever I'd done when I brought him back had broken something. His soul wasn't steady, his life literally fading away with every memory he'd had to string back together so far.

I needed to figure out why, so I could fix it.

"I understand why you're worried, I do, but I'm doing this." I tried to force as much confidence into my words as I could. "Mags said Prince needs to make it to First Rights. I might be able to help."

"Ali, we don't know what could happen if you go to the Void again. You've been on a thread ever since the shit with Sebek. It's not worth the risk," Fallon pressed, shaking his head, his expression seemingly cold, closed off in a way that would make others take a step back.

Fallon could act as high and mighty as he wanted, but at the end of the day, I'd grown very used to picking up on his more subtle cues. Like the flex of his hands when he wasn't in control of a situation or the hitch in his breath when he was scared.

The way he looked at me like he might lose me, the same look that had been cemented on his face after he'd found me that first time in the middle of the forest, after the *Rend*.

I'd never forget the tears in his eyes. Which was exactly why I couldn't back down now.

"It is to me," I said, gripping my hands tighter as I tried to level my breathing. Prince jolted back to his body, pulling in a haggard breath. His eyes rolled back, and Adrian had to go to his other side to keep him standing.

Never again.

"I can't sit idly by anymore." It wasn't a matter of fighting what I was, or being scared to face the reality that I was a Reaper. This was bigger than that, bigger than me. Prince was dying, and if I had the ability to help slow it down until Mags could stop it, then I would.

Eirik huffed, moving so fast I hadn't even realized it until he was hoisting me into his arms like he did. His eyes were clear blue pearls, his expression savage as he watched me. I felt him hunting for what I was worried he might find; indecision or fear. He sank a little when he didn't find it, leaning in to rub his nose against mine. "Are you sure?"

"I am," I said back, lifting my head as Prince's eyes cracked open again. They took a moment to clear, his head tipping forward as he coughed. I expected his protests to ring the loudest, but when his lips curled into that familiar Cheshire smile, I melted.

I loved seeing the colors that made him up. The copper tints in his red-brown hair, the flecks of soft blue in his silver eyes, which glowed so brightly against the tan of his skin. His moment of lucidity warmed me.

The pink of his tongue as he licked his lips, chuckling when I blushed.

Then I was stuck between him and Eirik. The warmth to my back, Prince to my front, caging me in. Someone made a noise in the background, likely to try to stop him from moving, but Prince wasn't one to be held down. Not by something as silly as death.

Though it was obvious Eirik was holding most of his weight, too.

"Stubborn," Prince whispered, his voice cracking a little. The first brush of his lips was a teasing caress, one I tried to chase as he pulled away.

"Maybe ... but I can't just watch you die," I pressed again. The protests were more muted this time, even Fallon sighing. I was going to do this either way, but having them on my side helped to take some of the weight from my shoulders. "Please, trust me."

"I don't think it could hurt," Prince said, and I felt Eirik's growl before I heard it. "Hey, let's not turn on me like some bad guy. I really do think it'll help. Trust me on this since I am also, you know, *deadish*. Aaliyah can do it, and besides, this isn't a *Rend*."

"No, I've gone before," I said, thinking back to the few times I'd found myself in Void while *not* dead. With Osiris after Kri'Valta's Gala ... and with Eirik sitting across from me, his eyes closed softly. The memory made me smile. "In the training room. I'll do it the same way I did before. See if I can get in touch with Azer."

I wasn't able to speak then, to interact with the Void. I'd have to find a way to go back in person, like I had the last few times. The only problem was I had no idea how. I'd only ever gotten out on purpose.

Eirik's eyes filled with recognition, his head tipping back. "You want to meditate?"

I nodded, and the tension seemed to drop. Prince brushed his hair back, shaking his head with a slight flinch. When his nose bled, I reached out. He got there before me, wiping it away with a harsh swipe.

"Are you going to be all right?" I asked, my heart sinking even as he smiled.

Because I felt the same pressure in my head. The *Rends* wouldn't stop coming, and I saw that same pain in Prince's gaze as he covered one of his eyes.

"One step at a time, Aaliyah. I'm fine," he responded, cupping my cheek in a cool palm.

I hated seeing it, knowing that we were waiting for a cure. It was just another push to get me moving. Eirik grunted, leaning in as Prince peeled away from me, Fallon taking his side, hauling one of his arms over his shoulders again.

It was shocking how quickly Prince sagged against Fallon, his entire body deflating as he closed his eyes. Always acting stronger for me, even now.

"We'll put him to bed, then be right there," Adrian whispered, and I shook my head.

"Stay with him? I won't be able to focus if he's alone." Fallon's jaw clenched as I spoke, and I quickly followed it with, "Please."

It was a long few seconds before they nodded. Fallon was slow to turn, his eyes lingering, another hint of protest caught behind the bite of his teeth as Prince was ripped out of himself again.

"I'll watch over her," Eirik affirmed, eyes a stormy sky as his face grew sharp. His nose brushed against the top of my head, and the rush of his breath tickled my temple.

Fallon's head dipped, and he said nothing else. All too soon, the door to the back room was sliding closed, leaving only Eirik and I here.

The beast part of him huffed, searching the room for threats. He was tense, his teeth flashing in a snarl as his eyes grew darker, the partial shift forcing his face to shudder.

In the next instant, I was in Eirik's arms. He stalked to the far door, the one nearest to the kitchen, shouldering it open. The last time I'd been in it, it had been a bedroom, the sheets a silken softness that had left me wrapped in warmth. Now, it reminded me of home in an entirely different way.

It was the training room, or close to it. As close as the Eternium could replicate. From the soft white floors to the tall windows on the far side of the room. Though, they didn't show the outside, the gentle moss gardens that I'd grown used to. It was just stone, as if the mountain was all it could see, hard and unyielding.

There was a brush of cold against me, the subtle hint of Red as I was set gently on my feet. Eirik's hands brushed over me, lingering on my exposed skin, my arms and neck. His face twitched, and he pulled in a steady breath, jumpy as his eyes bounced back and forth between sky and stormy blue.

This moment reminded me of something, of a time when I'd been just as pent up. I stepped away from him, jolting a bit when he held on to me. I sank to the floor anyway, turning so I was facing him.

"Sit," I whispered, and Eirik tilted his head, more beast than man.

He watched me like a hunter would prey, and I shivered. It was intoxicating, if not intimidating, the way his muscles flexed, the ripple of muscle against tanned skin. His tattoos, the dark marks that seemed carved into his flesh, flexed as he followed my lead in one swift movement.

"Do you remember when we meditated before?" I asked, and it took a second before Eirik nodded.

"**Yes**," he whispered with a distinctive growl to his words, one that sent a shiver down my spine.

His hands flexed on his thick thighs, his chest rumbling in a gentle purr. He didn't move, even though I could see the need to in the flex of his muscles, but he did inch closer to me, until our knees brushed against each other.

"Then close your eyes," I said, and Eirik huffed, his head shaking softly as he followed my direction.

"**You cannot escape this one just because we can't see you, *smár Valkyrja*,**" he purred, his eyes staying dutifully closed.

He leaned forward, his hand finding mine in an instant. I gasped when he lifted it, running his nose along my wrist. I knew this was his beast, that Eirik was there somewhere, but that didn't stop the thrill of the unknown that flooded me.

There was an air of mystery and danger that surrounded this version of Eirik. Like he'd try and devour me whole.

"You're ***ours***," he said, resolute as his hands settled.

His nose flared, his teeth flashing bright white. His tongue traced them slowly, and I was hooked on the move.

"And you're mine, Eirik," I said back without any hesitation.

"*Always*, my beautiful warrior," he whispered, then he was tugging me forward.

I landed in his lap, his firm chest to mine. I blushed when his hips pressed into me, but he didn't go any further, just held me close as he ran his nose over my neck. He was so large that I felt dwarfed completely by him, safe in his arms. The heat of him was addictive. "I'm with you, every step of the way."

He held me tightly, like he might shoulder this burden for me, his strength keeping me steady as I smiled. I took a deep breath, feeling a burn in my lungs as I focused on what I could feel, like he'd taught me before.

"I'll be back soon," I whispered, closing my eyes, using his heart as a guide. It was steady under my ear, a consistent thump I could feel in my bones. A purr caught in his chest, his arms squeezing tighter around me, preparing for what was coming.

I had to get to the Void.

One breath in, and I felt the world around me. The push and pull of Eirik's heartbeat, the subtle shift of the shadows under our prone forms. Azer's instructions came next, and I thought of that endless expanse of silver, saw Azer's lavender eyes, and tried to push the Void to let me in.

The shadows pulled around me, a frozen chill sinking down over the top of us, and I shivered against Eirik.

One breath out, and the air around me snapped taut, and magic so rich I could taste it flooded my senses. It was metallic, like the sour hint of iron buried in ozone, but as quickly as it had appeared, it was gone.

When I opened my eyes, I expected to find the Void, maybe Azer, looking on with mocking irritation. Or at least something like what I'd thought of.

Instead, I was alone in an empty hall. It had the same feeling as the rest of the Eternium, the same red accents and gold flare ... but it didn't move. There was no guiding force pushing me forward.

Just me and a singular door at the end of it, one that seemed to call to me.

The hair on my arms stood on end, and static clung to my skin, so different than when I'd tried this before. I could feel, looking down at my hands that were in full color, which meant I was here.

I just didn't understand how.

My entire body flushed with a steady fear that pooled like the sweat on the back of my neck. I'd felt hunted before, when Curtis had found me on the way to Fellow Manor and at Ascension when Nilus used to watch me through the glass of my cell, but nothing had felt quite like this.

My eyes never left that door, stuck in a fight-or-flight mode, my breath catching. Silence was suddenly my only goal.

Never make noise.

"*Aaliyah,*" a voice whispered.

It was soft, a breathy sound that was meant to entice. A normal, rational person would turn around, try to force themselves back into that room with Eirik. I could only imagine how panicked he'd gotten when I'd disappeared. I'd planned to do exactly that before I took a step forward, drawn like a moth to a raging fire.

Toward that door.

Every instinct in me warred, trapped between turning around and reaching the voice that called to me. It was like it was ingrained, like everything had led to this moment, to whoever was waiting on the other side.

"Hello?" I asked, the echo of my voice jarringly loud, ringing in my ears as it bounced down the hall.

There was no answer.

I walked until I was in front of the old oak, the barest whisper of a breeze sliding from underneath it. It cracked open as I got close, as if beckoning me in to play.

Inside was a tree, one that towered over the space, the rustling green leaves spread out along branches that spanned the entire cavern. They swayed as if caught in a soft summer breeze. Light filtered in from the cracks and fissures along the jagged rock face that made up the roof. The moon was out, illuminating the entire area, and the budding flowers and foliage that swallowed the floor.

"How did you get here?" I asked out loud, drawn inside.

The door clicked closed behind me. I shuddered and kept moving. Whatever this was, it wanted me here. The Eternium must have done something, interfered with my attempt to reach the Void.

The more that I experienced it, the more convinced I was that the Eternium wasn't taking us where *we* wanted to go. It seemed too alive for that, too pushy in the way it directed everyone to move.

It took us where we were needed, where it saw us being ... and this felt no different.

I walked to the tree, setting a hand against the aged wood. Its touch felt like that of a friend, a companion. I sank down to its roots, finding a seat in them. "Well, I hope you don't mind me stealing your space."

There was a rustle of leaves that lulled me into a comforted stupor as I closed my eyes. The ground, wet with a light mist, pulsed beneath my hands, and I felt it in the marrow of my bones, as if it was singing to me. It was almost like sending a ghost on, like the soft whisper of someone's last emotions before they passed through. It felt like the *Void*.

I took a steady breath, trying to hold on to that feeling. Trying to catch it. There was a pinch behind my eyes as my hands shook where they'd planted into the ground, digging into raw earth.

One more breath, the feeling ragged in my chest. A chill found its way into my blood, the reminder of Nero's fading body like a bucket of cold water, Crustava's face a movie that played behind my closed eyes.

My gifts danced along my skin, pushing me, the Void more insistent now. I just had to fall into it ...

So, why did I hesitate? Why was I so terrified now?

"Curious," a voice called, and I snapped my eyes open with a choked gasp.

A man sat cross-legged in front of me, one I'd never seen before, and I'd likely never see again, if he could even be called a *man*.

Broad twisting horns sprouted from his head, so much like the branches of the tree at my back. He had no face, lost under the cracked ivory of a clean skull. The rest of him was hidden by a cloak, only bits of dark black fur to be seen tucked underneath, peeking up toward his neck.

And he was huge, a literal beast that even sitting would tower over my standing form. Tall enough to reach the leaves that stood so far above my head, a wicked tail flicking behind him.

That feeling of being hunted grew so sharply I held my breath, as if trying to convince my body I was already dead. Whoever this man was, was the same person who'd called my name.

The same one that even my soul recognized as dangerous.

"Who are you?" I asked.

The Void pulsed again, and I almost listened, if only to escape the blank gaze of the skull. The pockets where the eyes should have been were deep black, endless pits of nothingness. Then, in an instant, they were filled with fire, a red so deep it might as well have been blood.

"Fear is unbecoming of death. Don't you think?" he asked. His voice was smooth, a gentleness to it that betrayed the precarious aura that surrounded him. "Tell me, Aaliyah. Why do you fear what lies on the other side of this life? Why does the Void burden you?"

The tree rustled again, leaves falling gently to the ground around us. The Void stopped pressing for a moment, as if listening for my answer.

The same one I'd been simmering on for days.

"Because it killed Prince," I whispered, flinching when his head tipped back up.

He didn't have emotions, the skull giving nothing away, but I could almost feel the disappointment in his gaze, the fire dimming in his eyes. He hunched lower as his tail flicked agitatedly behind him.

"He seems rather alive now," he whispered. "Yet your fear still lingers. The truth, this time."

I swallowed, rubbing my arm where the marks of my men lingered, the three that remained. I shouldn't have felt compelled to tell him ... but there was something curious about the way this beast spoke, the way he moved.

My mind didn't trust him, but the longer I was here, the more my soul did. The hunted feeling slipped by, lost in the sweat that clung to my skin, now cold. Again, I found myself opening my mouth, speaking. "I can't see it as anything other than the thing that has ruined my life. And ... it speaks. *Dark things.* It makes me want to hurt people."

I still couldn't rid myself of Crustava's face when I'd ripped out his soul. When I'd destroyed him. I never wanted to be in that position again, that overwhelming sense of power, the flood of it addicting and dangerous.

I didn't want to hurt anyone, and that had always been the problem.

"You fight the balance that comes with the dark. You fight when you should wield. The Void is an extension of yourself," he whispered, almost mirroring Osiris when he'd first tried to bring my gifts out.

"It's all here." His large hand, fingers tipped in deadly claws, reached up. He tapped at my chest, the spot where my heart was. I flinched when he got close, unable not to. He didn't react, just kept speaking. "Close your eyes, feel for it."

It was like a flood, something that I'd avoided as I shuddered under the Void. It washed through me from where his claw touched, and when he pulled back, I was left alone with that feeling.

Everything about this felt like a dream. The room, the beast. Yet, I didn't feel scared anymore. There was no fear clinging to me beyond the first burst that had come from being watched. Something tied me to this man, told me he was safe, even if he didn't look like it.

There was a drift of something in the air, a flower, I realized, as he plucked it out of the sky. He held it between his claws, showing me.

"For every light, there is dark. For every death, there is a life. Hold on to it, Reaper. It's not trying to hurt you," he said, just as cryptically as he set the bloom in my palm. It floated above my skin, a white bud that fell open as it twirled. "It *is* you."

The flower turned to dust in my hand.

"It is *yours*. Use it," His words came as a whisper, filling the room, the space, even my head. His chest expanded, a tender purr that someone without their own beast would likely be terrified of. "You are so much like I imagine *she*."

She?

"Thank you," I whispered as I took in his words. The calmness with which he spoke settled my resolve.

I sank back down to the ground. This time, when I breathed in, I let the Void sink deep. It filled my lungs, settled in my pours. I didn't struggle against it, forcing myself to let it linger. When it pricked at my skin, I didn't flinch at its touch.

"You never told me your name?" I whispered, peeking at him one last time as his head tilted again, mouth opening to show rows of jagged teeth as a rough chuckle spilled from him. I couldn't place what he felt like beyond that safety. My blood called to him, the Void slithering around our feet even now, as if caressing.

As if it *knew* him.

"My brothers favor Than," he said, dipping his head.

The tree moved with him, the branches swaying, the Void singing praise as his hand dipped back toward the earth, skimming over the shadows. He didn't move again, just looked up at the tree, at the branching light that had filtered in. I closed my eyes.

One breath, then the next.

The Void was to be my shield and my hope, and I would use it to *protect* the men I loved. The next breath I had, I opened my eyes to find an endless silver room.

"Well, I'll be," a voice called, the sarcastic crack to his words familiar.

I looked over my shoulder, from where I sat on the rippling silver ground. Azer smiled at me, pride shining in his lavender eyes. He tsked, shaking his head as he walked over. He extended a hand, and I took it, letting him drag me to my feet. "Didn't think you'd make it here. I'll give you one thing. You have spirit."

I panted, exertion already weighing down on me.

"Teach me?" I asked, thankful when my voice found itself, watching as his lips curled up in a pleased smile.

"Teach you what?" he pressed again, insisting I say it.

Thoughts of what this power had done to me, thoughts of everything else fled. The only thing that mattered was understanding, was learning how to use, not be used by the powers that my mother passed down to me.

The Void was my domain, the gifts parts of me that I needed to stop avoiding ...

"Teach me how to be a Reaper," I asked, keeping eye contact as Azer's eyes were slowly overtaken by an inky black. The shadows flexed under our feet, and the Void lit up. "Prince is dying. I need to know how to save him."

"Ah, looking for help on the soul side of things?" he pressed, a goading to his voice. "You know what you're asking, then? You understand that these aren't nice little tea party powers?"

I swallowed before nodding. I'd spent a lot of time thinking about what it meant to be a Reaper, about the powers I knew I held. They could destroy—they *would* destroy—but they could be so much more.

I'd like to think I was more.

Azer laughed, his head tipping back, before he nodded. "I was wondering when you'd get there. Get ready, little Imperial. This is going to be fun."

Azer watched me with a bored stare, his arms crossed over his chest. He had the same twist to the corner of his lips that my mother used to, the one when she was amused but didn't want to show it.

He huffed when I lifted my arms for the thousandth time, desperately trying to move the Void as he'd been doing. Trying to shift the shadows that lay at our feet, but even as I forced all my effort into them, they didn't move.

My hands shook, and the Void came, just a bit, brushing against my skin. It made the hair stand up on my arms, and I sucked in a harsh breath, trying to keep from flinching away.

I failed, and the Void kept back again, slinking away as my arms dropped.

"You know, darling, I, too, have a strenuous relationship with the Void, truly. But you treat it like it's going to reach out and bite you." Azer clicked his tongue before he flicked his hand, the shadow at his feet seeming to grow before wavering. It came alive under his touch, coming off the ground and condensing into a ball that settled above his hand. "Which, in all fairness, *it might*, but you don't have to be this skittish."

The mass of Void rolled over his fingers, seeming to play like a little creature as it bounced from one finger to the next. I tried to focus on my own, forcing Osiris's and Than's words to stay close to me. They'd said not to treat the Void like a monster, but that was what it felt like.

"How is this supposed to help Prince?" I mumbled. No matter how hard I tried, the cold brush of the Void still made my skin crawl. That voice in the back of my head came crawling forward, tempting me with things I didn't want to do.

"It would be so easy to let go," it whispered.

"Souls and Void are the same thing at their cores. You could even go as far as to say the Void *is* a soul. So, theoretically speaking, if you can control the Void, you can hold the pieces of your little lover together. I doubt for *long*, but you might be able to buy yourself a day or two." Azer dropped his hand, the shadow that had been there moving to dance around his head instead. "Either way, you need to accept it. Your powers are built in the Void; there's *no* escaping it."

"What I'm hearing is that you don't actually know," I said, letting my hands drop to my sides. They ached, my muscles screaming at me as I finally let them relax. My fingers were tense, and flexing my hands hurt.

Azer snorted, walking toward me as he shoved his hands into his pockets. "No, I don't. This is new territory for me. Bringing someone back from the dead isn't exactly our realm of expertise, and I'm still trying to figure out how you did it. I'm doing what I can here, to save your boy toy and to get you ready for everything else that's about to come your way."

I knew that. I hated that even knowing didn't make it any easier to reach for the Void.

"Are you always this much of an asshole?" I asked, and Azer's eyes rose with mocking surprise.

His mouth fell open, and he cupped his jaw. "Darling, if you think this is an attitude, you should see me without sleep. Which we are getting dangerously close to."

His hand flicked, and in an instant the little dancing blob of shadow that had clung to him turned into a blade. It thinned until I could barely see it, cutting through the open air with an audible slash. It went on, shooting into the Void until it faded from view. He shoved his hands back into his pockets after that, walking toward me, looking over the blank expanse in front of us. He reached up, snapping his fingers, and the Void listened, morphing into a target. "Would it help if I conjured up a dummy? Maybe we could put Sebek's face on it. Or Kri'-Valta's?"

His hand touched my head, awkwardly patting me like you might a dog or a toddler in distress. I could practically hear him gagging around a "there there."

"Wasn't Kri'Valta your father?" I asked, and Azer clicked his tongue.

He brushed his hair back, toying with the black chunk that stood out in the vibrant white. His eyes were brandished lavender with flecks of gold, and the sudden broken look on his face took me by surprise.

"Yes, and you'd be ecstatic to know how many times I've imagined killing him. It's become a bit of a wet dream that your devilish little man stole from me," he hummed. He brushed his arm, one now covered in a standoffish white shirt. He scoffed just as shiver bumps lined my arms. "Not that I'm complaining, being that I'm free and all."

The Void itself was cold, but when that chill deepened, I felt it like an extension of my own skin. I was turning before Azer felt it, the familiar chill shocking me.

"It seems we have a visitor," Azer said, just as surprised.

Red danced around, little more than shifting dust in the air, but I could see him. The outline of a body, the flash of a smile that was then lost to nothing.

"Red," I said, equal parts excited to see him and terrified, but the Void didn't seem to be plucking at him. It wasn't trying to drag him away.

Azer looked at the dust with mild interest. He didn't reach out to touch it, luckily, but I still tensed when he leaned forward. "Odd. Seems he's just a fragment, too small for the Void to take. I doubt it even sees him."

Red shimmered, and a flash of annoyance filled the air. Just as quickly, his emotions wavered, dashing between several over just a few seconds. Azer snapped his fingers. "This gives me a wonderful idea! Sit."

He didn't wait for me to do so, sinking to the ground in front of me with his legs crossed, his hands planted on his knees. I did the same, facing him.

We'd been at it for a while, a long while, but the actual time wasn't something I could place. It moved so much differently here, and I wondered what time it would be in the real world when I finally left.

"All right, here's what I need you to do," Azer started, closing his eyes and tipping his head from side to side. "Take a deep breath and imagine looking at your soul through a window. Imagine being *just* close enough to touch."

His hand extended out in front of him, and he took a deep breath. A glowing light started in the center of his chest before it expanded, eventually around him, then around me. It shimmered, with flecks of gold and black all stitched together in perfect harmony. The black battled with the gold, the hints of his heritage shining in the powerful slashes that came barreling off the gold edges, just for the power to be absorbed by the black. Demon meeting Reaper.

"Lovely, I know. I have quite the beautiful soul," Azer mused, his eyes open again, focused on me. "Give it a try."

I nodded, tensing my hands on my knees as I closed my eyes and tried to take level breaths. It was like meditating with Eirik all over again, the overbearing weight of the Void a distraction I couldn't rip my thoughts away from. I tried and failed to imagine what he'd said.

Even when I got close, it was like my soul revolted, shying away, shrinking in my chest. Sweat gathered on my forehead as I opened my eyes.

"This is going to be tougher than I thought," Azer mused. "Your soul is a *mess,* baby Imperial. Though, you did tie yourself to someone and ripped it apart to bring him back from the dead. Guess this is the best I can get."

"What else can we do?" I asked, letting my fingers go slack as they ached from how tightly I'd clenched them.

Azer grinned, bowing his head with a flourish. "Lucky for you, I should be able to pull it forward, and we can see what we're working with."

He reached out his hand, the majority of his arm covered with the cloth of his shirt, but it pulled back enough to see the golden runes that sat against his skin. They glowed, pulsing slightly, bringing attention to the scars that were buried inside of them.

I didn't comment on it, just took his hand, slowly. He flinched when we touched, before he relaxed into it. One second his soul danced around us; the next, mine was dragged out of my chest.

It sucked the breath right out of me so fast I couldn't even scream, the pain so focused I could feel the rush of unconsciousness in the black spots that danced in my eyes.

"Sorry about that. It's never quite as nice doing it to someone else," he said, completely unbothered by my shaking hand as he let me go. I glared at him, intent on giving him a piece of my mind, when I realized he was no longer looking at me.

He looked around the Void, to the soul that surrounded us. It was black, like his had been, mixed with a rolling, snapping red that I guessed was the Vampire half of me. Where his was an easy mix, mine was fractured. Huge fissures broke it apart, bits and pieces flaking off, others completely unmoving, as if dead.

"Holy hells," Azer whispered, running his hand through his hair as he searched my soul. "How are you alive?"

It may have been a question, but it wasn't one directed at me, not really. My soul jolted every few seconds, as if trying to find a bridge. Some bits stuck together, only to rattle violently apart.

"What are these gaps?" Azer asked as he reached out to the gray spaces that tied everything together.

"My memories, the ones I haven't gotten back yet," I guessed, and Azer nodded, moving around to the next odd piece.

A red flowing mass that differed from the Vampire side of my soul. It was rowdy, almost flashy, as it stuck to the other bits. The way it moved, the way it breathed, the gentle warmth I got from it when I reached out to touch it.

"And I take it this is ..." Azer said, not finishing as I nodded my head.

Where my soul was fractured, that piece did its best to hold it together, a stitch that kept things at least mostly contained.

"Prince," I whispered. "That's Prince."

It wasn't the only odd piece, as I lingered on another stretch of black, this one seemingly frozen, skating along the edges of the other bits. The Void. It was almost the exact same flowing black as my soul, which made it hard to recognize at first, but I *knew* it wasn't me. It solidified what Davi had said before, when I'd watched my mother bring back my father. The Void had been a part of me for centuries.

"Damn, this is a lot to unpack," Azer said with a whistle. "A person's soul is a mix of their entire life. Every memory, every moment. You shouldn't have this many lifetimes."

So much of my soul was made up of blank spots, memories I hadn't yet gotten back. Memories of a life that seemed fake. How many were good? How many would leave me smiling afterward? I wasn't sure I wanted to know.

I wasn't sure I had a choice.

"Azer, what would you say if I said I was born here? That I've been around for ... as long as you? Maybe longer," I asked, looking to him for guidance when I had none.

A surprisingly serious look took over his face, and he spent time searching my soul, too, his fingers touching the jagged edges as they flowed around us. Red shuffled nervously, wrapping himself around my shoulders.

"Born in the Void?" he asked, shaking his head. The black streak of hair tumbled down over his forehead, and for just a second, his skin glowed, the demonic runes there shimmering forward as he looked me in the eye. "Normally, I'd call you crazy and ask if you'd like a room with a window."

The Void flexed under us, rippling in what felt like a warning. Red grew more agitated, bounding around me now.

"But the Void? It seems to think you're right." Everything settled, and he huffed a dry laugh. "Guess you really are the favorite."

His bitter words echoed as the Void flexed underneath us again, more insistent this time, as though gently pointing me in the direction I should be going, like hands on my shoulders.

"Seems our time is up," Azer said, standing before he reached his hand down to help me to my feet.

I'd been here forever, it seemed like, but I didn't feel like I'd done anything. I was just as lost as I was when I first came here. No closer to a way to stitch Prince back together.

Just the realization that I was somehow more broken than I thought.

"Now stop that. What did I say? The Void *takes*, Aaliyah," Azer warned. "Don't forget it. We've already been here longer than we should have."

I nodded numbly, taking his hand and letting him pull me to my feet. Red made himself known again, sliding up close to me, passing on comfort as Azer stretched.

"Now, do you remember how to get back?"

"Yes," I whispered, tipping my head forward as I pressed a hand to my chest, searching for my home. I felt them immediately, my wrist tingling where their marks were. I was suddenly more than happy to leave here. I could only imagine how stressed they were after I'd disappeared. I needed to make sure they were all okay.

Prince was sick, Adrian and Fallon were fighting the *Call*, Osiris was in prison, and Eirik seemed to be in a constant fight with his beast. The fact that they were alone, even with each other, didn't sit right with me.

"Good. I bet your wild hunks are rather upset with your absence." His response was teased with a laugh as he threw his head back.

"Do you know how much time has passed?"

"No idea. You'll find out when you land. Time is a finicky bitch, but if I had to guess, it'll be exactly the time you need it to be. The Void's been kind about it so far," Azer said, as he winked my way, tipping his head in a flourish. "Until next time, darling."

The silver beneath him rippled, his shadow crawling up his body, cinching on his arms and legs, before it dragged him backwards into the floor. Then he was gone.

It didn't take much for me to get out this time, much like a breath as I thought of the others. One moment I was in the Void, staring at the obsidian sky; the next I was breathing in the scent of the sea, wrapped in arms that squeezed almost too tight. The force knocked away my breath as I wrapped myself around Eirik. His heat sank into me, helping to push away the chill that still lingered.

Red was back as well, moving joyfully around the room, and that helped to relax me the rest of the way.

Eirik grunted, his nose burying in my face, his chest rumbling in a deep purr. When he pulled back, his face was sharp. With the extension of his fangs over his lip and his eyes that deep shade of blue, he looked almost cute. I smiled as I reached up, pressing a finger to the sharp point.

I wasn't expecting him to shudder, his pupils growing. He nipped at my finger, playfully toying with it.

"This isn't meditating," he said, the husk of his words accenting the heat in his gaze.

"How long was I gone?" I asked, and he tilted his head, his eyes going crystal clear.

He held me closer, huffing against the top of my head. "I didn't know you were."

The time shift made my head hurt, my entire body feeling the ache that came with it. Yet nothing had passed here. I lifted a hand to my forehead, rubbing the sting away. "I was there for a while, an hour, at least. I should have disappeared, like I did after the ball."

Eirik grunted, "You never left my arms."

At least time slid to a stop, rather than rushing forward. But I felt it, the effects of the Void, the worries Azer had tried so hard to get me to see. It was like my soul ached, a hunger so vicious in my stomach it made me sick.

It takes, and it takes, and it takes.

I'd have to be more careful next time, not to push it too far.

The room grew quiet for a beat before another hand found my back. A second later, my head was being tilted, and my lips were claimed by the fresh press of Fallon's, unyielding as he dominated the exchange, stole every thought I had. The only other thing I could feel was the ache of Eirik's fingers as they dug into my hip.

"Be safe, Ali," he whispered, looking serious in a way that I couldn't help but smile at.

"I'm already back, Fal," I said, reaching up to grab his face again. I kissed him slowly and savored the way he softened against me.

He sighed, sagging into my hold, hugging me as tightly against him as he could while I was still in Eirik's lap. His arms shook, his heart echoing in my ear. "Was it supposed to be that fast?"

I let out a breath. "I don't know. I was there, in person. It was different from the last time I tried to go."

I saw the twitch of fear in Fallon's eyes, his jaw clenching like he was going to push more. Instead, he pressed his forehead to mine. "Proud of you, trouble."

His nickname sank straight to my core as I remembered the weight of him inside of me. I ached to get closer to him and find his lips again. I leaned forward as a whimper rose from my chest, and Fallon's eyes danced with mirthful heat.

I was waiting for the dizziness to wear off when the door swung open. I froze in Eirik's arms, suddenly feeling caught in a vulnerable position, even Eirik's growl picking up. Until I saw who it was.

Adrian was covered in blood, his eyes wide as he looked frantically around the room. The few moments I'd been away seemed to spiral down, and panic swallowed us. I didn't need to ask whose it was.

Pressure, I felt it grow the closer I looked at Adrian's stricken face, the harder I focused on the cool shifts in the air. The presence of a ghost popping in and out of existence.

I hadn't learned anything. I hadn't found a way to fix this ... and Prince was still dying.

He snapped out again, hard enough that I felt it in my chest, a wrecking gasp tearing out of me as I began to sweat. It was easier now to find the Void that lingered in the cracks of my soul, just like the pieces of Prince that bound the broken chunks together. I stumbled to my feet, finding Prince halfway through the bedroom door, curled up on the floor.

He gasped, dragging back to his body, arching off the ground. I felt that too, breathing into the pain as I searched ... for the bits of *me* that brought him back.

"Get Mags," I said, wiping the sweat from my brow, leaning on Eirik as he stepped to my side, and another tear ripped through me.

Another chill, another death. There was no way we'd make it even to the First Rights in this state. I reached for my chest, feeling for the parts of my soul that were Prince. He wobbled, the stitches that held me to him just as fragile as the rest of me.

I had to do something, anything.

We were out of time.

Chapter 44

Prince

God, I fucking hated the taste of my own blood.

I licked my lips, grunting when the cracked things split, sending even more into my mouth. I'd already coughed it up, had it sliding down my nose like an insufferable leak.

And now this. I was supposed to make it to the fucking Rights, and this all would have been fine. Instead, here I was, not even a full day after Mags told me in no uncertain terms that I would *stay* dead if I didn't rein this in, questioning why my soul was such a temperamental bitch.

I leaned into Eirik as he came to my side, my knee giving with a grunt as he hauled me to my feet. Pride be damned, I sank every spare ounce of weight I could onto him. He could make fun of me for it later. I'd even let him carry me again, if he offered, because I would *not* be giving Aaliyah anymore reason to worry.

She had enough on her plate, and I was already pissed she had to deal with this much.

I'd known this had been coming since I'd crawled out of the mausoleum and found myself in Mags's care. I knew I was on borrowed time, one memory after another, just like Aaliyah. I'd thought I'd managed to keep it under lock and key, but somehow it seemed I'd lost the fucking key.

I coughed again, blood splattering the front of my shirt.

"Hang on, Prince," Aaliyah whispered, the warmth of her hand against my abdomen breathing life back into me. She rubbed gently, back and forth, until my trembles faded, and my head stopped screaming at me.

We inched the last few feet into the living room, each one feeling like the greatest accomplishment I'd ever had. I slipped down the moment we hit the softness of a rug; the shivers becoming manic, the pressure in my head spiraling out of control.

More blood flowed from my nose, over my lips. Wetness on my ears told me there as well. At least hitting the floor instead of the nice bed.

Who the fuck decided we needed to go to the living room?

Oh, that was right. *Me.* I wanted to move.

Fuck me, I was an idiot.

Warm hands circled my neck, my head finding comfort over Aaliyah's legs on her lap. Lavender sweetness muddled the pain, and it was enough to let me focus for one second.

Enough to catch her eyes, see the worry in them, and hate myself a little more for being the cause of it.

I'd fought for so long to be someone who could help her, to be more than just a burden or a ghost she couldn't touch. Now that I was alive, I was little better than before.

On the fucking floor like some shitty rug with great hair and a blood fetish. Blood that was now getting all over Aaliyah.

I tried to jerk away, my brain rattling in my skull, bouncing and snapping. The pressure spiked, a sharp pain behind my eyes telling me that if it didn't stop soon, I'd be losing them. I gritted my teeth when Aaliyah didn't let go.

"I'm going to make a mess out of you, and not the fun kind," I mumbled, the joke coming out with a cry.

She didn't let go, her fingers brushing softly against my cheeks. Weakness stole my muscle movement, the tremors the only thing I could do as I sank into that feeling of her touch, more than happy to cling to her as she hummed.

I ignored the shake in her fingers. I ignored the pain I knew she could see as a scream caught behind my teeth, and the pressure in my head became overwhelming.

There was the tear of teeth into flesh, the sound of my brothers' choked protests, before a wrist hit my lips. Blood, floral and sweet, like the rivers of heaven had found a direct path to my lips.

I took several mouthfuls, soothed by her hand in my hair, before my eyes rolled back, and the blood turned sour in my stomach. My entire body contracted, my back bowing as everything came back up, and I was forced to choke on it.

"It's not working. My blood isn't working," Aaliyah whispered as the door flew open. She curled around me, hugging my shaking body to hers. "Where's Mags!"

I wanted to, more than anything, besides maybe stopping those tears that streaked down her face. Another appeared at my side, and God, I doubted I'd ever been happier to see Mags's crazed face, my brothers barreling in behind the scowling Sorceri. This time, they weren't even holding a skillet.

It was the little things.

"Thought you'd last longer," Mags snorted, shaking their head as if it were my fault that my soul was even more of a temperamental bitch than I was. "I said the *First Rights*. It is not time."

"Oh, Mags, just when I was starting to miss you," I grunted, shaking my head. "I really do love these chats."

I still wasn't used to the body they'd taken the shape of. Their black hair swooped away from their face, damp from either a shower or a dip in some forbidden pool somewhere. They wore simple clothes, a black T-shirt, and matching black slacks.

"And I was missing the quiet," Mags snapped, and I was too tired to say anything against it. My mouth went numb, my throat contracting as if trying to close. I felt the pulse behind my eyes like a heartbeat, the thud unending. *"It is not yet time."*

Mags shrugged as if there were nothing more to do. "Shame, such shame ... my favor will die with you."

Another bout of blood flooded my mouth, and it felt like my body was trying to rip itself apart at the seams. I seized in Aaliyah's arms, holding back a scream with only sheer will as a *Rend* tried to happen.

I felt the pull, the rip, but I stayed lodged firmly in my body. A fact that said body was not a fan of. That couldn't be good.

"He won't last any longer," Aaliyah whispered, no doubt having seen it, as well, a fine layer of sweat on her forehead as she brushed the hair away from mine. Her hands trembled against my skin, my only comfort in the place I'd found with my head in her lap. And her eyes, those lavender eyes that I'd learned were the best place to get lost in.

God, if I was going to die, at least it was in her arms.

"*No.* If he dies, it is because the Hallowed will it. It is not my time to intervene." Mags grunted after they spoke, turning to leave, even as Fallon and Eirik moved to stop them. "There is nothing to be done."

Nothing. Gravity might as well have fled the fucking room with the way the breaths around me stopped, the words a blow that I'd been expecting for weeks. Mags said them callously, as if my life didn't matter to them. I hated to admit how much that stung my budding friendship, seeming as nothing more than a nuisance. Not even enough to try to save me.

I'd known I was dying ever since I'd woken in that tomb, since I'd found Mags.

Since I'd found Aaliyah.

I was on borrowed time, time I never should have had to begin with. I'd gotten to live when any other would have stayed dead. I got to hold the woman I loved in my arms.

Got to say her name.

That was a life worth it for me. Even if we didn't get to finish it, that dream was still there. In a perfect world, we'd live together, with my brothers. She'd never want for anything. She'd curl up in the library with a good book, Adrian's food keeping her content. Eirik singing while Osiris and I picked at that damned old piano. Fallon always staying close to feed her another chocolate.

"Aaliyah," I said, hoping she heard it, the first word I'd needed to say when I woke, the only word that ever mattered to me. Her name was like a prayer.

Tears flooded her eyes, and she curled around my head, her hand still buried in my hair.

"No, not like this. I just got you," she whispered, her voice cracking as another fresh bout of hell had me seizing again. "You promised me forever, Prince. I'm not letting you take that back."

Another bout. Rip. Pull. *Rend.* The scream came out this time, spattered with the blood that caught in my throat. Aaliyah cradled me the entire time. Another of my brothers, maybe more than one, held my limbs to keep me from hurting her.

Hours, that was how long it seemed like it went. Each *Rend* was a blow that left me reeling. Aaliyah's hands were my single grounding point as my eyes closed, and I lost sight of her lavender gaze.

Then a soothing spread over my taut muscles and burst blood vessels, as though someone had placed me in a cool bath. Aaliyah's hands were on my chest, warming me through my shirt.

My soul expanded for her, the cracks that had come from being thrown back into my body after she'd brought me back filling but not closing. It was enough to breathe, to catch the look of concentration on her face as she grew pale, her eyes dimming.

Whatever she was doing was stemming it, but it was causing havoc on her as well. Her eyes rolled back, and her heart stopped beating as her hands went limp where they'd been pressed.

The *Rend* swallowed her, the stability that we'd given her seeming to have slipped away, and I jolted, trying desperately to catch her. My arms were little better than wet noodles, and Eirik was by my side in an instant, holding her up with me. I couldn't understand his words, my mind mush.

Minutes went by before Aaliyah sucked in a ragged breath. A memory played behind her eyes as the pressure in my skull grew again. The seams she'd sealed shut split open. She gritted her teeth, moving me again, holding her hands to my chest even as I tried to sit up and push her away.

The weakness of my own body was shown in how easily she kept me pinned down, another wave of ease shooting over me. The cracks sealed, and she coughed, blood sliding down her chin.

My protest died on the next *Rend* that had me looking over the scene, time slowing as the others rushed around us. Aaliyah went next, her body jolting as her soul ripped itself away. She looked at me, her gray reflection making me sick.

She smiled softly like she did, pressing her hand over her chest even as I screamed. Her ring and pinky finger were tucked away, and I could only watch in horror as her eyes rolled back, and I was slammed back into my gasping body.

Aaliyah might not be able to save me ... but it was easy to see that she would die trying.

CHAPTER 45

AALIYAH

Black shadows circled the floor around us, clinging to my skin, sinking into my bones and over Prince. I called them close, searching in myself for the fractured bits of my soul that held me to him, just like Azer had shown me.

My soul wasn't circling the room, but I could see it when I closed my eyes, the same broken parts of mine hiding in Prince's chest. His soul was just as cracked, black streaks in the red that looked dead. *Memories.*

I reached for them, soothing each one with shaking hands, forcing them to seal as the press of the Void made me sick. It helped, closing the wounds if only for a second longer. My stomach cramped, the Void demanding more for every bit I held closed, as if pulling on an empty well. A hand landed on my shoulder.

Adrian looked down at me, his eyes worried as he wiped the sweat from my brow, but he didn't try to move me. Not when I shook my head, my hands anchored to Prince.

"There is *nothing* to be done!" Magelav screamed, panic lacing their words, proving my theory right. "You'll only kill yourself."

My breaths were shaky, clouded with a wheeze. Adrian's hand tightened as a chill filled the air. I knew what death felt like, remembered it well.

Red. He settled over us, a blanket between Prince and I, taking some of the weight off me. The sweat on my neck cooled, and the little parts of him that were Void were easier to grasp than the bits that weren't.

I breathed, turning to Magelav with clear focus, unyielding as I gritted my teeth. The fear in their eyes was a driving force as pressure radiated in my skull, my eyes burning with the need to close them. I managed to get the words out past a cough as the taste of iron flooded my mouth. "You don't care what happens to him."

A *Rend,* just out of reach. Magelav strained toward me, frantically pacing when I didn't pull back.

"But I can't die, can I? That ruins your plans, doesn't it?" I asked, ignoring the sharp intake of breath as Adrian let out a choked sound.

"Aaliyah!" Fallon screamed, his voice cracking, body strung tight.

Adrian tugged on my shoulder, and I shook my head again just as Mags snapped.

"*Don't!*" Magelav screamed, their voice like a gavel as it slammed against the walls, shaking them and me. "If you take her now, you'll rip them both apart. Her soul is keeping him together. One without the other, and death will become them both."

Defeat burrowed in Mags's crazed eyes as a snarl built in their chest. The air filled with the scent of boggy water and burned sand.

"We're tied together. His soul is a part of me now." The shadows stuck to my arms like a black tar, pulsing with the beat of my heart. "You'll save him, or you'll lose me, too."

The threat was a vicious war cry, echoing softly.

"Impossible," Mags tried, seemingly hollow black eyes trying to call my bluff. "His soul, if nothing else, is a burden on yours."

The Void was a living thing, brushing against my wrists and skin, asking me to come and play or slide my way between the cracks of this world and the after. Prince shuddered under me, his eyes rolling back even with my soul stitching his together. Blood pooled in his mouth, his heart stuttering in his chest.

Red strained, and there was a ripple of pain from him that had my control over the cracks slipping.

"Is it? Because I've seen my soul, looked at the cracks that I can't fix, and seen that he was the only thing holding me together. I've died a thousand times," I whispered, my heart sinking as I leaned down and pressed a kiss to his forehead. Thoughts of the others were close to the surface, and I struggled to keep my gaze down as Adrian's hand grew shaky. Fallon heaved breaths hard enough for me to feel, and Eirik's beast hadn't stopped the keening cry that was buried behind a stifling growl. I could be wrong, but the threat was enough. It had to be.

I couldn't let Prince die.

Not again.

"I know what it feels like for my soul to be ready to pass on. I've known death, and I can promise you that if he goes, I will follow, one way or another," I said.

I promised the men I loved many things. Not dying had been at the top of the list. I broke it with those words that I would follow through on if it was the last thing I did. I'd save Prince.

Or I'd die with him.

"You risk much," Mags said, suddenly calm in the way they looked at me, hands flexing as a vacant stare took over their face. "Your mission, your Exilium. You could be *wrong*."

"Are you willing to risk the same?" was my only response.

Tense seconds passed, and no one breathed besides Prince, who struggled through his.

"Fine," Magelav finally consented, as their face twisted in unbridled rage. They nearly spit when they spoke next. "Sit him up. Reaper, you need to touch him. One without the other. I hope you're ready to face your demons, too."

I'd expected that, the gaps in my own memory swirling. Eirik helped pull me into a sitting position, my hands staying connected to Prince. Adrian was right there, holding me up as I wobbled, struggling to keep myself upright. I grunted as my hands peeled off Prince, the darkness of the Void pulling away.

I crawled into his lap, anchoring myself to him as his eyes lulled open again.

The others backed away, and I snuck the glance I'd been avoiding. Adrian and Eirik were looking anywhere but me, their faces grim. It was Fallon who caught me off guard, his green eyes so focused on me I nearly flinched.

I'd seen him angry before, like a beast that was preparing to strike.

This was something else entirely, something that struck a chord in my chest so sharply the guilt built until it hurt to breathe.

"We'll be talking about this later," he whispered before his eyes finally tipped away.

Dismissed, I deflated, clinging to Prince, keeping him stable as he coughed. He clung to me just as hard as I did to him.

"How do you feel?" Mags asked, and Prince snorted.

"Mags, are you just fucking with me?" he asked.

I gently rubbed his chest as another tremor took over, his entire body tensing as more blood splattered against my shoulder. The cold touch of it sank past my shirt.

"At least your spirits are up. Good, you'll need them. Now drink," Mags said, waving some concoction in front of my face, the rolling potion seeming to swirl even when not touched, glitter glowing in the neon blue depths. They handed the same one to Prince.

"Will this fix it?" I asked, and Mags shrugged.

"Maybe, maybe not. It's all Mags has," they said before sitting back on their heels.

"Tell me you're joking," Fallon bit out, glaring between the three of us.

"You can posture all you like. It's the only option," Mags snapped, turning to stare at the others. I hadn't realized before how close Eirik, Adrian, and Fallon were hovering. "How about you make yourselves useful and get what I need?"

Mags rattled off a few ingredients, the others watching hesitantly before shooting off to do as they had bid.

Mags stood, looking at us expectantly. "Drink, or Mags leave."

Prince's arms tightened around me, and I curled into his cool body, my voice steady against his neck. "Don't you have to wait for them to get back?"

"No. Wanted them gone. Too loud, breaking my concentration. They'll become beasts when you start screaming."

The idea of my memories was enough to get me there already. I clung to the scars that I had, the ones that I knew.

The ones that I didn't.

There were so many, so many years trapped in that glass cell, so many leers and prods. So many doctors. Bile slid up my throat, and I curled tighter around Prince.

"Hey, look at me," Prince said, pulling back just enough to catch my eyes. "I'm right here, Aaliyah."

I shivered, looking from him to the glass in my hand.

"I'm scared, Prince," I admitted after a long moment. Mags scoffed, and Prince flashed his teeth at them, furious that they thought they had the right to judge. "Ascension destroyed me. I don't know if I can handle seeing it all. Not again."

His breath skipped, and I saw the way he shut down his own pain when he cupped my cheek. I focused on the brush of his hand and the soft press of bloodied lips against my own.

"You're never alone again, Aaliyah. Your demons have always been my demons. We face them together, okay?" he said, pressing his forehead into mine. "Be scared, terrified, but never let go of me. No matter what happens, we walk out of this."

I laughed, a broken sound, but sank against him regardless. I kept my eyes closed as our cheeks pressed together, and I chose to hope that the wetness was from the blood and not the tears I knew I'd shed.

"I love you." I choked on the words, but I didn't pull away as I tipped my head back and downed the glass Mags had given us in one drink. I set it next to me, watching as Prince lifted it to his lips and did the same.

The effect was immediate, like a shot straight to the heart. Adrenaline flooded, and I sucked in a hard breath.

"I love you, too, Aaliyah," he said, pressing our foreheads back together, his hand coming to my chest above my heart, pinky and ring finger down. "Forever."

I expected the *Rend*, had been prepared for it, but this was so much different from what I'd grown used to. I snapped out of myself, hitting a silver room with a horrid breath. Only it wasn't endless like I was expecting, instead fissured and cracked. The black sky and flickering stars morphed and distorted, boxing in the room of silver. In it, was my soul.

Every broken piece of it, watching on as one of the shadowed bits hurtled toward me. It slammed into my chest, throwing me back, out of the room. Darkness embraced me as the memory hit, bits of a doctor I couldn't name and the cracking of a bone I felt viscerally.

One by one, they came fluttering back, the room that housed my soul like their playground. A lifetime of surviving, of barely existing.

A lifetime of scars, and then another, and *another.*

Until one life faded into the next, and I realized how right Azer had been, how right *Davi* had been. I'd lived so many lifetimes stuck in a cage, so many years trapped behind glass walls enduring cruel taunts from guards and doctors whose faces and names had long since been lost to me. I hadn't just been alive longer than I thought ... I'd been at *Ascension* for years. Decades.

Lifetimes.

And there was no escaping them now.

CHAPTER 46

OSIRIS

Magic crackled along my skin, digging in like the jagged rocks below me. I had a breath of confusion before my senses homed in, searching for threats as I lay vulnerable on the ground.

The Sage's magic had warped me here, precious seconds wasted as I recognized I was no longer in the Eternium halls. Seconds that were eaten up by the vicious swing of steel through heated air.

I pulled left, my entire body arching as a blade dug into the ground where I'd been, sinking several inches deep. The body holding it shimmered, a flash of white wings my only warning before the blade was pulled from the rocks, swinging at me again.

"*Rex interfectorem.*"

I rolled to my feet, face to face with a man that I never thought I'd see again.

The centuries since I'd seen him last had passed in the blink of an eye, and it was ironic that he was here now, standing in my way one last time. A man I'd met at my first Eternium, a man whom I'd helped to overthrow.

A man who gave me my name, as the first king I felled.

"It's been a long time, coward."

Cael. Angel of Diligence, and the first of the Angel Eternals.

His hair, once golden like the early rays of the sun on mountain peaks, was chopped to pieces, likely by the same dull sword he swung over his shoulder. Angels were large, and Cael was no different, standing at what I could only guess was just over eight feet tall.

It was going to be a fight I'd have to play carefully.

Contempt boiled in his eyes, his teeth exposed as he snarled, his wings snapping wide as he raised the sword again.

I reached for my magic, for *Echomancy*, or the *Flame*, and found both still too faded to use. The well that held my magic had run empty under the weight of the Sage's spell, and trying to draw up more was physically painful. Expected but inconvenient as I dodged another blow, my ears ringing at the deafening crack that came from it. The fact that he could swing at me at all meant this part of the Eternium bent rules that others didn't. Which meant that the weak point I'd been searching for all along had been the Pits. The spot where the Eternium was thinnest. Most fragile.

Which also meant it was entirely possible he'd be able to kill me here.

"Cael," I said, swiping my brow as I stood. We circled each other, the crevice we were in much like an arena. I hadn't been listening before, to the way the walls seemed to cheer. I looked up. A quick glance found empty air. "I thought you died."

He scoffed, as the tips of his wings went deep black, and wrath filled his eyes. "Did you really think Adathan would be able to kill me? No, that would be too cruel for an Angel of *Kindness*. He just locked me up here to fucking rot!"

The white ruins that traced his skin, shimmering like gems under the surface, warped as though filled with fire, bending to the rage that he gave off as he flew at me again.

I didn't manage to dodge as quickly as I had before, crippled by his Holy Aura and my loss of magic. The dull edge bit into my side, ripping flesh as I jerked away. His laugh was bitter as he dragged the bloodied blade across the ground.

"What? No fire without your magic?" he hissed, exposing his throat, where I knew a burn scar to be. One I'd left on him. "No words behind that *wicked silver tongue*!"

It had been centuries since I'd helped Adathan take the seat of Eternal, a move that was done mostly out of boredom and a desire to see Archon pay for the disrespect he had treated me to at my first Eternium. An Eternal spot taken, what I'd thought had been the death of a powerhouse, and a man trapped in his own lamp thinking the same.

Ironic, that the consequences would come back so viciously, now of all times.

He rushed again, and I continued the defense, hitting the edge of the platform, staring at the Void below it, stretching out as far as I could see. Like an island in an ocean that was the Pits.

One slip and I'd fall to who knew where. I had a feeling it was a direct line to the Void, and I wouldn't have an Imperial to guide me through this time.

"I can kill you, you know? Here, so close to the edge of the abyss. Where the Eternium meets the other side," Cael whispered, wiping the dirt off his face as I *flitted* away from the edge. "It's why I brought you here after the Sages dropped you off. Figured it was poetic."

"How are you still here? The Pits are for holding," I asked, stalling for time, searching for a way past him.

The path came in the form of my wrist, the one I reached to hide as he scanned me, sneering at what he saw.

The tattoo pulsed under my palm, Darius's brand holding just enough magic in it to call on, to breathe in. It wasn't like mine; it wasn't magic that came from me, but it was magic in me, regardless.

I struggled not to vomit at the thought of using his tools to help me. A normal tracking spell wouldn't work now, not when I was looking for something unknown. Like a needle in a haystack.

No, but I could still search for something that I knew, something that was a part of me. The tattoo on my wrist, the one now partially covered by the mark that Aaliyah had bestowed on me, was glaringly bright at the thought. My key to felling Darius was down here, and the only spell I could think to use to find it now needed a piece of him.

"The *Pits* decide how long you stay, and when no one comes looking for you? They're happy to keep you forever," Cael said, shaking his head like a voice had called something else in it. He slammed his palm against his ear, gritting his teeth as he turned to snarl at the Void. "They reek of death, flooded with it, so buried in the rot that it oozes from the walls."

I didn't have time for this. "You don't intend to let me get away, do you?"

Cael threw his head back in a laugh before preparing his sword to strike again. It may have looked like steel, but the holy blade he wielded stung, the wound on my stomach still throbbing, struggling to heal.

I gripped the tattoo, preparing for what I had to do. My ring and pinky finger stayed down as the next spell slipped past my lips.

It searched for the distinct pull of unfamiliar magic, and yet nothing came. Frustration was quick to follow as I was forced to dodge another blow.

I set my hand over the ink, the one that Darius had placed himself, winding Mythic energy inside of it. I shivered with disgust at the feeling of raised bumps, uneven ink from how I'd thrashed, trying to get away.

"Now, what would be the fun in that?" he asked, slinking forward as I called the magic again, asked for its help, begging, even as it made my skin crawl, imploring it to search. To pick apart the Pits until it found its other half, found itself in whatever idol Darius had thrown away. "You have centuries of pain to make up for, Vivas."

It came forward, sluggish and lazy, but it was enough. I felt it snap into place, beginning its search through the rubble, and all I could do now was wait.

I shrugged my suit coat off, letting it fall to the floor as I lifted my hands, balling them in a familiar stance that Nero had taught me so long ago. I cracked my neck, breathing in.

"Oh, so you're going to fight me with your hands?" Cael mocked before throwing his sword to the side. It clattered, crashing heavily into the dirt.

He raised his hands in a similar position, stalking around me with his lips pulled back, exposing teeth. "Fine. I'm happy to see the life drain from your eyes up close."

He flew at me, all power in the crack of his wings against the air. The mark on my wrist burned, and I could only hope it found its mark soon.

Until then, I had a fight on my hands.

CHAPTER 47

AALIYAH

The memory faded in, clinging to the walls like the red that painted them. Vicious lights blazed from above, and I waited in horrified silence as shuffling echoed around me.

The room warped, as if bending to the sound before a man appeared, one my brain struggled to place as he flashed glinting white teeth at me.

"What do you want to do today, Aaliyah?" he asked as he brushed gentle fingers against my cheek.

I struggled not to flinch away.

Flinn Ammerson. That was his name, standing proudly against his chest on a little white name tag. He wore black slacks and a blue button-down dress shirt, with two open buttons on the top. His hair was a messy mop of brown that called to the hazel in his earthy eyes.

Conventionally, he was attractive, something that always made my stomach sour. Because I knew what was coming next.

"Feeling shy on me today? That's okay. Leave it all up to me," he whispered, leaning in.

His tongue brushed my cheek, his hand skimming down my neck. He didn't dip farther, wouldn't dare. Sir Amoun made sure that was clear with the first doctor that had tried anything more. I couldn't remember his name, or his face, but I remembered the way his body contorted after *he'd been strung up, displayed in the halls like art made by a butcher. A warning to others. Small mercies in this hell.*

Not that my heart didn't jolt in my chest, and bile didn't build in my mouth when his fingers trailed along my collarbone.

Eyes alight, he pulled back. I did my best to brace, closing my eyes for whatever he had planned.

One breath in, another out.

"Now, just sit back for me," he hummed, and I heard him flip through his papers before his pen touched down. He scribbled something, voicing it out loud just seconds later. "Doctor Flinn Ammerson, starting trial thirteen forty-three, March sixth, nineteen..."

I didn't hear the rest, keeping my eyes closed. One breath in, one out.

I held it in, even as the first blade broke skin, hitting muscle and tendon, dancing along nerves that coiled every muscle I had. I held it in until I couldn't breathe past the agony anymore. His laugh was acidic until that first whimper broke through.

He slammed a hand over my mouth, and his manic voice came to my ear, genuine terror clinging to it. "Don't scream. He'll hear you."

The kind that made me stay silent as I listened for quiet footsteps, for the man who ran this place, the one who'd stolen me from my home. Sir Amoun.

I let out a breath, stilling like the dead on the table, even as everything in me ached and burned. It crawled up my throat, and I held it back with sheer will and tears, Flinn's hand still over my mouth.

Never make noise.

I choked on my blood, and Flinn pulled back, facing the door as it opened. I kept myself still, even as I wanted to thrash.

"Progress?" The sharp voice was hauntingly familiar, and the tears I'd held on to fell, mixing with the blood that painted me.

They get more violent when they hear noise.

One breath in, another out ... before sweet unconsciousness claimed me.

This one, like every memory before it, ended with the soft lull of my own heartbeat in my ears, and the building of a scream on my lips, one I didn't let go, even as it pressed on my lungs, and made it hard to breathe.

Never make noise.

The echoing of the memory slammed into me like the tremors that followed it. I gagged, sickened by the thought of Flinn. I'd forgotten about him. Even now that everything was fresh, he'd faded to the back of my mind. One of the first of *many* doctors I'd had.

Up to now, nearly all my memories had been centered on Nox and Castillion—or around *Prince*—but that moment, plucked from the seams of my consciousness, was before that. The years spent in that horrible cell were hard enough with him by my side ... the *decades* without him were much harder pills to swallow.

I felt the tears before they fell, struggling to keep them in as my breathing became labored, quietly rioting in my chest. I'd spent enough time remembering Ascension to know how little of a life I'd actually had, but this was too much.

They get more violent when they hear noise.

I was still in Prince's arms, wrapped around him as he twitched and flinched, his own memories coming back to him. His skin was warmed from my own, his body the only thing keeping me grounded as I waited for the next vile memory to take me, but it never came. The silver room that held my soul was blissfully silent.

I reached up, pressing a hand to my head, searching for the pressure that had been dragging me along for the past several hours. It was absent and left in the place that had been my lack of memories was now only dread.

A shiver rocked me as I leaned more fully into Prince. The room was silent, something that made my skin crawl as I closed my eyes. Even Red's emotions were pulled back, diluted by the tension in the air. I knew the others were here, but I couldn't bring myself to look at them, not yet.

Not when I was so close to broken.

Something wrapped around my shoulders a couple seconds later, the soft scent of ocean salt giving Eirik away. His shirt was large, soaked in the heat that poured from him. He sat next to us, his body thumping against the ground.

Sound burst from his chest, the purr that had brought me back so many times, seeming so loud now. I lifted my eyes, catching his crystal-clear ones.

"How long?" I whispered, habitually.

Eirik huffed, reaching out to tuck a stray piece of hair over my ear. "Six hours."

He kept his voice low, and as I looked around, I realized Adrian and Fallon were strewn across the ground just a couple of feet away, sleeping soundly.

The dark bags under their eyes were more pronounced, the *Calls* that still ailed them affecting them even now as Fallon's face contorted with a gnarled grimace. At least the marks left by the sun seemed to have faded, even Fallon moving more easily as he rolled over, tossing in his sleep.

Magelav, however, held no such subtly. Their black hair was ruffled, eyes dulled with a lack of sleep. Their hands, up in a spell-casting position, were shaking. "How do you feel? Any more pesky memories hiding away in there?"

Adrian shot up first, looking around with wide, startled eyes. He was quick to move, standing and coming close. Fallon was slower, and my heart stalled in my chest at the idea that he might not come, that what I'd done earlier might have broken that tie.

I'd deserved it. I'd done as I promised I never would. I'd been ready to die in front of them, and they had no chance or ability to stop it. I hadn't expected Magelav to do anything but cave, but had they ... I would have left the men I loved behind if it came to it.

Something that hurt me to admit.

But Fallon stood, still guarded as he narrowed his eyes, before he came to me. I reached for them, not getting out of Prince's lap, but getting close enough to touch. I ran gentle fingers over the creases on their faces, trying my best to keep my shaking down as they sighed into the touch.

"I don't think so," I said, looking around the room for Magelav, finding them at the table next to another familiar face.

Xander sat across from Mags, scowling as he tapped his finger against the wood. He wore a typical white suit, one leg crossed prissily over the other. Mags didn't give him the time of day, never taking their crazed eyes away from me.

Even when Xander whispered something I couldn't hear, and a vein popped on Magelav's neck.

"Good, then you're done here," Fallon grunted, his voice husky from sleep.

"What about Prince? We can't just leave him like this," I said.

His body still twitched under mine, and while I didn't see his soul snapping from the *Rends*, I could feel it happening. They echoed in the air, something almost audible, before fading away when more memories came to him.

It worried me that he was still out.

"He'll wake when he's done, a lot of memories in a mind like that. Or he'll die. Nothing more I can do." Mags's words hit the room like magic right before their arms finally dropped. They shook, almost violently, their eyes dulling further to a pasty white with bloodshot lines tracing them. They let out a weary sigh. "My part is done. With you awake, he just needs to remember."

My hand went to Prince's chest, searching for the thunder of his heart, and I only managed to open my mouth when I felt it.

"Why would he die?" I asked, and Mags shrugged.

"If he can't find his way out of the Void, it will claim him. Beg he's strong enough to come back to you." Mags didn't look worried, but at the same time I didn't expect them to. They were a wild card; that they helped at all was honestly a miracle. They tipped their head, humming as their eyes shot gold for just a moment. A flare of magic bursting into the air. "After all, it takes, and it takes, and it *takes*."

Just as quickly, their eyes were back to normal, and they were looking at me with a feral grin. I shivered, keeping my hand over Prince's heart.

It made sense that he'd take longer to wake. He had more life to live, more memories he likely wanted to savor. I didn't have the same luxury between Ascension and my time in the Void. I just had to hope he'd open his eyes soon, and we could put this behind us. *All of it.*

I wanted to bury Ascension back down, keep it locked up, thrown away. The last memory still rattled me, hitting my soul like a hammer hit bone.

"Don't look so despondent, Aaliyah. We've already learned that

Nero can't be held by something as simple as death," Xander said, nodding.

His words were meant to be encouraging, but the way he looked at us, like he might ask for Prince's body if he did die again, made the hairs on my neck stand on edge.

"Why are you here, Xander?" Fallon pressed, turning a cold stare to the volatile Dryad. "Don't you have someone else to bother?"

Xander chuckled, but didn't hide his sour glare, baring his teeth a bit too much in his smile. "Just checking on an old friend. Speaking of ... where is Osiris?"

I swallowed hard, nearly jolting out of Prince's arms when Red's familiar presence bled support into the air. It calmed me, but didn't take away from that feeling.

The thought of Osiris made my chest hurt, and it was painful as I looked around the room, knowing I wouldn't find him. I reached up, grabbing the necklace he'd made to replace the one Sebek had broken, finding comfort in the heat it gave off at my touch. He'd always been a quiet presence, but that almost made the loss of him hit that much harder.

I could feel him when he was around, and knew he was always watching over us. I always felt safer when he was near.

Xander's smile broadened when no one spoke; I wasn't willing to give an inch on it, even to him.

Especially to him.

"He's in the Pits, isn't he? Such a shame Darius is so cruel, unless of course ... Osiris planned this?" There was silence, the deadly kind that followed. Xander threw his head back and laughed.

The provocation masked his fear well ... but not well enough for me to miss the hints of it I saw in the way he tensed when Magelav coughed. He stood beside them, and for a second, there was something like compassion flashing across his face. Magelav was beautiful like this, in a savage way, even if they were terrifying.

"He'll wake when he wakes," Mags said, before dipping their head and turning toward the door.

Xander was quick to follow.

"Come, Mags. We have some catching up to do. Don't we?" The

words were purred, and Mags's face grew red, teeth bared like I'd seen Eirik do before.

They wobbled on their feet, though, seeming dazed as they leaned into Xander. He moved slowly, wrapping Mags's arm over his shoulder, and I was surprised that they allowed it.

"Piss off, you insufferable miscreant," they said, but didn't let go as Xander held them steady, more insults I couldn't quite hear following them out the door.

Silence met the room, and I sank farther into Prince's arms. Surrounded by the others, only missing one, was a balm to the chaos that still swirled in me. Memories replayed, and I was stuck counting the scars that lined my skin.

Saw.

I flinched.

Filet knife.

I trembled, unable to pull myself back, even as more hands found my skin. They covered the scars, but they were still there.

Dug so deep they'd never wash away.

"You promised," Fallon whispered, his voice cracking down the middle, the seams of his control splitting.

I looked up, catching his eyes, which had grown numb from where he sat on the floor.

"I know," I whispered.

I'd promised not to die, not to risk it, but this was something I couldn't have avoided. Even then, seeing the distraught look in his eyes was enough to hurt me.

"You were ready to die for Nero if it came to it. If you were wrong," he said, his face tensing up.

I turned back to Prince, his face serene. Magelav wouldn't have let me die. That much I'd known, I just had to convince them that saving Prince was the way to save me.

"I was ready to die for Prince if I was right," I responded, shaking my head. "And I can't apologize for it. I'd do it again, for any one of you."

Fallon let out a choked cry as he stood. The chair that he'd sat on flung back, hitting the floor with a crash.

"We don't want you to die for us, Aaliyah! We don't want you to sacrifice yourself. We want you to live." He nearly didn't get the last word out, his hand going to his hair, flinging the blond locks into disarray. "You didn't even give us a warning. Magelav could have called your bluff, and it would have been over."

The quick thinking, the look in Magelav's eyes. It was hard to remember that I found it much easier to read people than most. I'd seen their ticks, the bits of them that gave away their emotions. I hadn't had time to explain it ... "I took a bet on Mags's plan, but it wasn't a bluff. I wouldn't have done something so drastic if I wasn't expecting to win."

"How do you know?" Fallon pressed, shrugging off Adrian as he tried to calm him down. He wasn't screaming or thrashing; there wasn't a hint of rage on his face, but his disappointment was clear enough to see, and it stung. "What makes you so sure?"

I thought back to the Void, to Davi and the memory that had started this whole mess. To the tie that Prince and I shared.

"Because the same thing that ties me to Prince, is why my father survived the Natural War. My mom brought him back, not realizing it would use a piece of my soul to do so," I said, rubbing the space between my breasts as the thought of my mother made my heart ache. "Sebek didn't intend to kill his brother, but when my mother died at his hands? Arvand went with her. It's why he went so crazy. He didn't mean to kill him, not really."

I realized now how that had seemed to them, to Fallon, who'd already watched me die once, and almost die twice.

He twitched, scratching at the black marks that sat faded on his skin, the dark bags under his eyes suddenly so much more pronounced. Their time at Archon's, even the *Call*, had been pushed aside, but that didn't mean it wasn't affecting them.

I'd been such an idiot

"I'm sorry for scaring you," I whispered, curling into myself as I watched Fallon deflate, his hands going to his head as he tried to settle his breathing.

Quickened breaths, shaking hands, eyes that seemed to daze the longer he panted. I knew the signs of panic, and I was quick to move, standing in front of him. I reached up, cupping his cheeks to get him to look at me.

I struggled to open my mouth, words seeming useless.

"What do you see?" a voice whispered, Adrian to my left, helping to support Fallon as his legs quaked.

"Four walls, dark paint, brothers"—he pulled in a breath, this one steadier—"*Aaliyah*."

"What do you feel?" Another voice, a deep rumble. Eirik.

Fallon took another breath, his eyes on mine as he leaned into my palms. "Warm."

It took a few more minutes, but the shaking subsided, and Fallon seemed to get his grips. He kissed my palm, closing his eyes. "I'm trying, trouble, *so hard* to remember that you're strong. But I can't handle watching you die again. A thousand times dead is a thousand times too many. One more is too *fucking* many."

"Look at me," I whispered, holding his face in my hands with all the tenderness I could. He looked like I might fade away if he didn't cling hard enough. "What's going on, Fallon? Really?"

He shuddered, closing his eyes the same way I did when memories of Ascension came, no doubt seeing whatever it was that haunted him behind the dark sheen.

"I keep seeing you dead, keep seeing your blood on my hands," he whispered, shaking his head. "I keep seeing *Aislinn* in every face I see. Have since Archon stuck me in his fucking lamp. I've been trying to ignore it, but it has me so amped up, so paranoid. It's pathetic—"

I pulled him to me before he could get any more cruel words out, pressing my lips to his to silence the venom he was spewing about himself. I hadn't seen it before, how hard he'd been holding himself back to try to let me breathe while being strangled by his own fear.

"Thank you for caring about me. For everything," I whispered, smiling at the dazed look in his eyes and the way he looked back to my lips. "I'll try not to leave you in the dark again."

He swallowed, tapping his forehead against mine as he brushed scarred knuckles against my cheek. So gentle, so loving. "You could have died—"

"I love you," I whispered.

His eyes went comically wide before he looked away from me, my hands slipping off of his cheeks as he rubbed the back of his head. "Are you trying to distract me, trouble?"

"No. Just realized I needed to say it. *I love you*, Fallon. Thank you for caring about me, for standing by my side," I said, and he turned back to me again.

This time, he led the kiss, holding me close enough that I couldn't feel the ache of the day anymore. "I love you, too."

The room was surprisingly quiet following my confession, and Fallon seemed all the happier with it as he asked, "You all right?"

His face was still clinging to dark shadows, his eyes haunted by a past he struggled to outrun. I didn't want to lay more burden on him, not now.

"I'm fine," I whispered before I could think better of it.

We'd come so far, and saying it felt like a slap. Tears soured the taste in my mouth, and the back of my throat became heavy with them as I tried to find words.

"Don't lie to me, Aaliyah. We help each other with our burdens," he said—exactly what I'd been thinking.

Words I couldn't voice, a pain that was so fresh I could still feel the cuts. I wanted to share, to tell them, to find comfort in their arms. But that voice that came with my memories was little more than a curse now, telling me things I knew weren't true, things that damned me.

I wasn't whole, not anymore. I never had been. *I wasn't what they needed.*

They needed someone strong, someone who could stand by them. Who wouldn't buckle like I was.

Prince, as if even in his dreams realizing I needed him, tightened his arms. I felt his heart against my ear as his move jolted my head to his chest. The steady thump, the shallow breaths.

"Ascension," I started before I could stop myself, stomping on the thoughts of inadequacy. "I was there for a *long* time, longer than I ever thought. Getting my memories back—"

I bit my lip, a hand shooting to my shoulder, to an ache there I'd all but forgotten about. The first tear that fell opened a dam.

"I'm broken, Fallon. No piece of me is still intact, and I don't know what to do. I don't know how you could want me after—"

The words never finished, as Fallon was tipping his head down, sealing his lips to mine. He did exactly as I had to him and cut off the venom I spewed about myself.

He had never been one for words, so I listened. To the way he kissed me, to the achingly gentle slide of his tongue over my lips, to the look in his eyes that I knew was saved for me.

"Aaliyah, I will always want you. *Always*. And I will tell you as many times as you need to hear. I'll scream it if you need me to." Fallon's face was vibrant, and I choked on my tears at the devotion in his eyes.

"You're ours. Ours to love, ours to protect. Ours to treasure," Eirik added in, shocking me as his lips found my forehead.

"We are Vivas," Fallon finished, running his thumb across the scar on my lip. When he leaned in this time, his tongue traced it. The skin was thin there, sensitive, and I trembled at the delicate touch.

The vow that had been forged in fire, and that made them family.

"Bound by blood, *family* by choice," Adrian added softly, smiling when I looked his way.

"When one calls, the others follow." Eirik's words were softened by the purr of his beast.

They looked at me, watching me silently, and it was with unending joy that I realized they wanted me to finish it. The vow that they'd made. The bond that made them Vivas.

They wanted me in it.

"And when one fights, we fight with them," I finished, nearly breaking when Fallon's lips tilted in a soft smile.

"You're our family, love," Adrian said. "Through the good, and the bad. We're by your side."

Prince stirred under me, twitching again, this time his hands lifting. They found my cheeks, cool to the touch, pulling me away from Fallon's grip. There was a ghost of a breath before his lips slid over mine, and I gasped.

There was a sureness to his kiss, a confidence that felt new in the way he angled our heads, his fingers guiding our moves.

"Forever," he purred, his silver eyes opening.

The anxiety around regaining our memories was lost to me. Instead, there was only him.

"Prince," I whispered, following him as he pulled away, not ready to give up his lips just yet.

He laughed, stealing a few more kisses.

"Morning, my sweet Aaliyah," he whispered, knocking his forehead against mine.

"How are you feeling?" I asked, watching as he shrugged his shoulders and rolled his head from side to side.

I kept waiting for the other shoe to drop, for him to stand a different man than I knew. The fear that the few years we'd shared would be overshadowed by centuries of life wasn't new to me ... but he just smiled, the curl to his lips sinfully familiar.

"Better, now," he whispered.

He didn't look better, at least not his body, but it was nice to see his eyes clear. I settled my ear against his chest, listening to the steady beat of his heart and his easy breaths.

There was shuffling, and before I knew it, we were standing.

I was still wrapped up in Prince's arms, my head lying on his shoulder. Exhaustion was a beast that I'd pushed off for too long.

"Come on, let's get a few hours of actual rest, love," Adrian whispered, and I nodded, letting him gently comb his hands through my hair. "We're not going anywhere."

CHAPTER 48

ADRIAN

I'd *kill* for a coffee.

I rubbed my eyes, cracking my neck until I heard the pop as I shook off the sleepy haze that clung to me.

It was nearing noon, a fact that had me wanting to curl back up and continue to sleep the final day away before the vote. I wasn't used to being up now, and my mind was a hazy mess of tired and jittery. Normally, I'd still be curled up with Aaliyah, watching over her while she slept, just to get a few more hours near her.

She was pale when I'd left the bed, with shadows under her eyes a constant reminder of why I was doing this. Yesterday had taken its toll on her, the return of her memories hitting harder than she was letting on.

I saw it in every move she made, in the haunted looks she thought she hid so well. If we weren't so close to First Rights, I wouldn't have even dreamed of leaving her side.

But tensions were rising. Those on both sides would be looking for allies. I'd be looking for ammunition.

Unfortunately, those that could be used would be in the grand hall by now, schmoozing it up with the other bigwigs and trying to prove who had the biggest cock. The answer would always be the Three ... not that any of them would admit that.

"Headed out?" Eirik asked, nodding at me from where he stood by the island as I walked by.

The tension he held was a nasty thing, his shoulders bunched tight, his eyes shadowed. The weight of the world that had sunk so heavily on our eldest now sat with Eirik. He reached for his neck, hand finding air before he touched the scar that sliced across his throat.

"Yeah, have some allies to sway. Hold down the fort?" I asked.

Eirik just nodded absently. We hadn't heard anything yet from our eldest, after he'd descended into the Pits thanks to Darius's call for Retaliation, but his bond hadn't wavered. We could only hope he managed to find whatever it was he was looking for, and that it was enough to take down Darius the Great.

It would be a win like no other. Darius was old, pretty much evil-villain-level powerful, and his allies would be more likely to sway toward us with him out of the picture.

"Axius?" Eirik grunted, and I nodded once.

The wary Gargoyle was going to be a tough nut to crack. Axius was inflexible. From everything I'd read on him, he was staunchly protective of Hyland, no matter how terrible his brother grew to be. But something about him felt good. Stupid, and blindly loyal, sure.

But with the right push, he could be useful.

"I'll do what I can," I said, though, not really holding much hope for it.

Eirik surprised me when he spoke. "We don't want Hyland keeping the spot. Any ally we can get, we should take advantage of. Valen said the same."

The gravity of that sentiment didn't fall away, and now more than ever, that was true.

Our allies had been in shambles before this, held together by an idea that barely had enough weight to get off the ground. With the terror that had come after Sebek had exposed Aaliyah, it was a miracle there were allies left to be had. Sebek knew what he was doing.

He was crazy, bat shit and beyond the point of madness, something he'd proven when he'd outed Ali ... but there was no one else that could plan like he could. It was terrifying.

"I'll get it done," I said and turned toward the door.

"I know you will, Adrian." Eirik's vote of confidence helped to settle some of the worry that held me down. "Be safe, brother."

I smirked at him over my shoulder, waving as I walked out the door and into the hallway. "Always."

The door closed, and the mask fell away.

I rubbed my hands over my face, struggling to keep myself steady as I rocked my head from side to side again. I was exhausted, shaking, and, if I were honest, barely standing.

I made a rather piss-poor Collector right now.

My vision sharpened as the walls slowly shifted around me. It was a short walk to the main hall. The Eternium took me right there, thank God, the floor beneath my feet wavering as though it were only an illusion.

Then I was turning a corner, and there I was, in a sea of deceit. I was used to dealing with the power hungry, with those that thought themselves at the top of the world, but to see so many?

It was going to be a long day.

"Trouble sleeping?" a voice asked, and I turned to smile at Fallon as he stepped up to my side.

I snorted, taking a second to look at him. He was back in one of his signature white suits, though it varied from the one he wore day to day. This one seemed to add extra flair, a bit more gold and less green. The tie weaving the colors together against his dark undershirt.

A gift from the Eternium, no doubt.

"Something like that. You?" I asked, still warily searching the Eternals who had started to take notice of us.

"Something like that," he repeated, the extra weight to his words almost too slight to discern.

But I wouldn't have expected him to just come out and say anything, not directly, so I picked apart his words, his stance.

The *Call* still fought him, like it did me.

"Need any help?" I asked nonchalantly as I could when I smiled widely at Adathan as he passed, the Angel Eternal tipping his head in my direction, long blond hair bound in a tight bun. His white wings spawned out behind him, flexing before pulling close to his back.

"No, just wanted to check in before I lost you in the crowd," Fallon said. "You?"

Oh, I would take all the help I could get. I was practically shaking, sick to my stomach. But this was my problem, and Fallon had his own to deal with.

"No, I think I've got this," I said, shoving my hands into my pockets.

Fallon watched me for a moment before he nodded. "See you back safe, brother."

He walked away from my side, disappearing into the mass of people. I took a deep breath and let a smile slide onto my face.

Game time.

I moved my way through the crowd, as well, stopping to chat with those that Drakon had mentioned, and those that I knew were wavering on the edge of a decision. Most kept tight lips, and the more I tallied, the more dread set in. The vote for a passing Exilium was three-fourths, and the more I spoke to, the fewer we seemed to have on our side, even assuming all Challenges passed. Worse than that, even the allies we'd gained seemed to keep their distance. Faces turned up in disgust and in fear, but there was one I knew would always look my way.

Even if he rolled his eyes while doing so.

Amadeus, the Alderi Hordes Demon of Lust.

He saw me coming; he always did, his head tipping back as though he were praying. He was sitting at a large circular table with several empty chairs and I was more than happy to take one off his hands as I slid in beside him.

His hair was brushed back, exposing the gold to his eyes and the runes that traced his skin. He wore a suit, a simple one with no flashy accents, black and dull. He was still in his human body, at least the one that appeared human, anyway, beyond his slightly pointed ears. But there was an air about him, one that made sure no one would be getting too close, even as liquid lust dusted off him in gold puffs. Outwardly, he seemed like the type of man others would flock to, but *damn*, he put the prick in prickly personality.

It made sure the people realized who he was, as a Horde member of the new Demon Eternal, Vidius.

"Adrian," Amadeus said, not even bothering to look my way before tipping his drink toward me with a grumble.

I chuckled, shaking my head. "Amadeus, don't look so happy to see me, old friend."

He rolled his eyes, pulling the olive out of his drink before popping it into his mouth. "Maybe I would be, if you weren't so worn down. Troubled isn't a good look on you."

"And boorish isn't a good look on you. I expected you'd be more inclined to enjoy the festivities?"

"If you're asking why I'm not off fucking someone in a spare room, then you'd be pleased to know no one here meets my standards." He looked me up and down before grimacing like he was holding back a gag. I almost laughed. "No offense."

Oh, that was one hundred percent meant with *full* offense. It was one of the many things I loved about Amadeus; he was an asshole.

But he was a terrible liar.

"I wish I could help to settle that mind of yours. I see it racing, but unfortunately, I don't imagine any news I have will help you much," he said after, keeping his voice low as he inched a bit closer.

"Tell me, what are our odds? What do you think?" I pressed, and he scratched his jaw.

One of his runes glowed at the touch, faintly for just a moment, before settling back to a soft gold, and he waited a bit longer before responding. "If you want the honest answer? Exilium isn't going to pass, Adrian. At best, the Butcher might only kill some of you when this is over."

He shivered, glancing over his shoulder like even saying that might summon Sebek. He took another sip of his drink. "Word of your girl has gone around. The Eternals are terrified by what she represents. *True death*. Some that had been allied with Drakon before have pulled back, and the ones that stayed are in shambles. Then there's the issue with Kali and Osiris. Killing one Eternal, sure, but two? That's not a good look."

I nodded, but didn't really share that sentiment. Our odds without Kali seemed almost better than with her. It was one less monster on Osiris's back, one less chance for him to crack like Sebek had.

One less chance for the numb to live in his eyes forever.

"We planned for this," I said simply, and Amadeus nodded.

"Right, the Challenge," he whispered, tipping his head back, letting his hair fall loosely over his shoulders. "It may not be much, but you have the Alderi Horde on your side, even if I think it's stupid to get in the middle of this."

Probably right, but I appreciated the show of support, regardless. We needed it, and it was nice knowing that at least some people were on our side.

"You're Demons. You're always in the middle of the dark and dirty. Or did you forget how we grew acquainted already?" I asked, raising an eyebrow.

Amadeus blushed, covering his face with his hands. It had been quite the sight, finding the Lust of the Alderi Horde in a human prison. Getting him out hadn't been hard, but it had been a way to gain some leverage over him, even if it had long since been repaid.

Now we could be called acquaintances, maybe even friends, in the right light. One that had ample amounts of booze and music to drown out the sound of his whining.

"Yeah, yeah, go on, continue your scheming, Collector," Amadeus grumbled, shaking his head again as he finished off his drink.

"With pleasure," I said, scanning the room for the ones I needed to talk to tonight. "Any eyes on Axius?"

I'd caught a few already, ones that slid to the shadows, trying to stay hidden. They hadn't been that lucky.

"The Sentinel? Yeah, he's been on the fringes all night, watching over his brother. Hyland seems like quite the piece of work." He pointed to a table on the far side of the room, to a man who looked like he was somehow having less fun than him.

"So I've heard," I said, humming. I'd already thought of how I was going to handle Axius. It was just a matter of getting him alone. Really, he was just a way to bridge the conversation and to hide my true intentions as I whispered the next bit. "And what of Sadi?"

It took Amadeus a second to register my words, like he hadn't been expecting me to ask that. Archon was a small fry in the big picture, and while he was a nuisance, he was one that could be taken care of later. I didn't want later, couldn't last through later.

I itched my arm, gritting my teeth when I felt nothing from it. I had to stop before I drew blood.

"The Djinn?" he asked, his mouth opening slightly when I nodded my head. "I'm surprised you're even asking. She's only here because of her mating to a distant relation to the new Fae Eternal. She's not on our list."

I shook my head. "Call it curiosity."

Amadeus's eyes grew dark, a hint of his horns peeking through the illusion of his human flesh. "You don't *get* curious, Collector. What are you playing at?"

I couldn't risk saying it out loud, and I flagged down the nearest waiter, snagging a drink off his plate before taking a slow sip. Amadeus watched, unnerved.

"That's for me to know, and you to find out when the fireworks start," I said, grinning as he leaned back in his chair.

"She's *kind*, Adrian, kinder than any here deserves, especially after the loss of her sister," he said cautiously, his eyes lingering on where she was in the crowd.

No wonder he hadn't taken anyone to bed yet, and now I knew he wouldn't.

"Loliana, right? She'd been training under Archon last I heard, before her unfortunate passing," I asked, steering away from Sadi. Amadeus's shoulders dropped, and he was all too happy to move on.

"That's right. She'd been a promising candidate for the next Djinn Eternal." His words were forced, and I knew nothing else of use would come from him.

"You seem to know Sadi. Would you mind letting her know that I'd like to talk? I think we have a lot in common, her and I." I said it as I stood, and Amadeus didn't look at me beyond a sharp nod, passing me a look of regret that soured the feeling in my stomach. I brushed it off, for the sake of what I needed to do. The who had been decided. This wouldn't work without Sadi; Archon wouldn't fall without her. I just hoped he wouldn't take her down with him, or I might end up losing my connection to the Horde. "Have a good night, Amadeus. Axius seems rather lonely. I think I need to go make a new friend."

I walked away as Amadeus laughed behind me, the sound rotten in his chest. "May the devil help him."

It didn't take long to get to Axius. I'd seen him already, picked him out of the crowd, and knew now would be the best time to strike. He was large, Eirik's size from the look of it, with rich black hair and steely gray eyes that looked like freshly wet stone, muddled by his irritation as he glanced at me.

I stole one of the seats without asking, already preparing the start of my *amazing* speech when he grunted. "Not interested."

I hadn't gotten the warmest welcome here, being who I was, but I expected more than what he'd given me. There was a dance that those in the Eternium played, but it didn't seem that Axius was intent on joining in.

I leaned forward, chin on my palm. His entire body tensed, his tail slashing behind him loud enough to hear it split the air.

"While you're adorable, that's not why I'm here," I said with a wink.

There was an art to information collection, one I'd painstakingly learned over the years. Axius's agitation had been easy to see, even a mile away, but now the smaller ticks were coming to the surface.

Irritation bred contempt, contempt bred loose lips. Even if that wasn't what he wanted.

"You think I don't know why you're here, *Collector?*" he practically spit.

My, seems I was quite popular today.

My fangs ached, my vision flashing red for the briefest moment as I forced a steady smile while the *Call* fought tooth and nail in the back of my skull. I had to bite my tongue to stop my smile from shifting to a sneer.

" I already talked to *Challe* Osiris, and you can have the same answer as him. Whatever you want, whatever you have to say, I'm not interested. I'm not going to take the title from Hyland."

My mouth watered, my eyes blurring, but even when I lost some of the fight, and my body jerked, I didn't go for him. Bloodlust ravaged the *Call*, the Eternium keeping me locked down. I was thankful for it, even as it destroyed me.

The only relief came from the lack of pain that should have been there, eating at my stomach.

"Then why are you here?" I pressed.

"Because I'm required." Was his standard, shitty answer.

He picked up his drink, then sipped the sweet-smelling liquid. His eyes darted around the room, and I knew without looking they'd landed on Hyland. I'd done my research about the Gargoyle Eternal, Zercara, after I'd heard about his death. His sons, twins, had been joined at the hip. The familial bond still burned in Axius, even if Hyland's blood had been tainted by years of power and greed.

Axius still cared for him, and that was his weak point, the part I could dig into.

"No, *I'm* required. From the sour looks Hyland has been shooting you, I'd say he doesn't want you here at all. You're watching out for him," I said, tipping my head but not bothering to look over my shoulder.

Axius tensed, his eyes narrowing into silver slits. "Hyland doesn't need anyone to watch him."

"Yet you do anyway. A good brother. A good twin," I praised, almost mockingly. "You don't want to have to fight him. Even though you know what he's siding with isn't right."

The push was enough to cause a fissure in his expression, a flash of doubt. He swallowed, and it was masked in the next second. But it had been there, the seed of doubt, the worry.

"Leave," he growled, the tone an ominous thunder.

His face shifted, his skin pulling tight as stone replaced it. It rippled before it hardened. It might have intimidated a weaker man, but I'd lived with *Eirik*.

No amount of growling would get Axius his way.

"He plans to push for human enslavement. I've heard whispers, you know, that he intends to go even further. Genocide—"

Axius faltered, his jaw clenching as he stood abruptly. "What part of leave do you not understand, Vivas?"

I hummed, taking in my handiwork, and the riled state he was in now. The doubt I'd sowed would spread, would stick in his mind like sludge. I just needed one more push, one more hint to drive him over.

He wouldn't fight his brother without it. Wouldn't consider it.

"Seems I struck a nerve. Your Sentinel is showing," I said, and Axius's face molted into shame.

His shift back was slow, like he fought to dial it back in.

"I won't fight him, not like this," he whispered, his eyes again on Hyland. "He's the only family I have left."

I scoffed, shaking my head. Sometimes, this was too easy.

"Valen would be disappointed to hear you say that. He was the one who told us to come looking, after all. A worried brother." Axius flinched, as though struck. Valen was a well-kept secret, one so buried it had nearly slipped by even me. The bastard child spawned between a Sorceri and the Gargoyle Eternal. Hidden in the cracks where no one would go looking. I wasn't no one. "Fine, you've made your point, but keep that in mind if Hyland prevails, and Sebek lives ..."

I stood, brushing off my suit, straightening it. "Well, you won't have to worry about being the one to take down your brother. Sebek will do it for you."

I didn't bother waiting for a response, just turned away and left Axius at the table. His likelihood of Challenge was higher now. I'd say at least fifty percent, but still, our chances of Exilium passing weren't good.

Abysmal, really.

Even if everyone Drakon had scrounged up somehow did Challenge, and won, we'd still be a few votes short. Even if I managed to wangle a few extra spots, Archon's included. We needed Osiris, needed him to put Darius in his place once and for all. Needed a Challenge against the myth that was Sebek Ra.

If not ... well, odds had never been our strong suit.

* * *

Socializing was a *literal* nightmare.

It drained me, sucked the soul right out of my body in the worst possible way. Especially with the type of people that could be found lounging about in a place like the Eternium. The ones that were looking for the weak and the exploitable. The ones with thousand-watt smiles hiding rows and rows of dagger-like teeth.

God, they were insufferable.

I lugged my way through the halls, thankful that the Eternium's magic made the walk back short. My legs were heavy, something I could tell only by how often I found myself stumbling over my own feet. It distracted me, made me a damned good target if anyone wanted to try something. Lucky for me, that wasn't the case.

But the door I came upon, after my amble through the halls, wasn't our room. It was made of cloudy pane glass that fogged up slightly from whatever was behind it. A hint of steam seeped from the crack at the bottom.

Curiosity was a curse of mine, always had been, which meant I couldn't stop myself from opening it. If the Eternium brought me here, then it had a reason to. I just had to hope that the reason wasn't something I'd regret sticking my nose into.

A brush of air blew past me, and I breathed in deeply on instinct when I saw what was on the inside.

"Oh, Eternium, you sweet, beautiful thing," I whispered, stepping into what had to be the most indulgent pool room I'd ever seen. It was large, I'd assume Olympic-sized, with a slight misting coming off the surface. A small fountain sat to the side, flowing over several rocks and into the pool, creating just enough sound to be soothing. The water was perfectly still beyond that, like a sheet of glass on the side that I was on, just begging me to jump in. I was already shrugging my shirt off when the door slid closed behind me. "Praise the Hallowed Three. I am forever in your debt."

I managed to strip down to my underwear—almost taking them off in my haste—all but giddy to hit the water. I needed a good swim, more than anything else. The freeness; the ease.

The distraction.

I broke the surface with a splash, the feeling distinctly odd as my brain tried to tell me that I should be feeling it. The wet, and the slight chill, or the glossy film that coated your skin and made your hair soft and flowy. Even the slight burn of chlorine in my eyes.

Guess I should have realized I wouldn't be that lucky.

I sighed, dunking my head, flipping it back so my hair wasn't in my face. It killed my mood, making my stomach sink as I floated in the blissful water. Leave it to Archon to take even this from me.

Just another nightmare to add to the list. A bubbling rage settled in my heart, leaving a bitterness that I couldn't outrun, and I hated the loathing that came on like wildfire. More than that, I hated the person it made me, like I was filled to the brim with tar that only a death could wash away.

I was the Collector; I found secrets. I hid them ... because I'd never been the fighter. I didn't like to see people hurt, didn't like to see them bleed. Archon changed that, changed *me.*

"Fuck it," I growled, an impressive impersonation of Eirik as I slapped my cheeks, likely a bit harder than I should have. I flipped, treading water as I gauged the length of the pool again. Sensation or not, swimming was my escape, one of the few ways I truly felt free, and I wasn't going to let a rat bastard like Archon take that from me. "I'm going to enjoy this."

How often was it that we'd have time to play here, anyway? I could spare a few minutes to at least try to enjoy it. I moved, grabbing the wall. My legs bent, feet against the slick tile, and I took a breath on instinct, holding it in before I pushed off, sliding through the water in a familiar stroke. My breathing steadied, my eyes closing as instinct drove me forward, one move after another, until I reached the opposing wall.

I couldn't feel it, but I knew when to flip, ducking my head and rotating, using my legs to kick me off, and I was soaring.

Then again.

Even without the ability to feel, I lost myself in the movements, the swift way that I cut through the water. For a second, I wasn't broken.

For a second I forgot that I ever was.

My next lap went slower as I dragged it out, still searching for the comfort that swimming had always given me. I opened my eyes, just in time to see a pair of legs sticking in about knee deep, waving gently back and forth.

I shot up, half choking as I sucked in a panicked breath, and I raised my hands for a very bad attempt at a counterattack if whoever it was planned to ... well, *attack*.

"Aaliyah!" I gasped, dropping my hands with an audible splash.

Ali was grinning at me, an indulgently pleased look on her face. She swished her legs in the water, her pants pulled up so they wouldn't get wet. Even though she was this close, I could still see the hesitation in her movements, like she didn't want to risk falling in.

"Sorry, I didn't mean to scare you," she whispered, that easy tone settling me immediately.

I swam the rest of the way to her, perching on the side of the pool so I could peek up at her a bit easier through the steam. It reminded me of home, when I'd dragged her in with me and showed her there was nothing to be afraid of in the water.

Especially if I was there.

I reached for my lips, smiling at the memory of the way she'd breathed against me, the softness of a first kiss I'd remember forever. I dropped my hands, letting a goofy grin come to my face.

"Scare me? Please, I'll have you know I watched the *Exorcist* when it first came out and only cried once," I joked, smiling wider when she laughed. She swished her legs again, looking at the water with the same contemplative expression I had.

She gnawed at her lower lip, a spark of fear in her eyes.

"Care for a swim?" I asked, a distraction, offering her my hand.

There had been hesitation when I'd asked before, but that wasn't there now. Her shoulders dipped, tension leaving her hands as she reached for the hem of her shirt. It came over her head in a flash, her pants quickly following until she was only in a bra and her underwear. I swallowed once, then twice, my head growing light at the sight, the primal part of my brain all but demanding I throw her over my shoulder and run off into the night so we might have a different kind of fun.

Another part of my body wasn't as excited at all. Fucker.

"I'd love to," she said, interrupting my brooding as she took my hand, sliding into the water with a graceful dip. I let out a breath, pulling her arms to my shoulders so she was wrapped loosely around me. "Don't let me go?"

I waded easily, comforted by the steady beat of her heart. Her breath got lost in the steam in front of her, her cheeks flushing at the warm water. "Never, love."

Never again.

I held her gently against my chest, squeezing as tightly as I could without worrying I might hurt her. We floated like that, the water steaming slightly around us. Aaliyah's face flushed contentedly.

"How did you get here? Not that I'm complaining," I whispered against the top of her head, not wanting to break the moment.

She was quiet for a few seconds, humming softly under her breath. "I wanted to see you."

And the Eternium had brought her here, like a gift wrapped in lavender.

I groaned, curling into her, tucking my face into the curve of her neck, putting a kiss there. "You're going to make me blush, love."

She trailed a hand over my chest, lingering on the fluttering skin over my abdomen, before she traveled to my arm, touching the black marks like she had so many times.

"I know, not my best look," I said.

They were better than they were a few days ago, but by no means faded. They traveled up my arms, across my chest and even to my neck and face. I looked, for lack of a better word, *shitty.*

"I'm just glad they don't hurt. Though, I know that can't be easy either," she said, stopping her trail, glancing up at me with that all-knowing gaze.

It was like she could see right through me. She looked at me like she wanted to offer a hand if I needed it. Like she just wanted to stand by my side, to help not mock, even if that meant just standing in silence.

Or floating in a pool while I worked through an existential crisis.

I wanted her so badly in this moment. My heart thundered in my chest, eyes dilating until I could see every detail on her face. Every laugh line and perfect feature.

I reached up, brushing my hand against her cheek, mourning now more than ever the spark that I'd lost at the touch of her skin. Still, she stayed, easily accepting the contact that I'd feared she'd never not flinch away from.

She stayed by me, like a rock in a storm, and I knew in that moment I wanted her, all of her. Which meant she deserved all of me.

Every broken piece, even the ones that still lay on Archon's table.

"Ali ..." I started, choking on the words.

"I know, Adrian," she whispered, leaning back into my arms, her head against my chest.

But she didn't. I couldn't be anything more than this for her, not until I fixed what Archon broke. And that was assuming I fixed it at all.

I might not ever have the chance to make love to her, and that hurt worse than any pain. It made the understanding of my deal that much sourer.

"Archon took everything from me. I can't ... I *can't*—" I held her close, one hand on her neck, searching for her pulse. The other trailing a shaking path along her side, begging for the warmth to be there. "I can't feel you, Ali. Not in here, and not like this."

It hurt to say, but I realized as the words came out, it had hurt so much more to keep them in. Aaliyah was my other half, the piece of me I hadn't known I was missing, and I wanted to share it with her.

My pain. My joy. My laughter. The days when I didn't want to wake up and the days when all I could think about was getting to see her again. The triumphs and the burned risottos.

"I know, Adrian," she whispered, holding me so close, so gently.

She never stopped her trailing hand, always touching me, keeping it obvious so I could see it even when I couldn't feel it.

"You know?" I asked.

She nodded her head, looking me in the eye. "I could tell something else was wrong, that something was eating you. I just didn't want to make it worse by asking."

I shouldn't have been surprised. Ali had shown this talent before, had proven just how well she could read people.

"There's a chance I can never fix it, that I'll just be stuck like this," I said, grabbing her chin to keep her eyes on mine. I wanted to make it clear what she was getting into. That I would do everything in my power to be whole again, but there was always a chance I wouldn't be. "I understand if you'd rather shave off the dead weight."

I said it as a joke, masking the insecurity with a laugh that she caught immediately. Her hands reached up, cupping my cheeks as she pulled me down. Her eyes were lit like fire, a rare show of anger as she shook her head.

"You're *not* dead weight." She'd said it so vehemently I had no choice but to nod dumbly. She waited until she was sure I'd understood her, searching my soul with those violet eyes I loved so much.

She hauled me the rest of the way, giving me plenty of time to pull back if I didn't want her. Like I would ever deny a chance to taste her lips, even if I couldn't really savor it. She kissed me softly, and I kept my eyes open, taking in every expression she made as she moved against me. It was a kiss I'd dreaded, yet something about it made it the most important one we'd ever shared.

It made me feel loved.

She pulled away, panting, and I wasn't much better as my hands tightened on her hips.

"I'm in love with you, Adrian," she said, ripping away my breath so quickly I almost choked. "I'm in love with easy days in a kitchen covered in flour. With dance lessons and midnight cupcakes. I'm in love with the way you look at me, like I'll always be enough. Every broken piece of me."

I went to protest, when her hand cupped my cheek again. "That's why you'll *always* be enough, Adrian. Even if you never get it back."

Tears bubbled in my eyes, the weight of my failure heavy on my shoulders ... but for the first time since Archon's lamp, I wasn't drowning in it.

"I've never known a love like you, Aaliyah. You're my world, and there isn't a day that goes by that I'm not in awe of you," I whispered, setting my forehead on hers. "I will fix this," I said, resolve somehow even stronger. There was nothing I wouldn't do to get the chance to feel her touch again.

"I know," she said, nodding. "And I'm with you. No matter what."

"*I love you.*" The room seemed to brighten as I said it, the lavender in Aaliyah's eyes vivid and passionate.

She laughed softly, curling into my arms again. "I love you, too, Adrian."

Even with my lack of pleasure, lack of pain, there was no doubt that this was real. No question if Archon was playing the long game, and I was still stuck in that fucking lamp. Aaliyah's voice would live forever in my head.

She loved me ... and I *would* fix this.

It was time to beat Archon at his own goddamned game.

CHAPTER 49

FALLON

I was the first to admit that I could be seen as *unapproachable*. Adrian and Nero had always been the ones with flashy charm and winning personalities, their ability to play a room damned near unparalleled. I liked it that way, being able to fall into the background and have a godforsaken drink without needing to fend off the vultures that circled around me was better than any social standing.

I slipped through the crowd, ignoring the Eternals and their Secondaries talking in low tones, as they watched me out the sides of their eyes. It wasn't enough to warrant my attention, and most moved when I got too close, wary even when I was by myself. They knew better than to approach a member of the Vivas Crypt without reason, even having never seen me in person.

Thank God for small mercies.

I grabbed a drink off a passing server's tray—an aged scotch that went down smooth. I set the empty glass back down, not bothering to look as he bowed and ran off, too busy searching for a man I knew wasn't here.

Fae were unusual among the other Naturals, with their annoying tendency to somehow avoid crowds even more than I did. I'd been hoping that Koldan would be the exception to that.

Though, I wasn't surprised that he wasn't.

I reached for the winding ink that sat on my chest and over my ribs, itching, stretching. The ticking time bomb was enough to get me moving. I made it to the edge of the crowd in a flash, keeping my head high as the door I walked up to opened for me, and I slipped through.

"I don't know what you're trying to prove," a soft voice whispered, and I gritted my teeth, continuing to walk as Aislinn came to my side. The hall flexed, the golden accents lining red walls seeming to curl toward me as she stretched her arms above her head. She wasn't wearing anything unusual today, the normal hides and ornate beads ... but her neck was already torn, dried blood caked across her skin.

She'd come more and more often, her visions turning into something I never could have dreamed up before. Her cruel smile came with a trail of blood down her nose, which she swiped away with a calloused hand. "You're going to die. I don't know why you fight it."

I grunted, ignoring her, walking faster. The hall wound with no end in sight, and no other doors to take refuge in.

Fuck.

"The world would be better off without a *monster* like you," she whispered in a singsong voice, her laugh crackling like old wood in a hot fire. "You can't run from me, Fallon."

I held my breath, struggling to keep looking ahead and not slam my hands over my ears to block out the mocking.

"Fallon!" A hand landed on my arm, and I ripped away, jolting back with clenched teeth. A grunt of pain followed, one that made me so sick I almost puked, wrapped in a cold sweat that sank into my bones as I rubbed my face. Aislinn looked back at me for all of a second before lavender eyes took her place.

"Ali?" I asked as she took a step back from me. My blood went cold, my hands shaking.

She rubbed her hand, the one I'd just about pulled out of her damned wrist. "Fallon ...?"

My stomach dropped, sinking to the floor when I saw the first sign of a bruise across her pale skin. I backed up, heel cracking against the floorboard as my shoulder blades hit the wall.

"Sorry, I shouldn't have done that," she said, shaking her head.

She flinched as she rubbed her wrist, her fingers trembling as she pulled it to her chest.

What the fuck *was I doing?*

I had her hand in mine in the next second, rotating it gently so I could see if I'd done any damage. I searched for open wounds, for broken bones, all while Aislinn's laugh still echoed in my head. The image of blood sliding down her face burned into me. "No, *no.* You never have to apologize for touching me, Ali. I—"

I could have really hurt her.

Aislinn's smile was knowing, a dark whisper to what I already knew.

Fuck, I'd almost hurt *Ali.*

"Fallon?" Aaliyah whispered my name, her hands cupping my cheeks, forcing me to look away from Aislinn and into her eyes instead. Everything about her came forward, the curve of her lips and the nick of scars that I still hadn't avenged for her. "Don't look at her. Look at me."

Saliva filled my mouth as Aaliyah stared on, perfectly still, smelling slightly of chlorine. It blocked her sweet chocolate-tinted scent. I cleared my throat, acid burning down it. "You need to go, trouble."

To where she would be protected, safe. Away from *me.*

"No," Ali said, the confident tone clearing away Aislinn's words. She lifted her chin, chewing her bottom lip as she continued. "When I said that I won't let you face this alone, I meant it."

But how could she? Fear was alive and well in me, even as much as I wished it had died on that fucking roof. Just being close to her made me shake ... I couldn't kill someone I loved, not again. I wouldn't fucking survive it.

"What?" Aislinn whispered, and I bit my tongue so hard it bled. "I think she'd look so pretty in red."

"I killed Aislinn, Ali," I said, the cracked words that of a broken man I didn't even recognize.

I killed her, and then I watched her die, again and *again.*

Her blood stained me long before Archon had trapped me, but the memory was fresh now, as real as the hint of iron on my lips as I bit my tongue until I bled. "I deserve this. She's haunting me, and I *deserve* it."

"What happened was a tragedy, one brought on by a man that wanted to play God, not you. Aislinn wouldn't want this for you."

I struggled to swallow, to fight back the tears that burned in the back of my throat.

Taz.

I'd held Aislinn, comforted her while her blood spilled onto sand I'd never see as home again, dying from the gouge I'd put on her throat. She'd smiled at me, those endless ink-black eyes dulling as the press of night cast a shadow that would haunt me for the rest of my life. *Smiled* like she had every morning, beaming at me with a life I snuffed out.

"What was she like, Fallon?" Aaliyah's question split the air, and even Aislinn paused. "Aislinn, tell me about her?"

I pulled in a breath, my head thudding against the wall behind me. The room could have very well closed in on top of us, and I wouldn't have been able to look away from Aaliyah's eyes. I'd been attracted to the fire in them since the moment I'd seen her, drawn like a moth to an open flame. I wanted her to burn me and destroy the bits of myself that I'd left on that beach I once called my home.

"She was sweet, soft. Headstrong and ..." I rambled off, even as Aislinn snorted from beside me. I closed my eyes, remembering the way she used to *be*. It killed me to think about her; it always had. Now, more than ever, I struggled to remember how she was before, when she was still alive, but there was one thing she'd always been. "Kind. She was endlessly kind."

To everything and everyone. She'd loved helping people, and there were few creatures she wouldn't put her neck on the line for. Like the wily Tasmanian devil that had wandered into our home.

Good morning, Taz.

"In the entire time you knew her, would she ever say what she is now?" Ali asked, like a voice of reason, acting as the angel on my shoulder.

Such a simple question had never crossed my mind, not in any meaningful way. I hadn't thought about it, not when everything else pointed toward what I already knew ... that she was gone because of me.

"I don't—"

"This isn't Aislinn, Fallon," Aaliyah whispered, her hands never leaving me, like a bridge from the past to the present. "Her words hurt because they come with her face, but it's not her. She wouldn't do this to you."

I ripped myself away, breaking the contact Aaliyah had made. The loss of her touch, of that explosive warmth, made me shiver.

I looked at Aislinn, and she was smiling at me now. Like I'd somehow solved her riddle, my breath coming out in a soft apology. She snorted, raising an eyebrow, but she didn't speak again. Not outwardly, anyway, as she mouthed the words to me.

"See you on the other side, Taz."

I breathed out, and in that breath, the weight lifted off me. Aislinn was gone. I felt free in a way I hadn't in years. I sank back against the wall, rubbing my face with my hands. The constant state of fight-or-flight dimmed.

"Are you all right?" Aaliyah asked, always so open as she sat in front of me, patient, rubbing the hand that had found its way to hers. I flipped it, taking her wrist, tracing the empty space where my mark once was.

"Yes," I said as I stood. I dusted off the suit, cracking my knuckles as I cleared my throat. Emotion stuck clung to me in a way that made me feel sticky, almost like I was wading through a shallow pool of it. It dragged me down, and I shook my head, trying to clear it.

"Good, you're going to deal with the mark, right? Then let's go." She grabbed my hand again, intertwining our fingers, and staring straight ahead. It was crazy how much stronger I felt with her by my side. She took my silence as a refusal, gnawing on her bottom lip as she glanced up at me. "I'm going with, Fallon. The only question is, am I following behind and are you pretending not to see me, or are we walking into whatever this is together?"

I almost laughed. In one shocking breath, she'd managed to remind me why I'd fallen in love with her. She might breathe heavily, her hands shaking, but Ali *never* backed down. Not once in the time that I'd known her. She was a force to be reckoned with, and I pitied anyone that tried to get in her way.

"You really are trouble," I said, shaking my head, looking around the empty hall. Like the Eternium knew what to do, it shifted until just barely in the distance, I could see something. *Someone.* "Come on. We have a Fae to meet."

She didn't respond, looking ahead, learning with what she saw. We walked toward it, the door that appeared standing almost twice as tall as the guards that stood by it. Two, one on each side.

The left was an imposing figure, his black eyes steadfast and cold, like the frosty mist that hovered over his blue-tinted skin. His eyes were almost black, with a solid circle in the middle that looked like a new moon, beyond a slight sliver of light on the outside that matched the dusting of white stars across his high cheeks and the white lines that stretched from the corners of his mouth up to his pointed ears. An Unseelie Fae, and from the chill that leaked from him, it didn't take much to guess that he had an affinity for the cold.

To the right was one I wasn't expecting to see. About as large as his pair, with skin a pasty white, stars across his face just the same, and a bright full moon in the center of his black eyes, just slightly less than whole. His marks trailed up his neck, solid black lines that came out from under his armor, ending just below his eyes.

They had the same scattering of stars over their high cheeks, and if I was a betting man, I'd guess they were the opposite in every way. Two pieces of the same whole. A perfect combination, not that either of them mattered right now. They were little more than a show, standing like grunts in front of a door that likely saw no travelers.

Two Fae with near total moons in their eyes, and Koldan had them on door duty.

I rolled my shoulders, grunting as though preparing to go to blows. The Eternium felt it too, already shackling me with those invisible chains.

"I need to speak with Fae Eternal Koldan," I said as the guards stared dead ahead, not even looking down.

There was an air of superiority around them, the kind that I usually beat out of fuckers like them.

"Eternal Koldan, Bringer of Dusk, is not taking visitors," the one on the left said with a curt sneer, slamming his spear into the ground with a violent thud. "Leave."

Patience was a virtue I'd never learned. Anger rose hard and fast inside of me, catching my vocal cords as I bit out, "I won't ask again."

His face twitched, rage slipping into his eyes as his other half gritted his teeth. It was a fragile few seconds of silence before he lifted his spear and pointed it at us. "And I said leave, Fang."

He couldn't do anything with it, but I didn't like the threat for what it was. I moved Ali behind me as I stepped up to the spearhead, letting it sit against my chest, over the marking that Hadlie had left there.

I gripped the metal until it bit into my palm, pushing it to the side with a slam. The Fae holding it jolted back, teeth bared in a snarl. I braced, ready to deflect a blow if the Eternium found itself lacking, just as Ali peeked her head around me.

She hummed, catching my attention, and that of the Fae. "You're scared. You wouldn't resort to insults if you weren't," she said, simply. Watching carefully as the guard flinched and fell back into line with a straight face. "Is it of us or Koldan?"

One simple sentence gave her all she needed in a way I never would have thought to try. His eyes darted between us before landing on her, filled with contempt, hatred, and no small amount of *fear*.

"Us, then," she whispered, more confident now as she stepped fully around me. I nearly choked, watching the two guards warily, keeping my hand on her shoulder and biting back the need to push her behind me again. That need only grew when the Unseelie snarled. "But there's nothing to be afraid of here. The Eternium stops people from attacking others with bad intent."

She looked at the door, a bit longer than they were comfortable with. Her next words damned well could have been carved from ice. "So, what's going on behind that door that you don't want us to see?"

I was so *fucking* proud of her.

The Seelie Fae was the one to move, crossing his spear over the front of the door like he was trying to block her seeking gaze. He leaned down to speak, mockingly slow. "You don't know anything, Vampire *slut.*"

My fangs fell in an instant, my mouth filling with my blood as they pierced my bottom lip. I lost control in the blink of an eye, grabbing his spear, ripping it from his hands. He stumbled forward, shock clear in his expression as I sank the tip into the wall by his head.

The Eternium stopped me from doing what I really wanted, what I'd do the moment the spell let me go. Even then, I memorized his face, the cold scent of his fear as he bared his teeth in a fanged sneer. The wooden end wobbled, the marble by his face fissuring open.

"You're going to die for that," I snarled, clenching my fists. "Maybe not now, but I swear as soon as this Eternium is over, I'll find you."

The other guard was on edge now, his spear raised in a defensive position. My hands ached, the unholy desire to split his face all consuming.

Aaliyah didn't even flinch.

"Insults are a show of fear, so something we don't want to see, then. You're flushed, a sign of physical activity, and it smells like ... steel." Aaliyah was unrelenting, like a tidal wave as she rammed over and over into the guards' heads, battering them with information that she garnered just from watching. It was like art, to watch the way she broke them apart with soft words and sure confidence. The mix of psychological warfare and her collected tone broke them in real time. "It's odd how much something so small can tell you. Isn't it?"

The Unseelie shivered, the bravado now lost in the panic, his cheeks flushed a darker blue, the stars on his face glowing like that single crescent of white in his eyes.

"So, want to bring out Koldan so we can speak to him and be on our way?" Ali asked, giving them a way out, and it was too easy to spot the resigned breath. The Unseelie pulled his spear back, dropping his offensive stance. "Or do I need to keep guessing?"

Silence was a serenade, and I squeezed Ali's hand, smiling when she looked at me. Her cheeks flushed with unapologetic pride. That blush stretched down her neck, her pulse beating in my hand. There was a moment when she tipped her head down, biting her lip as she stared at the floor, before she seemed to rethink the move.

She took a breath, squaring her shoulders before tipping her chin up, flinching as the two Fae tensed. Even when their gazes turned sharp, she didn't look down again.

"What part of 'no visitors' do you not fucking understand?" another voice boomed as the door flew open.

The guards went ramrod straight, their eyes forward as frost spilled out of the entrance and into the hall. It overwhelmed and made the Fae guarding it look like children. The man who walked through oozed the kind of power you'd expect from an Eternal. His head was high, his nose turned down on us like we were filth.

The usual.

I straightened my tie, cracking my neck.

He was tall, I'd guess roughly eight feet, though not overly muscular. His long white hair was braided down his back in an intricate design that would have made Eirik jealous, and in his deep-black eyes there was a single solid circular outline of white.

Just like Hadlie.

It put me on edge, even remembering what she'd told me. *You can trust the Fae Eternal.*

I didn't place a lot of faith in words.

"My Lord," the Seelie Fae said, the tremble to his words lit by the smoke that slipped from his mouth as he breathed a little too hard. "I was just getting rid of them."

"I take it you're Koldan? I need to talk to you," I butted in.

Koldan rolled his eyes, leaning down to look me in mine like someone might a child. They were wide enough that I could see flecks of what I'd assume were more stars lingering behind it.

I bit my tongue, almost desperate to start shit with the tall Fae.

"How very Vampire of you," he said, clicking his tongue with an admonishing tone. "You were already told I'm not taking visitors, and the *last* thing I need on my door is a Reaper. Leave."

Aaliyah tensed next to me, and I gritted my teeth. "I need—"

"I said *leave*," he cut in, leaving no room for argument as he stood straight again. "I don't care what you have to say, Fang. I want you out of my sight and not sullying my air."

The Eternium dragged me to a stop as my blood roared, and if it hadn't been stopping me, I might have been going to blows with the Fae Eternal. The disrespect was growing old, *fast.*

If I didn't need to be here, I wouldn't be. This wasn't something that was worth my time, and whether or not Koldan believed it, neither was he.

Deep. Fucking. Breaths.

"Hadlie sent me," I growled, grinding my teeth as the mark on my side ached, pulsing like it was growing.

Koldan stood straight, his eyes going wide for only a second before they narrowed back down. His long ears twitched as he stepped forward until he was too fucking close. He had the same markings that Hadlie had, silver slashes down his forehead and over his eyes, sliding all the way into his obnoxious robes.

"Hadlie?" he asked, saying her name slowly, like I might have misspoken.

I snorted a laugh, shaking my head. "Oh, you seem *very* interested in talking now."

Koldan ground his teeth, the frost disappearing from the air at the snap of his fingers, all of his cavalier goading gone in a second. His attention was sharp. "Where was she?"

Aaliyah squeezed my hand, and I was quick to squeeze it back. "Archon's, in his—"

Koldan let out a breath, one faster than I would have expected. "Then she's still with him?"

His face fell when I nodded, his expression souring as he pushed a stray hair out of his eyes.

"Said you'd know what to do, whatever that means," I said.

He hummed, watching me carefully as he stood tall once again with his arms crossed behind his back. It exposed his throat, his demeanor shifting from tense to languid.

"Hadlie is my twin sister, second heir to the Unseelie Fae," he said, his eyes dulling. The silver ring in them seemed to glow. He was almost animated in his interest, his expression hopeful. "She's very important to me."

Fae couldn't lie, from what I remembered of Adrian's boring fucking lecture on them. It was against their nature, or something of the sort. So that, at least, had to be true.

I hesitated before answering, unsure how much I should share, as Ali squeezed my hand again. When I looked at her, her face was carefully blank, but she didn't stop tapping her pointer finger against my wrist.

"What do I need to do to finish the Bargain?" I asked, keeping my expression neutral.

Hadlie had sent me his way for a reason.

But what *was* the reason? Part of me wanted to believe it was because her brother had good intentions. The other half knew a snake when I saw one.

Koldan was quiet for a moment, smiling widely as he nodded his head, gritting his teeth. It set off warning signals in my mind when he tipped forward. "She wants out. That is why she sent you to me, and there is only one way to free her of that place."

The tree branches on my side lengthened, their limbs still moving, *still* stretching. I held in the gasp, strangling the need to reach up and touch it. Ali was my grounding force, the bit that kept me staring straight ahead as she leaned into my side.

"I don't have all day," I said, ignoring the glowers from the guards.

Koldan tipped forward, ignoring my sharp tongue. "You must kill Hadlie."

Ali froze, her hand squeezed tight in mine. Hadlie seemed like many things, but I hadn't taken her as suicidal. There was a fire in her eyes, a will to fight, a will to *live.*

"There's no way that's what she meant," I said, as Koldan stood straight, looking down on me from over his nose.

"I cannot lie, Vivas. You wished for an answer, yes?" he said, brushing me off, slinging his braid over his shoulder. "That's the only one I have to give. Hadlie wishes to be freed from Archon. This is how you do it."

It was all authority in his stuck up assurance, dismissing us with a bow of his head. "Now, it's best you go. No need to stir unwanted attention."

The door closed as he walked away, not even uttering a goodbye, and we were left with the two Fae guards. Ali never let go of my hand as we turned around. Her face was calm, her eyes straight ahead until we were far enough away for the Eternium to change our path.

Then she let out a breath. "Something about how he talked about her was off."

She said it so quietly I almost didn't hear her.

"I was thinking the same thing," I said.

There was too much excitement in the way he'd moved, and though nothing he said was a lie ... that didn't make me trust him, either.

The hall tapered off, and slowly, another body took shape, this one with auburn hair I knew well.

"Adrian," I said, startling him as he jolted and looked up at us. Then he was rushing forward, taking Aaliyah's face in his hands.

"Love! You disappeared on me. Are you all right?" he asked, letting out a breath as he leaned down and kissed her softly. There was a brightness back in him now, a life that had been ripped away at Archon's. It was nice to see some of that spark back. He looked at me. "Fally, you look rather shaken up."

"What do you know about Koldan?" I asked, getting straight to the point as his eyes narrowed.

"Very little. Fae are ... real pieces of work. All I know is that he took over for Frileti after Sebek killed her," he said, humming under his breath as he tapped his arm. "He seems like a wild card, killed nearly all of his competition to get to the top after spending most of his life promoting peace. Apparently, he was originally fifth in line."

"He wouldn't be the type to want one of his siblings freed, then, would he?" Aaliyah asked, quietly.

"Oh, not on his life." Adrian snorted, and my little problem grew a lot more complicated. "Why?"

Which meant that she didn't send me to Koldan because she thought he'd get her out. She sent me to him because he had gotten her locked in.

Her Fae Bargain wasn't with Archon; it was with Koldan. I had to figure out what it was and break it. Or I wouldn't see the end of my first Eternium.

"Think you could do some more digging on him?" I asked, and Adrian hesitated for a moment before he nodded sharply. "He's hiding something."

"I'll see what I can do," he said, his expression going harsh. He looked over his shoulder, checking that no one had drawn too close. "Relating to your mark, yeah?"

I nodded. "Something like that."

The air grew quiet then, and we walked in silence to the room. The halls moved, and we were quick to slip inside our little haven. We followed the sound of music as it blared from behind the door that was tucked away by the kitchen, hiding the replica training room behind it. We looked at each other as it flew open.

Nero was grinning from the other side, his expression vibrant and slightly bloodthirsty.

"Ah, just in time," he said through a pant. He still looked rough, his body lacking much of the muscle it had before, though it seemed it was getting better. He was covered in a fine layer of sweat and a few fresh cuts that looked like they were still healing. "Interested in a spar, Fally?"

CHAPTER 50

AALIYAH

"I regret ever asking you for help," I wheezed, lying back down on the ground.

Every muscle I had hurt. Every joint, every ligament, even my lungs. When Prince had asked Fallon for a spar, I'd thought it would be a great time to do some work of my own on that little trick Azer had shown me in the Void.

The only problem was, I forgot how much it drained me the last time I tried to work through Fallon's grueling training. At least then, it was *just* him.

With Prince and Eirik on his side? They were practically slave drivers. It had started with some kind of running exercise, something that kept me moving until my legs physically gave out. Then the push-ups, then something they, I hope jokingly, referred to as a dead hang. Now I was here, halfway through what *they* assumed was a reasonable number of sit ups, questioning if they would notice if I crawled away.

All of that in between trying to get the shadows to do as I asked ... which still hadn't bore any fruit.

"You'll thank me later," Fallon said with a chuckle, the deep timbre vibrating through me as he crouched by my side and extended a hand for me to take. "Strength training settles the body, should help you stay more in tune with yourself."

I groaned and covered my eyes, unwilling at this point to move. Sweat clung to me, and I doubted my ability to stand again, even if I wanted to.

"Come on, *smár Valkyrja*. One more." Eirik pushed from the side, his fingers hovering over the braids he'd wound into my hair before we'd begun.

"I liked it better the last time we trained," I grumbled, taking Fallon's hand. I'd like to say that I stood on my own, that I was ready to go another round ... but in reality, Fallon was the only thing that kept me standing, and my knees only grew weaker when his lips brushed my ear.

"I liked that, too. Maybe we can have another reward later," he whispered before he nipped the sensitive skin, and I shivered.

My cheeks flushed, and I looked around Fallon to find both Eirik and Prince watching me with suddenly heated gazes. As much as I wanted to follow up on that, my body wasn't in a place to *move*.

Not that I didn't think about it.

"One more try," I whispered.

Fallon searched my face before he backed up, sticking close as my legs trembled.

I closed my eyes, and Red moved around me like flowing water. His presence was soothing, a balm that I leaned on as I went searching for the Void. It had become easier these last couple of tries as I pushed back the dark voice and focused instead on what I could feel. *Red*. When I lifted my hand, a small sliver of shadow bloomed across my palm.

Sweat pooled down my back.

"There you go, Aaliyah. You've got this." Prince's quiet praise pushed me to hold on to the feeling.

Red danced around me, almost like he'd reached out and grabbed my hand, before I took a steading breath. The Void pressed, reminding me it was there, and I flinched hard enough that my control wavered. I held my breath, forcing it to stay solid.

I launched the shadow forward with a grunt, straining as I did. It hit the wall, the sound reverberating through the floor, and I sucked in a breath at what it left behind.

A gouge, the largest one I'd seen yet at *maybe* an inch. I threw my arms up and cheered.

The others followed, pride radiating from them as they moved toward me.

"Knew you could do it, trouble," Fallon whispered, his arms again encircling me.

I fell into him, literally, unable to keep my legs under me as they trembled. He held me, gentle hands rubbing circles on my back. Eirik and Prince were close by, whispering the same words of praise. Adrian wasn't here, but I knew he was close, in the kitchen making something to eat.

The only one missing, truly missing, was Osiris.

His absence hit in ways I never thought it would have. He was a presence, a man of few words that somehow managed to steal the entirety of whatever space he was in. I craved the gentle cadence of his words as he spoke, translating a book as he read.

His soft touch, the gentle press of hesitant lips. I missed him.

"What's on your mind?" Prince asked, tipping my head up with steady fingers.

His thumb brushed my jaw, his eyes searching mine.

"Just thinking about Osiris is all," I said. I knew he was okay, could feel him in the mark on my wrist, but that didn't help to lessen my worry. "I hope he's all right."

Prince's chest expanded in a soft chuckle before he leaned forward and pressed his lips to my forehead. "He is. Trust me on this. We'd know if he wasn't."

"Do you really think he'll find something down there?" I asked.

"I don't know. But if there's something to find, Osiris will find it," Eirik chimed in.

Fallon hummed at my back, his lips drawing a path down the column of my throat.

I was a sweaty mess, and I protested for just a second, until I was shocked silent by the press of his fangs against my pulse point, his tongue trailing a line that shot straight to my core.

"Now about that reward, Ali." His voice was followed by a rolling, husky moan. "I think you deserve one after that."

Prince moved in tandem, covering my front, claiming my lips in a fierce kiss. His fangs dropped, and his tongue must have hit one of them. Delicious ambrosia swapped between us, and I moaned at the taste of him.

"Hm, and some blood," he whispered, pulling back with a dark chuckle when I tried to follow him. "Let us take care of you?"

Like I'd ever be able to deny that.

The distraction was a welcome one, one I fell into as they both surrounded me. A rumble filled the air, and Eirik showed his presence with a soft brush of gentle fingers against the exposed skin at my throat.

In one move, I was lifted and turned. My legs wrapped around Prince's waist in a familiar position, Fallon to my back drawing breathless kisses against the expanse of my throat. I never expected that I would grow this ravenous for touch, but I needed it, wanted the press of their fingers into my skin, wanted to feel them for hours after, so I'd always remember how they'd moved against me.

I arched forward, my lips finding Prince's. It was a consuming kiss, one I savored as much as devoured, a needy pulse in my core making me cry out when Fallon's fingers dipped confidently under my shirt.

He toyed with the exposed skin, fingers brushing taut nipples as I shivered. Prince, my beautiful Prince, gripped my hips ferociously, grinding me perfectly against the budding arousal in his pants.

It was a perfect moment. It *should* have been the perfect moment.

Until I heard the first whisper, the first sickening voice in my ear, as if Nilus was right behind me. I froze at the hint of the depraved things he used to promise, leaving me cowering under my bed at night, watching Prince as he stood sentinel by my door, waiting for the monster to go away.

Then Hugo, a man that I'd only just remembered. He used to steal touches when no one was looking, his hands invoking a touch I remembered all too well, enough to make me sick as I fought the constricting arms that I suddenly found around me.

He'd done it enough that eventually Flinn noticed, and then Hugo wasn't there anymore.

I struggled to pull in breaths, my feet finally hitting the ground as I stumbled away, my vision blotting out. I hit the floor, palms first, then the rest of my body followed.

A hand reached for me, setting on my cheek, warm to the touch. I waited for it to bite into my skin as *Nilus* went flush in sick satisfaction.

"Don't touch me!" I screamed, jerking away, only finding breath when the hand shot back.

I curled up, desperately trying to hide away, frantically searching for the cool touch of Prince. I tried to count my breaths, to settle myself, but nothing seemed to work. Until the cold appeared, settling easily over my shoulders, like a weighted blanket.

Like a gentle hand on my back.

It was easier to breathe with each brush they gave me, my eyes clearing as the tears fell and weren't replaced with more. My surroundings came next, fading back in as I was able to pull in more steady breaths, and I remembered where I was.

I looked up, just in time to catch the horrified faces of Fallon, Prince, and Eirik. Red moved around me, the one whose touch dragged me back to the present, one soft comfort at a time.

They stared on, hands flexed at their sides, agony so open in their expressions I felt it in my chest. The worst, though, was Eirik, as his face morphed and pulled, his beast fighting under the surface of his skin and behind his eyes.

Like he was scared of me ... or terrified I was scared of *him*.

I reached out, my voice caught in my throat like the mantra that rang in my ears. He jerked away, his head darting back and forth as his eyes flushed between sky blue and ocean black. "Eirik—"

His pupils dilated, his nose flaring wide as he looked to the door.

Before he was gone.

CHAPTER 51

EIRIK

She flinched away from me.

I knew it was a response, a reaction to the trigger that had dragged her furiously into a panic attack, but I hadn't been ready for her to flinch away from my touch. For her words to burrow so deeply under my skin, ripping me to fucking shreds as they had.

Don't touch me!

I was going to be sick.

I tensed, my body pulsing with hunger and adrenaline as they collided with the surge of regret in my stomach. My wolf had gone feral with his need to burst out, the scent of sex still lingering on my skin. But my other half hadn't seen what I had, didn't understand why I ran from our mate when she was needing. His desire to be next to her was like a goddamned calling card that I nearly broke myself to resist. I slammed against a wall, grunting as a partial shift sent pain searing down my spine.

It was enough to ground me, to drown out the endless cries of my beast. His keening ended up vocal in my throat, and in my chest.

Mate. Mate. Mate.

"Mine."

I gritted my teeth, snarling through the gaps as claws burst from my fingers, gouging into the intricate walls, leaving long jagged scars in the red and gold.

"You look like you've been better, brother," a voice mused, and I flipped to them, not fully in control when I snapped in the familiar face of Yrsa.

She didn't flinch, scoffing with an eye roll. I wasn't sure how she got here, in this isolated hallway, but my beast didn't like her so close. My hackles rose, a growl building so viciously my vocal cords protested. All it took was one look at her face to shift from partially joking to serious.

"What's wrong?" she asked, reaching toward me with hands that I snapped at.

Words felt archaic, unnecessary, and my beast made a point to make it as difficult as he could for me to get them out. Words didn't matter, not when our mate needed us. He didn't understand why I left, and he fought it with every ounce of his strength.

"Scared—" The word ended in a growl that savaged my vocal cords, the shift moving to my shoulders as my spine popped. "**Her**. Scared her."

"I see ... Well, you've chosen a fantastic time to fully descend into a mating frenzy then, and by the sheer amount of pheromones you're pumping out, I'd say you haven't sealed the deal yet," she said. I couldn't answer as I bowed over, and another partial shift threatened to take me to my knees. "Word of advice. I'd remedy that before the start of this. It'll give her a layer of protection and get your wolf off your ass so you can focus on protecting her."

"I can't," I hissed, the words a gnarled mash of letters. "I *scared* her."

More than scared, terrified. I wouldn't be able to wash away that haunted look she gave me—there was no way I'd ever forget it. Bile rose in my throat, even my wolf calming for a blissful fucking second.

Any chance of mating her tonight was gone, and I would not put this decision on her now. What she'd experienced after getting back her memories had obviously taken more of a toll on her than she realized.

I couldn't ask this of her, *wouldn't*. Not now, not after smelling her fear in the air like a poison. Even if it meant fighting my wolf for the reins every spare second I had.

Yrsa watched me for a long second, her eyes narrowed on me like she hadn't heard what I'd said. "You are *Úlfhéðnar,* and *Úlfhéðnar* take what they want, brother. Your wolf has chosen a mate. You've given her time, given her your life. *Take her.*"

That was the way of our clan, the hunt, the chase. Yrsa had mentioned it to me before, and it filled me with a need so deep my wolf went silent.

For one blissful second, it was just me. The idea of running through the woods, listening to the soft breaths of Aaliyah as she ran, her eyes wide, adrenaline making her blood pump as she dashed through the underbrush.

Heightened by fear.

"I will *not* scare her again!" I snarled.

What my beast wanted to do was to go beyond a frolic through the woods. It was carnal, a claiming, and my sweet *Valkyrja* had been through enough. Tonight had proven that. I didn't need to add to the amount of shit already on her plate, no matter my desires.

Not now. Maybe not ever. Her pace, it would always be her pace.

I pushed it down, the wallowing cries of my wolf and the furious need that clung to my blood. Bolted it in place as sweat stuck to my skin. The effect was immediate, the block on my other half making me sick.

I can't fucking scare her again.

"Who says you will?" Yrsa growled.

It was a different kind of feeling, going toe to toe with a wolf again. My own instincts sparked, challenge rolling in my blood, as I stared down my elder. Her eyes, that stormy blue that gave away the beast, stayed trained on me.

"She's—" I started, but Yrsa didn't let me get any words out.

"A badass female capable of making her own goddamned choice! That's what you were going to say, right?" she asked, sarcastic, like I wouldn't agree with her. Like I didn't want to worship the ground Aaliyah fucking walked on. I grunted. "So, you scared her. It happens. I take it you also ran away before she could talk to you about it? She won't reject you, Eirik. You know that. Look at your arm, feel it in your chest where your wolf cries for her. You're letting fear talk because you don't know what to expect, either."

As if on cue, the mark at my wrist warmed, the flowing lavender band a constant tie to my chest. The bond was a comfort.

Think of how much we could feel tied to her forever. My beast pushed, slipping through the cracks, images of her pinned beneath us coming without warning. My fangs deep in her neck, a true mating bond sealing us together.

My mouth watered, and the scent of lavender flashed in the air.

My skin rippled again, my wolf nearly ripping away the reins as it tore through my mental defenses. I stumbled away from Yrsa in a desperate attempt at control. Another scent hit, one I wasn't expecting, one I couldn't place in this haze, as she grunted, waving me off.

"Fucking Odin's beard, get out of here. I'll deal with it. Just think of a nice forestry area to go to, but good luck getting your beast to calm down. You've waited far too long," she said.

I didn't have time to question her words as I shot down the hall. The first door I came to, I swung open. Just like Yrsa had said, a forest greeted me.

I breathed in the fresh air, lit by the crispness of salt that didn't quite taste right. I stumbled forward, another shutter.

The shift came like a wave. One second, I was standing.

The next, I was only *Úlfhéðinn*.

Aaliyah

I followed Eirik in a haze, rushing out after a quick word to Prince and Fallon, who looked on with worried eyes. They called something after me, but I was already out the door, the Eternium carting me away from them and toward what I hoped was Eirik. The halls weaved in front of me, each turn leading to another long hallway that had my heart sinking deeper into the pits of my chest.

My legs were still shaking from what had happened, the thoughts so close to the surface it hurt to breathe ... but seeing his face, the fear that flashed across it?

I needed to make sure he was okay.

I turned a blind corner, nearly running into a body that stopped me with two hands on my shoulders. I jerked away from them, their touch like a blow I couldn't fight again. I gritted my teeth, looking up as my legs prepared to run.

"Oh, my," a voice called, bringing me out of my thoughts. I flinched at the sound, curling in on myself instinctively as I swiveled to look up at the woman that had spoken. Not a man, not Nilus or Hugo. "You must be Aaliyah. You were just who I was hoping to run into. Crazy, how the Eternium works, isn't it?"

It only took one look to see the likeness in this woman to Eirik, enough to settle the raging beat of my heart, her sky-colored eyes holding a light flutter of curiosity. She had laugh lines framing the corners, and a broad smile that flashed white teeth. Her long blond hair was pulled up into a high ponytail that draped long over her exposed back. She wore a dress, the sharp blue of it accentuating her soft features and toned body.

"Yrsa?" I asked.

She was everything I'd imagined when Eirik had told me of his siblings, even more so when her head tipped back in a hearty laugh. Her whole body moved as she did, and I couldn't help but wonder if Eirik would do the same.

"So, my brother has told you about me! Only the best things, I'm sure," she said, rubbing some stray tears out of her eyes. "We'll have plenty of time to bond later, sister, but right now, I need your help. Eirik's in a frenzy."

I bit my lip at that, before looking down the long hall and pulling in an unsteady breath, wondering if I even had the strength to keep following him. I wanted to curl up, to force the memories away the only way I knew how.

"What can I do?" I asked, instead.

Yrsa stared at me, her expression shifting. There was a look of war in her eyes, a hardening that came with battle and sacrifice. She assessed me, the look so intense it made me shiver.

I felt inadequate under it, small.

"Do you love him?" she asked.

"I do," I whispered, not a breath of hesitation.

"I'm not asking if it's just a passing fling, or even the start of something more. Do you *love* him? With your entire soul, from your bones to your blood. Can you imagine a life not by his side?" Yrsa pressed.

Six months ago, I would have laughed at the thought. I would have cowered at the sight of Eirik, like I had that first day I'd seen him. My giant, *gentle* wolf. The Vivas family was so ingrained in my life now that there was no me without them. Their love was branded on my skin, their names etched into my fate.

So, it wasn't a question, not one I struggled with as I shook my head.

"No, I can't," I answered, as I straightened my spine, hopefully mirroring the severity of her eyes. "I love him with everything I am."

Yrsa was silent again before her lips split into a grin wide enough to show sharp fangs.

"Then listen to me very closely," she said. The edge to her stance softened, and her eyes lost their dark sheen—what I was now realizing had been her wolf. "Wolf Shifters, but especially *Úlfhéðnar*, are protective, possessive bastards. They don't do things in halves, and honestly, I'm surprised you've lasted this long without a mark on your shoulder. Eirik and his wolf have claimed you as theirs. In every way but one. It sounds like something happened when he was on the cusp of a full rut. He scared you, and he ran so he wouldn't hurt you. He's fighting his wolf now, because of it."

Yrsa stepped forward, and I flinched when she set her hand on my shoulder.

"If you want him, go to him. I'm not going to lie to you and say it will be easy. This isn't going to be the sweet love-making I'm sure you're used to with your other lovely men. It will be a claiming. He'll chase you, fuck you, and he'll mark you. Likely in the dirt or wherever else you land when he catches you, and he *will* catch you. If you don't want that, or can't handle it, go back to your room and wait it out."

That declaration was the first thing to cause me to pause. My heart sped up, a fear so bitter it made my mouth go dry, skittering over my skin like little bugs. My legs shook, and the idea of running like that *terrified* me. The idea of souring this moment that I wanted to be between us with memories of a place that broke me nearly enough to pull me away.

I gave myself a minute to think, to truly consider Yrsa's words. Could I handle this? I wasn't sure, not after everything that had happened. The only thing I really knew was that this was *Eirik*; and he wouldn't hurt me. But the act of it, the memories it might bring up ...

"What will happen if I don't?" I asked, ashamed the words even slipped out when Yrsa's eyes dimmed.

"Maybe he'll come to his senses. Calm down," she said, shrugging her shoulders, but I knew people, knew their tells. Her eyes dropped low, her hands tensing into fists as tension racked her body.

Eirik would be stuck like this. My Eirik. The man who'd held me so close it chased away the demons that haunted me. Who'd pulled away so quickly when I'd asked that I barely felt the heat of his touch. He treated me with care, always made sure I was in control, always made me feel so safe.

Raised his hands after I'd cut his skin with a knife I'd brought against him, palms facing me. He'd made me feel safe after an auction that I swore was going to be another hell.

I wanted him, all of him. I wasn't sure if I was completely ready for this, but I was out of time, and he was *mine*. I wouldn't let him suffer if I could help it.

"Thank you, Yrsa," I said with a smile. The abrupt change must have given her whiplash, as her eyes went wide. "I have to go."

"Good choice," she said with a nod. She crossed her arms over her chest. "See you soon, my *systur*!"

I waved at her over my shoulder, not letting myself think about what I was walking into, only focusing on putting one foot after the other. Each step filled me with determination, pushing me toward my goal.

When I finally came to a door, I pushed through before I could stop myself. It opened to a wide expanse of forest, stretched out from a single clearing. The grass was green, so different from the cold winter I knew existed outside of this mountain.

The entire room was blanketed with a soft light that almost seemed like it was coming from the moon, as an artificial wind blew past, the flowers and plants rustling under the soft onslaught.

Standing in the middle of the clearing was Eirik, just barely feet away. He tipped his head toward me, his eyes nearly midnight black, the color lost to the expansion of his pupils. He'd lost his shirt, his chest damp with sweat as he panted. Those dark tattoos that traced his body glowed like sigils in the low light, the ethereal accents giving him a godly look. His hair was pulled loose, no longer bound into intricate braids, falling over his head in unruly blond waves. He looked wild, *feral*, as he pulled in a breath that ended in a deep growl.

"**My *smár Valkyrja*,**" he rumbled, more beast than man, his chest expanding in a purr that sent a shock wave down my spine. He took a step toward me. His next words were spoken with savage pride. "**Our mate. Knew you'd come.**"

"Eirik, are you okay?" I asked carefully, muscles tensing when he took another step toward me.

His head was tilted to the side, his eyes locked in on me, unblinking.

"**Yes,**" he rumbled, taking another step. He was right there. I could reach out and touch him now. My breath caught.

This was it. I struggled to keep my cool as I looked him up and down. His stature really came to me now, his staggering height suddenly intimidating as I looked past him into the woods. It would take him no time at all to catch me in this chase.

That same fear came bubbling up inside me again, my vision blurring at the edges as I swallowed several times, trying to breathe away the sound of Nilus's voice.

Eirik's purr stumbled, and I looked back just in time to see his eyebrows cinch together. "**Why do you fear us? We will not harm you.**"

He lifted his hand, as if to reach out to me, before pulling it back to his chest. His rolling tattoos flexed across his bare skin, his body shivering as a fine layer of sweat coated it. Every bit of him tensed as he looked down, trying to make himself seem small.

Safe.

"Can you both see me?" I asked, relaxing as curled tighter, his chest vibrating in that comforting purr.

"**Yes,**" he grunted with a nod.

"Eirik ..." I started, reaching up to press my hand to his chest. His heart thundered under my palm, his skin vibrating with the captivating melody that only grew when I smiled. "My sweet, beautiful wolf."

That purr deepened, and Eirik leaned down, his nose brushing against the top of my head, his entire large body leaning over mine, encompassing me. His breath brushed against the skin of my temple. Little puffs.

"*Mine*," he growled, the sound bitingly dangerous. Another skitter of fear laced down my spine, blending with the lust that had been building between my legs. The serious edge to his word was the last push I needed. This was it. I lifted my hand higher, cupping his cheek. The rough stubble of his beard tickled my palm, but the warmth didn't scare me this time.

"Can I ask you a question?" I started, looking him in his blown eyes, searching for the Eirik I knew was buried there, finding him watching carefully alongside his beastly half.

"*Always*," he whispered, one of his hands finding my hair, toying with the braid he'd woven.

"If I leave, what will you do?" I asked, watching as his face scrunched up like he hadn't been expecting that. He pulled his hand up, showing me his wrist. The one that bore a single lavender line. When he responded, it was all wolf.

"**No mark?**"

I shook my head, pushing past the anxiety in my stomach. "No mark."

Eirik hummed as if contemplating it, gentle fingers caressing my cheek, his hand large enough to cup the entirety of my face. So much power held in him, and he used it to tuck the hair behind my ear.

"**Then we wait,**" his wolf whispered, and I froze, not expecting that he'd be the one that came forward. There was such sincerity in the words that I almost didn't hear him finish. "**Until you crave us again. Until the fear has settled, and you are ready for us.**"

I let out a breath, reaching up to cup his hand, savoring the warmth he gave off. I searched for the fear that had gripped me in the training room, dreading that it might come stumbling forward again, but for now, it stayed quiet.

"And if we start, and I need you to stop?" I pressed, and this time there was no waiting.

"I won't ever do something you aren't willing to, *Elskan*." Eirik said, vehemently, his eyes his again as they flashed sky blue. "No matter what. If you wish to stop, **we stop.**"

His beast closed it out, and they didn't let go of my eyes as they watched me carefully. Blissful silence filled my head, and the voices that had stolen my thoughts were nothing but a distant memory.

I wasn't sure if doing this would bring another up; I wasn't sure if I could handle this ... but I knew without a shadow of a doubt that Eirik would stop if I asked. I trusted him more than anything.

It was why I felt comfortable stepping back, keeping a bare point of contact with his cheek.

"I love you, Eirik," I said, and his expression melted, his lips tilting into an adorable smile that was so contrasting to what I was about to do with him. The fear that had swallowed me was washed away by the gentleness in his eyes, the caring words he said so fervently. "So, *chase me*. Mark me, please."

Time could have frozen with the way Eirik's face shifted, the skin under my palm bunching. His eyes rolled back, his teeth bared in a snarl before he spoke. "You're sure?"

It was Eirik's voice, not the beast. Still there enough to ask, to make sure.

He wouldn't hurt me in any way I didn't want, *not my Eirik.*

I didn't answer, not with words, but a nod as I stepped around him. His eyes traced me as I walked slowly, keeping my eyes on him until I hit the tree line.

My heart rate skyrocketed, adrenaline already soaring in my blood.

"Then run," he whispered, his words falling into a growl as his eyes flushed fully black again. The playful nature there fell completely to lust, and he shivered. **"You get a head start, little warrior."**

My heart jolted, adrenaline so clear in my blood it made my fingers tingle. His eyes narrowed, the look of a predator stalking prey as his purr shifted into an eager growl.

This was Eirik.

Fear came with the steps I took, but I didn't stop. I held my breath, flipping to face the trees.

And I *ran*.

I dashed through the thick underbrush, my legs catching the stray shrubs and branches. The stings started and ended on a breath, but I was so numb to the feeling I barely felt it as adrenaline kept me soaring forward. My heart was the only thing I could truly feel.

It thundered, a mix of foreboding and anticipation that kept me moving at full speed. My senses honed, my ears listening for every sound I could catch, the woods silent around me for all of a second.

A twig snapped to my right, cracking like gunfire in my ears as I gasped, jolting away from it, stumbling as I tried to move in the other direction. My knees hit the ground, the forest floor slick as I hauled myself back to my feet.

A growl filled the air, far enough away that it faded into the panicked breaths I let out. Close enough that I could feel it in my bones. The space between my legs ached, a deep emptiness in my core catching me off guard. My gait stuttered with each beat of my heart, and my rational brain urged caution while the primal side sought to run harder, knowing that he was close.

I stumbled again, hitting a tree hard enough to hurt. I swore I could feel hot breath on the back of my neck as I looked over my shoulder, finding empty forest. Like he was toying with me, playful and eager, while not wanting the chase to be over just yet. I knew it wouldn't last; it was only a matter of time before he caught me. I moved again, refusing to stay idle. It was freeing, in a way, how my mind cleared with the sole intention of running. There wasn't a worry beyond my next step, a fear beyond the one I knew wouldn't really hurt me.

I wanted this. I realized, and I trusted Eirik to not take it too far. Another snapping twig had me stumbling in another direction, then another, until I was in a field of familiar flowers.

The white buds of the moonflowers barely registered before a body hit me from behind. I fell to the ground with an oof, my front cushioned by the hand that now caged me possessively to a broad chest.

"Got you, *Elskan*," Eirik panted, his nose running along my neck, teeth quick to follow as a deep growl vibrated along my spine. He consumed me as he flexed, that rumbling growl mixing with a groan low in his chest. It went straight to my core, like a direct line. **"Now you're ours."**

He molded me to him, pressing every inch into me, including the thick length that settled against my back. I shivered at his size, the thought of it making me dizzy. It wasn't my first time, but Eirik was huge, and more than intimidating, especially with the frantic way he nipped at my neck, his large hand trailing down my lower stomach. His hand wandered, toying with the hem of my pants.

I didn't have time to worry, as Eirik moved, keeping me on my hands and knees as he ripped my pants and underwear down in one swift jerk. Next thing I knew, I was sitting, knees hitting the ground by his ears, my hands planted firmly on the ground above his head. Even like this, I wasn't in control. His hand dug into my thighs as he pulled me down to sit fully on his face. The first swipe of his tongue had me jerking forward. There was no room to move as his fingers tightened and his moan lit with a savage growl that sounded like a beast digging into its meal. The grunts and groans that spilled out of him would have been mortifying if I wasn't so completely lost in the haze of pleasure he brought. He sank a finger into me, testing me with smooth, gentle strokes that betrayed the nip of his teeth against the back of my thigh.

Then another joined it, and I cried out at the stretch. His mouth returned to its place, licking around his fingers, clinging to my clit as he continued to growl and snarl. He bucked hard enough for me to feel it. Then a third finger was joining the other two, until I was completely full of him and rocking back onto his hand and face with reckless abandonment. The stretch stung, but it was no more noticeable than the scrapes that lined my legs and arms from the run.

He didn't let go, not until I was a mess for him, the hint of an orgasm sitting just out of reach. Every time I got close, he pulled back, and I was left reeling, chasing the feeling as he shifted his movements to drag out the pleasure.

"Eirik?" I asked when he pulled away, a needy whine leaving my lips at the loss of his fingers. He moved me how he wanted, my hands still planted in the dewy underbrush, my cheek digging in as he kneeled behind me. I was so desperate for release that when I finally felt the brush of his cock head against my entrance, I jolted at the feeling, gasping when he ran it along my clit.

His chest rumbled, his body falling over mine again. One hand fell to my hip, the other landing on my neck in a hold that had me arching into him. He held me gently, but with purpose, a control that told me exactly what I needed.

He wouldn't push too far. He'd keep me safe.

But I wasn't going anywhere.

"Soon, you'll wear our mark," he whispered.

My body flushed, and I gasped, the strangled sound forcing my hips back, searching for something as I tilted in his hands. His mouth opened, a tongue trailing a line over my shoulder. When I felt his fangs, my own started burning.

"**Here**," he whispered, kissing the spot lovingly. The idea of a mark, one from him that I'd carry forever, appealed to me in a way I wasn't expecting.

It would *scar* no doubt, but I didn't hate that idea. If anything, I reveled in it. I wanted a good scar, like the one he wore on his face. I wanted one that I didn't have to flinch away from.

"Mine," he snarled, as his tip sank into me.

There was a burn, one I expected even with all of his preparation, but he didn't just slam into me, like I'd worried he might. The hand at my hip moved, settling on my clit as he gently rocked his hips. His entire body shook, little grunts of pleasure echoing in my ear as he nibbled on my earlobe and down my neck, sinking in inch by devastating inch.

The bites of pain were quickly washed away by the sheer fullness he left me with. I was encompassed by him, I wasn't sure where I ended and he began by the time I felt the front of his thighs meet the back of mine. He didn't give any leeway, pressing as deep as he could go until I was squirming in his arms, unable to move away. When his hand climbed, pressing on my abdomen, feeling himself through the muscle there, I groaned helplessly.

He'd stretched places that hadn't been before, pressed firm against my cervix, and it was daunting to feel him so fully.

His hand went back to stroking my hip, the other at my neck applying that ever so steady gentle pressure.

"You okay, *Elskan*?" he asked, his words coming between growls and pants.

I flexed around him, causing an answering groan from both of us.

"Move, Eirik. Please," I whimpered, nodding.

His entire body shivered, his breath stopping as the low rumble in his chest picked back up. His breath was a soft warning as he pulled out, leaving just the tip inside before he slammed back in. Yrsa's words fully registered at the impact of his hips against mine. It rattled my teeth, and he somehow seemed even deeper now, my vision blotting as I held my breath. There was no pause as he pulled out and snapped back forward with a heady grunt. He held me tightly, so close to him I had no choice but to surrender to the brutal pleasure his thrusts brought.

One after another, he overloaded my senses with him, never shying away from the depth he seemed desperate to get to. His hand fell to my clit, the shock of it enough to send me spiraling, dragging out an orgasm I hadn't seen coming as he sank deep and held himself there. He made sure every second of it was spent entirely on his thick cock, which still pulsed inside me.

He started moving again, a shift in his thrusts matching an erratic hitch in his purr as he continued to lick my neck. The sinful growl was a shock, almost as much as when his teeth bit down, the little love bites shifting into something more urgent. Not enough to break skin, but enough to send a sharp burst of pain down my spine. I gasped when his tongue covered the mark, soothing the ache.

I hadn't thought to ask if the marking would hurt. I'd been bitten before.

Eirik snapped his hips one more time, his thumb a constant pressure on my clit, sending me spiraling into an orgasm that my body tried desperately to give him. It was then that his fangs sank deep. It wasn't a feeding bite, the brutality of it taking my breath away as pain shot out from the wound. A cold shiver shot down my spine, spreading as though ice had entered my bloodstream.

I wiggled instinctively, trying to get away from the pressure, Eirik keeping me locked to him with his hands as a growl rocked his frame, ending in his teeth that were still locked in my neck. An unyielding panic started to build inside me when Eirik pressed deeper, *harder*. His feet dug into the ground, the arm at my waist dragging me back against him in the same movement. He strained against my cervix, my body not willing to yield.

Then, the base of him, which was just inside of me, past my pubic bone, started to grow.

I jolted, choking on my gasp at the sharp feeling, but there was no getting away from it. Eirik's teeth were still buried deep, and even his purr couldn't calm me as he continued to grow. Tears pooled in my eyes, and I sobbed when it finally stopped, seconds before I was sure it would be too late, sure he'd tear me.

My breathing was the only thing I could hear, ragged and panicked, as Eirik's fangs pulled from my neck, his tongue lapping up the blood that spilled from the wound.

"**Mine,**" Eirik whispered, his beast still firmly in control as he rocked his hips slightly. I flinched at the tight, tugging feeling, taken by surprise as the pain dulled to a pleasant ache. My shoulder went numb, a contented warmth flowing through me as he continued to move slightly back and forth.

"What's happening?" I asked, gasping as I spasmed around him, his purr making him vibrate inside.

"**The claiming,**" the beast said simply, continuing to lick and play. "**You're *mine*, little mate.**"

Warmth spread through me, and I arched involuntarily as I melted beneath him.

"**My other half has watched enough. He longs for you,**" he whispered, the raspy tone of his beast fading a bit. He kissed my neck again, lips pressed to the mark he'd left there. Sparks of pure euphoria danced beneath it.

It still ached, bleeding as my body worked on healing it, but that didn't stop me from reaching for it. My heart sped up at the idea of seeing it every day. The scar it would leave. Eirik had told me once that the scar on his face was a point of pride for him, and I hadn't understood.

I did now. I wanted the imprint of his teeth to remain on my skin forever.

"My beautiful, fierce *Valkyrja*," Eirik groaned, his voice his own again. "Are you okay?"

He licked the wound, and I gasped, still clenched around him, moaning as he pressed hard against my inner walls.

"Yeah, I am," I whispered, half whimpering when he shifted, grinding into me.

I didn't think I'd be able to come again, not after everything, but the gentle press of Eirik's lips against my neck, and the weight of him over me, told me I might be wrong.

"What is this?" I asked.

I hadn't been expecting this, even from what Yrsa had told me. It had been terrifying, at first, but now that it was there ... I could get used to it.

He ground again, catching something inside of me that had my eyes rolling back. Yes, I could *really* get used to this.

"Don't know," Eirik mumbled. "He didn't warn me."

The pull from inside had me gasping again, tensing when Eirik's deft fingers found my clit and began swirling in steady circles.

He kept his thrusts short and steady, gentle compared to how his beast had taken me, driving me up as my legs began to tremble, and I found myself arching back into him. "Eirik—"

A moan tore itself from my chest, muted against the ground as he nipped the newly healed mark.

"You are my sweetest treasure, Aaliyah," he whispered, pride stealing his words as his free hand found my lower stomach again, pressing above where we were joined, making me squirm. I reached up, grabbing the arm that was planted by my head. "My other half claimed you. Your last cries are mine."

He said it so sweetly while he did everything in his power to make me come undone again, and I was helpless to do anything but let him. I sobbed into the ground, his hand moving up, cupping my face, holding me reverently as he continued to move, and me doing the same.

Chasing a pleasure that would burn me to ashes.

"Feed," Eirik growled as I licked his palm. It was barely a question before I'd buried my fangs into him, pulling in a mouthful of sea-tinted blood.

The combination was all I needed, and I climaxed again, getting lost in the feel and taste of him as he grunted, continuing to grind. I felt his release bathing my insides for the second time, leaving me contently warm as he curled around me, holding me close, his nose brushing his mark every few seconds as if to make sure it was still there.

My wolf, my protector.

My *mate*.

CHAPTER 52

OSIRIS

I wiped the sweat from my brow, clutching the gaping wound that stretched across my abdomen. The slice of a holy sword seared the skin, burning right through tissue and a few of my ribs.

I had no idea how long I'd been here, long enough for my stomach to revolt and blood lust to leave me weakened. Unable to even heal. My mouth watered, my mind flipping to Aaliyah as I ducked into another cell, one of the many I'd found since I'd managed to slip away from Cael. Wherever we were was even deeper than the fighting ring we'd been in. There was a curiosity to the air, a plucking, almost taunting nature that had me constantly looking over my shoulder. It was a feeling I'd only ever experienced once before, and the drag that seemed to linger here, the way time seemed to slow ... it was like the Void.

The cells were laid out in a spiral, a decline looping them down into an expanse I couldn't see the bottom of. In the center was what looked to be liquid silver, falling down in endless waves from a place far above me, crashing into the limitless depths.

I moved my hand over the brand of Darius, urging it to keep searching for the steady hint of him, even as it made me physically ill. It was stronger now, the pulse more consistent as I wound my way down the spiraling cells.

A small spell lingered on the ground, like a trail of gold along the withered steps, sticking close to the cells and away from the emptiness that sat outside them. Away from the taunting calls of the furious Cael as he tried to find me a few rungs up.

He would. I didn't have any doubt about that. Angels were able to sense sin in a way that I'd never been able to rationalize. They were like bloodhounds, and I had more than enough innocent blood on my hands for him to track. I could see him now, his nose to the ground as he goaded and hunted me. It was only a matter of time, which had me picking up my pace, even as fresh hot agony shot down my spine. I couldn't handle another bout with him.

The first fight had been brutal, hours of trading blows and grievous wounds, neither strong enough to end the other. If I wasn't actively fighting without my magic, I might have had a better chance.

Lie. Steal. Cheat.

It didn't matter; all of it was a setback, one that the path I followed would clear. I needed to find Darius's tie.

The path glittered on the ground like little gems, shifting and moving as it led me along. Only bones remained in the cells here, proof that Cael wasn't the only one to be left abandoned, a desolate quiet dragging up the eeriness of the endless spire.

I went on, until the path grew hazy, and noises began to fill the air. Quiet at first, like the skitter of mice in rotten walls, before they grew savage. Until I was in front of another cage.

Another cell.

It was no different than the rest, not even at the end of this long line. Just a random set of bars that held more than bones ... another prisoner. A man, or rather what *used* to be a man, the path ending at his chest, his back against a crumbling wall of limestone and wood.

The thing in front of me now was nothing more than a feral beast. His head thrashed from side to side, foam on his mouth as he struggled against rusted chains that hung tightly to the wall. The skin on his wrists was long gone, bones showing where I could see, and his long, matted hair fell all the way to the floor, wrapping up and snagging in the links.

The words he spoke were foreign even to me, the guttural intonation not even sparking familiarity. The entire cell smelled of mold, feces, and decaying blood, its age showing in the fissure-like cracks that spanned the floor. It seemed to move, the entire thing swaying as though a ship in turbulent waters.

I'd expected an idol when I came looking for Darius's weak point. Kri'Valta had assumed the same. Not a *man*, let alone one so crazed and bumbling, one that reeked of power so vast it bled onto the ground with the rest of his blood.

Buried in it, as if entwined with the cells inside of him, was a scent like an arid desert oasis. It stuck to even his skin. Without a doubt, this man was who Kri'Valta had spoken of. The tie that gave Darius his endless supply of power and luck. The one obstacle between me and the fall of that monster.

I reached in myself, searching for more, hoping to find anything to allow me to break his bonds. My magic, as before, was barely a hint of what it could be, and even then whatever spell this was extended past what I could do. It wrapped around him, weaving between his breaths and the genetic makeup inside of him.

I lifted my hand, a different spell slipping out. Less like poison and more like habit again, the only one I could manage with as little power as I had. His speech slowly shifted, his words morphing into English.

It didn't clear up the meaning.

Useless.

I pressed on the laws of the Eternium, assessing the pressure that came with the intent to kill. It was there, but rather than an overbearing presence, it lingered like a devil on my shoulder.

I *could* kill him. Rid us of Darius's charm at the source and pave the path forward for a seamless Retaliation. It would be easy. Not my first kill, not my last.

But something about him made me pause. My fingers fell slack, my caster hand dropping as my final hints of magic fizzled away. This man, he'd been a victim as well. He'd fallen prey much like I had. This savage, feral beast had been someone once. He didn't deserve to die purely because of Darius's cruelty.

I sighed and reached for the bars, the rusted hinges turning to dust under the force as the magic crumbled. The shackles that held him fell apart next, but he was too far gone to have noticed it. He slid to the ground, his legs unable to hold him up. He grunted and groaned before he went silent, curling in on himself.

I reached down, hauling him over my shoulder, holding his weight long enough for me to go searching for my magic once again. It didn't respond beyond a quick flash that was swallowed by the Pits. Not near enough to teleport me out, and I hadn't expected it to.

I'd prepared accordingly.

I didn't look for the powers in me. I looked for the ones I'd made, for the necklace that Aaliyah had around her neck. I called for the spell I'd placed in it, benign, and waiting for activation.

One that allowed me to go to her, no matter where I was. I smiled when I found it, felt the heat of her skin through the stone like it was my own, and reveled in the weight of her breath. I pulled on it, allowing the flow of teleportation magic to wash over me and the man that was supposed to be the key to Darius's fall Kri'Valta had promised.

I was no fool. Getting him out didn't secure victory. The only thing it'd do was bring us closer to dragging Darius to heel, and that itself wasn't a certainty. I'd found no other allies, found no other way forward.

Which meant Exilium was going to fail. I hadn't wanted to say it before, but I'd seen the numbers, the panic that had risen with Sebek's announcement that first night. Some had turned against us when they'd been made aware of what Aaliyah was. Which meant there was no choice, no alternative, even if the others still wanted there to be. I needed to Challenge Sebek.

Or none of us would be leaving this Eternium alive.

"What do we have here?" Cael called, whistling a sharp tune. He was still bloodied from our bout, one of his eyes sealed closed as he spit a mouthful of blood onto the ground.

The sigil grew under my feet, red hot.

There was a flash of confusion when he saw the flux of teleportation, his wings flaring wide before a smile so foul it could have leaked poison crossed his face.

I pushed the will of the spell as hard as I could, forcing the bindings to close as he shot forward. The pull was vicious as we were dragged through the magical tar that was the Pits, the Eternium's magic fighting it every step of the way. The incantation was fast, reacting in an instant, cracking closed.

But *Cael* was faster. He touched me just as the magic binding me to Aaliyah strained tight, snapping before closing around me.

We left the Pits behind with a puff of arid dust.

Dragging Cael out with us.

CHAPTER 53

AALIYAH

Eirik's hands slid deftly through my hair, picking apart the knots and binds with gentle moves. I was boneless in front of him, humming softly as he continued to dote.

He'd insisted on it, eyes shining so brightly I couldn't have told him no. He wanted to take care of me, nursing the bruises he'd left and washing away the dirt and sex, all while singing that delightfully deep song for me.

We were back in the main living space the Eternium had deemed ours, lying across blankets on top of the couch. The others were close by, Prince seated next to us on the floor, rubbing out some of the tension in my hand with well-placed strokes. Fallon perched on a chair, watching with soft eyes as Eirik continued his after care. Adrian had slipped out just a few moments ago, after making sure I was fed.

"What time is it?" I asked, and Fallon moved until he was close enough to touch me.

I leaned into his hand, my eyes closing as his fingers traced a soft path down my face and over the mark Eirik had left on my neck. It was healed now, no longer even aching. It was odd, how freely Fallon touched me now. His hand found my hair, his fingers threading through the strands Eirik had smoothed out. His lips pressed against my forehead, then my temple, loving caresses that were so gentle I melted.

"Late," he whispered back. "You okay?"

I smiled at his worry as I stretched up.

It was hard lugging myself out of Eirik's arms, and I struggled not to laugh as he grunted and tried to pull me closer, scowling the entire time. It seemed so natural to be sprawled between them.

I could imagine warm Sunday mornings like this, the scent of freshly cooked breakfast blending seamlessly with the sound of laughter. My emotions were still reeling, my body worn out from the run, but there was nowhere I'd rather be. They made it worth it, made it easy to nod my head.

The auction, even Ascension, had led me to them. Every moment in my life, as shitty as it had been, had led me here. It was a trauma I'd always hold with me, my past a broken thing that still hurt. Like shards of glass that sank too deep.

But one day at a time, one word, one comforting embrace ... It'd begun to hurt less. While I'd never truly remove it, I knew I wasn't alone.

I had them. My family. My loves.

"Thank you for being my home," I whispered, and Fallon's breath caught.

Eirik's arm tightened around my midsection, his nose brushing against the mark he'd left on my neck.

"You brought the home, Aaliyah. You tied us back together, molded us into something new, something stronger than before. I can't wait to live this life with you. I won't allow anything less," Fallon said back, trying to hide the crack in his voice as he looked away.

He covered his smile with his hand as he ran his fingers over his jaw. One moment looking so at ease ... until the air cracked.

It wasn't a sound, not really, as electricity danced over my skin. The hair on my arms rose, static ringing in my ears. I reached up, grabbing the necklace Osiris had made to replace the one I'd lost to Sebek's violence. It was warm, almost to the point of being *too* hot, and it only calmed when I touched it.

"Do you feel that?" I asked, my nose scrunching as a slightly acidic scent filled the air. Something about it, the way the power crackled, didn't set me on edge like it should have.

"Stay down," Fallon grunted, standing in an instant, shielding me with his body as the room started to warp.

Eirik followed suit, rolling us so he was on top, covering me as the magic flexed, harder now. The walls groaned, seeming to wobble. Prince was the next to his feet, butting into Fallon's shoulder as he took up the space to his left.

Even Red took up arms, his presence brushing mine in a familiar violent cadence. His energy was explosive, his emotions all over the place.

Fear, excitement, and rage.

"What's going on?" Prince asked, brushing his eyes with the backs of his hands, looking around, confused.

Another crackle, then I felt it, like a brush against my own soul. The marks on my wrist warmed, the twisting black marks pulsing, and the feeling of safety that washed over me had me standing.

I stepped around Fallon. "Wait."

He grunted, his hands landing on my shoulders as figures began to take shape. The scent of metal filled the air, bitter and sharp, and I tilted my head, overjoyed when a familiar face came into view. "Osiris?"

He materialized seconds later, grunting under the weight of the body that he held up as another crashed onto the floor beside him. His clothing was battered, singe marks tracing his skin as ash fell from his hair when he shook his head. His body was bruised and bloody, much like his face, as he tipped his head up to look at us, his black hair brushed back, stark blue eyes searching the room.

As soon as he saw me, he dropped the person he was holding, the body hitting the ground with a thud, much like the first. The man didn't make a sound.

Then Osiris was on me.

I'd always treaded carefully with him, worried I'd bring up bad memories by moving too fast. Now, more than ever, I felt the need to hold myself back. My own memories were all too savage, a warning of how terrible the past could be ... but he didn't stop in front of me, didn't extend a hesitant hand.

He pulled me into his arms, breathing me in like I was the oxygen he needed to survive, and I did the same. He hissed when my hands found his face, the spark of contact like a drug, his body bowing when I searched him to see the damage.

His side was ripped apart, the slice of a dull blade, his abdomen quivering when I reached out to it.

His kiss came as a surprise, stopping my worried hands in their tracks, his soft lips chasing mine in a dance that left me breathless. I wrapped my arms around his shoulders, letting my tongue slide across one of his descended fangs, flooding our mouths with my blood.

Faster than he could have protested it.

He groaned into me, his hands tightening on my hips, a full body shiver tossing his head back as a drop slid down his chin, over his jaw and down the front of his neck. I traced his side again, humming, when I watched the festering wound begin to seal.

"*Lux mea*," he whispered, panting. He set his forehead on mine, keeping me in his arms, not yet letting me down. "I've missed you."

"Osiris," I said, brushing away tears as they clouded my eyes. I kissed him again, the taste of my blood in his mouth making me shiver. "You're back."

"Good to see you in one piece, brother," Prince said, walking up to Osiris and wrapping an arm around his shoulder. He did a once-over, as well, checking for the same things I had.

The wound was gone by the time he saw it, my fingertips now pressed against smooth skin. Prince didn't linger, his hand going to my head, weaving the strands of my hair into his grip before leaning in to press a chaste kiss to my lips.

I gasped when he pulled back, his tongue tracing a red line over his. He winked when he was done, chuckling when I blushed.

"Oh, isn't this darling?" a rasping voice whispered as the first man that had hit the ground stood on shaking legs. "Osiris found a *lover*? Never thought I'd see the day."

He was massive, with towering wings that touched the roof as he dragged his bloodied sword up, laying it across his shoulders. One of the wings was mangled, golden blood sliding down it, hitting the floor like acid, sizzling against the wood. Malice leaked from him, slamming into me.

He snarled, the ruins on his skin glowing white hot, even his eyes flushing of color.

"Cael," Osiris whispered, stepping in front of us and acting as a wall.

The man rolled his eyes, almost mocking, as he looked between us.

"Thanks for the out, *Rex interfectorem*," he said with a mocking smile as though indulging in a joke. The blood on his blade matched that which covered Osiris, the red staining the floor where it dripped from the edge. Rage was quick to find a place in my chest, but I didn't get a chance to even speak as Cael turned away. "Be seeing you around, I'm sure."

Then he limped out of the room, not looking back. Even with that, I couldn't shake the lingering fear that came with him, almost like my body was scared to get too close. No one moved to stop him, and it was only when the door closed that I was finally able to breathe. The voice in my head savaged me, pushed me to go after him for what he'd done to Osiris, even with the Eternium stamping down on the urge.

Make him pay.

"Well, I'll be the first to address the elephant in the room. Or should I say, the body in the room? Who the fuck was that, and do you want to explain the mostly dead man on the ground?" Prince asked.

Osiris looked at said body, and I peeked around him to do the same.

He hadn't moved, whoever he was, since Osiris had dropped him. I wiggled out of his arms, looking at what I assumed at first was a corpse.

The man was rail thin, bone poking through skin in several places, mostly along his wrists and ankles. His hair was matted, wrapping around him almost like a garment, his face completely covered in it. It was only when he breathed that I realized he was still *alive.*

"Cael was the first Angel Eternal. He'd been trapped in the Pits after I'd helped Adathan win his Challenge several Eterniums back. It was bad luck that he happened to find me. Nothing to be done about it now," he said, before turning his eyes to the body on the floor. He hesitated before sighing. "I believe this man is tied to Darius."

The man didn't stir, and the more I looked at him, the more my stomach dropped.

"Is he what you went down there for?" Fallon asked, rolling his shoulders as he glanced back at the door.

"Yes," Osiris added. "Though I was expecting an idol. A charm. Not—"

He paused, and Eirik was quick to follow up. "A man?"

"Right," Osiris finished. "He's a tie, a bridge of sorts. Darius trapped him in the Pits after he took over as Mythic Eternal. He can't lose a fight so long as the idol stays whole."

The man grunted, groaning low in his chest as he tried to rotate. He didn't have the strength to, or the strength to cry out as I heard a pop. Like the breaking of a bone or a dislocated joint.

"You're sure?" Eirik added, and Osiris dipped his head, the solemn way he watched the man telling enough.

"Kri'Valta told me before he died," Osiris said, his eyes clouding as if remembering the moment. He hadn't spoken of it much, barely at all, but something about it still clung to him now. "He was many things, but I don't believe him to be a liar."

How long had he spent down there? Locked away, unable to get out for *years*. It made me sick. Torture, pain. It was nothing new. I'd seen it myself, in the others that had lingered at Ascension.

This man knew torture, too. The sight of him, with crude scars circling his wrists. The thin frailness of his body so clearly led by starvation.

"So, we're fucked," Eirik chimed in, snapping his teeth.

He sought me out, walking behind me as he looked down at the body, too.

"We need to find a way to kill him and be done with it," Fallon finished, looking Osiris in the eye. There was a cruel detachment to his words, and he didn't even bother looking at the man he spoke about.

I froze.

"There has to be some way to, even past the Eternium rules. I'm sure Mags knows something," Prince added with a hum. "They owe me after leaving me to die like that. It'd be the least they could do."

He moved, intention clear, and none of the others went to stop him. They spoke about it so casually, so ruthlessly. The death of a man who didn't have any say in the matter, who didn't deserve it. At least not based on what we'd seen so far.

I'd seen enough innocent death, faced it, *done it*. My stomach twisted to the point of pain at the thought of watching it again.

"No!" I protested, moving to stand in front of the prone man, acting as a wall while the others looked on in shock. "He doesn't deserve to die, not because a madman decided to lock him up."

Darius ripped away his freedoms, trapped him where he'd never see the light of day again. I didn't move, even when Fallon scowled, and Eirik crossed his arms over his chest.

"I'm with Fallon. His death would serve us far better than his life," Eirik chimed in, the vicious swirl of his beast behind his eyes just adding fuel to his fire.

I reached for my neck, the mark he'd put there, stepping back until my heels touched skin.

There was an obstinate determination in their eyes, one that spoke of years of experience. I could see their reasoning, the cruel efficiency that it would bring. It was the easier path, and part of me understood that.

Death was easy, death was final, but this man had been through so much it showed in the scars on his wrists, the crazy I could feel still clinging to me after so many years trapped in my own personal hell.

"No, it's not right," I said, standing my ground. I took a deep breath, unwilling to budge. My legs shook, old habits dying hard as my throat closed around the words.

Never make noise.

"Ali—" Fallon started, his expression faltering.

This man had been tortured, locked away, and left to die ... like I had.

"I can't let you kill him, Fallon," I said, hoping he could see why I held on so tightly.

I'd been here once, strapped down and made to feel like less of a person and more like an object to be used. I saw myself in this man. I'd give on many things, but this was a hill I was ready to die on.

Ready to fight on.

"Our lives might depend on it, Ali! Don't be stubborn just because your heart bleeds for him," Fallon said, his face twisting into a rage that betrayed the ice in his voice. "For all we know, he could be worse than Darius!"

Still, I didn't back down, even at his snarling. There wasn't a hint of fear in me from him, and even now I knew that. It was what gave me the strength to take a step toward him until we were nose to nose. "You're ruling him out because the easier path is to deal with him. You're calling him a monster because it's easier to kill a monster! What if he isn't one?"

"Both of you need to calm down. Tension isn't the answer right now," Prince grunted, pushing between us.

His hands were steady weights as he urged us both back. He looked between us, grimacing before his head was tipping back with a groan. He glanced at the man that writhed again.

"Then we vote!" Fallon bit out, looking at Osiris, whose face twisted. My heart dropped, my chest suddenly aching as Prince's eyes hit the floor. Then Eirik's.

I covered the pain that bloomed with my palm, trembling as I shook my head. Osiris was quiet for a second before he sighed.

"Darius's cruel games should not damn him ... but I will not deny your right to a vote, Fallon," Osiris said, never looking away from me, putting the weight of the decision on his shoulders as he accepted it for what it was.

Osiris's eyes welled with apology, and it was like the ground gave out from under my feet. I turned my head to face the wall, suddenly sick at the thought of looking at them. Thoughts of my own memories sent a shiver down my spine, a reminder of the cold steel table that I still saw when I closed my eyes ... but it also gave me an idea.

Memories were tied to the Void, like the souls that wandered endlessly searching for it. I was intimately aware of them, how they worked and what they could do. Even now, I could see my own, compartmentalized as if I'd placed them myself.

Because I had. I saw that silver room, felt the bits of myself that I had put back together. One memory at a time.

"What if I can bring him back?" I said, snapping to look at them again, shifting from foot to foot. The others grew quiet, watching me with confused expressions. "Azer spoke to me about it, when I was trying to find a solution for Prince. I saw it after Mags brought back our memories. I might be able to tap into his soul, piece him back together. Then he can help. What if he knows more about Darius, about whatever is tying them together? He doesn't have to die."

I fought my way through the sentence. A sickening feeling of inadequacy flooded me, and the silly notion that I could help quickly fizzled. I blushed, my cheeks heating in embarrassment when no one spoke for a moment.

"It's too dangerous," Fallon added, looking as resolute as I felt.

"As opposed to what? Killing him?" I asked, gripping my hands together to stop the shaking. I knew the moment Fallon saw it, his shoulders deflating as I kept my head high. "We don't know anything about the binding between him and Darius. For all we know, killing him might not sever it. We don't have the time to waste on trying to find a way to kill him."

I looked, one more time, as the man suffered at our feet. For just a moment, I caught a glimpse of his eyes as they opened wide, a stark mix of blues and greens that choked me. He looked so afraid.

I turned back to Fallon, a man I loved, my head dipping. "I call a vote. The First Rights begin at midnight, Fallon. I can do this."

If I could save him, like I wished someone would have saved me ... that would be enough.

"I think it's worth a shot," Prince said with a softness I knew was reserved for me. He smiled, the way he always had, hiding his fears behind it as he nodded. I reached for my wrist, touching a scar that ran through the marks born from my ties to these men. Prince's expression dropped, catching the move. "I can see how much this means to you, Aaliyah. If you think you can do it, then you have my vote."

I could barely breathe, relief washing over me in a rush.

"And mine," Eirik grunted, moving to my side, always needing to touch. His nose brushed the silvery scar against my neck.

"This is ridiculous, please Ali. Not this." A hand cupped my cheek, lifting my head. Fallon's face was a mask, seemingly unfeeling as he ran his thumb over my cheek, wiping away the tears that fell. His eyes were still the most breathtaking I'd ever seen, so full of love, of life.

"Saving someone who needs saved is not ridiculous," I asked, hating the way Fallon's jaw clenched tightly. "He's just like me, Fallon. Trapped and scared. I can't just stand back and do nothing."

Not if I could help it.

Red fluttered around me, approval clear in his almost bouncing joy. He stopped by Prince, who swatted at the air with a twisted expression. Mirth clung to Red as he danced back to me.

"She has my vote as well," Osiris filled in, making it four.

I let out a breath and looked at the prone man. He was twisted up in his hair, his body contorted as he made another soft string of painful noises.

"What is your vote, Fallon?" Osiris asked, and Fallon's eyes slammed closed as he pulled away

Losing his touch burned, and when he opened his eyes again, there was a wall there, formed between him and I in a way that made my stomach ache.

"This is a mistake," he said, unwavering. He flexed his hands before running one through his hair. He took a second to fix his tie as he looked at the door. "You do what you need to do, but I won't accept this. I *can't* watch you die again, Ali."

He shuddered and moved to walk away.

"Fallon—" I started, cut off by his words as he slipped into the hall.

"You have your vote." The door closed behind him.

Silence descended on the room, and I shivered as a cold wave covered my shoulders, Red providing a comfort that Eirik matched with a soft purr.

"Let him go. He needs to get it out," Prince said, coming to my other side, looking down at the mass that went silent. "When he comes back, it will be with a clear head."

Some wretched part of my mind toyed with his words, and I continued to stare at the door.

If he comes back.

"That makes four," Osiris said, sighing as he glanced at his watch. "I'd normally wait for Adrian, but we don't have the time. What do you need from us, my dear?"

I shook my head, looking around as I tried to focus.

"Get him comfortable," I mumbled, crouching on the ground where the man lay. It wasn't necessarily a requirement, but I hated to see him so agonized on the floor.

Eirik did it himself, picking him up and moving him so he was less splattered to the ground. They even got him a blanket, as he began to shiver. I sat by his side, sinking thankfully onto a pillow that Prince snagged for me with a small smile.

"All right," I said, carefully lifting my hands. I flinched as I touched his warm skin, fighting the urge to pull away. Red fluttered around my head, poking at me in question. The shadows breathed, the Void sinking into my skin as I closed my eyes and reached out to it. "Red, I'm going to need a lot of help here."

He danced happily before wrapping around me like he did. He sank onto my shoulders, as if holding on tightly.

"Don't push yourself, Aaliyah. I couldn't give less shits about him. You come back to us safe, okay?" Prince said, his hands landing on my shoulders.

I shuddered, checking myself over like I used to do in my cell after every session with the doctors, cataloguing each ache and pain I felt. I was exhausted, my head pounding to the beat of my heart. The last time I'd been to the Void still clung to me, making my lungs hurt as I took a deep breath.

It takes, and it takes.

"Don't worry. I've got this." I pulled in another breath, forcing myself to hold it, feeling the pain for what it was, my focus solely on the man. His heart beat like a drum, quiet under the chill of his skin. I did as Azer had instructed, as I'd done with Prince and myself. I pressed my hands over his chest, searching for the warmth of a soul, and when I found the Void, I asked it to let me in. It was slow to do so, creaking open like a door. I wasn't sure if this would work, if it would even be the same as it had been for my own memories.

All I could do was see.

"I've never doubted you, Aaliyah, not once," Prince whispered, taking up the spot at my side. His arm wrapped around my shoulders, his weight soothing. "We'll be here when you get back."

CHAPTER 54

ADRIAN

"Well, seems I missed a party," I said dryly, looking at the body that was sprawled across the floor while rubbing the bridge of my nose.

This was not what I was expecting to find when I got back from my quick run to find some better bread. A man I didn't know propped up like some shitty center piece at an art show in the middle of our goddamned living room.

What I wouldn't give to skip whatever this was, crash into bed, and maybe cuddle with Aaliyah to clear my mind before the shit show that was going to be tonight. The First Rights, the starting call for Challenges, and Retaliation. For *Exilium,* even if it didn't pass.

Instead, here we were.

With a *body.*

Typical.

"Anyone want to explain what's going on? Or are we just going to leave me in suspense?" I asked, striding forward, then stopping next to Nero.

They were all standing around the man, watching intently at where Aaliyah sat at his side, her eyes closed. With the exception of Fallon, who seemed to be sulking on the far side of the room.

My heart clenched, and I listened for a heartbeat, only breathing again when I found it.

I plopped down next to her, brushing the hair away from her damp forehead, stricken when she didn't move.

"Osiris went looking for a charm in the Pits. Something to do with Darius's power," Eirik grunted, nodding toward the body. Like that explained everything, let alone how Osiris was here. "He found him."

Oh, well, it is what it is.

The man's eyes flashed behind closed lids, moving as though dreaming. He was ... something. Like what I imagined an old wizard in an ancient tower might look like, with a scraggly beard and frail frame. Straight down to the bone thinness. His hair had been chopped crudely, recently based on the remnants of the long strands on the floor, just enough to keep it out of his face.

Not to mention the smell. God, it was a good thing I wasn't hungry.

"Problem is, said charm is a man with a couple thousand screws loose. Aaliyah's in his head, trying to piece it back together," Nero added. He brushed his hair back, circling his ear with his pointer finger, the barest hint of his trickster personality shining through, covered almost entirely by worry as he searched Aaliyah's still face.

There went my cuddling plans, now well and *truly* dashed. I stretched out my muscles, giving my arms a good rotation as I settled into my seat on the hardwood, lucky I couldn't feel how uncomfortable it was. I shuffled again just as a crash rang through the air, and I had to look down to make sure my hand hadn't gone through the floor.

Only for the sound to ring again as Eirik snarled low in his chest. His face twisted as he turned to face the door, like a wall between us.

Whoever was on the other side of the door radiated heat, furious curses on his lips as he crashed into it again. From the scent of smoldering wood and volcanic ash, I'd say we just became hosts to a very pissed off Dragonkin. *Lovely.* While I didn't exactly know what could have brought Drakon so hot on our heels, I could wager a guess.

Another crash, more cursing.

"Osiris. Was this man the only thing you found in the Pits?" I asked.

I didn't need words. The shake of his head was enough. I sighed, rubbing my neck as I stood, preparing my best impression of a sleazy salesman's smile. I cracked my back, chuckling when the barest hint of a threat came muffled into the room. I walked to the door, then opened it to the fury-filled Dragonkin.

Drakon's eyes were lit with fire, the golden browns seeming almost red under the heat. He let out a breath, smoke fanning his face as red scales crawled up his neck.

"Drakon, just in time," I managed to get out as he barreled in like a crazed bat out of hell and went after probably the worst of us he could have.

"You slimy coward of a fucking man!" he screamed, grabbing Osiris by the collar, slamming him into the nearest wall like he was an unruly couch and not a walking embodiment of ancient death. "You just don't know when to stop!"

It was probably a good thing we couldn't kill each other right now.

I saw the moment Drakon's skin connected with Osiris's, his eyes darkening, the mismatching blue suddenly swirling. Lightning sparked in the air, the scent of electricity sending me into overdrive as I rushed forward, once again ready to play mediator.

"Tensions are obviously very high, but I would recommend airing your grievance say ... five feet away?"

But Drakon didn't let up, that persistent Dragon in him pushing him to get closer. I'd seen the markings of it nearly every day with Eirik, the sharpening of his pupils into hard-cut diamonds. More smoke billowed from his nose.

The air sparked again, my hair standing up.

"I think I'm perfectly happy right where I am. I should fucking gut all of you! You ruined everything!" Drakon snarled.

Osiris's eyes bled red, his fingers wrapping around Drakon's wrist, shaking as they squeezed hard enough to clash with the Eternium magic. "Kri'Valta was dealt with—"

"This isn't about Kri'Valta. This is about the monster you let out of the Pits!" Drakon pushed again before he dropped Osiris's shirt. "Cael is free, and he just Challenged Adathan! All of our planning for nothing! Our deal is over, our partnership, all of it. Fuck you, all of you. I should have known better than to trust the word of a Vivas."

The room fell silent, everyone waiting for Osiris to move as he stood straight once again.

There was a terrifying weight to Osiris's presence, one I tended to ignore since he was my family. But I saw that look now, that unearthly power that made people fear him so much.

He was well over two thousand years old. He held the magic of *Echomancy*, the strongest and most volatile of its kind, and he was a Vampire. The blood of Sebek Ra.

The fucking *Kingslayer*.

His head tipped to the side, and he moved, caging Drakon in with sure steps until they were away from where Aaliyah was. The others that had followed Drakon—Aldric, his second, like a ghost, he moved so deftly, and Cassius, his ruthless enforcer—tensed.

"If your plan is shallow enough to break under one man, then it is a worthless plan," Osiris said, deceptively calm. Until he took another step, and fire burned where his feet had been.

"The votes were already close, you know that—" Drakon snarled.

"And you knew that I would Challenge if Exilium failed. But this isn't about Exilium, is it? This was never just about Exilium, or did you think I didn't realize that?" Osiris asked.

Drakon paled as confusion spiked, even in my mind. Eirik was quick to capitalize, quick to move to stand by Osiris's side, staring down Cassius as the large Dragonkin sized up my brother.

He was big, damned fucking big, with black hair and a wiry smile that almost reminded me of Nero. His black eyes were calculating, testing if this were a fight he'd win, if the circumstances were different.

"So, he has something else planned, something dangerous?" Eirik added, looking to Drakon, digging into his soul with a flash of teeth as his wolf came to the fray.

Nero was next; like a well-oiled machine, they were a force, a monster, and with all three of them standing in front of him, Drakon's rage-filled facade crumbled. It was as impressive as it was daunting.

"No, something else. I'd place my bet on revolutionary," Nero pushed, chuckling when Drakon straightened at the accusation. "You do seem the type to hero worship. Let me guess, you'll be the hero of this story?"

"You have no idea what you're talking about," Drakon snarled, looking suddenly like a trapped dog, ready to bite.

I should have stepped in, but goddamn, even I was scared to get too close. Fallon moved to guard Aaliyah's body with his, simply watching the madness unfold as our brothers showed their age.

Their power.

"Tell me, with Sebek out of the way, what do you really want to vote on?" Osiris asked.

No, he *Charmed*. The weight of it, the unbearable force slamming Aldric and Cassius to their knees with startled gasps. Drakon stayed standing, barely, but that didn't stop the words from spilling out. "True equality. Eternals by popular vote, not power. Exposure to the humans."

What they meant couldn't be taken back now, a truth like none other. Drakon realized it just as fast, shaking his head. "You bastard—"

"A goal you can't accomplish without more power. Allies that we've supplied to your cause, but Cael can sway that with his age if he wins, can't he?" Osiris asked, with a finality more certain than death. "You think to play me at my own game, Drakon? That's dangerous for someone so young."

Whatever worry I'd had that he'd follow through with the threat died then as Drakon swallowed his pride, gritting his teeth. "I'll kill you for this. Maybe not now, but one day. I fucking swear it."

Osiris's head tilted, and he stood tall.

"There's a long line of shallow graves full of men that have vowed the same," he said, a spark of fire across his skin promising a fight if Drakon just asked for it.

He had the good sense to step back.

"And even if you do manage it, you still have to deal with the rest of us. Which I can't even say I'd be mad about. You look like you'd be a good fight," Nero added with a whistle, cracking his knuckles.

Drakon, faced with the elders of the Vivas Crypt—Osiris the Kingslayer, Nero the Emperor, and Eirik the Tactician, the fabled Emperor's shadow—dipped his head. He didn't try to go to blows like I half expected him to, even against what the Eternium was likely pushing on him. Instead, he looked over to the couch, to Aaliyah and the man she was trying to save.

"So, do you hold on to this righteous anger and hold out some paltry hope to try to kill us? Or do you trust that we still have the upper hand here?" Osiris pushed, giving him no time to recover from the onslaught of power that had been thrown at him.

Drakon contemplated it, his lips curling back as his tension showed in the flex of his hands and the clench of his jaw.

"I will kill you one day, Vivas. I fucking swear it." Drakon's promise went on deaf ears as Osiris raised a brow and didn't respond. Drakon ground his teeth as he moved on. "Do I even want to know what's happening right now?"

I hummed, happy to step forward and act as the distraction. Though that didn't mean I'd let him get close, still functioning as a block between him and Aaliyah. The last thing we needed was this place going up in flames with her still locked inside the head of a madman.

"Don't you know a human sacrifice when you see one? Such a young, innocent Dragonkin. Too pure for this world," I quipped, taking the moment to ease the tension, smiling widely when Drakon let out a long breath, as though searching for patience.

I flexed my hands, quelling the shaking, forcing a steady breath.

"What Adrian meant to say is Aaliyah is trying to desoupify this lovely gentleman's brain," Nero added, not at all helpfully.

Drakon grunted, rubbing his temples. "Fuck me, there's two of them. You can have a different shtick, you know."

Nero huffed, walking forward and wrapping an arm around Drakon's shoulders. He pulled the man down, acting as if he hadn't been ready to just rip his throat out. Drakon took offense, snarling and tensing up, though it wasn't enough to get Nero to let go. "Technically, if we want to promote accuracy, I'm *far* worse. I'm the original, after all."

Nero's merciless swagger was only accented by the smirk he plastered on as he pulled away, just as Drakon snapped his teeth at him. Drakon's wary eyes traced where he stood as Nero bowed low. "Now, did you come for an actual reason? Or, just to try to fight Osiris? Because honestly, it wasn't your best choice."

I still waited for more rage, for the crumbling of Drakon's already declining patience. Dragonkin weren't known for letting go of things, not like this, but he just crossed his arms. Seemed Osiris hit the nail on the head with his wants.

We could still help him, even if he fucking hated us, and that was the crux of all good deals.

"Unless the mystery man on your floor can scrounge us up five extra votes, Exilium is going to fail, even with our Challenges," Drakon said, grunting. "And with Cael running rampant, so will a vote on introduction to the human world."

"Not quite. Should only be four, assuming Axius does as I expect," I added, fully confident that he'd at the very least try to persuade Hyland away from his current path. "Then, three at least, assuming this guy is any help at all? If we wipe Darius out, that just might pull the leverage we need."

But that was, unfortunately, my only bit of good news.

Three votes down going into the night wasn't our best odds.

"We always knew it was going to be close," Fallon said, brushing his hair back.

I stole a second, just one, to check him over. The *Call* still clung to our minds, the nagging need to hunt like stepping on jagged rock but not being able to shake them off. He shook, his hands trembling as he flexed them, hiding that pain well. Even the marks of the sun, the jagged black lines, still hadn't fully faded. And that was nothing to say of the Fae Bargain on his chest, or the haunted look in his eyes.

Osiris was exhausted, his eyes dull as he shook off whatever he'd faced in the Pits. Darius was getting to him. Eirik was a mess, but at least his beast settled for the first time in what had to be ages. Nero was still dealing with the effects of getting his memories back, his mind still scrambled up, his body following closely behind.

We were in shambles, not a good look for a united front.

Especially not with the dilemma I was facing to add a cherry on top of our shit pie. My nails bit into my palm, and I longed for the sour hint of pain.

"If the vote fails, we still have this," Osiris said, producing the vial of High Fae Mana, as if on cue. The shimmery gold liquid sloshed in the small diamond glass. A possibility for a few more votes, but even that could go haywire. At the end of the day, who knew what would come spewing out of Sebek's mouth? "Sebek will tell the truth tonight, whether or not he desires to."

Nothing good, for sure.

Drakon nodded. "And you'll really do it if we come out on the losing side? Challenge him?"

Osiris's eyes flashed red, and he bared his teeth, but it was Nero who stepped forward. Always the gladiator, he didn't even look fazed, brushing his hair back, showing eyes that were only fire. It was one of the few times Nero would lose the bubbly face.

When a fight was coming.

"I'll be Challenging Sebek," he said, all bravado and strength. "Osiris will take out Darius. You worry about the rest."

My heart dropped, and Drakon narrowed his eyes, scrutinizing Nero's stance. Osiris stared on, as well, looking shocked yet unable to get any words out.

"Don't look at me like that. I'm of age, technically," Nero said with a click of his tongue when Osiris opened his mouth to protest. "And you and I both know the bureaucracies of the job would lead you to an early grave, Osi. I'll take on Sebek. I need to do this. It's my fight."

He glanced back then, to where Aaliyah still sat silent. For decades he'd watched her get torn apart, unable to do anything about it as our Maker, her Uncle, broke her down and ripped her open. That rage simmered in his eyes now, hidden behind his fragile smile.

"If we're really fucking lucky, it won't come to that," Drakon added. "But be prepared anyway. The last thing we need is dead weight."

"No, hopefully not. But if it does? *Gods*. I can't wait to punch that worthless fuck in the face." Nero chuckled. "You don't have to worry. If it comes to Challenge. I won't lose."

It hid the real worry in his words, the understanding that fighting Sebek was the last option, because it wasn't one we ever expected to survive. Aaliyah wouldn't like it. She barely accepted it with Osiris, since he was the eldest.

To lose Prince again?

"We need to tell her," Eirik said, voicing my thoughts with a grunt, and Nero hesitated.

"She'll hate it." He sighed as he rubbed the bridge of his nose.

"Yes, but she deserves to know," Eirik finished, the grumble of his wolf adding to his words.

Melancholy silence filled the room, the weight of the evening bearing down. I looked to Nero, to the brother we just got back, and tried to find it in me to accept this choice. It was the right move, strategically. Gave us the best odds at winning if it did come down to a fight.

That didn't make it sit any easier in my stomach.

"Nothing to be done about it now. Drakon, leave. We know our plan, you know your part. We need time to prepare." Osiris's words were final, and he turned away, giving the Dragonkin his back.

"Don't have to tell me twice," Drakon grumbled, his face pinching at the obvious disrespect, but he didn't fight it, just left, his second and enforcer following closely behind him.

Though not before Cassius gave one more look to Eirik, the feral hint of a challenge simmering there.

A problem to deal with later.

"What do we do now?" I asked.

Nero took a seat next to Aaliyah, taking her hand softly in his. Everyone was quick to follow, needing to be close to her. It was a mess of elbows and cursed words as we worked it out, sprawled around her where she sat.

"Wait for her. As long as we have to," Nero mumbled, never taking his eyes off her face.

As long as we had to.

Each second I got to look at her, to breathe her in, was more time than I'd thought I'd have, and I cherished every single one. Counting down the moments I had left.

Before the First Rights decided our fates.

CHAPTER 55

AALIYAH

The pull of the Void, like always, made the hair on the back of my neck stand. It was involuntary, a panicked response that came from my experience with the power that surrounded me. It picked at me even now, the touch teasing and curious. I opened my eyes slowly, prepared for the endless mercury, or even an orderly box with memories trapped about it. I found neither.

The room wasn't endless, which at least that was a comfort, but that was where the similarities between my mind and the man's ended. The ground was fragmented, the obsidian sky meshing into silver. The memories weren't orderly, as bits of them leaked onto the Void, flashes of people I didn't know sprinting past me before fading away. And the *screams*, they were so loud they drowned out my thoughts, made it hard to focus on anything.

How long had he been like this? Years of being trapped, decades, *centuries*. I'd barely survived mine with Prince by my side, and he'd likely been stuck down there for so much longer.

"I don't even know where to start," I mumbled, distraught by what I saw.

I looked to my hands, letting out a breath when I saw at least they were in color, and I could speak. I wasn't sure if that meant I was in the Void or not, but I'd take a physical form right now.

It made me feel safe.

It felt insurmountable, the task that I'd suddenly found myself in. I had no idea where to even start, what to *do*.

I might have been in a bit over my head.

"That makes two of us," a voice called, a mock kindness burrowed in a seething anger that made me flinch. "I don't know how you keep managing to drag me here, but you couldn't have worse timing."

My shoulders dropped as I looked over my shoulder, catching Azer's irritated scowl. His hair was wet, hanging loosely around his head, a towel covering the lower half of his body.

"Azer—" I stumbled, not even sure how to go about apologizing. I hadn't meant to bring him here, didn't even think of it. I looked away, giving him my back. "I'm sorry, I don't—"

He huffed, what sounded like a mumbled curse under his breath, before he snapped his fingers.

"Oh, calm down. I was wearing a *towel*. I'm decent, if you don't mind telling me what the fuck this is," he grumbled, as I turned back around. He was wearing a T-shirt now, loose pants around his hips, both of which looked like they were made of the shadows themselves, the material so black it seemed fake. He glared around the room at the memories that danced like icicles in the sky as he rubbed his temples. "Is this your boy? Damn, and I thought your soul was fucked up."

I let out a breath, following his gaze. "No, this is ... someone else. I'm trying to fix him."

Azer laughed, though it didn't reach his face or eyes. "Fix him? This is a mess, darling. There's no fixing this. I'm still trying to decide what *this* is."

Another figment dashed past, this time a young boy being chased by another as laughter filled the air.

"He's a man Osiris found in the Pits. I'm trying to save him," I said, watching as both boys faded away, their laughter going with them.

"Why in the devil would you do that?" Azer asked, his mouth open like I was crazy as he rubbed the bridge of his nose. "Look, I get it. You don't share my happily budding relationship with murder, and you'd rather not dabble in it, but I hate to tell you this: you're at the Eternium. I don't know if you realized this, but the Eternals called for your head on a pretty little spike. You need to get it out of your mind that you have the luxury of kindness, because you don't, Aaliyah. This is not what you should be focusing on right now."

His chastising words stung. I'd spent so long trying to figure out what I was, hoping that it would fix all my problems ... but then we found out, and I realized that nothing would ever be that simple.

Now I was faced with this. Hurting people wasn't something I ever wanted to do. It conflicted with my nature to just let this go. Would I even still be the same person if I did? If I backed away and let this man die.

Cold steel against my back, Castillion's laugh like a nightmare ringing in my ears.

The only way to do that was to turn into something I *promised* myself I wouldn't. I wasn't a monster, and I refused to be one. The powers that I had, the Void ... it didn't have to be evil.

"No, I'm going to help him. One way or another," I said, resolute. Azer actually jolted back, eyes narrowing when I turned away. I traced the floating memories, picking one in the distance that was close enough to the ground. "You can leave if you don't want to help."

Azer sighed, the sound turning into a groan as he stomped after me. "We've gone over that I leave when the Void wants me to leave. Gods, you're insufferable."

Red pulsed, irritation sparking in the air. His form was somehow more stable in the Void. His face came slightly into view, his eyes hollow bits of white in the air. He fluttered around before stopping by one of the many fissures that was spread across the room. The air cooled, and for a second his hand flashed over the surface, as if asking me to reach out and touch.

A starting point.

"What is he doing?" Azer asked, turning to me with a scowl that had me backing up. "Wait, actually, I think he might be on to something. Hold your hand out, would you?"

He made a grabbing motion with his hand, grumbling when I didn't follow his direction.

"I'm not touching Red," I said, gritting my teeth when Azer rolled his eyes.

"That wasn't what I was going to say," Azer said, Red lingering close to me as Azer crossed his arms. "You're scared of the Void, boring but understandable. But you're not scared of Red, and at this point, he's little more than a chunk of it that has some sentience. Wherever this is, it isn't the Void, not exactly. A piece of it maybe, but nowhere near whole, and you'll need whole to take care of this."

Red glowed, warmth starting at the tips of my fingers and lighting all the way up to my eyes. Azer saw it, grinning. "Red is your work-around, your bridge. He's how you use your gifts."

"Won't it hurt Red?" I asked, and Azer contemplated it for a second.

"Probably not. You won't actually touch him, and like I said, the Void doesn't even realize he's here." Azer's words did little to soothe my worried thoughts.

I could feel Red's excitement in the air, the emotion so potent it literally flashed along my mind, like a shot of dopamine directly to my brain. It had my entire body relaxing, and a smile curling onto my lips even as worry for him grew.

"Are you really okay with that?" I asked, turning to look at the mass that swirled in the air.

Dust danced in front of me, as if Red was swaying to the pulse of the Void. His emotions seemed clearer, more concise than they had been before. The one that stood out most, that hammered me down, was the pride.

Azer huffed, rolling his eyes. "Please. It's not like you can kill him. If anything, you should be worried about who you're trying to save. You want to piece this man back together? This is how. Different applications and all that."

I didn't like the idea of using Red like that, the risk of sending him on nagging at the back of my mind, especially considering what he was. What I was. That didn't stop him from fluttering around, almost like he was trying to boost my spirits. Like he was excited to try.

"Okay, Red," I said, smiling weakly as I walked up to the piece. "We'll try it your way."

It was small, barely a couple of inches long, and it hovered in the air, the sounds it made getting louder the closer I got. There were growled words, the pitches of an argument hitting me in the chest as I froze. Indecision warred as Red flashed again, just like he had in front of the cellar when we'd met.

I swallowed and reached out, running a tentative hand over the glassy surface. Red clung to the movement, swelling when I pulled everything forward. My gifts were warm, settling into my bones as black fissures spread across the glass.

The Void flowed around him, the silver of the floor wobbling as Red bounced. My thoughts were ended abruptly, a shiver of dread shooting down my spine as Azer clapped his hands.

I wasn't sure what I expected, but it shifted at my touch, cracking open. The flash of a memory that spilled out was little more than a fading sense of déjà vu. It was the man, screaming at another. His words were disjointed and completely unrecognizable. The only thing I got from it was emotion.

He was outraged.

Disappointed.

I shivered as the shard pulled away, hovering in the air for just a second longer before it shot off, crashing into another piece. The shards melded together, forming a new chunk. They shifted between several colors before it eventually settled on clear again. At least they didn't disappear.

"Wonderful," Azer said, dropping his hands. He watched me carefully, his next words measurably quieter. "I'm so glad that worked. All this stress isn't good for my skin."

He ran the back of his hand over his forehead, and I snorted at his cheeky smile. It was so odd, seeing him and catching the little ticks that reminded me of Mom. I didn't have many memories of her, not enough to paint a whole picture, but something about the way he moved told me it was the same.

The tilt of his nose, the way he started every laugh with a soft snort. It was comforting, and it helped to settle me as Red's presence grew

I hummed, following Red toward the new piece. It was louder now as the memory filled out, the words clearer, the emotions more vivid.

I won't speak of this again, Darius.

I had a feeling that was the voice of our tortured soul, the twisting to his words holding an accent I'd never heard. The visage of the small, angry man that had been Osiris's hell appeared for a second in the glass. The hint of it flashed in the space in front of me.

You've gone soft, Atlas.

I lifted my arms again, rocking my head back and forth. I reached for the Void, for the pit in me that called to the dark. This time, it was Red's presence I felt, the brush of his familiar cold bringing goosebumps to my skin.

It was easier to embrace, to hold on to when it was Red I felt.

His emotions seeped into me, and for a second it felt like his hands were on mine, like I could see more than just mist in the air where he was.

I shivered, touching the shard, watching as it shot off.

I followed the memory on instinct, chasing a puzzle that slowly played out in front of me. The fight grew more real, and each time I touched another shard, the memory felt less like Atlas's and more like mine. Until the entire thing flashed in front of me.

Darius had wanted to join in on the Natural war, wanted to fight to gain allies. He'd wanted to kill the Reapers, but Atlas, at the time the Mythic Eternal, had stopped him, had shot him down even when the fear for my kind was so strong it was splitting families.

He fought for us, even when no one else wanted to.

"All right then, what do you say to a divide and conquer?" Azer asked, touching his own shard, the Void obeying on command, dark shards splintering through his piece.

It dashed off, ramming into another. I nodded, Azer already ambling off.

I moved to the next memory, fixing as I went. My shadow deformed under my feet as power rose in me, flexing from the bottoms of my heels to the tips of my fingers. It sparked like fire, heating me up as Red's chill grew deeper.

Hours must have passed, days maybe, but time in the Void had never worked the same as time on the outside, and I could only hope the others weren't worried. I didn't feel the same pull I had before, the distinct feeling that it was time to go.

But the Void showed its presence in other ways, my arms growing heavy, my steps growing shorter and shorter. I kept trudging along. I wandered, until the shards had become few and far between, and the life of Atlas had played out before me. Even his years in the Pits, as his tortured descent into madness and endless hunger, ripped him apart. The way he'd beg for a death that wouldn't come, likely to do with what he was, the writhing animal seeming to appear out of nowhere in his memories. A part of him that was feral.

A beast with feline grace, his head shaped like that of an eagle, with large brown wings sprouting from its back.

Griffon. He was a Griffon.

I was lost in my thoughts, watching another bit of him struggling against his chains, my stomach twisting at the sight, when something cold pressed to my neck. I froze, eyes darting to Red, who fluttered nervously.

"Who are you?" the voice asked, gruff from misuse, his chill a living thing.

This was a soul, the characteristic flutter of emotions in the air like a whip. He shouldn't have been able to speak, but ... then again, neither should I. His words were clear, not like they'd been whispered in my head.

I jolted when he reached for me, pulling away from his hand so his soul didn't find contact with my skin.

"Don't, Atlas," I said, turning to look at him. His clear olive skin was a deeper shade of brown than how he looked outside of this place, his eyes a medley of blues and greens that sparkled with crazed rage. His hair, a rich black, was cut short, exposing high cheekbones and sharp, pointed ears. I expected him to look more human, but there was an ethereal grace to him when he stalked forward, his face distinctly avian. Something about it had my mind firing off warning signals, like it knew it was seeing something ... wrong. He was large, spanning a height that had me taking a step back, fear climbing up my throat unbidden. I swallowed when he bared his teeth in a growl. "I'm Aaliyah, I know you're scared—"

He screamed, and I covered my ears to hide from it. He cupped his own, the knife in his hand digging into his cheek. It bled, but when he pulled away to point it at me again, the mark was already gone.

In its place was a swift streak of light, like a nick on his soul that whispered to my blood and dragged up the call of the Void. He wasn't really here, his body was still in the real world, I assumed with mine, but that didn't mean he couldn't do damage. There was a very real chance he could hurt me here.

"What have you done to me?" he snarled, dipping low to the ground, looking less and less like a man and more like a monster.

I took several steps back, lifting my hand to stop his advance.

"Stop, you're not—" I managed, barely dodging his chaotic swing.

Red came to my call, like a vicious wave that Atlas didn't see coming. The Void sang as the shadows around the room dashed forward, and Red barreled into him, stopping his next slash. Atlas was thrown off me, crashing into the silver floor. Red, taking a full shape for the first time, glared on. I caught the sight of strong cheekbones and sharp eyes that seemed to bore into Atlas. He was there for just a second, wavering in his transparency, yet unyielding as Atlas stood again, wiping the blood from his face before it faded away.

Only he couldn't move toward me again.

"When a lady tells you to stop, you do," Azer cut in, his voice startlingly calm, a simmer of rage beneath his words as he stepped closer to me. The Void whipped angrily around his head, the hinting of two horns peeking out from his hair, the golden spirals riddled with black. "Rather rude to rush her like that, don't you think?"

Atlas snapped, his face contorting like Eirik's, sharpening into a vicious point as the Griffon behind his eyes shot forward.

"Calm down," I whispered.

The shadows stuck to his skin, like bindings, tying him to the floor. They moved as Azer did, pinching tighter when he clenched his fists.

Atlas's eyes cleared just enough for him to look at the bonds that held him still. "*Reapers.*"

"That's right," I whispered. He didn't struggle again, that clarity staying in his eyes as he looked around the Void. His face twisted, a dreadful fear boiling up there. "We're in your head right now, sifting through your memories to try to piece you back together enough to wake you up. Do you know where you've been the last few centuries?"

"Hell," he grunted, shaking his head as if trying to dislodge the thought. "Never heard of Reapers being able to do this. Another trick up your sleeve. Good. You need as many as you can get. If you're here to get me out, that must mean you're truly desperate."

There was a stark hope in his voice that hurt even more when I knew how much he'd lost to try to turn the outcome.

"Oh, isn't that cute? Where did you find this guy again?" Azer asked, snorting with a roll of his eyes.

I ignored him, gritting my teeth.

"The war went forward, after you were trapped in the Eternium Pits by Darius the Great," I explained, watching the emotions flicker over Atlas's face: confusion, disbelief, and finally rage. "I'm not here for your help to save the Reapers."

"Darius would never do something of the sort. He's my closest kin!" The disbelief was warped by the widening of his eyes, his breaths hard as he grimaced. His hands twitched, his eyes darting around the room. There was a panicked hilt to his voice, a stutter in his breath as his body revolted. "You *lie.*"

I knew that look well.

"You're scared," I whispered, carefully. The silence that flooded the room suddenly made me realize that the screaming was still going on in the background. Atlas's stance shifted, and he tensed against the bonds Azer kept him trapped in. "Scared that I'm right. You already had your doubts. I've seen the fights."

His head tipped back, and he laughed dryly. "Another Reaper power?"

I shook my head, clenching and unclenching my fists, thinking of all the time I spent in my own cell, watching the guards sneer from their side of the glass.

Red flowed around me, a comfort I breathed in.

"I spent a lot of my life locked up, too. I learned how to read quicker than most that a smile that hides malice cuts deeper than barely veiled disgust."

Castillion's cruel grin, like always, was the one I saw. His face twisted, his eyes alight with excitement as his knife dug deep. Still, he'd smile, cooing words like he wasn't flaying me alive.

Never make noise.

"He did it to take your spot, to help in the War," I said, gently.

Atlas's face shifted, his skin rolling against bone as his beast tried to force its way out.

"Then why are you here?" he asked, his eyes on the ground. Betrayal was a bitter thing, and Atlas's jaw clenched, a vein popping there as he gritted his teeth. "Why not leave me to rot?"

"Because we need your help. We need Darius removed as Mythic Eternal, and with your life tied to his—"

Atlas let out a barked laugh that crackled in his chest, cutting me off. "No one could beat him. Not with our *Inhama* feeding his luck."

The way he said that word, *Inhama,* carried a warmth. I reached for the *Hallen Bonds* on my wrist, finding comfort in the touch of them. He watched me do it, his head jerking away.

"Yes," I whispered.

"There is no undoing it," he said, shaking his head. "It is everlasting."

"We can cross that bridge when we get there," I responded, as the floor flexed beneath our feet. The hint of the Void pressed on me, like a whisper, a warning that we'd been here too long.

I looked around the room. A lot of his memories were still fragmented, but enough of them were pieced back together for him to be at least partially whole here ... and I just had to hope that it was enough to wake him up. Hopefully, his mind would heal the rest itself.

"Times up, baby Imperial," Azer said as he let the restraints holding Atlas fall. Red wasn't as quick to let him up, his presence like a live wire at my back. He stayed in that space in between me and the Void, ready to move if Atlas came at me again.

"We have to go," I whispered. "Are you coming with?"

Atlas eyed me cautiously before he sighed. "Do I have a choice?"

He rubbed his wrists, the skin clear here in the Void, so different from what he'd find outside of it. His autonomy had been ripped away, his pride dragged down by the weight of what should have been his family.

"You always have a choice," I whispered, giving him a moment to think on it.

He did, several seconds passing as I saw the weight on his shoulder bare down. There was a moment when I even thought he would choose to stay. He grunted, and reached out to take my hand, no longer reading like the dead when he did. I took it carefully, only breathing when I didn't feel the familiar pull of a spirit slipping past me. The touch of his skin made my stomach twist with dread, and sweat pooled on the back of my neck.

His eyes cleared before he nodded. Silence filled the room, Azer still watching me. He didn't look away, even when I caught his eyes fully.

"What is it?" I asked, shuffling on my feet as he huffed.

I was ready for the next insult, or for his gruff laugh to remind me that "death is always waiting!" Instead, he walked forward, placing his hand on my head, ruffling my hair. There was more weight to it this time, more conscious thought, before he pulled back. "Be safe out there, yeah?"

He grumbled it out, but the look of worry in his eyes was genuine.

"You, too," I whispered back, smiling as he stepped away.

His eyes rolled hard, a snort following it as he waved at me over his shoulder. I got one last look before the shadows at his feet shot up, dragging him into the silver below.

The Void flexed again, urging me to move, and Red grew anxious as he coiled around my shoulders. I let out a breath and closed my eyes, doing as I'd been taught, Azer's words guiding me where I wanted to go.

Home.

Back to the life I was determined not to lose again.

CHAPTER 56

FALLON

Hours had passed since we sat by Aaliyah's side, hours that had been filled with watching her, waiting for the moment when she'd open her eyes again, so I could take in the calming lavender of them.

I couldn't sleep, not until she was awake, not until I could *talk* to her. The fight we'd had left a sour taste in my mouth that was built on my own fears. This wasn't something I'd normally cave on, her safety something I held viciously close, but it seemed like the more I stepped back, the more I realized how stupid it'd been.

She was my everything. Her happiness was something I'd always been hunting to find, and this petty fight wasn't worth losing that. I trusted her, and she wanted to save him, this man who likely didn't deserve whatever the fuck it was Darius did to him. Would it be easier to find a way to kill him?

Absolutely.

But she thought there was another way, that resolution in her eyes strong even as she stared us all down, unwilling to let us dig ourselves into yet another grave, another rope around our necks, labeling us exactly what we'd been trying to avoid. Monsters.

She didn't want that for us. Who was I to tell her no?

Fuck, I'd been such an asshole. Such a controlling, bullheaded *asshole*.

My fight with my demons was my own, and while I was learning how to lean on people, that didn't make them any less mine.

I struggled with it as I brushed my knuckles over her cheek, checking again for warmth, to make sure her breathing was still steady. She didn't need someone who would tear her down; she needed someone to stand by her side.

Like she'd stood by mine. She deserved the best I could give her.

The room was silent, and I stewed in my thoughts, boiled alive by them. I was the only one still awake, the others exhausted to the point of collapse, leading up to the final hours before First Rights. Osiris had stayed the longest, but even he had faded to the call of sleep, sprawled across the floor, his hand touching hers. It was fine; they needed it for tonight.

We all did.

Her breathing hitched, and I sat up straight, my bones popping after hours of stagnancy. I waited, my entire body tense as Aaliyah's eyes opened slowly, her head dropping forward, a groan on her lips. Rich violet peeked through white lashes, and I heaved a sigh of relief.

"Welcome back, trouble," I whispered.

My fingers were still on her cheek when it flushed, the spark of her touch igniting there. When she beamed at me, it was with a look of pride telling me what I already knew. She'd done it, whatever she'd gone in there to do.

"Fallon—" she started.

"Wait, let me say something," I said, making sure her eyes stayed on mine so I couldn't hide myself behind the ice in my blood. I leaned in, pressing my forehead to hers. I wanted to kiss her, mindlessly, to remind myself that she was mine ... but didn't want to push that on her now. Instead, I ran my nose across the tip of hers, sighing as she hummed. She sank into the touch, not pulling away like she damned well could have. I'd have deserved it.

"I want to apologize for the way I acted. Things got heated. I got scared. It's no excuse, and I want you to know I'm sorry," I whispered, making sure she heard every word. They were just words for now, but they had intent, and I'd do whatever I could to prove I meant them.

"Your voice means just as much to this family as the rest, and you deserve to speak it. I never want to take that away from you."

She always seemed to know what to do, as she lifted her hand to my cheek, forcing me to look at her again. I hadn't even realized I'd looked away. The warmth of her reminded me I was alive ... reminding me she was too.

"Thank you, Fallon," she said, her thumb running over the back of my hand before she placed soft lips against the back. "I didn't mean to scare you."

I gave a tug, pulling her into my arms, wrapping myself securely around her. The way she molded to me cooled the fear that still bubbled inside of me. And it was fear. This Eternium had bred nothing but fear, and right at the top of that was losing her. To Sebek, to the Eternals.

To my own selfish whims.

"Scare me every day, Ali. I don't care. Just don't stop being mine," I whispered.

That was the only thing I couldn't take. I'd stand by her, against any fucker that dared to get in her way.

But I could only do it by her side.

When I pulled back, she was still smiling. The soft expression brightened every bit of her face, her cheeks more filled out now, her eyes cradled by laugh lines. I reached into my pocket on instinct, searching for one of the chocolates I kept there.

I pulled out two pieces. One with a familiar foil, the soft smell of strawberry slipping past it, the other the little golden piece Grigen had given me.

I'd found mine in the wreck that had been Archon's home and promptly forgotten I'd even found it. They'd taken them all when we'd been caught, eaten most of the ones I'd had on me, I'd guess. This was the only one I'd found there, likely one of the last I had. The stock had been getting low for some time, more so now that I had someone to give them to.

Part of me still wanted to hoard it, this delicacy that had reminded me so much of home, but Aldovin chocolate was just that, a memory I wanted to live through again, one I wanted to share with the woman I loved.

Just like she had that first time I'd offered her a piece, she looked up at me, wide violet eyes enough to bring me to my knees, and just like then, they took my breath away. My heart sped up, my stomach fluttering. I took her hand, chuckling like a boy with a budding crush, before I set the chocolate pieces in it. "One from me, and one from Grigen."

Aaliyah was protesting, but I was already closing her hand. "Take them, trouble. They were meant for you."

She opened her fingers and picked up Grigen's piece like she was going to hand it back. "Share them with me? I don't want to eat them alone," she whispered, opening the golden foil.

A soft emotion slipped over her face as she took the first bite, savoring it with a smile, before bringing the other half up to me. I took it from her fingers, tongue sliding across the tips. It was sweet, a light milk chocolate with a caramel center. I licked my lips, picking up the Aldovin chocolate when she didn't move for a second, chuckling at the blush on her face.

I took a bite, closing my eyes at the subtle sweetness, before holding up the other half to her lips. Aaliyah's eyes misted before she opened her mouth. I set the strawberry sweetness on her tongue. Watching the remains of that part of my life fade into her memories, as well, always to be there.

My time as a human haunted me, always would, but she held it with me now, remembered the taste and reminisced on the memories of a life that was still mine. Just new, bright, and when I thought of that time, it wasn't the nightmare that I saw. It wasn't the bloodied sandy beach stained with the sins of my turn. It was a smile and kindness in dark eyes that would be proud of me, that wanted me to do this. To live.

Aislinn would be proud.

"I love you, Aaliyah." *More than any treat, than any painting. More than anything in this world.*

Aaliyah's lips pressed against mine in a sugary sweet kiss, one I'd spend the rest of my long life savoring.

"I love you, too, Fallon," she whispered.

A few breathless moments more of silence were all we got before a groan filled the air. Adrian chose the perfect moment to stir, his eyes opening and his gasp making Aaliyah jolt. "Sweetheart, you're awake!"

Her sudden dose of fear faded, and she smiled as he pulled her into his arms.

"I leave for bread and come back to a dumpster fire." He touched her everywhere he could, placing an obnoxious number of kisses on her face, only stopping when she pulled away to laugh. Even then, he didn't quite let go of her, running his nose along her neck. "How was your trip, love? Tell me everything."

"It was divine." The body still plastered to the floor groaned.

The fact that he spoke at all was in improvement, and Aaliyah beamed at the sound of it as the man, all seven feet of him, sat up. He stretched, showing ribs that poked a bit too close to the surface, his bones cracking, his still-open wounds oozing.

He looked like hell. His hair was a matted mess, his eyes dimmed with pain and a crazy that nothing would ever solve, but he was coher-ent, awake.

Fucking *talking*.

Aaliyah had worked a goddamned miracle.

"Well, you're already doing better than I expected. Not that I trust that as a measure of your sanity," I said.

He grunted, the sound half laugh, half gasp as he clutched his ribs.

"Easy, Atlas," Aaliyah said as she pulled out of Adrian's arms, going to the wounded man's side, checking over the lesions that had split back open. Jealousy bubbled in my chest, and had I sensed even a touch of attraction between them, I would have pulled her away.

Caveman accusations be fucking damned.

But there was only worry there, Aaliyah and her caring nature. I loved it about her, but Christ was it a danger to her. Eirik stirred, and Osiris was quick to follow, then Nero. Safety in numbers, knowing each of us were here settled me a bit.

At least she had a few of us to pay attention, to watch out for her.

"Fear not for my mind," Atlas hissed when Aaliyah pressed on a tender rib. His teeth flashed, the mark of a beast behind his eyes as his face contorted. "Aaliyah has already told me of your plight. I'll take the seat when Darius has been bested. Hopefully, sway the vote your way for Exilium. If Sebek is as rotten now as he was then, I imagine he deserves this."

Adrian snorted, seemingly at ease, as he inched closer to the two. He made a big show of slinging his arm over Aaliyah's shoulder, putting himself between her and Atlas. "Oh, he's about one wrong turn away from a full train wreck, friend. Pretty sure he plans to kill all the Eternals that oppose him."

Atlas nodded, unshaken by the words. He popped his jaw, a sick crack sounding in the air as he grunted. A tooth landed in his hand a second later, rotted and broken.

"Glad to see at least one thing hasn't changed. Hopefully, my word is still worth something," he said, looking down at himself for just long enough to grimace. "But that isn't the issue we need to focus on now."

He was rod thin, in absolutely no condition to fight, and wouldn't be this Eternium. I still wasn't sure it was worth keeping him alive, even like this ...

Aaliyah looked at him with another worried hum, and I held my tongue.

"You're tied to him," Osiris voiced, stepping forward. "Darius."

"Right." Atlas's head dipped. He lifted his arm, showing a shallow vein of gold that traced it. "We have been since we were but boys. It was a way to foster a strong bond, common among my tribe to do with those born on the same day—brothers of one sun. Never could I have expected him to turn on me like this. We'll need to break it before we can take him down."

The gold veins flexed, and he hid them like I'd seen Osiris do so many times. The mark like a brand. Osiris watched it, but for once, he didn't cover his wrist. The marks there, the swirling, clashing bands of lavender and black, were displayed.

"You sure you're up to facing his Retaliation alone?" Nero asked, pointing his look at Osiris. "I'm sure we could find another way."

I'd never seen Osiris's eyes so viciously bright before, a determination in them that was typically reserved for Nero and I. That blood-thirsty need to fight.

"I will not lose." Was his unflinching answer.

"What about Sebek? You can't do it all," Aaliyah chimed in. "We still need to figure something out if Exilium fails."

There was silence, the room's tension amping up. Aaliyah noticed it, her eyes narrowing as she looked around the room. For once, I wished she couldn't read people like she could. Her perceptiveness meant you couldn't slide anything past her, not that this was something I'd want to keep from her.

But it made it difficult, and it meant giving her a pain she didn't deserve.

"I'll be Challenging him if it comes to it," Nero said quietly, watching Aaliyah carefully as her eyes flew wide.

She stood up on shaking legs, stepping toward him, into his arms as he wrapped himself around her. "This wasn't the plan."

Nero took her face in his steady palms, studying every inch of her expression as his own strong act crumbled.

"We don't have a choice, Aaliyah. Hopefully, it doesn't even come to it, but if it does—" He took a breath. "Then I'll be sure to make him pay for everything he ever did to you, for every scream he tried to silence and every bit of blood he spilled. I need this, Aaliyah. He let you suffer for years, decades. If he doesn't pay with Exilium, then he'll pay by my hand."

Aaliyah's head dipped as she thought through the same options we had, no doubt narrowing down to the exact situation we were in now.

"I don't like this," she whispered, eventually folding her arms around Nero, hugging him so tightly he grunted against the top of her head.

"I know." Was his solemn reply.

Here was to hoping, for the first time, that tonight didn't end in a fight.

Atlas grunted, drawing attention to him as he picked at the sodden clothes that clung to his body. In a blink, it seemed like he'd gained ten pounds, his cheeks losing some of the hollowness. He flexed his shoulders, groaning as another bone popped. "Right. I do hate to intrude, but do you have something I could wear?"

He was skin and bones and wearing precisely nothing but the blanket he held to his front. Not to mention his size. He was big, slightly larger than Eirik, who stepped in front of him. They stared each other down, for a long second just sizing each other up, like two circling beasts.

Eirik was the first to break, grinning with all teeth as he reached a hand out, one Atlas took. Unflinching. Watching their other halves come to play was a horrifying fucking sight. Their skin pulled taut, their jaws and chins sharpening, and their eyes filling with savage intelligence that made my skin crawl.

It was a good thing Eirik's wolf had settled down. I couldn't handle any more close calls.

"Eirik," my brother grunted, his face falling back into place. He kept his head high, dipping it just once.

"Atlas," the Mythic replied back, his voice twisted from years of screaming.

No other words, no other noises. They just let go and ambled off toward the back room, Eirik supporting Atlas so he didn't have to limp.

"Well, they're going to make fast friends," Adrian said, whistling. He was quick to find Aaliyah's side again before looking at the clock on the wall. All of us did, though no one said anything about it.

Adrian just smiled, that easy way he did, hiding the fear in his eyes as he took her hand. "Come on, sweetheart, time to get ready."

Chapter 57

Aaliyah

The Eternium moved like something that sought attention, the walls wobbling just out of view, like the Void when I was close enough to touch. Now was no exception, walking into the large open ballroom, staring down from the staircase after the Sage had announced us again, and finding it decorated with a vintage flair. Tables were strewn about, a low warm light giving it an almost ominous presence.

There were so many I couldn't see the end of them as we walked silently down to find our own table. The air was somber, even the other Eternals keeping to themselves as they shuffled past to find seats. A hand settled on my shoulder, and I looked up at Eirik as he watched me.

His silent confidence had always bolstered my own, made me feel like I could take on the world with him at my side. His hand moved higher, brushing against the silvery scar on my shoulder, a comfort to us both. No matter what today brought, we would get through it.

We had to.

"Ali!" A voice cut through the crowd, followed by the sound of grunting as a body shoved their way through a throng of some of the most powerful people I'd ever seen. They stumbled apart, audible gasps of outrage swallowed by my *oomph* as Eliza ran directly into my arms.

I smiled, wrapping her in a hug. "Liz!"

I caught eyes with Dezen and Carter as they stepped up, looking at us, and then at the rest of my men. They wore the same suit, a simple black design with red bow ties to match Eliza's glittering dress. She was too busy giving me a bear hug to notice anything else.

"You're okay," she whispered, pulling back, examining me like she had Grigen after he'd slipped on his way down the stairs one day, scraping his knees on the floor. "God, you had me so worried."

It was probably bad that I wasn't sure which life-changing event she was talking about. I smiled, refusing to let her go, not ready to lose the touch of my friend yet. "I'm okay. How are you? How's Grigen?"

She snorted before pulling back, running a hand through the longer part of her red hair, making her eyes sparkle in the dim light. She was dressed well, even for the occasion, in a sharp red dress that hugged her form and showed off the delicate curves of her body.

"Probably snuggled up, watching a movie with Carter's sister, waiting for us to come home," she said, her eyes dimming as she reached for the little shell necklace around her neck. She ran a thumb over it, sighing. "You don't have to worry about me. *Baba* isn't one to be messed with."

That determination I knew so well started in the curve of her lips as she looked me up and down again. "You look rough, Ali. More *Rends*?"

For once, I searched for a pressure that wasn't there. I waited for the dragging feeling and the ache behind my eyes, the tingling sensation that made my lips go numb and my head hurt, but it never came forward. In its place were the memories, the bits that I still struggled to reconcile as mine. I forced a smile as I swallowed back my mantra, hiding the faces of my past as I took her hands. I hid the shaking well, but obviously not well enough, as she frowned.

This was what we'd wanted, what that walk through Century Side had been for, and somehow ... it almost seemed worse now.

A part of me missed the unknown, missed not knowing what happened.

"The *Rends* are gone, Liz. Mags helped get my memories back. I'm fine," I said, even if I didn't feel it right now. The voices of my past lingered—would always linger—but I could handle their taunts for now. Eliza's face twisted, the same haunted look in her eyes that I imagined mirrored my own.

Osiris stepped to my side, placing a hand on my lower back, using his touch to ground me as I let go of Eliza. Just in time for another group to come barreling forward.

The room filled slowly, overwhelming me with sounds and scents as I shuffled closer to Osiris.

"I see the gangs all here," a familiar voice called, echoing over the crowd.

Three walked forward, two men and a woman. The men were dressed in suits of their own, navy blue with open collars and silver chains around their necks. The woman, Rose, wore a simple black dress that extended slightly behind her and seemed anything but, with how she swayed through the room, captivating anyone that looked her way. It had bare shoulders that were instead covered in a light shawl.

"Milo!" Prince said, dashing through Adrian and Fallon, the two grunting on impact, a laugh coming forward as he power-walked toward his friend. There wasn't any hesitation as he reached out and grabbed Milo's forearm. "Come here, you bastard."

He leaned forward, kissing Milo's cheeks three times. It was like watching Milo reset, his eyes going wide as he held perfectly still. When he jerked back, he grabbed Nero's shoulder, gasping like a fish for a moment.

"Nero?" he asked, watching as Prince grinned, dipping his head once. That was all Milo needed, before he was pulling Prince into a bone-crushing hug. "Nero! You asshole, took you long enough to remember who the fuck I am!"

Nero laughed, patting Milo on the back with a few hard slaps. "Please, like I'd actually forget that face."

They continued to babble on, Fallon, Adrian, Osiris and Eirik stepping in as well. Even Will added a few jabs, blending seamlessly as they joked, speaking in a language that seemed as old as time. The kind that came with long-standing friendships that lasted well into the centuries.

"Nice to see you again, Aaliyah," Rose said, stepping up to my side, looking over me with that same worried expression she'd had at Eliza's.

"Same, Rose," I said, easing into our conversation as she looked at our men. It was as easy as breathing to relax around her, Eliza stepping up and passing us both a glass of what looked like white wine.

It bubbled on my lips, the sweet taste refreshing as I took a sip.

"I swear. He's all Milo's been talking about," Rose mused, looking smitten at the animated expressions Milo shot Prince's way. He had his arms wrapped around Prince's shoulders, speaking loudly about some story that had everyone laughing.

"You sure you're okay?" Liz asked, taking my hand in a show of support, keeping her head high as she looked around the room.

I nodded, pulling the sleeve of my dress to cover more of my arm, of the scars that slid across the skin from my collarbone over my shoulder. "Yeah, I'm fine."

"We've got your back, Ali," she whispered, pulling me into a hug again. Eliza was always so warm, so open. It was like her arms were a safety net. She gave the best hugs. "So, let's give 'em hell?"

"Let's hope this time there aren't any more dark alleys," I mumbled, and she choked before heaving a laugh.

When she pulled back for the last time, it was to brush the hair out of my face, tucking in a piece that had come undone from the braid Eirik had weaved before coming here.

A loud ringing filled the air, consistent with the sway of a large bell that was out of sight. It rocked the room, making my legs shake as the conversation fell quiet. "What's happening?"

"That means it's time," Dezen added, flashing a tight smile as he came to Eliza's side again, Carter taking up the other in a protective stance. Milo and Will were quick to do the same with Rose. "The Call for Challenges and Retaliations is starting."

"Stay strong, Ali. You've got this," Liz said, before her face switched, becoming something stoic and powerful. There was a breath of sea water in the air as she looked at Osiris as he came back to my side. "Take care of her, okay? I'll have your ass if she gets hurt again."

Each of my men nodded, huddling close as we watched Eliza walk away, waving at us as she went to Eternal Ilenia's table. Rose and her band did the same, nods of support following them until they disappeared into the crowd.

It wasn't much longer before we found our seats, and the room that had been alight with chatter grew silent.

Food had been laid out, something that hadn't been on the tables before, dishes I couldn't place or even think to name. Something that smelled like sage wrapped in cooked meat and covered in a red sauce.

Not that I was in any state to eat. Several glasses sat empty there, as well, a Sage sliding by, filling them with a crimson liquid that smelled of iron.

Just as another Sage took to the pedestal.

They looked exactly like the one that had invited us in, wearing a long robe that obscured part of their blank face. They were emotionless as a lengthy scroll unfurled in front of them. It floated in the air, suspended under an overhead light. They glanced it over before beginning, "For Dragonkin Eternal, Drakon Halsen is presented. Is there a contest?"

The monotone of its voice brought goosebumps to my arms, and I reached for someone, settling only when a hand slid into mine. Our fingers interlaced, and Osiris was quick to bring it up to his lips, pressing a soft kiss to my knuckles.

"I, Marietta Halsen, Challenge," a voice called from across the room, seemingly from nowhere.

The Sage tilted its head, her name etching onto the scroll in golden ink, before the stage shook, and a woman appeared next to him, along with Drakon. They faded in, settling softly to the ground, the familiar itch of a teleportation spell filling the room, a ring of blue under their feet.

Both Dragonkin looked at each other, the similarities blinding as any hint of familial bond faded away. The Sage moved them silently, until both their palms were over the water. One quick slash, and their blood pooled in it, staining the clear liquid red.

"So, it is sealed," the Sage whispered as their hands healed, and a mark took the spot there.

They were simple black designs. Drakon's a set of two overlapping triangles, slightly offset to the left, the points matching up. Marietta's had one of the triangles facing down, the bottoms not quite lining up to make a diamond.

Drakon watched Marietta carefully, his face twisting with confusion, but she showed no remorse. Her brown hair was strung back, her eyes high and cold.

They faded from the stage. Quick, efficient, and just like that the Sage continued.

"For Sorceri Eternal, Magelav Rourovic is presented. Is there a contest?"

I wasn't expecting anyone to come forward, not after seeing what Mags could do, so I nearly jumped when a voice echoed above the crowd just a few feet from us. "I'd like to Challenge."

He was scraggly, almost ancient, the kind of stature that reminded me of the professors in those movies that Eliza liked to watch. He had graying hair, and a long beard that was trimmed neatly. Glasses sat over his eyes, the color hidden by the distance between us, and he pushed them up as he waited for the Sage to acknowledge him.

"Warlow Emigrand Challenges," the Sage whispered, calling them both to the floor. Warlow stood tall, his head held above the rest as he stared at what should have been a powerful opponent.

But Magelav looked haunted.

Their eyes were sunken, their body trembling as they swayed on their feet. They held their hand above the water and accepted the mark, the same that Drakon had. It left a sour feeling in my stomach when they wiped away a slash of blood as it slid down their nose.

"So, it is sealed," the Sage called, the names scrawling in that large scroll. The ink on it turned gold as they wrote before fading away entirely.

"What happened to Mags?" Prince asked as he continued to stare at the pool with an almost lost look.

He searched the room, trying to find where Mags had slipped back to. I searched with him, but the rows and rows of tables made it impossible to pick anyone out.

"I don't know," Osiris replied, tapping his fingers against the table. A soft knock echoed, dampened by the soft cloth that sat over it. "That was odd, even for them."

The Sage moved on.

A man with savage red eyes and ashen gray skin came forward when Alderi'Vidius was called. His ears were sharply pointed, his expression almost bored as he was pulled onto the stage. There was something distinct about him that reminded me of Osiris, the twirl in his long suit coat and the way he watched the rest of the room.

"Bradsai'Crimson," Osiris mumbled, his hand stopping on the table as Vidius took up the spot across from the dapper man. I hadn't seen Vidius in person, just heard whispers that hadn't done him justice. His black hair was styled deftly around his head, an air of power that befitted someone with the title of Eternal ... but I wasn't expecting him to look so scared.

"Who's he?" I asked as the Sage pulled their hands over the water, slicing a wound onto their palms. Vidius's blood fed into the pool, Crimson's next, staining the well a deep gold.

"A Pride Demon. He reigned with Lucifer over the hells for centuries, before he grew bored with it. Last I'd heard, he was traveling the world. Of anyone to Challenge, I wasn't expecting him," Osiris said, never looking away as the two were teleported back.

"Can Vidius win?" Fallon pressed, running his hand over his face, itching one of the dull gray lines that was still etched into it.

Osiris was quiet for a long moment, his jaw clenched, before he shook his head. "Crimson is older than Kri'Valta by several thousand years. If he wants the seat, Vidius will give it to him. Or he'll die."

I gripped my wrist, keeping my head low as the Sage's voice called out again.

"For Titan Eternal, Jerick is presented. Is there a contest?" Its voice grated in my head, making my teeth hurt as silence stretched over the room.

The Fae Eternal seat was the last to be called, and the man that Fallon and I had seen, Koldan, went uncontested. The Sage tapped the scroll as it floated above the pool, lingering there as they dipped their head.

All the names they'd called were related to spots that had been freed, either from someone stepping down or from the death of another. Now they just stood, their tentacle arms waving around them. "Are there any other rulings?"

Osiris's hand tensed in mine, and before the Sage had even finished speaking, a voice boomed throughout the room. "Osiris Vivas. You're supposed to be in the Pits."

Darius was easy to pick out, sitting on his seat like it was a throne. He leaned back, a woman I didn't recognize on his knee, her golden hair pulled tightly in his hand, his other on her leg in a grip that looked painful.

"The Pits are holding ground, nothing more. I've been held, Darius," Osiris called back, swallowing hard as a *Charm* inched out with the last few words. It made me shiver, the people next to us scooting away. "Do you have something to say or not?"

Darius stood up, knocking the woman off him as he slammed his hands down on the table, rattling the center piece that decorated it. Osiris flinched, and I held him steady as Darius spoke. "I call for Retaliation against Osiris Vivas. For the death of my dearest Kali. The prior Sorceri Eternal."

The Sage was impartial, its body turning to face us, without even having to guess where we might be. "Osiris Vivas, do you deny these claims?"

My heart was in my throat as Osiris stood, dusting off his suit, letting go of my hand. I hated it, hated the way he moved under Darius's gaze like he was trying to prepare himself for hell.

"I do," he whispered, yet even with Darius snarling at him, he kept his head high. "But I accept his Retaliation. Darius wishes for a fight. I'm happy to give him one."

Darius's expression contorted, his face sharpening as the hint of a beast peeked through, egged on by the words Osiris spoke and the mocking whispers of the crowd. The Sage was quiet for a moment, more words flashing across the scroll. "Retaliation accepted."

Osiris faded from view in the next second, shimmering into place next to the Sage, across the pool from Darius. The process was the same, their blood lingering in the water, and a mark appearing on Osiris's hand. The black glyph glowed as he clenched his fist. This time, the mark was circular, with a diamond in the middle.

I couldn't hear what Darius said, but I saw how Osiris reacted to it, like he'd been struck.

He returned to us moments later, his head dipped low, the Sage already moving. I didn't have time to ask him what had been said, his eyes clouded as he looked ahead. That blank stare was back, and he clutched his wrist tightly.

"Are there any other rulings?"

A few more voices filled the crowd. They mentioned names I knew, like a Siren calling for Ilenia, who looked like she might eat the brave male for dinner. Another Lycan, a woman with shiny black hair and a devious smile, Challenged Yrsa. Cael for Adathan, a move that had the entire room flooding with gasps and shock at the sight of the old Eternal back in the flesh.

When no one else spoke, Osiris stood again.

Eirik took a deep breath at my side, his chest rumbling with the starting of a growl as the other tables leaned close, like vultures looking for rotting meat when Osiris spoke. "For his crimes against the Eternals, and his willful ignorance toward their laws by the killing of Fae Eternal Frileti and Titan Eternal Roderick, we, the Vivas Crypt, put Sebek Ra, the Vampire Eternal, up for Exilium. An Honored Death."

Just the word was enough to bring the Eternals to arms, the ones that were in the dark panicking the hardest. Their voices raised above the rest, one leading to two, then many. Until screams filled the air.

"Have you gone completely mad?"

"This is an outrage. Exilium is not done!"

"You cannot call for Exilium as a man facing Retaliation!"

"Enough," the Sage called, their voice in my head, vibrating my skull hard enough to clatter my teeth. The room quieted before shaking again as a light darted across the floor, separating it into two halves.

"Exilium has been called. Cast your votes." The Sage lifted one waving appendage. It fluttered in the air, pointing out the sides. "To the left, yes. To the right, no."

There was a fearful shuffle as everyone stood, and the Eternals searched the room for the man who faced the charges, looking over shoulders, hiding their eyes.

Sebek was the bogeyman, even in a room full of monsters.

We followed, taking the front row on the left-hand side of the mark. It fissured in the marble, almost pulsing as we stepped up to it, toeing the line.

At first, I wasn't sure if anyone else would follow, a fear ingrained in the way I moved and breathed. Then Liz took up our side.

She smiled at me boldly, unwilling to falter as Ilenia took her right. The Siren Eternal was every bit the intimidating presence she was when I first met her, the ice in her eyes so sharp it damned well could have cut.

"Eternal Ilenia," Osiris said, dipping his head as the Siren Eternal raised a brow. Her long aqua hair was down her back, untied, flowing across the open expanse of her dress.

"Vivas," she bit out, staring straight ahead, not bothering to look our way. "Aaliyah, I see you didn't take my advice."

Her words of warning, the ones that she'd shared at her home in her attempt to sway me away from the men at my back. Eirik's hands fell on my shoulders, his nose running against my hair as I smiled.

"No, I didn't."

Unlike last time, there was more than simmering disgust and disappointment in the way she looked at me. Her head tipped up, a flash of light blue scales across her neck and a hint of pride in her eyes as she turned back to center.

A shadow cast over me, darkening the room and stealing my breath. All it took was one brush of it to send my mind spiraling. Eirik's hands tightened on my shoulders, and I bit my tongue.

Never make noise.

"You intend to stand against me, Ilenia?" Sebek asked, his hands shoved into the pockets of his black suit.

He watched on with clear irritation, his black hair messy around his head, that comforting red in his eyes fiendish. A cold wind blew, making me shiver as Red fluttered over, lingering near my shoulders. He was as anxious as I was, clinging to me as we both waited to see what Sebek would do.

"Was it ever a question, Butcher?" Ilenia responded with a cold glare, tensions spiraling as Sebek grinned.

More Eternals and their secondaries filled the sides, and though there seemed to be more with us ... only the Eternals votes would matter in the end. Milo, Adathan, Avedal, Drakon, and Vidius, were a few that I saw standing proudly with us. One was slower, starting off across the line. He was large, his skin a silvery gray that looked rocky like stone. His large wings on his back stretched upward above his head, and his face reminded me of Valen.

He looked at the fissure and back at the men and women that made up the people on his side. It was a long few seconds before the stone man stepped over the line, his wings curling close to his back as he did, as if ashamed.

Adrian breathed out, and Eirik clapped him on the back.

"Axius, what the *fuck* are you doing?" another hissed, looking exactly like the man now on our side.

They stared in opposition, one all fury and the other looking more and more worn.

"I can't let you do this, Hyland," Axius said but didn't falter. His tail whipped behind him, his eyes broken but firm. "I've watched long enough, but I can't stand by on this. Father would have never stood on that side with that *monster*. I can't either."

He took a breath, crossing his arms and strengthening his stance. "Consider this my Challenge."

More whispers filled the air as others danced the line, a few more shuffling across before another familiar face was by our side. Magelav looked like they'd been through hell, even worse up close, their eyes dulled and far off, the same way they'd been after helping Prince and I with our memories. Guilt started low when they wiped away another swath of blood from under their nose. They didn't say anything, just stood by Prince's side, Xander taking up the other with a man I hadn't seen before.

"Mags," Xander purred, that same expression of want lingering in the way he looked them up and down. He wore the same white suit I'd always seen him in, the glittering of forest green accenting it.

Mags snorted, shaking their head with a mocking grin. "*Rat*."

The more people moved, the less equal the sides became, until everyone stopped. The Sage waited precious few seconds, and we all collectively held our breaths. "Current vote, eighty-seven of one hundred and sixteen. The total votes required for a pass is ninety-three. Exilium does not pass under current conditions."

I swallowed the failure, already expecting it before the Challenges, but that didn't make it seem any more attainable. It felt like a loser's game, a checkmate.

"There's still a chance," Drakon said, grunted as he looked at me and the others. It filled me with warmth, a hope I hadn't realized I'd let go of. Sebek sneered, clicking his tongue.

"A wolf in sheep's clothing stands among us," Mags said, mumbled behind closed teeth as they pitched forward, staring straight ahead.

It wasn't often they had an expression that was readable. Most of the time, I'd compare the way they surveyed and moved to *Sebek*. They had the same type of mannerism, the same crazed look in their eyes.

That wasn't the case now as Prince looked down at the Sorceri with narrowed brows. Mags closed their eyes, their hands shaking as they gritted their teeth. I could almost see the dread coming off their shoulders, sinking into their skin as *Xander* stepped forward.

Drakon cursed, held back only by his Enforcer, Cassius, as Xander eyed the gouge in the marble. He looked down at the line, humming as I choked on my next breath.

"Always so perceptive, Mags." He whistled, dipping his head as if conceding a victory to a game no one knew they'd been playing.

He stepped over the line, followed by who I now assumed was another Dryad, likely the Eternal, with wispy green hair and matching green eyes. It was like watching our hope crumble in front of us. He caught my eyes last, smiling that gentle way, like he hadn't just tightened the noose around our necks. "Don't look at me like that. It's just business."

Mags didn't give him a response, just kept their eyes closed as Nero jolted forward. His eyes shot red. "You're a godforsaken coward, Axandre."

Xander hummed, still looking at Mags. For a moment he looked sorry, swallowing hard before he was shaking his head, grief washed away by his smile, cleansed by his laugh. "A practical one. I like to be on the winning side of things. You won't win Exilium. You never stood a chance."

Sebek seemed to know this was coming, pulling what looked to be a book out of his suit pocket. It was small, leather bound, and Xander looked downright gleeful when Sebek set it in his hands.

Payment for his switching of sides, no doubt. I hadn't ever trusted Xander, but this seemed like too much ... he'd been so strong in his opposition, his hatred in the way Sebek had killed the other Reapers. But it seemed that hatred would only go so far when faced with something he truly wanted.

The Sage called out again, breaking up the rage in Prince as he jolted back, continuing to bare his teeth. "Current vote, eighty-five of one hundred and sixteen. Exilium does not pass under current conditions."

Drakon didn't move, his eyes going blank as he gritted his teeth. We'd relied on the Dryad's vote, who now stood by Xander's side with his head held high. Even if everyone passed their Challenges and Retaliations ... that made six votes needed.

We only had *five* Challenges lined up. We wouldn't make Exilium like this.

"We offer evidence to sway," Osiris said, steadily calm. He reached into his pocket, pulling out the vial that Adrian had found before. The swirling liquid was like gold in the diamond flask. "This is High Fae Mana, truth in its highest form. Sebek intends to destroy the Eternals, something he'd already started before coming here. Frileti was one of the first of his kills. Roderick the second. Both who opposed him. He plans to do more, with none other than Reaper blood."

I struggled to stay sitting as Sebek scowled. I waited, watching as he pushed back his hair, barely even looking at Osiris. I expected a rebuke, some kind of words, but he just grabbed the vial, snapping the cap, and drinking it down in one go.

It happened so fast I almost missed it, the way he moved so uncaring, tossing the vial to the ground and watching it shatter. It made my instincts scream, had me looking closer as he narrowed his eyes at Osiris.

Red turned frantic, and I struggled to breathe as his emotions seemed to outweigh my own. I couldn't even tell what he was trying to say. His form was sporadic, broken down into little more than dust, not even an outline to guess at.

"Ask," Sebek pushed, and Osiris didn't hesitate.

"Do you, Sebek Ra, intend to destroy the Eternals?"

I shook, trying to shrug off the bad feeling, my unease only growing when it worsened. Sebek cracked his neck, his eyes shimmering as if back lit as the potion sifted its way through his body. He let a breath out, a dusting of gold slipping out with it.

"No," he responded, clear and articulate, no room to second guess what he'd said. Eirik jolted next to me.

Most on our side froze, and the taunting jeers started from the other. I'd seen Sebek kill that man at Ascension, watched for a soul that never appeared. His potion destroyed him.

"Impossible," Prince whispered as Mags shook.

"Do you intend harm upon them?" Osiris tried again, his eyes narrowing, differing pools of blue that didn't hide his surprise when Sebek answered again, this time with a smile that made me ill.

"No, I do not intend to harm the Eternals in any way."

Everything that we'd thought about Sebek's plans crumbled. If he wasn't intending on using my blood to kill them, to control them ... then what was he going to do?

He turned to look at me, like he could feel the way I watched him, catching my gaze in the crowd of people.

"Ask, I see it in your eyes," he said, clearly pointed at me.

With every move he made, we were seven behind. Every step we took felt like a step in the wrong direction. He knew about Exilium, knew about our plans, and he shut them all down with a ruthless efficiency.

"What's your plan with Aaliyah's blood?" Osiris pressed, and finally, Sebek turned back to face him.

The mention of me, of what I could do, snapped the attention of the rabid crowd our way.

Everything he'd said, every interaction with him, raced across my mind. The thought of it was so simple now that the idea of death had been pushed to the side. Sebek could kill whoever he wanted. He didn't need my blood to do it, something he'd proven when he'd taken down two Eternals and still had an army of loyal followers at his back.

"To bring back true immortality. To reverse death, in the truest sense. Aaliyah's blood, Reaper blood, is the key, and I can prove it," he said, and I knew it was the moment we'd lost.

Sebek didn't want to kill the Eternals, not with this. None of this had *ever* been about killing, but rather who he'd already killed. Who we wanted back more than anything.

I sucked in a breath, suddenly sweating.

He wasn't supposed to die.

Sebek wanted to bring back my father, the man he'd killed when my mother died. Their souls bound together, her death leading to his. Sebek wanted to undo his mistake.

My vision narrowed, the thought of it almost a dream, especially knowing exactly how I was brought back the first time. Sebek wouldn't succeed, even if that was his goal. He'd ruined his chances the moment he'd taken me ... because after I'd died at his doctor's hands, it was my father's soul that was used to bring me back.

Like my mother had used me for him all those years ago. Like Davi had shown me.

Like Crustava's had been for Prince.

I was going to be sick.

Sebek reached into his coat, pulling out a vial I recognized. The liquid in it sloshed around, an inky black that stuck to the walls. Another man I didn't know came to his side, with blue eyes and silvery hair that matched his suit. He had scales along his skin, not quite like I'd seen on Dragonkin, more aquatic. A Mer, like Eliza, I'd guess based on the way Ilenia stiffened. Sebek handed it to him, not even touching him.

"You can't kill someone in the Eternium, not with feats of strength, but they can still die," Sebek said, nodding once.

The man didn't hesitate before crushing the vial in his palm. "For true eternal life."

It took all of a few seconds before his eyes rolled back, his body slumping to the floor. Just like before, no spirit came up from his body. Red was the first to move toward it, his apprehension alive in the air as he circled the man who'd dropped dead. It was like he was prodding him, looking for the same thing I was.

Nothing happened.

The crowd came alive with whispers, shock stealing words as the writhing turned to screams ... before it went silent. Sebek pulled another vial from his coat, this one clear with flecks of familiar silver.

Bile rose in my throat.

"Aaliyah?" Fallon asked.

"It was tricky finding it at first, but the tie of Reaper blood to the Void is there. They can send souls on or repurpose them. *Rebirth* them." Sebek took a step, rolling the man over with his foot. His eyes moved back to me, and then to Prince as he opened the vial, taking great care to touch the man as little as possible as he poured the concoction down his throat. "Now, they can also bring them back. My once dead Turned is proof of that."

The rumbles in the room grew louder and louder. The crumbling remains of our plan slipped from our hands as several bodies from our side passed over the fissure. The Sage called out new tallies, our odds dropping lower and lower.

Eighty votes.

Seventy-six votes.

Sixty-eight votes ...

Which meant there was only one way.

I looked at Prince, his face set in stone, his expression giving nothing away. He wore the look of a gladiator going to war.

"I have no desire to kill you. I wish to bring back those that were lost. To restore order, to purge the world of the filth that stains it. And I'll do so, even if I have to drag you along with me," Sebek yelled above the chaos, and the Eternals rallied around him.

No ghost appeared, washed away by the potion ... but this time, he didn't stay dead. The body flinched, twitching, no doubt filled with a heartbeat they could suddenly hear loud and clear again. None of them paid any further attention, not noticing when he stopped twitching again.

And they *cheered* for the man who would see them all dead if it meant the ability to bring back my father. This man who'd killed so many just like them, Naturals that didn't deserve the deaths that they were dealt. This idea that he could better them washed away any semblance of moral decency.

Osiris tugged at the sleeves of his dress shirt, hiding the marks on his wrist. Sebek smiled, gloating as he watched the frantic trading of sides around us. He didn't have to speak as he looked at me one last time, eyes vicious.

He knew he won.

Your move, Glass.

"Current vote, fifty-two of one hundred and sixteen. An eighty percent majority needed for a passing vote. *Failure* for Exilium."

I could have heard a pin drop.

Sebek was so confident in the way he moved after the announcement, the way he stood tall and looked on like we were nothing but pawns. Like he never had anything to worry about to begin with.

Our goal was Exilium, but if that failed, Prince was going to Challenge, and it only made sense at this point to believe that Sebek knew that, too. It was like it didn't bother him in the grand scheme of things. This was all just a setback, just another game.

He knew what was coming, and nothing else would get in his way.

"Are there any more issues to address?" The Sage whispered, like a gavel falling.

Exilium will not save you.

"You've already lost," he said, and Osiris's face flushed red with rage.

All of our planning led here, to the moment I'd begged would never come to be. Sebek turned his back, walking away as the fissure of light disappeared from the center of the room. There was no fear in him, no more hesitancy in the way he moved.

You've already lost.

Words got lodged in my throat, silence stealing my voice as panic became understanding.

Prince stepped forward, head held high, staring down the Sage with the confidence of a king. Of the Gladiator I knew he was.

"I Challenge Sebek Ra, for the spot of Vampire Eternal."

Chapter 58

Prince

Somehow, hearing the words was worse than what they represented. The soft echo, followed by the unnerving silence as everyone held their breath, trying to decide if their ears had made some terrible mistake. No one even moved.

Because it wasn't Osiris, *Rex interfectorem,* that had called the Challenge.

It wasn't *me.*

Aaliyah stood with that driven confidence that could only come from years of facing monsters. I took her in slowly, her eyes wide but unrelenting, her focus forward on where the Sage sat just as quiet as the rest.

She stood in front of us, like a guard, keeping Sebek at bay with the steely look in her lavender eyes.

"I, *Aaliyah Ra Imperial,* Challenge Sebek for the title of Vampire Eternal," she said again, and hearing it a second time did nothing to help me understand the words.

Aaliyah Challenged Sebek.

Aaliyah. *My* Aaliyah.

A swirling of magic started under her feet, the will of the Sage sending a wave of discomfort down my spine as Aaliyah disappeared, just to flash into position in the middle of the room. Next to the bowl that had been conjured up, the liquid in it a silvery white again. I couldn't catch her eye, as Sebek appeared in front of her, looking like a beast himself, his face an impassible mask of rage.

She was so close yet so far away, *too* far. The need to be by her side was a fucking drive in my brain, but I couldn't move. My feet anchored to the floor as the Eternium locked us all in place.

She'd Challenged Sebek. The battles ahead, the obstacles ... They would be ruthless. Savage. I'd seen events that had torn down so many men and women that I'd lost count. Only their names lived on now.

She'd taken that on without flinching. What was supposed to be my burden. Why, *why*?

Eirik snarled viciously, Osiris's magic touching the air with the soft scent of fire. Even our allies watched with barely contained shock. It had all been a mess, Xander's betrayal, Sebek's show ...

Now this.

"No," Sebek snarled, the first to break that unholy silence, his eyes flashing a dangerous red, his mouth nearly foaming as he leaned over the bowl. His hands slammed to the sides, the liquid inside sloshing. "Impossible. You're a Reaper, and a *babe*. You cannot Challenge me."

Aaliyah shivered, shaking her head as she clenched her hands tightly against her sides.

"I'm half Vampire. I was born in the Void nearly three thousand years ago," she said, unwavering. More whispers wrapped around us from the filled stands, no one willing to get any louder, like it might incur the wrath of the Butcher.

Or the Reaper.

"I am fit to Challenge," she said, not backing down even as he snarled in her face.

Un. Fucking. Relenting.

Whatever was left of Sebek's composure fractured, and his eyes went red as his fangs fell. They sliced his lip, and blood splattered across the Sage's pool.

"I won't allow it!" he screamed, managing a step forward.

His power, even put on a leash by the Eternium, swallowed the room, trying to force her to bow to it. Those same rules tied me down, even standing a chore as I tried to force myself to move. Osiris was by my side, his face sweating as he did the same.

There was a moment when I thought Sebek might try to attack, and I was disgusted with the way hatred rotted out what was left of the man behind his eyes. His hand twitched, his face contorted in pain and rage.

"That is quite enough," a voice echoed, and the room that I hadn't realized had fallen into complete bedlam fell silent again.

The Eternals were outraged, their heavy fearful breaths the only thing that could be heard now. Osiris grabbed my arm, the sharp chill of his exposed hand making me curse as I snapped my attention to him. I was fully ready to give him a piece of my mind until I saw his fucking face. Pallid, a fear that felt bone deep, as he looked toward that center stage.

Suddenly, the hair on the back of my neck stood, my blood pulsing so hard it was all I could hear. Saliva flooded my mouth, my vision tunneling. Eirik cowered, his eyes the clearest blue I'd ever seen. Adrian sank to the ground like so many others, his face so ashen I thought he might pass out. Fallon stood, barely, just enough to keep himself from falling as sweat slid down his gray-lined skin.

And I shook, too afraid to breathe, as I turned back to look at whoever had spoken.

"You have caused quite the stir, tiny death," another voice called. The gravelly tone carried something that shot me with a primal fear, forcing my heart to speed up. Power coated the room. Bathed it, swallowed it whole and spit it out.

"Is that ..." Adrian whispered, swallowing several times as he tried to force himself to speak. Like he was calling the boogeyman forward. "Jesus Christ, *they're* here."

They were three of the most imposing creatures I'd ever had the misfortune of seeing. They stood on that center ground, in front of the Sage, looking down at Aaliyah. They towered above her and Sebek, so still they could have been mistaken for statues. The one that had spoken last resonated something in me, singing with my blood. He was a monster, with grotesque horns sprouting from his head, curling up and away from a wicked animal skull that sat where his face was. White eyes stared back at us. His skin was inky black, everything but his skull and eyes looking like it was dipped in midnight. His legs were long, double-jointed with ghastly clawed feet at the ends. Behind him sat a twisting thin tail that slashed through the air, making an audible whip sound. Loud enough that Eirik flinched.

This man, this *beast* ... he was the Hallowed of *Death*.

Jesus fucking Christ, Adrian was right. *They* were here. The Hallowed Three were in front of us.

In front of Aaliyah.

"Quite the interesting turn of events. I wonder, how will they play out?" The next to speak was an opposing force to the first. Seeming to be the light in the darkness. He was almost human shaped, with the exception of his four arms and the wings that sprouted from his back that housed more eyes than I could count. He was missing a face, something that he made up for with wicked horns that sprouted up around his head, circling it like a corrupted crown. His bottom hands held something made of glittering gold that seemed so small in his deft fingers, an hourglass.

The Hallowed of Time.

"Davi. Than," Aaliyah said, breaking the silence in the way only she could. She didn't back down as she turned to them, the same way she had anyone she spoke to. Completely unbothered by their appearance, at least at first glance.

I let out a breath, so desperate to be by her side for this. Aaliyah had never been fearless ... but she never backed down.

"This was what you wanted, wasn't it?" she asked, and I held my breath, watching as the two goliaths dipped their heads, the third and final chuckling.

The sound crackled in the air, like lightning about to strike.

"Clever is the beast that hides in the shadows," he said, to the right of Death. He was less a person and more a shapeless being. Every time he moved, the pieces that made up his body shifted oddly with him, like he could move them independently. His skin looked like it was painted with stars, almost fake with how oily it appeared ... but the closer I watched, the more I realized the stars were moving. His eyes were black voids, no trace of light to be found. "Aaliyah, The Hallowed accept your right to Challenge."

The Hallowed of Space.

You could have heard a fucking pin drop, not even the likes of Darius making a mockery of themselves as we all just watched. Some neanderthal parts of our brains told us we shouldn't speak, shouldn't move, shouldn't *breathe* out of line. That if we wanted to live, we needed to wait for the danger to leave.

So, none of us did.

Aaliyah shivered, but she didn't hold that same fear. The shadows on the ground seemed to pull closer to her, breathing the same way she was. She'd said their names; I assumed ones they'd given her.

She saw them; she knew them.

And this had been their plan all along.

"Impossible," Osiris whispered beside me, his hand clenched so tightly I caught the faint hint of blood in the air.

"She meets the criteria set by the Eternals. This is final," Death called, almost daring someone to deny it.

His head dipped low, the hollow sockets that held his eyes flashing red as he bared rows and rows of dagger-like teeth. I wouldn't have been brave enough to flip him off behind his back ...

"No, no! I won't allow it!" Sebek screamed, somehow not cowed like the rest of us were, something knocked loose in that brain of his, as if he could deny the will of the gods, *our* gods.

The ones we were born from, the Original Naturals. The fucking *Hallowed*.

They had come forward to allow this. Aaliyah was going to have to fight Sebek ... One way or another. A battle of Wits, a battle of Endurance, or a battle of Strength.

She looked to the floor, then to the frothing mass that was Sebek. I would admit, it was nice to see him dragged through the dirt a bit. She lifted her hand, cutting her thumb on one of her fangs before extending it over the pool that the Sage had summoned. The Hallowed looked on, silent again like the crowd around us.

Her blood hit the water with a splash, Sebek's snarls lost behind the surge of magic that filled the air, a binding sliding over her open palm. The mark of a *Challe,* two triangles, points opposing. Sebek fought it all he could, his own blood already in the pool. The mark of the Challenged surging against his hand, burning.

The Sage marked their long scroll, the Hallowed dipping their heads, before Sebek and Aaliyah faded from the Sage. They appeared again in the crowd, Aaliyah next to us with a graceful sway, and Sebek just several feet from us in a furious heap that I couldn't find the will to worry about.

"Aaliyah ... why?" I asked, ashamed by the brokenness in my voice.

I wanted to protect her. It was all I wanted. I spent so long having to watch her suffer, having to fight my guilt to smile for her when she did the same for me. I didn't want to be useless anymore.

This was supposed to be my fight.

Aaliyah smiled as she turned her head to look at me, as if taking the world on her shoulders didn't bother her. The sadness in her eyes was drowned out by the love there as she lifted her hand. The marks on her wrist glowed, and she glanced among us.

Her eyes lingered, settling on each of the men that she'd caught in her tender web.

"Because you can't fight him," she said with a steadfast certainty that made me damned well believe her.

"What do you mean?" Osiris asked, that same cracking in his voice.

"He's not scared, not at all. Because you *can't* fight him," she said, and Sebek froze.

There was a methodical calculation in her eyes when she said it, the way she watched him turn to her. His face twisted, a mix between pride and rage.

"I don't think Turned can hurt their Makers. He wouldn't be treating you so offhandedly if you stood a chance. Why else would he keep you all alive when he'd already killed the rest?"

Her words were a smoking gun that was set off by the way Sebek tried to rush at us, caught in the ties of the Eternium. He strained against them, his eyes red, blood slipping down his nose and over his top lip as he fought a magic that outweighed even him.

"Because we'd never be a threat to him," Osiris added, shaking his head.

"Exactly," she said, nodding one more time. "If you fight him, you die. He doesn't want to kill me. That gives us more time."

"Time. Always *time*," Mags whispered, butting in and silencing the conversation, looking more wrecked than ever as they came to my side. Their hair, now that inky black, was frayed, waving chaotically around their head, matching the sunken gray under their eyes. "One soul mirrors the other, and another piece of you to be made whole lives again. Oh, what fun we'll have."

They sucked in a hard breath, head snapping to the center, eyes landing on the Three, though none of them paid the fevered Sorceri any mind.

Always so helpful, really. What would we do without them?

"Mags—" I started, exasperated, only to be cut off by a devastating *crack*.

A deep groan filled the air, one that came from the body that had been lying prone on the ground. The one that had been conveniently forgotten about after Sebek's little magic trick failed ... or that we'd thought failed.

Everyone's attention snapped to him as he writhed, spewing groans like he was dying all over again as he stood, almost like a zombie. Just as soon as it started, all sound from him stopped, his body twitching as if trying to figure out how to move.

Whoever the fuck this was, wasn't the man that had sacrificed himself for Sebek's *glorious foolproof plan* or whatever. His hair was charcoal black, skin so white it was nearly transparent, covered in a fine layer of blood that he seemed all too happy to spread across his face. But it was his eyes that really drew me in, made me pause. They were a wispy white, with a haze that came off them, fluttering around his head like smoke. When he smiled at us, he flashed fangs.

Fucking hell, I was going to be sick at the thought of Aaliyah's soul being tied to someone so fucking savage.

"Xiang," Sebek muttered, seeming as caught off guard as he had been when he'd first seen me again.

The man stumbled forward, and the Eternals gasped around us, staring on like onlookers to a slaughter in what was to be my new Colosseum.

"My *sweet* little one," Xiang purred, in broken English that seemed like it was tied together by loose string, pretending to be words. As though he'd never actually spoken the language, just heard it, and did his best to copy it.

He didn't look at Sebek, the man who seemed like he might be seeing a ghost, his eyes on the one *fucking* thing they shouldn't be on.

He was looking directly at Aaliyah.

Chapter 59

???

I lifted my hands to the sky, savoring the feeling of the cool red mist that stuck to skin. *My* skin.

The Void staggered through my head, searching for something I didn't have to give. None of it mattered, not now, not with the life that breathed into my lungs.

I was nothing, and it was perfect, a symphony of vibrancy. The sights, with broad arrays of colors decorating dresses and suits. The array of lights that flickered across hard marble, glittering and glowing. The sounds, the quickening of heartbeats and intakes of breath, stuttering and begging to be chased. The scents I'd surely never enjoyed before, sucking in a lungful of the fresh air that mingled so sweetly with the fear and outrage of those around me. The touch of my skin against the silken clothes I wore.

I was *free.*

My heart thundered at the sight of my purpose, the same sight I'd followed since I found her. Elation was a blow to the chest, the pain a welcome delight as I purred.

She had bled life back into my soul, brought me back to the world of the living.

Aaliyah. My sweet Aaliyah.

My sweet obsession. The reason I breathed, the reason I lived.

Memories of a past that was no longer mine fractured in my skull, fading entirely as I took a step toward her. I didn't need them; they were useless in comparison to her. Her eyes went wide with a fear that was misplaced, one I sought to wash away.

I cracked my neck, wiping that drying mist from my face, metallic and so delicious. A blood that was my own? The room narrowed on her, the pulsing vein in her neck, the men that stood by her side like warning signs that I was all too ready to ignore.

Thud. I licked my lips. *Thud.* My breath quickened. *Thud.* My mouth watered, my eyes rolling back at the delicate scent of her as I realized that the consistent sound was her heart.

Outcry echoed, and I was on her in a flash, pulling her into my arms and savoring that warmth. Something tried to stop me, something that reached for the same thing the Void had ... meaning to control me.

It found nothing.

I sank fangs deep into the thin flesh of her neck, feeling whole for what had to be the first time, the drag of her blood down my throat enough to make me moan against her skin, drowning in the ecstasy of her sugary sweetness.

She gasped, held tightly in my arms, safe only when close to me, and I could hear the sound of her heart more clearly.

I split my tongue open, allowing our blood to mix as her wound started to close. I felt her in my chest, in my heart, and in my *skull.* Pulsing like that strange beat that didn't feel real in my veins. My vision went red, and I licked my lips again.

Exactly as it should be.

Her other men tried to stop me, too slow. Hands on my body that weren't able to hurt, digging as deep as they were able. They tried and failed to pull us apart. My wrist burned, and I watched with glee as a mark slowly grew across it, my entire body aching for one glorious moment.

A lavender band shined back at me.

She clutched her own wrist, staring up at me with those wide eyes I'd coveted. She slid to the ground, and I followed, ripping out of the arms that thought to hold me back. I reached for her, needing to be the comfort she went to. I needed it. More than I needed to be alive, there was no me without her.

She was everything, as she had been before. She was my beating heart and my reason to be. I was her Void and her anchor. I was the one who'd protect her.

I was her *Red*.

To Be Continued

Need more to sink your teeth into?

Then come and join my newsletter! You'll get exclusive chapters about how the guys found and built their home. Along with this, you can expect to be the first to hear about all things book (and sometimes life) related. Including being the first to see cover reveals, exclusive commissioned art, and new ideas in the works!

You can find the sign on my website!: https://krrainbolt.com

A Note For You, Dear Reader

If you've made it this far, then this is for you, dear reader. Thank you for jumping into this story and enjoying the twists and turns that Ali and the guys' adventure has taken so far. Book two was a wild ride to write, and I hope, for a while at least, I gave you someplace new and exciting to explore. I can't say how excited I am to continue this series and this experience with you.

Thank you for being you.

With that being said, it would mean the world to me if you could take a second to leave a review on this book's Amazon or Goodreads page. Reviews are like lifeblood for many indie authors, me included, and your support—with even just a sentence—would help me leaps and bounds.

Thank you so very much for your support. I couldn't do this without you guys!

About the Author

Born and raised in the Wyoming Rocky Mountains, K. R. Rainbolt, or Kennady, is a lover of cakes and all things sweet. She also has a *minor* obsession with suits, but who doesn't love a nice, crisp waistcoat, right? She has been crafting stories for as long as she can remember, and nothing makes her happier than bringing a character to life. Now, as a first-time publisher, she's excited to share them with everyone else as well.

Kennady spends a lot of time writing, both for her novels and the occasional video game mod. When she's not immersed in one of her stories, she can be found spending time with the love of her life Dominic or playing with her fur baby Marlie.

Kennady loves to bowl, fish, play video games, and watch movies (the spookier, the better). Along with this, she is big on the world of science and research, and as a Chemical Engineer, she loves to include hints of her studies in her novels.

Lastly, a word of advice that her grandmother used to say: *Remember, live life.*

After all, you only have one, so you better spend it doing something you love!

Want to know more about Kennady? Then stalk her on social media! You can find her Official Facebook group, TikTok, Instagram and more on her Linktree: https://linktr.ee/k.r.rainboltauthor

Glossary

Latin

Vivas — To live

Lux mea — My light

Et in domum suam in solem — Home of the sun

Frater — Brother

Te desum — I miss you

Rex interfectorem — Kingslayer

Servatum — The Saved

Fabula Fortium — A Tale of the Brave

Mortui carmen — Song of the Dead

Meus sermo obligat — My word is binding

Perdita — The Lost

Icelandic/Norse

Elskan — Darling (term of endearment)

Fífl — Idiot or Fool

Úlfhéðinn (singular)/*Úlfhéðnar* (plural) — Wearers of the wolf skin, or Odin's special warriors

Smár Valkyrja — Small Valkyrie, or tiny warrior.

Muna langt fram — Remember from a long time back

Dreyrugr — Bloodstained

Lítár hana — Look at her

Ég elska þig — I love you

Systur — Sister

Geit — In Old Norse, geit referred to a she-goat—but as an insult, the same word could also be used for a cowardly, gutless person

Bróðir — Brother

Aboriginal Australian

Mob — Family

Nimanburru — The Tribe that Fallon grew up in

Greek

Vrykólakas — Loosely translated to vampires

COPTIC

Ab — My heart and soul

WORLD SPECIFIC

Baba — Old Siren dialect meaning grandmother, or matriarch.

Challe — Someone with the ability to Challenge the current Eternal of their species for the right to be Eternal. This range varies per species.

Challenge — A Challenge is a formal fight between a current Eternal and a Challe, done at the Eternium where the others can bare witness to either a new Eternal, or the continued reign of one.

Charm — A Vampire ability.

Chronomancer — A Sorceri that can control the flow of time to a degree. They can often look into the future a short distance and read someone's past with a touch. They can also slow and speed up time in an area.

Clutch — A grouping of Dragonkin, typically living together.

Crypt — A grouping of Vampires, typically living together. A Crypt does not have to contain Vampires of only one Maker.

Demon Core — The life source for demons, typically an object smaller than a quarter. It has to be kept close to them, but not necessarily on their body.

Echomancer — A Sorceri that can mimic the abilities of the other Sorceri classes to a degree. They are a jack of all trades but master of none.

Eternal — A leader of a Natural Race. Each defined Natural Race has an Eternal.

Eternium — A celebration and reconvening of the Eternals that takes place once every 250 years, at the start of the Gregorian year.

Exilium — The honored death. A way to remove an Eternal without needing them to lose to a Challenge. This has to be passed by the other Eternals at an 80/20 majority.

Flit — A Vampire ability that allows them to move at extremely fast speeds. Their physical form warps when flitting, making them appear as little more than a burst of ashes.

Forgemancer — A Sorceri with the ability to enchant or craft magical items. They specialize in charm and ward making.

Hallen Bond — The name of a bond between typically two Vampires, that ties them so closely they are able to feed off of each other. This bond typically shows as a mark on each person (in Aaliyah and the boy's case, it shows as lavender bands on the guys' wrists, and intricate black bands on Aaliyah's)

Hemomancer — A Sorceri with the ability to manipulate blood cells, and in some cases, other cells as well.

Himal — A figure that most Waterborne Naturals consider to be their primary deity.

Horde — A grouping of Demons (consisting of one of each sin), typically living together. They share a common name (ex. Kri'Valta – Valta of the Kri Horde).

Inhama — A bond formed between Mythics born on the same day. This is an ancient tradition that was thought lost to time.

Maker — A Vampire that has transitioned another person into a Vampire.

Maker's Call (often called The Call) — This is an undeniable pull that a Vampire Maker can place on his spawn. It is a Charm that they must follow. As time goes on, this pull can lessen, and they can resist it. It doesn't go away, unless the one who placed it dies.

Natural — The term for supernatural beings in this universe.

Rend — Aaliyah's affliction. The first part of a Rend is her soul leaving her body for a time. This time grows in length with each Rend she has. The second part of a Rend is the memory. Rends are often brought on by 'triggers' or events that remind her brain of something from the past.

Siren's Call — The Sirens' ability to muddle minds. This often makes people forget periods of time or do small things at the Sirens' behest.

Sorceri — They are human wielders of magic, though they are still considered Naturals.

Swell - A grouping of Waterborn Naturals (including but not limited to Sirens, Mermaids, Selkies, etc.).

The Flame — A gift passed down the Vivas bloodline from one of the original six Vampires, Ferrion.

Turned — The term Maker's use when referring to people they have changed into Vampires.

Venomcaller — A shifter with the ability to turn into a spider.

Prince's Code

You okay? — Pointer finger to the nose while nodding.

Danger — Crossing arms over chest in an 'x' formation.

All clear — Pointer and middle finger pointed at the eyes.

Quiet — Pointer finger over lips in 'shush' motion.

Tell me? — Middle finger dragged from lips to left ear.

Sorry — Hands with interlaced fingers brought from chest to lips.

Forever — Hand settled over the heart, with the pinky and ring finger tucked underneath the hand.

Idiot — Swirling a finger around the ear.

Rend — Hands together, palms against one another, before they are pulled slowly apart.

Important Characters
Beware of possible spoilers ahead!

Aaliyah — The main character. She escaped Ascension Rising after years of torture and is now dealing with both memory loss and *Rends* as a side effect. She ended up with the Vivas Crypt after getting sold at auction, and found out that they stabilize her, keeping her soul intact while they try to find a solution to her impending death. Book 2 ended with her getting taken by Sebek, her blood uncle and the leader of Ascension Rising.

Prince — Aaliyah's best friend and first love. He's a Ghost and is found to be Nero in book 2 after an incident that leads to Aaliyah thinking she sent him on when, in reality, she brought him back from the dead.

Red — The Ghost of the armory. He's a fragment of a Ghost that's tied to a red cloth that Aaliyah keeps on her person. He helps Aaliyah through her grief the incident in book 2 where she believes she sent Prince on.

The Vivas Crypt (Main MCs)

Adrian — The youngest of the Vivas Crypt, he born in Victorian Era London before he was Turned. He was labeled Jack the Ripper due to the traumatic nature of his Turn, and those he killed during it. He's also called The Collector.

Eirik — The third eldest of the Vivas Crypt. He's a Vampire and Lycan (*Úlfhéðinn* (singular)/*Úlfhéðnar* (plural)) Norseman. He spent several years as a slave under Brazen after being stolen from his home before he was killed. Sebek Turned him on a whim to see if he could, since Eirik wasn't human before the Turn. He's also called The Emperor's Shadow.

Fallon — The fourth eldest of the Vivas Crypt. He's a Vampire who was born in Australia and grew up in the Nimanburru tribe. He was married Aislinn before he was Turned, after which he was forced to kill her and the rest of his tribe.

Nero — The second eldest of the Vivas Crypts. He's a Vampire, and before he was Turned, he was a Roman Gladiator, the bastard son of Emperor Claudius Nero. A notorious flirt and who many considered to be the glue that held the Vivas Crypt together. He died in Russia about 100 years before the start of book 1, after a mission had gone wrong. He's also called The Emperor (mostly as an insult).

Osiris — The eldest of the Crypt and fourth Turned of Sebek Ra. He's Vampire and Echomancer Sorceri who was born in ancient Egypt. He hates touch after his past with Kali and Darius the Great (where he was forced into Darius's Harem). He's struggled extensively with suicidal thoughts after the loss of Nero and has had to work to get himself back after Ali came into their lives. He's also called *Rex interfectorem* (or Kingslayer).

ELIZA AND COMPANY

Carter Halsen — Eliza's second husband. He's a Dragonkin, and one of the many sons of Dragonkin Eternal Teviticus Halsen.

Dezen Lal — Eliza's first husband. He's a Hemomancer Sorceri.

Eliza Barlow — Aaliyah's friend, a Siren who is trying to help her figure out who/what she is before Aaliyah meets the boys. She's a Siren and the granddaughter of Siren Eternal Ilenia.

Grigen Barlow — Eliza, Dezen and Carter's young son. He's assumed to be a Dragonkin. He has a particular soft spot for Aaliyah and Fallon.

THE HALSEN CLUTCH

Aldric — Second in command of Drakon's Clutch. He's considered akin to Adrian when it comes to information gathering/tracking.

Cassius — Enforcer of Drakon's Clutch.

Drakon Halsen — Son of Teviticus Halsen and head of the Clutch. After he killed his father he became the standing Dragonkin Eternal. He made a deal with Osiris to have Kri'Valta killed for his part in the murder of his Pearl.

THE ALDERI HORDE

Alderi'Amadeus — The Alderi Hordes Demon of Lust. He's Adrian's contact within the Horde.

Alderi'Theodious — The Alderi Hordes Demon of Wrath.

Alderi'Vidius — The Alderi Hordes Demon of Greed. He's gives Osiris the tickets to Kri'Valta's Gala after Adrian and Osiris meet him at The Altar (the nightclub owned by his Horde). He's a direct descendent of Mammon, the original Demon of Greed, and intends to take the spot of Eternal after Kri'Valta is killed.

ETERNALS

Archon Sewire — The Djinn Eternal and also speculated to be the one that tipped off

Curtis when Ali and Eliza would be going through Century Side. Eirik, Adrian and Fallon end book 2 being captured by him.

Avedal — The Basilisk Eternal, and long-standing ally to the Vivas Crypt. He gives them information on Sebek's latest killings, before promising to meet them at the Eternium.

Darius the Great — The Mythic Eternal. He owned Osiris before he was Turned by Sebek. He's still seeking, even decades later, to bring Osiris back into his bed and arms.

Frileti — The old Fae Eternal. She was killed by Sebek.

Ilenia Barlow — The Siren Eternal and grandmother/matriarch to Eliza. Also called *baba*, and The Red Witch of the Atlantic. She staunching anti Vampire, but is willing to help the Vivas Crypt if it means unseating Sebek.

Kali Rourovic — The Sorceri Eternal. She's an Echomancer, and the one who found Osiris when he was human. Drawn by his power that rivaled hers, she brought him into the company of Darius the Great and spent many of his human years violating him to turn him into the perfect pet.

Kri'Valta — The Demon Eternal, and Demon of Lust. He's been allies with Sebek for centuries and is the target of Drakon after it's believed he helped Teviticus with the murder of Darkon's Pearl. Killing him is how the Vivas Crypt is supposed to ensure the support of Drakon and his allies. He's also referred to as The Horror of the Depths.

Milo King — Selkie Eternal and best friend to Nero (and one of the main characters from the lovely Gisele Briseia's *The Golden Isles Series).*

Roderick — The old Titan Eternal. He was killed by Sebek.

Sebek Ra — The Vampire Eternal, Maker of everyone in the Vivas Crypt and Uncle of Aaliyah. Also referred to as *Amoun*, and is the leader of Ascension Rising. His twin brother, Arvand, is Aaliyah's father. Many consider his final decent into madness as beginning with Arvand's death at the hands of Escandric in the Natural War.

Teviticus Halsen — The Dragonkin Eternal. He's killed by his son, Drakon, after he kills Drakon's Pearl (wife) and unborn twins.

The Hallowed Three

The Hallowed of Death — No more information is known at this time.
The Hallowed of Life — No more information is known at this time.
The Hallowed of Time — No more information is known at this time.

Ascension Rising

Castillion — One of the researchers in charge of getting Aaliyah's blood. He's the one Aaliyah sees most often in her memories. He dies before the events of book 1.

Donavan — One of Aaliyah's former guards. He dies before the events of book 1.

Nilus — One of Aaliyah's former guards. He stumbles on Aaliyah while she's on an outing with Adrian and Fallon. After they drag him back to their home, he's tortured for information, before he's eventually killed by Osiris.

Nox — One of the researchers in charge of getting Aaliyah's blood. She dies before the events of book 1.

Side Characters

Aislinn — Fallon's wife from when he was a human. She was killed by Fallon while he was under the influence of Sebek's *Makers Call*.

Arvand Ra — Aaliyah's father, and twin brother to Sebek. He was killed before the events of book 1. In his human life, he was called *Usire* (the Coptic translation of Osiris). His name is the reason that Sebek Turned Osiris.

Audric — A Venomcaller informant for the Vivas Crypt, and fantastic tailor at his shop The Weathered Needle. He gives Adrian some information on the current state of the Eternal's, and tells of their fear of Sebek.

Axandre (Xander) — Also called the Keeper, he's a hoarder of information and a Nymph Dryad. The Vivas Crypt goes to him to see if he knows what Aaliyah is. He's able to tell them she's a Reaper and gives them his tentative support in the Exilium of Sebek.

Aya — A Banshee that owns a noodle shop in Treten. Osiris, Nero and Eirik helped her escape Japan during a Natural Revolt, and she's been loyal to them since.

Brazen — The man who bought Eirik and is responsible for a large majority of the scars on him.

Curtis Hadfall — A Dragonkin, and bastard son of Teviticus. He stole Ali off the street to sell her at auction. He's partner to Darius Verslini, and co owner of *The Devil's Details*. He dies to Osiris after the auction.

Darius Verslini — The owner of *The Devil's Details*. He's a Vampire, and the one who officially sold Ali. He's found dead in book 2 due to Aaliyah's blood being in his system.

Hillam — Avedal's Mate, mentioned briefly in book 2. A Kraken Mythic.

Iris Imperial — Aaliyah's mother, and one of the last members of the Reaper Imperial Royals. She was killed before the events of book 1.

Magelav — A Chronomancer Sorceri that the Vivas Crypt considering going to for information. They end up finding Prince after he wakes in the Roman Crypt, and help to nurse him back to help as he suffers through his own *Rends*. They are also called The Bog Sorceri.

Valen — A Gargoyle Sentinel and Entromancer Sorceri blacksmith who made Aaliyah's courting gift for Eirik. He's dying, as he's currently unable to turn back into his human form (which means his Gargoyle is slowly crumbling). He's one of Eirik's closest friends.

Yrsa — Eirik's eldest sister. The last time he saw her was before he was turned.

THE GOLDEN ISLES SERIES
BY GISELE BRISEIA

Do you guys remember Milo and company? The suave and sassy Selkie and his two beautiful mates that helps out the boys at Eliza's (and just so happens to be Prince's best friend/brother in all but blood)? If yes, then I have some great news!

You can read all about their story in the Golden Isles Series, one that's particularly close to my heart and written by one of my best friends. If you enjoyed his particular banter (and are looking for another angsty, raw why choose to dive into) then I'd recommend you give it a shot! You won't be disappointed.